A ROOM
WITH A VIEW

HOWARDS END

MAURICE

A ROOM
WITH A VIEW

❧

HOWARDS END

❧

MAURICE

❧

E. M. Forster

QUALITY PAPERBACK BOOK CLUB
New York

A ROOM
WITH A VIEW

To
H. O. M.

Contents

Part One

Part Two

Contents

Part One

Chapter I: The Bertolini

"THE Signora had no business to do it," said Miss Bartlett, "no business at all. She promised us south rooms with a view close together, instead of which here are north rooms, looking into a courtyard, and a long way apart. Oh, Lucy!"

"And a Cockney, besides!" said Lucy, who had been further saddened by the Signora's unexpected accent. "It might be London." She looked at the two rows of English people who were sitting at the table; at the row of white bottles of water and red bottles of wine that ran between the English people; at the portraits of the late Queen and the late Poet Laureate that hung behind the English people, heavily framed; at the notice of the English church (Rev. Cuthbert Eager, M. A. Oxon.), that was the only other decoration of the wall. "Charlotte, don't you feel, too, that we might be in London? I can hardly believe that all kinds of other things are just outside. I suppose it is one's being so tired."

"This meat has surely been used for soup," said Miss Bartlett, laying down her fork.

"I want so to see the Arno. The rooms the

Signora promised us in her letter would have looked over the Arno. The Signora had no business to do it at all. Oh, it is a shame!"

"Any nook does for me," Miss Bartlett continued; "but it does seem hard that you shouldn't have a view."

Lucy felt that she had been selfish. "Charlotte, you mustn't spoil me: of course, you must look over the Arno, too. I meant that. The first vacant room in the front—"

"You must have it," said Miss Bartlett, part of whose travelling expenses were paid by Lucy's mother—a piece of generosity to which she made many a tactful allusion.

"No, no. You must have it."

"I insist on it. Your mother would never forgive me, Lucy."

"She would never forgive *me*."

The ladies' voices grew animated, and—if the sad truth be owned—a little peevish. They were tired, and under the guise of unselfishness they wrangled. Some of their neighbours interchanged glances, and one of them—one of the ill-bred people whom one does meet abroad—leant forward over the table and actually intruded into their argument. He said:

"I have a view, I have a view."

Miss Bartlett was startled. Generally at a pension people looked them over for a day or two before speaking, and often did not find out that they would "do" till they had gone. She knew that the intruder was ill-bred, even before she glanced at him. He was an old man, of heavy build, with a fair, shaven face and large eyes. There was something childish in those eyes, though it was not the childishness of senility. What exactly it was Miss Bartlett did not stop to consider, for her glance passed on to his clothes. These did not attract her. He was probably trying to become acquainted with them before they got into the swim. So she assumed a dazed expression when he spoke to her, and then said: "A view? Oh, a view! How delightful a view is!"

"This is my son," said the old man; "his name's George. He has a view too."

"Ah," said Miss Bartlett, repressing Lucy, who was about to speak.

"What I mean," he continued, "is that you can have our rooms, and we'll have yours. We'll change."

The better class of tourist was shocked at this, and sympathized with the new-comers. Miss Bartlett, in reply, opened her mouth as little as possible, and said:

"Thank you very much indeed; that is out of the question."

"Why?" said the old man, with both fists on the table.

"Because it is quite out of the question, thank you."

"You see, we don't like to take—" began Lucy. Her cousin again repressed her.

"But why?" he persisted. "Women like looking at a view; men don't." And he thumped with his fists like a naughty child, and turned to his son, saying, "George, persuade them!"

"It's so obvious they should have the rooms," said the son. "There's nothing else to say."

He did not look at the ladies as he spoke, but his voice was perplexed and sorrowful. Lucy, too, was perplexed; but she saw that they were in for what is known as "quite a scene," and she had an odd feeling that whenever these ill-bred tourists spoke the contest widened and deepened till it dealt, not with rooms and views, but with—well, with something quite different, whose existence she had not realized before. Now the old man attacked Miss Bartlett almost violently: Why should she not change? What possible objection had she? They would clear out in half an hour.

Miss Bartlett, though skilled in the delicacies of conversation, was powerless in the presence of brutality. It was impossible to snub any one so gross. Her face reddened with displeasure. She looked around as much as to say, "Are you all like this?" And two little old ladies, who were sitting further up the table, with shawls hanging over the backs of the chairs, looked back, clearly indicating "We are not; we are genteel."

"Eat your dinner, dear," she said to Lucy, and began to toy again with the meat that she had once censured.

Lucy mumbled that those seemed very odd people opposite.

"Eat your dinner, dear. This pension is a failure. To-morrow we will make a change."

Hardly had she announced this fell decision when she reversed it. The curtains at the end of the room parted, and revealed a clergyman, stout but attractive, who hurried forward to take his place at the table, cheerfully apologizing for his lateness. Lucy, who had not yet acquired decency, at once rose to her feet, exclaiming: "Oh, oh! Why, it's Mr. Beebe! Oh, how perfectly lovely! Oh, Charlotte, we must stop now, however bad the rooms are. Oh!"

Miss Bartlett said, with more restraint:

"How do you do, Mr. Beebe? I expect that you have forgotten us: Miss Bartlett and Miss Honeychurch, who were at Tunbridge Wells when you helped the Vicar of St. Peter's that very cold Easter."

The clergyman, who had the air of one on a holiday, did not remember the ladies quite as clearly as they remembered him. But he came forward pleasantly enough and accepted the chair into which he was beckoned by Lucy.

"I *am* so glad to see you," said the girl, who was in a state of spiritual starvation, and would have been glad to see the waiter if her cousin had permitted it. "Just fancy how small the world is. Summer Street, too, makes it so specially funny."

"Miss Honeychurch lives in the parish of Summer Street," said Miss Bartlett, filling up the gap, "and she happened to tell me in the course of conversation that you have just accepted the living—"

"Yes, I heard from mother so last week. She didn't know that I knew you at Tunbridge Wells; but I wrote back at once, and I said: 'Mr. Beebe is—' "

"Quite right," said the clergyman. "I move into the Rectory at Summer Street next June. I am lucky to be appointed to such a charming neighbourhood."

"Oh, how glad I am! The name of our house is Windy Corner."

Mr. Beebe bowed.

"There is mother and me generally, and my brother, though it's not often we get him to ch— The church is rather far off, I mean."

"Lucy, dearest, let Mr. Beebe eat his dinner."

"I am eating it, thank you, and enjoying it."

He preferred to talk to Lucy, whose playing he remembered, rather than to Miss Bartlett, who probably remembered his sermons. He asked the girl whether she knew Florence well, and was informed at some length that she had never been there before. It is delightful to advise a newcomer, and he was first in the field.

"Don't neglect the country round," his advice concluded. "The first fine afternoon drive up to Fiesole, and round by Settignano, or something of that sort."

"No!" cried a voice from the top of the table. "Mr. Beebe, you are wrong. The first fine afternoon your ladies must go to Prato."

"That lady looks so clever," whispered Miss Bartlett to her cousin. "We are in luck."

And, indeed, a perfect torrent of information burst on them. People told them what to see, when to see it, how to stop the electric trams, how to get rid of the beggars, how much to give for a vellum blotter, how much the place would grow upon them. The Pension Bertolini had decided, almost enthusiastically, that they would do. Whichever way they looked, kind ladies smiled and shouted at them. And above all rose the voice of the clever lady, crying: "Prato! They must go to Prato. That place is too sweetly squalid for words. I love it; I revel in shaking off the trammels of respectability, as you know."

The young man named George glanced at the clever lady, and then returned moodily to his plate. Obviously he and his father did not do. Lucy, in the midst of her success, found time to wish they did. It gave her no extra pleasure that any one should be left in the cold; and when she rose to go, she turned back and gave the two outsiders a nervous little bow.

The father did not see it; the son acknowledged

it, not by another bow, but by raising his eyebrows and smiling; he seemed to be smiling across something.

She hastened after her cousin, who had already disappeared through the curtains—curtains which smote one in the face, and seemed heavy with more than cloth. Beyond them stood the unreliable Signora, bowing good-evening to her guests, and supported by 'Enery, her little boy, and Victorier, her daughter. It made a curious little scene, this attempt of the Cockney to convey the grace and geniality of the South. And even more curious was the drawing-room, which attempted to rival the solid comfort of a Bloomsbury boarding-house. Was this really Italy?

Miss Bartlett was already seated on a tightly stuffed arm-chair, which had the colour and the contours of a tomato. She was talking to Mr. Beebe, and as she spoke, her long narrow head drove backwards and forwards, slowly, regularly, as though she were demolishing some invisible obstacle. "We are most grateful to you," she was saying. "The first evening means so much. When you arrived we were in for a peculiarly *mauvais quart d'heure.*"

He expressed his regret.

"Do you, by any chance, know the name of an old man who sat opposite us at dinner?"

"Emerson."

"Is he a friend of yours?"

"We are friendly—as one is in pensions."

"Then I will say no more."

He pressed her very slightly, and she said more.

"I am, as it were," she concluded, "the chaperon of my young cousin, Lucy, and it would be a serious thing if I put her under an obligation to people of whom we know nothing. His manner was somewhat unfortunate. I hope I acted for the best."

"You acted very naturally," said he. He seemed thoughtful, and after a few moments added: "All the same, I don't think much harm would have come of accepting."

"No *harm,* of course. But we could not be under an obligation."

"He is rather a peculiar man." Again he hesitated, and then said gently: "I think he would not take advantage of your acceptance, nor expect you to show gratitude. He has the merit—if it is one —of saying exactly what he means. He has rooms he does not value, and he thinks you would value them. He no more thought of putting you under an obligation than he thought of being polite. It is so difficult—at least, I find it difficult—to understand people who speak the truth."

Lucy was pleased, and said: "I was hoping that he was nice; I do so always hope that people will be nice."

"I think he is; nice and tiresome. I differ from him on almost every point of any importance, and so, I expect—I may say I hope—you will differ.

But his is a type one disagrees with rather than deplores. When he first came here he not unnaturally put people's backs up. He has no tact and no manners—I don't mean by that that he has bad manners—and he will not keep his opinions to himself. We nearly complained about him to our depressing Signora, but I am glad to say we thought better of it."

"Am I to conclude," said Miss Bartlett, "that he is a Socialist?"

Mr. Beebe accepted the convenient word, not without a slight twitching of the lips.

"And presumably he has brought up his son to be a Socialist, too?"

"I hardly know George, for he hasn't learnt to talk yet. He seems a nice creature, and I think he has brains. Of course, he has all his father's mannerisms, and it is quite possible that he, too, may be a Socialist."

"Oh, you relieve me," said Miss Bartlett. "So you think I ought to have accepted their offer? You feel I have been narrow-minded and suspicious?"

"Not at all," he answered; "I never suggested that."

"But ought I not to apologize, at all events, for my apparent rudeness?"

He replied, with some irritation, that it would be quite unnecessary, and got up from his seat to go to the smoking-room.

"Was I a bore?" said Miss Bartlett, as soon as he had disappeared. "Why didn't you talk, Lucy? He prefers young people, I'm sure. I do hope I haven't monopolized him. I hoped you would have him all the evening, as well as all dinner-time."

"He is nice," exclaimed Lucy. "Just what I remember. He seems to see good in every one. No one would take him for a clergyman."

"My dear Lucia—"

"Well, you know what I mean. And you know how clergymen generally laugh; Mr. Beebe laughs just like an ordinary man."

"Funny girl! How you do remind me of your mother. I wonder if she will approve of Mr. Beebe."

"I'm sure she will; and so will Freddy."

"I think every one at Windy Corner will approve; it is the fashionable world. I am used to Tunbridge Wells, where we are all hopelessly behind the times."

"Yes," said Lucy despondently.

There was a haze of disapproval in the air, but whether the disapproval was of herself, or of Mr. Beebe, or of the fashionable world at Windy Corner, or of the narrow world at Tunbridge Wells, she could not determine. She tried to locate it, but as usual she blundered. Miss Bartlett sedulously denied disapproving of any one, and added: "I am afraid you are finding me a very depressing companion."

And the girl again thought: "I must have been selfish or unkind; I must be more careful. It is so dreadful for Charlotte, being poor."

Fortunately one of the little old ladies, who for some time had been smiling very benignly, now approached and asked if she might be allowed to sit where Mr. Beebe had sat. Permission granted, she began to chatter gently about Italy, the plunge it had been to come there, the gratifying success of the plunge, the improvement in her sister's health, the necessity of closing the bed-room windows at night, and of thoroughly emptying the water-bottles in the morning. She handled her subjects agreeably, and they were, perhaps, more worthy of attention than the high discourse upon Guelfs and Ghibellines which was proceeding tempestuously at the other end of the room. It was a real catastrophe, not a mere episode, that evening of hers at Venice, when she had found in her bedroom something that is one worse than a flea, though one better than something else.

"But here you are as safe as in England. Signora Bertolini is so English."

"Yet our rooms smell," said poor Lucy. "We dread going to bed."

"Ah, then you look into the court." She sighed. "If only Mr. Emerson was more tactful! We were so sorry for you at dinner."

"I think he was meaning to be kind."

"Undoubtedly he was," said Miss Bartlett.

"Mr. Beebe has just been scolding me for my suspicious nature. Of course, I was holding back on my cousin's account."

"Of course," said the little old lady; and they murmured that one could not be too careful with a young girl.

Lucy tried to look demure, but could not help feeling a great fool. No one was careful with her at home; or, at all events, she had not noticed it.

"About old Mr. Emerson—I hardly know. No, he is not tactful; yet, have you ever noticed that there are people who do things which are most indelicate, and yet at the same time—beautiful?"

"Beautiful?" said Miss Bartlett, puzzled at the word. "Are not beauty and delicacy the same?"

"So one would have thought," said the other helplessly. "But things are so difficult, I sometimes think."

She proceeded no further into things, for Mr. Beebe reappeared, looking extremely pleasant.

"Miss Bartlett," he cried, "it's all right about the rooms. I'm so glad. Mr. Emerson was talking about it in the smoking-room, and knowing what I did, I encouraged him to make the offer again. He has let me come and ask you. He would be so pleased."

"Oh, Charlotte," cried Lucy to her cousin, "we must have the rooms now. The old man is just as nice and kind as he can be."

Miss Bartlett was silent.

"I fear," said Mr. Beebe, after a pause, "that I have been officious. I must apologize for my interference."

Gravely displeased, he turned to go. Not till then did Miss Bartlett reply: "My own wishes, dearest Lucy, are unimportant in comparision with yours. It would be hard indeed if I stopped you doing as you liked at Florence, when I am only here through your kindness. If you wish me to turn these gentlemen out of their rooms, I will do it. Would you then, Mr. Beebe, kindly tell Mr. Emerson that I accept his kind offer, and then conduct him to me, in order that I may thank him personally?"

She raised her voice as she spoke; it was heard all over the drawing-room, and silenced the Guelfs and the Ghibellines. The clergyman, inwardly cursing the female sex, bowed, and departed with her message.

"Remember, Lucy, I alone am implicated in this. I do not wish the acceptance to come from you. Grant me that, at all events."

Mr. Beebe was back, saying rather nervously:

"Mr. Emerson is engaged, but here is his son instead."

The young man gazed down on the three ladies, who felt seated on the floor, so low were their chairs.

"My father," he said, "is in his bath, so you cannot thank him personally. But any message

given by you to me will be given by me to him as
soon as he comes out."

Miss Bartlett was unequal to the bath. All her
barbed civilities came forth wrong end first. Young
Mr. Emerson scored a notable triumph to the delight of Mr. Beebe and to the secret delight of
Lucy.

"Poor young man!" said Miss Bartlett, as soon
as he had gone. "How angry he is with his father
about the rooms! It is all he can do to keep
polite."

"In half an hour or so your rooms will be
ready," said Mr. Beebe. Then looking rather
thoughtfully at the two cousins, he retired to
his own rooms, to write up his philosophic diary.

"Oh, dear!" breathed the little old lady, and
shuddered as if all the winds of heaven had entered
the apartment. "Gentlemen sometimes do not
realize—" Her voice faded away, but Miss Bartlett seemed to understand and a conversation developed, in which gentlemen who did not thoroughly
realize played a principal part. Lucy, not realizing
either, was reduced to literature. Taking up Baedeker's *Handbook to Northern Italy,* she committed
to memory the most important dates of Florentine
History. For she was determined to enjoy herself on the morrow. Thus the half-hour crept
profitably away, and at last Miss Bartlett rose
with a sigh, and said:

"I think one might venture now. No, Lucy, do not stir. I will superintend the move."

"How you do do everything," said Lucy.

"Naturally, dear. It is my affair."

"But I would like to help you."

"No, dear."

Charlotte's energy! And her unselfishness! She had been thus all her life, but really, on this Italian tour, she was surpassing herself. So Lucy felt, or strove to feel. And yet—there was a rebellious spirit in her which wondered whether the acceptance might not have been less delicate and more beautiful. At all events, she entered her own room without any feeling of joy.

"I want to explain," said Miss Bartlett, "why it is that I have taken the largest room. Naturally, of course, I should have given it to you; but I happen to know that it belongs to the young man, and I was sure your mother would not like it."

Lucy was bewildered.

"If you are to accept a favour it is more suitable you should be under an obligation to his father than to him. I am a woman of the world, in my small way, and I know where things lead to. However, Mr. Beebe is a guarantee of a sort that they will not presume on this."

"Mother wouldn't mind I'm sure," said Lucy, but again had the sense of larger and unsuspected issues.

Miss Bartlett only sighed, and enveloped her in

a protecting embrace as she wished her good-night. It gave Lucy the sensation of a fog, and when she reached her own room she opened the window and breathed the clean night air, thinking of the kind old man who had enabled her to see the lights dancing in the Arno and the cypresses of San Miniato, and the foot-hills of the Apennines, black against the rising moon.

Miss Bartlett, in her room, fastened the window-shutters and locked the door, and then made a tour of the apartment to see where the cupboards led, and whether there were any oubliettes or secret entrances. It was then that she saw, pinned up over the washstand, a sheet of paper on which was scrawled an enormous note of interrogation. Nothing more.

"What does it mean?" she thought, and she examined it carefully by the light of a candle. Meaningless at first, it gradually became menacing, obnoxious, portentous with evil. She was seized with an impulse to destroy it, but fortunately remembered that she had no right to do so, since it must be the property of young Mr. Emerson. So she unpinned it carefully, and put it between two pieces of blotting-paper to keep it clean for him. Then she completed her inspection of the room, sighed heavily according to her habit, and went to bed.

Chapter II: In Santa Croce with No Baedeker

IT was pleasant to wake up in Florence, to open the eyes upon a bright bare room, with a floor of red tiles which look clean though they are not; with a painted ceiling whereon pink griffins and blue amorini sport in a forest of yellow violins and bassoons. It was pleasant, too, to fling wide the windows, pinching the fingers in unfamiliar fastenings, to lean out into sunshine with beautiful hills and trees and marble churches opposite, and close below, the Arno, gurgling against the embankment of the road.

Over the river men were at work with spades and sieves on the sandy foreshore, and on the river was a boat, also diligently employed for some mysterious end. An electric tram came rushing underneath the window. No one was inside it, except one tourist; but its platforms were overflowing with Italians, who preferred to stand. Children tried to hang on behind, and the conductor, with no malice, spat in their faces to make them let go. Then soldiers appeared—good-looking, undersized men —wearing each a knapsack covered with mangy fur, and a great-coat which had been cut for some larger soldier. Beside them walked officers, looking foolish and fierce, and before them went little boys, turning somersaults in time with the band. The tramcar became entangled in their ranks, and moved on painfully, like a caterpillar in a swarm of ants. One of the little boys fell down, and some white bullocks came out of an archway. Indeed, if it had not been for the good advice of an old man who was selling button-hooks, the road might never have got clear.

Over such trivialities as these many a valuable hour may slip away, and the traveller who has gone to Italy to study the tactile values of Giotto, or the corruption of the Papacy, may return remembering nothing but the blue sky and the men and women who live under it. So it was as well that Miss Bartlett should tap and come in, and having commented on Lucy's leaving the door unlocked, and on her leaning out of the window before she was fully dressed, should urge her to hasten herself, or the best of the day would be gone. By the time Lucy was ready her cousin had done her breakfast, and was listening to the clever lady among the crumbs.

A conversation then ensued, on not unfamiliar lines. Miss Bartlett was, after all, a wee bit tired, and thought they had better spend the morning settling in; unless Lucy would at all like to go out? Lucy would rather like to go out, as it was her first day in Florence, but, of course, she could go alone. Miss Bartlett could not allow this. Of course she would accompany Lucy everywhere. Oh, certainly not; Lucy would stop with her cousin. Oh, no! that would never do. Oh, yes!

At this point the clever lady broke in.

"If it is Mrs. Grundy who is troubling you, I do assure you that you can neglect the good person. Being English, Miss Honeychurch will be perfectly safe. Italians understand. A dear friend of mine, Contessa Baroncelli, has two daughters, and when she cannot send a maid to school with them, she lets them go in sailor-hats instead. Every one takes them for English, you see, especially if their hair is strained tightly behind."

Miss Bartlett was unconvinced by the safety of Contessa Baroncelli's daughters. She was determined to take Lucy herself, her head not being so very bad. The clever lady then said that she was going to spend a long morning in Santa Croce, and if Lucy would come too, she would be delighted.

"I will take you by a dear dirty back way, Miss Honeychurch, and if you bring me luck, we shall have an adventure."

Lucy said that this was most kind, and at once opened the Baedeker, to see where Santa Croce was.

"Tut, tut! Miss Lucy! I hope we shall soon emancipate you from Baedeker. He does but touch the surface of things. As to the true Italy —he does not even dream of it. The true Italy is only to be found by patient observation."

In Santa Croce with No Baedeker

This sounded very interesting, and Lucy hurried over her breakfast, and started with her new friend in high spirits. Italy was coming at last. The Cockney Signora and her works had vanished like a bad dream.

Miss Lavish—for that was the clever lady's name—turned to the right along the sunny Lung' Arno. How delightfully warm! But a wind down the side streets cut like a knife, didn't it? Ponte alle Grazie—particularly interesting, mentioned by Dante. San Miniato—beautiful as well as interesting; the crucifix that kissed a murderer—Miss Honeychurch would remember the story. The men on the river were fishing. (Untrue; but then, so is most information.) Then Miss Lavish darted under the archway of the white bullocks, and she stopped, and she cried:

"A smell! a true Florentine smell! Every city, let me teach you, has its own smell."

"Is it a very nice smell?" said Lucy, who had inherited from her mother a distaste to dirt.

"One doesn't come to Italy for niceness," was the retort; "one comes for life. Buon giorno! Buon giorno!" bowing right and left. "Look at that adorable wine-cart! How the driver stares at us, dear, simple soul!"

So Miss Lavish proceeded through the streets of the city of Florence, short, fidgety, and playful as a kitten, though without a kitten's grace. It was a treat for the girl to be with any one so clever

and so cheerful; and a blue military cloak, such as
an Italian officer wears, only increased the sense of
festivity.

"Buon giorno! Take the word of an old woman, Miss Lucy: you will never repent of a little
civility to your inferiors. *That* is the true democracy. Though I am a real Radical as well. There,
now you're shocked."

"Indeed, I'm not!" exclaimed Lucy. "We are
Radicals, too, out and out. My father always
voted for Mr. Gladstone, until he was so dreadful
about Ireland."

"I see, I see. And now you have gone over to
the enemy."

"Oh, please—! If my father was alive, I am
sure he would vote Radical again now that Ireland
is all right. And as it is, the glass over our front-
door was broken last election, and Freddy is sure
it was the Tories; but mother says nonsense, a
tramp."

"Shameful! A manufacturing district, I suppose?"

"No—in the Surrey hills. About five miles from
Dorking, looking over the Weald."

Miss Lavish seemed interested, and slackened
her trot.

"What a delightful part; I know it so well. It
is full of the very nicest people. Do you know Sir
Harry Otway—a Radical if ever there was?"

"Very well indeed."

"And old Mrs. Butterworth the philanthropist?"

"Why, she rents a field of us! How funny!"

Miss Lavish looked at the narrow ribbon of sky, and murmured:

"Oh, you have property in Surrey?"

"Hardly any," said Lucy, fearful of being thought a snob. "Only thirty acres—just the garden, all downhill, and some fields."

Miss Lavish was not disgusted, and said it was just the size of her aunt's Suffolk estate. Italy receded. They tried to remember the last name of Lady Louisa some one, who had taken a house near Summer Street the other year, but she had not liked it, which was odd of her. And just as Miss Lavish had got the name, she broke off and exclaimed:

"Bless us! Bless us and save us! We've lost the way."

Certainly they had seemed a long time in reaching Santa Croce, the tower of which had been plainly visible from the landing window. But Miss Lavish had said so much about knowing her Florence by heart, that Lucy had followed her with no misgivings.

"Lost! lost! My dear Miss Lucy, during our political diatribes we have taken a wrong turning. How those horrid Conservatives would jeer at us! What are we to do? Two lone females in an unknown town. Now, this is what *I* call an adventure."

Lucy, who wanted to see Santa Croce, suggested, as a possible solution, that they should ask the way there.

"Oh, but that is the word of a craven! And no, you are not, not, *not* to look at your Baedeker. Give it to me; I shan't let you carry it. We will simply drift."

Accordingly they drifted through a series of those grey-brown streets, neither commodious nor picturesque, in which the eastern quarter of the city abounds. Lucy soon lost interest in the discontent of Lady Louisa, and became discontented herself. For one ravishing moment Italy appeared. She stood in the Square of the Annunziata and saw in the living terra-cotta those divine babies whom no cheap reproduction can ever stale. There they stood, with their shining limbs bursting from the garments of charity, and their strong white arms extended against circlets of heaven. Lucy thought she had never seen anything more beautiful; but Miss Lavish, with a shriek of dismay, dragged her forward, declaring that they were out of their path now by at least a mile.

The hour was approaching at which the continental breakfast begins, or rather ceases, to tell, and the ladies bought some hot chestnut paste out of a little shop, because it looked so typical. It tasted partly of the paper in which it was wrapped, partly of hair oil, partly of the great unknown. But it gave them strength to drift into another Piazza,

In Santa Croce with No Baedeker

large and dusty, on the farther side of which rose a black-and-white façade of surpassing ugliness. Miss Lavish spoke to it dramatically. It was Santa Croce. The adventure was over.

"Stop a minute; let those two people go on, or I shall have to speak to them. I do detest conventional intercourse. Nasty! they are going into the church, too. Oh, the Britisher abroad!"

"We sat opposite them at dinner last night. They have given us their rooms. They were so very kind."

"Look at their figures!" laughed Miss Lavish. "They walk through my Italy like a pair of cows. It's very naughty of me, but I would like to set an examination paper at Dover, and turn back every tourist who couldn't pass it."

"What would you ask us?"

Miss Lavish laid her hand pleasantly on Lucy's arm, as if to suggest that she, at all events, would get full marks. In this exalted mood they reached the steps of the great church, and were about to enter it when Miss Lavish stopped, squeaked, flung up her arms, and cried:

"There goes my local-colour box! I must have a word with him!"

And in a moment she was away over the Piazza, her military cloak flapping in the wind; nor did she slacken speed till she caught up an old man with white whiskers, and nipped him playfully upon the arm.

Lucy waited for nearly ten minutes. Then she began to get tired. The beggars worried her, the dust blew in her eyes, and she remembered that a young girl ought not to loiter in public places. She descended slowly into the Piazza with the intention of rejoining Miss Lavish, who was really almost too original. But at that moment Miss Lavish and her local-colour box moved also, and disappeared down a side street, both gesticulating largely.

Tears of indignation came to Lucy's eyes— partly because Miss Lavish had jilted her, partly because she had taken her Baedeker. How could she find her way home? How could she find her way about in Santa Croce? Her first morning was ruined, and she might never be in Florence again. A few minutes ago she had been all high spirits, talking as a woman of culture, and half persuading herself that she was full of originality. Now she entered the church depressed and humiliated, not even able to remember whether it was built by the Franciscans or the Dominicans.

Of course, it must be a wonderful building. But how like a barn! And how very cold! Of course, it contained frescoes by Giotto, in the presence of whose tactile values she was capable of feeling what was proper. But who was to tell her which they were? She walked about disdainfully, unwilling to be enthusiastic over monuments of uncertain authorship or date. There was no one even to tell her which, of all the sepulchral slabs that paved the nave and transepts, was the one that was really beautiful, the one that had been most praised by Mr. Ruskin.

Then the pernicious charm of Italy worked on her, and, instead of acquiring information, she began to be happy. She puzzled out the Italian notices—the notices that forbade people to introduce dogs into the church—the notice that prayed people, in the interest of health and out of respect to the sacred edifice in which they found themselves, not to spit. She watched the tourists; their noses were as red as their Baedekers, so cold was Santa Croce. She beheld the horrible fate that overtook three Papists—two he-babies and a she-baby—who began their career by sousing each other with the Holy Water, and then proceeded to the Machiavelli memorial, dripping but hallowed. Advancing towards it very slowly and from immense distances, they touched the stone with their fingers, with their handkerchiefs, with their heads, and then retreated. What could this mean? They did it again and again. Then Lucy realized that they had mistaken Machiavelli for some saint, hoping to acquire virtue. Punishment followed quickly. The smallest he-baby stumbled over one of the sepulchral slabs so much admired by Mr. Ruskin, and entangled his feet in the features of a recumbent bishop. Protestant as she was, Lucy darted forward. She was too late. He fell heavily upon the prelate's upturned toes.

"Hateful bishop!" exclaimed the voice of old Mr. Emerson, who had darted forward also. "Hard in life, hard in death. Go out into the sunshine, little boy, and kiss your hand to the sun, for that is where you ought to be. Intolerable bishop!"

The child screamed frantically at these words, and at these dreadful people who picked him up, dusted him, rubbed his bruises, and told him not to be superstitious.

"Look at him!" said Mr. Emerson to Lucy. "Here's a mess: a baby hurt, cold, and frightened! But what else can you expect from a church?"

The child's legs had become as melting wax. Each time that old Mr. Emerson and Lucy set it erect it collapsed with a roar. Fortunately an Italian lady, who ought to have been saying her prayers, came to the rescue. By some mysterious virtue, which mothers alone possess, she stiffened the little boy's back-bone and imparted strength to his knees. He stood. Still gibbering with agitation, he walked away.

"You are a clever woman," said Mr. Emerson. "You have done more than all the relics in the world. I am not of your creed, but I do believe in those who make their fellow-creatures happy. There is no scheme of the universe——"

He paused for a phrase.

"Niente," said the Italian lady, and returned to her prayers.

"I'm not sure she understands English," suggested Lucy.

In her chastened mood she no longer despised the Emersons. She was determined to be gracious to them, beautiful rather than delicate, and, if possible, to erase Miss Bartlett's civility by some gracious reference to the pleasant rooms.

"That woman understands everything," was Mr. Emerson's reply. "But what are you doing here? Are you doing the church? Are you through with the church?"

"No," cried Lucy, remembering her grievance. "I came here with Miss Lavish, who was to explain everything; and just by the door—it is too bad!—she simply ran away, and after waiting quite a time, I had to come in by myself."

"Why shouldn't you?" said Mr. Emerson.

"Yes, why shouldn't you come by yourself?" said the son, addressing the young lady for the first time.

"But Miss Lavish has even taken away Baedeker."

"Baedeker?" said Mr. Emerson. "I'm glad it's *that* you minded. It's worth minding, the loss of a Baedeker. *That's* worth minding."

Lucy was puzzled. She was again conscious of some new idea, and was not sure whither it would lead her.

"If you've no Baedeker," said the son, "you'd better join us."

Was this where the idea would lead? She took refuge in her dignity.

"Thank you very much, but I could not think of that. I hope you do not suppose that I came to join on to you. I really came to help with the child, and to thank you for so kindly giving us your rooms last night. I hope that you have not been put to any great inconvenience."

"My dear," said the old man gently, " I think that you are repeating what you have heard older people say. You are pretending to be touchy; but you are not really. Stop being so tiresome, and tell me instead what part of the church you want to see. To take you to it will be a real pleasure."

Now, this was abominably impertinent, and she ought to have been furious. But it is sometimes as difficult to lose one's temper as it is difficult at other times to keep it. Lucy could not get cross. Mr. Emerson was an old man, and surely a girl might humour him. On the other hand, his son was a young man, and she felt that a girl ought to be offended with him, or at all events be offended before him. It was at him that she gazed before replying.

"I am not touchy, I hope. It is the Giottos that I want to see, if you will kindly tell me which they are."

The son nodded. With a look of sombre satisfaction, he led the way to the Peruzzi Chapel.

There was a hint of the teacher about him. She felt like a child in school who had answered a question rightly.

The chapel was already filled with an earnest congregation, and out of them rose the voice of a lecturer, directing them how to worship Giotto, not by tactful valuations, but by the standards of the spirit.

"Remember," he was saying, "the facts about this church of Santa Croce; how it was built by faith in the full fervour of medievalism, before any taint of the Renaissance had appeared. Observe how Giotto in these frescoes—now, unhappily, ruined by restoration—is untroubled by the snares of anatomy and perspective. Could anything be more majestic, more pathetic, beautiful, true? How little, we feel, avails knowledge and technical cleverness against a man who truly feels!"

"No!" exclaimed Mr. Emerson, in much too loud a voice for church. "Remember nothing of the sort! Built by faith indeed! That simply means the workmen weren't paid properly. And as for the frescoes, I see no truth in them. Look at that fat man in blue! He must weigh as much as I do, and he is shooting into the sky like an air-balloon."

He was referring to the fresco of the "Ascension of St. John." Inside, the lecturer's voice faltered, as well it might. The audience shifted uneasily, and so did Lucy. She was sure that she ought not to be with these men; but they had cast a spell over her. They were so serious and so strange that she could not remember how to behave.

"Now, did this happen, or didn't it? Yes or no?"

George replied:

"It happened like this, if it happened at all. I would rather go up to heaven by myself than be pushed by cherubs; and if I got there I should like my friends to lean out of it, just as they do here."

"You will never go up," said his father. "You and I, dear boy, will lie at peace in the earth that bore us, and our names will disappear as surely as our work survives."

"Some of the people can only see the empty grave, not the saint, whoever he is, going up. It did happen like that, if it happened at all."

"Pardon me," said a frigid voice. "The chapel is somewhat small for two parties. We will incommode you no longer."

The lecturer was a clergyman, and his audience must be also his flock, for they held prayer-books as well as guide-books in their hands. They filed out of the chapel in silence. Amongst them were the two little old ladies of the Pension Bertolini —Miss Teresa and Miss Catherine Alan.

"Stop!" cried Mr. Emerson. "There's plenty of room for us all. Stop!"

The procession disappeared without a word.

Soon the lecturer could be heard in the next chapel, describing the life of St. Francis.

"George, I do believe that clergyman is the Brixton curate."

George went into the next chapel and returned, saying, "Perhaps he is. I don't remember."

"Then I had better speak to him and remind him who I am. It's that Mr. Eager. Why did he go? Did we talk too loud? How vexatious. I shall go and say we are sorry. Hadn't I better? Then perhaps he will come back."

"He will not come back," said George.

But Mr. Emerson, contrite and unhappy, hurried away to apologize to the Rev. Cuthbert Eager. Lucy, apparently absorbed in a lunette, could hear the lecture again interrupted, the anxious, aggressive voice of the old man, the curt, injured replies of his opponent. The son, who took every little contretemps as if it were a tragedy, was listening also.

"My father has that effect on nearly every one," he informed her. "He will try to be kind."

"I hope we all try," said she, smiling nervously.

"Because we think it improves our characters. But he is kind to people because he loves them; and they find him out, and are offended, or frightened."

"How silly of them!" said Lucy, though in her heart she sympathized; "I think that a kind action done tactfully—"

"Tact!"

He threw up his head in disdain. Apparently she had given the wrong answer. She watched the singular creature pace up and down the chapel. For a young man his face was rugged, and—until the shadows fell upon it—hard. Enshadowed, it sprang into tenderness. She saw him once again at Rome, on the ceiling of the Sistine Chapel, carrying a burden of acorns. Healthy and muscular, he yet gave her the feeling of greyness, of tragedy that might only find solution in the night. The feeling soon passed; it was unlike her to have entertained anything so subtle. Born of silence and of unknown emotion, it passed when Mr. Emerson returned, and she could re-enter the world of rapid talk, which was alone familiar to her.

"Were you snubbed?" asked his son tranquilly.

"But we have spoilt the pleasure of I don't know how many people. They won't come back."

". . . full of innate sympathy . . . quickness to perceive good in others . . . vision of the brotherhood of man . . ." Scraps of the lecture on St. Francis came floating round the partition wall.

"Don't let us spoil yours," he continued to Lucy. "Have you looked at those saints?"

"Yes," said Lucy. "They are lovely. Do you know which is the tombstone that is praised in Ruskin?"

He did not know, and suggested that they should try to guess it. George, rather to her relief, refused to move, and she and the old man wandered not unpleasantly about Santa Croce, which, though it is like a barn, has harvested many beautiful things inside its walls.   There were also beggars to avoid, and guides to dodge round the pillars, and an old lady with her dog, and here and there a priest modestly edging to his Mass through the groups of tourists.   But Mr. Emerson was only half interested.   He watched the lecturer, whose success he believed he had impaired, and then he anxiously watched his son.

"Why will he look at that fresco?" he said uneasily.   "I saw nothing in it."

"I like Giotto," she replied.   "It is so wonderful what they say about his tactile values.   Though I like things like the Della Robbia babies better."

"So you ought.   A baby is worth a dozen saints. And my baby's worth the whole of Paradise, and as far as I can see he lives in Hell."

Lucy again felt that this did not do.

"In Hell," he repeated.   "He's unhappy."

"Oh, dear!' said Lucy.

"How can he be unhappy when he is strong and alive?   What more is one to give him?   And think how he has been brought up—free from all the superstition and ignorance that lead men to hate one another in the name of God.   With such an education as that, I thought he was bound to grow up happy."

She was no theologian, but she felt that here

was a very foolish old man, as well as a very irreligious one. She also felt that her mother might not like her talking to that kind of person, and that Charlotte would object most strongly.

"What are we to do with him?" he asked. "He comes out for his holiday to Italy, and behaves—like that; like the little child who ought to have been playing, and who hurt himself upon the tombstone. Eh? What did you say?"

Lucy had made no suggestion. Suddenly he said:

"Now don't be stupid over this. I don't require you to fall in love with my boy, but I do think you might try and understand him. You are nearer his age, and if you let yourself go I am sure you are sensible. You might help me. He has known so few women, and you have the time. You stop here several weeks, I suppose? But let yourself go. You are inclined to get muddled, if I may judge from last night. Let yourself go. Pull out from the depths those thoughts that you do not understand, and spread them out in the sunlight and know the meaning of them. By understanding George you may learn to understand yourself. It will be good for both of you."

To this extraordinary speech Lucy found no answer.

"I only know what it is that's wrong with him; not why it is "

"And what is it?" asked Lucy fearfully, expecting some harrowing tale.

"The old trouble; things won't fit."

"What things?"

"The things of the universe. It is quite true. They don't."

"Oh, Mr. Emerson, whatever do you mean?"

In his ordinary voice, so that she scarcely realized he was quoting poetry, he said:

> " 'From far, from eve and morning,
> And yon twelve-winded sky,
> The stuff of life to knit me
> Blew hither: here am I.'

George and I both know this, but why does it distress him? We know that we come from the winds, and that we shall return to them; that all life is perhaps a knot, a tangle, a blemish in the eternal smoothness. But why should this make us unhappy? Let us rather love one another, and work and rejoice. I don't believe in this world sorrow."

Miss Honeychurch assented.

"Then make my boy think like us. Make him realize that by the side of the everlasting Why there is a Yes—a transitory Yes if you like, but a Yes."

Suddenly she laughed; surely one ought to laugh. A young man melancholy because the universe wouldn't fit, because life was a tangle or a wind, or a Yes, or something!

"I'm very sorry," she cried. "You'll think me unfeeling, but—but—" Then she became matronly. "Oh, but your son wants employment. Has he no particular hobby? Why, I myself have worries, but I can generally forget them at the piano; and collecting stamps did no end of good for my brother. Perhaps Italy bores him; you ought to try the Alps or the Lakes."

The old man's face saddened, and he touched her gently with his hand. This did not alarm her; she thought that her advice had impressed him and that he was thanking her for it. Indeed, he no longer alarmed her at all; she regarded him as a kind thing, but quite silly. Her feelings were as inflated spiritually as they had been an hour ago æsthetically, before she lost Baedeker. The dear George, now striding towards them over the tombstones, seemed both pitiable and absurd. He approached, his face in the shadow. He said:

"Miss Bartlett."

"Oh, good gracious me!" said Lucy, suddenly collapsing and again seeing the whole of life in a new perspective. "Where? Where?"

"In the nave."

"I see. Those gossiping little Miss Alans must have—" She checked herself.

"Poor girl!" exploded Mr. Emerson. "Poor girl!"

She could not let this pass, for it was just what she was feeling herself.

"Poor girl? I fail to understand the point of that remark. I think myself a very fortunate girl, I assure you. I'm thoroughly happy, and having a splendid time. Pray don't waste time mourning over *me*. There's enough sorrow in the world, isn't there, without trying to invent it. Good-bye. Thank you both so much for all your kindness. Ah, yes! there does come my cousin. A delightful morning! Santa Croce is a wonderful church."

She joined her cousin.

Chapter III: Music, Violets, and the Letter "S"

IT so happened that Lucy, who found daily life rather chaotic, entered a more solid world when she opened the piano. She was then no longer either deferential or patronizing; no longer either a rebel or a slave. The kingdom of music is not the kingdom of this world; it will accept those whom breeding and intellect and culture have alike rejected. The commonplace person begins to play, and shoots into the empyrean without effort, whilst we look up, marvelling how he has escaped us, and thinking how we could worship him and love him, would he but translate his visions into human words, and his experiences into human actions. Perhaps he cannot; certainly he does not, or does so very seldom. Lucy had done so never.

She was no dazzling *exécutante;* her runs were not at all like strings of pearls. and she struck no more right notes than was suitable for one of her age and situation. Nor was she the passionate young lady, who performs so tragically on a summer's evening with the window open. Passion was there, but it could not be easily labelled; it slipped between love and hatred and jealousy, and all the furniture of the pictorial style. And she was tragical only in the sense that she was great, for she loved to play on the side of Victory. Victory of what and over what—that is more than the words of daily life can tell us. But that some sonatas of Beethoven are written tragic no one can gainsay; yet they can triumph or despair as the player decides, and Lucy had decided that they should triumph.

A very wet afternoon at the Bertolini permitted her to do the thing she really liked, and after lunch she opened the little draped piano. A few people lingered round and praised her playing, but finding that she made no reply, dispersed to their rooms to write up their diaries or to sleep. She took no notice of Mr. Emerson looking for his son, nor of Miss Bartlett looking for Miss Lavish, nor of Miss Lavish looking for her cigarette-case. Like every true performer, she was intoxicated by the mere feel of the notes: they were fingers caressing her own; and by touch, not by sound alone, did she come to her desire.

Mr. Beebe, sitting unnoticed in the window, pondered over this illogical element in Miss Honeychurch, and recalled the occasion at Tunbridge Wells when he had discovered it. It was at one of those entertainments where the upper classes entertain the lower. The seats were filled with a respectful audience, and the ladies and gentlemen of the parish, under the auspices of their vicar, sang, or recited, or imitated the drawing of a champagne cork.

Among the promised items was "Miss Honeychurch. Piano. Beethoven," and Mr. Beebe was wondering whether it would be *Adelaida,* or the march of *The Ruins of Athens,* when his composure was disturbed by the opening bars of Opus III. He was in suspense all through the introduction, for not until the pace quickens does one know what the performer intends. With the roar of the opening theme he knew that things were going extraordinarily; in the chords that herald the conclusion he heard the hammer strokes of victory. He was glad that she only played the first movement, for he could have paid no attention to the winding intricacies of the measures of nine-sixteen. The audience clapped, no less respectful. It was Mr. Beebe who started the stamping; it was all that one could do.

"Who is she?" he asked the vicar afterwards.

"Cousin of one of my parishioners. I do not consider her choice of a piece happy. Beethoven is so usually simple and direct in his appeal that it is sheer perversity to choose a thing like that, which, if anything, disturbs."

"Introduce me."

"She will be delighted. She and Miss Bartlett are full of the praises of your sermon."

"My sermon?" cried Mr. Beebe. "Why ever did she listen to it?"

When he was introduced he understood why, for Miss Honeychurch, disjoined from her music-stool, was only a young lady with a quantity of dark hair and a very pretty, pale, undeveloped face. She loved going to concerts, she loved stopping with her cousin, she loved iced coffee and meringues. He did not doubt that she loved his sermon also. But before he left Tunbridge Wells he made a remark to the vicar, which he now made to Lucy herself when she closed the little piano and moved dreamily towards him:

"If Miss Honeychurch ever takes to live as she plays, it will be very exciting—both for us and for her."

Lucy at once re-entered daily life.

"Oh, what a funny thing! Some one said just the same to mother, and she said she trusted I should never live a duet."

"Doesn't Mrs. Honeychurch like music?"

"She doesn't mind it. But she doesn't like one to get excited over anything; she thinks I am silly about it. She thinks—I can't make out. Once, you know, I said that I liked my own playing better than any one's. She has never got over it. Of course, I didn't mean that I played well; I only meant—"

"Of course," said he, wondering why she bothered to explain.

"Music—" said Lucy, as if attempting some generality. She could not complete it, and looked out absently upon Italy in the wet. The whole life of the South was disorganized, and the most graceful nation in Europe had turned into formless lumps of clothes. The street and the river were dirty yellow, the bridge was dirty grey, and the hills were dirty purple. Somewhere in their folds were concealed Miss Lavish and Miss Bartlett, who had chosen this afternoon to visit the Torre del Gallo.

"What about music?" said Mr. Beebe.

"Poor Charlotte will be sopped," was Lucy's reply.

The expedition was typical of Miss Bartlett, who would return cold, tired, hungry, and angelic, with a ruined skirt, a pulpy Baedeker, and a tickling cough in her throat. On another day, when the whole world was singing and the air ran into the mouth like wine, she would refuse to stir from the drawing-room, saying that she was an old thing, and no fit companion for a hearty girl.

"Miss Lavish has led your cousin astray. She hopes to find the true Italy in the wet I believe."

"Miss Lavish is so original," murmured Lucy. This was a stock remark, the supreme achievement of the Pension Bertolini in the way of definition. Miss Lavish was so original. Mr. Beebe had his doubts, but they would have been put down to clerical narrowness. For that, and for other reasons, he held his peace.

"Is it true," continued Lucy in awe-struck tones, "that Miss Lavish is writing a book?"

"They do say so."

"What is it about?"

"It will be a novel," replied Mr. Beebe, "dealing with modern Italy. Let me refer you for an account to Miss Catharine Alan, who uses words herself more admirably than any one I know."

"I wish Miss Lavish would tell me herself. We started such friends. But I don't think she ought to have run away with Baedeker that morning in Santa Croce. Charlotte was most annoyed at finding me practically alone, and so I couldn't help being a little annoyed with Miss Lavish."

"The two ladies, at all events, have made it up."

He was interested in the sudden friendship between women so apparently dissimilar as Miss Bartlett and Miss Lavish. They were always in each other's company, with Lucy a slighted third. Miss Lavish he believed he understood, but Miss Bartlett might reveal unknown depths of strangeness, though not, perhaps, of meaning. Was Italy deflecting her from the path of prim chaperon, which he had assigned to her at Tunbridge Wells? All his life he had loved to study maiden ladies; they were his specialty, and his profession had provided him with ample opportunities for the work. Girls like Lucy were charming to look at, but Mr. Beebe was, from rather profound reasons, somewhat chilly in his attitude towards the other sex, and preferred to be interested rather than enthralled.

Lucy, for the third time, said that poor Charlotte would be sopped. The Arno was rising in flood, washing away the traces of the little carts upon the foreshore. But in the south-west there had appeared a dull haze of yellow, which might mean better weather if it did not mean worse. She opened the window to inspect, and a cold blast entered the room, drawing a plaintive cry from Miss Catharine Alan, who entered at the same moment by the door.

"Oh, dear Miss Honeychurch, you will catch a chill! And Mr. Beebe here besides. Who would suppose this is Italy? There is my sister actually nursing the hot-water can; no comforts or proper provisions."

She sidled towards them and sat down, self-conscious as she always was on entering a room which contained one man, or a man and one woman.

"I could hear your beautiful playing, Miss Honeychurch, though I was in my room with the door shut. Doors shut; indeed, most necessary. No one has the least idea of privacy in this country. And one person catches it from another."

Lucy answered suitably. Mr. Beebe was not able to tell the ladies of his adventure at Modena, where the chambermaid burst in upon him in his bath, exclaiming cheerfully, "Fa niente, sono vecchia." He contented himself with saying: "I quite agree with you, Miss Alan. The Italians are a most unpleasant people. They pry everywhere, they see everything, and they know what we want before we know it ourselves. We are at their mercy. They read our thoughts, they foretell our desires. From the cab-driver down to—to Giotto, they turn us inside out, and I resent it. Yet in their heart of hearts they are—how superficial! They have no conception of the intellectual life. How right is Signora Bertolini, who exclaimed to me the other day: 'Ho, Mr. Beebe, if you knew what I suffer over the children's edjucaishion! *Hi* won't 'ave my little Victorier taught by a hignorant Italian what can't explain nothink!' "

Miss Alan did not follow, but gathered that she was being mocked in an agreeable way. Her sister was a little disappointed in Mr. Beebe, having expected better things from a clergyman whose head was bald and who wore a pair of russet whiskers. Indeed, who would have supposed that tolerance, sympathy, and a sense of humour would inhabit that militant form?

In the midst of her satisfaction she continued to sidle, and at last the cause was disclosed. From the chair beneath her she extracted a gun-metal cigarette-case, on which were powdered in turquoise the initials "E. L."

"That belongs to Lavish," said the clergyman. "A good fellow, Lavish, but I wish she'd start a pipe."

"Oh, Mr. Beebe," said Miss Alan, divided between awe and mirth. "Indeed, though it is dreadful for her to smoke, it is not quite as dreadful as you suppose. She took to it, practically in despair, after her life's work was carried away in a landslip. Surely that makes it more excusable."

"What was that?" asked Lucy.

Mr. Beebe sat back complacently, and Miss Alan began as follows:

"It was a novel—and I am afraid, from what I can gather, not a very nice novel. It is so sad when people who have abilities misuse them, and I must say they nearly always do. Anyhow, she left it almost finished in the Grotto of the Calvary at the Capuccini Hotel at Amalfi while she went for a little ink. She said: 'Can I have a little ink, please?' But you know what Italians are, and meanwhile the Grotto fell roaring on to the beach, and the saddest thing of all is that she cannot remember what she has written. The poor thing was very ill after it, and so got tempted into cigarettes. It is a great secret, but I am glad to say that she is writing another novel. She told Teresa and Miss Pole the other day that she had got up all the local colour—this novel is to be about modern Italy; the other was historical—but that she could not start till she had an idea. First she tried Perugia for an inspiration, then she came here— this must on no account get round. And so cheerful through it all! I cannot help thinking that there is something to admire in every one, even if you do not approve of them."

Miss Alan was always thus being charitable against her better judgment. A delicate pathos perfumed her disconnected remarks, giving them unexpected beauty, just as in the decaying autumn woods there sometimes rise odours reminiscent of spring. She felt she had made almost too many allowances, and apologized hurriedly for her toleration.

"All the same, she is a little too—I hardly like to say unwomanly, but she behaved most strangely when the Emersons arrived."

Mr. Beebe smiled as Miss Alan plunged into an anecdote which he knew she would be unable to finish in the presence of a gentleman.

"I don't know, Miss Honeychurch, if you have noticed that Miss Pole, the lady who has so much yellow hair, takes lemonade. That old Mr. Emerson, who puts things very strangely—"

Her jaw dropped. She was silent. Mr. Beebe, whose social resources were endless, went out to order some tea, and she continued to Lucy in a hasty whisper:

"Stomach. He warned Miss Pole of her stomach—acidity, he called it—and he may have meant to be kind. I must say I forgot myself and laughed; is was so sudden. As Teresa truly said, it was no laughing matter. But the point is that Miss Lavish was positively *attracted* by his mentioning S., and said she liked plain speaking, and meeting different grades of thought. She thought they were commercial travellers—'drummers' was the word she used—and all through dinner she tried to prove that England, our great and beloved country, rests on nothing but commerce. Teresa was very much an-

noyed, and left the table before the cheese, saying
as she did so: 'There, Miss Lavish, is one who
can confute you better than I,' and pointed to that
beautiful picture of Lord Tennyson. Then Miss
Lavish said: 'Tut! The early Victorians.' Just
imagine! 'Tut! The early Victorians.' My sister had gone, and I felt bound to speak. I said:
'Miss Lavish, *I* am an early Victorian; at least, that
is to say, I will hear no breath of censure against our
dear Queen.' It was horrible speaking. I reminded her how the Queen had been to Ireland when
she did not want to go, and I must say she was
dumbfounded, and made no reply. But, unluckily,
Mr. Emerson overheard this part, and called in his
deep voice: 'Quite so, quite so! I honour the
woman for her Irish visit.' The woman! I tell
things so badly; but you see what a tangle we were
in by this time, all on account of S. having been
mentioned in the first place. But that was not all.
After dinner Miss Lavish actually came up and said:
'Miss Alan, I am going into the smoking-room to
talk to those two nice men. Come, too.' Need-
less to say, I refused such an unsuitable invitation,
and she had the impertinence to tell me that it
would broaden my ideas, and said that she had four
brothers, all University men, except one who was in
the army, who always made a point of talking to
commercial travellers."

"Let me finish the story," said Mr. Beebe, who
had returned. "Miss Lavish tried Miss Pole, my-

self, every one, and finally said: 'I shall go alone.'
She went. At the end of five minutes she returned
unobtrusively with a green baize board, and began
playing patience."

"Whatever happened?" cried Lucy.

"No one knows. No one will ever know. Miss
Lavish will never dare to tell, and Mr. Emerson
does not think it worth telling."

"Mr. Beebe—old Mr. Emerson, is he nice or not
nice? I do so want to know."

Mr. Beebe laughed and suggested that she should
settle the question for herself.

"No; but it is so difficult. Sometimes he is so
silly, and then I do not mind him. Miss Alan, what
do you think? Is he nice?"

The little old lady shook her head, and sighed
disapprovingly. Mr. Beebe, whom the conversation amused, stirred her up by saying:

"I consider that you are bound to class him as
nice, Miss Alan, after that business of the violets."

"Violets? Oh, dear! Who told you about the
violets? How do things get round? A pension is
a sad place for gossips. No, I cannot forget how
they behaved at Mr. Eager's lecture at Santa Croce.
Oh, poor Miss Honeychurch! It really was too
bad! No, I have quite changed. I do *not* like the
Emersons. They are not nice."

Mr. Beebe smiled nonchalantly. He had made
a gentle effort to introduce the Emersons into
Bertolini society, and the effort had failed. He was

almost the only person who remained friendly to them. Miss Lavish, who represented intellect, was avowedly hostile, and now the Miss Alans, who stood for good breeding, were following her. Miss Bartlett, smarting under an obligation, would scarcely be civil. The case of Lucy was different. She had given him a hazy account of her adventures in Santa Croce, and he gathered that the two men had made a curious and possibly concerted attempt to annex her, to show her the world from their own strange standpoint, to interest her in their private sorrows and joys. This was impertinent; he did not wish their cause to be championed by a young girl: he would rather it should fail. After all, he knew nothing about them, and pension joys, pension sorrows, are flimsy things; whereas Lucy would be his parishioner.

Lucy, with one eye upon the weather, finally said that she thought the Emersons were nice; not that she saw anything of them now. Even their seats at dinner had been moved.

"But aren't they always waylaying you to go out with them, dear?" said the little lady inquisitively.

"Only once. Charlotte didn't like it, and said something—quite politely, of course."

"Most right of her. They don't understand our ways. They must find their level."

Mr. Beebe rather felt that they had gone under. They had given up their attempt—if it was one—to conquer society, and now the father was almost as silent as the son. He wondered whether he would not plan a pleasant day for these folk before they left—some expedition, perhaps, with Lucy well chaperoned to be nice to them. It was one of Mr. Beebe's chief pleasures to provide people with happy memories.

Evening approached while they chatted; the air became brighter; the colours on the trees and hills were purified, and the Arno lost its muddy solidity and began to twinkle. There were a few streaks of bluish-green among the clouds, a few patches of watery light upon the earth, and then the dripping façade of San Miniato shone brilliantly in the declining sun.

"Too late to go out," said Miss Alan in a voice of relief. "All the galleries are shut."

"I think I shall go out," said Lucy. "I want to go round the town in the circular tram—on the platform by the driver."

Her two companions looked grave. Mr. Beebe, who felt responsible for her in the absence of Miss Bartlett, ventured to say:

"I wish we could. Unluckily I have letters. If you do want to go out alone, won't you be better on your feet?"

"Italians, dear, you know," said Miss Alan.

"Perhaps I shall meet some one who reads me through and through!"

But they still looked disapproval, and she so far conceded to Mr. Beebe as to say that she would only

go for a little walk, and keep to the street frequented by tourists.

"She oughtn't really to go at all," said Mr. Beebe,
as they watched her from the window, "and she
knows it. I put it down to too much Beethoven."

Chapter IV: Fourth Chapter

MR. BEEBE was right. Lucy never knew her desires so clearly as after music. She had not really appreciated the clergyman's wit, nor the suggestive twitterings of Miss Alan. Conversation was tedious; she wanted something big, and she believed that it would have come to her on the wind-swept platform of an electric tram.

This she might not attempt. It was unladylike. Why? Why were most big things unladylike? Charlotte had once explained to her why. It was not that ladies were inferior to men; it was that they were different. Their mission was to inspire others to achievement rather than to achieve themselves. Indirectly, by means of tact and a spotless name, a lady could accomplish much. But if she rushed into the fray herself she would be first censured, then despised, and finally ignored. Poems had been written to illustrate this point.

There is much that is immortal in this medieval lady. The dragons have gone, and so have the knights, but still she lingers in our midst. She reigned in many an early Victorian castle, and was Queen of much early Victorian song. It is sweet to protect her in the intervals of business, sweet to pay her honour when she has cooked our dinner well. But alas! the creature grows degenerate. In her heart also there are springing up strange desires. She too is enamoured of heavy winds, and vast panoramas, and green expanses of the sea. She has marked the kingdom of this world, how full it is of wealth, and beauty, and war—a radiant crust, built around the central fires, spinning towards the receding heavens. Men, declaring that she inspires them to it, move joyfully over the surface, having the most delightful meetings with other men, happy, not because they are masculine, but because they are alive. Before the show breaks up she would like to drop the august title of the Eternal Woman, and go there as her transitory self.

Lucy does not stand for the medieval lady, who was rather an ideal to which she was bidden to lift her eyes when feeling serious. Nor has she any system of revolt. Here and there a restriction annoyed her particularly, and she would transgress it, and perhaps be sorry that she had done so. This afternoon she was peculiarly restive. She would really like to do something of which her well-wishers disapproved. As she might not go on the electric tram, she went to Alinarl's shop.

There she bought a photograph of Botticelli's "Birth of Venus." Venus, being a pity, spoilt the picture, otherwise so charming, and Miss Bartlett had persuaded her to do without it. (A pity in art of course signified the nude.) Giorgione's "Tempestà," the "Idolino," some of the Sistine frescoes and the Apoxyomenos, were added to it. She felt a little calmer then, and bought Fra Angelico's "Coronation," Giotto's "Ascension of St. John," some Della Robbia babies, and some Guido Reni Madonnas. For her taste was catholic, and she extended uncritical approval to every well-known name.

But though she spent nearly seven lire, the gates of liberty seemed still unopened. She was conscious of her discontent; it was new to her to be conscious of it. "The world," she thought, "is certainly full of beautiful things, if only I could come across them." It was not surprising that Mrs. Honeychurch disapproved of music, declaring that it always left her daughter peevish, unpractical, and touchy.

"Nothing ever happens to me," she reflected, as she entered the Piazza Signoria and looked nonchalantly at its marvels, now fairly familiar to her. The great square was in shadow; the sunshine had come too late to strike it. Neptune was already unsubstantial in the twilight, half god, half ghost, and his fountain plashed dreamily to the men and satyrs who idled together on its marge. The Loggia showed as the triple entrance of a cave, wherein dwelt many a deity, shadowy, but immortal, looking forth upon the arrivals and departures of mankind. It was the hour of unreality—the hour, that is, when unfamiliar things are real. An older person at such an hour and in such a place might think that sufficient was happening to him, and rest content. Lucy desired more.

She fixed her eyes wistfully on the tower of the palace, which rose out of the lower darkness like a pillar of roughened gold. It seemed no longer a tower, no longer supported by earth, but some unattainable treasure throbbing in the tranquil sky. Its brightness mesmerized her, still dancing before her eyes when she bent them to the ground and started towards home.

Then something did happen.

Two Italians by the Loggia had been bickering about a debt. "Cinque lire," they had cried, "cinque lire!" They sparred at each other, and one of them was hit lightly upon the chest. He frowned; he bent towards Lucy with a look of interest, as if he had an important message for her. He opened his lips to deliver it, and a stream of red came out between them and trickled down his unshaven chin.

That was all. A crowd rose out of the dusk. It hid this extraordinary man from her, and bore him away to the fountain. Mr. George Emerson happened to be a few paces away, looking at her across the spot where the man had been. How very odd! Across something. Even as she caught sight of him he grew dim; the palace itself grew dim, swayed above her, fell on to her softly, slowly, noiselessly, and the sky fell with it.

She thought: "Oh, what have I done?"

"Oh, what have I done?" she murmured, and opened her eyes.

George Emerson still looked at her, but not across anything. She had complained of dullness, and lo! one man was stabbed, and another held her in his arms.

They were sitting on some steps in the Uffizi Arcade. He must have carried her. He rose when she spoke, and began to dust his knees. She repeated:

"Oh, what have I done?"

"You fainted."

"I—I am very sorry."

"How are you now?"

"Perfectly well—absolutely well." And she began to nod and smile.

"Then let us come home. There's no point in our stopping."

He held out his hand to pull her up. She pretended not to see it. The cries from the fountain— they had never ceased—rang emptily. The whole world seemed pale and void of its original meaning.

"How very kind you have been! I might have hurt myself falling. But now I am well. I can go alone, thank you."

His hand was still extended.

"Oh, my photographs!" she exclaimed suddenly.

"What photographs?"

"I bought some photographs at Alinari's. I must have dropped them out there in the square." She looked at him cautiously. "Would you add to your kindness by fetching them?"

He added to his kindness. As soon as he had turned his back, Lucy arose with the cunning of a maniac and stole down the arcade towards the Arno.

"Miss Honeychurch!"

She stopped with her hand on her heart.

"You sit still; you aren't fit to go home alone."

"Yes, I am, thank you so very much."

"No, you aren't. You'd go openly if you were."

"But I had rather—"

"Then I don't fetch your photographs."

"I had rather be alone."

He said imperiously: "The man is dead—the man is probably dead; sit down till you are rested." She was bewildered, and obeyed him. "And don't move till I come back."

In the distance she saw creatures with black hoods, such as appear in dreams. The palace tower had lost the reflection of the declining day, and joined itself to earth. How should she talk to Mr. Emerson when he returned from the shadowy square? Again the thought occurred to her, "Oh, what have I done?"—the thought that she, as well as the dying man, had crossed some spiritual boundary.

He returned, and she talked of the murder. Oddly enough, it was an easy topic. She spoke of the Italian character; she became almost garrulous over the incident that had made her faint five minutes before. Being strong physically, she soon overcame the horror of blood. She rose without his assistance, and though wings seemed to flutter inside her, she walked firmly enough towards the Arno. There a cabman signalled to them; they refused him.

"And the murderer tried to kiss him, you say —how very odd Italians are!—and gave himself up to the police! Mr. Beebe was saying that Italians know everything, but I think they are rather childish. When my cousin and I were at the Pitti yesterday— What was that?"

He had thrown something into the stream.

"What did you throw in?"

"Things I didn't want," he said crossly.

"Mr. Emerson!"

"Well?"

"Where are the photographs?"

He was silent.

"I believe it was my photographs that you threw away."

"I didn't know what to do with them," he cried, and his voice was that of an anxious boy. Her heart warmed towards him for the first time. "They were covered with blood. There! I'm glad I've told you; and all the time we were making conversation I was wondering what to do with them." He pointed down-stream. "They've gone." The river swirled under the bridge. "I did mind them so, and one is so foolish, it seemed better that they should go out to the sea—I don't know; I may just mean that they frightened me." Then the boy verged into a man. "For something tremendous has happened; I must face it without getting muddled. It isn't exactly that a man has died."

Something warned Lucy that she must stop him.

"It has happened," he repeated, "and I mean to find out what it is."

"Mr. Emerson—"

He turned towards her frowning, as if she had disturbed him in some abstract quest.

"I want to ask you something before we go in."

They were close to their pension. She stopped and leant her elbows against the parapet of the embankment. He did likewise. There is at times a magic in identity of position; it is one of the things that have suggested to us eternal comradeship. She moved her elbows before saying:

"I have behaved ridiculously."

He was following his own thoughts.

"I was never so much ashamed of myself in my life; I cannot think what came over me."

"I nearly fainted myself," he said; but she felt that her attitude repelled him.

"Well, I owe you a thousand apologies."

"Oh, all right."

"And—this is the real point—you know how silly people are gossiping—ladies especially, I am afraid—you understand what I mean?"

"I'm afraid I don't."

"I mean, would you not mention it to any one, my foolish behaviour?"

"Your behaviour? Oh, yes, all right—all right."

"Thank you so much. And would you—"

She could not carry her request any further. The river was rushing below them, almost black in the advancing night. He had thrown her photographs into it, and then he had told her the reason. It struck her that it was hopeless to look for chivalry in such a man. He would do her no harm by idle gossip; he was trustworthy, intelligent, and even kind; he might even have a high opinion of her. But he lacked chivalry; his thoughts, like his behaviour, would not be modified by awe. It was useless to say to him, "And would you—" and hope that he would complete the sentence for himself, averting his eyes from her nakedness like the knight in that beautiful picture. She had been in his arms, and he remembered it, just as he remembered the blood on the photographs that she had bought in Alinari's shop. It was not exactly that a man had died; something had happened to the living: they had come to a situation where character tells, and where Childhood enters upon the branching paths of Youth.

"Well, thank you so much," she repeated. "How quickly these accidents do happen, and then one returns to the old life!"

"I don't."

Anxiety moved her to question him.

His answer was puzzling: "I shall probably want to live."

"But why, Mr. Emerson? What do you mean?"

"I shall want to live, I say."

Leaning her elbows on the parapet, she contemplated the River Arno, whose roar was suggesting some unexpected melody to her ears.

Chapter V: Possibilities of a Pleasant Outing

IT was a family saying that "you never knew which way Charlotte Bartlett would turn." She was perfectly pleasant and sensible over Lucy's adventure, found the abridged account of it quite adequate, and paid suitable tribute to the courtesy of Mr. George Emerson. She and Miss Lavish had had an adventure also. They had been stopped at the Dazio coming back, and the young officials there, who seemed impudent and *désœuvré*, had tried to search their reticules for provisions. It might have been most unpleasant. Fortunately Miss Lavish was a match for any one.

For good or for evil, Lucy was left to face her problem alone. None of her friends had seen her, either in the Piazza or, later on, by the embankment. Mr. Beebe, indeed, noticing her startled eyes at dinner-time, had again passed to himself the remark of "Too much Beethoven." But he only supposed that she was ready for an adventure, not that she had encountered it. This solitude oppressed her; she was accustomed to have her thoughts confirmed by others or, at all events, contradicted; it was too dreadful not to know whether she was thinking right or wrong.

At breakfast next morning she took decisive action. There were two plans between which she had to choose. Mr. Beebe was walking up to the Torre del Gallo with the Emersons and some American ladies. Would Miss Bartlett and Miss Honeychurch join the party? Charlotte declined for herself; she had been there in the rain the previous afternoon. But she thought it an admirable idea for Lucy, who hated shopping, changing money, fetching letters, and other irksome duties—all of which Miss Bartlett must accomplish this morning and could easily accomplish alone.

"No, Charlotte!" cried the girl, with real warmth. "It's very kind of Mr. Beebe, but I am certainly coming with you. I had much rather."

"Very well, dear," said Miss Bartlett, with a faint flush of pleasure that called forth a deep flush of shame on the cheeks of Lucy. How abominably she behaved to Charlotte, now as always! But now she should alter. All morning she would be really nice to her.

She slipped her arm into her cousin's, and they started off along the Lung' Arno. The river was a lion that morning in strength, voice, and colour. Miss Bartlett insisted on leaning over the parapet to look at it. She then made her usual remark, which was:

"How I do wish Freddy and your mother could see this, too!"

Lucy fidgeted; it was tiresome of Charlotte to have stopped exactly where she did.

"Look, Lucia! Oh, you are watching for the Torre del Gallo party. I feared you would repent you of your choice."

Serious as the choice had been, Lucy did not repent. Yesterday had been a muddle—queer and odd, the kind of thing one could not write down easily on paper—but she had a feeling that Charlotte and her shopping were preferable to George Emerson and the summit of the Torre del Gallo. Since she could not unravel the tangle, she must take care not to re-enter it. She could protest sincerely against Miss Bartlett's insinuations.

But though she had avoided the chief actor, the scenery unfortunately remained. Charlotte, with the complacency of fate, led her from the river to the Piazza Signoria. She could not have believed that stones, a Loggia, a fountain, a palace tower, would have such significance. For a moment she understood the nature of ghosts.

The exact site of the murder was occupied, not by a ghost, but by Miss Lavish, who had the morning newspaper in her hand. She hailed them briskly. The dreadful catastrophe of the previous day had given her an idea which she thought would work up into a book.

"Oh, let me congratulate you!" said Miss Bartlett. "After your despair of yesterday! What a fortunate thing!"

"Aha! Miss Honeychurch, come you here! I am in luck. Now, you are to tell me absolutely everything that you saw from the beginning."

Lucy poked at the ground with her parasol.

"But perhaps you would rather not?"

"I'm sorry—if you could manage without it, I think I would rather not."

The elder ladies exchanged glances, not of disapproval; it is suitable that a girl should feel deeply.

"It is I who am sorry," said Miss Lavish. "We literary hacks are shameless creatures. I believe there's no secret of the human heart into which we wouldn't pry."

She marched cheerfully to the fountain and back, and did a few calculations in realism. Then she said that she had been in the Piazza since eight o'clock collecting material. A good deal of it was unsuitable, but of course one always had to adapt. The two men had quarrelled over a five-franc note. For the five-franc note she should substitute a young lady, which would raise the tone of the tragedy, and at the same time furnish an excellent plot.

"What is the heroine's name?" asked Miss Bartlett.

"Leonora," said Miss Lavish; her own name was Eleanor.

"I do hope she's nice."

That desideratum would not be omitted.

"And what is the plot?"

Love, murder, abduction, revenge, was the plot. Out it all came while the fountain plashed to the satyrs in the morning sun.

"I hope you will excuse me for boring on like this," Miss Lavish concluded. "It is so tempting to talk to really sympathetic people. Of course, this is the barest outline. There will be a deal of local colouring, descriptions of Florence and the neighbourhood, and I shall also introduce some humorous characters. And let me give you all fair warning: I intend to be unmerciful to the British tourist."

"Oh, you wicked woman," cried Miss Bartlett. "I am sure you are thinking of the Emersons."

Miss Lavish gave a Machiavellian smile.

"I confess that in Italy my sympathies are not with my own countrymen. It is the neglected Italians who attract me, and whose lives I am going to paint so far as I can. For I repeat and I insist, and I have always held most strongly, that a tragedy such as yesterday's is not the less tragic because it happened in humble life."

There was a fitting silence when Miss Lavish had concluded. Then the cousins wished success to her labours, and walked slowly away across the square.

"She is my idea of a really clever woman," said Miss Bartlett. "That last remark struck me as so particularly true. It should be a most pathetic novel."

Lucy assented. At present her great aim was not to get put into it. Her perceptions this morning were curiously keen, and she believed that Miss Lavish had her on trial for an *ingénue*.

"She is emancipated, but only in the very best sense of the word," continued Miss Bartlett slowly. "None but the superficial would be shocked at her. We had a long talk yesterday. She believes in justice and truth and human interest. She told me also that she has a high opinion of the destiny of woman— Mr. Eager! Why, how nice! What a pleasant surprise!"

"Ah, not for me," said the chaplain blandly, "for I have been watching you and Miss Honeychurch for quite a little time."

"We were chatting to Miss Lavish."

His brow contracted.

"So I saw. Were you indeed? Andate via! sono occupato!" The last remark was made to a vender of panoramic photographs who was approaching with a courteous smile. "I am about to venture a suggestion. Would you and Miss Honeychurch be disposed to join me in a drive some day this week—a drive in the hills? We might go up by Fiesole and back by Settignano. There is a point on that road where we could get down and have an hour's ramble on the hillside. The view thence of Florence is most beautiful—far better than the hackneyed view of Fiesole. It is the view that Alessio Baldovinetti is fond of introducing in-

to his pictures. That man had a decided feeling
for landscape. Decidedly. But who looks at it
to-day? Ah, the world is too much for us."

Miss Bartlett had not heard of Alessio Baldovinetti, but she knew that Mr. Eager was no commonplace chaplain. He was a member of the residential colony who had made Florence their home.
He knew the people who never walked about with
Baedekers, who had learnt to take a siesta after
lunch, who took drives the pension tourists had
never heard of, and saw by private influence galleries which were closed to them. Living in delicate
seclusion, some in furnished flats, others in Renaissance villas on Fiesole's slope, they read, wrote,
studied, and exchanged ideas, thus attaining to that
intimate knowledge, or rather perception, of
Florence which is denied to all who carry in their
pockets the coupons of Cook.

Therefore an invitation from the chaplain was
something to be proud of. Between the two sections of his flock he was often the only link, and
it was his avowed custom to select those of his
migratory sheep who seemed worthy, and give them
a few hours in the pastures of the permanent. Tea
at a Renaissance villa? Nothing had been said
about it yet. But if it did come to that—how Lucy
would enjoy it!

A few days ago and Lucy would have felt the
same. But the joys of life were grouping themselves anew. A drive in the hills with Mr. Eager

and Miss Bartlett—even if culminating in a residential tea-party—was no longer the greatest of them. She echoed the raptures of Charlotte somewhat faintly. Only when she heard that Mr. Beebe was also coming did her thanks become more sincere.

"So we shall be a *partie carrée,*" said the chaplain. "In these days of toil and tumult one has great needs of the country and its message of purity. Andate via! andate presto, presto! Ah, the town! Beautiful as it is, it is the town."

They assented.

"This very square—so I am told—witnessed yesterday the most sordid of tragedies. To one who loves the Florence of Dante and Savonarola there is something portentous in such desecration —portentous and humiliating."

"Humiliating indeed," said Miss Bartlett. "Miss Honeychurch happened to be passing through as it happened. She can hardly bear to speak of it." She glanced at Lucy proudly.

"And how came we to have you here?" asked the chaplain paternally.

Miss Bartlett's recent liberalism oozed away at the question.

"Do not blame her, please, Mr. Eager. The fault is mine: I left her unchaperoned."

"So you were here alone, Miss Honeychurch?" His voice suggested sympathetic reproof but at the same time indicated that a few harrowing details would not be unacceptable. His dark, handsome face drooped mournfully towards her to catch her reply.

"Practically."

"One of our pension acquaintances kindly brought her home," said Miss Bartlett, adroitly concealing the sex of the preserver.

"For her also it must have been a terrible experience. I trust that neither of you was at all—that it was not in your immediate proximity."

Of the many things Lucy was noticing to-day, not the least remarkable was this: the ghoulish fashion in which respectable people will nibble after blood. George Emerson had kept the subject strangely pure.

"He died by the fountain, I believe," was her reply.

"And you and your friend——"

"Were over at the Loggia."

"That must have saved you much. You have not, of course, seen the disgraceful illustrations which the gutter Press— This man is a public nuisance; he knows that I am a resident perfectly well, and yet he goes on worrying me to buy his vulgar views."

Surely the vendor of photographs was in league with Lucy—in the eternal league of Italy with youth. He had suddenly extended his book before Miss Bartlett and Mr. Eager, binding their hands together by a long glossy ribbon of churches, pictures, and views.

"This is too much!" cried the chaplain, striking petulantly at one of Fra Angelico's angels. She tore. A shrill cry rose from the vendor. The book it seemed, was more valuable than one would have supposed.

"Willingly would I purchase—" began Miss Bartlett.

"Ignore him," said Mr. Eager sharply, and they all walked rapidly away from the square.

But an Italian can never be ignored, least of all when he has a grievance. His mysterious persecution of Mr. Eager became relentless; the air rang with his threats and lamentations. He appealed to Lucy; would not she intercede? He was poor—he sheltered a family—the tax on bread. He waited, he gibbered, he was recompensed, he was dissatisfied, he did not leave them until he had swept their minds clean of all thoughts whether pleasant or unpleasant.

Shopping was the topic that now ensued. Under the chaplain's guidance they selected many hideous presents and mementoes—florid little picture-frames that seemed fashioned in gilded pastry; other little frames, more severe, that stood on little easels, and were carven out of oak; a blotting book of vellum; a Dante of the same material; cheap mosaic brooches, which the maids, next Christmas, would never tell from real; pins, pots, heraldic saucers, brown art-photographs; Eros and Psyche in alabaster; St. Peter to match—all of which would have cost less in London.

This successful morning left no pleasant impressions on Lucy. She had been a little frightened, both by Miss Lavish and by Mr. Eager, she knew not why. And as they frightened her, she had, strangely enough, ceased to respect them. She doubted that Miss Lavish was a great artist. She doubted that Mr. Eager was as full of spirituality and culture as she had been led to suppose. They were tried by some new test, and they were found wanting. As for Charlotte—as for Charlotte she was exactly the same. It might be possible to be nice to her; it was impossible to love her.

"The son of a labourer; I happen to know it for a fact. A mechanic of some sort himself when he was young; then he took to writing for the Socialistic Press. I came across him at Brixton."

They were talking about the Emersons.

"How wonderfully people rise in these days!" sighed Miss Bartlett, fingering a model of the leaning Tower of Pisa.

"Generally," replied Mr. Eager, "one has only sympathy for their success. The desire for education and for social advance—in these things there is something not wholly vile. There are some working men whom one would be very willing to see out here in Florence—little as they would make of it."

"Is he a journalist now?" Miss Bartlett asked.

"He is not; he made an advantageous marriage."

He uttered this remark with a voice full of meaning, and ended with a sigh.

"Oh, so he has a wife."

"Dead, Miss Bartlett, dead. I wonder—yes, I wonder how he has the effrontery to look me in the face, to dare to claim acquaintance with me. He was in my London parish long ago. The other day in Santa Croce, when he was with Miss Honeychurch, I snubbed him. Let him beware that he does not get more that a snub."

"What?" cried Lucy, flushing.

"Exposure!" hissed Mr. Eager.

He tried to change the subject; but in scoring a dramatic point he had interested his audience more than he had intended. Miss Bartlett was full of very natural curiosity. Lucy, though she wished never to see the Emersons again, was not disposed to condemn them on a single word.

"Do you mean," she asked, "that he is an irreligious man? We know that already."

"Lucy, dear—" said Miss Bartlett, gently reproving her cousin's penetration.

"I should be astonished if you knew all. The boy—an innocent child at the time—I will exclude. God knows what his education and his inherited qualities may have made him."

"Perhaps," said Miss Bartlett, "it is something that we had better not hear."

Possibilities of a Pleasant Outing

"To speak plainly," said Mr. Eager, "it is. I will say no more."

For the first time Lucy's rebellious thoughts swept out in words—for the first time in her life.

"You have said very little."

"It was my intention to say very little," was his frigid reply.

He gazed indignantly at the girl, who met him with equal indignation. She turned towards him from the shop counter; her breast heaved quickly. He observed her brow, and the sudden strength of her lips. It was intolerable that she should disbelieve him.

"Murder, if you want to know," he cried angrily. "That man murdered his wife!"

"How?" she retorted.

"To all intents and purposes he murdered her. That day in Santa Croce—did they say anything against me?"

"Not a word, Mr. Eager—not a single word."

"Oh, I thought they had been libelling me to you. But I suppose it is only their personal charms that makes you defend them."

"I'm not defending them," said Lucy, losing her courage, and relapsing into the old chaotic methods. "They're nothing to me."

"How could you think she was defending them?" said Miss Bartlett, much discomfited by the unpleasant scene. The shopman was possibly listening.

"She will find it difficult. For that man has murdered his wife in the sight of God."

The addition of God was striking. But the chaplain was really trying to qualify a rash remark. A silence followed which might have been impressive, but was merely awkward. Then Miss Bartlett hastily purchased the Leaning Tower, and led the way into the street.

"I must be going," said he, shutting his eyes and taking out his watch.

Miss Bartlett thanked him for his kindness, and spoke with enthusiasm of the approaching drive.

"Drive? Oh, is our drive to come off?"

Lucy was recalled to her manners, and after a little exertion the complacency of Mr. Eager was restored.

"Bother the drive!" exclaimed the girl, as soon as he had departed. "It is just the drive we had arranged with Mr. Beebe without any fuss at all. Why should he invite us in that absurd manner? We might as well invite him. We are each paying for ourselves."

Miss Bartlett, who had intended to lament over the Emersons, was launched by this remark into unexpected thoughts.

"If that is so, dear—if the drive we and Mr. Beebe are going with Mr. Eager is really the same as the one we are going with Mr. Beebe, then I foresee a sad kettle of fish."

"How?"

Possibilities of a Pleasant Outing

"Because Mr. Beebe has asked Eleanor Lavish to come, too."

"That will mean another carriage."

"Far worse. Mr. Eager does not like Eleanor. She knows it herself. The truth must be told; she is too unconventional for him."

They were now in the newspaper-room at the English bank. Lucy stood by the central table, heedless of Punch and the Graphic, trying to answer, or at all events to formulate the questions rioting in her brain. The well-known world had broken up, and there emerged Florence, a magic city where people thought and did the most extraordinary things. Murder, accusations of murder, a lady clinging to one man and being rude to another—were these the daily incidents of her streets? Was there more in her frank beauty than met the eye—the power, perhaps, to evoke passions, good and bad, and to bring them speedily to a fulfillment?

Happy Charlotte, who, though greatly troubled over things that did not matter, seemed oblivious to things that did; who could conjecture with admirable delicacy "where things might lead to," but apparently lost sight of the goal as she approached it! Now she was crouching in the corner trying to extract a circular note from a kind of linen nose-bag which hung in chaste concealment round her neck. She had been told that this was the only safe way to carry money in Italy; it must only be broached within the walls of the English bank. As she groped she murmured: "Whether it is Mr. Beebe who forgot to tell Mr. Eager, or Mr. Eager who forgot when he told us, or whether they have decided to leave Eleanor out altogether—which they could scarcely do—but in any case we must be prepared. It is you they really want; I am only asked for appearances. You shall go with the two gentlemen, and I and Eleanor will follow behind. A one-horse carriage would do for us. Yet how difficult it is!"

"It is indeed," replied the girl, with a gravity that sounded sympathetic.

"What do you think about it?" asked Miss Bartlett, flushed from the struggle, and buttoning up her dress.

"I don't know what I think, nor what I want."

"Oh, dear, Lucy! I do hope Florence isn't boring you. Speak the word, and, as you know, I would take you to the ends of the earth to-morrow."

"Thank you, Charlotte," said Lucy, and pondered over the offer.

There were letters for her at the bureau—one from her brother, full of athletics and biology; one from her mother, delightful as only her mother's letters could be. She had read in it of the crocuses which had been bought for yellow and were coming up puce, of the new parlour-maid, who had watered the ferns with essence of lemonade, of the semi-detached cottages which were ruining Summer Street, and breaking the heart of Sir Harry Otway.

Possibilities of a Pleasant Outing

She recalled the free, pleasant life of her home, where she was allowed to do everything, and where nothing ever happened to her. The road up through the pine-woods, the clean drawing-room, the view over the Sussex Weald—all hung before her bright and distinct, but pathetic as the pictures in a gallery to which, after much experience, a traveller returns.

"And the news?" asked Miss Bartlett.

"Mrs. Vyse and her son have gone to Rome," said Lucy, giving the news that interested her least. "Do you know the Vyses?"

"Oh, not that way back. We can never have too much of the dear Piazza Signoria."

"They're nice people, the Vyses. So clever —my idea of what's really clever. Don't you long to be in Rome?"

"I die for it!"

The Piazza Signoria is too stony to be brilliant. It has no grass, no flowers, no frescoes, no glittering walls of marble or comforting patches of ruddy brick. By an odd chance—unless we believe in a presiding genius of places—the statues that relieve its severity suggest, not the innocence of childhood, nor the glorious bewilderment of youth, but the conscious achievements of maturity. Perseus and Judith, Hercules and Thusnelda, they have done or suffered something, and though they are immortal, immortality has come to them after experience, not before. Here, not only in the solitude of Nature, might a hero meet a goddess, or a heroine a god.

"Charlotte!" cried the girl suddenly. "Here's an idea. What if we popped off to Rome to-morrow—straight—to the Vyses' hotel? For I do know what I want. I'm sick of Florence. Now, you said you'd go to the ends of the earth! Do! Do!"

Miss Bartlett, with equal vivacity, replied:

"Oh, you droll person! Pray, what would become of your drive in the hills?"

They passed together through the gaunt beauty of the square, laughing over the unpractical suggestion.

Chapter VI: The Reverend Arthur Beebe, the Reverend Cuthbert Eager, Mr. Emerson, Mr. George Emerson, Miss Eleanor Lavish, Miss Charlotte Bartlett, and Miss Lucy Honeychurch Drive Out in Carriages to See a View; Italians Drive Them.

IT was Phaethon who drove them to Fiesole that memorable day, a youth all irresponsibility and fire, recklessly urging his master's horses up the stony hill. Mr. Beebe recognized him at once. Neither the Ages of Faith nor the Age of Doubt had touched him; he was Phaethon in Tuscany driving a cab. And it was Persephone whom he asked leave to pick up on the way, saying that she was his sister—Persephone, tall and slender and pale, returning with the Spring to her mother's cottage, and still shading her eyes from the unaccustomed light. To her Mr. Eager objected, saying that here was the thin edge of the wedge, and one must guard against imposition. But the ladies interceded, and when it had been made clear that it was a very great favour, the goddess was allowed to mount beside the god.

Phaethon at once slipped the left rein over her

head, thus enabling himself to drive with his arm round her waist. She did not mind. Mr. Eager, who sat with his back to the horses, saw nothing of the indecorous proceeding, and continued his conversation with Lucy. The other two occupants of the carriage were old Mr. Emerson and Miss Lavish. For a dreadful thing had happened: Mr. Beebe, without consulting Mr. Eager, had doubled the size of the party. And though Miss Bartlett and Miss Lavish had planned all the morning how the people were to sit, at the critical moment when the carriages came round they lost their heads, and Miss Lavish got in with Lucy, while Miss Bartlett, with George Emerson and Mr. Beebe, followed on behind.

It was hard on the poor chaplain to have his *partie carrée* thus transformed. Tea at a Renaissance villa, if he had ever meditated it, was now impossible. Lucy and Miss Bartlett had a certain style about them, and Mr. Beebe, though unreliable, was a man of parts. But a shoddy lady writer and a journalist who had murdered his wife in the sight of God—they should enter no villa at his introduction.

Lucy, elegantly dressed in white, sat erect and nervous amid these explosive ingredients, attentive to Mr. Eager, repressive towards Miss Lavish, watchful of old Mr. Emerson, hitherto fortunately asleep, thanks to a heavy lunch and the drowsy atmosphere of Spring. She looked on the expedition as the work of Fate. But for it she would have avoided George Emerson successfully. In an open manner he had shown that he wished to continue their intimacy. She had refused, not because she disliked him, but because she did not know what had happened, and suspected that he did know. And this frightened her.

For the real event—whatever it was—had taken place, not in the Loggia, but by the river. To behave wildly at the sight of death is pardonable. But to discuss it afterwards, to pass from discussion into silence, and through silence into sympathy, that is an error, not of a startled emotion, but of the whole fabric. There was really something blameworthy (she thought) in their joint contemplation of the shadowy stream, in the common impulse which had turned them to the house without the passing of a look or word. This sense of wickedness had been slight at first. She had nearly joined the party to the Torre del Gallo. But each time that she avoided George it became more imperative that she should avoid him again. And now celestial irony, working through her cousin and two clergymen, did not suffer her to leave Florence till she had made this expedition with him through the hills.

Meanwhile Mr. Eager held her in civil converse; their little tiff was over.

"So, Miss Honeychurch, you are travelling? As a student of art?"

"Oh, dear me, no—oh, no!"

"Perhaps as a student of human nature," interposed Miss Lavish, "like myself?"

"Oh, no. I am here as a tourist."

"Oh, indeed," said Mr. Eager. "Are you indeed? If you will not think me rude, we residents sometimes pity you poor tourists not a little —handed about like a parcel of goods from Venice to Florence, from Florence to Rome, living herded together in pensions or hotels, quite unconscious of anything that is outside Baedeker, their one anxiety to get 'done' or 'through' and go on somewhere else. The result is, they mix up towns, rivers, palaces in one inextricable whirl. You know the American girl in *Punch* who says: 'Say, poppa, what did we see at Rome?' And the father replies: 'Why, guess Rome was the place where we saw the yaller dog.' There's travelling for you. Ha! ha! ha!"

"I quite agree," said Miss Lavish, who had several times tried to interrupt his mordant wit. "The narrowness and superficiality of the Anglo-Saxon tourist is nothing less than a menace."

"Quite so. Now, the English colony at Florence, Miss Honeychurch—and it is of considerable size, though, of course, not all equally—a few are here for trade, for example. But the greater part are students. Lady Helen Laverstock is at present busy over Fra Angelico. I mention her name because we are passing her villa on the left.

No, you can only see it if you stand—no, do not stand; you will fall. She is very proud of that thick hedge. Inside, perfect seclusion. One might have gone back six hundred years. Some critics believe that her garden was the scene of *The Decameron,* which lends it an additional interest, does it not?"

"It does indeed!" cried Miss Lavish. "Tell me, where do they place the scene of that wonderful seventh day?"

But Mr. Eager proceeded to tell Miss Honeychurch that on the right lived Mr. Someone Something, an American of the best type—so rare!—and that the Somebody Elses were farther down the hill. "Doubtless you know her monographs in the series of 'Mediæval Byways'? He is working at *Gemistus Pletho.* Sometimes as I take tea in their beautiful grounds I hear, over the wall, the electric tram squealing up the new road with its loads of hot, dusty, unintelligent tourists who are going to 'do' Fiesole in an hour in order that they may say they have been there, and I think—I think—I think how little they think what lies so near them."

During this speech the two figures on the box were sporting with each other disgracefully. Lucy had a spasm of envy. Granted that they wished to misbehave, it was pleasant for them to be able to do so. They were probably the only people enjoying the expedition. The carriage

swept with agonizing jolts up through the Piazza
of Fiesole and into the Settignano road.

"Piano! piano!" said Mr. Eager, elegantly
waving his hand over his head.

"Va bene, signore, va bene, va bene," crooned
the driver, and whipped his horses up again.

Now Mr. Eager and Miss Lavish began to talk
against each other on the subject of Alessio Baldovinetti. Was he a cause of the Renaissance, or
was he one of its manifestations? The other
carriage was left behind. As the pace increased
to a gallop the large, slumbering form of Mr.
Emerson was thrown against the chaplain with the
regularity of a machine.

"Piano! piano!" said he, with a martyred look
at Lucy.

An extra lurch made him turn angrily in his seat.
Phaethon, who for some time had been endeavouring to kiss Persephone, had just succeeded.

A little scene ensued, which, as Miss Bartlett
said afterwards, was most unpleasant. The horses
were stopped, the lovers were ordered to disentangle
themselves, the boy was to lose his *pourboire*, the
girl was immediately to get down.

"She is my sister," said he, turning round on
them with piteous eyes.

Mr. Eager took the trouble to tell him that he
was a liar. Phaethon hung down his head, not
at the matter of the accusation, but at its manner.
At this point Mr. Emerson, whom the shock of

stopping had awoke, declared that the lovers must on no account be separated, and patted them on the back to signify his approval. And Miss Lavish, though unwilling to ally him, felt bound to support the cause of Bohemianism.

"Most certainly I would let them be," she cried. "But I dare say I shall receive scant support. I have always flown in the face of the conventions all my life. This is what *I* call an adventure."

"We must not submit," said Mr. Eager. "I knew he was trying it on. He is treating us as if we were a party of Cook's tourists."

"Surely no!" said Miss Lavish, her ardour visibly decreasing.

The other carriage had drawn up behind, and sensible Mr. Beebe called out that after this warning the couple would be sure to behave themselves properly.

"Leave them alone," Mr. Emerson begged the chaplain, of whom he stood in no awe. "Do we find happiness so often that we should turn it off the box when it happens to sit there? To be driven by lovers— A king might envy us, and if we part them it's more like sacrilege than anything I know."

Here the voice of Miss Bartlett was heard saying that a crowd had begun to collect.

Mr. Eager, who suffered from an over-fluent tongue rather than a resolute will, was determined to make himself heard. He addressed the driver again. Italian in the mouth of Italians is a deep-voiced stream, with unexpected cataracts and boulders to preserve it from monotony. In Mr. Eager's mouth it resembled nothing so much as an acid whistling fountain which played ever higher and higher, and quicker and quicker, and more and more shrilly, till abruptly it was turned off with a click.

"Signorina!" said the man to Lucy, when the display had ceased. Why should he appeal to Lucy?

"Signorina!" echoed Persephone in her glorious contralto. She pointed at the other carriage. Why?

For a moment the two girls looked at each other. Then Persephone got down from the box.

"Victory at last!" said Mr. Eager, smiting his hands together as the carriages started again.

"It is not victory," said Mr. Emerson. "It is defeat. You have parted two people who were happy."

Mr. Eager shut his eyes. He was obliged to sit next to Mr. Emerson, but he would not speak to him. The old man was refreshed by sleep, and took up the matter warmly. He commanded Lucy to agree with him; he shouted for support to his son.

"We have tried to buy what cannot be bought with money. He has bargained to drive us, and he is doing it. We have no rights over his soul."

Miss Lavish frowned. It is hard when a person you have classed as typically British speaks out of his character.

"He was not driving us well," she said. "He jolted us."

"That I deny. It was as restful as sleeping. Aha! he is jolting us now. Can you wonder? He would like to throw us out, and most certainly he is justified. And if I were superstitious I'd be frightened of the girl, too. It doesn't do to injure young people. Have you ever heard of Lorenzo de Medici?"

Miss Lavish bristled.

"Most certainly I have. Do you refer to Lorenzo il Magnifico, or to Lorenzo, Duke of Urbino, or to Lorenzo surnamed Lorenzino on account of his diminutive stature?"

"The Lord knows. Possibly he does know, for I refer to Lorenzo the poet. He wrote a line—so I heard yesterday—which runs like this: 'Don't go fighting against the Spring.'"

Mr. Eager could not resist the opportunity for erudition.

"Non fate guerra al Maggio," he murmured. "'War not with the May' would render a correct meaning."

"The point is, we have warred with it. Look." He pointed to the Val d' Arno, which was visible far below them, through the budding trees. "Fifty miles of Spring, and we've come up to admire them. Do you suppose there's any difference between Spring in nature and Spring in man? But there we go, praising the one and condemning the other as improper, ashamed that the same laws work eternally through both."

No one encouraged him to talk. Presently Mr. Eager gave a signal for the carriages to stop, and marshalled the party for their ramble on the hill. A hollow like a great amphitheatre, full of terraced steps and misty olives, now lay between them and the heights of Fiesole, and the road, still following its curve, was about to sweep on to a promontory which stood out in the plain. It was this promontory, uncultivated, wet, covered with bushes and occasional trees, which had caught the fancy of Alessio Baldovinetti nearly five hundred years before. He had ascended it, that diligent and rather obscure master, possibly with an eye to business, possibly for the joy of ascending. Standing there, he had seen that view of the Val d' Arno and distant Florence, which he afterwards had introduced not very effectively into his work. But where exactly had he stood? That was the question which Mr. Eager hoped to solve now. And Miss Lavish, whose nature was attracted by anything problematical, had become equally enthusiastic.

But it is not easy to carry the pictures of Alessio Baldovinetti in your head, even if you have remembered to look at them before starting. And the haze in the valley increased the difficulty of the quest. The party sprang about from tuft to tuft of grass, their anxiety to keep together being only equalled by their desire to go different directions. Finally they split into groups. Lucy clung to Miss Bartlett and Miss Lavish; the Emersons returned to hold laborious converse with the drivers; while the two clergymen, who were expected to have topics in common, were left to each other.

The two elder ladies soon threw off the mask. In the audible whisper that was now so familiar to Lucy they began to discuss, not Alessio Baldovinetti, but the drive. Miss Bartlett had asked Mr. George Emerson what his profession was, and he had answered "the railway." She was very sorry that she had asked him. She had no idea that it would be such a dreadful answer, or she would not have asked him. Mr. Beebe had turned the conversation so cleverly, and she hoped that the young man was not very much hurt at her asking him.

"The railway!" gasped Miss Lavish. "Oh, but I shall die! Of course it was the railway!" She could not control her mirth. "He is the image of a porter—on, on the South-Eastern."

"Eleanor, be quiet," plucking at her vivacious companion. "Hush! They'll hear—the Emersons—"

"I can't stop. Let me go my wicked way. A porter—"

"Eleanor!"

"I'm sure it's all right," put in Lucy. "The

Emersons won't hear, and they wouldn't mind if they did."

Miss Lavish did not seem pleased at this.

"Miss Honeychurch listening!" she said rather crossly. "Pouf! wouf! You naughty girl! Go away!"

"Oh, Lucy, you ought to be with Mr. Eager, I'm sure."

"I can't find them now, and I don't want to either."

"Mr. Eager will be offended. It is your party."

"Please, I'd rather stop here with you."

"No, I agree," said Miss Lavish. "It's like a school feast; the boys have got separated from the girls. Miss Lucy, you are to go. We wish to converse on high topics unsuited for your ear."

The girl was stubborn. As her time at Florence drew to its close she was only at ease amongst those to whom she felt indifferent. Such a one was Miss Lavish, and such for the moment was Charlotte. She wished she had not called attention to herself; they were both annoyed at her remark and seemed determined to get rid of her.

"How tired one gets," said Miss Bartlett. "Oh, I do wish Freddy and your mother could be here."

Unselfishness with Miss Bartlett had entirely usurped the functions of enthusiasm. Lucy did not look at the view either. She would not enjoy anything till she was safe at Rome.

"Then sit you down," said Miss Lavish. "Observe my foresight."

With many a smile she produced two of those mackintosh squares that protect the frame of the tourist from damp grass or cold marble steps. She sat on one; who was to sit on the other?

"Lucy; without a moment's doubt, Lucy. The ground will do for me. Really I have not had rheumatism for years. If I do feel it coming on I shall stand. Imagine your mother's feelings if I let you sit in the wet in your white linen." She sat down heavily where the ground looked particularly moist. "Here we are, all settled delightfully. Even if my dress is thinner it will not show so much, being brown. Sit down, dear; you are too unselfish; you don't assert yourself enough." She cleared her throat. "Now don't be alarmed; this isn't a cold. It's the tiniest cough, and I have had it three days. It's nothing to do with sitting here at all."

There was only one way of treating the situation. At the end of five minutes Lucy departed in search of Mr. Beebe and Mr. Eager, vanquished by the mackintosh square.

She addressed herself to the drivers, who were sprawling in the carriages, perfuming the cushions with cigars. The miscreant, a bony young man scorched black by the sun, rose to greet her with the courtesy of a host and the assurance of a relative.

"Dove?" said Lucy, after much anxious thought.

His face lit up. Of course he knew where. Not so far either. His arm swept three-fourths of the horizon. He should just think he did know where. He pressed his finger-tips to his forehead and then pushed them towards her, as if oozing with visible extract of knowledge.

More seemed necessary. What was the Italian for "clergyman"?

"Dove buoni uomini?" said she at last.

Good? Scarcely the adjective for those noble beings! He showed her his cigar.

"Uno—piu—piccolo," was her next remark, implying "Has the cigar been given to you by Mr. Beebe, the smaller of the two good men?"

She was correct as usual. He tied the horse to a tree, kicked it to make it stay quiet, dusted the carriage, arranged his hair, remoulded his hat, encouraged his moustache, and in rather less than a quarter of a minute was ready to conduct her. Italians are born knowing the way. It would seem that the whole earth lay before them, not as a map, but as a chess-board, whereon they continually behold the changing pieces as well as the squares. Any one can find places, but the finding of people is a gift from God.

He only stopped once, to pick her some great blue violets. She thanked him with real pleasure. In the company of this common man the world was beautiful and direct. For the first time she felt the influence of Spring. His arm swept the horizon gracefully; violets, like other things, existed in great profusion there; would she like to see them?

"Ma buoni uomini."

He bowed. Certainly. Good men first, violets afterwards. They proceeded briskly through the undergrowth, which became thicker and thicker. They were nearing the edge of the promontory, and the view was stealing round them, but the brown network of the bushes shattered it into countless pieces. He was occupied in his cigar, and in holding back the pliant boughs. She was rejoicing in her escape from dullness. Not a step, not a twig, was unimportant to her.

"What is that?"

There was a voice in the wood, in the distance behind them. The voice of Mr. Eager? He shrugged his shoulders. An Italian's ignorance is sometimes more remarkable than his knowledge. She could not make him understand that perhaps they had missed the clergymen. The view was forming at last; she could discern the river, the golden plain, other hills.

"Eccolo!" he exclaimed.

At the same moment the ground gave way, and with a cry she fell out of the wood. Light and beauty enveloped her. She had fallen on to a little open terrace, which was covered with violets from end to end.

"Courage!" cried her companion, now standing some six feet above. "Courage and love."

She did not answer. From her feet the ground sloped sharply into view, and violets ran down in rivulets and streams and cataracts, irrigating the hillside with blue, eddying round the tree stems, collecting into pools in the hollows, covering the grass with spots of azure foam. But never again were they in such profusion; this terrace was the well-head, the primal source whence beauty gushed out to water the earth.

Standing at its brink, like a swimmer who prepares, was the good man. But he was not the good man that she had expected, and he was alone.

George had turned at the sound of her arrival. For a moment he contemplated her, as one who had fallen out of heaven. He saw radiant joy in her face, he saw the flowers beat against her dress in blue waves. The bushes above them closed. He stepped quickly forward and kissed her.

Before she could speak, almost before she could feel, a voice called, "Lucy! Lucy! Lucy!" The silence of life had been broken by Miss Bartlett, who stood brown against the view.

Chapter VII: They Return

SOME complicated game had been playing up and down the hillside all the afternoon. What it was and exactly how the players had sided, Lucy was slow to discover. Mr. Eager had met them with a questioning eye. Charlotte had repulsed him with much small talk. Mr. Emerson, seeking his son, was told whereabouts to find him. Mr. Beebe, who wore the heated aspect of a neutral, was bidden to collect the factions for the return home. There was a general sense of groping and bewilderment. Pan had been amongst them—not the great god Pan, who has been buried these two thousand years, but the little god Pan, who presides over social contretemps and unsuccessful picnics. Mr. Beebe had lost every one, and had consumed in solitude the tea-basket which he had brought up as a pleasant surprise. Miss Lavish had lost Miss Bartlett. Lucy had lost Mr. Eager. Mr. Emerson had lost George. Miss Bartlett had lost a mackintosh square. Phaethon had lost the game.

That last fact was undeniable. He climbed on to the box shivering, with his collar up, prophesying the swift approach of bad weather.

"Let us go immediately," he told them. "The signorino will walk."

"All the way? He will be hours," said Mr. Beebe.

"Apparently. I told him it was unwise." He would look no one in the face; perhaps defeat was particularly mortifying for him. He alone had played skilfully, using the whole of his instinct, while the others had used scraps of their intelligence. He alone had divined what things were, and what he wished them to be. He alone had interpreted the message that Lucy had received five days before from the lips of a dying man. Persephone, who spends half her life in the grave— she could interpret it also. Not so these English. They gain knowledge slowly, and perhaps too late.

The thoughts of a cab-driver, however just, seldom affect the lives of his employers. He was the most competent of Miss Bartlett's opponents, but infinitely the least dangerous. Once back in the town, he and his insight and his knowledge would trouble English ladies no more. Of course, it was most unpleasant; she had seen his black head in the bushes; he might make a tavern story out of it. But after all, what have we to do with taverns? Real menace belongs to the drawing-room. It was of drawing-room people that Miss Bartlett thought as she journeyed downwards towards the fading sun. Lucy sat beside her; Mr. Eager sat opposite, trying to catch her eye; he was vaguely suspicious. They spoke of Alessio Baldovinetti.

Rain and darkness came on together. The two

ladies huddled together under an inadequate parasol. There was a lightning flash, and Miss Lavish, who was nervous, screamed from the carriage
in front. At the next flash, Lucy screamed also.
Mr. Eager addressed her professionally:

"Courage, Miss Honeychurch, courage and faith.
If I might say so, there is something almost blas-
phemous in this horror of the elements. Are we
seriously to suppose that all these clouds, all this
immense electrical display, is simply called into existence to extinguish you or me?"

"No—of course—"

"Even from the scientific standpoint the chances
against our being struck are enormous. The steel
knives, the only articles which might attract the
current, are in the other carriage. And, in any
case, we are infinitely safer than if we were walking. Courage—courage and faith."

Under the rug, Lucy felt the kindly pressure
of her cousin's hand. At times our need for a
sympathetic gesture is so great that we care not
what exactly it signifies or how much we may have
to pay for it afterwards. Miss Bartlett, by this
timely exercise of her muscles, gained more than
she would have got in hours of preaching or cross-
examination.

She renewed it when the two carriages stopped,
half into Florence.

"Mr. Eager!" called Mr. Beebe. "We want
your assistance. Will you interpret for us?"

"George!" cried Mr. Emerson. "Ask your driver which way George went. The boy may lose his way. He may be killed."

"Go, Mr. Eager," said Miss Bartlett. "No, don't ask our driver; our driver is no help. Go and support poor Mr. Beebe; he is nearly demented."

"He may be killed!" cried the old man. "He may be killed!"

"Typical behaviour," said the chaplain, as he quitted the carriage. "In the presence of reality that kind of person invariably breaks down."

"What does he know?" whispered Lucy as soon as they were alone. "Charlotte, how much does Mr. Eager know?"

"Nothing, dearest; he knows nothing. But—" she pointed at the driver—"*he* knows everything. Dearest, had we better? Shall I?" She took out her purse. "It is dreadful to be entangled with low-class people. He saw it all." Tapping Phaethon's back with her guide-book, she said, "Silenzio!" and offered him a franc.

"Va bene," he replied, and accepted it. As well this ending to his day as any. But Lucy, a mortal maid, was disappointed in him.

There was an explosion up the road. The storm had struck the overhead wire of the tramline, and one of the great supports had fallen. If they had not stopped perhaps they might have been hurt. They chose to regard it as a miraculous preservation, and the floods of love and sincerity, which fructify every hour of life, burst forth in tumult. They descended from the carriages; they embraced each other. It was as joyful to be forgiven past unworthinesses as to forgive them. For a moment they realized vast possibilities of good.

The older people recovered quickly. In the very height of their emotion they knew it to be unmanly or unladylike. Miss Lavish calculated that, even if they had continued, they would not have been caught in the accident. Mr. Eager mumbled a temperate prayer. But the drivers, through miles of dark squalid road, poured out their souls to the dryads and the saints, and Lucy poured out hers to her cousin.

"Charlotte, dear Charlotte, kiss me. Kiss me again. Only you can understand me. You warned me to be careful. And I—I thought I was developing."

"Do not cry, dearest. Take your time."

"I have been obstinate and silly—worse than you know, far worse. Once by the river—Oh, but he isn't killed—he wouldn't be killed, would he?"

The thought disturbed her repentance. As a matter of fact, the storm was worst along the road; but she had been near danger, and so she thought it must be near to every one.

"I trust not. One would always pray against that."

"He is really—I think he was taken by surprise,

just as I was before. But this time I'm not to
blame; I want you to believe that. I simply slipped
into those violets. No, I want to be really truthful. I am a little to blame. I had silly thoughts.
The sky, you know, was gold, and the ground all
blue, and for a moment he looked like some one
in a book."

"In a book?"

"Heroes—gods—the nonsense of schoolgirls."

"And then?"

"But, Charlotte, you know what happened then."

Miss Bartlett was silent. Indeed, she had little
more to learn. With a certain amount of insight
she drew her young cousin affectionately to her.
All the way back Lucy's body was shaken by deep
sighs, which nothing could repress.

"I want to be truthful," she whispered. "It is
so hard to be absolutely truthful."

"Don't be troubled, dearest. Wait till you are
calmer. We will talk it over before bed-time in
my room."

So they re-entered the city with hands clasped.
It was a shock to the girl to find how far emotion
had ebbed in others. The storm had ceased, and
Mr. Emerson was easier about his son. Mr. Beebe
had regained good humour, and Mr. Eager was
already snubbing Miss Lavish. Charlotte alone
she was sure of—Charlotte, whose exterior concealed so much insight and love.

The luxury of self-exposure kept her almost

happy through the long evening. She thought not so much of what had happened as of how she should describe it. All her sensations, her spasms of courage, for moments of unreasonable joy, her mysterious discontent, should be carefully laid before her cousin. And together in divine confidence they would disentangle and interpret them all.

"At last," thought she, "I shall understand myself. I shan't again be troubled by things that come out of nothing, and mean I don't know what."

Miss Alan asked her to play. She refused vehemently. Music seemed to her the employment of a child. She sat close to her cousin, who, with commendable patience, was listening to a long story about lost luggage. When it was over she capped it by a story of her own. Lucy became rather hysterical with the delay. In vain she tried to check, or at all events to accelerate, the tale. It was not till a late hour that Miss Bartlett had recovered her luggage and could say in her usual tone of gentle reproach: "Well, dear, I at all events am ready for Bedfordshire. Come into my room, and I will give a good brush to your hair."

With some solemnity the door was shut, and a cane chair placed for the girl. Then Miss Bartlett said:

"So what is to be done?"

She was unprepared for the question. It had not occurred to her that she would have to do anything. A detailed exhibition of her emotions was all that she had counted upon.

"What is to be done? A point, dearest, which you alone can settle."

The rain was streaming down the black windows, and the great room felt damp and chilly. One candle burnt trembling on the chest of drawers close to Miss Bartlett's toque, which cast monstrous and fantastic shadows on the bolted door. A tram roared by in the dark, and Lucy felt unaccountably sad, though she had long since dried her eyes. She lifted them to the ceiling, where the griffins and bassoons were colourless and vague, the very ghosts of joy.

"It has been raining for nearly four hours," she said at last.

Miss Bartlett ignored the remark.

"How do you propose to silence him?"

"The driver?"

"My dear girl, no; Mr. George Emerson."

Lucy began to pace up and down the room.

"I don't understand," she said at last.

She understood very well, but she no longer wished to be absolutely truthful.

"How are you going to stop him talking about it?"

"I have a feeling that talk is a thing he will never do."

"I, too, intend to judge him charitably. But

unfortunately I have met the type before. They seldom keep their exploits to themselves."

"Exploits?" cried Lucy, wincing under the horrible plural.

"My poor dear, did you suppose that this was his first? Come here and listen to me. I am only gathering it from his own remarks. Do you remember that day at lunch when he argued with Miss Alan that liking one person is an extra reason for liking another?"

"Yes," said Lucy, whom at the time the argument had pleased.

"Well, I am no prude. There is no need to call him a wicked young man, but obviously he is thoroughly unrefined. Let us put it down to his deplorable antecedents and education, if you wish. But we are no farther on with our question. What do you propose to do?"

An idea rushed across Lucy's brain, which, had she thought of it sooner and made it part of her, might have proved victorious.

"I propose to speak to him," said she.

Miss Bartlett uttered a cry of genuine alarm.

"You see, Charlotte, your kindness—I shall never forget it. But—as you said—it is my affair. Mine and his."

"And you are going to *implore* him, to *beg* him to keep silence?"

"Certainly not. There would be no difficulty.

Whatever you ask him he answers, yes or no; then it is over. I have been frightened of him. But now I am not one little bit."

"But we fear him for you, dear. You are so young and inexperienced, you have lived among such nice people, that you cannot realize what men can be—how they can take a brutal pleasure in insulting a woman whom her sex does not protect and rally round. This afternoon, for example, if I had not arrived, what would have happened?"

"I can't think," said Lucy gravely.

Something in her voice made Miss Bartlett repeat her question, intoning it more vigorously.

"What would have happened if I hadn't arrived?"

"I can't think," said Lucy again.

"When he insulted you, how would you have replied?"

"I hadn't time to think. You came."

"Yes, but won't you tell me now what you would have done?"

"I should have—" She checked herself, and broke the sentence off. She went up to the dripping window and strained her eyes into the darkness. She could not think what she would have done.

"Come away from the window, dear," said Miss Bartlett. "You will be seen from the road."

Lucy obeyed. She was in her cousin's power. She could not modulate out the key of self-abasement in which she had started. Neither of them referred again to her suggestion that she should speak to George and settle the matter, whatever it was, with him.

Miss Bartlett became plaintive.

"Oh, for a real man! We are only two women, you and I. Mr. Beebe is hopeless. There is Mr. Eager, but you do not trust him. Oh, for your brother! He is young, but I know that his sister's insult would rouse in him a very lion. Thank God, chivalry is not yet dead. There are still left some men who can reverence woman."

As she spoke, she pulled off her rings, of which she wore several, and ranged them upon the pincushion. Then she blew into her gloves and said:

"It will be a push to catch the morning train, but we must try."

"What train?"

"The train to Rome." She looked at her gloves critically.

The girl received the announcement as easily as it had been given.

"When does the train to Rome go?"

"At eight."

"Signora Bertolini would be upset."

"We must face that," said Miss Bartlett, not liking to say that she had given notice already.

"She will make us pay for a whole week's pension."

"I expect she will. However, we shall be much

more comfortable at the Vyses' hotel. Isn't afternoon tea given there for nothing?"

"Yes, but they pay extra for wine."

After this remark she remained motionless and silent. To her tired eyes Charlotte throbbed and swelled like a ghostly figure in a dream.

They began to sort their clothes for packing, for there was no time to lose, if they were to catch the train to Rome. Lucy, when admonished, began to move to and fro between the rooms, more conscious of the discomforts of packing by candlelight than of a subtler ill. Charlotte, who was practical without ability, knelt by the side of an empty trunk, vainly endeavouring to pave it with books of varying thickness and size. She gave two or three sighs, for the stooping posture hurt her back, and, for all her diplomacy, she felt that she was growing old. The girl heard her as she entered the room, and was seized with one of those emotional impulses to which she could never attribute a cause. She only felt that the candle would burn better, the packing go easier, the world be happier, if she could give and receive some human love. The impulse had come before to-day, but never so strongly. She knelt down by her cousin's side and took her in her arms.

Miss Bartlett returned the embrace with tenderness and warmth. But she was not a stupid woman, and she knew perfectly well that Lucy did not

love her, but needed her to love. For it was in
ominous tones that she said, after a long pause:

"Dearest Lucy, how will you ever forgive me?"

Lucy was on her guard at once, knowing by
bitter experience what forgiving Miss Bartlett
meant. Her emotion relaxed, she modified her
embrace a little, and she said:

"Charlotte dear, what do you mean? As if I
have anything to forgive!"

"You have a great deal, and I have a very great
deal to forgive myself, too. I know well how much
I vex you at every turn."

"But no——"

Miss Bartlett assumed her favourite rôle, that
of the prematurely aged martyr.

"Ah, but yes! I feel that our tour together
is hardly the success I had hoped. I might have
known it would not do. You want some one
younger and stronger and more in sympathy with
you. I am too uninteresting and old-fashioned—
only fit to pack and unpack your things."

"Please——"

"My only consolation was that you found people
more to your taste, and were often able to leave
me at home. I had my own poor ideas of what
a lady ought to do, but I hope I did not inflict
them on you more than was necessary. You had
your own way about these rooms, at all events."

"You mustn't say these things," said Lucy softly.

She still clung to the hope that she and Charlotte loved each other, heart and soul. They continued to pack in silence.

"I have been a failure," said Miss Bartlett, as she struggled with the straps of Lucy's trunk instead of strapping her own. "Failed to make you happy; failed in my duty to your mother. She has been so generous to me; I shall never face her again after this disaster."

"But mother will understand. It is not your fault, this trouble, and it isn't a disaster either."

"It is my fault, it is a disaster. She will never forgive me, and rightly. For instance, what right had I to make friends with Miss Lavish?"

"Every right."

"When I was here for your sake? If I have vexed you it is equally true that I have neglected you. Your mother will see this as clearly as I do, when you tell her."

Lucy, from a cowardly wish to improve the situation, said:

"Why need mother hear of it?"

"But you tell her everything?"

"I suppose I do generally."

"I dare not break your confidence. There is something sacred in it. Unless you feel that it is a thing you could not tell her."

The girl would not be degraded to this.

"Naturally I should have told her. But in case she should blame you in any way, I promise I will not. I am very willing not to. I will never speak of it either to her or to any one."

Her promise brought the long-drawn interview to a sudden close. Miss Bartlett pecked her smartly on both cheeks, wished her good-night, and sent her to her own room.

For a moment the original trouble was in the background. George would seem to have behaved like a cad throughout; perhaps that was the view which one would take eventually. At present she neither acquitted nor condemned him; she did not pass judgment. At the moment when she was about to judge him her cousin's voice had intervened, and, ever since, it was Miss Bartlett who had dominated; Miss Bartlett who, even now, could be heard sighing into a crack in the partition wall; Miss Bartlett, who had really been neither pliable nor humble nor inconsistent. She had worked like a great artist; for a time—indeed, for years—she had been meaningless, but at the end there was presented to the girl the complete picture of a cheerless, loveless world in which the young rush to destruction until they learn better—a shamefaced world of precautions and barriers which may avert evil, but which do not seem to bring good, if we may judge from those who have used them most.

Lucy was suffering from the most grievous wrong which this world has yet discovered: diplomatic advantage had been taken of her sincerity, of her craving for sympathy and love. Such a wrong is not easily forgotten. Never again did she expose herself without due consideration and precaution against rebuff. And such a wrong may react disastrously upon the soul.

The door-bell rang, and she started to the shutters. Before she reached them she hesitated, turned, and blew out the candle. Thus it was that, though she saw some one standing in the wet below, he, though he looked up, did not see her.

To reach his room he had to go by hers. She was still dressed. It struck her that she might slip into the passage and just say that she would be gone before he was up, and that their extraordinary intercourse was over.

Whether she would have dared to do this was never proved. At the critical moment Miss Bartlett opened her own door, and her voice said:

"I wish one word with you in the drawing-room, Mr. Emerson, please."

Soon their footsteps returned, and Miss Bartlett said: "Good-night, Mr. Emerson."

His heavy, tired breathing was the only reply; the chaperon had done her work.

Lucy cried aloud: "It isn't true. It can't all be true. I want not to be muddled. I want to grow older quickly."

Miss Bartlett tapped on the wall.

"Go to bed at once, dear. You need all the rest you can get."

In the morning they left for Rome.

Part Two

Chapter VIII: Mediæval

THE drawing-room curtains at Windy Corner had been pulled to meet, for the carpet was new and deserved protection from the August sun. They were heavy curtains, reaching almost to the ground, and the light that filtered through them was subdued and varied. A poet—none was present—might have quoted, "Life like a dome of many coloured glass," or might have compared the curtains to sluice-gates, lowered against the intolerable tides of heaven. Without was poured a sea of radiance; within, the glory, though visible, was tempered to the capacities of man.

Two pleasant people sat in the room. One—a boy of nineteen—was studying a small manual of anatomy, and peering occasionally at a bone which lay upon the piano. From time to time he bounced in his chair and puffed and groaned, for the day was hot and the print small, and the human frame fearfully made; and his mother, who was writing a letter, did continually read out to him what she had written. And continually did she rise from her seat and part the curtains so that a rivulet of light fell across the carpet, and make the remark that they were still there.

"Where aren't they?" said the boy, who was Freddy, Lucy's brother. "I tell you I'm getting fairly sick."

"For goodness' sake go out of my drawing-room, then?" cried Mrs. Honeychurch, who hoped to cure her children of slang by taking it literally.

Freddy did not move or reply.

"I think things are coming to a head," she observed, rather wanting her son's opinion on the situation if she could obtain it without undue supplication.

"Time they did."

"I am glad that Cecil is asking her this once more."

"It's his third go, isn't it?"

"Freddy I do call the way you talk unkind."

"I didn't mean to be unkind." Then he added: "But I do think Lucy might have got this off her chest in Italy. I don't know how girls manage things, but she can't have said 'No' properly before, or she wouldn't have to say it again now. Over the whole thing—I can't explain—I do feel so uncomfortable."

"Do you indeed, dear? How interesting!"

"I feel—never mind."

He returned to his work.

"Just listen to what I have written to Mrs. Vyse. I said: 'Dear Mrs. Vyse'—"

"Yes, mother, you told me. A jolly good letter."

"I said: 'Dear Mrs. Vyse, Cecil has just asked my permission about it, and I should be delighted, if Lucy wishes it. But—'" She stopped reading. "I was rather amused at Cecil asking my permission at all. He has always gone in for unconventionality, and parents nowhere, and so forth. When it comes to the point, he can't get on without me."

"Nor me."

"You?"

Freddy nodded.

"What do you mean?"

"He asked me for my permission also."

She exclaimed: "How very odd of him!"

"Why so?" asked the son and heir. "Why shouldn't my permission be asked?"

"What do you know about Lucy or girls or anything? What ever did you say?"

"I said to Cecil, 'Take her or leave her; it's no business of mine!'"

"What a helpful answer!" But her own answer, though more normal in its wording, had been to the same effect.

"The bother is this," began Freddy.

Then he took up his work again, too shy to say what the bother was. Mrs. Honeychurch went back to the window.

"Freddy, you must come. There they still are!"

"I don't see you ought to go peeping like that."

"Peeping like that! Can't I look out of my own window?"

But she returned to the writing-table, observing, as she passed her son, "Still page 322?" Freddy snorted, and turned over two leaves. For a brief space they were silent. Close by, beyond the curtains, the gentle murmur of a long conversation had never ceased.

"The bother is this: I have put my foot in it with Cecil most awfully." He gave a nervous gulp. "Not content with 'permission,' which I did give—that is to say, I said, 'I don't mind'—well, not content with that, he wanted to know whether I wasn't off my head with joy. He practically put it like this: Wasn't it a splendid thing for Lucy and for Windy Corner generally if he married her? And he would have an answer—he said it would strengthen his hand."

"I hope you gave a careful answer, dear."

"I answered 'No'" said the boy, grinding his teeth. "There! Fly into a stew! I can't help it— I had to say it. I had to say no. He ought never to have asked me."

"Ridiculous child!" cried his mother. "You think you're so holy and truthful, but really it's only abominable conceit. Do you suppose that a man like Cecil would take the slightest notice of anything you say? I hope he boxed your ears. How dare you say no?"

"Oh, do keep quiet, mother! I had to say no when I couldn't say yes. I tried to laugh as if I didn't mean what I said, and, as Cecil laughed too, and went away, it may be all right. But I feel my foot's in it. Oh, do keep quiet, though, and let a man do some work."

"No," said Mrs. Honeychurch, with the air of one who has considered the subject, "I shall not keep quiet. You know all that has passed between them in Rome; you know why he is down here, and yet you deliberately insult him, and try to turn him out of my house."

"Not a bit!" he pleaded. "I only let out I didn't like him. I don't hate him, but I don't like him. What I mind is that he'll tell Lucy."

He glanced at the curtains dismally.

"Well, I like him," said Mrs. Honeychurch. "I know his mother; he's good, he's clever, he's rich, he's well connected— Oh, you needn't kick the piano! He's well connected—I'll say it again if you like: he's well connected." She paused, as if rehearsing her eulogy, but her face remained dissatisfied. She added: "And he has beautiful manners."

"I liked him till just now. I suppose it's having him spoiling Lucy's first week at home; and it's also something that Mr. Beebe said, not knowing."

"Mr. Beebe?" said his mother, trying to conceal her interest. "I don't see how Mr. Beebe comes in."

"You know Mr. Beebe's funny way, when you never quite know what he means. He said: 'Mr. Vyse is an ideal bachelor.' I was very cute. I asked him what he meant. He said 'Oh, he's like me—better detached.' I couldn't make him say any more, but it set me thinking. Since Cecil has come after Lucy he hasn't been so pleasant, at least—I can't explain."

"You never can, dear. But I can. You are jealous of Cecil because he may stop Lucy knitting you silk ties."

The explanation seemed plausible, and Freddy tried to accept it. But at the back of his brain there lurked a dim mistrust. Cecil praised one too much for being athletic. Was that it? Cecil made one talk in one's own way. This tired one. Was that it? And Cecil was the kind of fellow who would never wear another fellow's cap. Unaware of his own profundity, Freddy checked himself. He must be jealous, or he would not dislike a man for such foolish reasons.

"Will this do?" called his mother. " 'Dear Mrs. Vyse,—Cecil has just asked my permission about it, and I should be delighted if Lucy wishes it.' Then I put in at the top, 'and I have told Lucy so.' I must write the letter out again—'and I have told Lucy so. But Lucy seems very uncertain, and in these days young people must decide for themselves.' I said that because I didn't want Mrs. Vyse to think us old-fashioned. She goes in for lectures and improving her mind, and all the time a thick layer of flue under the beds, and the maid's dirty thumb-marks where you turn on the electric light. She keeps that flat abominably—"

"Suppose Lucy marries Cecil, would she live in a flat, or in the country?"

"Don't interrupt so foolishly. Where was I? Oh yes—'Young people must decide for themselves. I know that Lucy likes your son, because she tells me everything, and she wrote to me from Rome when he asked her first.' No, I'll cross that last bit out—it looks patronizing. I'll stop at 'because she tells me everything.' Or shall I cross that out, too?"

"Cross it out, too," said Freddy.

Mrs. Honeychurch left it in.

"Then the whole things runs: 'Dear Mrs. Vyse, —Cecil has just asked my permission about it, and I should be delighted if Lucy wishes it, and I have told Lucy so. But Lucy seems very uncertain, and in these days young people must decide for themselves. I know that Lucy likes your son, because she tells me everything. But I do not know—' "

"Look out!" cried Freddy.

The curtains parted.

Cecil's first movement was one of irritation. He couldn't bear the Honeychurch habit of sitting in the dark to save the furniture. Instinctively he gave the curtains a twitch, and sent them swinging down their poles. Light entered. There was revealed a terrace, such as is owned by many villas, with trees each side of it, and on it a little rustic seat, and two flower-beds. But it was transfigured by the view beyond, for Windy Corner was built on the range that overlooks the Sussex Weald. Lucy, who was in the little seat, seemed on the edge of a green magic carpet which hovered in the air above the tremulous world.

Cecil entered.

Appearing thus late in the story, Cecil must be at once described. He was mediæval. Like a Gothic statue. Tall and refined, with shoulders that seemed braced square by an effort of the will, and a head that was tilted a little higher than the usual level of vision, he resembled those fastidious saints who guard the portals of a French cathedral. Well educated, well endowed, and not deficient physically, he remained in the grip of a certain devil whom the modern world knows as self-consciousness, and whom the mediæval, with dimmer vision, worshipped as asceticism. A Gothic statue implies celibacy, just as a Greek statue implies fruition, and perhaps this was what Mr. Beebe meant. And Freddy, who ignored history and art, perhaps meant the same when he failed to imagine Cecil wearing another fellow's cap.

Mrs. Honeychurch left her letter on the writing-table and moved towards her young acquaintance.

"Oh, Cecil!" she exclaimed—"oh, Cecil, do tell me!"

"I promessi sposi," said he.

They stared at him anxiously.

"She has accepted me," he said, and the sound of the thing in English made him flush and smile with pleasure, and look more human.

"I am so glad," said Mrs. Honeychurch, while Freddy proffered a hand that was yellow with chemicals. They wished that they also knew Italian, for our phrases of approval and of amazement are so connected with little occasions that we fear to use them on great ones. We are obliged to become vaguely poetic, or to take refuge in Scriptural reminiscences.

"Welcome as one of the family!" said Mrs. Honeychurch, waving her hand at the furniture. "This is indeed a joyous day! I feel sure that you will make our dear Lucy happy."

"I hope so," replied the young man, shifting his eyes to the ceiling.

"We mothers—" simpered Mrs. Honeychurch, and then realized that she was affected, sentimental, bombastic—all the things she hated most. Why could she not be Freddy, who stood stiff in the middle of the room, looking very cross and almost handsome?

"I say, Lucy!" called Cecil, for conversation seemed to flag.

Lucy rose from the seat. She moved across the lawn and smiled in at them, just as if she was going to ask them to play tennis. Then she saw

her brother's face. Her lips parted, and she took
him in her arms. He said, "Steady on!"

"Not a kiss for me?" asked her mother.

Lucy kissed her also.

"Would you take them into the garden and tell
Mrs. Honeychurch all about it?" Cecil suggested.
"And I'd stop here and tell my mother."

"We go with Lucy?" said Freddy, as if taking
orders.

"Yes, you go with Lucy."

They passed into the sunlight. Cecil watched
them cross the terrace, and descend out of sight
by the steps. They would descend—he knew their
ways—past the shrubbery, and past the tennis-lawn
and the dahlia-bed, until they reached the kitchen-
garden, and there, in the presence of the potatoes
and the peas, the great event would be discussed.

Smiling indulgently, he lit a cigarette, and rehearsed the events that had led to such a happy
conclusion.

He had known Lucy for several years, but only
as a commonplace girl who happened to be musical. He could still remember his depression that
afternoon at Rome, when she and her terrible
cousin fell on him out of the blue, and demanded
to be taken to St. Peter's. That day she had
seemed a typical tourist—shrill, crude, and gaunt
with travel. But Italy worked some marvel in her.
It gave her light, and—which he held more precious—it gave her shadow. Soon he detected in

her a wonderful reticence. She was like a woman of Leonardo da Vinci's, whom we love not so much for herself as for the things that she will not tell us. The things are assuredly not of this life; no woman of Leonardo's could have anything so vulgar as a "story." She did develop most wonderfully day by day.

So it happened that from patronizing civility he had slowly passed if not to passion, at least to a profound uneasiness. Already at Rome he had hinted to her that they might be suitable for each other. It had touched him greatly that she had not broken away at the suggestion. Her refusal had been clear and gentle; after it—as the horrid phrase went—she had been exactly the same to him as before. Three months later, on the margin of Italy, among the flower-clad Alps, he had asked her again in bald, traditional language. She reminded him of a Leonardo more than ever; her sunburnt features were shadowed by fantastic rock; at his words she had turned and stood between him and the light with immeasurable plains behind her. He walked home with her unashamed, feeling not at all like a rejected suitor. The things that really mattered were unshaken.

So now he had asked her once more, and, clear and gentle as ever, she had accepted him, giving no coy reasons for her delay, but simply saying that she loved him and would do her best to make him happy. His mother, too, would be pleased; she had counselled the step; he must write her a long account.

Glancing at his hand, in case any of Freddy's chemicals had come off on it, he moved to the writing table. There he saw "Dear Mrs. Vyse," followed by many erasures. He recoiled without reading any more, and after a little hesitation sat down elsewhere, and pencilled a note on his knee.

Then he lit another cigarette, which did not seem quite as divine as the first, and considered what might be done to make Windy Corner drawing-room more distinctive. With that outlook it should have been a successful room, but the trail of Tottenham Court Road was upon it; he could almost visualize the motor-vans of Messrs. Shoolbred and Messrs. Maple arriving at the door and depositing this chair, those varnished book-cases, that writing-table. The table recalled Mrs. Honeychurch's letter. He did not want to read that letter—his temptations never lay in that direction; but he worried about it none the less. It was his own fault that she was discussing him with his mother; he had wanted her support in his third attempt to win Lucy; he wanted to feel that others, no matter who they were, agreed with him, and so he had asked their permission. Mrs. Honeychurch had been civil, but obtuse in essentials, while as for Freddy—

"He is only a boy," he reflected. "I represent

all that he despises. Why should he want me for a brother-in-law?"

The Honeychurches were a worthy family, but he began to realize that Lucy was of another clay; and perhaps—he did not put it very definitely— he ought to introduce her into more congenial circles as soon as possible.

"Mr. Beebe!" said the maid, and the new rector of Summer Street was shown in; he had at once started on friendly relations, owing to Lucy's praise of him in her letters from Florence.

Cecil greeted him rather critically.

"I've come for tea, Mr. Vyse. Do you suppose that I shall get it?"

"I should say so. Food is the thing one does get here— Don't sit in that chair; young Honeychurch has left a bone in it."

"Pfui!"

"I know," said Cecil. "I know. I can't think why Mrs. Honeychurch allows it."

For Cecil considered the bone and the Maples' furniture separately; he did not realize that, taken together, they kindled the room into the life that he desired.

"I've come for tea and for gossip. Isn't this news?"

"News? I don't understand you," said Cecil. "News?"

Mr. Beebe, whose news was of a very different nature, prattled forward.

"I met Sir Harry Otway as I came up; I have every reason to hope that I am first in the field. He has bought Cissie and Albert from Mr. Flack!"

"Has he indeed?" said Cecil, trying to recover himself. Into what a grotesque mistake had he fallen! Was it likely that a clergyman and a gentleman would refer to his engagement in a manner so flippant? But his stiffness remained, and, though he asked who Cissie and Albert might be, he still thought Mr. Beebe rather a bounder.

"Unpardonable question! To have stopped a week at Windy Corner and not to have met Cissie and Albert, the semi-detached villas that have been run up opposite the church! I'll set Mrs. Honeychurch after you."

"I'm shockingly stupid over local affairs," said the young man languidly. "I can't even remember the difference between a Parish Council and a Local Government Board. Perhaps there is no difference, or perhaps those aren't the right names. I only go into the country to see my friends and to enjoy the scenery. It is very remiss of me. Italy and London are the only places where I don't feel to exist on sufferance."

Mr. Beebe, distressed at this heavy reception of Cissie and Albert, determined to shift the subject.

"Let me see, Mr. Vyse—I forget—what is your profession?"

"I have no profession," said Cecil. "It is another example of my decadence. My attitude—

quite an indefensible one—is that so long as I am no trouble to any one I have a right to do as I like. I know I ought to be getting money out of people, or devoting myself to things I don't care a straw about, but somehow, I've not been able to begin."

"You are very fortunate," said Mr. Beebe. "It is a wonderful opportunity, the possession of leisure."

His voice was rather parochial, but he did not quite see his way to answering naturally. He felt, as all who have regular occupation must feel, that others should have it also.

"I am glad that you approve. I daren't face the healthy person—for example, Freddy Honeychurch."

"Oh, Freddy's a good sort, isn't he?"

"Admirable. The sort who has made England what she is."

Cecil wondered at himself. Why, on this day of all others, was he so hopelessly contrary? He tried to get right by inquiring effusively after Mr. Beebe's mother, an old lady for whom he had no particular regard. Then he flattered the clergyman, praised his liberal-mindedness, his enlightened attitude towards philosophy and science.

"Where are the others?" said Mr. Beebe at last. "I insist on extracting tea before evening service."

"I suppose Anne never told them you were here.

In this house one is so coached in the servants the day one arrives. The fault of Anne is that she begs your pardon when she hears you perfectly, and kicks the chair-legs with her feet. The faults of Mary—I forget the faults of Mary, but they are very grave. Shall we look in the garden?"

"I know the faults of Mary. She leaves the dust-pans standing on the stairs."

"The fault of Euphemia is that she will not, simply will not, chop the suet sufficiently small."

They both laughed, and things began to go better.

"The faults of Freddy—" Cecil continued.

"Ah, he has too many. No one but his mother can remember the faults of Freddy. Try the faults of Miss Honeychurch; they are not innumerable."

"She has none," said the young man, with grave sincerity.

"I quite agree. At present she has none."

"At present?"

"I'm not cynical. I'm only thinking of my pet theory about Miss Honeychurch. Does it seem reasonable that she should play so wonderfully, and live so quietly? I suspect that one day she will be wonderful in both. The water-tight compartments in her will break down, and music and life will mingle. Then we shall have her heroically good, heroically bad—too heroic, perhaps, to be good or bad."

Mediæval

Cecil found his companion interesting.

"And at present you think her not wonderful as far as life goes?"

"Well, I must say I've only seen her at Tunbridge Wells, where she was not wonderful, and at Florence. Since I came to Summer Street she has been away. You saw her, didn't you, at Rome and in the Alps. Oh, I forgot; of course, you knew her before. No, she wasn't wonderful in Florence either, but I kept on expecting that she would be."

"In what way?"

Conversation had become agreeable to them, and they were pacing up and down the terrace.

"I could as easily tell you what tune she'll play next. There was simply the sense that she had found wings, and meant to use them. I can show you a beautiful picture in my Italian diary: Miss Honeychurch as a kite, Miss Bartlett holding the string. Picture number two: the string breaks."

The sketch was in his diary, but it had been made afterwards, when he viewed things artistically. At the time he had given surreptitious tugs to the string himself.

"But the string never broke?"

"No. I mightn't have seen Miss Honeychurch rise, but I should certainly have heard Miss Bartlett fall."

"It has broken now," said the young man in low, vibrating tones.

Immediately he realized that of all the conceited, ludicrous, contemptible ways of announcing an engagement this was the worst. He cursed his love of metaphor; had he suggested that he was a star and that Lucy was soaring up to reach him?

"Broken? What do you mean?"

"I meant," said Cecil stiffly, "that she is going to marry me."

The clergyman was conscious of some bitter disappointment which he could not keep out of his voice.

"I am sorry; I must apologize. I had no idea you were intimate with her, or I should never have talked in this flippant, superficial way. Mr. Vyse, you ought to have stopped me." And down the garden he saw Lucy herself; yes, he was disappointed.

Cecil, who naturally preferred congratulations to apologies, drew down his mouth at the corners. Was this the reception his action would get from the world? Of course, he despised the world as a whole; every thoughtful man should; it is almost a test of refinement. But he was sensitive to the successive particles of it which he encountered.

Occasionally he could be quite crude.

"I am sorry I have given you a shock," he said dryly. "I fear that Lucy's choice does not meet with your approval."

"Not that. But you ought to have stopped me. I know Miss Honeychurch only a little as time goes. Perhaps I oughtn't to have discussed her so freely with any one; certainly not with you."

"You are conscious of having said something indiscreet?"

Mr. Beebe pulled himself together. Really, Mr. Vyse had the art of placing one in the most tiresome positions. He was driven to use the prerogatives of his profession.

"No, I have said nothing indiscreet. I foresaw at Florence that her quiet, uneventful childhood must end, and it has ended. I realized dimly enough that she might take some momentous step. She has taken it. She has learnt—you will let me talk freely, as I have begun freely—she has learnt what it is to love: the greatest lesson, some people will tell you, that our earthly life provides." It was now time for him to wave his hat at the approaching trio. He did not omit to do so. "She has learnt through you," and if his voice was still clerical, it was now also sincere; "let it be your care that her knowledge is profitable to her."

"Grazie tante!" said Cecil, who did not like parsons.

"Have you heard?" shouted Mrs. Honeychurch as she toiled up the sloping garden. "Oh, Mr. Beebe, have you heard the news?"

Freddy, now full of geniality, whistled the wedding march. Youth seldom criticizes the accomplished fact.

"Indeed I have!" he cried. He looked at Lucy. In her presence he could not act the parson any longer—at all events not without apology. "Mrs. Honeychurch, I'm going to do what I am always supposed to do, but generally I'm too shy. I want to invoke every kind of blessing on them, grave and gay, great and small. I want them all their lives to be supremely good and supremely happy as husband and wife, as father and mother. And now I want my tea."

"You only asked for it just in time," the lady retorted. "How dare you be serious at Windy Corner?"

He took his tone from her. There was no more heavy beneficence, no more attempts to dignify the situation with poetry or the Scriptures. None of them dared or was able to be serious any more.

An engagement is so potent a thing that sooner or later it reduces all who speak of it to this state of cheerful awe. Away from it, in the solitude of their rooms, Mr. Beebe, and even Freddy, might again be critical. But in its presence and in the presence of each other they were sincerely hilarious. It has a strange power, for it compels not only the lips, but the very heart. The chief parallel— to compare one great thing with another—is the power over us of a temple of some alien creed. Standing outside, we deride or oppose it, or at the most feel sentimental. Inside, though the saints and gods are not ours, we become true believers, in case any true believer should be present.

So it was that after the gropings and the misgivings of the afternoon they pulled themselves together and settled down to a very pleasant tea-party. If they were hypocrites they did not know it, and their hypocrisy had every chance of setting and of becoming true. Anne, putting down each plate as if it were a wedding present, stimulated them greatly. They could not lag behind that smile of hers which she gave them ere she kicked the drawing-room door. Mr. Beebe chirruped. Freddy was at his wittiest, referring to Cecil as the "Fiasco"—family honoured pun on fiancé. Mrs. Honeychurch, amusing and portly, promised well as a mother-in-law. As for Lucy and Cecil, for whom the temple had been built, they also joined in the merry ritual, but waited, as earnest worshippers should, for the disclosure of some holier shrine of joy.

Chapter IX: Lucy as a Work of Art

A FEW days after the engagement was announced Mrs. Honeychurch made Lucy and her Fiasco come to a little garden-party in the neighbourhood, for naturally she wanted to show people that her daughter was marrying a presentable man.

Cecil was more than presentable; he looked distinguished, and it was very pleasant to see his slim figure keeping step with Lucy, and his long, fair face responding when Lucy spoke to him. People congratulated Mrs. Honeychurch, which is, I believe, a social blunder, but it pleased her, and she introduced Cecil rather indiscriminately to some stuffy dowagers.

At tea a misfortune took place: a cup of coffee was upset over Lucy's figured silk, and though Lucy feigned indifference, her mother feigned nothing of the sort but dragged her indoors to have the frock treated by a sympathetic maid. They were gone some time, and Cecil was left with the dowagers. When they returned he was not as pleasant as he had been.

"Do you go to much of this sort of thing?" he asked when they were driving home.

"Oh, now and then," said Lucy, who had rather enjoyed herself.

"Is it typical of country society?"

"I suppose so.   Mother, would it be?"

"Plenty of society," said Mrs. Honeychurch, who was trying to remember the hang of one of the dresses.

Seeing that her thoughts were elsewhere, Cecil bent towards Lucy and said:

"To me it seemed perfectly appalling, disastrous, portentous."

"I am so sorry that you were stranded."

"Not that, but the congratulations.   It is so disgusting, the way an engagement is regarded as public property—a kind of waste place where every outsider may shoot his vulgar sentiment.   All those old women smirking!"

"One has to go through it, I suppose.   They won't notice us so much next time."

"But my point is that their whole attitude is wrong.   An engagement—horrid word in the first place—is a private matter, and should be treated as such."

Yet the smirking old women, however wrong individually, were racially correct.   The spirit of the generations had smiled through them, rejoicing in the engagement of Cecil and Lucy because it promised the continuance of life on earth.   To Cecil and Lucy it promised something quite different

—personal love. Hence Cecil's irritation and Lucy's belief that his irritation was just.

"How tiresome!" she said. "Couldn't you have escaped to tennis?"

"I don't play tennis—at least, not in public. The neighbourhood is deprived of the romance of me being athletic. Such romance as I have is that of the Inglese Italianato."

"Inglese Italianato?"

"E un diavolo incarnato! You know the proverb?"

She did not. Nor did it seem applicable to a young man who had spent a quiet winter in Rome with his mother. But Cecil, since his engagement, had taken to affect a cosmopolitan naughtiness which he was far from possessing.

"Well," said he, "I cannot help it if they do disapprove of me. There are certain irremovable barriers between myself and them, and I must accept them."

"We all have our limitations, I suppose," said wise Lucy.

"Sometimes they are forced on us, though," said Cecil, who saw from her remark that she did not quite understand his position.

"How?"

"It makes a difference doesn't it, whether we fence ourselves in, or whether we are fenced out by the barriers of others?"

She thought a moment, and agreed that it did make a difference.

"Difference?" cried Mrs. Honeychurch, suddenly alert. "I don't see any difference. Fences are fences, especially when they are in the same place."

"We were speaking of motives," said Cecil, on whom the interruption jarred.

"My dear Cecil, look here." She spread out her knees and perched her card-case on her lap. "This is me. That's Windy Corner. The rest of the pattern is the other people. Motives are all very well, but the fence comes here."

"We weren't talking of real fences," said Lucy, laughing.

"Oh, I see, dear—poetry."

She leant placidly back. Cecil wondered why Lucy had been amused.

"I tell you who has no 'fences,' as you call them," she said, "and that's Mr. Beebe."

"A parson fenceless would mean a parson defenceless."

Lucy was slow to follow what people said, but quick enough to detect what they meant. She missed Cecil's epigram, but grasped the feeling that prompted it.

"Don't you like Mr. Beebe?" she asked thoughtfully.

"I never said so!" he cried. "I consider him far above the average. I only denied—" And he swept off on the subject of fences again, and was brilliant.

"Now, a clergyman that I do hate," said she, wanting to say something sympathetic, "a clergyman that does have fences, and the most dreadful ones, is Mr. Eager, the English chaplain at Florence. He was truly insincere—not merely the manner unfortunate. He was a snob, and so conceited, and he did say such unkind things."

"What sort of things?"

"There was an old man at the Bertolini whom he said had murdered his wife."

"Perhaps he had."

"No!"

"Why 'no'?"

"He was such a nice old man, I'm sure."

Cecil laughed at her feminine inconsequence.

"Well, I did try to sift the thing. Mr. Eager would never come to the point. He prefers it vague—said the old man had 'practically' murdered his wife—had murdered her in the sight of God."

"Hush, dear!" said Mrs. Honeychurch absently.

"But isn't it intolerable that a person whom we're told to imitate should go round spreading slander? It was, I believe, chiefly owing to him that the old man was dropped. People pretended he was vulgar, but he certainly wasn't that."

"Poor old man! What was his name?"

"Harris," said Lucy glibly.

"Let's hope that Mrs. Harris there warn't no sich person," said her mother.

Cecil nodded intelligently.

"Isn't Mr. Eager a parson of the cultured type?" he asked.

"I don't know. I hate him. I've heard him lecture on Giotto. I hate him. Nothing can hide a petty nature. I *hate* him."

"My goodness gracious me, child!" said Mrs. Honeychurch. "You'll blow my head off! Whatever is there to shout over? I forbid you and Cecil to hate any more clergymen."

He smiled. There was indeed something rather incongruous in Lucy's moral outburst over Mr. Eager. It was as if one should see the Leonardo on the ceiling of the Sistine. He longed to hint to her that not here lay her vocation; that a woman's power and charm reside in mystery, not in muscular rant. But possibly rant is a sign of vitality: it mars the beautiful creature, but shows that she is alive. After a moment, he contemplated her flushed face and excited gestures with a certain approval. He forebore to repress the sources of youth.

Nature—simplest of topics, he thought—lay around them. He praised the pine-woods, the deep lakes of bracken, the crimson leaves that spotted the hurt-bushes, the serviceable beauty of the turnpike road. The outdoor world was not very familiar to him, and occasionally he went wrong in a question of fact. Mrs. Honeychurch's mouth twitched when he spoke of the perpetual green of the larch.

"I count myself a lucky person," he concluded. "When I'm in London I feel I could never live out of it. When I'm in the country I feel the same about the country. After all, I do believe that birds and trees and the sky are the most wonderful things in life, and that the people who live amongst them must be the best. It's true that in nine cases out of ten they don't seem to notice anything. The country gentleman and the country labourer are each in their way the most depressing of companions. Yet they may have a tacit sympathy with the workings of Nature which is denied to us of the town. Do you feel that, Mrs. Honeychurch?"

Mrs. Honeychurch started and smiled. She had not been attending. Cecil, who was rather crushed on the front seat of the victoria, felt irritable, and determined not to say anything interesting again.

Lucy had not attended either. Her brow was wrinkled, and she still looked furiously cross—the result, he concluded, of too much moral gymnastics. It was sad to see her thus blind to the beauties of an August wood.

" 'Come down, O maid, from yonder mountain height,' " he quoted, and touched her knee with his own.

She flushed again and said: "What height?"

" 'Come down, O maid, from yonder mountain height,
What pleasure lives in height (the shepherd sang),

In height and in the splendour of the hills?'

Let us take Mrs. Honeychurch's advice and hate clergymen no more. What's this place?"

"Summer Street, of course," said Lucy, and roused herself.

The woods had opened to leave space for a sloping triangular meadow. Pretty cottages lined it on two sides, and the upper and third side was occupied by a new stone church, expensively simple, with a charming shingled spire. Mr. Beebe's house was near the church. In height it scarcely exceeded the cottages. Some great mansions were at hand, but they were hidden in the trees. The scene suggested a Swiss Alp rather than the shrine and centre of a leisured world, and was marred only by two ugly little villas—the villas that had competed with Cecil's engagement, having been acquired by Sir Harry Otway the very afternoon that Lucy had been acquired by Cecil.

"Cissie" was the name of one of these villas, "Albert" of the other. These titles were not only picked out in shaded Gothic on the garden gates, but appeared a second time on the porches, where they followed the semicircular curve of the entrance arch in block capitals. "Albert" was inhabited. His tortured garden was bright with geraniums and lobelias and polished shells. His little windows were chastely swathed in Nottingham lace. "Cissie" was to let. Three notice-boards, belonging to Dorking agents, lolled on her fence and announced the not surprising fact. Her paths were already weedy; her pocket-handkerchief of a lawn was yellow with dandelions.

"The place is ruined!" said the ladies mechanically. "Summer Street will never be the same again."

As the carriage passed, "Cissie's" door opened, and a gentleman came out of her.

"Stop!" cried Mrs. Honeychurch, touching the coachman with her parasol. "Here's Sir Harry. Now we shall know. Sir Harry, pull those things down at once!"

Sir Harry Otway—who need not be described —came to the carriage and said:

"Mrs. Honeychurch, I meant to. I can't, I really can't turn out Miss Flack."

"Am I not always right? She ought to have gone before the contract was signed. Does she still live rent free, as she did in her nephew's time?"

"But what can I do?" He lowered his voice. "An old lady, so very vulgar, and almost bedridden."

"Turn her out," said Cecil bravely.

Sir Harry sighed, and looked at the villas mournfully. He had had full warning of Mr. Flack's intentions, and might have bought the plot before building commenced: but he was apathetic and dilatory. He had known Summer Street for so many years that he could not imagine it being spoilt. Not till Mrs. Flack had laid the foundation stone, and the apparition of red and cream brick began to rise, did he take alarm. He called on Mr. Flack, the local builder,—a most reasonable and respectful man—who agreed that tiles would have made a more artistic roof, but pointed out that slates were cheaper. He ventured to differ, however, about the Corinthian columns which were to cling like leeches to the frames of the bow windows, saying that, for his part, he liked to relieve the façade by a bit of decoration. Sir Harry hinted that a column, if possible, should be structural as well as decorative. Mr. Flack replied that all the columns had been ordered, adding, "and all the capitals different—one with dragons in the foliage, another approaching to the Ionian style, another introducing Mrs. Flack's initials—every one different." For he had read his Ruskin. He built his villas according to his desire; and not until he had inserted an immovable aunt into one of them did Sir Harry buy.

This futile and unprofitàble transaction filled the knight with sadness as he leant on Mrs. Honeychurch's carriage. He had failed in his duties to the country-side, and the country-side was laughing at him as well. He had spent money, and yet Summer Street was spoilt as much as ever. All he could do now was to find a desirable tenant for "Cissie"—some one really desirable.

"The rent is absurdly low," he told them, "and perhaps I am an easy landlord. But it is such an awkward size. It is too large for the peasant class, and too small for any one the least like ourselves."

Cecil had been hesitating whether he should despise the villas or despise Sir Harry for despising them. The latter impulse seemed the more fruitful.

"You ought to find a tenant at once," he said maliciously. "It would be a perfect paradise for a bank clerk."

"Exactly!" said Sir Harry excitedly. "That is exactly what I fear, Mr. Vyse. It will attract the wrong type of people. The train service has improved—a fatal improvement, to my mind. And what are five miles from a station in these days of bicycles?"

"Rather a strenuous clerk it would be," said Lucy.

Cecil, who had his full share of mediæval mischievousness, replied that the physique of the lower middle classes was improving at a most appalling rate. She saw that he was laughing at their harmless neighbour, and roused herself to stop him.

"Sir Harry!" she exclaimed, "I have an idea. How would you like spinsters?"

"My dear Lucy, it would be splendid. Do you know any such?"

"Yes; I met them abroad."

"Gentlewomen?" he asked tentatively.

"Yes, indeed, and at the present moment homeless. I heard from them last week—Miss Teresa and Miss Catharine Alan. I'm really not joking. They are quite the right people. Mr. Beebe knows them, too. May I tell them to write to you?"

"Indeed you may!" he cried. "Here we are with the difficulty solved already. How delightful it is! Extra facilities—please tell them they shall have extra facilities, for I shall have no agents' fees. Oh, the agents! The appalling people they have sent me! One woman, when I wrote—a tactful letter, you know—asking her to explain her social position to me, replied that she would pay the rent in advance. As if one cares about that! And several references I took up were most unsatisfactory—people swindlers, or not respectable. And oh, the deceit! I have seen a good deal of the seamy side this last week. The deceit of the most promising people. My dear Lucy, the deceit!"

She nodded.

"My advice," put in Mrs. Honeychurch, "is to have nothing to do with Lucy and her decayed gentlewomen at all. I know the type. Preserve me from people who have seen better days, and bring heirlooms with them that make the house smell stuffy. It's a sad thing, but I'd far rather let to some one who is going up in the world than to some one who has come down."

"I think I follow you," said Sir Harry; "but it is, as you say, a very sad thing."

"The Misses Alan aren't that!" cried Lucy.

"Yes, they are," said Cecil. "I haven't met them but I should say they were a highly unsuitable addition to the neighbourhood."

"Don't listen to him, Sir Harry—he's tiresome."

"It's I who am tiresome," he replied. "I oughtn't to come with my troubles to young people. But really I am so worried, and Lady Otway will only say that I cannot be too careful, which is quite true, but no real help."

"Then may I write to my Misses Alan?"

"Please!"

But his eye wavered when Mrs. Honeychurch exclaimed:

"Beware! They are certain to have canaries. Sir Harry, beware of canaries: they spit the seed out through the bars of the cages and then the mice come. Beware of women altogether. Only let to a man."

"Really—" he murmured gallantly, though he saw the wisdom of her remark.

"Men don't gossip over tea-cups. If they get drunk, there's an end of them—they lie down comfortably and sleep it off. If they're vulgar, they somehow keep it to themselves. It doesn't spread so. Give me a man—of course, provided he's clean."

Sir Harry blushed. Neither he nor Cecil enjoyed these open compliments to their sex. Even the exclusion of the dirty did not leave them much distinction. He suggested that Mrs. Honeychurch, if she had time, should descend from the carriage and inspect "Cissie" for herself. She was delighted. Nature had intended her to be poor and to live in such a house. Domestic arrangements always attracted her, especially when they were on a small scale.

Cecil pulled Lucy back as she followed her mother.

"Mrs. Honeychurch," he said, "what if we two walk home and leave you?"

"Certainly!" was her cordial reply.

Sir Harry likewise seemed almost too glad to get rid of them. He beamed at them knowingly, said, "Aha! young people, young people!" and then hastened to unlock the house.

"Hopeless vulgarian!" exclaimed Cecil, almost before they were out of earshot.

"Oh, Cecil!"

"I can't help it. It would be wrong not to loathe that man."

"He isn't clever, but really he is nice."

"No, Lucy he stands for all that is bad in country life. In London he would keep his place. He would belong to a brainless club, and his wife would give brainless dinner parties. But down here he acts the little god with his gentility, and his patronage, and his sham æsthetics, and every one—even your mother—is taken in."

"All that you say is quite true," said Lucy, though she felt discouraged. "I wonder whether— whether it matters so very much."

"It matters supremely. Sir Harry is the essence of that garden-party. Oh, goodness, how cross I feel! How I do hope he'll get some vulgar tenant in that villa—some woman so really vulgar that he'll notice it. *Gentlefolks!* Ugh! with his bald head and retreating chin! But let's forget him."

This Lucy was glad enough to do. If Cecil disliked Sir Harry Otway and Mr. Beebe, what guarantee was there that the people who really mattered to her would escape? For instance, Freddy. Freddy was neither clever, nor subtle, nor beautiful, and what prevented Cecil from saying, any minute, "It would be wrong not to loathe Freddy"? And what would she reply? Further than Freddy she did not go, but he gave her anxiety enough. She could only assure herself that Cecil had known Freddy some time, and that they had always got on pleasantly, except, perhaps, during the last few days, which was an accident, perhaps.

"Which way shall we go?" she asked him.

Nature—simplest of topics, she thought—was around them. Summer Street lay deep in the woods, and she had stopped where a footpath diverged from the highroad.

"Are there two ways?"

"Perhaps the road is more sensible, as we're got up smart."

"I'd rather go through the wood," said Cecil, with that subdued irritation that she had noticed in him all the afternoon. "Why is it, Lucy, that you always say the road? Do you know that you have never once been with me in the fields or the wood since we were engaged?"

"Haven't I? The wood, then," said Lucy, startled at his queerness, but pretty sure that he would explain later; it was not his habit to leave her in doubt as to his meaning.

She led the way into the whispering pines, and sure enough he did explain before they had gone a dozen yards.

"I had got an idea—I dare say wrongly—that you feel more at home with me in a room."

"A room?" she echoed, hopelessly bewildered.

"Yes. Or, at the most, in a garden, or on a road. Never in the real country like this."

"Oh, Cecil, whatever do you mean? I have never felt anything of the sort. You talk as if I was a kind of poetess sort of person."

"I don't know that you aren't. I connect you with a view—a certain type of view. Why shouldn't you connect me with a room?"

She reflected a moment, and then said, laughing:

"Do you know that you're right? I do. I must be a poetess after all. When I think of you it's always as in a room. How funny!"

To her surprise, he seemed annoyed.

"A drawing-room, pray? With no view?"

"Yes, with no view, I fancy. Why not?"

"I'd rather," he said reproachfully, "that you connected me with the open air."

She said again, "Oh, Cecil, whatever do you mean?"

As no explanation was forthcoming, she shook off the subject as too difficult for a girl, and led him further into the wood, pausing every now and then at some particularly beautiful or familiar combination of the trees. She had known the wood between Summer Street and Windy Corner ever since she could walk alone; she had played at losing Freddy in it, when Freddy was a purple-faced baby; and though she had been to Italy, it had lost none of its charm.

Presently they came to a little clearing among the pines—another tiny green alp, solitary this time, and holding in its bosom a shallow pool.

She exclamed, "The Sacred Lake!"

"Why do you call it that?"

"I can't remember why. I suppose it comes out of some book. It's only a puddle now, but you see that stream going through it? Well, a good deal of water comes down after heavy rains, and can't get away at once, and the pool becomes quite large and beautiful. Then Freddy used to bathe there. He is very fond of it."

"And you?"

He meant, "Are you fond of it?" But she answered dreamily, "I bathed here, too, till I was found out. Then there was a row."

At another time he might have been shocked, for he had depths of prudishness within him. But now, with his momentary cult of the fresh air, he was delighted at her admirable simplicity. He looked at her as she stood by the pool's edge. She was got up smart, as she phrased it, and she reminded him of some brilliant flower that has no leaves of its own, but blooms abruptly out of a world of green.

"Who found you out?"

"Charlotte," she murmured. "She was stopping with us. Charlotte—Charlotte."

"Poor girl!"

She smiled gravely. A certain scheme, from which hitherto he had shrank, now appeared practical.

"Lucy!"

"Yes, I suppose we ought to be going," was her reply.

"Lucy, I want to ask something of you that I have never asked before."

At the serious note in his voice she stepped frankly and kindly towards him.

"What, Cecil?"

"Hitherto never—not even that day on the lawn when you agreed to marry me—"

He became self-conscious and kept glancing

round to see if they were observed. His courage had gone.

"Yes?"

"Up to now I have never kissed you."

She was as scarlet as if he had put the thing most indelicately.

"No—more you have," she stammered.

"Then I ask you—may I now?"

"Of course, you may, Cecil. You might before. I can't run at you, you know."

At that supreme moment he was conscious of nothing but absurdities. Her reply was inadequate. She gave such a business-like lift to her veil. As he approached her he found time to wish that he could recoil. As he touched her, his gold pince-nez became dislodged and was flattened between them.

Such was the embrace. He considered, with truth, that it had been a failure. Passion should believe itself irresistible. It should forget civility and consideration and all the other curses of a refined nature. Above all, it should never ask for leave where there is a right of way. Why could he not do as any labourer or navvy—nay, as any young man behind the counter would have done? He recast the scene. Lucy was standing flowerlike by the water, he rushed up and took her in his arms; she rebuked him, permitted him and revered him ever after for his manliness. For he believed that women revere men for their manliness.

They left the pool in silence, after this one salutation. He waited for her to make some remark which should show him her inmost thoughts. At last she spoke, and with fitting gravity.

"Emerson was the name, not Harris."

"What name?"

"The old man's."

"What old man?"

"That old man I told you about. The one Mr. Eager was so unkind to."

He could not know that this was the most intimate conversation they had ever had.

Chapter X: Cecil as a Humourist

THE society out of which Cecil proposed to rescue Lucy was perhaps no very splendid affair, yet it was more splendid than her antecedents entitled her to. Her father, a prosperous local solicitor, had built Windy Corner, as a speculation at the time the district was opening up, and, falling in love with his own creation, had ended by living there himself. Soon after his marriage, the social atmosphere began to alter. Other houses were built on the brow of that steep southern slope, and others, again, among the pine-trees behind, and northward on the chalk barrier of the downs. Most of these houses were larger than Windy Corner, and were filled by people who came, not from the district, but from London, and who mistook the Honeychurches for the remnants of an indigenous aristocracy. He was inclined to be frightened, but his wife accepted the situation without either pride or humility. "I cannot think what people are doing," she would say, "but it is extremely fortunate for the children." She called everywhere; her calls were returned with enthusiasm, and by the time people found out that she was not exactly of their *milieu*, they liked her,

and it did not seem to matter. When Mr. Honeychurch died, he had the satisfaction—which few
honest solicitors despise—of leaving his family
rooted in the best society obtainable.

The best obtainable. Certainly many of the im-
migrants were rather dull, and Lucy realized this
more vividly since her return from Italy. Hitherto she had accepted their ideals without questioning
—their kindly affluence, their inexplosive religion,
their dislike of paper-bags, orange-peel, and broken
bottles. A Radical out and out, she learnt to speak
with horror of Suburbia. Life, so far as she
troubled to conceive it, was a circle of rich, pleasant
people, with identical interests and identical foes.
In this circle, one thought, married, and died. Outside it were poverty and vulgarity for ever trying
to enter, just as the London fog tries to enter the
pine-woods pouring through the gaps in the northern
hills. But, in Italy, where any one who chooses
may warm himself in equality, as in the sun, this conception of life vanished. Her senses expanded; she
felt that there was no one whom she might not
get to like, that social barriers were irremovable,
doubtless, but not particularly high. You jump over
them just as you jump into a peasant's olive-yard
in the Apennines, and he is glad to see you. She
returned with new eyes.

So did Cecil; but Italy had quickened Cecil, not
to tolerance, but to irritation. He saw that the
local society was narrow, but, instead of saying,

"Does that very much matter?" he rebelled, and tried to substitute for it the society he called broad. He did not realize that Lucy had consecrated her environment by the thousand little civilities that create a tenderness in time, and that though her eyes saw its defects, her heart refused to despise it entirely. Nor did he realize a more important point—that if she was too great for this society, she was too great for all society, and had reached the stage where personal intercourse would alone satisfy her. A rebel she was, but not of the kind he understood—a rebel who desired, not a wider dwelling-room, but equality beside the man she loved. For Italy was offering her the most priceless of all possessions—her own soul.

Playing bumble-puppy with Minnie Beebe, niece to the rector, and aged thirteen—an ancient and most honourable game, which consists in striking tennis-balls high into the air, so that they fall over the net and immoderately bounce; some hit Mrs. Honeychurch; others are lost. The sentence is confused, but the better illustrates Lucy's state of mind, for she was trying to talk to Mr. Beebe at the same time.

"Oh, it has been such a nuisance—first he, then they—no one knowing what they wanted, and every one so tiresome."

"But they really are coming now," said Mr. Beebe. "I wrote to Miss Teresa a few days ago—she was wondering how often the butcher called, and my reply of once a month must have impressed her favourably. They are coming. I heard from them this morning."

"I shall hate those Miss Alans!" Mrs. Honeychurch cried. "Just because they're old and silly one's expected to say 'How sweet!' I hate their 'if'-ing and 'but'-ing and 'and'-ing. And poor Lucy —serve her right—worn to a shadow."

Mr. Beebe watched the shadow springing and shouting over the tennis-court. Cecil was absent— one did not play bumble-puppy when he was there.

"Well, if they are coming— No, Minnie, not Saturn." Saturn was a tennis-ball whose skin was partially unsewn. When in motion his orb was en- circled by a ring. "If they are coming, Sir Harry will let them move in before the twenty-ninth, and he will cross out the clause about whitewashing the ceilings, because it made them nervous, and put in the fair wear and tear one.—That doesn't count. I told you not Saturn."

"Saturn's all right for bumble-puppy," cried Freddy, joining them. "Minnie, don't you listen to her."

"Saturn doesn't bounce."

"Saturn bounces enough."

"No, he doesn't."

"Well, he bounces better than the Beautiful White Devil."

"Hush, dear," said Mrs. Honeychurch.

"But look at Lucy—complaining of Saturn, and

all the time's got the Beautiful White Devil in her hand, ready to plug it in. That's right, Minnie, go for her—get her over the shins with the racquet—get her over the shins!"

Lucy fell, the Beautiful White Devil rolled from her hand.

Mr. Beebe picked it up, and said: "The name of this ball is Vittoria Corombona, please." But his correction passed unheeded.

Freddy possessed to a high degree the power of lashing little girls to fury, and in half a minute he had transformed Minnie from a well-mannered child into a howling wilderness. Up in the house Cecil heard them, and, though he was full of entertaining news, he did not come down to impart it, in case he got hurt. He was not a coward and bore necessary pain as well as any man. But he hated the physical violence of the young. How right it was! Sure enough it ended in a cry.

"I wish the Miss Alans could see this," observed Mr. Beebe, just as Lucy, who was nursing the injured Minnie, was in turn lifted off her feet by her brother.

"Who are the Miss Alans?" Freddy panted.

"They have taken Cissie Villa."

"That wasn't the name—"

Here his foot slipped, and they all fell most agreeably on to the grass. An interval elapses.

"Wasn't what name?" asked Lucy, with her brother's head in her lap.

"Alan wasn't the name of the people Sir Harry's let to."

"Nonsense, Freddy! You know nothing about it."

"Nonsense yourself! I've this minute seen him. He said to me: 'Ahem! Honeychurch,' "—Freddy was an indifferent mimic—" 'ahem! ahem! I have at last procured really dee-sire-rebel tenants.' I said, 'Hooray, old boy!' and slapped him on the back."

"Exactly. The Miss Alans?"

"Rather not. More like Anderson."

"Oh, good gracious, there isn't going to be another muddle!" Mrs. Honeychurch exclaimed. "Do you notice, Lucy, I'm always right? I *said* don't interfere with Cissie Villa. I'm always right. I'm quite uneasy at being always right so often."

"It's only another muddle of Freddy's. Freddy doesn't even know the name of the people he pretends have taken it instead."

"Yes, I do. I've got it. Emerson."

"What name?"

"Emerson. I'll bet you anything you like."

"What a weathercock Sir Harry is," said Lucy quietly. "I wish I had never bothered over it at all."

Then she lay on her back and gazed at the cloudless sky. Mr. Beebe, whose opinion of her rose daily, whispered to his niece that *that* was the proper way to behave if any little thing went wrong.

Meanwhile the name of the new tenants had diverted Mrs. Honeychurch from the contemplation of her own abilities.

"Emerson, Freddy? Do you know what Emersons they are?"

"I don't know whether they're any Emersons," retorted Freddy, who was democratic. Like his sister and like most young people, he was naturally attracted by the idea of equality, and the undeniable fact that there are different kinds of Emersons annoyed him beyond measure.

"I trust they are the right sort of person. All right, Lucy"—she was sitting up again—"I see you looking down your nose and thinking your mother's a snob. But there *is* a right sort and a wrong sort, and it's affectation to pretend there isn't."

"Emerson's a common enough name," Lucy remarked.

She was gazing sideways. Seated on a promontory herself, she could see the pine-clad promontories descending one beyond another into the Weald. The further one descended the garden, the more glorious was this lateral view.

"I was merely going to remark, Freddy, that I trusted they were no relations of Emerson the philosopher, a most trying man. Pray, does that satisfy you?"

"Oh, yes," he grumbled. "And you will be satisfied, too, for they're friends of Cecil; so"—

with elaborate irony—"you and the other country families will be able to call in perfect safety."

"*Cecil?*" exclaimed Lucy.

"Don't be rude, dear," said his mother placidly. "Lucy, don't screech. It's a new bad habit you're getting into."

"But has Cecil—"

"Friends of Cecil's," he repeated, " 'and so really dee-sire-rebel. Ahem! Honeychurch, I have just telegraphed to them.' "

She got up from the grass.

It was hard on Lucy. Mr. Beebe sympathized with her very much. While she believed that her snub about the Miss Alans came from Sir Harry Otway, she had borne it like a good girl. She might well "screech" when she heard that it came partly from her lover. Mr. Vyse was a tease— something worse than a tease: he took a malicious pleasure in thwarting people. The clergyman, knowing this, looked at Miss Honeychurch with more than his usual kindness.

When she exclaimed, "But Cecil's Emersons— they can't possibly be the same ones—there is that—" he did not consider that the exclamation was strange, but saw in it an opportunity of diverting the conversation while she recovered her composure. He diverted it as follows:

"The Emersons who were at Florence, do you mean? No, I don't suppose it will prove to be them. It is probably a long cry from them to friends of Mr. Vyse's. Oh, Mrs. Honeychurch, the oddest people! The queerest people! For our part we liked them, didn't we?" He appealed to Lucy. "There was a great scene over some violets. They picked violets and filled all the vases in the room of these very Miss Alans who have failed to come to Cissie Villa. Poor little ladies! So shocked and so pleased. It used to be one of Miss Catharine's great stories. 'My dear sister loves flowers,' it began. They found the whole room a mass of blue—vases and jugs—and the story ends with 'So ungentlemanly and yet so beautiful.' It is all very difficult. Yes, I always connect those Florentine Emersons with violets."

"Fiasco's done you this time," remarked Freddy, not seeing that his sister's face was very red. She could not recover herself. Mr. Beebe saw it, and continued to divert the conversation.

"These particular Emersons consisted of a father and a son—the son a goodly, if not a good young man; not a fool, I fancy, but very immature— pessimism, et cetera. Our special joy was the father—such a sentimental darling, and people declared he had murdered his wife."

In his normal state Mr. Beebe would never have repeated such gossip, but he was trying to shelter Lucy in her little trouble. He repeated any rubbish that came into his head.

"Murdered his wife?" said Mrs. Honeychurch.

"Lucy, don't desert us—go on playing bumble-puppy. Really, the Pension Bertolini must have been the oddest place. That's the second murderer I've heard of as being there. Whatever was Charlotte doing to stop? By-the-by, we really must ask Charlotte here some time."

Mr. Beebe could recall no second murderer. He suggested that his hostess was mistaken. At the hint of opposition she warmed. She was perfectly sure that there had been a second tourist of whom the same story had been told. The name escaped her. What was the name? Oh, what was the name? She clasped her knees for the name. Something in Thackeray. She struck her matronly forehead.

Lucy asked her brother whether Cecil was in.

"Oh, don't go!" he cried, and tried to catch her by the ankles.

"I must go," she said gravely. "Don't be silly. You always overdo it when you play."

As she left them her mother's shout of "Harris!" shivered the tranquil air, and reminded her that she had told a lie and had never put it right. Such a senseless lie, too, yet it shattered her nerves and made her connect these Emersons, friends of Cecil's, with a pair of nondescript tourists. Hitherto truth had come to her naturally. She saw that for the future she must be more vigilant, and be—absolutely truthful? Well, at all events, she must not tell lies. She hurried up the garden, still flushed with shame. A word from Cecil would soothe her, she was sure.

"Cecil!"

"Hullo!" he called, and leant out of the smoking-room window. He seemed in high spirits. "I was hoping you'd come. I heard you all bear-gardening, but there's better fun up here. I, even I, have won a great victory for the Comic Muse. George Meredith's right—the cause of Comedy and the cause of Truth are really the same; and I, even I, have found tenants for the distressful Cissie Villa. Don't be angry! Don't be angry! You'll forgive me when you hear it all."

He looked very attractive when his face was bright, and he dispelled her ridiculous forebodings at once.

"I have heard," she said. "Freddy has told us. Naughty Cecil! I suppose I must forgive you. Just think of all the trouble I took for nothing! Certainly the Miss Alans are a little tiresome, and I'd rather have nice friends of yours. But you oughtn't to tease one so."

"Friends of mine?" he laughed. "But, Lucy, the whole joke is to come! Come here." But she remained standing where she was. "Do you know where I met these desirable tenants? In the National Gallery, when I was up to see my mother last week."

"What an odd place to meet people!" she said nervously. "I don't quite understand."

"In the Umbrian Room. Absolute strangers. They were admiring Luca Signorelli—of course, quite stupidly. However, we got talking, and they refreshed me not a little. They had been to Italy."

"But, Cecil—"

He proceeded hilariously.

"In the course of conversation they said that they wanted a country cottage—the father to live there, the son to run down for week-ends. I thought, 'What a chance of scoring off Sir Harry!' and I took their address and a London reference, found they weren't actual blackguards—it was great sport—and wrote to him, making out—"

"Cecil! No, it's not fair. I've probably met them before—"

He bore her down.

"Perfectly fair. Anything is fair that punishes a snob. That old man will do the neighbourhood a world of good. Sir Harry is too disgusting with his 'decayed gentlewomen.' I meant to read him a lesson some time. No, Lucy, the classes ought to mix, and before long you'll agree with me. There ought to be intermarriage—all sorts of things. I believe in democracy—"

"No, you don't," she snapped. "You don't know what the word means."

He stared at her, and felt again that she had

failed to be Leonardesque. "No, you don't!"
Her face was inartistic—that of a peevish virago.

"It isn't fair, Cecil. I blame you—I blame you
very much indeed. You had no business to undo
my work about the Miss Alans, and make me look
ridiculous. You call it scoring off Sir Harry, but
do you realize that it is all at my expense? I consider it most disloyal of you."

She left him.

"Temper!" he thought, raising his eyebrows.

No, it was worse than temper—snobbishness. As
long as Lucy thought that his own smart friends
were supplanting the Miss Alans, she had not
minded. He perceived that these new tenants
might be of value educationally. He would tolerate the father and draw out the son, who was
silent. In the interests of the Comic Muse and
of Truth, he would bring them to Windy Corner.

Chapter XI: In Mrs. Vyse's Well-Appointed Flat

THE Comic Muse, though able to look after her own interests, did not disdain the assistance of Mr. Vyse. His idea of bringing the Emersons to Windy Corner struck her as decidedly good, and she carried through the negotiations without a hitch. Sir Harry Otway signed the agreement, met Mr. Emerson, who was duly disillusioned. The Miss Alans were duly offended, and wrote a dignified letter to Lucy, whom they held responsible for the failure. Mr. Beebe planned pleasant moments for the new-comers, and told Mrs. Honeychurch that Freddy must call on them as soon as they arrived. Indeed, so ample was the Muse's equipment that she permitted Mr. Harris, never a very robust criminal, to droop his head, to be forgotten, and to die.

Lucy—to descend from bright heaven to earth, whereon there are shadows because there are hills —Lucy was at first plunged into despair, but settled after a little thought that it did not matter in the very least. Now that she was engaged, the Emersons would scarcely insult her and were welcome to come into the neighbourhood. And Cecil was welcome to bring whom he would into the neighbourhood. Therefore Cecil was welcome to bring the Emersons into the neighbourhood. But, as I say, this took a little thinking, and—so illogical are girls—the event remained rather greater and rather more dreadful than it should have done. She was glad that a visit to Mrs. Vyse now fell due; the tenants moved into Cissie Villa while she was safe in the London flat.

"Cecil—Cecil darling," she whispered the evening she arrived, and crept into his arms.

Cecil, too, became demonstrative. He saw that the needful fire had been kindled in Lucy. At last she longed for attention, as a woman should, and looked up to him because he was a man.

"So you do love me, little thing?" he murmured.

"Oh, Cecil, I do, I do! I don't know what I should do without you."

Several days passed. Then she had a letter from Miss Bartlett.

A coolness had sprung up between the two cousins, and they had not corresponded since they parted in August. The coolness dated from what Charlotte would call "the flight to Rome," and in Rome it had increased amazingly. For the companion who is merely uncongenial in the mediæval world becomes exasperating in the classical. Charlotte, unselfish in the Forum, would have tried a sweeter temper than Lucy's, and once, in the Baths of Caracalla, they had doubted whether they could continue their tour. Lucy had said she would join the Vyses—Mrs. Vyse was an acquaintance of her mother, so there was no impropriety in the plan— and Miss Bartlett had replied that she was quite used to being abandoned suddenly. Finally nothing happened; but the coolness remained, and, for Lucy, was even increased when she opened the letter and read as follows. It had been forwarded from Windy Corner.

> "Tunbridge Wells,
> "*September*.
>
> "Dearest Lucia,
>
> "I have news of you at last! Miss Lavish has been bicycling in your parts, but was not sure whether a call would be welcome. Puncturing her tire near Summer Street, and it being mended while she sat very woebegone in that pretty churchyard, she saw to her astonishment, a door open opposite and the younger Emerson man come out. He said his father had just taken the house. He *said* he did not know that you lived in the neighbourhood(?). He never suggested giving Eleanor a cup of tea. Dear Lucy, I am much worried, and I advise you to make a clean breast of his past behaviour to your mother, Freddy, and Mr. Vyse, who will forbid him to enter the house, etc. That was a great misfortune, and I dare say you have told them already. Mr. Vyse is so sensitive. I remember how I used to get on his nerves at Rome. I am very sorry about it all, and should not feel easy unless I warned you.
>
> "Believe me,
> "Your anxious and loving cousin,
> "Charlotte."

Lucy was much annoyed, and replied as follows:

"BEAUCHAMP MANSIONS, S. W.

"DEAR CHARLOTTE,

"Many thanks for your warning. When Mr. Emerson forgot himself on the mountain, you made me promise not to tell mother, because you said she would blame you for not being always with me. I have kept that promise, and cannot possibly tell her now. I have said both to her and Cecil that I met the Emersons at Florence, and that they are respectable people—which I *do* think—and the reason that he offered Miss Lavish no tea was probably that he had none himself. She should have tried at the Rectory. I cannot begin making a fuss at this stage. You must see that it would be too absurd. If the Emersons heard I had complained of them, they would think themselves of importance, which is exactly what they are not. I like the old father, and look forward to seeing him again. As for the son, I am sorry for *him* when we meet, rather than for myself. They are known to Cecil, who is very well and spoke of you the other day. We expect to be married in January.

"Miss Lavish cannot have told you much about me, for I am not at Windy Corner at all, but here. Please do not put 'Private' outside your envelope again. No one opens my letters.

"Yours affectionately,

"L. M. HONEYCHURCH."

Secrecy has this disadvantage: we lose the sense of proportion; we cannot tell whether our secret is important or not. Were Lucy and her cousin closeted with a great thing which would destroy

Cecil's life if he discovered it, or with a little thing which he would laugh at? Miss Bartlett suggested the former. Perhaps she was right. It had become a great thing now. Left to herself, Lucy would have told her mother and her lover ingenuously, and it would have remained a little thing. "Emerson, not Harris"; it was only that a few weeks ago. She tried to tell Cecil even now when they were laughing about some beautiful lady who had smitten his heart at school. But her body behaved so ridiculously that she stopped.

She and her secret stayed ten days longer in the deserted Metropolis visiting the scenes they were to know so well later on. It did her no harm, Cecil thought, to learn the framework of society, while society itself was absent on the golf-links or the moors. The weather was cool, and it did her no harm. In spite of the season, Mrs. Vyse managed to scrape together a dinner-party consisting entirely of the grandchildren of famous people. The food was poor, but the talk had a witty weariness that impressed the girl. One was tired of everything, it seemed. One launched into enthusiasms only to collapse gracefully, and pick oneself up amid sympathetic laughter. In this atmosphere the Pension Bertolini and Windy Corner appeared equally crude, and Lucy saw that her London career would estrange her a little from all that she had loved in the past.

The grandchildren asked her to play the piano.

She played Schumann. "Now some Beethoven," called Cecil, when the querulous beauty of the music had died. She shook her head and played Schumann again. The melody rose, unprofitably magical. It broke; it was resumed broken, not marching once from the cradle to the grave. The sadness of the incomplete—the sadness that is often Life, but should never be Art—throbbed in its disjected phrases, and made the nerves of the audience throb. Not thus had she played on the little draped piano at the Bertolini, and "Too much Schumann" was not the remark that Mr. Beebe had passed to himself when she returned.

When the guests were gone, and Lucy had gone to bed, Mrs. Vyse paced up and down the drawing-room, discussing her little party with her son. Mrs. Vyse was a nice woman, but her personality, like many another's, had been swamped by London, for it needs a strong head to live among many people. The too vast orb of her fate had crushed her; and she had seen too many seasons, too many cities, too many men, for her abilities, and even with Cecil she was mechanical, and behaved as if he was not one son, but, so to speak, a filial crowd.

"Make Lucy one of us," she said, looking round intelligently at the end of each sentence, and straining her lips apart until she spoke again. "Lucy is becoming wonderful—wonderful."

"Her music always was wonderful."

"Yes, but she is purging off the Honeychurch

taint—most excellent Honeychurches, but you know what I mean. She is not always quoting servants, or asking one how the pudding is made."

"Italy has done it."

"Perhaps," she murmured, thinking of the museum that represented Italy to her. "It is just possible. Cecil, mind you marry her next January. She is one of us already."

"But her music!" he exclaimed. "The style of her! How she kept to Schumann when, like an idiot, I wanted Beethoven. Schumann was right for this evening. Schumann was the thing. Do you know, mother, I shall have our children educated just like Lucy. Bring them up among honest country folks for freshness, send them to Italy for subtlety, and then—not till then—let them come to London. I don't believe in these London educations—" He broke off, remembering that he had had one himself, and concluded, "At all events, not for women."

"Make her one of us," repeated Mrs. Vyse, and processed to bed.

As she was dozing off, a cry—the cry of nightmare—rang from Lucy's room. Lucy could ring for the maid if she liked but Mrs. Vyse thought it kind to go herself. She found the girl sitting upright with her hand on her cheek.

"I am so sorry, Mrs. Vyse—it is these dreams."

"Bad dreams?"

"Just dreams."

The elder lady smiled and kissed her, saying very distinctly: "You should have heard us talking about you, dear. He admires you more than ever. Dream of that."

Lucy returned the kiss, still covering one cheek with her hand. Mrs. Vyse recessed to bed. Cecil, whom the cry had not awoke, snored. Darkness enveloped the flat.

Chapter XII: Twelfth Chapter

IT was a Saturday afternoon, gay and brilliant after abundant rains, and the spirit of youth dwelt in it, though the season was now autumn. All that was gracious triumphed. As the motor-cars passed through Summer Street they raised only a little dust, and their stench was soon dispersed by the wind and replaced by the scent of the wet birches or of the pines. Mr. Beebe, at leisure for life's amenities, leant over his Rectory gate. Freddy leant by him, smoking a pendant pipe.

"Suppose we go and hinder those new people opposite for a little."

"M'm."

"They might amuse you."

Freddy, whom his fellow-creatures never amused, suggested that the new people might be feeling a bit busy, and so on, since they had only just moved in.

"I suggested we should hinder them," said Mr. Beebe. "They are worth it." Unlatching the gate, he sauntered over the triangular green to Cissie Villa. "Hullo!" he cried, shouting in at the open door, through which much squalor was visible.

A grave voice replied, "Hullo!"

"I've brought some one to see you."

"I'll be down in a minute."

The passage was blocked by a wardrobe, which the removal men had failed to carry up the stairs. Mr. Beebe edged round it with difficulty. The sitting-room itself was blocked with books.

"Are these people great readers?" Freddy whispered. "Are they that sort?"

"I fancy they know how to read—a rare accomplishment. What have they got? Byron. Exactly. *A Shropshire Lad.* Never heard of it. *The Way of All Flesh.* Never heard of it. Gibbon. Hullo! dear George reads German. Um—um—Schopenhauer, Nietzsche, and so we go on. Well, I suppose your generation knows its own business, Honeychurch."

"Mr. Beebe, look at that," said Freddy in awestruck tones.

On the cornice of the wardrobe, the hand of an amateur had painted this inscription: "Mistrust all enterprises that require new clothes."

"I know. Isn't it jolly? I like that. I'm certain that's the old man's doing."

"How very odd of him!"

"Surely you agree?"

But Freddy was his mother's son and felt that one ought not to go on spoiling the furniture.

"Pictures!" the clergyman continued, scrambling about the room. "Giotto—they got that at Florence, I'll be bound."

"The same as Lucy's got."

Twelfth Chapter

"Oh, by-the-by, did Miss Honeychurch enjoy London?"

"She came back yesterday."

"I suppose she had a good time?"

"Yes, very," said Freddy, taking up a book. "She and Cecil are thicker than ever."

"That's good hearing."

"I wish I wasn't such a fool, Mr. Beebe."

Mr. Beebe ignored the remark.

"Lucy used to be nearly as stupid as I am, but it'll be very different now, mother thinks. She will read all kinds of books."

"So will you."

"Only medical books. Not books that you can talk about afterwards. Cecil is teaching Lucy Italian, and he says her playing is wonderful. There are all kinds of things in it that we have never noticed. Cecil says—"

"What on earth are those people doing upstairs? Emerson—we think we'll come another time."

George ran down-stairs and pushed them into the room without speaking.

"Let me introduce Mr. Honeychurch, a neighbour."

Then Freddy hurled one of the thunderbolts of youth. Perhaps he was shy, perhaps he was friendly, or perhaps he thought that George's face wanted washing. At all events he greeted him with, "How d'ye do? Come and have a bathe."

"Oh, all right," said George, impassive.

Mr. Beebe was highly entertained.

" 'How d' ye do? how d'ye do? Come and have a bathe,' " he chuckled. "That's the best conversational opening I've ever heard. But I'm afraid it will only act between men. Can you picture a lady who has been introduced to another lady by a third lady opening civilities with 'How do you do? Come and have a bathe'? And yet you will tell me that the sexes are equal."

"I tell you that they shall be," said Mr. Emerson, who had been slowly descending the stairs. "Good-afternoon, Mr. Beebe. I tell you they shall be comrades, and George thinks the same."

"We are to raise ladies to our level?" the clergyman inquired.

"The Garden of Eden," pursued Mr. Emerson, still descending, "which you place in the past, is really yet to come. We shall enter it when we no longer despise our bodies."

Mr. Beebe disclaimed placing the Garden of Eden anywhere.

"In this—not in other things—we men are ahead. We despise the body less than women do. But not until we are comrades shall we enter the garden."

"I say, what about this bathe?" murmured Freddy, appalled at the mass of philosophy that was approaching him.

"I believed in a return to Nature once. But how can we return to Nature when we have never been with her? To-day, I believe that we must discover Nature. After many conquests we shall attain simplicity. It is our heritage."

"Let me introduce Mr. Honeychurch, whose sister you will remember at Florence."

"How do you do? Very glad to see you, and that you are taking George for a bathe. Very glad to hear that your sister is going to marry. Marriage is a duty. I am sure that she will be happy, for we know Mr. Vyse, too. He has been most kind. He met us by chance in the National Gallery, and arranged everything about this delightful house. Though I hope I have not vexed Sir Harry Otway. I have met so few Liberal landowners, and I was anxious to compare his attitude towards the game laws with the Conservative attitude. Ah, this wind! You do well to bathe. Yours is a glorious country, Honeychurch!"

"Not a bit!" mumbled Freddy. "I must —that is to say, I have to—have the pleasure of calling on you later on, my mother says, I hope."

"*Call,* my lad? Who taught us that drawing-room twaddle? Call on your grandmother! Listen to the wind among the pines! Yours is a glorious country."

Mr. Beebe came to the rescue.

"Mr. Emerson, he will call, I shall call; you or your son will return our calls before ten days have elapsed. I trust that you have realized about the

ten days' interval. It does not count that I helped
you with the stair-eyes yesterday. It does not count
that they are going to bathe this afternoon."

"Yes, go and bathe, George. Why do you
dawdle talking? Bring them back to tea. Bring
back some milk, cakes, honey. The change will do
you good. George has been working very hard at
his office. I can't believe he's well."

George bowed his head, dusty and sombre, exhaling the peculiar smell of one who has handled furniture.

"Do you really want this bathe?" Freddy asked
him. "It is only a pond, don't you know. I dare
say you are used to something better."

"Yes—I have said 'Yes' already."

Mr. Beebe felt bound to assist his young friend,
and led the way out of the house and into the pine-
woods. How glorious it was! For a little time
the voice of old Mr. Emerson pursued them dispens-
ing good wishes and philosophy. It ceased, and
they only heard the fair wind blowing the bracken
and the trees.

Mr. Beebe, who could be silent, but who could
not bear silence, was compelled to chatter, since the
expedition looked like a failure, and neither of his
companions would utter a word. He spoke of
Florence. George attended gravely, assenting or
dissenting with slight but determined gestures that
were as inexplicable as the motions of the tree-tops
above their heads.

"And what a coincidence that you should meet Mr. Vyse! Did you realize that you would find all the Pension Bertolini down here?"

"I did not. Miss Lavish told me."

"When I was a young man, I always meant to write a 'History of Coincidence.'"

No enthusiasm.

"Though, as a matter of fact, coincidences are much rarer than we suppose. For example, it isn't purely coincidentality that you are here now, when one comes to reflect."

To his relief, George began to talk.

"It is. I have reflected. It is Fate. Everything is Fate. We are flung together by Fate, drawn apart by Fate—flung together, drawn apart. The twelve winds blow us—we settle nothing—"

"You have not reflected at all," rapped the clergyman. "Let me give you a useful tip, Emerson: attribute nothing to Fate. Don't say, 'I didn't do this,' for you did it, ten to one. Now I'll cross-question you. Where did you first meet Miss Honeychurch and myself?"

"Italy."

"And where did you meet Mr. Vyse, who is going to marry Miss Honeychurch?"

"National Gallery."

"Looking at Italian art. There you are, and yet you talk of coincidence and Fate! You naturally seek out things Italian, and so do we and our

friends.   This narrows the field immeasurably, and
we meet again in it."

"It is Fate that I am here," persisted George.
"But you can call it Italy if it makes you less unhappy."

Mr. Beebe slid away from such heavy treatment
of the subject.   But he was infinitely tolerant of the
young, and had no desire to snub George.

"And so for this and for other reasons my 'History of Coincidence' is still to write."

Silence.

Wishing to round off the episode, he added;

"We are all so glad that you have come."

Silence.

"Here we are!" called Freddy.

"Oh, good!" exclaimed Mr. Beebe, mopping his
brow.

"In there's the pond.   I wish it was bigger," he
added apologetically.

They climbed down a slippery bank of pine-need-
les.   There lay the pond, set in its little alp of green
—only a pond, but large enough to contain the human body, and pure enough to reflect the sky.   On account of the rains, the waters had flooded the surrounding grass, which showed like a beautiful emer-
ald path, tempting the feet towards the central
pool.

"It's distinctly successful, as ponds go," said Mr.
Beebe.   "No apologies are necessary for the pond."

Twelfth Chapter

George sat down where the ground was dry, and drearily unlaced his boots.

"Aren't those masses of willow-herb splendid? I love willow-herb in seed. What's the name of this aromatic plant?"

No one knew, or seemed to care.

"These abrupt changes of vegetation—this little spongeous tract of water plants, and on either side of it all the growths are tough or brittle—heather, bracken, hurts, pines. Very charming, very charming."

"Mr. Beebe, aren't you bathing?" called Freddy, as he stripped himself.

Mr. Beebe thought he was not.

"Water's wonderful!" cried Freddy, prancing in.

"Water's water," murmured George. Wetting his hair first—a sure sign of apathy—he followed Freddy into the divine, as indifferent as if he were a statue and the pond a pail of soapsuds. It was necessary to use his muscles. It was necessary to keep clean. Mr. Beebe watched them, and watched the seeds of the willow-herb dance chorically above their heads.

"Apooshoo, apooshoo, apooshoo," went Freddy, swimming for two strokes in either direction, and then becoming involved in reeds or mud.

"Is it worth it?" asked the other, Michelangelesque on the flooded margin.

The bank broke away, and he fell into the pool

before he had weighed the question properly.

"Hee—poof—I've swallowed a pollywog. Mr. Beebe, water's wonderful, water's simply ripping."

"Water's not so bad," said George, reappearing from his plunge, and sputtering at the sun.

"Water's wonderful. Mr. Beebe, do."

"Apooshoo, kouf."

Mr. Beebe, who was hot, and who always acquiesced where possible, looked around him. He could detect no parishioners except the pine-trees, rising up steeply on all sides, and gesturing to each other against the blue. How glorious it was! The world of motor-cars and rural Deans receded illimitably. Water, sky, evergreens, a wind— these things not even the seasons can touch, and surely they lie beyond the intrusion of man?

"I may as well wash too"; and soon his garments made a third little pile on the sward, and he too asserted the wonder of the water.

It was ordinary water, nor was there very much of it, and, as Freddy said, it reminded one of swimming in a salad. The three gentlemen rotated in the pool breast high, after the fashion of the nymphs in Götterdämmerung. But either because the rains had given a freshness or because the sun was shedding a most glorious heat, or because two of the gentlemen were young in years and the third young in spirit—for some reason or other a change came over them, and they forgot Italy and Botany

and Fate. They began to play. Mr. Beebe and
Freddy splashed each other. A little deferentially,
they splashed George. He was quiet: they feared
they had offended him. Then all the forces of
youth burst out. He smiled, flung himself at them,
splashed them, ducked them, kicked them, muddied
them, and drove them out of the pool.

"Race you round it, then," cried Freddy, and
they raced in the sunshine, and George took a short
cut and dirtied his shins, and had to bathe a second
time. Then Mr. Beebe consented to run—a memorable sight.

They ran to get dry, they bathed to get cool,
they played at being Indians in the willow-herbs
and in the bracken, they bathed to get clean. And
all the time three little bundles lay discreetly on
the sward, proclaiming:

"No. We are what matters. Without us shall
no enterprise begin. To us shall all flesh turn in
the end."

"A try! A try!" yelled Freddy, snatching up
George's bundle and placing it beside an imaginary
goal-post.

"Socker rules," George retorted, scattering
Freddy's bundle with a kick.

"Goal!"

"Goal!"

"Pass!"

"Take care my watch!" cried Mr. Beebe.

Clothes flew in all directions.

"Take care my hat! No, that's enough, Freddy. Dress now. No, I say!"

But the two young men were delirious. Away they twinkled into the trees, Freddy with a clerical waistcoat under his arm, George with a wide-awake hat on his dripping hair.

"That'll do!" shouted Mr. Beebe, remembering that after all he was in his own parish. Then his voice changed as if every pine-tree was a Rural Dean. "Hi! Steady on! I see people coming, you fellows!"

Yells, and widening circles over the dappled earth.

"Hi! hi! *Ladies!*"

Neither George nor Freddy was truly refined. Still, they did not hear Mr. Beebe's last warning or they would have avoided Mrs. Honeychurch, Cecil, and Lucy, who were walking down to call on old Mrs. Butterworth. Freddy dropped the waistcoat at their feet, and dashed into some bracken. George whooped in their faces, turned and scudded away down the path to the pond, still clad in Mr. Beebe's hat.

"Gracious alive!" cried Mrs. Honeychurch. "Whoever were those unfortunate people? Oh, dears, look away! And poor Mr. Beebe, too! Whatever has happened?"

"Come this way immediately," commanded Cecil, who always felt that he must lead women, though

Twelfth Chapter

he knew not whither, and protect them, though he knew not against what. He led them now towards the bracken where Freddy sat concealed.

"Oh, poor Mr. Beebe! Was that his waistcoat we left in the path? Cecil, Mr. Beebe's waist-coat—"

"No business of ours," said Cecil, glancing at Lucy, who was all parasol and evidently "minded."

"I fancy Mr. Beebe jumped back into the pond."

"This way, please, Mrs. Honeychurch, this way."

They followed him up the bank attempting the tense yet nonchalant expression that is suitable for ladies on such occasions.

"Well, *I* can't help it," said a voice close ahead, and Freddy reared a freckled face and a pair of snowy shoulders out of the fronds. "I can't be trodden on, can I?"

"Good gracious me, dear; so it's you! What miserable management! Why not have a com-fortable bath at home, with hot and cold laid on?"

"Look here, mother, a fellow must wash, and a fellow's got to dry, and if another fellow—"

"Dear, no doubt you're right as usual, but you are in no position to argue. Come, Lucy." They turned. "Oh, look—don't look! Oh, poor Mr. Beebe! How unfortunate again—"

For Mr. Beebe was just crawling out of the pond, on whose surface garments of an intimate nature did float; while George, the world-weary George, shouted to Freddy that he had hooked a fish.

"And me, I've swallowed one," answered he of the bracken. "I've swallowed a pollywog. It wriggleth in my tummy. I shall die—Emerson, you beast, you've got on my bags."

"Hush, dears," said Mrs. Honeychurch, who found it impossible to remain shocked. "And do be sure you dry yourselves thoroughly first. All these colds come of not drying thoroughly."

"Mother, do come away," said Lucy. "Oh, for goodness' sake, do come."

"Hullo!" cried George, so that again the ladies stopped.

He regarded himself as dressed. Barefoot, bare-chested, radiant and personable against the shadowy woods, he called:

"Hullo, Miss Honeychurch! Hullo!"

"Bow, Lucy; better bow. Whoever is it? I shall bow."

Miss Honeychurch bowed.

That evening and all that night the water ran away. On the morrow the pool had shrunk to its old size and lost its glory. It had been a call to the blood and to the relaxed will, a passing benediction whose influence did not pass, a holiness, a spell, a momentary chalice for youth.

Chapter XIII: How Miss Bartlett's Boiler Was So Tiresome

HOW often had Lucy rehearsed this bow, this interview! But she had always rehearsed them indoors, and with certain accessories, which surely we have a right to assume. Who could foretell that she and George would meet in the rout of a civilization, amidst an army of coats and collars and boots that lay wounded over the sunlit earth? She had imagined a young Mr. Emerson, who might be shy or morbid or indifferent or furtively impudent. She was prepared for all of these. But she had never imagined one who would be happy and greet her with the shout of the morning star.

Indoors herself, partaking of tea with old Mrs. Butterworth, she reflected that it is impossible to foretell the future with any degree of accuracy, that it is impossible to rehearse life. A fault in the scenery, a face in the audience, an irruption of the audience on to the stage, and all our carefully planned gestures mean nothing, or mean too much. "I will bow," she had thought. "I will not shake hands with him. That will be just the proper thing." She had bowed—but to whom? To gods, to heroes, to the nonsense of school-girls!

She had bowed across the rubbish that cumbers the world.

So ran her thoughts, while her faculties were busy with Cecil. It was another of those dreadful engagement calls. Mrs. Butterworth had wanted to see him, and he did not want to be seen. He did not want to hear about hydrangeas, why they change their colour at the seaside. He did not want to join the C. O. S. When cross he was always elaborate, and made long, clever answers where "Yes" or "No" would have done. Lucy soothed him and tinkered at the conversation in a way that promised well for their married peace. No one is perfect, and surely it is wiser to discover the imperfections before wedlock. Miss Bartlett, indeed, though not in word, had taught the girl that this our life contains nothing satisfactory. Lucy, though she disliked the teacher, regarded the teaching as profound, and applied it to her lover.

"Lucy," said her mother, when they got home, "is anything the matter with Cecil?"

The question was ominous; up till now Mrs. Honeychurch had behaved with charity and restraint.

"No, I don't think so, mother; Cecil's all right."

"Perhaps he's tired."

Lucy compromised: perhaps Cecil was a little tired.

"Because otherwise"—she pulled out her bonnet-pins with gathering displeasure—"because otherwise I cannot account for him."

"I do think Mrs. Butterworth is rather tiresome, if you mean that."

"Cecil has told you to think so. You were devoted to her as a little girl, and nothing will describe her goodness to you through the typhoid fever. No—it is just the same thing everywhere."

"Let me just put your bonnet away, may I?"

"Surely he could answer her civilly for one half-hour?"

"Cecil has a very high standard for people," faltered Lucy, seeing trouble ahead. "It's part of his ideals—it is really that that makes him sometimes seem—"

"Oh, rubbish! If high ideals make a young man rude, the sooner he gets rid of them the better," said Mrs. Honeychurch, handing her the bonnet.

"Now, mother! I've seen you cross with Mrs. Butterworth yourself!"

"Not in that way. At times I could wring her neck. But not in that way. No. It is the same with Cecil all over."

"By-the-by—I never told you. I had a letter from Charlotte while I was away in London."

This attempt to divert the conversation was too puerile, and Mrs. Honeychurch resented it.

"Since Cecil came back from London, nothing appears to please him. Whenever I speak he winces;—I see him, Lucy; it is useless to contradict me. No doubt I am neither artistic nor literary nor intellectual nor musical, but I cannot help the drawing-room furniture; your father bought it and we must put up with it, will Cecil kindly remember."

"I—I see what you mean, and certainly Cecil oughtn't to. But he does not mean to be uncivil —he once explained—it is the *things* that upset him—he is easily upset by ugly things—he is not uncivil to *people*."

"Is it a thing or a person when Freddy sings?"

"You can't expect a really musical person to enjoy comic songs as we do."

"Then why didn't he leave the room? Why sit wriggling and sneering and spoiling everyone's pleasure?"

"We mustn't be unjust to people," faltered Lucy. Something had enfeebled her, and the case for Cecil, which she had mastered so perfectly in London, would not come forth in an effective form. The two civilizations had clashed—Cecil hinted that they might—and she was dazzled and bewildered, as though the radiance that lies behind all civilization had blinded her eyes. Good taste and bad taste were only catchwords, garments of diverse cut; and music itself dissolved to a whisper through pine-trees, where the song is not distinguishable from the comic song.

She remained in much embarrassment, while Mrs.

Miss Bartlett's Boiler

Honeychurch changed her frock for dinner; and every now and then she said a word, and made things no better. There was no concealing the fact—Cecil had meant to be supercilious, and he had succeeded. And Lucy—she knew not why— wished that the trouble could have come at any other time.

"Go and dress, dear; you'll be late."

"All right, mother—"

"Don't say 'All right' and stop. Go."

She obeyed, but loitered disconsolately at the landing window. It faced north, so there was little view, and no view of the sky. Now, as in the winter, the pine-trees hung close to her eyes. One connected the landing window with depression. No definite problem menaced her, but she sighed to herself, "Oh, dear, what shall I do, what shall I do?" It seemed to her that every one else was behaving very badly. And she ought not to have mentioned Miss Bartlett's letter. She must be more careful; her mother was rather inquisitive, and might have asked what it was about. Oh, dear, what should she do?—and then Freddy came bounding up-stairs, and joined the ranks of the ill-behaved.

"I say, those are topping people."

"My dear baby, how tiresome you've been! You had no business to take them bathing in the Sacred Lake; it's much too public. It was all right for you, but most awkward for every one else. Do be more careful. You forget the place is growing half suburban."

"I say, is anything on to-morrow week?"

"Not that I know of."

"Then I want to ask the Emersons up to Sunday tennis."

"Oh, I wouldn't do that, Freddy, I wouldn't do that with all this muddle."

"What's wrong with the court? They won't mind a bump or two, and I've ordered new balls."

"I meant *it's* better not. I really mean it."

He seized her by the elbows and humorously danced her up and down the passage. She pretended not to mind, but she could have screamed with temper. Cecil glanced at them as he proceeded to his toilet and they impeded Mary with her brood of hot-water cans. Then Mrs. Honeychurch opened her door and said: "Lucy, what a noise you're making! I have something to say to you. Did you say you had had a letter from Charlotte?" and Freddy ran away.

"Yes. I really can't stop. I must dress too."

"How's Charlotte?"

"All right."

"Lucy!"

The unfortunate girl returned.

"You've a bad habit of hurrying away in the middle of one's sentences. Did Charlotte mention her boiler?"

"Her *what?*"

"Don't you remember that her boiler was to be had out in October, and her bath cistern cleaned out, and all kinds of terrible to-doings?"

"I can't remember all Charlotte's worries," said Lucy bitterly. "I shall have enough of my own, now that you are not pleased with Cecil."

Mrs. Honeychurch might have flamed out. She did not. She said: "Come here, old lady—thank you for putting away my bonnet—kiss me." And, though nothing is perfect, Lucy felt for the moment that her mother and Windy Corner and the Weald in the declining sun were perfect.

So the grittiness went out of life. It generally did at Windy Corner. At the last minute, when the social machine was clogged hopelessly, one member or other of the family poured in a drop of oil. Cecil despised their methods—perhaps rightly. At all events, they were not his own.

Dinner was at half-past seven. Freddy gabbled a grace, and they drew up their heavy chairs and fell to. Fortunately, the men were hungry. Nothing untoward occurred until the pudding. Then Freddy said:

"Lucy, what's Emerson like?"

"I saw him in Florence," said Lucy, hoping that this would pass for a reply.

"Is he the clever sort, or is he a decent chap?"

"Ask Cecil; it is Cecil who brought him here."

"He is the clever sort, like myself," said Cecil.

Freddy looked at him doubtfully.

"How well did you know them at the Bertolini?" asked Mrs. Honeychurch.

"Oh, very slightly. I mean, Charlotte knew them even less than I did."

"Oh, that reminds me—you never told me what Charlotte said in her letter."

"One thing and another," said Lucy, wondering whether she would get through the meal without a lie. "Among other things, that an awful friend of hers had been bicycling through Summer Street, wondered if she'd come up and see us, and mercifully didn't."

"Lucy, I do call the way you talk unkind."

"She was a novelist," said Lucy craftily. The remark was a happy one, for nothing roused Mrs. Honeychurch so much as literature in the hands of females. She would abandon every topic to inveigh against those women who (instead of minding their houses and their children) seek notoriety by print. Her attitude was: "If books must be written, let them be written by men"; and she developed it at great length, while Cecil yawned and Freddy played at "This year, next year, now, never," with his plum-stones, and Lucy artfully fed the flames of her mother's wrath. But soon the conflagration died down, and the ghosts began to gather in the darkness. There were too many ghosts about. The original ghost—that touch of lips on her cheek—had surely been laid long ago; it could be nothing to her that a man had kissed her on a mountain once. But it had begotten a spectral family—Mr. Harris, Miss Bartlett's letter, Mr. Beebe's memories of violets—and one or other of these was bound to haunt her before Cecil's very eyes. It was Miss Bartlett who returned now, and with appalling vividness.

"I have been thinking, Lucy, of that letter of Charlotte's. How is she?"

"I tore the thing up."

"Didn't she say how she was? How does she sound? Cheerful?"

"Oh, yes, I suppose so—no—not very cheerful, I suppose."

"Then, depend upon it, it *is* the boiler. I know myself how water preys upon one's mind. I would rather anything else—even a misfortune with the meat."

Cecil laid his hand over his eyes.

"So would I," asserted Freddy, backing his mother up—backing up the spirit of her remark rather than the substance.

"And I have been thinking," she added rather nervously, "surely we could squeeze Charlotte in here next week, and give her a nice holiday while the plumbers at Tunbridge Wells finish. I have not seen poor Charlotte for so long."

It was more than her nerves could stand. And yet she could not protest violently after her mother's goodness to her upstairs.

"Mother, no!" she pleaded. "It's impossible.

We can't have Charlotte on the top of the other things; we're squeezed to death as it is. Freddy's got a friend coming Tuesday, there's Cecil, and you've promised to take in Minnie Beebe because of the diphtheria scare. It simply can't be done."

"Nonsense! It can."

"If Minnie sleeps in the bath. Not otherwise."

"Minnie can sleep with you."

"I won't have her."

"Then, if you're so selfish, Mr. Floyd must share a room with Freddy."

"Miss Bartlett, Miss Bartlett, Miss Bartlett," moaned Cecil, again laying his hand over his eyes.

"It's impossible," repeated Lucy. "I don't want to make difficulties, but it really isn't fair on the maids to fill up the house so."

Alas!

"The truth is, dear, you don't like Charlotte."

"No, I don't. And no more does Cecil. She gets on our nerves. You haven't seen her lately, and don't realize how tiresome she can be, though so good. So please, mother, don't worry us this last summer; but spoil us by not asking her to come."

"Hear, hear!" said Cecil.

Mrs. Honeychurch, with more gravity than usual, and with more feeling than she usually permitted herself, replied: "This isn't very kind of you two. You have each other and all these woods to walk in, so full of beautiful things; and poor

Charlotte has only the water turned off and plumbers. You are young, dears, and however clever young people are, and however many books they read, they will never guess what it feels like to grow old."

Cecil crumbled his bread.

"I must say Cousin Charlotte was very kind to me that year I called on my bike," put in Freddy. "She thanked me for coming till I felt like such a fool, and fussed round no end to get an egg boiled for my tea just right."

"I know, dear. She is kind to every one, and yet Lucy makes this difficulty when we try to give her some little return."

But Lucy hardened her heart. It was no good being kind to Miss Bartlett. She had tried herself too often and too recently. One might lay up treasure in heaven by the attempt, but one enriched neither Miss Bartlett nor any one else upon earth. She was reduced to saying: "I can't help it, mother. I don't like Charlotte. I admit it's horrid of me."

"From your own account, you told her as much."

"Well, she would leave Florence so stupidly. She flurried—"

The ghosts were returning; they filled Italy, they were even usurping the places she had known as a child. The Sacred Lake would never be the same again, and, on Sunday week, something would even happen to Windy Corner. How would she fight against ghosts? For a moment the visible world faded away, and memories and emotions alone seemed real.

"I suppose Miss Bartlett must come, since she boils eggs so well," said Cecil, who was in rather a happier frame of mind, thanks to the admirable cooking.

"I didn't mean the egg was *well* boiled," corrected Freddy, "because in point of fact she forgot to take it off, and as a matter of fact I don't care for eggs. I only meant how jolly kind she seemed."

Cecil frowned again. Oh, these Honeychurches! Eggs, boilers, hydrangeas, maids—of such were their lives compact. "May me and Lucy get down from our chairs?" he asked, with scarcely veiled insolence. "We don't want no dessert."

Chapter XIV: How Lucy Faced the External Situation Bravely

OF course Miss Bartlett accepted. And, equally of course, she felt sure that she would prove a nuisance, and begged to be given an inferior spare room—something with no view, anything. Her love to Lucy. And, equally of course, George Emerson could come to tennis on the Sunday week.

Lucy faced the situation bravely, though, like most of us, she only faced the situation that encompassed her. She never gazed inwards. If at times strange images rose from the depths, she put them down to nerves. When Cecil brought the Emersons to Summer Street, it had upset her nerves. Charlotte would burnish up past foolishness, and this might upset her nerves. She was nervous at night. When she talked to George— they met again almost immediately at the Rectory —his voice moved her deeply, and she wished to remain near him. How dreadful if she really wished to remain near him! Of course, the wish was due to nerves, which love to play such perverse tricks upon us. Once she had suffered from "things that came out of nothing and meant she didn't know what." Now Cecil had explained psychology to her one wet afternoon, and all the troubles of youth in an unknown world could be dismissed.

It is obvious enough for the reader to conclude, "She loves young Emerson." A reader in Lucy's place would not find it obvious. Life is easy to chronicle, but bewildering to practice, and we welcome "nerves" or any other shibboleth that will cloak our personal desire. She loved Cecil; George made her nervous; will the reader explain to her that the phrases should have been reversed?

But the external situation—she will face that bravely.

The meeting at the Rectory had passed off well enough. Standing between Mr. Beebe and Cecil, she had made a few temperate allusions to Italy, and George had replied. She was anxious to show that she was not shy, and was glad that he did not seem shy either.

"A nice fellow," said Mr. Beebe afterwards. "He will work off his crudities in time. I rather mistrust young men who slip into life gracefully."

Lucy said, "He seems in better spirits. He laughs more."

"Yes," replied the clergyman. "He is waking up."

That was all. But, as the week wore on, more of her defences fell, and she entertained an image that had physical beauty.

In spite of the clearest directions, Miss Bartlett

contrived to bungle her arrival. She was due at the South-Eastern station at Dorking, whither Mrs. Honeychurch drove to meet her. She arrived at the London and Brighton station, and had to hire a cab up. No one was at home except Freddy and his friend, who had to stop their tennis and to entertain her for a solid hour. Cecil and Lucy turned up at four o'clock, and these, with little Minnie Beebe, made a somewhat lugubrious sextette upon the upper lawn for tea.

"I shall never forgive myself," said Miss Bartlett, who kept on rising from her seat, and had to be begged by the united company to remain. "I have upset everything. Bursting in on young people! But I insist on paying for my cab up. Grant me that, at any rate."

"Our visitors never do such dreadful things," said Lucy, while her brother, in whose memory the boiled egg had already grown unsubstantial, exclaimed in irritable tones: "Just what I've been trying to convince Cousin Charlotte of, Lucy, for the last half hour."

"I do not feel myself an ordinary visitor," said Miss Bartlett, and looked at her frayed gloves.

"All right, if you'd really rather. Five shillings, and I gave a bob to the driver."

Miss Bartlett looked in her purse. Only sovereigns and pennies. Could any one give her change? Freddy had half a quid and his friend had four half-crowns. Miss Bartlett accepted their moneys and then said: "But who am I to give the sovereign to?"

"Let's leave it all till mother comes back," suggested Lucy.

"No, dear; your mother may take quite a long drive now that she is not hampered with me. We all have our little foibles, and mine is the prompt settling of accounts."

Here Freddy's friend, Mr. Floyd, made the one remark of his that need be quoted: he offered to toss Freddy for Miss Bartlett's quid. A solution seemed in sight, and even Cecil, who had been ostentatiously drinking his tea at the view, felt the eternal attraction of Chance, and turned round.

But this did not do, either.

"Please—please—I know I am a sad spoilsport, but it would make me wretched. I should practically be robbing the one who lost."

"Freddy owes me fifteen shillings," interposed Cecil. "So it will work out right if you give the pound to me."

"Fifteen shillings," said Miss Bartlett dubiously. "How is that, Mr. Vyse?"

"Because, don't you see, Freddy paid your cab. Give me the pound, and we shall avoid this deplorable gambling."

Miss Bartlett, who was poor at figures, became bewildered and rendered up the sovereign, amidst the suppressed gurgles of the other youths. For a moment Cecil was happy. He was playing at nonsense among his peers. Then he glanced at Lucy, in whose face petty anxieties had marred the smiles. In January he would rescue his Leonardo from this stupefying twaddle.

"But I don't see that!" exclaimed Minnie Beebe who had narrowly watched the iniquitous transaction. "I don't see why Mr. Vyse is to have the quid."

"Because of the fifteen shillings and the five," they said solemnly. "Fifteen shillings and five shillings make one pound, you see."

"But I don't see—"

They tried to stifle her with cake.

"No, thank you. I'm done. I don't see why— Freddy, don't poke me. Miss Honeychurch, your brother's hurting me. Ow! What about Mr. Floyd's ten shillings? Ow! No, I don't see and I never shall see why Miss What's-her-name should-n't pay that bob for the driver."

"I had forgotten the driver," said Miss Bartlett, reddening. "Thank you, dear, for reminding me. A shilling was it? Can any one give me change for half a crown?"

"I'll get it," said the young hostess, rising with decision. "Cecil, give me that sovereign. No— give me up that sovereign. I'll get Euphemia to change it, and we'll start the whole thing again from the beginning."

"Lucy—Lucy—what a nuisance I am!" protested Miss Bartlett, and followed her across the lawn. Lucy tripped ahead, simulating hilarity. When they were out of earshot Miss Bartlett stopped her wails and said quite briskly: "Have you told him about him yet?"

"No, I haven't," replied Lucy, and then could have bitten her tongue for understanding so quickly what her cousin meant. "Let me see—a sovereign's worth of silver."

She escaped into the kitchen. Miss Bartlett's sudden transitions were too uncanny. It sometimes seemed as if she planned every word she spoke or caused to be spoken; as if all this worry about cabs and change had been a ruse to surprise the soul.

"No, I haven't told Cecil or any one," she remarked, when she returned. "I promised you I shouldn't. Here is your money—all shillings, except two half-crowns. Would you count it? You can settle your debt nicely now."

Miss Bartlett was in the drawing-room, gazing at the photograph of St. John ascending, which had been framed.

"How dreadful!" she murmured, "how more than dreadful, if Mr. Vyse should come to hear of it from some other source."

"Oh, no, Charlotte," said the girl, entering the battle. "George Emerson is all right, and what other source is there?"

Miss Bartlett considered. "For instance, the

driver. I saw him looking through the bushes at you. I remember he had a violet between his teeth."

Lucy shuddered a little. "We shall get the silly affair on our nerves if we aren't careful. How could a Florentine cab-driver ever get hold of Cecil?"

"We must think of every possibility."

"Oh, it's all right."

"Or perhaps old Mr. Emerson knows. In fact, he is certain to know."

"I don't care if he does. I was grateful to you for your letter, but even if the news does get round, I think I can trust Cecil to laugh at it."

"To contradict it?"

"No, to laugh at it." But she knew in her heart that she could not trust him, for he desired her untouched.

"Very well, dear, you know best. Perhaps gentlemen are different to what they were when I was young. Ladies are certainly different."

"Now, Charlotte!" She struck at her playfully. "You kind, anxious thing! What *would* you have me do? First you say, 'Don't tell'; and then you say, 'Tell.' Which is it to be? Quick!"

Miss Bartlett sighed. "I am no match for you in conversation, dearest. I blush when I think how I interfered at Florence, and you so well able to look after yourself, and so much cleverer in all ways than I am. You will never forgive me."

"Shall we go out, then. They will smash all the china if we don't."

For the air rang with the shrieks of Minnie, who was being scalped with a teaspoon.

"Dear, one moment—we may not have this chance for a chat again. Have you seen the young one yet?"

"Yes, I have."

"What happened?"

"We met at the Rectory."

"What line is he taking up?"

"No line. He talked about Italy, like any other person. It is really all right. What advantage would he get from being a cad, to put it bluntly? I do wish I could make you see it my way. He really won't be any nuisance, Charlotte."

"Once a cad, always a cad. That is my poor opinion."

Lucy paused. "Cecil said one day—and I thought it so profound—that there are two kinds of cads—the conscious and the subconscious." She paused again, to be sure of doing justice to Cecil's profundity. Through the window she saw Cecil himself, turning over the pages of a novel. It was a new one from Smith's library. Her mother must have returned from the station.

"Once a cad, always a cad," droned Miss Bartlett.

"What I mean by subconscious is that Mr.

Emerson lost his head. I fell into all those violets, and he was silly and surprised. I don't think we ought to blame him very much. It makes such a difference when you see a person with beautiful things behind him unexpectedly. It really does; it makes an enormous difference, and he lost his head: he doesn't admire me, or any of that nonsense, one straw. Freddy rather likes him, and has asked him up here on Sunday, so you can judge for yourself. He has improved; he doesn't always look as if he's going to burst into tears. He is a clerk in the General Manager's office at one of the big railways—not a porter! and runs down to his father for week-ends. Papa was to do with journalism, but is rheumatic and has retired. There! Now for the garden." She took hold of her guest by the arm. "Suppose we don't talk about this silly Italian business any more. We want you to have a nice restful visit at Windy Corner, with no worriting."

Lucy thought this rather a good speech. The reader may have detected an unfortunate slip in it. Whether Miss Bartlett detected the slip one cannot say, for it is impossible to penetrate into the minds of elderly people. She might have spoken further, but they were interrupted by the entrance of her hostess. Explanations took place, and in the midst of them Lucy escaped, the images throbbing a little more vividly in her brain.

Chapter XV: The Disaster Within

THE Sunday after Miss Bartlett's arrival was a glorious day, like most of the days of that year. In the Weald, autumn approached, breaking up the green monotony of summer, touching the parks with the grey bloom of mist, the beech-trees with russet, the oak-trees with gold. Up on the heights, battalions of black pines witnessed the change, themselves unchangeable. Either country was spanned by a cloudless sky, and in either arose the tinkle of church bells.

The garden of Windy Corners was deserted except for a red book, which lay sunning itself upon the gravel path. From the house came incoherent sounds, as of females preparing for worship. "The men say they won't go"— "Well, I don't blame them"— "Minnie says, need she go?" — "Tell her, no nonsense"— "Anne! Mary! Hook me behind!"— "Dearest Lucia, may I trespass upon you for a pin?" For Miss Bartlett had announced that she at all events was one for church.

The sun rose higher on its journey, guided, not by Phaethon, but by Apollo, competent, unswerving, divine. Its rays fell on the ladies whenever they advanced towards the bedroom windows; on

The Disaster Within

Mr. Beebe down at Summer Street as he smiled over a letter from Miss Catharine Alan; on George Emerson cleaning his father's boots; and lastly, to complete the catalogue of memorable things, on the red book mentioned previously. The ladies move, Mr. Beebe moves, George moves, and movement may engender shadow. But this book lies motionless, to be caressed all the morning by the sun and to raise its covers slightly, as though acknowledging the caress.

Presently Lucy steps out of the drawing-room window. Her new cerise dress has been a failure, and makes her look tawdry and wan. At her throat is a garnet brooch, on her finger a ring set with rubies—an engagement ring. Her eyes are bent to the Weald. She frowns a little—not in anger, but as a brave child frowns when he is trying not to cry. In all that expanse no human eye is looking at her, and she may frown unrebuked and measure the spaces that yet survive between Apollo and the western hills.

"Lucy! Lucy! What's that book? Who's been taking a book out of the shelf and leaving it about to spoil?"

"It's only the library book that Cecil's been reading."

"But pick it up, and don't stand idling there like a flamingo."

Lucy picked up the book and glanced at the title listlessly, *Under a Loggia.* She no longer read novels herself, devoting all her spare time to solid literature in the hope of catching Cecil up. It was dreadful how little she knew, and even when she thought she knew a thing, like the Italian painters, she found she had forgotten it. Only this morning she had confused Francesco Francia with Piero della Francesca, and Cecil had said, "What! you aren't forgetting your Italy already?" And this too had lent anxiety to her eyes when she saluted the dear view and the dear garden in the foreground, and above them, scarcely conceivable elsewhere, the dear sun.

"Lucy—have you a sixpence for Minnie and a shilling for yourself?"

She hastened in to her mother, who was rapidly working herself into a Sunday fluster.

"It's a special collection—I forget what for. I do beg, no vulgar clinking in the plate with half-pennies; see that Minnie has a nice bright sixpence. Where is the child? Minnie! That book's all warped. (Gracious, how plain you look!) Put it under the Atlas to press. Minnie!"

"Oh, Mrs. Honeychurch—" from the upper regions.

"Minnie, don't be late. Here comes the horse" —it was always the horse, never the carriage. "Where's Charlotte? Run up and hurry her. Why is she so long? She had nothing to do. She never brings anything but blouses. Poor Charlotte — How I do detest blouses! Minnie!"

The Disaster Within

Paganism is infectious—more infectious than diphtheria or piety—and the Rector's niece was taken to church protesting. As usual, she didn't see why. Why shouldn't she sit in the sun with the young men? The young men, who had now appeared, mocked her with ungenerous words. Mrs. Honeychurch defended orthodoxy, and in the midst of the confusion Miss Bartlett, dressed in the very height of the fashion, came strolling down the stairs.

"Dear Marian, I am very sorry, but I have no small change—nothing but sovereigns and half-crowns. Could any one give me—"

"Yes, easily. Jump in. Gracious me, how smart you look! What a lovely frock! You put us all to shame."

"If I did not wear my best rags and tatters now, when should I wear them?" said Miss Bartlett reproachfully. She got into the victoria and placed herself with her back to the horse. The necessary uproar ensued, and then they drove off.

"Good-bye! Be good!" called out Cecil.

Lucy bit her lip, for the tone was sneering. On the subject of "church and so on" they had had rather an unsatisfactory conversation. He had said that people ought to overhaul themselves, and she did not want to overhaul herself; she did not know how it was done. Honest orthodoxy Cecil respected, but he always assumed that honesty is the result of a spiritual crisis; he could not imagine

it as a natural birthright, that might grow heavenward like flowers. All that he said on this subject
pained her, though he exuded tolerance from
every pore; somehow the Emersons were different.

She saw the Emersons after church. There was
a line of carriages down the road, and the Honeychurch vehicle happened to be opposite Cissie Villa.
To save time, they walked over the green to it, and
found father and son smoking in the garden.

"Introduce me," said her mother. "Unless the
young man considers that he knows me already."

He probably did; but Lucy ignored the Sacred
Lake and introduced them formally. Old Mr.
Emerson claimed her with much warmth, and said
how glad he was that she was going to be married.
She said yes, she was glad too; and then, as Miss
Bartlett and Minnie were lingering behind with Mr.
Beebe, she turned the conversation to a less dis-
turbing topic, and asked him how he liked his new
house.

"Very much," he replied, but there was a note
of offence in his voice; she had never known him
offended before. He added: "We find, though,
that the Miss Alans were coming, and that we have
turned them out. Women mind such a thing. I
am very much upset about it."

"I believe that there was some misunderstanding," said Mrs. Honeychurch uneasily.

"Our landlord was told that we should be a different type of person," said George, who seemed disposed to carry the matter further. "He thought we should be artistic. He is disappointed."

"And I wonder whether we ought to write to the Miss Alans and offer to give it up. What do you think?" He appealed to Lucy.

"Oh, stop now you have come," said Lucy lightly. She must avoid censuring Cecil. For it was on Cecil that the little episode turned, though his name was never mentioned.

"So George says. He says that the Miss Alans must go to the wall. Yet it does seem so unkind."

"There is only a certain amount of kindness in the world," said George, watching the sunlight flash on the panels of the passing carriages.

"Yes!" exclaimed Mrs. Honeychurch. "That's exactly what I say. Why all this twiddling and twaddling over two Miss Alans?"

"There is a certain amount of kindness, just as there is a certain amount of light," he continued in measured tones. "We cast a shadow on something wherever we stand, and it is no good moving from place to place to save things; because the shadow always follows. Choose a place where you won't do harm—yes, choose a place where you won't do very much harm, and stand in it for all you are worth, facing the sunshine."

"Oh, Mr. Emerson, I see you're clever!"

"Eh—?"

"I see you're going to be clever. I hope you didn't go behaving like that to poor Freddy."

George's eyes laughed, and Lucy suspected that he and her mother would get on rather well.

"No, I didn't," he said. "He behaved that way to me. It is his philosophy. Only he starts life with it; and I have tried the Note of Interrogation first."

"What *do* you mean? No, never mind what you mean. Don't explain. He looks forward to seeing you this afternoon. Do you play tennis? Do you mind tennis on Sunday—?"

"George mind tennis on Sunday! George, after his education, distinguish between Sunday—"

"Very well, George doesn't mind tennis on Sunday. No more do I. That's settled. Mr. Emerson, if you could come with your son we should be so pleased."

He thanked her, but the walk sounded rather far; he could only potter about in these days.

She turned to George: "And then he wants to give up his house to the Miss Alans."

"I know," said George, and put his arm round his father's neck. The kindness that Mr. Beebe and Lucy had always known to exist in him came out suddenly, like sunlight touching a vast landscape—a touch of the morning sun? She remembered that in all his perversities he had never spoken against affection.

Miss Bartlett approached.

The Disaster Within

"You know our cousin, Miss Bartlett," said Mrs. Honeychurch pleasantly. "You met her with my daughter in Florence."

"Yes, indeed!" said the old man, and made as if he would come out of the garden to meet the lady. Miss Bartlett promptly got into the victoria. Thus entrenched, she emitted a formal bow. It was the Pension Bertolini again, the dining-table with the decanters of water and wine. It was the old, old battle of the room with the view.

George did not respond to the bow. Like any boy, he blushed and was ashamed; he knew that the chaperon remembered. He said: "I—I'll come up to tennis if I can manage it," and went into the house. Perhaps anything that he did would have pleased Lucy, but his awkwardness went straight to her heart; men were not gods after all, but as human and as clumsy as girls; even men might suffer from unexplained desires, and need help. To one of her upbringing, and of her destination, the weakness of men was a truth unfamiliar, but she had surmised it at Florence, when George threw her photographs into the River Arno.

"George, don't go," cried his father, who thought it a great treat for people if his son would talk to them. "George has been in such good spirits to-day, and I am sure he will end by coming up this afternoon."

Lucy caught her cousin's eye. Something in its mute appeal made her reckless. "Yes," she said, raising her voice, "I do hope he will." Then she went to the carriage and murmured, "The old man hasn't been told; I knew it was all right." Mrs. Honeychurch followed her, and they drove away.

Satisfactory that Mr. Emerson had not been told of the Florence escapade; yet Lucy's spirits should not have leapt up as if she had sighted the ramparts of heaven. Satisfactory; yet surely she greeted it with disproportionate joy. All the way home the horses' hoofs sang a tune to her: "He has not told, he has not told." Her brain expanded the melody: "He has not told his father—to whom he tells all things. It was not an exploit. He did not laugh at me when I had gone." She raised her hand to her cheek. "He does not love me. No. How terrible if he did! But he has not told. He will not tell."

She longed to shout the words: "It is all right. It's a secret between us two for ever. Cecil will never hear." She was even glad that Miss Bartlett had made her promise secrecy, that last dark evening at Florence, when they had knelt packing in his room. The secret, big or little, was guarded. Only three English people knew of it in the world.

Thus she interpreted her joy. She greeted Cecil with unusual radiance, because she felt so safe. As he helped her out of the carriage, she said:

"The Emersons have been so nice. George Emerson has improved enormously."

The Disaster Within

"Oh, how are my protégés?" asked Cecil, who took no real interest in them, and had long since forgotten his resolution to bring them to Windy Corner for educational purposes.

"Protégés!" she exclaimed with some warmth.

For the only relationship which Cecil conceived was feudal: that of protector and protected. He had no glimpse of the comradeship after which the girl's soul yearned.

"You shall see for yourself how your protégés are. George Emerson is coming up this afternoon. He is a most interesting man to talk to. Only don't—" She nearly said, "Don't protect him." But the bell was ringing for lunch, and, as often happened, Cecil had paid no great attention to her remarks. Charm, not argument, was to be her forte.

Lunch was a cheerful meal. Generally Lucy was depressed at meals. Some one had to be soothed—either Cecil or Miss Bartlett or a Being not visible to the mortal eye—a Being who whispered to her soul: "It will not last, this cheerfulness. In January you must go to London to entertain the grandchildren of celebrated men." But to-day she felt she had received a guarantee. Her mother would always sit there, her brother here. The sun, though it had moved a little since the morning, would never be hidden behind the western hills. After luncheon they asked her to play. She had seen Gluck's *Armide* that year, and played from memory the music of the enchanted garden—the music to which Renaud approaches, beneath the light of an eternal dawn, the music that never gains, never wanes, but ripples for ever like the tideless seas of fairyland. Such music is not for the piano, and her audience began to get restive, and Cecil, sharing the discontent, called out: "Now play us the other garden—the one in *Parsifal*."

She closed the instrument.

"Not very dutiful," said her mother's voice.

Fearing that she had offended Cecil, she turned quickly round. There George was. He had crept in without interrupting her.

"Oh, I had no idea!" she exclaimed, getting very red; and then, without a word of greeting, she re-opened the piano. Cecil should have the *Parsifal*, and anything else that he liked.

"Our performer has changed her mind," said Miss Bartlett, perhaps implying, she will play the music to Mr. Emerson. Lucy did not know what to do nor even what she wanted to do. She played a few bars of the Flower Maidens' song very badly and then she stopped.

"I vote tennis," said Freddy, disgusted at the scrappy entertainment.

"Yes, so do I." Once more she closed the unfortunate piano. "I vote you have a men's four."

"All right."

"Not for me, thank you," said Cecil. "I will not spoil the set." He never realized that it may be an act of kindness in a bad player to make up a fourth.

"Oh, come along Cecil. I'm bad, Floyd's rotten, and so I dare say's Emerson."

George corrected him: "I am not bad."

One looked down one's nose at this. "Then certainly I won't play," said Cecil, while Miss Bartlett, under the impression that she was snubbing George, added: "I agree with you, Mr. Vyse. You had much better not play. Much better not."

Minnie, rushing in where Cecil feared to tread, announced that she would play. "I shall miss every ball anyway, so what does it matter?" But Sunday intervened and stamped heavily upon the kindly suggestion.

"Then it will have to be Lucy," said Mrs. Honeychurch; "you must fall back on Lucy. There is no other way out of it. Lucy, go and change your frock."

Lucy's Sabbath was generally of this amphibious nature. She kept it without hypocrisy in the morning, and broke it without reluctance in the afternoon. As she changed her frock, she wondered whether Cecil was sneering at her; really she must overhaul herself and settle everything up before she married him.

Mr. Floyd was her partner. She liked music, but how much better tennis seemed. How much better to run about in comfortable clothes than to sit at the piano and feel girt under the arms. Once

more music appeared to her the employment of a
child. George served, and surprised her by his
anxiety to win. She remembered how he had sighed
among the tombs at Santa Croce because things
wouldn't fit; how after the death of that obscure
Italian he had leant over the parapet by the Arno
and said to her: "I shall want to live, I tell you."
He wanted to live now, to win at tennis, to stand for
all he was worth in the sun—in the sun which had
begun to decline and was shining in her eyes; and he
did win.

Ah, how beautiful the Weald looked! The hills
stood out above its radiance, as Fiesole stands above
the Tuscan Plain, and the South Downs, if one
chose, were the mountains of Carrara. She might
be forgetting her Italy, but she was noticing more
things in her England. One could play a new game
with the view, and try to find in its innumerable
folds some town or village that would do for Florence. Ah, how beautiful the Weald looked!

But now Cecil claimed her. He chanced to be in
a lucid critical mood, and would not sympathize
with exaltation. He had been rather a nuisance
all through the tennis, for the novel that he was
reading was so bad that he was obliged to read
it aloud to others. He would stroll round the pre-
cincts of the court and call out: "I say, listen to this,
Lucy. Three split infinitives." "Dreadful!" said
Lucy, and missed her stroke. When they had finished their set, he still went on reading; there was

some murder scene, and really every one must listen to it. Freddy and Mr. Floyd were obliged to hunt for a lost ball in the laurels, but the other two acquiesced.

"The scene is laid in Florence."

"What fun, Cecil! Read away. Come, Mr. Emerson, sit down after all your energy." She had "forgiven" George, as she put it, and she made a point of being pleasant to him.

He jumped over the net and sat down at her feet, asking: "You—and are you tired?"

"Of course I'm not!"

"Do you mind being beaten?"

She was going to answer, "No," when it struck her that she did mind, so she answered, "Yes." She added merrily, "I don't see *you're* such a splendid player, though. The light was behind you, and it was in my eyes."

"I never said I was."

"Why, you did!"

"You didn't attend."

"You said—oh, don't go in for accuracy at this house. We all exaggerate, and we get very angry with people who don't."

'The scene is laid in Florence," repeated Cecil, with an upward note.

Lucy recollected herself.

" 'Sunset. Leonora was speeding—' "

Lucy interrupted. "Leonora? Is Leonora the heroine? Who's the book by?"

"Joseph Emery Prank. 'Sunset. Leonora was speeding across the square. Pray the saints she might not arrive too late. Sunset—the sunset of Italy. Under Orcagna's Loggia—the Loggia de' Lanzi, as we sometimes call it now—' "

Lucy burst into laughter. " 'Joseph Emery Prank' indeed! Why it's Miss Lavish! It's Miss Lavish's novel, and she's publishing it under somebody else's name."

"Who may Miss Lavish be?"

"Oh, a dreadful person—Mr. Emerson, you remember Miss Lavish?" Excited by her pleasant afternoon, she clapped her hands.

George looked up. "Of course I do. I saw her the day I arrived at Summer Street. It was she who told me that you lived here."

"Weren't you pleased?" She meant—"to see Miss Lavish," but when he bent down to the grass without replying, it struck her that she could mean something else. She watched his head, which was almost resting against her knee, and she thought that the ears were reddening. "No wonder the novel's bad," she added. "I never liked Miss Lavish. But I suppose one ought to read it as one's met her."

"All modern books are bad," said Cecil, who was annoyed at her inattention, and vented his annoyance on literature. "Every one writes for money in these days."

"Oh, Cecil—!"

"It is so. I will inflict Joseph Emery Prank on you no longer."

Cecil, this afternoon, seemed such a twittering sparrow. The ups and downs in his voice were noticeable, but they did not affect her. She had dwelt amongst melody and movement, and her nerves refused to answer to the clang of his. Leaving him to be annoyed, she gazed at the black head again. She did not want to stroke it, but she saw herself wanting to stroke it; the sensation was curious.

"How do you like this view of ours, Mr. Emerson?"

"I never notice much difference in views."

"What do you mean?"

"Because they're all alike. Because all that matters in them is distance and air."

"H'm!" said Cecil, uncertain whether the remark was striking or not.

"My father"—he looked up at her (and he was a little flushed)—"says that there is only one perfect view—the view of the sky straight over our heads, and that all these views on earth are but bungled copies of it."

"I expect your father has been reading Dante," said Cecil, fingering the novel, which alone permitted him to lead the conversation.

"He told us another day that views are really crowds—crowds of trees and houses and hills—and are bound to resemble each other, like human crowds

—and that the power they have over us is sometimes supernatural, for the same reason."

Lucy's lips parted.

"For a crowd is more than the people who make it up. Something gets added to it—no one knows how—just as something has got added to those hills."

He pointed with his racquet to the South Downs.

"What a splendid idea!" she murmured. "I shall enjoy hearing your father talk again. I'm so sorry he's not so well."

"No, he isn't well."

"There's an absurd account of a view in this book," said Cecil.

"Also that men fall into two classes—those who forget views and those who remember them, even in small rooms."

"Mr. Emerson, have you any brothers or sisters?"

"None. Why?"

"You spoke of 'us.'"

"My mother, I was meaning."

Cecil closed the novel with a bang.

"Oh, Cecil—how you made me jump!"

"I will inflict Joseph Emery Prank on you no longer."

"I can just remember us all three going into the country for the day and seeing as far as Hindhead. It is the first thing that I remember."

Cecil got up; the man was ill-bred—he hadn't put on his coat after tennis—he didn't do. He would have strolled away if Lucy had not stopped him.

"Cecil, do read the thing about the view."

"Not while Mr. Emerson is here to entertain us."

"No—read away. I think nothing's funnier than to hear silly things read out loud. If Mr. Emerson thinks us frivolous, he can go."

This struck Cecil as subtle, and pleased him. It put their visitor in the position of a prig. Somewhat mollified, he sat down again.

"Mr. Emerson, go and find tennis balls." She opened the book. Cecil must have his reading and anything else that he liked. But her attention wandered to George's mother, who—according to Mr. Eager—had been murdered in the sight of God—according to her son—had seen as far as Hindhead.

"Am I really to go?" asked George.

"No, of course not really," she answered.

"Chapter two," said Cecil, yawning. "Find me chapter two, if it isn't bothering you."

Chapter two was found, and she glanced at its opening sentences.

She thought she had gone mad.

"Here—hand me the book."

She heard her voice saying: "It isn't worth reading—it's too silly to read—I never saw such rubbish—it oughtn't to be allowed to be printed."

He took the book from her.

" 'Leonora,' " he read, " 'sat pensive and alone.

Before her lay the rich champaign of Tuscany, dotted over with many a smiling village. The season was spring.' "

Miss Lavish knew, somehow, and had printed the past in draggled prose, for Cecil to read and for George to hear.

" 'A golden haze,' " he read. He read: " 'Afar off the towers of Florence, while the bank on which she sat was carpeted with violets. All unobserved Antonio stole up behind her—' "

Lest Cecil should see her face she turned to George and she saw his face.

He read: " 'There came from his lips no wordy protestation such as formal lovers use. No eloquence was his, nor did he suffer from the lack of it. He simply enfolded her in his manly arms.' "

There was a silence.

"This isn't the passage I wanted," he informed them. "There is another much funnier, further on." He turned over the leaves.

"Should we go in to tea?" said Lucy, whose voice remained steady.

She led the way up the garden, Cecil following her, George last. She thought a disaster was averted. But when they entered the shrubbery it came. The book, as if it had not worked mischief enough, had been forgotten, and Cecil must go back for it; and George, who loved passionately, must blunder against her in the narrow path.

"No—" she gasped, and, for the second time, was kissed by him.

As if no more was possible, he slipped back; Cecil rejoined her; they reached the upper lawn alone.

Chapter XVI: Lying to George

BUT Lucy had developed since the spring. That is to say, she was now better able to stifle the emotions of which the conventions and the world disapprove. Though the danger was greater, she was not shaken by deep sobs. She said to Cecil, "I am not coming in to tea—tell mother—I must write some letters," and went up to her room. Then she prepared for action. Love felt and returned, love which our bodies exact and our hearts have transfigured, love which is the most real thing that we shall ever meet, reappeared now as the world's enemy, and she must stifle it.

She sent for Miss Bartlett.

The contest lay not between love and duty. Perhaps there never is such a contest. It lay between the real and the pretended, and Lucy's first aim was to defeat herself. As her brain clouded over, as the memory of the views grew dim and the words of the book died away, she returned to her old shibboleth of nerves. She "conquered her breakdown." Tampering with the truth, she forgot that the truth had ever been. Remembering that she was engaged to Cecil, she compelled herself to confused remembrances of George; he was nothing to her; he never had been anything; he had behaved abominably; she had never encouraged him. The armour of falsehood is subtly wrought out of darkness, and hides a man not only from others, but from his own soul. In a few moments Lucy was equipped for battle.

"Something too awful has happened," she began, as soon as her cousin arrived. "Do you know anything about Miss Lavish's novel?"

Miss Bartlett looked surprised, and said that she had not read the book, nor known that it was published; Eleanor was a reticent woman at heart.

"There is a scene in it. The hero and heroine make love. Do you know about that?"

"Dear—?"

"Do you know about it, please?" she repeated. "They are on a hillside, and Florence is in the distance."

"My good Lucia, I am all at sea. I know nothing about it whatever."

"There are violets. I cannot believe it is a coincidence. Charlotte, Charlotte, how *could* you have told her? I have thought before speaking; it *must* be you."

"Told her what?" she asked, with growing agitation.

"About that dreadful afternoon in February."

Miss Bartlett was genuinely moved. "Oh, Lucy, dearest girl—she hasn't put that in her book?"

Lucy nodded.

"Not so that one could recognize it?"

"Yes."

"Then never—never—never more shall Eleanor Lavish be a friend of mine."

"So you did tell?"

"I did just happen—when I had tea with her at Rome—in the course of conversation—"

"But Charlotte—what about the promise you gave me when we were packing? Why did you tell Miss Lavish, when you wouldn't even let me tell mother?"

"I will never forgive Eleanor. She has betrayed my confidence."

"Why did you tell her, though? This is a most serious thing."

Why does any one tell anything? The question is eternal, and it was not surprising that Miss Bartlett should only sigh faintly in response. She had done wrong—she admitted it, she only hoped that she had not done harm; she had told Eleanor in the strictest confidence.

Lucy stamped with irritation.

"Cecil happened to read out the passage aloud to me and to Mr. Emerson; it upset Mr. Emerson and he insulted me again. Behind Cecil's back. Ugh! Is it possible that men are such brutes? Behind Cecil's back as we were walking up the garden."

Miss Bartlett burst into self-accusations and regrets.

"What is to be done now? Can you tell me?"

"Oh, Lucy—I shall never forgive myself, never to my dying day. Fancy if your prospects—"

"I know," said Lucy, wincing at the word. "I see now why you wanted me to tell Cecil, and what you meant by 'some other source.' You knew that you had told Miss Lavish, and that she was not reliable."

It was Miss Bartlett's turn to wince.

"However," said the girl, despising her cousin's shiftiness, "what's done's done. You have put me in a most awkward position. How am I to get out of it?"

Miss Bartlett could not think. The days of her energy were over. She was a visitor, not a chaperon, and a discredited visitor at that. She stood with clasped hands while the girl worked herself into the necessary rage.

"He must—that man must have such a setting down that he won't forget. And who's to give it him? I can't tell mother now—owing to you. Nor Cecil, Charlotte, owing to you. I am caught up every way. I think I shall go mad. I have no one to help me. That's why I've sent for you. What's wanted is a man with a whip."

Miss Bartlett agreed: one wanted a man with a whip.

"Yes—but it's no good agreeing. What's to be *done?* We women go maundering on. What *does* a girl do when she comes across a cad?"

"I always said he was a cad, dear. Give me

credit for that, at all events. From the very first moment—when he said his father was having a bath."

"Oh, bother the credit and who's been right or wrong! We've both made a muddle of it. George Emerson is still down the garden there, and is he to be left unpunished, or isn't he? I want to know."

Miss Bartlett was absolutely helpless. Her own exposure had unnerved her, and thoughts were colliding painfully in her brain. She moved feebly to the window, and tried to detect the cad's white flannels among the laurels.

"You were ready enough at the Bertolini when you rushed me off to Rome. Can't you speak again to him now?"

"Willingly would I move heaven and earth—"

"I want something more definite," said Lucy contemptuously. "Will you speak to him? It is the least you can do, surely, considering it all happened because you broke your word."

"Never again shall Eleanor Lavish be a friend of mine."

Really, Charlotte was outdoing herself.

"Yes or no, please; yes or no."

"It is the kind of thing that only a gentleman can settle."

George Emerson was coming up the garden with a tennis ball in his hand.

"Very well," said Lucy, with an angry gesture.

"No one will help me. I will speak to him myself."
And immediately she realized that this was what
her cousin had intended all along.

"Hullo, Emerson!" called Freddy from below.
"Found the lost ball? Good man! Want any
tea?" And there was an irruption from the house
on to the terrace.

"Oh, Lucy, but that is brave of you! I admire
you—"

They had gathered round George, who beckoned,
she felt, over the rubbish, the sloppy thoughts, the
furtive yearnings that were beginning to cumber her
soul. Her anger faded at the sight of him. Ah!
the Emersons were fine people in their way. She
had to subdue a rush in her blood before saying:

"Freddy has taken him into the dining-room.
The others are going down the garden. Come.
Let us get this over quickly. Come. I want you
in the room, of course."

"Lucy, do you mind doing it?"

"How can you ask such a ridiculous question?"

"Poor Lucy—" She stretched out her hand.
"I seem to bring nothing but misfortune wherever
I go." Lucy nodded. She remembered their last
evening at Florence—the packing, the candle, the
shadow of Miss Bartlett's toque on the door. She
was not to be trapped by pathos a second time.
Eluding her cousin's caress, she led the way downstairs.

"Try the jam," Freddy was saying. "The jam's jolly good."

George, looking big and dishevelled, was pacing up and down the dining-room. As she entered he stopped, and said:

"No—nothing to eat."

"You go down to the others," said Lucy; "Charlotte and I will give Mr. Emerson all he wants. Where's mother?"

"She's started on her Sunday writing. She's in the drawing-room."

"That's all right. You go away."

He went off singing.

Lucy sat down at the table. Miss Bartlett, who was thoroughly frightened, took up a book and pretended to read.

She would not be drawn into an elaborate speech. She just said: "I can't have it, Mr. Emerson. I cannot even talk to you. Go out of this house, and never come into it again as long as I live here"—flushing as she spoke and pointing to the door. "I hate a row. Go please."

"What—"

"No discussion."

"But I can't—"

She shook her head. "Go, please. I do not want to call in Mr. Vyse."

"You don't mean," he said, absolutely ignoring Miss Bartlett—"you don't mean that you are going to marry that man?"

The line was unexpected.

She shrugged her shoulders, as if his vulgarity wearied her. "You are merely ridiculous," she said quietly.

Then his words rose gravely over hers: "You cannot live with Vyse. He's only for an acquaintance. He is for society and cultivated talk. He should know no one intimately, least of all a woman."

It was a new light on Cecil's character.

"Have you ever talked to Vyse without feeling tired?"

"I can scarcely discuss—"

"No, but have you ever? He is the sort who are all right so long as they keep to things— books, pictures—but kill when they come to people. That's why I'll speak out through all this muddle even now. It's shocking enough to lose you in any case, but generally a man must deny himself joy, and I would have held back if your Cecil had been a different person. I would never have let myself go. But I saw him first in the National Gallery, when he winced because my father mispronounced the names of great painters. Then he brings us here, and we find it is to play some silly trick on a kind neighbour. That is the man all over—playing tricks on people, on the most sacred form of life that he can find. Next, I meet you together, and find him protecting and teaching you and your mother to be shocked, when it was for *you* to settle whether you were

shocked or no. Cecil all over again. He daren't
let a woman decide. He's the type who's kept
Europe back for a thousand years. Every moment of his life he's forming you, telling you what's
charming or amusing or ladylike, telling you what
a man thinks womanly; and you, you of all women,
listen to his voice instead of to your own. So it
was at the Rectory, when I met you both again; so
it has been the whole of this afternoon. Therefore
—not 'therefore I kissed you,' because the book
made me do that, and I wish to goodness I had more
self-control. I'm not ashamed. I don't apologize.
But it has frightened you, and you may not have
noticed that I love you. Or would you have told
me to go, and dealt with a tremendous thing so
lightly? But therefore—therefore I settled to
fight him."

Lucy thought of a very good remark.

"You say Mr. Vyse wants me to listen to him,
Mr. Emerson. Pardon me for suggesting that you
have caught the habit."

And he took the shoddy reproof and touched it
into immortality. He said:

"Yes, I have," and sank down as if suddenly
weary. "I'm the same kind of brute at bottom.
This desire to govern a woman—it lies very deep,
and men and women must fight it together before
they shall enter the garden. But I do love you—
surely in a better way than he does." He thought.
"Yes—really in a better way. I want you to have

your own thoughts even when I hold you in my arms." He stretched them towards her. "Lucy, be quick—there's no time for us to talk now— come to me as you came in the spring, and afterwards I will be gentle and explain. I have cared for you since that man died. I cannot live without you. 'No good,' I thought; 'she is marrying some one else'; but I meet you again when all the world is glorious water and sun. As you came through the wood I saw that nothing else mattered. I called. I wanted to live and have my chance of joy."

"And Mr. Vyse?" said Lucy, who kept commendably calm. "Does he not matter? That I love Cecil and shall be his wife shortly? A detail of no importance, I suppose?"

But he stretched his arms over the table towards her.

"May I ask what you intend to gain by this exhibition?"

He said: "It is our last chance. I shall do all that I can." And as if he had done all else, he turned to Miss Bartlett, who sat like some portent against the skies of the evening. "You wouldn't stop us this second time if you understood," he said. "I have been into the dark, and I am going back into it, unless you will try to understand."

Her long, narrow head drove backwards and forwards, as though demolishing some invisible obstacle. She did not answer.

"'It is being young," he said quietly, picking up his racquet from the floor and preparing to go. "It is being certain that Lucy cares for me really. It is that love and youth matter intellectually."

In silence the two women watched him. His last remark, they knew, was nonsense, but was he going after it or not? Would not he, the cad, the charlatan, attempt a more dramatic finish? No. He was apparently content. He left them, carefully closing the front-door; and when they looked through the hall window, they saw him go up the drive and begin to climb the slopes of withered fern behind the house. Their tongues were loosed, and they burst into stealthy rejoicings.

"Oh, Lucia—come back here—oh, what an awful man!"

Lucy had no reaction—at least, not yet. "Well, he amuses me," she said. "Either I'm mad, or else he is, and I'm inclined to think it's the latter. One more fuss through with you, Charlotte. Many thanks. I think, though, that this is the last. My admirer will hardly trouble me again."

And Miss Bartlett, too, essayed the roguish:

"Well, it isn't every one who could boast such a conquest, dearest, is it? Oh, one oughtn't to laugh, really. It might have been very serious. But you were so sensible and brave—so unlike the girls of my day."

"Let's go down to them."

But, once in the open air, she paused. Some

emotion—pity, terror, love, but the emotion was strong—seized her, and she was aware of autumn. Summer was ending, and the evening brought her odours of decay, the more pathetic because they were reminiscent of spring. That something or other mattered intellectually? A leaf, violently agitated, danced past her, while other leaves lay motionless. That the earth was hastening to re-enter darkness, and the shadows of those trees to creep over Windy Corner?

"Hullo, Lucy! There's still light enough for another set, if you two'll hurry."

"Mr. Emerson has had to go."

"What a nuisance! That spoils the four. I say, Cecil, do play, do, there's a good chap. It's Floyd's last day. Do play tennis with us, just this once."

Cecil's voice came: "My dear Freddy, I am no athlete. As you well remarked this very morning, 'There are some chaps who are no good for anything but books'; I plead guilty to being such a chap, and will not inflict myself on you."

The scales fell from Lucy's eyes. How had she stood Cecil for a moment? He was absolutely intolerable, and the same evening she broke off her engagement.

Chapter XVII: Lying to Cecil

HE was bewildered. He had nothing to say. He was not even angry, but stood, with a glass of whiskey between his hands, trying to think what had led her to such a conclusion.

She had chosen the moment before bed, when, in accordance with their bourgeois habit, she always dispensed drinks to the men. Freddy and Mr. Floyd were sure to retire with their glasses, while Cecil invariably lingered, sipping at his while she locked up the sideboard.

"I am very sorry about it," she said; "I have carefully thought things over. We are too different. I must ask you to release me, and try to forget that there ever was such a foolish girl."

It was a suitable speech, but she was more angry than sorry, and her voice showed it.

"Different—how—how—"

"I haven't had a really good education, for one thing," she continued, still on her knees by the sideboard. "My Italian trip came too late, and I am forgetting all that I learnt there. I shall never be able to talk to your friends, or behave as a wife of yours should."

"I don't understand you. You aren't like yourself. You're tired. Lucy."

"Tired!" she retorted, kindling at once. "That is exactly like you. You always think women don't mean what they say."

"Well, you sound tired, as if something has worried you."

"What if I do? It doesn't prevent me from realizing the truth. I can't marry you, and you will thank me for saying so some day."

"You had that bad headache yesterday— All right"—for she had exclaimed indignantly: "I see it's much more than headaches. But give me a moment's time." He closed his eyes. "You must excuse me if I say stupid things, but my brain has gone to pieces. Part of it lives three minutes back, when I was sure that you loved me, and the other part—I find it difficult—I am likely to say the wrong thing."

It struck her that he was not behaving so badly, and her irritation increased. She again desired a struggle, not a discussion. To bring on the crisis, she said:

"There are days when one sees clearly, and this is one of them. Things must come to a breaking-point some time, and it happens to be to-day. If you want to know, quite a little thing decided me to speak to you—when you wouldn't play tennis with Freddy."

"I never do play tennis," said Cecil, painfully bewildered; "I never could play. I don't understand a word you say."

"You can play well enough to make up a four. I thought it abominably selfish of you."

"No, I can't—well, never mind the tennis. Why couldn't you—couldn't you have warned me if you felt anything wrong? You talked of our wedding at lunch—at least, you let me talk."

"I knew you wouldn't understand," said Lucy quite crossly. "I might have known there would have been these dreadful explanations. Of course, it isn't the tennis—that was only the last straw to all I have been feeling for weeks. Surely it was better not to speak until I felt certain." She developed this position. "Often before I have wondered if I was fitted for your wife—for instance, in London; and are you fitted to be my husband? I don't think so. You don't like Freddy, nor my mother. There was always a lot against our engagement, Cecil, but all our relations seemed pleased, and we met so often, and it was no good mentioning it until—well, until all things came to a point. They have to-day. I see clearly. I must speak. That's all."

"I cannot think you were right," said Cecil gently. "I cannot tell why, but though all that you say sounds true, I feel that you are not treating me fairly. It's all too horrible."

"What's the good of a scene?"

"No good. But surely I have a right to hear a little more."

He put down his glass and opened the window.

From where she knelt, jangling her keys, she could see a slit of darkness, and, peering into it, as if it would tell him that "little more," his long, thoughtful face.

"Don't open the window; and you'd better draw the curtain, too; Freddy or any one might be outside." He obeyed. "I really think we had better go to bed, if you don't mind. I shall only say things that will make me unhappy afterwards. As you say it is all too horrible, and it is no good talking."

But to Cecil, now that he was about to lose her, she seemed each moment more desirable. He looked at her, instead of through her, for the first time since they were engaged. From a Leonardo she had become a living woman, with mysteries and forces of her own, with qualities that even eluded art. His brain recovered from the shock, and, in a burst of genuine devotion, he cried: "But I love you, and I did think you loved me!"

"I did not," she said. "I thought I did at first. I am sorry, and ought to have refused you this last time, too."

He began to walk up and down the room, and she grew more and more vexed at his dignified behaviour. She had counted on his being petty. It would have made things easier for her. By a cruel irony she was drawing out all that was finest in his disposition.

"You don't love me, evidently. I dare say you

are right not to. But it would hurt a little less if I knew why."

"Because"—a phrase came to her, and she accepted it—"you're the sort who can't know any one intimately."

A horrified look came into his eyes.

"I don't mean exactly that. But you will question me, though I beg you not to, and I must say something. It is that, more or less. When we were only acquaintances, you let me be myself, but now you're always protecting me." Her voice swelled. "I won't be protected. I will choose for myself what is ladylike and right. To shield me is an insult. Can't I be trusted to face the truth but I must get it second-hand through you? A woman's place! You despise my mother—I know you do—because she's conventional and bothers over puddings; but, oh goodness!"—she rose to her feet—"conventional, Cecil, you're that, for you may understand beautiful things, but you don't know how to use them; and you wrap yourself up in art and books and music, and would try to wrap up me. I won't be stifled, not by the most glorious music, for people are more glorious, and you hide them from me. That's why I break off my engagement. You were all right as long as you kept to things, but when you came to people—" She stopped.

There was a pause. Then Cecil said with great emotion:

"It is true."

"True on the whole," she corrected, full of some vague shame.

"True, every word. It is a revelation. It is —I."

"Anyhow, those are my reasons for not being your wife."

He repeated: " 'The sort that can know no one intimately.' It is true. I fell to pieces the very first day we were engaged. I behaved like a cad to Beebe and to your brother. You are even greater than I thought." She withdrew a step. "I'm not going to worry you. You are far too good to me. I shall never forget your insight; and, dear, I only blame you for this: you might have warned me in the early stages, before you felt you wouldn't marry me, and so have given me a chance to improve. I have never known you till this evening. I have just used you as a peg for my silly notions of what a woman should be. But this evening you are a different person: new thoughts—even a new voice—"

"What do you mean by a new voice?" she asked, seized with incontrollable anger.

"I mean that a new person seems speaking through you," said he.

Then she lost her balance. She cried: "If you think I am in love with some one else, you are very much mistaken."

"Of course I don't think that. You are not that kind, Lucy."

"Oh, yes, you do think it. It's your old idea, the idea that has kept Europe back—I mean the idea that women are always thinking of men. If a girl breaks off her engagement, every one says: 'Oh, she had some one else in her mind; she hopes to get some one else.' It's disgusting, brutal! As if a girl can't break it off for the sake of freedom."

He answered reverently: "I may have said that in the past. I shall never say it again. You have taught me better."

She began to redden, and pretended to examine the windows again.

"Of course, there is no question of 'some one else' in this, no 'jilting' or any such nauseous stupidity. I beg your pardon most humbly if my words suggested that there was. I only meant that there was a force in you that I hadn't known of up till now."

"All right, Cecil, that will do. Don't apologize to me. It was my mistake."

"It is a question between ideals, yours and mine—pure abstract ideals, and yours are the nobler. I was bound up in the old vicious notions, and all the time you were splendid and new." His voice broke. "I must actually thank you for what you have done—for showing me what I really am. Solemnly, I thank you for showing me a true woman. Will you shake hands?"

"Of course I will," said Lucy, twisting up her other hand in the curtains. "Good-night, Cecil. Good-bye. That's all right. I'm sorry about it. Thank you very much for your gentleness."

"Let me light your candle, shall I?"

They went into the hall.

"Thank you. Good-night again. God bless you, Lucy!"

"Good-bye, Cecil."

She watched him steal up-stairs, while the shadows from the banisters passed over her face like the beat of wings. On the landing he paused strong in his renunciation, and gave her a look of memorable beauty. For all his culture, Cecil was an ascetic at heart, and nothing in his love became him like the leaving of it.

She could never marry. In the tumult of her soul, that stood firm. Cecil believed in her; she must some day believe in herself. She must be one of the women whom she had praised so eloquently, who care for liberty and not for men; she must forget that George loved her, that George had been thinking through her and gained her this honourable release, that George had gone away into—what was it?—the darkness.

She put out the lamp.

It did not do to think, nor, for the matter of that to feel. She gave up trying to understand herself, and joined the vast armies of the benighted, who follow neither the heart nor the brain, and march to their destiny by catch-words. The armies are full of pleasant and pious folk. But they have yielded to the only enemy that matters—the enemy within. They have sinned against passion and truth, and vain will be their strife after virtue. As the years pass, they are censured. Their pleasantry and their piety show cracks, their wit becomes cynicism, their unselfishness hypocrisy; they feel and produce discomfort wherever they go. They have sinned against Eros and against Pallas Athene, and not by any heavenly intervention, but by the ordinary course of nature, those allied deities will be avenged.

Lucy entered this army when she pretended to George that she did not love him, and pretended to Cecil that she loved no one. The night received her, as it had received Miss Bartlett thirty years before.

Chapter XVIII: Lying to Mr. Beebe, Mrs. Honeychurch, Freddy, and the Servants

WINDY CORNER lay, not on the summit of the ridge, but a few hundred feet down the southern slope, at the springing of one of the great buttresses that supported the hill. On either side of it was a shallow ravine, filled with ferns and pine-trees, and down the ravine on the left ran the highway into the Weald.

Whenever Mr. Beebe crossed the ridge and caught sight of these noble dispositions of the earth, and, poised in the middle of them, Windy Corner, —he laughed. The situation was so glorious, the house so commonplace, not to say impertinent. The late Mr. Honeychurch had affected the cube, because it gave him the most accommodation for his money, and the only addition made by his widow had been a small turret, shaped like a rhinoceros' horn, where she could sit in wet weather and watch the carts going up and down the road. So impertinent—and yet the house "did," for it was the home of people who loved their surroundings honestly. Other houses in the neighborhood had been built by expensive architects, over others their inmates had fidgeted sedulously, yet all these suggested the accidental, the temporary; while Windy

Corner seemed as inevitable as an ugliness of Nature's own creation. One might laugh at the house, but one never shuddered.

Mr. Beebe was bicycling over this Monday afternoon with a piece of gossip. He had heard from the Miss Alans. These admirable ladies, since they could not go to Cissie Villa, had changed their plans. They were going to Greece instead.

"Since Florence did my poor sister so much good," wrote Miss Catharine, "we do not see why we should not try Athens this winter. Of course, Athens is a plunge, and the doctor has ordered her special digestive bread; but, after all, we can take that with us, and it is only getting first into a steamer and then into a train. But is there an English Church?" And the letter went on to say: "I do not expect we shall go any further than Athens, but if you knew of a really comfortable pension at Constantinople, we should be so grateful."

Lucy would enjoy this letter, and the smile with which Mr. Beebe greeted Windy Corner was partly for her. She would see the fun of it, and some of its beauty, for she must see some beauty. Though she was hopeless about pictures, and though she dressed so unevenly—oh, that cerise frock yesterday at church!—she must see some beauty in life, or she could not play the piano as she did. He had a theory that musicians are incredibly complex, and know far less than other artists what they want and what they are; that they puzzle themselves as well as their friends; that their psychology is a modern development, and has not yet been understood. This theory, had he known it, had possibly just been illustrated by facts. Ignorant of the events of yesterday he was only riding over to get some tea, to see his niece, and to observe whether Miss Honeychurch saw anything beautiful in the desire of two old ladies to visit Athens.

A carriage was drawn up outside Windy Corner, and just as he caught sight of the house it started, bowled up the drive, and stopped abruptly when it reached the main road. Therefore it must be the horse, who always expected people to walk up the hill in case they tired him. The door opened obediently, and two men emerged, whom Mr. Beebe recognized as Cecil and Freddy. They were an odd couple to go driving; but he saw a trunk beside the coachman's legs. Cecil, who wore a bowler, must be going away, while Freddy—(a cap)—was seeing him to the station. They walked rapidly, taking the short cuts, and reached the summit while the carriage was still pursuing the windings of the road.

They shook hands with the clergyman, but did not speak.

"So you're off for a minute, Mr. Vyse?" he asked.

Cecil said, "Yes," while Freddy edged away.

"I was coming to show you this delightful letter

from those friends of Miss Honeychurch's." He
quoted from it. "Isn't it wonderful? Isn't it
romance? most certainly they will go to Constantinople. They are taken in a snare that cannot fail.
They will end by going round the world."

Cecil listened civilly, and said he was sure that
Lucy would be amused and interested.

"Isn't Romance capricious! I never notice it in
you young people; you do nothing but play lawn
tennis, and say that romance is dead, while the Miss
Alans are struggling with all the weapons of propriety against the terrible thing. 'A really comfortable pension at Constantinople!' So they call it out
of decency, but in their hearts they want a pension
with magic windows opening on the foam of perilous
seas in fairyland forlorn! No ordinary view will
content the Miss Alans. They want the Pension
Keats."

"I'm awfully sorry to interrupt, Mr. Beebe,"
said Freddy, "but have you any matches?"

"I have," said Cecil, and it did not escape Mr.
Beebe's notice that he spoke to the boy more kindly.

"You have never met these Miss Alans, have you,
Mr. Vyse?"

"Never."

"Then you don't see the wonder of this Greek
visit. I haven't been to Greece myself, and don't
mean to go, and I can't imagine any of my friends
going. It is altogether too big for our little lot.
Don't you think so? Italy is just about as much as

we can manage. Italy is heroic, but Greece is god-
like or devilish—I am not sure which, and in either
case absolutely out of our suburban focus. All
right, Freddy—I am not being clever, upon my word
I am not—I took the idea from another fellow;
and give me those matches when you've done with
them." He lit a cigarette, and went on talking to
the two young men. "I was saying, if our poor
little Cockney lives must have a background, let it be
Italian. Big enough in all conscience. The ceiling
of the Sistine Chapel for me. There the contrast is
just as much as I can realize. But not the Parthe-
non, not the frieze of Phidias at any price; and here
comes the victoria."

"You're quite right," said Cecil. "Greece is
not for our little lot"; and he got in. Freddy followed, nodding to the clergyman, whom he trusted
not to be pulling one's leg, really. And before they
had gone a dozen yards he jumped out, and came
running back for Vyse's match-box, which had not
been returned. As he took it, he said: "I'm so
glad you only talked about books. Cecil's hard hit.
Lucy won't marry him. If you'd gone on about her,
as you did about them, he might have broken
down."

"But when—"

"Late last night. I must go."

"Perhaps they won't want me down there."

"No—go on. Good-bye."

"Thank goodness!" exclaimed Mr. Beebe to him-

self, and struck the saddle of his bicycle approvingly.
"It was the one foolish thing she ever did. Oh,
what a glorious riddance!" And, after a little
thought, he negotiated the slope into Windy Corner,
light of heart. The house was again as it ought
to be—cut off for ever from Cecil's pretentious
world.

He would find Miss Minnie down in the garden.
In the drawing-room Lucy was tinkling at a
Mozart Sonata. He hesitated a moment, but went
down the garden as requested. There he found a
mournful company. It was a blustering day, and
the wind had taken and broken the dahlias. Mrs.
Honeychurch, who looked cross, was tying them up,
while Miss Bartlett, unsuitably dressed, impeded her
with offers of assistance. At a little distance stood
Minnie and the "garden-child," a minute importation, each holding either end of a long piece of bass.

"Oh, how do you do, Mr. Beebe? Gracious
what a mess everything is! Look at my scarlet
pompons, and the wind blowing your skirts about,
and the ground so hard that not a prop will stick in,
and then the carriage having to go out, when I had
counted on having Powell, who—give every one
their due—does tie up dahlias properly."

Evidently Mrs. Honeychurch was shattered.

"How do you do?" said Miss Bartlett, with a
meaning glance, as though conveying that more
than dahlias had been broken off by the autumn
gales.

Lying to Mr. Beebe

"Here, Lennie, the bass," cried Mrs. Honey-church. The garden-child, who did not know what bass was, stood rooted to the path with horror. Minnie slipped to her uncle and whispered that every one was very disagreeable to-day, and that it was not her fault if dahlia-strings would tear longways instead of across.

"Come for a walk with me," he told her. "You have worried them as much as they can stand. Mrs. Honeychurch, I only called in aimlessly. I shall take her up to tea at the Beehive Tavern, if I may."

"Oh, must you? Yes do.—Not the scissors, thank you, Charlotte, when both my hands are full already— I'm perfectly certain that the orange cactus will go before I can get to it."

Mr. Beebe, who was an adept at relieving situations, invited Miss Bartlett to accompany them to this mild festivity.

"Yes, Charlotte, I don't want you—do go; there's nothing to stop about for, either in the house or out of it."

Miss Bartlett said that her duty lay in the dahlia-bed, but when she had exasperated every one, except Minnie, by a refusal, she turned round and exasperated Minnie by an acceptance. As they walked up the garden, the orange cactus fell, and Mr. Beebe's last vision was of the garden-child clasping it like a lover, his dark head buried in a wealth of blossom.

"It is terrible, this havoc among the flowers," he remarked.

"It is always terrible when the promise of months is destroyed in a moment," enunciated Miss Bartlett.

"Perhaps we ought to send Miss Honeychurch down to her mother. Or will she come with us?"

"I think we had better leave Lucy to herself, and to her own pursuits."

"They're angry with Miss Honeychurch because she was late for breakfast," whispered Minnie, "and Floyd has gone, and Mr. Vyse has gone, and Freddy won't play with me. In fact, Uncle Arthur, the house is not *at all* what it was yesterday."

"Don't be a prig," said her Uncle Arthur. "Go and put on your boots."

He stepped into the drawing-room, where Lucy was still attentively pursuing the Sonatas of Mozart. She stopped when he entered.

"How do you do? Miss Bartlett and Minnie are coming with me to tea at the Beehive. Would you come too?"

"I don't think I will, thank you."

"No, I didn't suppose you would care to much."

Lucy turned to the piano and struck a few chords.

"How delicate those Sonatas are!" said Mr. Beebe, though at the bottom of his heart, he thought them silly little things.

Lucy passed into Schumann.

"Miss Honeychurch!"

"Yes."

"I met them on the hill. Your brother told me."

"Oh he did?" She sounded annoyed. Mr. Beebe felt hurt, for he had thought that she would like him to be told.

"I needn't say that it will go no further."

"Mother, Charlotte, Cecil, Freddy, you," said Lucy, playing a note for each person who knew, and then playing a sixth note.

"If you'll let me say so, I am very glad, and I am certain that you have done the right thing."

"So I hoped other people would think, but they don't seem to."

"I could see that Miss Bartlett thought it unwise."

"So does mother. Mother minds dreadfully."

"I am very sorry for that," said Mr. Beebe with feeling.

Mrs. Honeychurch, who hated all changes, did mind, but not nearly as much as her daughter pretended, and only for the minute. It was really a ruse of Lucy's to justify her despondency—a ruse of which she was not herself conscious, for she was marching in the armies of darkness.

"And Freddy minds."

"Still, Freddy never hit it off with Vyse much, did he? I gathered that he disliked the engagement, and felt it might separate him from you."

"Boys are so odd."

Minnie could be heard arguing with Miss Bartlett through the floor. Tea at the Beehive apparently involved a complete change of apparel. Mr.

Beebe saw that Lucy—very properly—did not wish to discuss her action, so after a sincere expression of sympathy, he said, "I have had an absurd letter from Miss Alan.   That was really what brought me over.   I thought it might amuse you all."

"How delightful!" said Lucy, in a dull voice.

For the sake of something to do, he began to read her the letter.   After a few words her eyes grew alert, and soon she interrupted him with— "Going abroad?   When do they start?"

"Next week, I gather."

"Did Freddy say whether he was driving straight back?"

"No, he didn't."

"Because I do hope he won't go gossiping."

So she did want to talk about her broken engagement.   Always complaisant, he put the letter away. But she at once exclaimed in a high voice, "Oh, do tell me more about the Miss Alans!   How perfectly splendid of them to go abroad!"

"I want them to start from Venice, and go in a cargo steamer down the Illyrian coast!"

She laughed heartily.   "Oh, delightful!   I wish they'd take me."

"Has Italy filled you with the fever of travel? Perhaps George Emerson is right.   He says that 'Italy is only an euphuism for Fate.' "

"Oh, not Italy, but Constantinople.   I have always longed to go to Constantinople.   Constantinople is practically Asia, isn't it?"

Lying to Mr. Beebe

Mr. Beebe reminded her that Constantinople was still unlikely, and that the Miss Alans only aimed at Athens, "with Delphi, perhaps, if the roads are safe." But this made no difference to her enthusiasm. She had always longed to go to Greece even more, it seemed. He saw, to his surprise, that she was apparently serious.

"I didn't realize that you and the Miss Alans were still such friends, after Cissie Villa."

"Oh, that's nothing; I assure you Cissie Villa's nothing to me; I would give anything to go with them."

"Would your mother spare you again so soon? You have scarcely been home three months."

"She *must* spare me!" cried Lucy, in growing excitement. "I simply *must* go away. I have to." She ran her fingers hysterically through her hair. "Don't you see that I *have* to go away? I didn't realize at the time—and of course I want to see Constantinople so particularly."

"You mean that since you have broken off your engagement you feel—"

"Yes, yes. I knew you'd understand."

Mr. Beebe did not quite understand. Why could not Miss Honeychurch repose in the bosom of her family? Cecil had evidently taken up the dignified line, and was not going to annoy her. Then it struck him that her family itself might be annoying. He hinted this to her, and she accepted the hint eagerly.

"Yes, of course; to go to Constantinople until they are used to the idea and everything has calmed down."

"I am afraid it has been a bothersome business," he said gently.

"No, not at all. Cecil was very kind indeed; only—I had better tell you the whole truth, since you have heard a little—it was that he is so masterful. I found that he wouldn't let me go my own way. He would improve me in places where I can't be improved. Cecil won't let a woman decide for herself—in fact, he daren't. What nonsense I do talk! but that is the kind of thing."

"It is what I gathered from my own observation of Mr. Vyse; it is what I gather from all that I have known of you. I do sympathize and agree most profoundly. I agree so much that you must let me make one little criticism: Is it worth while rushing off to Greece?"

"But I must go somewhere!" she cried. "I have been worrying all the morning, and here comes the very thing." She struck her knees with clenched fists, and repeated: "I must! And the time I shall have with mother, and all the money she spent on me last spring. You all think much too highly of me. I wish you weren't so kind." At this moment Miss Bartlett entered, and her nervousness increased. "I must get away, ever so far. I must know my own mind and where I want to go."

"Come along; tea, tea, tea," said Mr. Beebe, and

hustled his guests out of the front-door. He hustled them so quickly that he forgot his hat. When he returned for it he heard, to his relief and surprise, the tinkling of a Mozart Sonata.

"She is playing again," he said to Miss Bartlett.

"Lucy can always play," was the acid reply.

"One is very thankful that she has such a resource. She is evidently much worried, as, of course, she ought to be. I know all about it. The marriage was so near that it must have been a hard struggle before she could wind herself up to speak."

Miss Bartlett gave a kind of wriggle, and he prepared for a discussion. He had never fathomed Miss Bartlett. As he had put it to himself at Florence, "she might yet reveal depths of strangeness, if not of meaning." But she was so unsympathetic that she must be reliable. He assumed that much, and he had no hesitation in discussing Lucy with her. Minnie was fortunately collecting ferns.

She opened the discussion with: "We had much better let the matter drop."

"I wonder."

"It is of the highest importance that there should be no gossip in Summer Street. It would be *death* to gossip about Mr. Vyse's dismissal at the present moment."

Mr. Beebe rased his eyebrows. Death is a strong word—surely too strong. There was no question of tragedy. He said: "Of course, Miss Honeychurch will make the fact public in her own way, and when she chooses. Freddy only told me because he knew she would not mind."

"I know," said Miss Bartlett civilly. "Yet Freddy ought not to have told even you. One cannot be too careful."

"Quite so."

"I do implore absolute secrecy. A chance word to a chattering friend, and—"

"Exactly." He was used to these nervous old maids and to the exaggerated importance that they attach to words. A rector lives in a web of petty secrets, and confidences and warnings, and the wiser he is the less he will regard them. He will change the subject, as did Mr. Beebe, saying cheerfully: "Have you heard from any Bertolini people lately? I believe you keep up with Miss Lavish. It is odd how we of that pension, who seemed such a fortuitous collection, have been working into one another's lives. Two, three, four, six of us—no, eight; I had forgotten the Emersons—have kept more or less in touch. We must really give the Signora a testimonial."

And, Miss Bartlett not favouring the scheme, they walked up the hill in a silence which was only broken by the rector naming some fern. On the summit they paused. The sky had grown wilder since he stood there last hour, giving to the land a tragic greatness that is rare in Surrey. Grey clouds were charging across tissues of white, which stretched and shredded and tore slowly, until through their final layers there gleamed a hint of the disappearing blue. Summer was retreating. The wind roared, the trees groaned, yet the noise seemed insufficient for those vast operations in heaven. The weather was breaking up, breaking, broken, and it is a sense of the fit rather than of the supernatural that equips such crises with the salvos of angelic artillery. Mr. Beebe's eyes rested on Windy Corner, where Lucy sat, practising Mozart. No smile came to his lips, and, changing the subject again, he said: "We shan't have rain, but we shall have darkness, so let us hurry on. The darkness last night was appalling."

They reached the Beehive Tavern at about five o'clock. That amiable hostelry possesses a verandah, in which the young and the unwise do dearly love to sit, while guests of more mature years seek a pleasant sanded room, and have tea at a table comfortably. Mr. Beebe saw that Miss Bartlett would be cold if she sat out, and that Minnie would be dull if she sat in, so he proposed a division of forces. They would hand the child her food through the window. Thus he was incidentally enabled to discuss the fortunes of Lucy.

"I have been thinking, Miss Bartlett," he said, "and, unless you very much object, I would like to reopen that discussion." She bowed. "Nothing about the past. I know little and care less about that; I am absolutely certain that it is to your cousin's credit. She has acted loftily and rightly, and it

is like her gentle modesty to say that we think too
highly of her. But the future. Seriously, what do
you think of this Greek plan?" He pulled out the
letter again. "I don't know whether you overheard, but she wants to join the Miss Alans in their
mad career. It's all—I can't explain—it's wrong."

Miss Bartlett read the letter in silence, laid it
down, seemed to hesitate, and then read it again.

"I can't see the point of it myself."

To his astonishment, she replied: "There I cannot agree with you. In it I spy Lucy's salvation."

"Really. Now, why?"

"She wanted to leave Windy Corner."

"I know—but it seems so odd, so unlike her, so—
I was going to say—selfish."

"It is natural, surely—after such painful scenes—
that she should desire a change."

Here, apparently, was one of those points that
the male intellect misses. Mr. Beebe exclaimed:
"So she says herself, and since another lady agrees
with her, I must own that I am partially convinced.
Perhaps she must have a change. I have no sisters
or—and I don't understand these things. But why
need she go as far as Greece?"

"You may well ask that," replied Miss Bartlett,
who was evidently interested, and had almost
dropped her evasive manner. "Why Greece?
(What is it, Minnie dear—jam?) Why not Tunbridge Wells? Oh, Mr. Beebe! I had a long and
most unsatisfactory interview with dear Lucy this

morning. I cannot help her. I will say no more. Perhaps I have already said too much. I am not to talk. I wanted her to spend six months with me at Tunbridge Wells, and she refused."

Mr. Beebe poked at a crumb with his knife.

"But my feelings are of no importance. I know too well that I get on Lucy's nerves. Our tour was a failure. She wanted to leave Florence, and when we got to Rome she did not want to be in Rome, and all the time I felt that I was spending her mother's money——."

"Let us keep to the future, though," interrupted Mr. Beebe. "I want your advice."

"Very well," said Charlotte, with a choky abruptness that was new to him, though familiar to Lucy. "I for one will help her to go to Greece. Will you?"

Mr. Beebe considered.

"It is absolutely necessary," she continued, lowering her veil and whispering through it with a passion, an intensity, that surprised him. "I know——I *know*." The darkness was coming on, and he felt that this odd woman really did know. "She must not stop here a moment, and we must keep quiet till she goes. I trust that the servants know nothing. Afterwards——but I may have said too much already. Only, Lucy and I are helpless against Mrs. Honeychurch alone. If you help we may succeed. Otherwise——"

"Otherwise——?"

"Otherwise," she repeated as if the word held finality.

"Yes, I will help her," said the clergyman, setting his jaw firm. "Come, let us go back now, and settle the whole thing up."

Miss Bartlett burst into florid gratitude. The tavern sign—a beehive trimmed evenly with bees—creaked in the wind outside as she thanked him. Mr. Beebe did not quite understand the situation; but then, he did not desire to understand it, nor to jump to the conclusion of "another man" that would have attracted a grosser mind. He only felt that Miss Bartlett knew of some vague influence from which the girl desired to be delivered, and which might well be clothed in the fleshly form. Its very vagueness spurred him into knight-errantry. His belief in celibacy, so reticent, so carefully concealed beneath his tolerance and culture, now came to the surface and expanded like some delicate flower. "They that marry do well, but they that refrain do better." So ran his belief, and he never heard that an engagement was broken off but with a slight feeling of pleasure. In the case of Lucy, the feeling was intensified through dislike of Cecil; and he was willing to go further—to place her out of danger until she could confirm her resolution of virginity. The feeling was very subtle and quite undogmatic, and he never imparted it to any other of the characters in this entanglement. Yet it existed, and it alone explains his action subsequently, and his influence on the action of others. The compact that he made with Miss Bartlett in the tavern, was to help not only Lucy, but religion also.

They hurried home through a world of black and grey. He conversed on indifferent topics: the Emersons' need of a housekeeper; servants; Italian servants; novels about Italy; novels with a purpose; could literature influence life? Windy Corner glimmered. In the garden, Mrs. Honeychurch, now helped by Freddy, still wrestled with the lives of her flowers.

"It gets too dark," she said hopelessly. "This comes of putting off. We might have known the weather would break up soon; and now Lucy wants to go to Greece. I don't know what the world's coming to."

"Mrs. Honeychurch," he said, "go to Greece she must. Come up to the house and let's talk it over. Do you, in the first place, mind her breaking with Vyse?"

"Mr. Beebe, I'm thankful—simply thankful."

"So am I," said Freddy.

"Good. Now come up to the house."

They conferred in the dining-room for half an hour.

Lucy would never have carried the Greek scheme alone. It was expensive and dramatic—both qualities that her mother loathed. Nor would Charlotte have succeeded. The honours of the day rested with Mr. Beebe. By his tact and common sense, and by his influence as a clergyman—for a clergyman who was not a fool influenced Mrs. Honeychurch greatly—he bent her to their purpose.

"I don't see why Greece is necessary," she said; "but as you do, I suppose it is all right. It must be something I can't understand. Lucy! Let's tell her. Lucy!"

"She is playing the piano," Mr. Beebe said. He opened the door, and heard the words of a song:

"Look not thou on beauty's charming."

"I didn't know that Miss Honeychurch sang, too."

"Sit thou still when kings are arming,
Taste not when the wine-cup glistens —"

"It's a song that Cecil gave her. How odd girls are!"

"What's that?" called Lucy, stopping short.

"All right, dear,'" said Mrs. Honeychurch kindly. She went into the drawing-room, and Mr. Beebe heard her kiss Lucy and say: "I am sorry I was so cross about Greece, but it came on the top of the dahlias."

Rather a hard voice said: "Thank you, mother; that doesn't matter a bit."

"And you are right, too—Greece will be all right; you can go if the Miss Alans will have you."

"Oh, splendid! Oh, thank you!"

Mr. Beebe followed. Lucy still sat at the piano with her hands over the keys. She was glad, but he had expected greater gladness. Her mother bent over her. Freddy, to whom she had been singing, reclined on the floor with his head against her, and an unlit pipe between his lips. Oddly enough, the group was beautiful. Mr. Beebe, who loved the art of the past, was reminded of a favourite theme, the *Santa Conversazione,* in which people who care for one another are painted chatting together about noble things—a theme neither sensual nor sensational, and therefore ignored by the art of to-day. Why should Lucy want either to marry or to travel when she had such friends at home?

> "Taste not when the wine-cup glistens,
> Speak not when the people listens,"

she continued.

"Here's Mr. Beebe."

"Mr. Beebe knows my rude ways."

"It's a beautiful song and a wise one," said he. "Go on."

"It isn't very good," she said listlessly. "I forget why—harmony or something."

"I suspected it was unscholarly. It's so beautiful."

"The tune's right enough," said Freddy, "but the words are rotten. Why throw up the sponge?"

"How stupidly you talk!" said his sister. The *Santa Conversazione* was broken up. After all, there was no reason that Lucy should talk about Greece or thank him for persuading her mother, so he said good-bye.

Freddy lit his bicycle lamp for him in the porch, and with his usual felicity of phrase, said: "This has been a day and a half."

"Stop thine ear against the singer—"

"Wait a minute; she is finishing."

> "From the red gold keep thy finger;
> Vacant heart and hand and eye
> Easy live and quiet die."

"I love weather like this," said Freddy.

Mr. Beebe passed into it.

The two main facts were clear. She had behaved splendidly, and he had helped her. He could not expect to master the details of so big a change in a girl's life. If here and there he was dissatisfied or puzzled, he must acquiesce; she was choosing the better part.

> "Vacant heart and hand and eye——"

Perhaps the song stated "the better part" rather too strongly. He half fancied that the soaring accompaniment—which he did not lose in the shout of the gale—really agreed with Freddy, and was gently criticizing the words that it adorned:

> "Vacant heart and hand and eye
> Easy live and quiet die."

However, for the fourth time Windy Corner lay poised below him—now as a beacon in the roaring tides of darkness.

Chapter XIX: Lying to Mr. Emerson

THE Miss Alans were found in their beloved temperance hotel near Bloomsbury—a clean, airless establishment much patronized by provincial England. They always perched there before crossing the great seas, and for a week or two would fidget gently over clothes, guide-books, mackintosh squares, digestive bread, and other Continental necessaries. That there are shops abroad, even in Athens, never occurred to them, for they regarded travel as a species of warfare, only to be undertaken by those who have been fully armed at the Haymarket Stores. Miss Honeychurch, they trusted, would take care to equip herself duly. Quinine could now be obtained in tabloids; paper soap was a great help towards freshening up one's face in the train. Lucy promised, a little depressed.

"But, of course, you know all about these things, and you have Mr. Vyse to help you. A gentleman is such a stand-by."

Mrs. Honeychurch, who had come up to town with her daughter, began to drum nervously upon her card-case.

"We think it so good of Mr. Vyse to spare you," Miss Catharine continued. "It is not every young

man who would be so unselfish. But perhaps he
will come out and join you later on."

"Or does his work keep him in London?" said
Miss Teresa, the more acute and less kindly of the
two sisters.

"However, we shall see him when he sees you off.
I do so long to see him."

"No one will see Lucy off," interposed Mrs.
Honeychurch. "She doesn't like it."

"No, I hate seeings-off," said Lucy.

"Really? How funny! I should have thought
that in this case—"

"Oh, Mrs. Honeychurch, you aren't going? It
is such a pleasure to have met you!"

They escaped, and Lucy said with relief: "That's
all right. We just got through that time."

But her mother was annoyed. "I should be told,
dear, that I am unsympathetic. But I cannot see
why you didn't tell your friends about Cecil and be
done with it. There all the time we had to
sit fencing, and almost telling lies, and be seen
through, too, I dare say, which is most unpleasant."

Lucy had plenty to say in reply. She described
the Miss Alans' character: they were such gossips,
and if one told them, the news would be everywhere
in no time.

"But why shouldn't it be everywhere in no time?"

"Because I settled with Cecil not to announce it
until I left England. I shall tell them then. It's

much pleasanter. How wet it is! Let's turn in here."

"Here" was the British Museum. Mrs. Honeychurch refused. If they must take shelter, let it be in a shop. Lucy felt contemptuous, for she was on the tack of caring for Greek sculpture, and had already borrowed a mythical dictionary from Mr. Beebe to get up the names of the goddesses and gods.

"Oh, well, let it be shop, then. Let's go to Mudie's. I'll buy a guide-book."

"You know, Lucy, you and Charlotte and Mr. Beebe all tell me I'm so stupid, so I suppose I am, but I shall never understand this hole-and-corner work. You've got rid of Cecil—well and good, and I'm thankful he's gone, though I did feel angry for the minute. But why not announce it? Why this hushing up and tip-toeing?"

"It's only for a few days."

"But why at all?"

Lucy was silent. She was drifting away from her mother. It was quite easy to say, "Because George Emerson has been bothering me, and if he hears I've given up Cecil may begin again"—quite easy, and it had the incidental advantage of being true. But she could not say it. She disliked confidences, for they might lead to self-knowledge and to that king of terrors—Light. Ever since that last evening at Florence she had deemed it unwise to reveal her soul.

Mrs. Honeychurch, too, was silent. She was thinking, "My daughter won't answer me; she would rather be with those inquisitive old maids than with Freddy and me. Any rag, tag, and bob-tail apparently does if she can leave her home." And as in her case thoughts never remained un-spoken long, she burst out with: "You're tired of Windy Corner."

This was perfectly true. Lucy had hoped to return to Windy Corner when she escaped from Cecil, but she discovered that her home existed no longer. It might exist for Freddy, who still lived and thought straight, but not for one who had deliberately warped the brain. She did not acknowledge that her brain was warped, for the brain itself must assist in that acknowledgment, and she was disordering the very instruments of life. She only felt, "I do not love George; I broke off my engagement because I did not love George; I must go to Greece because I do not love George; it is more important that I should look up gods in the dictionary than that I should help my mother; every one else is behaving very badly." She only felt irritable and petulant, and anxious to do what she was not expected to do, and in this spirit she proceeded with the conversation.

"Oh, mother, what rubbish you talk! Of course I'm not tired of Windy Corner."

"Then why not say so at once, instead of con-sidering half an hour?"

She laughed faintly, "Half a *minute* would be nearer."

"Perhaps you would like to stay away from your home altogether?"

"Hush, mother! People will hear you"; for they had entered Mudie's. She bought Baedeker, and then continued: "Of course I want to live at home; but as we are talking about it, I may as well say that I shall want to be away in the future more than I have been. You see, I come into my money next year."

Tears came into her mother's eyes.

Driven by nameless bewilderment, by what is in older people termed "eccentricity," Lucy determined to make this point clear. "I've seen the world so little—I felt so out of things in Italy. I have seen so little of life; one ought to come up to London more—not a cheap ticket like to-day, but to stop. I might even share a flat for a little with some other girl."

"And mess with typewriters and latch-keys," exploded Mrs. Honeychurch. "And agitate and scream, and be carried off kicking by the police. And call it a Mission—when no one wants you! And call it Duty—when it means that you can't stand your own home! And call it Work—when thousands of men are starving with the competition as it is! And then to prepare yourself, find two doddering old ladies, and go abroad with them."

"I want more independence," said Lucy lamely; she knew that she wanted something, and independence is a useful cry; we can always say that we have not got it. She tried to remember her emotions in Florence: those had been sincere and passionate, and had suggested beauty rather than short skirts and latch-keys. But independence was certainly her cue.

"Very well. Take your independence and be gone. Rush up and down and round the world, and come back as thin as a lath with the bad food. Despise the house that your father built and the garden that he planted, and our dear view —and then share a flat with another girl."

Lucy screwed up her mouth and said: "Perhaps I spoke hastily."

"Oh, goodness!" her mother flashed. "How you do remind me of Charlotte Bartlett!"

"*Charlotte?*" flashed Lucy in her turn, pierced at last by a vivid pain.

"More every moment."

"I don't know what you mean, mother; Charlotte and I are not the very least alike."

"Well, I see the likeness. The same eternal worrying, the same taking back of words. You and Charlotte trying to divide two apples among three people last night might be sisters."

"What rubbish! And if you dislike Charlotte so, it's rather a pity you asked her to stop. I warned you about her; I begged you, implored you not to, but of course it was not listened to."

"There you go."

"I beg your pardon?"

"Charlotte again, my dear; that's all; her very words."

Lucy clenched her teeth. "My point is that you oughtn't to have asked Charlotte to stop. I wish you would keep to the point." And the conversation died off into a wrangle.

She and her mother shopped in silence, spoke little in the train, little again in the carriage, which met them at Dorking Station. It had poured all day and as they ascended through the deep Surrey lanes showers of water fell from the over-hanging beech-trees and rattled on the hood. Lucy complained that the hood was stuffy. Leaning forward, she looked out into the steaming dusk, and watched the carriage-lamp pass like a search-light over mud and leaves, and reveal nothing beautiful. "The crush when Charlotte gets in will be abominable," she remarked. For they were to pick up Miss Bartlett at Summer Street, where she had been dropped as the carriage went down, to pay a call on Mr. Beebe's old mother. "We shall have to sit three a side, because the trees drop, and yet it isn't raining. Oh, for a little air!" Then she listened to the horse's hoofs—"He has not told— he has not told." That melody was blurred by the soft road. "*Can't* we have the hood down?" she demanded, and her mother, with sudden tenderness, said: "Very well, old lady, stop the horse." And the horse was stopped, and Lucy and Powell wrestled with the hood, and squirted water down Mrs. Honeychurch's neck. But now that the hood was down, she did see something that she would have missed—there were no lights in the windows of Cissie Villa, and round the garden gate she fancied she saw a padlock.

"Is that house to let again, Powell?" she called.

"Yes, miss," he replied.

"Have they gone?"

"It is too far out of town for the young gentleman, and his father's rheumatism has come on, so he can't stop on alone, so they are trying to let furnished," was the answer.

"They have gone, then?"

"Yes, miss, they have gone."

Lucy sank back. The carriage stopped at the Rectory. She got out to call for Miss Bartlett. So the Emersons had gone, and all this bother about Greece had been unnecessary. Waste! That word seemed to sum up the whole of life. Wasted plans, wasted money, wasted love, and she had wounded her mother. Was it possible that she had muddled things away? Quite possible. Other people had. When the maid opened the door, she was unable to speak, and stared stupidly into the hall.

Miss Bartlett at once came forward, and after a long preamble asked a great favour: might she go to church? Mr. Beebe and his mother had already gone, but she had refused to start until she obtained her hostess's full sanction, for it would mean keeping the horse waiting a good ten minutes more.

"Certainly," said the hostess wearily. "I forgot it was Friday. Let's all go. Powell can go round to the stables."

"Lucy dearest—"

"No church for me, thank you."

A sigh, and they departed. The church was invisible, but up in the darkness to the left there was a hint of colour. This was a stained window, through which some feeble light was shining, and when the door opened Lucy heard Mr. Beebe's voice running through the litany to a minute congregation. Even their church, built upon the slope of the hill so artfully, with its beautiful raised transept and its spire of silvery shingle—even their church had lost its charm; and the thing one never talked about—religion—was fading like all the other things.

She followed the maid into the Rectory.

Would she object to sitting in Mr. Beebe's study? There was only that one fire.

She would not object.

Some one was there already, for Lucy heard the words: "A lady to wait, sir."

Old Mr. Emerson was sitting by the fire, with his foot upon a gout-stool.

"Oh, Miss Honeychurch, that you should come!"

he quavered; and Lucy saw an alteration in him since last Sunday.

Not a word would come to her lips. George she had faced, and could have faced again, but she had forgotten how to treat his father.

"Miss Honeychurch, dear, we are so sorry! George is so sorry! He thought he had a right to try. I cannot blame my boy, and yet I wish he had told me first. He ought not to have tried. I knew nothing about it at all."

If only she could remember how to behave!

He held up his hand. "But you must not scold him."

Lucy turned her back, and began to look at Mr. Beebe's books.

"I taught him," he quavered, "to trust in love. I said: 'When love comes, that is reality.' I said: 'Passion does not blind. No. Passion is sanity, and the woman you love, she is the only person you will ever really understand.'" He sighed: "True, everlastingly true, though my day is over, and though there is the result. Poor boy! He is so sorry! He said he knew it was madness when you brought your cousin in; that whatever you felt you did not mean. Yet"—his voice gathered strength; he spoke out to make certain—"Miss Honeychurch, do you remember Italy?"

Lucy selected a book—a volume of Old Testament commentaries. Holding it up to her eyes, she said: "I have no wish to discuss Italy or any subject connected with your son."

"But you do remember it?"

"He has misbehaved himself from the first."

"I only was told that he loved you last Sunday. I never could judge behaviour. I—I—suppose he has."

Feeling a little steadier, she put the book back and turned round to him. His face was drooping and swollen, but his eyes, though they were sunken deep, gleamed with a child's courage.

"Why, he has behaved abominably," she said. "I am glad he is sorry. Do you know what he did?"

"Not 'abominably,'" was the gentle correction. "He only tried when he should not have tried. You have all you want, Miss Honeychurch: you are going to marry the man you love. Do not go out of George's life saying he is abominable."

"No, of course," said Lucy, ashamed at the reference to Cecil. "'Abominable' is much too strong. I am sorry I used it about your son. I think I will go to church, after all. My mother and my cousin have gone. I shall not be so very late—"

"Especially as he has gone under," he said quietly.

"What was that?"

"Gone under naturally." He beat his palms together in silence; his head fell on his chest.

"I don't understand."

"As his mother did."

"But, Mr. Emerson—*Mr. Emerson*—what are you talking about?"

"When I wouldn't have George baptized," said he.

Lucy was frightened.

"And she agreed that baptism was nothing, but he caught that fever when he was twelve and she turned round. She thought it a judgment." He shuddered. "Oh, horrible, when we had given up that sort of thing and broken away from her parents. Oh, horrible—worst of all—worse than death, when you have made a little clearing in the wilderness, planted your little garden, let in your sunlight, and then the weeds creep in again! A judgment! And our boy had typhoid because no clergyman had dropped water on him in church! Is it possible, Miss Honeychurch? Shall we slip back into the darkness for ever?"

"I don't know," gasped Lucy. "I don't understand this sort of thing. I was not meant to understand it."

"But Mr. Eager—he came when I was out, and acted according to his principles. I don't blame him or any one . . . but by the time George was well she was ill. He made her think about sin, and she went under thinking about it."

It was thus that Mr. Emerson had murdered his wife in the sight of God.

"Oh, how terrible!" said Lucy, forgetting her own affairs at last.

"He was not baptized," said the old man. "I did hold firm." And he looked with unwavering eyes at the rows of books, as if—at what cost!— he had won a victory over them. "My boy shall go back to the earth untouched."

She asked whether young Mr. Emerson was ill.

"Oh—last Sunday." He started into the present. "George last Sunday—no, not ill: just gone under. He is never ill. But he is his mother's son. Her eyes were his, and she had that forehead that I think so beautiful, and he will not think it worth while to live. It was always touch and go. He will live; but he will not think it worth while to live. He will never think anything worth while. You remember that church at Florence?"

Lucy did remember, and how she had suggested that George should collect postage stamps.

"After you left Florence—horrible. Then we took the house here, and he goes bathing with your brother, and became better. You saw him bathing?"

"I am so sorry, but it is no good discussing this affair. I am deeply sorry about it."

"Then there came something about a novel. I didn't follow it at all; I had to hear so much, and he minded telling me; he finds me too old. Ah, well, one must have failures. George comes down to-morrow, and takes me up to his London rooms. He can't bear to be about here, and I must be where he is."

"Mr. Emerson," cried the girl, "don't leave— at least, not on my account. I am going to Greece. Don't leave your comfortable house."

It was the first time her voice had been kind and he smiled. "How good every one is! And look at Mr. Beebe housing me—came over this morning and heard I was going! Here I am so comfortable with a fire."

"Yes, but you won't go back to London. It's absurd."

"I must be with George; I must make him care to live, and down here he can't. He says the thought of seeing you and of hearing about you— I am not justifying him: I am only saying what has happened."

"Oh, Mr. Emerson"—she took hold of his hand — "you mustn't. I've been bother enough to the world by now. I can't have you moving out of your house when you like it, and perhaps losing money through it—all on my account. You must stop! I am just going to Greece."

"All the way to Greece?"

Her manner altered.

"To Greece?"

"So you must stop. You won't talk about this business, I know. I can trust you both."

"Certainly you can. We either have you in our

lives, or leave you to the life that you have chosen."

"I shouldn't want—"

"I suppose Mr. Vyse is very angry with George? No, it was wrong of George to try. We have pushed our beliefs too far. I fancy that we deserve sorrow."

She looked at the books again—black, brown, and that acrid theological blue. They surrounded the visitors on every side; they were piled on the tables, they pressed against the very ceiling. To Lucy—who could not see that Mr. Emerson was profoundly religious, and differed from Mr. Beebe chiefly by his acknowledgment of passion—it seemed dreadful that the old man should crawl into such a sanctum, when he was unhappy, and be dependent on the bounty of a clergyman.

More certain than ever that she was tired, he offered her his chair.

"No, please sit still. I think I will sit in the carriage."

"Miss Honeychurch, you do sound tired."

"Not a bit," said Lucy, with trembling lips.

"But you are, and there's a look of George about you. And what were you saying about going abroad?"

She was silent.

"Greece"—and she saw that he was thinking the word over—"Greece; but you were to be married this year, I thought."

"Not till January, it wasn't," said Lucy, clasping

her hands. Would she tell an actual lie when it came to the point?

"I suppose that Mr. Vyse is going with you. I hope—it isn't because George spoke that you are both going?"

"No."

"I hope that you will enjoy Greece with Mr. Vyse."

"Thank you."

At that moment Mr. Beebe came back from church. His cassock was covered with rain. "That's all right," he said kindly. "I counted on you two keeping each other company. It's pouring again. The entire congregation, which consists of your cousin, your mother, and my mother, stands waiting in the church, till the carriage fetches it. Did Powell go round?"

"I think so; I'll see."

"No—of course, I'll see. How are the Miss Alans?"

"Very well, thank you."

"Did you tell Mr. Emerson about Greece?"

"I—I did."

"Don't you think it very plucky of her, Mr. Emerson, to undertake the two Miss Alans? Now, Miss Honeychurch, go back—keep warm. I think three is such a courageous number to go travelling." And he hurried off to the stables.

"He is not going," she said hoarsely. "I made a slip. Mr. Vyse does stop behind in England."

Lying to Mr. Emerson

Somehow it was impossible to cheat this old man. To George, to Cecil, she would have lied again; but he seemed so near the end of things, so dignified in his approach to the gulf, of which he gave one account, and the books that surrounded him another, so mild to the rough paths that he had traversed, that the true chivalry—not the worn-out chivalry of sex, but the true chivalry that all the young may show to all the old—awoke in her, and, at whatever risk, she told him that Cecil was not her companion to Greece. And she spoke so seriously that the risk became a certainty, and he, lifting his eyes, said: "You are leaving him? You are leaving the man you love?"

"I—I had to."

"Why, Miss Honeychurch, why?"

Terror came over her, and she lied again. She made the long, convincing speech that she had made to Mr. Beebe, and intended to make to the world when she announced that her engagement was no more. He heard her in silence, and then said: "My dear, I am worried about you. It seems to me"—dreamily; she was not alarmed—"that you are in a muddle."

She shook her head.

"Take an old man's word; there's nothing worse than a muddle in all the world. It is easy to face Death and Fate, and the things that sound so dreadful. It is on my muddles that I look back with horror—on the things that I might have avoided.

We can help one another but little. I used to think I could teach young people the whole of life, but I know better now, and all my teaching of George has come down to this: beware of muddle. Do you remember in that church, when you pretended to be annoyed with me and weren't? Do you remember before, when you refused the room with the view? Those were muddles—little, but ominous—and I am fearing that you are in one now." She was silent. "Don't trust me, Miss Honeychurch. Though life is very glorious, it is difficult." She was still silent. " 'Life' wrote a friend of mine, 'is a public performance on the violin, in which you must learn the instrument as you go along.' I think he puts it well. Man has to pick up the use of his functions as he goes along—especially the function of Love." Then he burst out excitedly; "That's it; that's what I mean. You love George!" And after his long preamble, the three words burst against Lucy like waves from the open sea.

"But you do," he went on, not waiting for contradiction. "You love the boy body and soul, plainly, directly, as he loves you, and no other word expresses it. You won't marry the other man for his sake."

"How dare you!" gasped Lucy, with the roaring of waters in her ears. "Oh, how like a man!—I mean, to suppose that a woman is always thinking about a man."

"But you are."

Lying to Mr. Emerson

She summoned physical disgust.

"You're shocked, but I mean to shock you. It's the only hope at times. I can reach you no other way. You must marry, or your life will be wasted. You have gone too far to retreat. I have no time for the tenderness, and the comradeship, and the poetry, and the things that really matter, and *for which* you marry. I know that, with George, you will find them, and that you love him. Then be his wife. He is already part of you. Though you fly to Greece, and never see him again, or forget his very name, George will work in your thoughts till you die. It isn't possible to love and to part. You will wish that it was. You can transmute love, ignore it, muddle it, but you can never pull it out of you. I know by experience that the poets are right: love is eternal."

Lucy began to cry with anger, and though her anger passed away soon, her tears remained.

"I only wish poets would say this, too: love is of the body; not the body, but of the body. Ah! the misery that would be saved if we confessed that! Ah! for a little directness to liberate the soul! Your soul, dear Lucy! I hate the word now, because of all the cant with which superstition has wrapped it round. But we have souls. I cannot say how they came nor whither they go, but we have them, and I see you ruining yours. I cannot bear it. It is again the darkness creeping in; it is hell." Then he checked himself. "What nonsense

I have talked—how abstract and remote! And I have made you cry! Dear girl, forgive my prosiness; marry my boy. When I think what life is, and how seldom love is answered by love— Marry him; it is one of the moments for which the world was made."

She could not understand him; the words were indeed remote. Yet as he spoke the darkness was withdrawn, veil after veil, and she saw to the bottom of her soul.

"Then, Lucy—"

"You've frightened me," she moaned. "Cecil —Mr. Beebe—the ticket's bought—everything." She fell sobbing into the chair. "I'm caught in the tangle. I must suffer and grow old away from him. I cannot break the whole of life for his sake. They trusted me."

A carriage drew up at the front-door.

"Give George my love—once only. Tell him 'muddle.'" Then she arranged her veil, while the tears poured over her cheeks inside.

"Lucy—"

"No—they are in the hall—oh, please not, Mr. Emerson—they trust me—"

"But why should they, when you have deceived them?"

Mr. Beebe opened the door, saying: "Here's my mother."

"You're not worthy of their trust."

"What's that?" said Mr. Beebe sharply.

"I was saying, why should you trust her when she deceived you?"

"One minute, mother." He came in and shut the door.

"I don't follow you, Mr. Emerson. To whom do you refer? Trust whom?"

"I mean she has pretended to you that she did not love George. They have loved one another all along."

Mr. Beebe looked at the sobbing girl. He was very quiet, and his white face, with its ruddy whiskers, seemed suddenly inhuman. A long black column, he stood and awaited her reply.

"I shall never marry him," quavered Lucy.

A look of contempt came over him, and he said, "Why not?"

"Mr. Beebe—I have misled you—I have misled myself—"

"Oh, rubbish, Miss Honeychurch!"

"It is not rubbish!" said the old man hotly. "It's the part of people that you don't understand."

Mr. Beebe laid his hand on the old man's shoulder pleasantly.

"Lucy! Lucy!" called voices from the carriage.

"Mr. Beebe, could you help me?"

He looked amazed at the request, and said in a low, stern voice: "I am more grieved than I can possibly express. It is lamentable, lamentable—incredible."

"What's wrong with the boy?" fired up the other again.

"Nothing, Mr. Emerson, except that he no longer interests me. Marry George, Miss Honeychurch. He will do admirably."

He walked out and left them. They heard him guiding his mother up-stairs.

"Lucy!" the voices called.

She turned to Mr. Emerson in despair. But his face revived her. It was the face of a saint who understood.

"Now it is all dark. Now Beauty and Passion seem never to have existed. I know. But remember the mountains over Florence and the view. Ah, dear, if I were George, and gave you one kiss, it would make you brave. You have to go cold into a battle that needs warmth, out into the muddle that you have made yourself; and your mother and all your friends will despise you, oh, my darling, and rightly, if it is ever right to despise. George still dark, all the tussle and the misery without a word from him. Am I justified?" Into his own eyes tears came. "Yes, for we fight for more than Love or Pleasure; there is Truth. Truth counts, Truth does count."

"You kiss me," said the girl. "You kiss me. I will try."

He gave her a sense of deities reconciled, a feeling that, in gaining the man she loved, she would gain something for the whole world. Throughout the squalor of her homeward drive—she spoke at once—his salutation remained. He had robbed the body of its taint, the world's taunts of their sting; he had shown her the holiness of direct desire. She "never exactly understood," she would say in after years, "how he managed to strengthen her. It was as if he had made her see the whole of everything at once."

Chapter XX: The End of the Middle Ages

THE Miss Alans did go to Greece, but they went by themselves. They alone of this little company will double Malea and plough the waters of the Saronic gulf. They alone will visit Athens and Delphi, and either shrine of intellectual song—that upon the Acropolis, encircled by blue seas; that under Parnassus, where the eagles build and the bronze charioteer drives undismayed towards infinity. Trembling, anxious, cumbered with much digestive bread, they did proceed to Constantinople, they did go round the world. The rest of us must be contented with a fair, but a less arduous, goal. Italiam petimus: we return to the Pension Bertolini.

George said it was his old room.

"No, it isn't," said Lucy; "because it is the room I had, and I had your father's room. I forget why; Charlotte made me, for some reason."

He knelt on the tiled floor, and laid his face in her lap.

"George, you baby, get up."

"Why shouldn't I be a baby?" murmured George.

Unable to answer this question, she put down his sock, which she was trying to mend, and gazed out through the window. It was evening and again the spring.

"Oh, bother Charlotte," she said thoughtfully. "What can such people be made of?"

"Same stuff as parsons are made of."

"Nonsense!"

"Quite right. It is nonsense."

"Now you get up off the cold floor, or you'll be starting rheumatism next, and you stop laughing and being so silly."

"Why shouldn't I laugh?" he asked, pinning her with his elbows, and advancing his face to hers. "What's there to cry at? Kiss me here." He indicated the spot where a kiss would be welcome.

He was a boy after all. When it came to the point, it was she who remembered the past, she into whose soul the iron had entered, she who knew whose room this had been last year. It endeared him to her strangely that he should be sometimes wrong.

"Any letters?" he asked.

"Just a line from Freddy."

"Now kiss me here; then here."

Then, threatened again with rheumatism, he strolled to the window, opened it (as the English will), and leant out. There was the parapet, there the river, there to the left the beginnings of the hills. The cab-driver, who at once saluted him with the hiss of a serpent, might be that very Phaethon who had set this happiness in motion twelve months ago. A passion of gratitude—all feelings grow to passions in the South—came over the husband, and he blessed the people and the things who had taken so much trouble about a young fool He had helped himself, it is true, but how stupidly! All the fighting that mattered had been done by others—by Italy, by his father, by his wife.

"Lucy, you come and look at the cypresses; and the church, whatever its name is, still shows."

"San Miniato. I'll just finish your sock."

"Signorino, domani faremo uno giro," called the cabman, with engaging certainty.

George told him that he was mistaken; they had no money to throw away on driving.

And the people who had not meant to help—the Miss Lavishes, the Cecils, the Miss Bartletts! Ever prone to magnify Fate, George counted up the forces that had swept him into this contentment.

"Anything good in Freddy's letter?"

"Not yet."

His own content was absolute, but hers held bitterness: the Honeychurches had not forgiven them; they were disgusted at her past hypocrisy; she had alienated Windy Corner, perhaps for ever.

"What does he say?"

"Silly boy! He thinks he's being dignified. He knew we should go off in the spring—he has known it for six months—that if mother wouldn't give her consent we should take the thing into our own hands.

They had fair warning, and now he calls it an elope-
ment. Ridiculous boy—"

"Signorino, domani faremo unogiro—"

"But it will all come right in the end. He has to
build us both up from the beginning again. I wish,
though, that Cecil had not turned so cynical about
women. He has, for the second time, quite altered.
Why will men have theories about women? I
haven't any about men. I wish, too, that Mr.
Beebe—"

"You may well wish that."

"He will never forgive us—I mean, he will never
be interested in us again. I wish that he did not
influence them so much at Windy Corner. I wish
he hadn't— But if we act the truth, the people who
really love us are sure to come back to us in the long-
run."

"Perhaps." Then he said more gently: "Well,
I acted the truth—the only thing I did do—and you
came back to me. So possibly you know." He
turned back into the room. "Nonsense with that
sock." He carried her to the window, so that she,
too, saw all the view. They sank upon their knees,
invisible from the road, they hoped, and began to
whisper one another's names. Ah! it was worth
while; it was the great joy that they had expected,
and countless little joys of which they had never
dreamt. They were silent.

"Signorino, domani faremo—"

"Oh, bother that man!"

But Lucy remembered the vendor of photographs and said, "No, don't be rude to him." Then with a catching of her breath, she murmured: "Mr. Eager and Charlotte, dreadful frozen Charlotte! How cruel she would be to a man like that!"

"Look at the lights going over the bridge."

"But this room reminds me of Charlotte. How horrible to grow old in Charlotte's way! To think that evening at the rectory that she shouldn't have heard your father was in the house. For she would have stopped me going in, and he was the only person alive who could have made me see sense. You couldn't have made me. When I am very happy" —she kissed him—"I remember on how little it all hangs. If Charlotte had only known, she would have stopped me going in, and I should have gone to silly Greece, and become different for ever."

"But she did know," said George; "she did see my father, surely. He said so."

"Oh, no, she didn't see him. She was upstairs with old Mrs. Beebe, don't you remember, and then went straight to the church. She said so."

George was obstinate again. "My father," said he, "saw her, and I prefer his word. He was dozing by the study fire, and he opened his eyes, and there was Miss Bartlett. A few minutes before you came in. She was turning to go as he woke up. He didn't speak to her."

Then they spoke of other things—the desultory talk of those who have been fighting to reach one another, and whose reward is to rest quietly in each other's arms. It was long ere they returned to Miss Bartlett, but when they did her behaviour seemed more interesting. George, who disliked any darkness, said: "It's clear that she knew. Then, why did she risk the meeting? She knew he was there, and yet she went to church."

They tried to piece the thing together.

As they talked, an incredible solution came into Lucy's mind. She rejected it, and said: "How like Charlotte to undo her work by a feeble muddle at the last moment." But something in the dying evening, in the roar of the river, in their very embrace warned them that her words fell short of life, and George whispered: "Or did she mean it?"

"Mean what?"

"Signorino, domani faremo uno giro—"

Lucy bent forward and said with gentleness: "Lascia, prego, lascia. Siamo sposati."

"Scusi tanto, signora," he replied in tones as gentle and whipped up his horse.

"Buona sera—e grazie."

"Niente."

The cabman drove away singing.

"Mean what, George?"

He whispered: "Is it this? Is this possible? I'll put a marvel to you. That your cousin has always hoped. That from the very first moment we met, she hoped, far down in her mind, that we should be like this—of course, very far down. That she fought us on the surface, and yet she hoped. I can't explain her any other way. Can you? Look how she kept me alive in you all the summer; how she gave you no peace; how month after month she became more eccentric and unreliable. The sight of us haunted her—or she couldn't have described us as she did to her friend. There are details—it burnt. I read the book afterwards. She is not frozen, Lucy, she is not withered up all through. She tore us apart twice, but in the rectory that evening she was given one more chance to make us happy. We can never make friends with her or thank her. But I do believe that, far down in her heart, far below all speech and behaviour, she is glad."

"It is impossible," murmured Lucy, and then, remembering the experiences of her own heart, she said: "No—it is just possible."

Youth enwrapped them; the song of Phaethon announced passion requited, love attained. But they were conscious of a love more mysterious than this. The song died away; they heard the river, bearing down the snows of winter into the Mediterranean.

THE END

HOWARDS
END

"Only connect . . ."

Chapter I

ONE may as well begin with Helen's letters to her sister.

"HOWARDS END,
"*Tuesday*.

"DEAREST MEG,

"It isn't going to be what we expected. It is old and little, and altogether delightful — red brick. We can scarcely pack in as it is, and the dear knows what will happen when Paul (younger son) arrives tomorrow. From hall you go right or left into dining-room or drawing-room. Hall itself is practically a room. You open another door in it, and there are the stairs going up in a sort of tunnel to the first-floor. Three bed-rooms in a row there, and three attics in a row above. That isn't all the house really, but it's all that one notices — nine windows as you look up from the front garden.

"Then there's a very big wych-elm — to the left as you look up — leaning a little over the house, and standing on the boundary between the garden and meadow. I quite love that tree already. Also ordinary elms, oaks — no nastier than ordinary oaks — pear-trees, apple-trees, and a vine. No silver birches, though. However, I must get on to my host and hostess. I only wanted to show that it isn't the least what we expected. Why did we settle that their house would be all gables and wiggles, and their garden all gamboge-coloured paths? I believe simply because we associate them with expensive hotels — Mrs. Wilcox trailing in beautiful dresses down long corridors, Mr. Wilcox bullying porters, etc. We females are that unjust.

"I shall be back Saturday; will let you know train later. They are as angry as I am that you did not come too; really Tibby is too tiresome, he starts a new mortal disease every month. How could he have got hay fever in London? and even if he could, it seems hard that you should give up a visit to hear a schoolboy sneeze. Tell him that Charles Wilcox

—7—

(the son who is here) has hay fever too, but he's brave, and gets quite cross when we inquire after it. Men like the Wilcoxes would do Tibby a power of good. But you won't agree, and I'd better change the subject.

"This long letter is because I'm writing before breakfast. Oh, the beautiful vine leaves! The house is covered with a vine. I looked out earlier, and Mrs. Wilcox was already in the garden. She evidently loves it. No wonder she sometimes looks tired. She was watching the large red poppies come out. Then she walked off the lawn to the meadow, whose corner to the right I can just see. Trail, trail, went her long dress over the sopping grass, and she came back with her hands full of the hay that was cut yesterday—I suppose for rabbits or something, as she kept on smelling it. The air here is delicious. Later on I heard the noise of croquet balls, and looked out again, and it was Charles Wilcox practising; they are keen on all games. Presently he started sneezing and had to stop. Then I hear more clicketing, and it is Mr. Wilcox practising, and then, 'a-tissue, a-tissue': he has to stop too. Then Evie comes out, and does some calisthenic exercises on a machine that is tacked on to a greengage-tree—they put everything to use—and then she says 'a-tissue,' and in she goes. And finally Mrs. Wilcox reappears, trail, trail, still smelling hay and looking at the flowers. I inflict all this on you because once you said that life is sometimes life and sometimes only a drama, and one must learn to distinguish t'other from which, and up to now I have always put that down as 'Meg's clever nonsense.' But this morning, it really does seem not life but a play, and it did amuse me enormously to watch the W's. Now Mrs. Wilcox has come in.

"I am going to wear [omission]. Last night Mrs. Wilcox wore an [omission], and Evie [omission]. So it isn't exactly a go-as-you-please place, and if you shut your eyes it still seems the wiggly hotel that we expected. Not if you open them. The dog-roses are too sweet. There is a great hedge of them over the lawn—magnificently tall, so that they fall down in garlands, and nice and thin at the bottom, so that you can see ducks through it and a cow. These belong to the farm, which is the only house near us. There goes the breakfast gong. Much love. Modified love to Tibby. Love to Aunt Juley; how good of her to come and keep you company, but what a bore. Burn this. Will write again Thursday.

"Helen."

"DEAREST MEG,

"I am having a glorious time. I like them all. Mrs. Wilcox, if quieter than in Germany, is sweeter than ever, and I never saw anything like her steady unselfishness, and the best of it is that the others do not take advantage of her. They are the very happiest, jolliest family that you can imagine. I do really feel that we are making friends. The fun of it is that they think me a noodle, and say so — at least, Mr. Wilcox does — and when that happens, and one doesn't mind, it's a pretty sure test, isn't it? He says the most horrid things about women's suffrage so nicely, and when I said I believed in equality he just folded his arms and gave me such a setting down as I've never had. Meg, shall we ever learn to talk less? I never felt so ashamed of myself in my life. I couldn't point to a time when men had been equal, nor even to a time when the wish to be equal had made them happier in other ways. I couldn't say a word. I had just picked up the notion that equality is good from some book — probably from poetry, or you. Anyhow, it's been knocked into pieces, and, like all people who are really strong, Mr. Wilcox did it without hurting me. On the other hand, I laugh at them for catching hay fever. We live like fighting-cocks, and Charles takes us out every day in the motor — a tomb with trees in it, a hermit's house, a wonderful road that was made by the Kings of Mercia — tennis — a cricket match — bridge — and at night we squeeze up in this lovely house. The whole clan's here now — it's like a rabbit warren. Evie is a dear. They want me to stop over Sunday — I suppose it won't matter if I do. Marvellous weather and the view's marvellous — views westward to the high ground. Thank you for your letter. Burn this.

"Your affectionate

"HELEN."

"HOWARDS END,

"*Sunday.*

"Dearest, dearest Meg,— I do not know what you will say: Paul and I are in love — the younger son who only came here Wednesday."

Chapter II

MARGARET glanced at her sister's note and pushed it over the breakfast-table to her aunt. There was a moment's hush, and then the flood-gates opened.

" I can tell you nothing, Aunt Juley. I know no more than you do. We met — we only met the father and mother abroad last spring. I know so little that I didn't even know their son's name. It's all so —" She waved her hand and laughed a little.

" In that case it is far too sudden."

" Who knows, Aunt Juley, who knows?"

" But, Margaret dear, I mean we mustn't be unpractical now that we've come to facts. It is too sudden, surely."

" Who knows! "

" But Margaret dear —"

"I'll go for her other letters," said Margaret. " No, I won't, I'll finish my breakfast. In fact, I haven't them. We met the Wilcoxes on an awful expedition that we made from Heidelberg to Speyer. Helen and I had got it into our heads that there was a grand old cathedral at Speyer — the Archbishop of Speyer was one of the seven electors — you know —' Speyer, Maintz, and Köln.' Those three sees once commanded the Rhine Valley and got it the name of Priest Street."

" I still feel quite uneasy about this business, Margaret."

" The train crossed by a bridge of boats, and at first sight it looked quite fine. But oh, in five minutes we had seen the whole thing. The cathedral had been ruined, absolutely ruined, by restoration; not an inch left of the original structure. We wasted a whole day, and came across the Wilcoxes as we were eating our sandwiches in the public gardens. They too, poor things, had been taken in — they were actually stopping at Speyer — and they rather liked Helen insisting that they must fly with us to Heidelberg. As a matter of fact, they did come on next day. We all took some drives together. They knew us well enough to ask Helen to come and see them — at least, I was asked too, but Tibby's illness prevented me, so last Monday she went alone. That's all. You know as much as I do now. It's a young man out the unknown. She was to have come back Saturday, but put off till Monday, perhaps on account of — I don't know."

She broke off, and listened to the sounds of a London morning. Their house was in Wickham Place, and fairly quiet, for a lofty promontory of buildings separated it from the main thoroughfare. One had the sense of a backwater, or rather of an estuary, whose waters flowed in from the invisible sea, and ebbed into a profound silence while the waves without were still beating. Though the promontory consisted of flats — expensive, with cavernous entrance halls, full of concierges and palms — it fulfilled its purpose, and gained for the older houses opposite a certain measure of peace. These, too, would be swept away in time, and another promontory would rise upon their site, as humanity piled itself higher and higher on the precious soil of London.

Mrs. Munt had her own method of interpreting her nieces. She decided that Margaret was a little hysterical, and was trying to gain time by a torrent of talk. Feeling very diplomatic, she lamented the fate of Speyer, and declared that never, never should she be so misguided as to visit it, and added of her own accord that the principles of restoration were ill understood in Germany. "The Germans," she said, "are too thorough, and this is all very well sometimes, but at other times it does not do."

"Exactly," said Margaret; "Germans are too thorough." And her eyes began to shine.

"Of course I regard you Schlegels as English," said Mrs. Munt hastily —"English to the backbone."

Margaret leaned forward and stroked her hand.

"And that reminds me — Helen's letter —"

"Oh, yes, Aunt Juley, I am thinking all right about Helen's letter. I know — I must go down and see her. I am thinking about her all right. I am meaning to go down."

"But go with some plan," said Mrs. Munt, admitting into her kindly voice a note of exasperation. "Margaret, if I may interfere, don't be taken by surprise. What do you think of the Wilcoxes? Are they our sort? Are they likely people? Could they appreciate Helen, who is to my mind a very special sort of person? Do they care about Literature and Art? That is most important when you come to think of it. Literature and Art. Most important. How old would the son be? She says 'younger son.' Would he be in a position to marry? Is he likely to make Helen happy? Did you gather —"

"I gathered nothing."

They began to talk at once.

"Then in that case —"

"In that case I can make no plans, don't you see."

"On the contrary —"

"I hate plans. I hate lines of action. Helen isn't a baby."

"Then in that case, my dear, why go down?"

Margaret was silent. If her aunt could not see why she must go down, she was not going to tell her. She was not going to say "I love my dear sister; I must be near her at this crisis of her life." The affections are more reticent than the passions, and their expression more subtle. If she herself should ever fall in love with a man, she, like Helen, would proclaim it from the house-tops, but as she only loved a sister she used the voiceless language of sympathy.

"I consider you odd girls," continued Mrs. Munt, " and very wonderful girls, and in many ways far older than your years. But — you won't be offended? — frankly I feel you are not up to this business. It requires an older person. Dear, I have nothing to call me back to Swanage." She spread out her plump arms. " I am all at your disposal. Let me go down to this house whose name I forget instead of you."

"Aunt Juley "— she jumped up and kissed her — "I must, must go to Howards End myself. You don't exactly understand, though I can never thank you properly for offering."

"I do understand," retorted Mrs. Munt, with immense confidence. " I go down in no spirit of interference, but to make inquiries. Inquiries are necessary. Now, I am going to be rude. You would say the wrong thing; to a certainty you would. In your anxiety for Helen's happiness you would offend the whole of these Wilcoxes by asking one of your impetuous questions — not that one minds offending them."

"I shall ask no questions. I have it in Helen's writing that she and a man are in love. There is no question to ask as long as she keeps to that. All the rest isn't worth a straw. A long engagement if you like, but inquiries, questions, plans, lines of action — no, Aunt Juley, no."

Away she hurried, not beautiful, not supremely brilliant, but filled with something that took the place of both qualities — something best described as a profound vivacity, a continual and sincere response to all that she encountered in her path through life.

"If Helen had written the same to me about a shop-assistant or a penniless clerk —"

"Dear Margaret, do come into the library and shut the door. Your good maids are dusting the banisters."

"— or if she had wanted to marry the man who calls for Carter Paterson, I should have said the same." Then, with one of those turns that convinced her aunt that she was not mad really and convinced observers of another type that she was not a barren theorist, she added: "Though in the case of Carter Paterson I should want it to be a very long engagement indeed, I must say."

"I should think so," said Mrs. Munt; "and, indeed, I can scarcely follow you. Now, just imagine if you said anything of that sort to the Wilcoxes. I understand it, but most good people would think you mad. Imagine how disconcerting for Helen! What is wanted is a person who will go slowly, slowly in this business, and see how things are and where they are likely to lead to."

Margaret was down on this.

"But you implied just now that the engagement must be broken off."

"I think probably it must; but slowly."

"Can you break an engagement off slowly?" Her eyes lit up. "What's an engagement made of, do you suppose? I think it's made of some hard stuff, that may snap, but can't break. It is different to the other ties of life. They stretch or bend. They admit of degree. They're different."

"Exactly so. But won't you let me just run down to Howards House, and save you all the discomfort? I will really not interfere, but I do so thoroughly understand the kind of thing you Schlegels want that one quiet look round will be enough for me."

Margaret again thanked her, again kissed her, and then ran upstairs to see her brother.

He was not so well.

The hay fever had worried him a good deal all night. His head ached, his eyes were wet, his mucous membrane, he informed her, was in a most unsatisfactory condition. The only thing that made life worth living was the thought of Walter Savage Landor, from whose " Imaginary Conversations " she had promised to read at frequent intervals during the day.

It was rather difficult. Something must be done about Helen. She must be assured that it is not a criminal offence to love at first sight. A telegram to this effect would be cold and cryptic, a personal visit seemed each moment more impossible. Now the doctor arrived, and said that Tibby was quite bad. Might it really be best to accept Aunt Juley's kind offer, and to send her down to Howards End with a note?

Certainly Margaret was impulsive. She did swing rapidly from one decision to another. Running downstairs into the library, she cried: " Yes, I have changed my mind; I do wish that you would go."

There was a train from King's Cross at eleven. At half-past ten Tibby, with rare self-effacement, fell asleep, and Margaret was able to drive her aunt to the station.

" You will remember, Aunt Juley, not to be drawn into discussing the engagement. Give my letter to Helen, and say whatever you feel yourself, but do keep clear of the relatives. We have scarcely got their names straight yet, and besides, that sort of thing is so uncivilized and wrong."

" So uncivilized?" queried Mrs. Munt, fearing that she was losing the point of some brilliant remark.

" Oh, I used an affected word. I only meant would you please only talk the thing over with Helen."

" Only with Helen."

" Because —" But it was no moment to expound the personal nature of love. Even Margaret shrank from it, and contented herself with stroking her good aunt's hand, and with meditating, half sensibly and half poetically, on the journey that was about to begin from King's Cross.

Like many others who have lived long in a great capital, she had strong feelings about the various railway termini. They are our gates to the glorious and the unknown. Through them we pass out into adventure and sunshine, to them, alas! we return. In Paddington all Cornwall is latent and the remoter west; down the inclines of Liverpool Street lie fenlands and the illimitable Broads; Scotland is through the pylons of Euston; Wessex behind the poised chaos of Waterloo. Italians realize this, as is natural; those of them who are so unfortunate as to serve as waiters in Berlin call the Anhalt Bahnhof the Stazione d'Italia, because by it they must return to their homes. And he is a chilly Londoner who does not endow his stations with some personality, and extend to them, however shyly, the emotions of fear and love.

To Margaret — I hope that it will not set the reader against her — the station of King's Cross had always suggested Infinity. Its very situation — withdrawn a little behind the facile splendours of St. Pancras — implied a comment on the materialism of life. Those two great arches, colourless, indifferent, shouldering between them an unlovely clock, were fit portals for some eternal adventure, whose issue might be prosperous, but would certainly not be expressed in the ordinary language of prosperity. If you think this ridiculous, remember that it is not Margaret who is telling you about it; and let me hasten to add that they were in plenty of time for the train; that Mrs. Munt, though she took a second-class ticket, was put by the guard into a first (only two seconds on the train, one smoking and the other babies — one cannot be expected to travel with babies); and that Margaret, on her return to

Wickham Place, was confronted with the following telegram:

"All over. Wish I had never written. Tell no one.—HELEN."

But Aunt Juley was gone — gone irrevocably, and no power on earth could stop her.

Chapter III

MOST complacently did Mrs. Munt rehearse her mission. Her nieces were independent young women, and it was not often that she was able to help them. Emily's daughters had never been quite like other girls. They had been left motherless when Tibby was born, when Helen was five and Margaret herself but thirteen. It was before the passing of the Deceased Wife's Sister Bill, so Mrs. Munt could without impropriety offer to go and keep house at Wickham Place. But her brother-in-law, who was peculiar and a German, had referred the question to Margaret, who with the crudity of youth had answered, 'No, they could manage much better alone.' Five years later Mr. Schlegel had died too, and Mrs. Munt had repeated her offer. Margaret, crude no longer, had been grateful and extremely nice, but the substance of her answer had been the same. "I must not interfere a third time," thought Mrs. Munt. However, of course she did. She learnt, to her horror, that Margaret, now of age, was taking her money out of the old safe investments and putting it into Foreign Things, which always smash. Silence would have been criminal. Her own fortune was invested in Home Rails, and most ardently did she beg her niece to imitate her. "Then we should be together, dear." Margaret, out of politeness, invested a few hundreds in the Nottingham and Derby Railway, and though the Foreign Things did admirably and the Nottingham and Derby declined with the steady dignity of which only Home

Rails are capable, Mrs. Munt never ceased to rejoice, and to say, "I did manage that, at all events. When the smash comes poor Margaret will have a nest-egg to fall back upon." This year Helen came of age, and exactly the same thing happened in Helen's case; she also would shift her money out of Consols, but she, too, almost without being pressed, consecrated a fraction of it to the Nottingham and Derby Railway. So far so good, but in social matters their aunt had accomplished nothing. Sooner or later the girls would enter on the process known as throwing themselves away, and if they had delayed hitherto, it was only that they might throw themselves more vehemently in the future. They saw too many people at Wickham Place — unshaven musicians, an actress even, German cousins (one knows what foreigners are), acquaintances picked up at Continental hotels (one knows what they are too). It was interesting, and down at Swanage no one appreciated culture more than Mrs. Munt; but it was dangerous, and disaster was bound to come. How right she was, and how lucky to be on the spot when the disaster came!

The train sped northward, under innumerable tunnels. It was only an hour's journey, but Mrs. Munt had to raise and lower the window again and again. She passed through the South Welwyn Tunnel, saw light for a moment, and entered the North Welwyn Tunnel, of tragic fame. She traversed the immense viaduct, whose arches span untroubled meadows and the dreamy flow of Tewin Water. She skirted the parks of politicians. At times the Great North Road accompanied her, more suggestive of infinity than any railway, awakening, after a nap of a hundred years, to such life as is conferred by the stench of motor-cars, and to such culture as is implied by the advertisements of antibilious pills. To history, to tragedy, to the past, to the future, Mrs. Munt remained equally indifferent;

hers but to concentrate on the end of her journey, and to rescue poor Helen from this dreadful mess.

The station for Howards End was at Hilton, one of the large villages that are strung so frequently along the North Road, and that owe their size to the traffic of coaching and pre-coaching days. Being near London, it had not shared in the rural decay, and its long High Street had budded out right and left into residential estates. For about a mile a series of tiled and slated houses passed before Mrs. Munt's inattentive eyes, a series broken at one point by six Danish tumuli that stood shoulder to shoulder along the highroad, tombs of soldiers. Beyond these tumuli habitations thickened, and the train came to a standstill in a tangle that was almost a town.

The station, like the scenery, like Helen's letters, struck an indeterminate note. Into which country will it lead, England or Suburbia? It was new, it had island platforms and a subway, and the superficial comfort exacted by business men. But it held hints of local life, personal intercourse, as even Mrs. Munt was to discover.

"I want a house," she confided to the ticket boy. "Its name is Howards Lodge. Do you know where it is?"

"Mr. Wilcox!" the boy called.

A young man in front of them turned round.

"She's wanting Howards End."

There was nothing for it but to go forward, though Mrs. Munt was too much agitated even to stare at the stranger. But remembering that there were two brothers, she had the sense to say to him, "Excuse me asking, but are you the younger Mr. Wilcox or the elder?"

"The younger. Can I do anything for you?"

"Oh, well"—she controlled herself with difficulty

" Really. Are you? I —" She moved away from the ticket boy and lowered her voice. " I am Miss Schlegel's aunt. I ought to introduce myself, oughtn't I? My name is Mrs. Munt."

She was conscious that he raised his cap and said quite coolly, " Oh, rather; Miss Schlegel is stopping with us. Did you want to see her?"

" Possibly —"

" I'll call you a cab. No; wait a mo—" He thought. " Our motor's here. I'll run you up in it."

" That is very kind —"

" Not at all, if you'll just wait till they bring out a parcel from the office. This way."

" My niece is not with you by any chance?"

" No; I came over with my father. He has gone on north in your train. You'll see Miss Schlegel at lunch. You're coming up to lunch, I hope?"

" I should like to come *up*," said Mrs. Munt, not committing herself to nourishment until she had studied Helen's lover a little more. He seemed a gentleman, but had so rattled her round that her powers of observation were numbed. She glanced at him stealthily. To a feminine eye there was nothing amiss in the sharp depressions at the corners of his mouth, nor in the rather box-like construction of his forehead. He was dark, clean-shaven and seemed accustomed to command.

" In front or behind? Which do you prefer? It may be windy in front."

" In front if I may; then we can talk."

" But excuse me one moment — I can't think what they're doing with that parcel." He strode into the booking-office, and called with a new voice: " Hi! hi, you there! Are you going to keep me waiting all day? Parcel for Wilcox, Howards End. Just look sharp!" Emerging, he said in quieter tones: " This station's abominably organized; if I had my way, the whole lot of 'em should get the sack. May I help you in?"

"This is very good of you," said Mrs. Munt, as she settled herself into a luxurious cavern of red leather, and suffered her person to be padded with rugs and shawls. She was more civil than she had intended, but really this young man was very kind. Moreover, she was a little afraid of him: his self-possession was extraordinary. "Very good indeed," she repeated, adding: "It is just what I should have wished."

"Very good of you to say so," he replied, with a slight look of surprise, which, like most slight looks, escaped Mrs. Munt's attention. "I was just tooling my father over to catch the down train."

"You see, we heard from Helen this morning."

Young Wilcox was pouring in petrol, starting his engine, and performing other actions with which this story has no concern. The great car began to rock, and the form of Mrs. Munt, trying to explain things, sprang agreeably up and down among the red cushions. "The mater will be very glad to see you," he mumbled. "Hi! I say. Parcel for Howards End. Bring it out. Hi!"

A bearded porter emerged with the parcel in one hand and an entry book in the other. With the gathering whir of the motor these ejaculations mingled: "Sign, must I? Why the —— should I sign after all this bother? Not even got a pencil on you? Remember next time I report you to the station-master. My time's of value, though yours mayn't be. Here" — here being a tip.

"Extremely sorry, Mrs. Munt."

"Not at all, Mr. Wilcox."

"And do you object to going through the village? It is rather a longer spin, but I have one or two commissions."

"I should love going through the village. Naturally I am very anxious to talk things over with you."

As she said this she felt ashamed, for she was disobeying Margaret's instructions. Only disobeying them in the letter, surely. Margaret had only warned her against discussing the incident with outsiders. Surely it was not 'uncivilized or wrong' to discuss it with the young man himself, since chance had thrown them together.

A reticent fellow, he made no reply. Mounting by her side, he put on gloves and spectacles, and off they drove, the bearded porter — life is a mysterious business — looking after them with admiration.

The wind was in their faces down the station road, blowing the dust into Mrs. Munt's eyes. But as soon as they turned into the Great North Road she opened fire. "You can well imagine," she said, "that the news was a great shock to us."

"What news?"

"Mr. Wilcox," she said frankly. "Margaret has told me everything — everything. I have seen Helen's letter."

He could not look her in the face, as his eyes were fixed on his work; he was travelling as quickly as he dared down the High Street. But he inclined his head in her direction, and said, "I beg your pardon; I didn't catch."

"About Helen. Helen, of course. Helen is a very exceptional person — I am sure you will let me say this, feeling towards her as you do — indeed, all the Schlegels are exceptional. I come in no spirit of interference, but it was a great shock."

They drew up opposite a draper's. Without replying, he turned round in his seat, and contemplated the cloud of dust that they had raised in their passage through the village. It was settling again, but not all into the road from which he had taken it. Some of it had percolated through the open windows, some had whitened the roses and gooseberries of the wayside gardens, while a certain proportion had entered the lungs of the villagers. "I wonder when they'll learn wisdom and tar the roads," was his comment. Then a man ran out of the draper's with a roll of oilcloth, and off they went again.

"Margaret could not come herself, on account of poor Tibby, so I am here to represent her and to have a good talk."

"I'm sorry to be so dense," said the young man, again drawing up outside a shop. "But I still haven't quite understood."

"Helen, Mr. Wilcox — my niece and you."

He pushed up his goggles and gazed at her, absolutely bewildered. Horror smote her to the heart, for even she began to suspect that they were at cross-purposes, and that she had commenced her mission by some hideous blunder.

"Miss Schlegel and myself?" he asked, compressing his lips.

"I trust there has been no misunderstanding," quavered Mrs. Munt. "Her letter certainly read that way."

"What way?"

"That you and she —" She paused, then drooped her eyelids.

"I think I catch your meaning," he said stickily. "What an extraordinary mistake!"

"Then you didn't the least —" she stammered, getting blood-red in the face, and wishing she had never been born.

"Scarcely, as I am already engaged to another lady." There was a moment's silence, and then he caught his breath and exploded with, "Oh, good God! Don't tell me it's some silliness of Paul's."

"But you are Paul."

" I'm not."

" Then why did you say so at the station? "

" I said nothing of the sort."

" I beg your pardon, you did."

" I beg your pardon, I did not. My name is Charles."

" Younger " may mean son as opposed to father, or second brother as opposed to first. There is much to be said for either view, and later on they said it. But they had other questions before them now.

" Do you mean to tell me that Paul —"

But she did not like his voice. He sounded as if he was talking to a porter, and, certain that he had deceived her at the station, she too grew angry.

" Do you mean to tell me that Paul and your niece —"

Mrs. Munt — such is human nature — determined that she would champion the lovers. She was not going to be bullied by a severe young man. " Yes, they care for one another very much indeed," she said. " I dare say they will tell you about it by-and-by. We heard this morning."

And Charles clenched his fist and cried, " The idiot, the idiot, the little fool! "

Mrs. Munt tried to divest herself of her rugs. " If that is your attitude, Mr. Wilcox, I prefer to walk."

" I beg you will do no such thing. I'll take you up this moment to the house. Let me tell you the thing's impossible, and must be stopped."

Mrs. Munt did not often lose her temper, and when she did it was only to protect those whom she loved. On this occasion she blazed out. " I quite agree, sir. The thing is impossible, and I will come up and stop it. My niece is a very exceptional person, and I am not inclined to sit still while she throws herself away on those who will not appreciate her."

Charles worked his jaws.

" Considering she has only known your brother

since Wednesday, and only met your father and mother at a stray hotel —"

"Could you possibly lower your voice? The shop-man will overhear."

"Esprit de classe "— if one may coin the phrase — was strong in Mrs. Munt. She sat quivering while a member of the lower orders deposited a metal funnel, a saucepan, and a garden squirt beside the roll of oil-cloth.

"Right behind?"

"Yes, sir." And the lower orders vanished in a cloud of dust.

"I warn you: Paul hasn't a penny; it's useless."

"No need to warn us, Mr. Wilcox, I assure you. The warning is all the other way. My niece has been very foolish, and I shall give her a good scolding and take her back to London with me."

"He has to make his way out in Nigeria. He couldn't think of marrying for years, and when he does it must be a woman who can stand the climate, and is in other ways— Why hasn't he told us? Of course he's ashamed. He knows he's been a fool. And so he has—a damned fool."

She grew furious.

"Whereas Miss Schlegel has lost no time in publish-ing the news."

"If I were a man, Mr. Wilcox, for that last remark I'd box your ears. You're not fit to clean my niece's boots, to sit in the same room with her, and you dare — you actually dare— I decline to argue with such a person."

"All I know is, she's spread the thing and he hasn't, and my father's away and I —"

"And all that I know is —"

"Might I finish my sentence, please?"

"No."

Charles clenched his teeth and sent the motor swerving all over the lane.

She screamed.

So they played the game of Capping Families, a round of which is always played when love would unite two members of our race. But they played it with unusual vigour, stating in so many words that Schlegels were better than Wilcoxes, Wilcoxes better than Schlegels. They flung decency aside. The man was young, the woman deeply stirred; in both a vein of coarseness was latent. Their quarrel was no more surprising than are most quarrels — inevitable at the time, incredible afterwards. But it was more than usually futile. A few minutes, and they were enlightened. The motor drew up at Howards End, and Helen, looking very pale, ran out to meet her aunt.

" Aunt Juley, I have just had a telegram from Margaret; I — I meant to stop your coming. It isn't — it's over."

The climax was too much for Mrs. Munt. She burst into tears.

"Aunt Juley dear, don't. Don't let them know I've been so silly. It wasn't anything. Do bear up for my sake."

" Paul," cried Charles Wilcox, pulling his gloves off.

" Don't let them know. They are never to know."

" Oh, my darling Helen —"

" Paul! Paul ! "

A very young man came out of the house.

" Paul, is there any truth in this? "

" I didn't — I don't —"

" Yes or no, man; plain question, plain answer. Did or didn't Miss Schlegel —"

" Charles dear," said a voice from the garden. " Charles, dear Charles, one doesn't ask plain questions. There aren't such things."

They were all silent. It was Mrs. Wilcox.

She approached just as Helen's letter had described her, trailing noiselessly over the lawn, and there was actually a wisp of hay in her hands. She seemed to belong not to the young people and their motor, but to the house, and to the tree that overshadowed it. One knew that she worshipped the past, and that the instinctive wisdom the past can alone bestow had descended upon her — that wisdom to which we give the clumsy name of aristocracy. High born she might not be. But assuredly she cared about her ancestors, and let them help her. When she saw Charles angry, Paul frightened, and Mrs. Munt in tears, she heard her ancestors say, " Separate those human beings who will hurt each other most. The rest can wait." So she did not ask questions. Still less did she pretend that nothing had happened, as a competent society hostess would have done. She said, " Miss Schlegel, would you take your aunt up to your room or to my room, whichever you think best. Paul, do find Evie, and tell her lunch for six, but I'm not sure whether we shall all be downstairs for it." And when they had obeyed her, she turned to her elder son, who still stood in the throbbing stinking car, and smiled at him with tenderness, and without a word, turned away from him towards her flowers.

" Mother," he called, " are you aware that Paul has been playing the fool again?"

" It's all right, dear. They have broken off the engagement."

" Engagement — ! "

" They do not love any longer, if you prefer it put that way," said Mrs. Wilcox, stooping down to smell a rose.

Chapter IV

HELEN and her aunt returned to Wickham Place in a state of collapse, and for a little time Margaret had three invalids on her hands. Mrs. Munt soon recovered. She possessed to a remarkable degree the power of distorting the past, and before many days were over she had forgotten the part played by her own imprudence in the catastrophe. Even at the crisis she had cried, " Thank goodness, poor Margaret is saved this ! " which during the journey to London evolved into, " It had to be gone through by some one," which in its turn ripened into the permanent form of " The one time I really did help Emily's girls was over the Wilcox business." But Helen was a more serious patient. New ideas had burst upon her like a thunder clap, and by them and by her reverberations she had been stunned.

The truth was that she had fallen in love, not with an individual, but with a family.

Before Paul arrived she had, as it were, been tuned up into his key. The energy of the Wilcoxes had fascinated her, had created new images of beauty in her responsive mind. To be all day with them in the open air, to sleep at night under their roof, had seemed the supreme joy of life, and had led to that abandonment of personality that is a possible prelude to love. She had liked giving in to Mr. Wilcox, or Evie, or Charles; she had liked being told that her notions of life were sheltered or academic; that Equality was nonsense, Votes for Women nonsense, Socialism nonsense,

Art and Literature, except when conducive to strengthening the character, nonsense. One by one the Schlegel fetiches had been overthrown, and, though professing to defend them, she had rejoiced. When Mr. Wilcox said that one sound man of business did more good
to the world than a dozen of your social reformers, she
had swallowed the curious assertion without a gasp,
and had leant back luxuriously among the cushions of
his motor-car. When Charles said. "Why be so
polite to servants? they don't understand it," she had
not given the Schlegel retort of, "If they don't understand it, I do." No; she had vowed to be less polite
to servants in the future. "I am swathed in cant,"
she thought, "and it is good for me to be stripped of
it." And all that she thought or did or breathed was
a quiet preparation for Paul. Paul was inevitable.
Charles was taken up with another girl, Mr. Wilcox
was so old, Evie so young, Mrs. Wilcox so different.
Round the absent brother she began to throw the halo
of Romance, to irradiate him with all the splendour
of those happy days, to feel that in him she should draw
nearest to the robust ideal. He and she were about
the same age, Evie said. Most people thought Paul
handsomer than his brother. He was certainly a better
shot, though not so good at golf. And when Paul appeared, flushed with the triumph of getting through
an examination, and ready to flirt with any pretty girl,
Helen met him halfway, or more than halfway, and
turned towards him on the Sunday evening.

He had been talking of his approaching exile in
Nigeria, and he should have continued to talk of it, and
allowed their guest to recover. But the heave of her
bosom flattered him. Passion was possible, and he became passionate. Deep down in him something whispered, "This girl would let you kiss her; you might not
have such a chance again."

That was "how it happened," or, rather, how Helen

described it to her sister, using words even more unsympathetic than my own. But the poetry of that kiss, the wonder of it, the magic that there was in life for hours after it — who can describe that? It is so easy for an Englishman to sneer at these chance collisions of human beings. To the insular cynic and the insular moralist they offer an equal opportunity. It is so easy to talk of " passing emotion," and how to forget how vivid the emotion was ere it passed. Our impulse to sneer, to forget, is at root a good one. We recognize that emotion is not enough, and that men and women are personalities capable of sustained relations, not mere opportunities for an electrical discharge. Yet we rate the impulse too highly. We do not admit that by collisions of this trivial sort the doors of heaven may be shaken open. To Helen, at all events, her life was to bring nothing more intense than the embrace of this boy who played no part in it. He had drawn her out of the house, where there was danger of surprise and light; he had led her by a path he knew, until they stood under the column of the vast wych-elm. A man in the darkness, he had whispered " I love you " when she was desiring love. In time his slender personality faded, the scene that he had evoked endured. In all the variable years that followed she never saw the like of it again.

" I understand," said Margaret —" at least, I understand as much as ever is understood of these things. Tell me now what happened on the Monday morning."

" It was over at once."

" How, Helen? "

" I was still happy while I dressed, but as I came downstairs I got nervous, and when I went into the dining-room I knew it was no good. There was Evie — I can't explain — managing the tea-urn, and Mr. Wilcox reading the *Times*."

" Was Paul there? "

"Yes; and Charles was talking to him about Stocks and Shares, and he looked frightened."

By slight indications the sisters could convey much to each other. Margaret saw horror latent in the scene, and Helen's next remark did not surprise her.

"Somehow, when that kind of man looks frightened it is too awful. It is all right for us to be frightened, or for men of another sort — father, for instance; but for men like that! When I saw all the others so placid, and Paul mad with terror in case I said the wrong thing, I felt for a moment that the whole Wilcox family was a fraud, just a wall of newspapers and motor-cars and golf-clubs, and that if it fell I should find nothing behind it but panic and emptiness."

"I don't think that. The Wilcoxes struck me as being genuine people, particularly the wife."

"No, I don't really think that. But Paul was so broad-shouldered; all kinds of extraordinary things made it worse, and I knew that it would never do — never. I said to him after breakfast, when the others were practising strokes, 'We rather lost our heads,' and he looked better at once, though frightfully ashamed. He began a speech about having no money to marry on, but it hurt him to make it, and I stopped him. Then he said, 'I must beg your pardon over this, Miss Schlegel; I can't think what came over me last night.' And I said, 'Nor what over me; never mind.' And then we parted — at least, until I remembered that I had written straight off to tell you the night before, and that frightened him again. I asked him to send a telegram for me, for he knew you would be coming or something; and he tried to get hold of the motor, but Charles and Mr. Wilcox wanted it to go to the station; and Charles offered to send the telegram for me, and then I had to say that the telegram was of no consequence, for Paul said Charles might read it, and though I wrote it out several times, he always said

people would suspect something. He took it himself
at last, pretending that he must walk down to get
cartridges, and, what with one thing and the other,
it was not handed in at the Post Office until too late.
It was the most terrible morning. Paul disliked me
more and more, and Evie talked cricket averages till
I nearly screamed. I cannot think how I stood her all
the other days. At last Charles and his father started
for the station, and then came your telegram warning
me that Aunt Juley was coming by that train, and Paul
— oh, rather horrible — said that I had muddled it.
But Mrs. Wilcox knew."

" Knew what ? "

" Everything; though we neither of us told her a
word, and had known all along, I think."

" Oh, she must have overheard you."

" I suppose so, but it seemed wonderful. When
Charles and Aunt Juley drove up, calling each other
names, Mrs. Wilcox stepped in from the garden and
made everything less terrible. Ugh! but it has been a
disgusting business. To think that —" She sighed.

" To think that because you and a young man meet
for a moment, there must be all these telegrams and
anger," supplied Margaret.

Helen nodded.

" I've often thought about it, Helen. It's one of the
most interesting things in the world. The truth is
that there is a great outer life that you and I have
never touched — a life in which telegrams and anger
count. Personal relations, that we think supreme, are
not supreme there. There love means marriage settle-
ments, death, death duties. So far I'm clear. But
here my difficulty. This outer life, though obviously
horrid, often seems the real one — there's grit in it.
It does breed character. Do personal relations lead
to sloppiness in the end?"

" Oh, Meg, that's what I felt, only not so clearly,

when the Wilcoxes were so competent, and seemed to have their hands on all the ropes."

"Don't you feel it now?"

"I remember Paul at breakfast," said Helen quietly. "I shall never forget him. He had nothing to fall back upon. I know that personal relations are the real life, for ever and ever."

"Amen!"

So the Wilcox episode fell into the background, leaving behind it memories of sweetness and horror that mingled, and the sisters pursued the life that Helen had commended. They talked to each other and to other people, they filled the tall thin house at Wickham Place with those whom they liked or could befriend. They even attended public meetings. In their own fashion they cared deeply about politics, though not as politicians would have us care; they desired that public life should mirror whatever is good in the life within. Temperance, tolerance, and sexual equality were intelligible cries to them; whereas they did not follow our Forward Policy in Thibet with the keen attention that it merits, and would at times dismiss the whole British Empire with a puzzled, if reverent, sigh. Not out of them are the shows of history erected: the world would be a grey, bloodless place were it entirely composed of Miss Schlegels. But the world being what it is, perhaps they shine out in it like stars.

A word on their origin. They were not " English to the backbone," as their aunt had piously asserted. But, on the other hand, they were not " Germans of the dreadful sort." Their father had belonged to a type that was more prominent in Germany fifty years ago than now. He was not the aggressive German, so dear to the English journalist, nor the domestic German, so dear to the English wit. If one classed him at all it would be as the countryman of Hegel and Kant, as the idealist, inclined to be dreamy, whose Imperialism was the Imperialism of the air. Not that his life had been inactive. He had fought like blazes against Denmark, Austria, France. But he had fought without visualizing the results of victory. A hint of the truth broke on him after Sedan, when he saw the dyed moustaches of Napoleon going grey; another when he entered Paris, and saw the smashed windows of the Tuileries. Peace came — it was all very immense, one had turned into an Empire — but he knew that some quality had vanished for which not all Alsace-Lorraine could compensate him. Germany a commercial Power, Germany a naval Power, Germany with colonies here and a Forward Policy there, and legitimate aspirations in the other place, might appeal to others, and be fitly served by them; for his own part, he abstained from the fruits of victory, and naturalized himself in England. The more earnest members of his family never forgave him, and knew that his children, though scarcely English of the dreadful sort, would never be German to the backbone. He had obtained work in one of our provincial Universities, and there married Poor Emily (or Die Engländerin as the case may be), and as she had money, they proceeded to London, and came to know a good many people. But his gaze was always fixed beyond the sea. It was his hope that the clouds of materialism obscuring the Fatherland would part in time, and the mild intellectual light re-emerge. "Do you imply that we Germans are stupid, Uncle Ernst?" exclaimed a haughty and magnificent nephew. Uncle Ernst replied, "To my mind. You use the intellect, but you no longer care about it. That I call stupidity." As the haughty nephew did not follow, he continued, "You only care about the things that you can use, and therefore arrange them in the following order: Money, supremely useful; intellect, rather useful; imagination, of no use at all. No "— for the other had protested —" your Pan-Germanism is no more imaginative than is our Imperialism over here. It is the vice of a vulgar mind to be thrilled by bigness, to think that a thousand square miles are a thousand times more wonderful than one square mile, and that a million square miles are almost the same as heaven. That is not imagination. No, it kills it. When their poets over here try to celebrate bigness they are dead at once, and naturally. Your poets too are dying, your philosophers, your musicians, to whom Europe has listened for two hundred years. Gone. Gone with the little courts that nurtured them — gone with Esterhaz and Weimar. What? What's that? Your Universities? Oh, yes, you have learned men, who collect more facts than do the learned men of England. They collect facts, and facts, and empires of facts. But which of them will rekindle the light within?"

To all this Margaret listened, sitting on the haughty nephew's knee.

It was a unique education for the little girls. The haughty nephew would be at Wickham Place one day, bringing with him an even haughtier wife, both convinced that Germany was appointed by God to govern the world. Aunt Juley would come the next day, convinced that Great Britain had been appointed to the same post by the same authority. Were both these loud-voiced parties right? On one occasion they had met, and Margaret with clasped hands had implored them to argue the subject out in her presence. Whereat they blushed, and began to talk about the weather. "Papa," she cried — she was a most offensive child —" why will they not discuss this most clear question?" Her father, surveying the parties grimly, replied that he did not know. Putting her head on one side, Margaret then remarked, " To me one of two things is very clear; either God does not know his own mind about England and Germany, or else these do not know the mind of God." A hateful little girl, but at thirteen she had grasped a dilemma that most people travel through life without perceiving. Her brain darted up and down; it grew pliant and strong. Her conclusion was, that any human being lies nearer to the unseen than any organization, and from this she never varied.

Helen advanced along the same lines, though with a more irresponsible tread. In character she resembled her sister, but she was pretty, and so apt to have a more amusing time. People gathered round her more readily, especially when they were new acquaintances, and she did enjoy a little homage very much. When their father died and they ruled alone at Wickham Place, she often absorbed the whole of the company, while Margaret — both were tremendous talkers — fell flat. Neither sister bothered about this. Helen never apologized afterwards, Margaret did not feel the slightest rancour. But looks have their influence upon character. The sisters were alike as little girls, but at the time of the Wilcox episode their methods were beginning to diverge; the younger was rather apt to entice people, and, in enticing them, to be herself enticed; the elder went straight ahead, and accepted an occasional failure as part of the game.

Little need be premised about Tibby. He was now an intelligent man of sixteen, but dyspeptic and difficile.

Chapter V

IT will be generally admitted that Beethoven's Fifth Symphony is the most sublime noise that has ever penetrated into the ear of man. All sorts and conditions are satisfied by it. Whether you are like Mrs. Munt, and tap surreptitiously when the tunes come — of course, not so as to disturb the others —; or like Helen, who can see heroes and shipwrecks in the music's flood; or like Margaret, who can only see the music; or like Tibby, who is profoundly versed in counterpoint, and holds the full score open on his knee; or like their cousin, Fräulein Mosebach, who remembers all the time that Beethoven is "echt Deutsch"; or like Fräulein Mosebach's young man, who can remember nothing but Fräulein Mosebach: in any case, the passion of your life becomes more vivid, and you are bound to admit that such a noise is cheap at two shillings. It is cheap, even if you hear it in the Queen's Hall, dreariest music-room in London, though not as dreary as the Free Trade Hall, Manchester; and even if you sit on the extreme left of that hall, so that the brass bumps at you before the rest of the orchestra arrives, it is still cheap.

"Who is Margaret talking to?" said Mrs. Munt, at the conclusion of the first movement. She was again in London on a visit to Wickham Place.

Helen looked down the long line of their party, and said that she did not know.

"Would it be some young man or other whom she takes an interest in?"

"I expect so," Helen replied. Music enwrapped

her, and she could not enter into the distinction that divides young men whom one takes an interest in from young men whom one knows.

"You girls are so wonderful in always having — Oh dear! one mustn't talk."

For the Andante had begun — very beautiful, but bearing a family likeness to all the other beautiful Andantes that Beethoven had written, and, to Helen's mind, rather disconnecting the heroes and shipwrecks of the first movement from the heroes and goblins of the third. She heard the tune through once, and then her attention wandered, and she gazed at the audience, or the organ, or the architecture. Much did she censure the attenuated Cupids who encircle the ceiling of the Queen's Hall, inclining each to each with vapid gesture, and clad in sallow pantaloons, on which the October sunlight struck. "How awful to marry a man like those Cupids!" thought Helen. Here Beethoven started decorating his tune, so she heard him through once more, and then she smiled at her cousin Frieda. But Frieda, listening to Classical Music, could not respond. Herr Liesecke, too, looked as if wild horses could not make him inattentive; there were lines across his forehead, his lips were parted, his pince-nez at right angles to his nose, and he had laid a thick, white hand on either knee. And next to her was Aunt Juley, so British, and wanting to tap. How interesting that row of people was! What diverse influences had gone to the making! Here Beethoven, after humming and hawing with great sweetness, said "Heigho," and the Andante came to an end. Applause, and a round of "wunderschöning" and "prachtvolleying" from the German contingent. Margaret started talking to her new young man; Helen said to her aunt: "Now comes the wonderful movement: first of all the goblins, and then a trio of elephants dancing;" and Tibby implored the company generally to look out for the transitional passage on the drum.

" On the what, dear? "

" On the *drum*, Aunt Juley."

" No; look out for the part where you think you have done with the goblins and they come back," breathed Helen, as the music started with a goblin walking quietly over the universe, from end to end. Others followed him. They were not aggressive creatures; it was that that made them so terrible to Helen. They merely observed in passing that there was no such thing as splendour or heroism in the world. After the interlude of elephants dancing, they returned and made the observation for the second time. Helen could not contradict them, for, once at all events, she had felt the same, and had seen the reliable walls of youth collapse. Panic and emptiness! Panic and emptiness! The goblins were right.

Her brother raised his finger: it was the transitional passage on the drum.

For, as if things were going too far, Beethoven took hold of the goblins and made them do what he wanted. He appeared in person. He gave them a little push, and they began to walk in major key instead of in a minor, and then — he blew with his mouth and they were scattered! Gusts of splendour, gods and demi-gods contending with vast swords, colour and fragrance broadcast on the field of battle, magnificent victory, magnificent death! Oh, it all burst before the girl, and she even stretched out her gloved hands as if it was tangible. Any fate was titanic; any contest desirable; conqueror and conquered would alike be applauded by the angels of the utmost stars.

And the goblins — they had not really been there at all? They were only the phantoms of cowardice and unbelief? One healthy human impulse would dispel them? Men like the Wilcoxes, or President Roosevelt, would say yes. Beethoven knew better. The goblins really had been there. They might return — and they did. It was as if the splendour of life might boil over and waste to steam and froth. In its dissolution one heard the terrible, ominous note, and a goblin, with increased malignity, walked quietly over the universe from end to end. Panic and emptiness! Panic and emptiness! Even the flaming ramparts of the world might fall.

Beethoven chose to make all right in the end. He built the ramparts up. He blew with his mouth for the second time, and again the goblins were scattered. He brought back the gusts of splendour, the heroism, the youth, the magnificence of life and of death, and, amid vast roarings of a superhuman joy, he led his Fifth Symphony to its conclusion. But the goblins were there. They could return. He had said so bravely, and that is why one can trust Beethoven when he says other things.

Helen pushed her way out during the applause. She desired to be alone. The music summed up to her all that had happened or could happen in her career. She read it as a tangible statement, which could never be superseded. The notes meant this and that to her, and they could have no other meaning, and life could have no other meaning. She pushed right out of the building, and walked slowly down the outside staircase, breathing the autumnal air, and then she strolled home.

" Margaret," called Mrs. Munt, " is Helen all right ? "

" Oh yes."

" She is always going away in the middle of a programme," said Tibby.

" The music has evidently moved her deeply," said Fräulein Mosebach.

" Excuse me," said Margaret's young man, who had

for some time been preparing a sentence, " but that lady has, quite inadvertently, taken my umbrella."

" Oh, good gracious me! — I am so sorry. Tibby, run after Helen."

" I shall miss the Four Serious Songs if I do."

" Tibby love, you must go."

" It isn't of any consequence," said the young man, in truth a little uneasy about his umbrella.

" But of course it is. Tibby! Tibby! "

Tibby rose to his feet, and wilfully caught his person on the backs of the chairs. By the time he had tipped up the seat and had found his hat, and had deposited his full score in safety, it was " too late " to go after Helen. The Four Serious Songs had begun, and one could not move during their performance.

" My sister is so careless," whispered Margaret.

" Not at all," replied the young man; but his voice was dead and cold.

" If you would give me your address —"

" Oh, not at all, not at all; " and he wrapped his greatcoat over his knees.

Then the Four Serious Songs rang shallow in Margaret's ears. Brahms, for all his grumbling and grizzling, had never guessed what it felt like to be suspected of stealing an umbrella. For this fool of a young man thought that she and Helen and Tibby had been playing the confidence trick on him, and that if he gave his address they would break into his rooms some midnight or other and steal his walking-stick too. Most ladies would have laughed, but Margaret really minded, for it gave her a glimpse into squalor. To trust people is a luxury in which only the wealthy can indulge; the poor cannot afford it. As soon as Brahms had grunted himself out, she gave him her card and said, " That is where we live; if you preferred, you could call for the umbrella after the concert, but I didn't like to trouble you when it has all been our fault."

His face brightened a little when he saw that Wickham Place was W. It was sad to see him corroded with suspicion, and yet not daring to be impolite, in case these well-dressed people were honest after all. She took it as a good sign that he said to her, " It's a fine programme this afternoon, is it not? " for this was the remark with which he had originally opened, before the umbrella intervened.

" The Beethoven's fine," said Margaret, who was not a female of the encouraging type. " I don't like the Brahms, though, nor the Mendelssohn that came first — and ugh! I don't like this Elgar that's coming."

" What, what? " called Herr Liesecke, overhearing. " The 'Pomp and Circumstance' will not be fine? "

" Oh, Margaret, you tiresome girl! " cried her aunt. " Here have I been persuading Herr Liesecke to stop for 'Pomp and Circumstance,' and you are undoing all my work. I am so anxious for him to hear what *we* are doing in music. Oh, you mustn't run down our English composers, Margaret."

" For my part, I have heard the composition at Stettin," said Fräulein Mosebach. " On two occasions. It is dramatic, a little."

" Frieda, you despise English music. You know you do. And English art. And English Literature, except Shakespeare and he's a German. Very well, Frieda, you may go."

The lovers laughed and glanced at each other. Moved by a common impulse, they rose to their feet and fled from 'Pomp and Circumstance.'

" We have this call to play in Finsbury Circus, it is true," said Herr Liesecke, as he edged past her and reached the gangway just as the music started.

" Margaret —" loudly whispered by Aunt Juley.

"Margaret, Margaret! Fräulein Mosebach has left her beautiful little bag behind her on the seat."

Sure enough, there was Frieda's reticule, containing her address book, her pocket dictionary, her map of London, and her money.

"Oh, what a bother — what a family we are! Fr — Frieda!"

"Hush!" said all those who thought the music fine.

"But it's the number they want in Finsbury Circus —"

"Might I — couldn't I —" said the suspicious young man, and got very red.

"Oh, I would be so grateful."

He took the bag — money clinking inside it — and slipped up the gangway with it. He was just in time to catch them at the swing-door, and he received a pretty smile from the German girl and a fine bow from her cavalier. He returned to his seat up-sides with the world. The trust that they had reposed in him was trivial, but he felt that it cancelled his mistrust for them, and that probably he would not be "had" over his umbrella. This young man had been "had" in the past — badly, perhaps overwhelmingly — and now most of his energies went in defending himself against the unknown. But this afternoon — perhaps on account of music — he perceived that one must slack off occasionally, or what is the good of being alive? Wickham Place, W., though a risk, was as safe as most things, and he would risk it.

So when the concert was over and Margaret said, "We live quite near; I am going there now. Could you walk around with me, and we'll find your umbrella?" he said, "Thank you," peaceably, and followed her out of the Queen's Hall. She wished that he was not so anxious to hand a lady downstairs, or to carry a lady's programme for her — his class was near enough her own for its manners to vex her. But she found him interesting on the whole —every one interested the Schlegels on the whole at that time — and while her lips talked culture, her heart was planning to invite him to tea.

" How tired one gets after music! " she began.

" Do you find the atmosphere of Queen's Hall oppressive? "

" Yes, horribly."

" But surely the atmosphere of Covent Garden is even more oppressive."

" Do you go there much? "

" When my work permits, I attend the gallery for the Royal Opera."

Helen would have exclaimed, " So do I. I love the gallery," and thus have endeared herself to the young man. Helen could do these things. But Margaret had an almost morbid horror of " drawing people out," of " making things go." She had been to the gallery at Covent Garden, but she did not " attend " it, preferring the more expensive seats; still less did she love it. So she made no reply.

" This year I have been three times — to ' Faust,' ' Tosca,' and —" Was it " Tannhouser " or " Tannhoyser "? Better not risk the word.

Margaret disliked " Tosca " and " Faust." And so, for one reason and another, they walked on in silence, chaperoned by the voice of Mrs. Munt, who was getting into difficulties with her nephew.

" I do in a *way* remember the passage, Tibby, but when every instrument is so beautiful, it is difficult to pick out one thing rather than another. I am sure that you and Helen take me to the very nicest concerts. Not a dull note from beginning to end. I only wish that our German friends would have stayed till it finished."

"But surely you haven't forgotten the drum steadily beating on the low C, Aunt Juley?" came Tibby's voice. "No one could. It's unmistakable."

"A specially loud part?" hazarded Mrs. Munt. "Of course I do not go in for being musical," she added, the shot failing. "I only care for music — a very different thing. But still I will say this for myself — I do know when I like a thing and when I don't. Some people are the same about pictures. They can go into a picture gallery — Miss Conder can — and say straight off what they feel, all round the wall. I never could do that. But music is so different to pictures, to my mind. When it comes to music I am as safe as houses, and I assure you, Tibby, I am by no means pleased by everything. There was a thing — something about a faun in French — which Helen went into ecstasies over, but I thought it most tinkling and superficial, and said so, and I held to my opinion too."

"Do you agree?" asked Margaret. "Do you think music is so different to pictures?"

"I — I should have thought so, kind of," he said.

"So should I. Now, my sister declares they're just the same. We have great arguments over it. She says I'm dense; I say she's sloppy." Getting under way, she cried: "Now, doesn't it seem absurd to you? What *is* the good of the Arts if they're interchangeable? What *is* the good of the ear if it tells you the same as the eye? Helen's one aim is to translate tunes into the language of painting, and pictures into the language of music. It's very ingenious, and she says several pretty things in the process, but what's gained, I'd like to know? Oh, it's all rubbish, radically false. If Monet's really Debussy, and Debussy's really Monet, neither gentleman is worth his salt — that's my opinion."

Evidently these sisters quarrelled.

" Now, this very symphony that we've just been having — she won't let it alone. She labels it with meanings from start to finish; turns it into literature. I wonder if the day will ever return when music will be treated as music. Yet I don't know. There's my brother — behind us. He treats music as music, and oh, my goodness! He makes me angrier than any one, simply furious. With him I daren't even argue."

An unhappy family, if talented.

" But, of course, the real villain is Wagner. He has done more than any man in the nineteenth century towards the muddling of arts. I do feel that music is in a very serious state just now, though extraordinarily interesting. Every now and then in history there do come these terrible geniuses, like Wagner, who stir up all the wells of thought at once. For a moment it's splendid. Such a splash as never was. But afterwards — such a lot of mud; and the wells — as it were, they communicate with each other too easily now, and not one of them will run quite clear. That's what Wagner's done."

Her speeches fluttered away from the young man like birds. If only he could talk like this, he would have caught the world. Oh to acquire culture! Oh, to pronounce foreign names correctly! Oh, to be well informed, discoursing at ease on every subject that a lady started! But it would take one years. With an hour at lunch and a few shattered hours in the evening, how was it possible to catch up with leisured women, who had been reading steadily from childhood? His brain might be full of names, he might have even heard of Monet and Debussy; the trouble was that he could not string them together into a sentence, he could not make them " tell," he could not quite forget about his stolen umbrella. Yes, the umbrella was the real trouble. Behind Monet and Debussy the umbrella persisted, with the steady beat of

a drum. "I suppose my umbrella will be all right,"
he was thinking. "I don't really mind about it. I
will think about music instead. I suppose my umbrella
will be all right." Earlier in the afternoon he had
worried about seats. Ought he to have paid as much
as two shillings? Earlier still he had wondered,
"Shall I try to do without a programme?" There had
always been something to worry him ever since he
could remember, always something that distracted
him in the pursuit of beauty. For he did pursue
beauty, and, therefore, Margaret's speeches did flutter
away from him like birds.

Margaret talked ahead, occasionally saying, "Don't
you think so? don't you feel the same?" And once
she stopped, and said, "Oh, do interrupt me!" which
terrified him. She did not attract him, though she
filled him with awe. Her figure was meagre, her
face seemed all teeth and eyes, her references to her
sister and brother were uncharitable. For all her
cleverness and culture, she was probably one of those
soulless, atheistical women who have been so shown
up by Miss Corelli. It was surprising (and alarming)
that she should suddenly say, "I do hope that you'll
come in and have some tea."

"I do hope that you'll come in and have some tea.
We should be so glad. I have dragged you so far
out of your way."

They had arrived at Wickham Place. The sun had
set, and the backwater, in deep shadow, was filling
with a gentle haze. To the right the fantastic sky-
line of the flats towered black against the hues of
evening; to the left the older houses raised a square-
cut, irregular parapet against the grey. Margaret
fumbled for her latchkey. Of course she had forgotten it. So, grasping her umbrella by its ferrule,
she leant over the area and tapped at the dining-room
window.

"Helen! Let us in!"

"All right," said a voice.

"You've been taking this gentleman's umbrella."

"Taken a what?" said Helen, opening the door. "Oh, what's that? Do come in! How do you do?"

"Helen, you must not be so ramshackly. You took this gentleman's umbrella away from Queen's Hall, and he has had the trouble of coming for it."

"Oh, I am so sorry!" cried Helen, all her hair flying. She had pulled off her hat as soon as she returned, and had flung herself into the big dining-room chair. "I do nothing but steal umbrellas. I am so very sorry! Do come in and choose one. Is yours a hooky or a nobbly? Mine's a nobbly — at least, I *think* it is."

The light was turned on, and they began to search the hall, Helen, who had abruptly parted with the Fifth Symphony, commenting with shrill little cries.

"Don't you talk, Meg! You stole an old gentleman's silk top-hat. Yes, she did, Aunt Juley. It is a positive fact. She thought it was a muff. Oh, heavens! I've knocked the In and Out card down. Where's Frieda? Tibby, why don't you ever — No, I can't remember what I was going to say. That wasn't it, but do tell the maids to hurry tea up. What about this umbrella?" She opened it. "No, it's all gone along the seams. It's an appalling umbrella. It must be mine."

But it was not.

He took it from her, murmured a few words of thanks, and then fled, with the lilting step of the clerk.

"But if you will stop —" cried Margaret. "Now, Helen, how stupid you've been!"

"Whatever have I done?"

"Don't you see that you've frightened him away? I meant him to stop to tea. You oughtn't to talk about stealing or holes in an umbrella. I saw his nice eyes getting so miserable. No, it's not a bit of good now." For Helen had darted out into the street, shouting, " Oh, do stop ! "

" I dare say it is all for the best," opined Mrs. Munt. " We know nothing about the young man, Margaret, and your drawing-room is full of very tempting little things."

But Helen cried: "Aunt Juley, how can you! You make me more and more ashamed. I'd rather he *had* been a thief and taken all the apostle spoons than that I — Well, I must shut the front-door, I suppose. One more failure for Helen."

" Yes, I think the apostle spoons could have gone as rent," said Margaret. Seeing that her aunt did not understand, she added: " You remember ' rent.' It was one of father's words — Rent to the ideal, to his own faith in human nature. You remember how he would trust strangers, and if they fooled him he would say, ' It's better to be fooled than to be suspicious ' — that the confidence trick is the work of man, but the want-of-confidence-trick is the work of the devil."

" I remember something of the sort now," said Mrs. Munt, rather tartly, for she longed to add, " It was lucky that your father married a wife with money." But this was unkind, and she contented herself with, " Why, he might have stolen the little Ricketts picture as well."

" Better that he had," said Helen stoutly.

" No, I agree with Aunt Juley," said Margaret. " I'd rather mistrust people than lose my little Ricketts. There are limits."

Their brother, finding the incident commonplace, had stolen upstairs to see whether there were scones for tea. He warmed the teapot — almost too deftly — rejected the Orange Pekoe that the parlour-maid had provided, poured in five spoonfuls of a superior blend, filled up with really boiling water, and now called to the ladies to be quick or they would lose the aroma.

"All right, Auntie Tibby," called Helen, while Margaret, thoughtful again, said: "In a way, I wish we had a real boy in the house — the kind of boy who cares for men. It would make entertaining so much easier."

"So do I," said her sister. "Tibby only cares for cultured females singing Brahms." And when they joined him she said rather sharply: "Why didn't you make that young man welcome, Tibby? You must do the host a little, you know. You ought to have taken his hat and coaxed him into stopping, instead of letting him be swamped by screaming women."

Tibby sighed, and drew a long strand of hair over his forehead.

"Oh, it's no good looking superior. I mean what I say."

"Leave Tibby alone!" said Margaret, who could not bear her brother to be scolded.

"Here's the house a regular hen-coop!" grumbled Helen.

"Oh, my dear!" protested Mrs. Munt. "How can you say such dreadful things! The number of men you get here has always astonished me. If there is any danger it's the other way round."

"Yes, but it's the wrong sort of men, Helen means."

"No, I don't," corrected Helen. "We get the right sort of man, but the wrong side of him, and I say that's Tibby's fault. There ought to be a something about the house — an — I don't know what."

"A touch of the W.'s, perhaps?"

Helen put out her tongue.

"Who are the W.'s?" asked Tibby.

"The W.'s are things I and Meg and Aunt Juley know about and you don't, so there!"

"I suppose that ours is a female house," said Margaret, "and one must just accept it. No, Aunt Juley, I don't mean that this house is full of women. I am trying to say something much more clever. I mean that it was irrevocably feminine, even in father's time. Now I'm sure you understand! Well, I'll give you another example. It'll shock you, but I don't care. Suppose Queen Victoria gave a dinner-party, and that the guests had been Leighton, Millais, Swinburne, Rossetti, Meredith, Fitzgerald, etc. Do you suppose that the atmosphere of that dinner would have been artistic? Heavens, no! The very chairs on which they sat would have seen to that. So with our house — it must be feminine, and all we can do is to see that it isn't effeminate. Just as another house that I can mention, but I won't, sounded irrevocably masculine, and all its inmates can do is to see that it isn't brutal."

"That house being the W.'s house, I presume," said Tibby.

"You're not going to be told about the W.'s, my child," Helen cried, "so don't you think it. And on the other hand, I don't the least mind if you find out, so don't you think you've done anything clever, in either case. Give me a cigarette."

"You do what you can for the house," said Margaret. "The drawing-room reeks of smoke."

"If you smoked too, the house might suddenly turn masculine. Atmosphere is probably a question of touch and go. Even at Queen Victoria's dinner-party — if something had been just a little different — perhaps if she'd worn a clinging Liberty tea-gown instead of a magenta satin —"

"With an Indian shawl over her shoulders —"

"Fastened at the bosom with a Cairngorm-pin —"

Bursts of disloyal laughter — you must remember that they are half German — greeted these suggestions, and Margaret said pensively, "How inconceivable it would be if the Royal Family cared about Art." And the conversation drifted away and away, and Helen's cigarette turned to a spot in the darkness, and the great flats opposite were sown with lighted windows, which vanished and were relit again, and vanished incessantly. Beyond them the thoroughfare roared gently — a tide that could never be quiet, while in the east, invisible behind the smokes of Wapping, the moon was rising.

"That reminds me, Margaret. We might have taken that young man into the dining-room, at all events. Only the majolica plate — and that is so firmly set in the wall. I am really distressed that he had no tea."

For that little incident had impressed the three women more than might be supposed. It remained as a goblin football, as a hint that all is not for the best in the best of all possible worlds, and that beneath these superstructures of wealth and art there wanders an ill-fed boy, who has recovered his umbrella indeed, but who has left no address behind him, and no name.

Chapter VI

WE are not concerned with the very poor. They are unthinkable, and only to be approached by the statistician or the poet. This story deals with gentlefolk, or with those who are obliged to pretend that they are gentlefolk.

The boy, Leonard Bast, stood at the extreme verge of gentility. He was not in the abyss, but he could see it, and at times people whom he knew had dropped in, and counted no more. He knew that he was poor, and would admit it: he would have died sooner than confess any inferiority to the rich. This may be splendid of him. But he was inferior to most rich people, there is not the least doubt of it. He was not as courteous as the average rich man, nor as intelligent, nor as healthy, nor as lovable. His mind and his body had been alike underfed, because he was poor, and because he was modern they were always craving better food. Had he lived some centuries ago, in the brightly coloured civilizations of the past, he would have had a definite status, his rank and his income would have corresponded. But in his day the angel of Democracy had arisen, enshadowing the classes with leathern wings, and proclaiming, "All men are equal — all men, that is to say, who possess umbrellas," and so he was obliged to assert gentility, lest he slipped into the abyss where nothing counts, and the statements of Democracy are inaudible.

As he walked away from Wickham Place, his first care was to prove that he was as good as the Miss Schlegels. Obscurely wounded in his pride, he tried to

wound them in return. They were probably not ladies.
Would real ladies have asked him to tea? They were
certainly ill-natured and cold. At each step his feeling
of superiority increased. Would a real lady have
talked about stealing an umbrella? Perhaps they were
thieves after all, and if he had gone into the house they
would have clapped a chloroformed handkerchief over
his face. He walked on complacently as far as the
Houses of Parliament. There an empty stomach
asserted itself, and told him that he was a fool.

" Evening, Mr. Bast."

" Evening, Mr. Dealtry."

" Nice evening."

" Evening."

Mr. Dealtry, a fellow clerk, passed on, and Leonard
stood wondering whether he would take the tram as
far as a penny would take him, or whether he would
walk. He decided to walk — it is no good giving in,
and he had spent money enough at Queen's Hall — and
he walked over Westminster Bridge, in front of St.
Thomas's Hospital, and through the immense tunnel·
that passes under the South-Western main line at
Vauxhall. In the tunnel he paused and listened to the
roar of the trains. A sharp pain darted through his
head, and he was conscious of the exact form of his
eye sockets. He pushed on for another mile, and did
not slacken speed until he stood at the entrance of a
road called Camelia Road, which was at present his
home.

Here he stopped again, and glanced suspiciously to
right and left, like a rabbit that is going to bolt into
its hole. A block of flats, constructed with extreme
cheapness, towered on either hand. Farther down
the road two more blocks were being built, and beyond
these an old house was being demolished to accommo-
date another pair. It was the kind of scene that may
be observed all over London, whatever the locality —

bricks and mortar rising and falling with the restlessness of the water in a fountain, as the city receives more and more men upon her soil. Camelia Road would soon stand out like a fortress, and command, for a little, an extensive view. Only for a little. Plans were out for the erection of flats in Magnolia Road also. And again a few years, and all the flats in either road might be pulled down, and new buildings, of a vastness at present unimaginable, might arise where they had fallen.

" Evening, Mr. Bast."

" Evening, Mr. Cunningham."

" Very serious thing this decline of the birth-rate in Manchester."

" I beg your pardon? "

" Very serious thing this decline of the birth-rate in Manchester," repeated Mr. Cunningham, tapping the Sunday paper, in which the calamity in question had just been announced to him.

" Ah, yes," said Leonard, who was not going to let on that he had not bought a Sunday paper.

" If this kind of thing goes on the population of England will be stationary in 1960."

" You don't say so."

" I call it a very serious thing, eh? "

" Good-evening, Mr. Cunningham."

" Good-evening, Mr. Bast."

Then Leonard entered Block B of the flats, and turned, not upstairs, but down, into what is known to house agents as a semi-basement, and to other men as a cellar. He opened the door, and cried " Hullo! " with the pseudo-geniality of the Cockney. There was no reply. " Hullo! " he repeated. The sitting-room was empty, though the electric light had been left burning. A look of relief came over his face, and he flung himself into the armchair.

The sitting-room contained, besides the armchair,

two other chairs, a piano, a three-legged table, and a cosy corner. Of the walls, one was occupied by the window, the other by a draped mantelshelf bristling with Cupids. Opposite the window was the door, and beside the door a bookcase, while over the piano there extended one of the masterpieces of Maud Goodman. It was an amorous and not unpleasant little hole when the curtains were drawn, and the lights turned on, and the gas-stove unlit. But it struck that shallow make-shift note that is so often heard in the modern dwelling-place. It had been too easily gained, and could be re-linquished too easily.

As Leonard was kicking off his boots he jarred the three-legged table, and a photograph frame, honourably poised upon it, slid sideways, fell off into the fireplace, and smashed. He swore in a colourless sort of way, and picked the photograph up. It represented a young lady called Jacky, and had been taken at the time when young ladies called Jacky were often photographed with their mouths open. Teeth of dazzling whiteness extended along either of Jacky's jaws, and positively weighed her head sideways, so large were they and so numerous. Take my word for it, that smile was simply stunning, and it is only you and I who will be fastidious, and complain that true joy begins in the eyes, and that the eyes of Jacky did not accord with her smile, but were anxious and hungry.

Leonard tried to pull out the fragments of glass, and cut his fingers and swore again. A drop of blood fell on the frame, another followed, spilling over on to the exposed photograph. He swore more vigor-ously, and dashed into the kitchen, where he bathed his hands. The kitchen was the same size as the sitting-room; through it was a bedroom. This completed his home. He was renting the flat furnished: of all the objects that encumbered it none were his own except the photograph frame, the Cupids, and the books.

"Damn, damn, damnation!" he murmured, together with such other words as he had learnt from older men. Then he raised his hand to his forehead and said, "Oh, damn it all —" which meant something different. He pulled himself together. He drank a little tea, black and silent, that still survived upon an upper shelf. He swallowed some dusty crumbs of a cake. Then he went back to the sitting-room, settled himself anew, and began to read a volume of Ruskin.

" Seven miles to the north of Venice —"

How perfectly the famous chapter opens! How supreme its command of admonition and of poetry! The rich man is speaking to us from his gondola.

" Seven miles to the north of Venice the banks of sand which nearer the city rise little above low-water mark attain by degrees a higher level, and knit themselves at last into fields of salt morass, raised here and there into shapeless mounds, and intercepted by narrow creeks of sea."

Leonard was trying to form his style on Ruskin: he understood him to be the greatest master of English Prose. He read forward steadily, occasionally making a few notes.

" Let us consider a little each of these characters in succession, and first (for of the shafts enough has been said already), what is very peculiar to this church — its luminousness."

Was there anything to be learnt from this fine sentence? Could he adapt it to the needs of daily life? Could he introduce it, with modifications, when he next wrote a letter to his brother, the lay-reader? For example —

" Let us consider a little each of these characters in succession, and first (for of the absence of ventilation enough has been said already), what is very peculiar to this flat — its obscurity."

Something told him that the modifications would not do; and that something, had he known it, was the spirit of English Prose. " My flat is dark as well as stuffy." Those were the words for him.

And the voice in the gondola rolled on, piping melodiously of Effort and Self-Sacrifice, full of high purpose, full of beauty, full even of sympathy and the love of men, yet somehow eluding all that was actual and insistent in Leonard's life. For it was the voice of one who had never been dirty or hungry, and had not guessed successfully what dirt and hunger are.

Leonard listened to it with reverence. He felt that he was being done good to, and that if he kept on with Ruskin, and the Queen's Hall Concerts, and some pictures by Watts, he would one day push his head out of the grey waters and see the universe. He believed in sudden conversion, a belief which may be right, but which is peculiarly attractive to a half-baked mind. It is the basis of much popular religion: in the domain of business it dominates the Stock Exchange, and becomes that " bit of luck " by which all successes and failures are explained. " If only I had a bit of luck, the whole thing would come straight. . . . He's got a most magnificent place down at Streatham and a 20 h.-p. Fiat, but then, mind you, he's had luck. . . . I'm sorry the wife's so late, but she never has any luck over catching trains." Leonard was superior to these people; he did believe in effort and in a steady preparation for the change that he desired. But of a heritage that may expand gradually, he had no conception: he hoped to come to Culture suddenly, much as the Revivalist hopes to come to Jesus. Those Miss Schlegels had come to it; they had done the trick; their hands were upon the ropes, once and for all. And meanwhile, his flat was dark, as well as stuffy.

Presently there was a noise on the staircase. He shut up Margaret's card in the pages of Ruskin, and opened the door. A woman entered, of whom it is simplest to say that she was not respectable. Her appearance was awesome. She seemed all strings and bell-pulls — ribbons, chains, bead necklaces that clinked and caught — and a boa of azure feathers hung round her neck, with the ends uneven. Her throat was bare, wound with a double row of pearls, her arms were bare to the elbows, and might again be detected at the shoulder, through cheap lace. Her hat, which was flowery, resembled those punnets, covered with flannel, which we sowed with mustard and cress in our childhood, and which germinated here yes, and there no. She wore it on the back of her head. As for her hair, or rather hairs, they are too complicated to describe, but one system went down her back, lying in a thick pad there, while another, created for a lighter destiny, rippled around her forehead. The face — the face does not signify. It was the face of the photograph, but older, and the teeth were not so numerous as the photographer had suggested, and certainly not so white. Yes, Jacky was past her prime, whatever that prime may have been. She was descending quicker than most women into the colourless years, and the look in her eyes confessed it.

" What ho ! " said Leonard, greeting the apparition with much spirit, and helping it off with its boa.

Jacky, in husky tones, replied, " What ho ! "

" Been out ? " he asked. The question sounds superfluous, but it cannot have been really, for the lady answered, " No," adding, " Oh, I am so tired."

" You tired ? "

" Eh ? "

" I'm tired," said he, hanging the boa up.

" Oh, Len, I am so tired."

" I've been to that classical concert I told you about," said Leonard.

" What's that ? "

" I came back as soon as it was over."

" Any one been round to our place? " asked Jacky.

" Not that I've seen. I met Mr. Cunningham outside, and we passed a few remarks."

" What, not Mr. Cunningham? "

" Yes."

" Oh, you mean Mr. Cunningham."

" Yes. Mr. Cunningham."

" I've been out to tea at a lady friend's."

Her secret being at last given to the world, and the name of the lady-friend being even adumbrated, Jacky made no further experiments in the difficult and tiring art of conversation. She never had been a great talker. Even in her photographic days she had relied upon her smile and her figure to attract, and now that she was —

> " On the shelf,
> On the shelf,
> Boys, boys, I'm on the shelf,"

she was not likely to find her tongue. Occasional bursts of song (of which the above is an example) still issued from her lips, but the spoken word was rare.

She sat down on Leonard's knee, and began to fondle him. She was now a massive woman of thirty-three, and her weight hurt him, but he could not very well say anything. Then she said, " Is that a book you're reading? " and he said, " That's a book," and drew it from her unreluctant grasp. Margaret's card fell out of it. It fell face downwards, and he murmured, " Bookmarker."

" Len — "

" What is it? " he asked, a little wearily, for she only had one topic of conversation when she sat upon his knee.

" You do love me? "

" Jacky, you know that I do. How can you ask such questions ! "

" But you do love me, Len, don't you ? "

" Of course I do."

A pause. The other remark was still due.

" Len —"

" Well? What is it ? "

" Len, you will make it all right ? "

" I can't have you ask me that again," said the boy, flaring up into a sudden passion. " I've promised to marry you when I'm of age, and that's enough. My word's my word. I've promised to marry you as soon as ever I'm twenty-one, and I can't keep on being worried. I've worries enough. It isn't likely I'd throw you over, let alone my word, when I've spent all this money. Besides, I'm an Englishman, and I never go back on my word. Jacky, do be reasonable. Of course I'll marry you. Only do stop badgering me."

" When's your birthday, Len ? "

" I've told you again and again, the eleventh of November next. Now get off my knee a bit; some one must get supper, I suppose."

Jacky went through to the bedroom, and began to see to her hat. This meant blowing at it with short sharp puffs. Leonard tidied up the sitting-room, and began to prepare their evening meal. He put a penny into the slot of the gas-meter, and soon the flat was reeking with metallic fumes. Somehow he could not recover his temper, and all the time he was cooking he continued to complain bitterly.

" It really is too bad when a fellow isn't trusted. It makes one feel so wild, when I've pretended to the people here that you're my wife — all right, you *shall* be my wife — and I've bought you the ring to wear, and I've taken this flat furnished, and it's far more than I can afford, and yet you aren't content, and I've also not told the truth when I've written home." He lowered his voice. "He'd stop it." In a tone of horror, that was a little luxurious, he repeated: "My brother'd stop it. I'm going against the whole world, Jacky.

"That's what I am, Jacky. I don't take any heed of what any one says. I just go straight forward, I do. That's always been my way. I'm not one of your weak knock-kneed chaps. If a woman's in trouble, I don't leave her in the lurch. That's not my street. No, thank you.

"I'll tell you another thing too. I care a good deal about improving myself by means of Literature and Art, and so getting a wider outlook. For instance, when you came in I was reading Ruskin's 'Stones of Venice.' I don't say this to boast, but just to show you the kind of man I am. I can tell you, I enjoyed that classical concert this afternoon."

To all his moods Jacky remained equally indifferent. When supper was ready — and not before — she emerged from the bedroom, saying: "But you do love me, don't you?"

They began with a soup square, which Leonard had just dissolved in some hot water. It was followed by the tongue — a freckled cylinder of meat, with a little jelly at the top, and a great deal of yellow fat at the bottom — ending with another square dissolved in water (jelly: pineapple), which Leonard had prepared earlier in the day. Jacky ate contentedly enough, occasionally looking at her man with those anxious eyes, to which nothing else in her appearance corresponded, and which yet seemed to mirror her soul. And Leonard managed to convince his stomach that it was having a nourishing meal.

After supper they smoked cigarettes and exchanged a few statements. She observed that her "likeness" had been broken. He found occasion to remark, for the second time, that he had come straight back home after the concert at Queen's Hall. Presently she sat upon his knee. The inhabitants of Camelia Road tramped to and fro outside the window, just on a level with their heads, and the family in the flat on the ground-floor began to sing, " Hark, my soul, it is the Lord."

" That tune fairly gives me the hump," said Leonard.

Jacky followed this, and said that, for her part, she thought it a lovely tune.

" No; I'll play you something lovely. Get up, dear, for a minute."

He went to the piano and jingled out a little Grieg. He played badly and vulgarly, but the performance was not without its effect, for Jacky said she thought she'd be going to bed. As she receded, a new set of interests possessed the boy, and he began to think of what had been said about music by that odd Miss Schlegel — the one that twisted her face about so when she spoke. Then the thoughts grew sad and envious. There was the girl named Helen, who had pinched his umbrella, and the German girl who had smiled at him pleasantly, and Herr some one, and Aunt some one, and the brother — all, all with their hands on the ropes. They had all passed up that narrow, rich staircase at Wickham Place, to some ample room, whither he could never follow them, not if he read for ten hours a day. Oh, it was no good, this continual aspiration. Some are born cultured; the rest had better go in for whatever comes easy. To see life steadily and to see it whole was not for the likes of him.

From the darkness beyond the kitchen a voice called, " Len?"

" You in bed?" he asked, his forehead twitching.

" M'm."

" All right."

Presently she called him again.

"I must clean my boots ready for the morning," he answered.

Presently she called him again.

"I rather want to get this chapter done."

"What?"

He closed his ears against her.

"What's that?"

"All right, Jacky, nothing; I'm reading a book."

"What?"

"What?" he answered, catching her degraded deafness.

Presently she called him again.

Ruskin had visited Torcello by this time, and was ordering his gondoliers to take him to Murano. It occurred to him, as he glided over the whispering lagoons, that the power of Nature could not be shortened by the folly, nor her beauty altogether saddened by the misery, of such as Leonard.

Chapter VII

"OH, Margaret," cried her aunt next morning, "such a most unfortunate thing has happened. I could not get you alone."
The most unfortunate thing was not very serious. One of the flats in the ornate block opposite had been taken furnished by the Wilcox family, " coming up, no doubt, in the hope of getting into London society." That Mrs. Munt should be the first to discover the misfortune was not remarkable, for she was so interested in the flats, that she watched their every mutation with unwearying care. In theory she despised them — they took away that old-world look — they cut off the sun — flats house a flashy type of person. But if the truth had been known, she found her visits to Wickham Place twice as amusing since Wickham Mansions had arisen, and would in a couple of days learn more about them than her nieces in a couple of months, or her nephew in a couple of years. She would stroll across and make friends with the porters, and inquire what the rents were, exclaiming for example: "What! a hundred and twenty for a basement? You'll never get it!" And they would answer: "One can but try, madam." The passenger lifts, the provision lifts, the arrangement for coals (a great temptation for a dishonest porter), were all familiar matters to her, and perhaps a relief from the politico-economical-aesthetic atmosphere that reigned at the Schlegels'.
Margaret received the information calmly, and did

not agree that it would throw a cloud over poor Helen's life.

"Oh, but Helen isn't a girl with no interests," she explained. "She has plenty of other things and other people to think about. She made a false start with the Wilcoxes, and she'll be as willing as we are to have nothing more to do with them."

"For a clever girl, dear, how very oddly you do talk. Helen'll *have* to have something more to do with them, now that they're all opposite. She may meet that Paul in the street. She cannot very well not bow."

"Of course she must bow. But look here; let's do the flowers. I was going to say, the will to be interested in him has died, and what else matters? I look on that disastrous episode (over which you were so kind) as the killing of a nerve in Helen. It's dead, and she'll never be troubled with it again. The only things that matter are the things that interest one. Bowing, even calling and leaving cards, even a dinner-party — we can do all those things to the Wilcoxes, if they find it agreeable; but the other thing, the one important thing — never again. Don't you see?"

Mrs. Munt did not see, and indeed Margaret was making a most questionable statement — that any emotion, any interest once vividly aroused, can wholly die.

"I also have the honour to inform you that the Wilcoxes are bored with us. I didn't tell you at the time — it might have made you angry, and you had enough to worry you — but I wrote a letter to Mrs. W., and apologized for the trouble that Helen had given them. She didn't answer it."

"How very rude!"

"I wonder. Or was it sensible?"

"No, Margaret, most rude."

"In either case one can class it as reassuring."

Mrs. Munt sighed. She was going back to Swanage on the morrow, just as her nieces were wanting her most. Other regrets crowded upon her : for instance, how magnificently she would have cut Charles if she had met him face to face. She had already seen him, giving an order to the porter — and very common he looked in a tall hat. But unfortunately his back was turned to her, and though she had cut his back, she could not regard this as a telling snub.

" But you will be careful, won't you ? " she exhorted.

" Oh, certainly. Fiendishly careful."

" And Helen must be careful, too."

" Careful over what ? " cried Helen, at that moment coming into the room with her cousin.

" Nothing," said Margaret, seized with a momentary awkwardness.

" Careful over what, Aunt Juley ? "

Mrs. Munt assumed a cryptic air. " It is only that a certain family, whom we know by name but do not mention, as you said yourself last night after the concert, have taken the flat opposite from the Mathesons — where the plants are in the balcony."

Helen began some laughing reply, and then disconcerted them all by blushing. Mrs. Munt was so disconcerted that she exclaimed, " What, Helen, you don't mind them coming, do you ? " and deepened the blush to crimson.

" Of course I don't mind," said Helen a little crossly. " It is that you and Meg are both so absurdly grave about it, when there's nothing to be grave about at all."

" I'm not grave," protested Margaret, a little cross in her turn.

" Well, you look grave ; doesn't she, Frieda ? "

" I don't feel grave, that's all I can say ; you're going quite on the wrong tack."

" No, she does not feel grave," echoed Mrs. Munt. " I can bear witness to that. She disagrees —"

" Hark!" interrupted Fräulein Mosebach. "I hear Bruno entering the hall."

For Herr Liesecke was due at Wickham Place to call for the two younger girls. He was not entering the hall — in fact, he did not enter it for quite five minutes. But Frieda detected a delicate situation, and said that she and Helen had much better wait for Bruno down below, and leave Margaret and Mrs. Munt to finish arranging the flowers. Helen acquiesced. But, as if to prove that the situation was not delicate really, she stopped in the doorway and said:

"Did you say the Mathesons' flat, Aunt Juley? How wonderful you are! *I* never knew that the woman who laced too tightly's name was Matheson."

"Come, Helen," said her cousin.

"Go, Helen," said her aunt; and continued to Margaret almost in the same breath: "Helen cannot deceive me. She does mind."

"Oh, hush!" breathed Margaret. "Frieda'll hear you, and she can be so tiresome."

"She minds," persisted Mrs. Munt, moving thoughtfully about the room, and pulling the dead chrysanthemums out of the vases. "I knew she'd mind — and I'm sure a girl ought to! Such an experience! Such awful coarse-grained people! I know more about them than you do, which you forget, and if Charles had taken you that motor drive — well, you'd have reached the house a perfect wreck. Oh, Margaret, you don't know what you are in for. They're all bottled up against the drawing-room window. There's Mrs. Wilcox — I've seen her. There's Paul. There's Evie, who is a minx. There's Charles — I saw him to start with. And who would an elderly man with a moustache and a copper-coloured face be?"

"Mr. Wilcox, possibly."

"I knew it. And there's Mr. Wilcox."

"It's a shame to call his face copper colour," complained Margaret. "He has a remarkably good complexion for a man of his age."

Mrs. Munt, triumphant elsewhere, could afford to concede Mr. Wilcox his complexion. She passed on from it to the plan of campaign that her nieces should pursue in the future. Margaret tried to stop her.

"Helen did not take the news quite as I expected, but the Wilcox nerve is dead in her really, so there's no need for plans."

"It's as well to be prepared."

"No — it's as well not to be prepared."

"Why?"

"Because —"

Her thought drew being from the obscure borderland. She could not explain in so many words, but she felt that those who prepare for all the emergencies of life beforehand may equip themselves at the expense of joy. It is necessary to prepare for an examination, or a dinner-party, or a possible fall in the price of stock: those who attempt human relations must adopt another method, or fail. "Because I'd sooner risk it," was her lame conclusion.

"But imagine the evenings," exclaimed her aunt, pointing to the Mansions with the spout of the watering-can. "Turn the electric light on here or there, and it's almost the same room. One evening they may forget to draw their blinds down, and you'll see them; and the next, you yours, and they'll see you. Impossible to sit out on the balconies. Impossible to water the plants, or even speak. Imagine going out of the front-door, and they come out opposite at the same moment. And yet you tell me that plans are unnecessary, and you'd rather risk it."

"I hope to risk things all my life."

"Oh, Margaret, most dangerous."

"But after all," she continued with a smile, "there's

never any great risk as long as you have money."

" Oh, shame! What a shocking speech!"

" Money pads the edges of things," said Miss Schlegel. " God help those who have none."

" But this is something quite new!" said Mrs. Munt, who collected new ideas as a squirrel collects nuts, and was especially attracted by those that are portable.

" New for me; sensible people have acknowledged it for years. You and I and the Wilcoxes stand upon money as upon islands. It is so firm beneath our feet that we forget its very existence. It's only when we see some one near us tottering that we realize all that an independent income means. Last night, when we were talking up here round the fire, I began to think that the very soul of the world is economic, and that the lowest abyss is not the absence of love, but the absence of coin."

" I call that rather cynical."

" So do I. But Helen and I, we ought to remember, when we are tempted to criticize others, that we are standing on these islands, and that most of the others, are down below the surface of the sea. The poor cannot always reach those whom they want to love, and they can hardly ever escape from those whom they love no longer. We rich can. Imagine the tragedy last June, if Helen and Paul Wilcox had been poor people, and couldn't invoke railways and motor-cars to part them."

" That's more like Socialism," said Mrs. Munt suspiciously.

" Call it what you like. I call it going through life with one's hand spread open on the table. I'm tired of these rich people who pretend to be poor, and think it shows a nice mind to ignore the piles of money that keep their feet above the waves. I stand each year upon six hundred pounds, and Helen upon the same, and Tibby will stand upon eight, and as fast as our

pounds crumble away into the sea they are renewed —
from the sea, yes, from the sea. And all our thoughts
are the thoughts of six-hundred-pounders, and all our
speeches; and because we don't want to steal um-
brellas ourselves, we forget that below the sea people
do want to steal them, and do steal them sometimes,
and that what's a joke up here is down there reality
—"

"There they go — there goes Fräulein Mosebach.
Really, for a German she does dress charmingly. Oh
—!"

"What is it?"

"Helen was looking up at the Wilcoxes' flat."

"Why shouldn't she?"

"I beg your pardon, I interrupted you. What was
it you were saying about reality?"

"I had worked round to myself, as usual," answered Margaret in tones that were suddenly pre-
occupied.

"Do tell me this, at all events. Are you for the
rich or for the poor?"

"Too difficult. Ask me another. Am I for poverty or for riches? For riches. Hurrah for riches!"

"For riches!" echoed Mrs. Munt, having, as it were,
at last secured her nut.

"Yes. For riches. Money for ever!"

"So am I, and so, I am afraid, are most of my acquaintances at Swanage, but I am surprised that you
agree with us."

"Thank you so much, Aunt Juley. While I have
talked theories, you have done the flowers."

"Not at all, dear. I wish you would let me help
you in more important things."

"Well, would you be very kind? Would you come
round with me to the registry office? There's a housemaid who won't say yes but doesn't say no."

On their way thither they too looked up at the Wilcoxes' flat. Evie was in the balcony, "staring most rudely," according to Mrs. Munt. Oh yes, it was a nuisance, there was no doubt of it. Helen was proof against a passing encounter but — Margaret began to lose confidence. Might it reawake the dying nerve if the family were living close against her eyes? And Frieda Mosebach was stopping with them for another fortnight, and Frieda was sharp, abominably sharp, and quite capable of remarking, "You love one of the young gentlemen opposite, yes?" The remark would be untrue, but of the kind which, if stated often enough, may become true; just as the remark, "England and Germany are bound to fight," renders war a little more likely each time that it is made, and is therefore made the more readily by the gutter press of either nation. Have the private emotions also their gutter press? Margaret thought so, and feared that good Aunt Juley and Frieda were typical specimens of it. They might, by continual chatter, lead Helen into a repetition of the desires of June. Into a repetition — they could not do more; they could not lead her into lasting love. They were — she saw it clearly — Journalism; her father, with all his defects and wrong-headedness, had been Literature, and had he lived, he would have persuaded his daughter rightly.

The registry office was holding its morning reception. A string of carriages filled the street. Miss Schlegel waited her turn, and finally had to be content with an insidious "temporary," being rejected by genuine housemaids on the ground of her numerous stairs. Her failure depressed her, and though she forgot the failure, the depression remained. On her way home she again glanced up at the Wilcoxes' flat, and took the rather matronly step of speaking about the matter to Helen.

"Helen, you must tell me whether this thing worries you."

"If what?" said Helen, who was washing her hands for lunch.

"The W.'s coming."

"No, of course not."

"Really?"

"Really." Then she admitted that she was a little worried on Mrs. Wilcox's account; she implied that Mrs. Wilcox might reach backward into deep feelings, and be pained by things that never touched the other members of that clan. "I shan't mind if Paul points at our house and says, 'There lives the girl who tried to catch me.' But she might."

"If even that worries you, we could arrange something. There's no reason we should be near people who displease us or whom we displease, thanks to our money. We might even go away for a little."

"Well, I am going away. Frieda's just asked me to Stettin, and I shan't be back till after the New Year. Will that do? Or must I fly the country altogether? Really, Meg, what has come over you to make such a fuss?"

"Oh, I'm getting an old maid, I suppose. I thought I minded nothing, but really I — I should be bored if you fell in love with the same man twice and " — she cleared her throat — " you did go red, you know, when Aunt Juley attacked you this morning. I shouldn't have referred to it otherwise."

But Helen's laugh rang true, as she raised a soapy hand to heaven and swore that never, nowhere and nohow, would she again fall in love with any of the Wilcox family, down to its remotest collaterals.

Chapter VIII

THE friendship between Margaret and Mrs. Wilcox, which was to develop so quickly and with such strange results, may perhaps have had its beginnings at Speyer, in the spring. Perhaps the elder lady, as she gazed at the vulgar, ruddy cathedral, and listened to the talk of Helen and her husband, may have detected in the other and less charming of the sisters a deeper sympathy, a sounder judgment. She was capable of detecting such things. Perhaps it was she who had desired the Miss Schlegels to be invited to Howards End, and Margaret whose presence she had particularly desired. All this is speculation: Mrs. Wilcox has left few clear indications behind her. It is certain that she came to call at Wickham Place a fortnight later, the very day that Helen was going with her cousin to Stettin.

"Helen!" cried Fräulein Mosebach in awestruck tones (she was now in her cousin's confidence)—"his mother has forgiven you!" And then, remembering that in England the new-comer ought not to call before she is called upon, she changed her tone from awe to disapproval, and opined that Mrs. Wilcox was "keine Dame."

"Bother the whole family!" snapped Margaret. "Helen, stop giggling and pirouetting, and go and finish your packing. Why can't the woman leave us alone?"

"I don't know what I shall do with Meg," Helen retorted, collapsing upon the stairs. "She's got Wilcox and Box upon the brain. Meg, Meg, I don't love

the young gentleman; I don't love the young genter-
man, Meg, Meg. Can a body speak plainer?"

"Most certainly her love has died," asserted Fräulein Mosebach.

"Most certainly it has, Frieda, but that will not
prevent me from being bored with the Wilcoxes if I
return the call."

Then Helen simulated tears, and Fräulein Mosebach, who thought her extremely amusing, did the
same. "Oh, boo hoo! boo hoo hoo! Meg's going to
return the call, and I can't. 'Cos why? 'Cos I'm going to German-eye."

"If you are going to Germany, go and pack; if you
aren't, go and call on the Wilcoxes instead of me."

"But, Meg, Meg, I don't love the young gentleman; I don't love the young — O lud, who's that coming down the stairs? I vow 'tis my brother. O crim-
ini!"

A male — even such a male as Tibby — was enough
to stop the foolery. The barrier of sex, though decreasing among the civilized, is still high, and higher
on the side of women. Helen could tell her sister all,
and her cousin much about Paul; she told her brother
nothing. It was not prudishness, for she now spoke
of "the Wilcox ideal" with laughter, and even with a
growing brutality. Nor was it precaution, for Tibby
seldom repeated any news that did not concern himself.
It was rather the feeling that she betrayed a secret
into the camp of men, and that, however trivial it was
on this side of the barrier, it would become important
on that. So she stopped, or rather began to fool on
other subjects, until her long-suffering relatives drove
her upstairs. Fräulein Mosebach followed her, but
lingered to say heavily over the banisters to Margaret,
"It is all right — she does not love the young man —
he has not been worthy of her."

"Yes, I know; thanks very much."

"I thought I did right to tell you."

"Ever so many thanks."

"What's that?" asked Tibby. No one told him, and he proceeded into the dining-room, to eat Elvas plums.

That evening Margaret took decisive action. The house was very quiet, and the fog — we are in November now — pressed against the windows like an excluded ghost. Frieda and Helen and all their luggages had gone. Tibby, who was not feeling well, lay stretched on a sofa by the fire. Margaret sat by him, thinking. Her mind darted from impulse to impulse, and finally marshalled them all in review. The practical person, who knows what he wants at once, and generally knows nothing else, will excuse her of indecision. But this was the way her mind worked. And when she did act, no one could accuse her of indecision then. She hit out as lustily as if she had not considered the matter at all. The letter that she wrote Mrs. Wilcox glowed with the native hue of resolution. The pale cast of thought was with her a breath rather than a tarnish, a breath that leaves the colours all the more vivid when it has been wiped away.

"DEAR MRS. WILCOX,

"I have to write something discourteous. It would be better if we did not meet. Both my sister and my aunt have given displeasure to your family, and, in my sister's case, the grounds for displeasure might recur. As far as I know, she no longer occupies her thoughts with your son. But it would not be fair, either to her or to you, if they met, and it is therefore right that our acquaintance which began so pleasantly, should end.

"I fear that you will not agree with this; indeed, I know that you will not, since you have been good enough to call on us. It is only an instinct on my part, and no doubt the instinct is wrong. My sister would, undoubtedly, say that it

is wrong. I write without her knowledge, and I hope that
you will not associate her with my discourtesy.
                    "Believe me,
                        "Yours truly,
                            "M. J. SCHLEGEL."

Margaret sent this letter round by the post. Next
morning she received the following reply by hand:

"DEAR MISS SCHLEGEL,
    "You should not have written me such a letter. I
called to tell you that Paul has gone abroad.
                            "RUTH WILCOX."

Margaret's cheeks burnt. She could not finish her
breakfast. She was on fire with shame. Helen had
told her that the youth was leaving England, but other
things had seemed more important, and she had forgotten. All her absurd anxieties fell to the ground,
and in their place arose the certainty that she had been
rude to Mrs. Wilcox. Rudeness affected Margaret
like a bitter taste in the mouth. It poisoned life. At
times it is necessary, but woe to those who employ it
without due need. She flung on a hat and shawl,
just like a poor woman, and plunged into the fog,
which still continued. Her lips were compressed, the
letter remained in her hand, and in this state she
crossed the street, entered the marble vestibule of the
flats, eluded the concierges, and ran up the stairs till
she reached the second-floor.

She sent in her name, and to her surprise was shown
straight into Mrs. Wilcox's bedroom.

"Oh, Mrs. Wilcox, I have made the baddest blunder. I am more, more ashamed and sorry than I can
say."

Mrs. Wilcox bowed gravely. She was offended,
and did not pretend to the contrary. She was sitting
up in bed, writing letters on an invalid table that
spanned her knees. A breakfast tray was on another

table beside her. The light of the fire, the light from the window, and the light of a candle-lamp, which threw a quivering halo round her hands, combined to create a strange atmosphere of dissolution.

"I knew he was going to India in November, but I forgot."

"He sailed on the 17th for Nigeria, in Africa."

"I knew — I know. I have been too absurd all through. I am very much ashamed."

Mrs. Wilcox did not answer.

"I am more sorry than I can say, and I hope that you will forgive me."

"It doesn't matter, Miss Schlegel. It is good of you to have come round so promptly."

"It does matter," cried Margaret. "I have been rude to you; and my sister is not even at home, so there was not even that excuse."

"Indeed?"

"She has just gone to Germany."

"She gone as well," murmured the other. "Yes, certainly, it is quite safe — safe, absolutely, now."

"You've been worrying too!" exclaimed Margaret, getting more and more excited, and taking a chair without invitation. "How perfectly extraordinary! I can see that you have. You felt as I do; Helen mustn't meet him again."

"I did think it best."

"Now why?"

"That's a most difficult question," said Mrs. Wilcox, smiling, and a little losing her expression of annoyance. "I think you put it best in your letter — it was an instinct, which may be wrong."

"It wasn't that your son still —"

"Oh no; he often — my Paul is very young, you see."

"Then what was it?"

She repeated: "An instinct which may be wrong."

"In other words, they belong to types that can fall in love, but couldn't live together. That's dreadfully probable. I'm afraid that in nine cases out of ten Nature pulls one way and human nature another."

"These are indeed ' other words,' " said Mrs. Wilcox. "I had nothing so coherent in my head. I was merely alarmed when I knew that my boy cared for your sister."

"Ah, I have always been wanting to ask you. How *did* you know? Helen was so surprised when our aunt drove up, and you stepped forward and arranged things. Did Paul tell you?"

"There is nothing to be gained by discussing that," said Mrs. Wilcox after a moment's pause.

"Mrs. Wilcox, were you very angry with us last June? I wrote you a letter and you didn't answer it."

"I was certainly against taking Mrs. Matheson's flat. I knew it was opposite your house."

"But it's all right now?"

"I think so."

"You only think? You aren't sure? I do love these little muddles tidied up?"

"Oh yes, I'm sure," said Mrs. Wilcox, moving with uneasiness beneath the clothes. "I always sound uncertain over things. It is my way of speaking."

"That's all right, and I'm sure too."

Here the maid came in to remove the breakfast-tray. They were interrupted, and when they resumed conversation it was on more normal lines.

"I must say good-bye now — you will be getting up."

"No — please stop a little longer — I am taking a day in bed. Now and then I do."

"I thought of you as one of the early risers."

"At Howards End — yes; there is nothing to get up for in London."

"Nothing to get up for?" cried the scandalized

Margaret. "When there are all the autumn exhibitions, and Ysaye playing in the afternoon! Not to mention people."

"The truth is, I am a little tired. First came the wedding, and then Paul went off, and, instead of resting yesterday, I paid a round of calls."

"A wedding?"

"Yes; Charles, my elder son, is married."

"Indeed!"

"We took the flat chiefly on that account, and also that Paul could get his African outfit. The flat belongs to a cousin of my husband's, and she most kindly offered it to us. So before the day came we were able to make the acquaintance of Dolly's people, which we had not yet done."

Margaret asked who Dolly's people were.

"Fussell. The father is in the Indian army — retired; the brother is in the army. The mother is dead."

So perhaps these were the "chinless sunburnt men" whom Helen had espied one afternoon through the window. Margaret felt mildly interested in the fortunes of the Wilcox family. She had acquired the habit on Helen's account, and it still clung to her. She asked for more information about Miss Dolly Fussell that was, and was given it in even, unemotional tones. Mrs. Wilcox's voice, though sweet and compelling, had little range of expression. It suggested that pictures, concerts, and people are all of small and equal value. Only once had it quickened — when speaking of Howards End.

"Charles and Albert Fussell have known one another some time. They belong to the same club, and are both devoted to golf. Dolly plays golf too, though I believe not so well, and they first met in a mixed foursome. We all like her, and are very much pleased. They were married on the 11th, a few days before

Paul sailed. Charles was very anxious to have his brother as best man, so he made a great point of having it on the 11th. The Fussells would have preferred it after Christmas, but they were very nice about it. There is Dolly's photograph — in that double frame."

"Are you quite certain that I'm not interrupting, Mrs. Wilcox?"

"Yes, quite."

"Then I will stay. I'm enjoying this."

Dolly's photograph was now examined. It was signed "For dear Mims," which Mrs. Wilcox interpreted as "the name she and Charles had settled that she should call me." Dolly looked silly, and had one of those triangular faces that so often prove attractive to a robust man. She was very pretty. From her Margaret passed to Charles, whose features prevailed opposite. She speculated on the forces that had drawn the two together till God parted them. She found time to hope that they would be happy.

"They have gone to Naples for their honeymoon."

"Lucky people!"

"I can hardly imagine Charles in Italy."

"Doesn't he care for travelling?"

"He likes travel, but he does see through foreigners so. What he enjoys most is a motor tour in England, and I think that would have carried the day if the weather had not been so abominable. His father gave him a car of his own for a wedding present, which for the present is being stored at Howards End."

"I suppose you have a garage there?"

"Yes. My husband built a little one only last month, to the west of the house, not far from the wych-elm, in what used to be the paddock for the pony."

The last words had an indescribable ring about them.

"Where's the pony gone?" asked Margaret after a pause.

"The pony? Oh, dead, ever so long ago."

"The wych-elm I remember. Helen spoke of it as a very splendid tree."

"It is the finest wych-elm in Hertfordshire. Did your sister tell you about the teeth?"

"No."

"Oh, it might interest you. There are pigs' teeth stuck into the trunk, about four feet from the ground. The country people put them in long ago, and they think that if they chew a piece of the bark, it will cure the toothache. The teeth are almost grown over now, and no one comes to the tree."

"I should. I love folklore and all festering superstitions."

"Do you think that the tree really did cure toothache, if one believed in it?"

"Of course it did. It would cure anything — once."

"Certainly I remember cases — you see I lived at Howards End long, long before Mr. Wilcox knew it. I was born there."

The conversation again shifted. At the time it seemed little more than aimless chatter. She was interested when her hostess explained that Howards End was her own property. She was bored when too minute an account was given of the Fussell family, of the anxieties of Charles concerning Naples, of the movements of Mr. Wilcox and Evie, who were motoring in Yorkshire. Margaret could not bear being bored. She grew inattentive, played with the photograph frame, dropped it, smashed Dolly's glass, apologized, was pardoned, cut her finger thereon, was pitied, and finally said she must be going — there was all the housekeeping to do, and she had to interview Tibby's riding-master.

Then the curious note was struck again.

"Good-bye, Miss Schlegel, good-bye. Thank you for coming. You have cheered me up."

"I'm so glad!"

"I — I wonder whether you ever think about yourself?"

"I think of nothing else," said Margaret, blushing, but letting her hand remain in that of the invalid.

"I wonder. I wondered at Heidelberg."

"*I'm* sure!"

"I almost think—"

"Yes?" asked Margaret, for there was a long pause — a pause that was somehow akin to the flicker of the fire, the quiver of the reading-lamp upon their hands, the white blur from the window; a pause of shifting and eternal shadows.

"I almost think you forget you're a girl."

Margaret was startled and a little annoyed. "I'm twenty-nine," she remarked. "That not so wildly girl-ish."

Mrs. Wilcox smiled.

"What makes you say that? Do you mean that I have been gauche and rude?"

A shake of the head. "I only meant that I am fifty-one, and that to me both of you — Read it all in some book or other; I cannot put things clearly."

"Oh, I've got it — inexperience. I'm no better than Helen, you mean, and yet I presume to advise her."

"Yes. You have got it. Inexperience is the word."

"Inexperience," repeated Margaret, in serious yet buoyant tones. "Of course, I have everything to learn — absolutely everything — just as much as Helen. Life's very difficult and full of surprises. At all events, I've got as far as that. To be humble and kind, to go straight ahead, to love people rather than pity them, to remember the submerged — well, one can't do all these things at once, worse luck, because they're so contradictory. It's then that proportion comes in — to live by proportion. Don't *begin* with proportion. Only prigs do that. Let proportion come in as a last resource, when the better things have failed, and a deadlock — Gracious me, I've started preaching!"

"Indeed, you put the difficulties of life splendidly," said Mrs. Wilcox, withdrawing her hand into the deeper shadows. "It is just what I should have liked to say about them myself."

Chapter IX

MRS. WILCOX cannot be accused of giving Margaret much information about life. And Margaret, on the other hand, has made a fair show of modesty, and has pretended to an inexperience that she certainly did not feel. She had kept house for over ten years; she had entertained, almost with distinction; she had brought up a charming sister, and was bringing up a brother. Surely, if experience is attainable, she had attained it.

Yet the little luncheon-party that she gave in Mrs. Wilcox's honour was not a success. The new friend did not blend with the " one or two delightful people " who had been asked to meet her, and the atmosphere was one of polite bewilderment. Her tastes were simple, her knowledge of culture slight, and she was not interested in the New English Art Club, nor in the dividing-line between Journalism and Literature, which was started as a conversational hare. The delightful people darted after it with cries of joy, Margaret leading them, and not till the meal was half over did they realize that the principal guest had taken no part in the chase. There was no common topic. Mrs. Wilcox, whose life had been spent in the service of husband and sons, had little to say to strangers who had never shared it, and whose age was half her own. Clever talk alarmed her, and withered her delicate imaginings; it was the social counterpart of a motor-car, all jerks, and she was a wisp of hay, a flower. Twice she deplored the weather, twice criticized the train service on the Great Northern Railway. They vigorously assented, and rushed on, and when she inquired whether there was any news of Helen, her hostess was too much occupied in placing Rothenstein to answer. The question was repeated: " I hope that your sister is safe in Germany by now." Margaret checked herself and said " Yes, thank you; I heard on Tuesday." But the demon of vociferation was in her, and the next moment she was off again.

" Only on Tuesday, for they live right away at Stettin. Did you ever know any one living at Stettin? "

" Never," said Mrs. Wilcox gravely, while her neighbour, a young man low down in the Education Office, began to discuss what people who lived at Stettin ought to look like. Was there such a thing at Stettininity? Margaret swept on.

" People at Stettin drop things into boats out of overhanging warehouses. At least, our cousins do, but aren't particularly rich. The town isn't interesting, except for a clock that rolls its eyes, and the view of the Oder, which truly is something special. Oh, Mrs. Wilcox, you would love the Oder! The river, or rather rivers — there seem to be dozens of them — are intense blue, and the plain they run through an intensest green."

" Indeed! That sounds like a most beautiful view, Miss Schlegel."

" So I say, but Helen, who will muddle things, says no, it's like music. The course of the Oder is to be like music. It's obliged to remind her of a symphonic poem. The part by the landing-stage is in B minor, if I remember rightly, but lower down things get extremely mixed. There is a slodgy theme in several keys at once, meaning mud-banks, and another for the navigable canal, and the exit into the Baltic is in C sharp major, pianissimo."

" What do the overhanging warehouses make of that? " asked the man, laughing.

"They make a great deal of it," replied Margaret, unexpectedly rushing off on a new track. "I think it's affectation to compare the Oder to music, and so do you, but the overhanging warehouses of Stettin take beauty seriously, which we don't, and the average Englishman doesn't, and despises all who do. Now don't say 'Germans have no taste,' or I shall scream. They haven't. But — but — such a tremendous but! — they take poetry seriously. They do take poetry seriously."

"Is anything gained by that?"

"Yes, yes. The German is always on the lookout for beauty. He may miss it through stupidity, or misinterpret it, but he is always asking beauty to enter his life, and I believe that in the end it will come. At Heidelberg I met a fat veterinary surgeon whose voice broke with sobs as he repeated some mawkish poetry. So easy for me to laugh — I, who never repeat poetry, good or bad, and cannot remember one fragment of verse to thrill myself with. My blood boils — well, I'm half German, so put it down to patriotism — when I listen to the tasteful contempt of the average islander for things Teutonic, whether they're Böcklin or my veterinary surgeon. 'Oh, Böcklin,' they say; 'he strains after beauty, he peoples Nature with gods too consciously.' Of course Böcklin strains, because he wants something — beauty and all the other intangible gifts that are floating about the world. So his landscapes don't come off, and Leader's do."

"I am not sure that I agree. Do you?" said he, turning to Mrs. Wilcox.

She replied: "I think Miss Schlegel puts everything splendidly"; and a chill fell on the conversation.

"Oh, Mrs. Wilcox, say something nicer than that. It's such a snub to be told you put things splendidly."

"I do not mean it as a snub. Your last speech interested me so much. Generally people do not seem quite to like Germany. I have long wanted to hear what is said on the other side."

"The other side? Then you do disagree. Oh, good! Give us your side."

"I have no side. But my husband"—her voice softened, the chill increased—"has very little faith in the Continent, and our children have all taken after him."

"On what grounds? Do they feel that the Continent is in bad form?"

Mrs. Wilcox had no idea; she paid little attention to grounds. She was not intellectual, nor even alert, and it was odd that, all the same, she should give the idea of greatness. Margaret, zig-zagging with her friends over Thought and Art, was conscious of a personality that transcended their own and dwarfed their activities. There was no bitterness in Mrs. Wilcox; there was not even criticism; she was lovable, and no ungracious or uncharitable word had passed her lips. Yet she and daily life were out of focus: one or the other must show blurred. And at lunch she seemed more out of focus than usual, and nearer the line that divides daily life from a life that may be of greater importance.

"You will admit, though, that the Continent—it seems silly to speak of 'the Continent,' but really it is all more like itself than any part of it is like England. England is unique. Do have another jelly first. I was going to say that the Continent, for good or for evil, is interested in ideas. Its Literature and Art have what one might call the kink of the unseen about them, and this persists even through decadence and affectation. There is more liberty of action in England, but for liberty of thought go to bureaucratic Prussia. People will there discuss with humility vital questions that we here think ourselves too good to touch with tongs."

"I do not want to go to Prussia," said Mrs. Wilcox—"not even to see that interesting view that you were describing. And for discussing with humility I am too old. We never discuss anything at Howards End."

"Then you ought to!" said Margaret. "Discussion keeps a house alive. It cannot stand by bricks and mortar alone."

"It cannot stand without them," said Mrs. Wilcox, unexpectedly catching on to the thought, and rousing, for the first and last time, a faint hope in the breasts of the delightful people. "It cannot stand without them, and I sometimes think — But I cannot expect your generation to agree, for even my daughter disagrees with me here."

"Never mind us or her. Do say!"

"I sometimes think that it is wiser to leave action and discussion to men."

There was a little silence.

"One admits that the arguments against the suffrage *are* extraordinarily strong," said a girl opposite, leaning forward and crumbling her bread.

"Are they? I never follow any arguments. I am only too thankful not to have a vote myself."

"We didn't mean the vote, though, did we?" supplied Margaret. "Aren't we differing on something much wider, Mrs. Wilcox? Whether women are to remain what they have been since the dawn of history; or whether, since men have moved forward so far, they too may move forward a little now. I say they may. I would even admit a biological change."

"I don't know, I don't know."

"I must be getting back to my overhanging warehouse," said the man. "They've turned disgracefully strict."

Mrs. Wilcox also rose.

"Oh, but come upstairs for a little. Miss Quested

plays. Do you like MacDowell? Do you mind him only having two noises? If you must really go, I'll see you out. Won't you even have coffee?"

They left the dining-room, closing the door behind them, and as Mrs. Wilcox buttoned up her jacket, she said: "What an interesting life you all lead in London!"

"No, we don't," said Margaret, with a sudden revulsion. "We lead the lives of gibbering monkeys. Mrs. Wilcox — really — We have something quiet and stable at the bottom. We really have. All my friends have. Don't pretend you enjoyed lunch, for you loathed it, but forgive me by coming again, alone, or by asking me to you."

"I am used to young people," said Mrs. Wilcox, and with each word she spoke the outlines of known things grew dim. "I hear a great deal of chatter at home, for we, like you, entertain a great deal. With us it is more sport and politics, but — I enjoyed my lunch very much, Miss Schlegel, dear, and am not pretending, and only wish I could have joined in more. For one thing, I'm not particularly well just today. For another, you younger people move so quickly that it dazes me. Charles is the same, Dolly the same. But we are all in the same boat, old and young. I never forget that."

They were silent for a moment. Then, with a newborn emotion, they shook hands. The conversation ceased suddenly when Margaret re-entered the dining-room: her friends had been talking over her new friend, and had dismissed her as uninteresting.

Chapter X

EVERAL days passed.

Was Mrs. Wilcox one of the unsatisfactory people — there are many of them — who dangle intimacy and then withdraw it? They evoke our interests and affections, and keep the life of the spirit dawdling round them. Then they withdraw. When physical passion is involved, there is a definite name for such behaviour — flirting — and if carried far enough it is punishable by law. But no law — not public opinion even — punishes those who coquette with friendship, though the dull ache that they inflict, the sense of misdirected effort and exhaustion, may be as intolerable. Was she one of these?

Margaret feared so at first, for, with a Londoner's impatience, she wanted everything to be settled up immediately. She mistrusted the periods of quiet that are essential to true growth. Desiring to book Mrs. Wilcox as a friend, she pressed on the ceremony, pencil, as it were, in hand, pressing the more because the rest of the family were away, and the opportunity seemed favourable. But the elder woman would not be hurried. She refused to fit in with the Wickham Place set, or to reopen discussion of Helen and Paul, whom Margaret would have utilized as a short-cut. She took her time, or perhaps let time take her, and when the crisis did come all was ready.

The crisis opened with a message: would Miss Schlegel come shopping? Christmas was nearing, and Mrs. Wilcox felt behind-hand with the presents. She had taken some more days in bed, and must make up for lost time. Margaret accepted, and at eleven o'clock one cheerless morning they started out in a brougham.

"First of all," began Margaret, "we must make a list and tick off the people's names. My aunt always does, and this fog may thicken up any moment. Have you any ideas?"

"I thought we would go to Harrod's or the Haymarket Stores," said Mrs. Wilcox rather hopelessly. "Everything is sure to be there. I am not a good shopper. The din is so confusing, and your aunt is quite right — one ought to make a list. Take my note-book, then, and write your own name at the top of the page."

"Oh, hooray!" said Margaret, writing it. "How very kind of you to start with me!" But she did not want to receive anything expensive. Their acquaintance was singular rather than intimate, and she divined that the Wilcox clan would resent any expenditure on outsiders; the more compact families do. She did not want to be thought a second Helen, who would snatch presents since she could not snatch young men, nor to be exposed, like a second Aunt Juley, to the insults of Charles. A certain austerity of demeanour was best, and she added: "I don't really want a Yuletide gift, though. In fact, I'd rather not."

"Why?"

"Because I've odd ideas about Christmas. Because I have all that money can buy. I want more people, but no more things."

"I should like to give you something worth your acquaintance, Miss Schlegel, in memory of your kindness to me during my lonely fortnight. It has so happened that I have been left alone, and you have stopped me from brooding. I am too apt to brood."

"If that is so," said Margaret, "if I have happened

to be of use to you, which I didn't know, you cannot pay me back with anything tangible."

" I suppose not, but one would like to. Perhaps I shall think of something as we go about."

Her name remained at the head of the list, but nothing was written opposite it. They drove from shop to shop. The air was white, and when they alighted it tasted like cold pennies. At times they passed through a clot of grey. Mrs. Wilcox's vitality was low that morning, and it was Margaret who decided on a horse for this little girl, a golliwog for that, for the rector's wife a copper warming-tray. " We always give the servants money." " Yes, do you, yes, much easier," replied Margaret, but felt the grotesque impact of the unseen upon the seen, and saw issuing from a forgotten manger at Bethlehem this torrent of coins and toys. Vulgarity reigned. Public-houses, besides their usual exhortation against temperance reform, invited men to " Join our Christmas goose club "— one bottle of gin, etc., or two, according to subscription. A poster of a woman in tights heralded the Christmas pantomime, and little red devils, who had come in again that year, were prevalent upon the Christmas-cards. Margaret was no morbid idealist. She did not wish this spate of business and self-advertisement checked. It was only the occasion of it that struck her with amazement annually. How many of these vacillating shoppers and tired shop-assistants realized that it was a divine event that drew them together ? She realized it, though standing outside in the matter. She was not a Christian in the accepted sense ; she did not believe that God had ever worked among us as a young artisan. These people, or most of them, believed it, and if pressed, would affirm it in words. But the visible signs of their belief were Regent Street or Drury Lane, a little mud displaced, a little money spent, a little food cooked, eaten, and forgotten. Inadequate. But in public who shall express the unseen adequately? It is private life that holds out the mirror to infinity; personal intercourse, and that alone, that ever hints at a personality beyond our daily vision.

"No, I do like Christmas on the whole," she announced. "In its clumsy way, it does approach Peace and Goodwill. But oh, it is clumsier every year."

"Is it? I am only used to country Christmases."

"We are usually in London, and play the game with vigour — carols at the Abbey, clumsy midday meal, clumsy dinner for the maids, followed by Christmas-tree and dancing of poor children, with songs from Helen. The drawing-room does very well for that. We put the tree in the powder-closet, and draw a curtain when the candles are lighted, and with the looking-glass behind it looks quite pretty. I wish we might have a powder-closet in our next house. Of course, the tree has to be very small, and the presents don't hang on it. No; the presents reside in a sort of rocky landscape made of crumpled brown paper."

"You spoke of your 'next house,' Miss Schlegel. Then are you leaving Wickham Place?"

"Yes, in two or three years, when the lease expires. We must."

"Have you been there long?"

"All our lives."

"You will be very sorry to leave it."

"I suppose so. We scarcely realize it yet. My father —" She broke off, for they had reached the stationary department of the Haymarket Stores, and Mrs. Wilcox wanted to order some private greeting cards.

"If possible, something distinctive," she sighed. At the counter she found a friend, bent on the same errand, and conversed with her insipidly, wasting much time. "My husband and our daughter are motoring."

"Bertha too? Oh, fancy, what a coincidence!"
Margaret, though not practical, could shine in such
company as this. While they talked, she went through
a volume of specimen cards, and submitted one for
Mrs. Wilcox's inspection. Mrs. Wilcox was delighted
— so original, words so sweet; she would order a
hundred like that, and could never be sufficiently grateful. Then, just as the assistant was booking the order,
she said: "Do you know, I'll wait. On second
thoughts, I'll wait. There's plenty of time still, isn't
there, and I shall be able to get Evie's opinion."

They returned to the carriage by devious paths;
when they were in, she said, "But couldn't you get it
renewed?"

"I beg your pardon?" asked Margaret.

"The lease, I mean."

"Oh, the lease! Have you been thinking of that
all the time? How very kind of you!"

"Surely something could be done."

"No; values have risen too enormously. They
mean to pull down Wickham Place, and build flats like
yours."

"But how horrible!"

"Landlords are horrible."

Then she said vehemently: "It is monstrous, Miss
Schlegel; it isn't right. I had no idea that this was
hanging over you. I do pity you from the bottom of
my heart. To be parted from your house, your
father's house — it oughtn't to be allowed. It is worse
than dying. I would rather die than — Oh, poor
girls! Can what they call civilization be right, if
people mayn't die in the room where they were born?
My dear, I am so sorry —"

Margaret did not know what to say. Mrs. Wilcox
had been overtired by the shopping, and was inclined
to hysteria.

"Howards End was nearly pulled down once. It would have killed me."

"Howards End must be a very different house to ours. We are fond of ours, but there is nothing distinctive about it. As you saw, it is an ordinary London house. We shall easily find another."

"So you think."

"Again my lack of experience, I suppose!" said Margaret, easing away from the subject. "I can't say anything when you take up that line, Mrs. Wilcox. I wish I could see myself as you see me — foreshortened into a backfisch. Quite the ingénue. Very charming — wonderfully well read for my age, but incapable —"

Mrs. Wilcox would not be deterred. "Come down with me to Howards End now," she said, more vehemently than ever. "I want you to see it. You have never seen it. I want to hear what you say about it, for you do put things so wonderfully."

Margaret glanced at the pitiless air and then at the tired face of her companion. "Later on I should love it," she continued, "but it's hardly the weather for such an expedition, and we ought to start when we're fresh. Isn't the house shut up, too?"

She received no answer. Mrs. Wilcox appeared to be annoyed.

"Might I come some other day?"

Mrs. Wilcox bent forward and tapped the glass. "Back to Wickham Place, please!" was her order to the coachman. Margaret had been snubbed.

"A thousand thanks, Miss Schlegel, for all your help."

"Not at all."

"It is such a comfort to get the presents off my mind — the Christmas-cards especially. I do admire your choice."

It was her turn to receive no answer. In her turn Margaret became annoyed.

"My husband and Evie will be back the day after tomorrow. That is why I dragged you out shopping today. I stayed in town chiefly to shop, but got through nothing, and now he writes that they must cut their tour short, the weather is so bad, and the police-traps have been so bad — nearly as bad as in Surrey. Ours is such a careful chauffeur, and my husband feels it particularly hard that they should be treated like road-hogs."

"Why?"

"Well, naturally he — he isn't a road-hog."

"He was exceeding the speed-limit, I conclude. He must expect to suffer with the lower animals."

Mrs. Wilcox was silenced. In growing discomfort they drove homewards. The city seemed Satanic, the narrower streets oppressing like the galleries of a mine. No harm was done by the fog to trade, for it lay high, and the lighted windows of the shops were thronged with customers. It was rather a darkening of the spirit which fell back upon itself, to find a more grievous darkness within. Margaret nearly spoke a dozen times, but something throttled her. She felt petty and awkward, and her meditations on Christmas grew more cynical. Peace? It may bring other gifts, but is there a single Londoner to whom Christmas is peaceful? The craving for excitement and for elaboration has ruined that blessing. Goodwill? Had she seen any example of it in the hordes of purchasers? Or in herself? She had failed to respond to this invitation merely because it was a little queer and imaginative — she, whose birthright it was to nourish imagination! Better to have accepted, to have tired themselves a little by the journey, than coldly to reply, "Might I come some other day?" Her cynicism left her. There would be no other day. This shadowy woman would never ask her again.

They parted at the Mansions. Mrs. Wilcox went in after due civilities, and Margaret watched the tall, lonely figure sweep up the hall to the lift. As the glass doors closed on it she had the sense of an imprisonment. The beautiful head disappeared first, still buried in the muff; the long trailing skirt followed. A woman of undefinable rarity was going up heavenward, like a specimen in a bottle. And into what a heaven — a vault as of hell, sooty black, from which soots descended!

At lunch her brother, seeing her inclined for silence, insisted on talking. Tibby was not ill-natured, but from babyhood something drove him to do the unwelcome and the unexpected. Now he gave her a long account of the day-school that he sometimes patronized. The account was interesting, and she had often pressed him for it before, but she could not attend now, for her mind was focussed on the invisible. She discerned that Mrs. Wilcox, though a loving wife and mother, had only one passion in life — her house — and that the moment was solemn when she invited a friend to share this passion with her. To answer "another day" was to answer as a fool. "Another day" will do for brick and mortar, but not for the Holy of Holies into which Howards End had been transfigured. Her own curiosity was slight. She had heard more than enough about it in the summer. The nine windows, the vine, and the wych-elm had no pleasant connections for her, and she would have preferred to spend the afternoon at a concert. But imagination triumphed. While her brother held forth she determined to go, at whatever cost, and to compel Mrs. Wilcox to go, too. When lunch was over she stepped over to the flats.

Mrs. Wilcox had just gone away for the night.

Margaret said that it was of no consequence, hurried downstairs, and took a hansom to King's Cross. She was convinced that the escapade was important, though it would have puzzled her to say why. There was a question of imprisonment and escape, and though she did not know the time of the train, she strained her eyes for the St. Pancras' clock.

Then the clock of King's Cross swung into sight, a second moon in that infernal sky, and her cab drew up at the station. There was a train for Hilton in five minutes. She took a ticket, asking in her agitation for a single. As she did so, a grave and happy voice saluted her and thanked her.

"I will come if I still may," said Margaret, laughing nervously.

"You are coming to sleep, dear, too. It is in the morning that my house is most beautiful. You are coming to stop. I cannot show you my meadow properly except at sunrise. These fogs"— she pointed at the station roof —"never spread far. I dare say they are sitting in the sun in Hertfordshire, and you will never repent joining them."

"I shall never repent joining you."

"It is the same."

They began the walk up the long platform. Far at its end stood the train, breasting the darkness without. They never reached it. Before imagination could triumph, there were cries of "Mother! mother!" and a heavy-browed girl darted out of the cloak-room and seized Mrs. Wilcox by the arm.

"Evie!" she gasped —"Evie, my pet —"

The girl called, "Father! I say! look who's here."

"Evie, dearest girl, why aren't you in Yorkshire?"

"No — motor smash — changed plans — father's coming."

"Why, Ruth!" cried Mr. Wilcox, joining them.

" What in the name of all that's wonderful are you doing here, Ruth?"

Mrs. Wilcox had recovered herself.

" Oh, Henry dear!— here's a lovely surprise — but let me introduce — but I think you know Miss Schlegel."

" Oh, yes," he replied, not greatly interested. " But how's yourself, Ruth?"

" Fit as a fiddle," she answered gaily.

" So are we and so was our car, which ran A1 as far as Ripon, but there a wretched horse and cart which a fool of a driver —"

" Miss Schlegel, our little outing must be for another day."

" I was saying that this fool of a driver, as the policeman himself admits —"

" Another day, Mrs. Wilcox. Of course."

"— But as we've insured against third party risks, it won't so much matter —"

"— Cart and car being practically at right angles —"

The voices of the happy family rose high. Margaret was left alone. No one wanted her. Mrs. Wilcox walked out of King's Cross between her husband and her daughter, listening to both of them.

Chapter XI

THE funeral was over. The carriages rolled away through the soft mud, and only the poor remained. They approached to the newly-dug shaft and looked their last at the coffin, now almost hidden beneath the spadefuls of clay. It was their moment. Most of them were women from the dead woman's district, to whom black garments had been served out by Mr. Wilcox's orders. Pure curiosity had brought others. They thrilled with the excitement of a death, and of a rapid death, and stood in groups or moved between the graves, like drops of ink. The son of one of them, a wood-cutter, was perched high above their heads, pollarding one of the churchyard elms. From where he sat he could see the village of Hilton, strung upon the North Road, with its accreting suburbs; the sunset beyond, scarlet and orange, winking at him beneath brows of grey; the church; the plantations; and behind him an unspoilt country of fields and farms. But he, too, was rolling the event luxuriously in his mouth. He tried to tell his mother down below all that he had felt when he saw the coffin approaching: how he could not leave his work, and yet did not like to go on with it; how he had almost slipped out of the tree, he was so upset; the rooks had cawed, and no wonder — it was as if rooks knew too. His mother claimed the prophetic power herself — she had seen a strange look about Mrs. Wilcox for some time. London had done the mischief, said others. She had been a kind lady; her grandmother had been kind, too — a plainer person, but very kind. Ah, the old sort was dying out! Mr. Wilcox, he was a kind gentleman. They advanced to the topic again and again, dully, but with exaltation. The funeral of a rich person was to them what the funeral of Alcestis of Ophelia is to the educated. It was Art; though remote from life, it enhanced life's values, and they witnessed it avidly.

The grave-diggers, who had kept up an undercurrent of disapproval — they disliked Charles; it was not a moment to speak of such things, but they did not like Charles Wilcox — the grave-diggers finished their work and piled up the wreaths and crosses above it. The sun set over Hilton: the grey brows of the evening flushed a little, and were cleft with one scarlet frown. Chattering sadly to each other, the mourners passed through the lych-gate and traversed the chestnut avenues that led down to the village. The young wood-cutter stayed a little longer, poised above the silence and swaying rhythmically. At last the bough fell beneath his saw. With a grunt, he descended, his thoughts dwelling no longer on death, but on love, for he was mating. He stopped as he passed the new grave; a sheaf of tawny chrysanthemums had caught his eye. "They didn't ought to have coloured flowers at buryings," he reflected. Trudging on a few steps, he stopped again, looked furtively at the dusk, turned back, wrenched a chrysanthemum from the sheaf, and hid it in his pocket.

After him came silence absolute. The cottage that abutted on the churchyard was empty, and no other house stood near. Hour after hour the scene of the interment remained without an eye to witness it. Clouds drifted over it from the west; or the church may have been a ship, high-prowed, steering with all its company towards infinity. Towards morning the air grew colder, the sky clearer, the surface of the earth hard and sparkling above the prostrate dead.

The wood-cutter, returning after a night of joy, re-flected: "They lilies, they chrysants; it's a pity I didn't take them all."

Up at Howards End they were attempting breakfast. Charles and Evie sat in the dining-room, with Mrs. Charles. Their father, who could not bear to see a face, breakfasted upstairs. He suffered acutely. Pain came over him in spasms, as if it was physical, and even while he was about to eat, his eyes would fill with tears, and he would lay down the morsel untasted.

He remembered his wife's even goodness during thirty years. Not anything in detail — not courtship or early raptures — but just the unvarying virtue, that seemed to him a woman's noblest quality. So many women are capricious, breaking into odd flaws of passion or frivolity. Not so his wife. Year after year, summer and winter, as bride and mother, she had been the same, he had always trusted her. Her tenderness! Her innocence! The wonderful inno-cence that was hers by the gift of God. Ruth knew no more of worldly wickedness and wis-dom than did the flowers in her garden, or the grass in her field. Her idea of business —"Henry, why do people who have enough money try to get more money?" Her idea of politics — "I am sure that if the mothers of various nations could meet, there would be no more wars." Her idea of religion — ah, this had been a cloud, but a cloud that passed. She came of Quaker stock, and he and his family, formerly Dissenters, were now members of the Church of England. The rector's sermons had at first repelled her, and she had ex-pressed a desire for "a more inward light," adding, "not so much for myself as for baby" (Charles). Inward light must have been granted, for he heard no complaints in later years. They brought up their three children without dispute. They had never disputed.

She lay under the earth now. She had gone, and as if to make her going the more bitter, had gone with a touch of mystery that was all unlike her. "Why didn't you tell me you knew of it?" he had moaned, and her faint voice had answered: "I didn't want to, Henry — I might have been wrong — and every one hates illnesses." He had been told of the horror by a strange doctor, whom she had consulted during his absence from town. Was this altogether just? Without fully explaining, she had died. It was a fault on her part, and — tears rushed into his eyes — what a little fault! It was the only time she had deceived him in those thirty years.

He rose to his feet and looked out of the window, for Evie had come in with the letters, and he could meet no one's eye. Ah yes — she had been a good woman — she had been steady. He chose the word deliberately. To him steadiness included all praise.

He himself, gazing at the wintry garden, is in appearance a steady man. His face was not as square as his son's, and, indeed, the chin, though firm enough in outline, retreated a little, and the lips, ambiguous, were curtained by a moustache. But there was no external hint of weakness. The eyes, if capable of kindness and good-fellowship, if ruddy for the moment with tears, were the eyes of one who could not be driven. The forehead, too, was like Charles's. High and straight, brown and polished, merging abruptly into temples and skull, it had the effect of a bastion that protected his head from the world. At times it had the effect of a blank wall. He had dwelt behind it, intact and happy, for fifty years.

"The post's come, father," said Evie awkwardly.

"Thanks. Put it down."

"Has the breakfast been all right?"

"Yes, thanks."

The girl glanced at him and at it with constraint. She did not know what to do.

"Charles says do you want the *Times?*"

"No, I'll read it later."

"Ring if you want anything, father, won't you?"

"I've all I want."

Having sorted the letters from the circulars, she went back to the dining-room.

"Father's eaten nothing," she announced, sitting down with wrinkled brows behind the tea-urn.

Charles did not answer, but after a moment he ran quickly upstairs, opened the door, and said: "Look here, father, you must eat, you know"; and having paused for a reply that did not come, stole down again. "He's going to read his letters first, I think," he said evasively; "I dare say he will go on with his breakfast afterwards." Then he took up the *Times,* and for some time there was no sound except the clink of cup against saucer and of knife on plate.

Poor Mrs. Charles sat between her silent companions, terrified at the course of events, and a little bored. She was a rubbishy little creature, and she knew it. A telegram had dragged her from Naples to the death-bed of a woman whom she had scarcely known. A word from her husband had plunged her into mourning. She desired to mourn inwardly as well, but she wished that Mrs. Wilcox, since fated to die, could have died before the marriage, for then less would have been expected of her. Crumbling her toast, and too nervous to ask for the butter, she remained almost motionless, thankful only for this, that her father-in-law was having his breakfast upstairs.

At last Charles spoke. "They had no business to be pollarding those elms yesterday," he said to his sister.

"No indeed."

"I must make a note of that," he continued. "I am surprised that the rector allowed it."

"Perhaps it may not be the rector's affair."

"Whose else could it be?"

"The lord of the manor."

"Impossible."

"Butter, Dolly?"

"Thank you, Evie dear. Charles—"

"Yes, dear?"

"I didn't know one could pollard elms. I thought one only pollarded willows."

"Oh no, one can pollard elms."

"Then why oughtn't the elms in the churchyard to be pollarded?" Charles frowned a little, and turned again to his sister.

"Another point. I must speak to Chalkeley."

"Yes, rather; you must complain to Chalkeley."

"It's no good him saying he is not responsible for those men. He is responsible."

"Yes, rather."

Brother and sister were not callous. They spoke thus, partly because they desired to keep Chalkeley up to the mark—a healthy desire in its way—partly because they avoided the personal note in life. All Wilcoxes did. It did not seem to them of supreme importance. Or it may be as Helen supposed: they realized its importance, but were afraid of it. Panic and emptiness, could one glance behind. They were not callous, and they left the breakfast-table with aching hearts. Their mother never had come in to breakfast. It was in the other rooms, and especially in the garden, that they felt her loss most. As Charles went out to the garage, he was reminded at every step of the woman who had loved him and whom he could never replace. What battles he had fought against her gentle conservatism! How she had disliked improvements, yet how loyally she had accepted them when made! He and his father — what trouble they had had to get this very garage! With what difficulty had they persuaded her to yield them to the paddock for it — the paddock that she loved more dearly than the garden itself! The vine — she had got her way about the vine. It still encumbered the south wall with its unproductive branches. And so with Evie, as she stood talking to the cook. Though she could take up her mother's work inside the house, just as the man could take it up without, she felt that something unique had fallen out of her life. Their grief, though less poignant than their father's, grew from deeper roots, for a wife may be replaced; a mother never.

Charles would go back to the office. There was little to do at Howards End. The contents of his mother's will had been long known to them. There were no legacies, no annuities, none of the posthumous bustle with which some of the dead prolong their activities. Trusting her husband, she had left him everything without reserve. She was quite a poor woman — the house had been all her dowry, and the house would come to Charles in time. Her watercolours Mr. Wilcox intended to reserve for Paul, while Evie would take the jewellery and lace. How easily she slipped out of life! Charles thought the habit laudable, though he did not intend to adopt it himself, whereas Margaret would have seen in it an almost culpable indifference to earthly fame. Cynicism — not the superficial cynicism that snarls and sneers, but the cynicism that can go with courtesy and tenderness — that was the note of Mrs. Wilcox's will. She wanted not to vex people. That accomplished, the earth might freeze over her for ever.

No, there was nothing for Charles to wait for. He could not go on with his honeymoon, so he would go up to London and work — he felt too miserable hanging about. He and Dolly would have the furnished flat while his father rested quietly in the country with Evie. He could also keep an eye on his own little house, which was being painted and decorated for him in one of the Surrey suburbs, and in which he hoped to instal himself soon after Christmas. Yes, he would go up after lunch in his new motor, and the town servants, who had come down for the funeral, would go up by train.

He found his father's chauffeur in the garage, said " Morning " without looking at the man's face, and, bending over the car, continued: " Hullo! my new car's been driven! "

" Has it, sir? "

" Yes," said Charles, getting rather red; " and whoever's driven it hasn't cleaned it properly, for there's mud on the axle.   Take it off."

The man went for the cloths without a word. He was a chauffeur as ugly as sin — not that this did him disservice with Charles, who thought charm in a man rather rot, and had soon got rid of the little Italian beast with whom they had started.

" Charles —" His bride was tripping after him over the hoar-frost, a dainty black column, her little face and elaborate mourning hat forming the capital thereof.

" One minute, I'm busy. Well, Crane, who's been driving it, do you suppose? "

" Don't know, I'm sure, sir. No one's driven it since I've been back, but, of course, there's the fortnight I've been away with the other car in Yorkshire."

The mud came off easily.

" Charles, your father's down. Something's happened. He wants you in the house at once. Oh, Charles! "

" Wait, dear, wait a minute. Who had the key to the garage while you were away, Crane? "

" The gardener, sir."

" Do you mean to tell me that old Penny can drive a motor?"

" No, sir; no one's had the motor out, sir."

" Then how do you account for the mud on the axle?"

"I can't, of course, say for the time I've been in Yorkshire. No more mud now, sir."

Charles was vexed. The man was treating him as a fool, and if his heart had not been so heavy he would have reported him to his father. But it was not a morning for complaints. Ordering the motor to be round after lunch, he joined his wife, who had all the while been pouring out some incoherent story about a letter and a Miss Schlegel.

" Now, Dolly, I can attend to you. Miss Schlegel? What does she want?"

When people wrote a letter Charles always asked what they wanted. Want was to him the only cause of action. And the question in this case was correct, for his wife replied, " She wants Howards End."

" Howards End? Now, Crane, just don't forget to put on the Stepney wheel."

" No, sir."

" Now, mind you don't forget, for I — Come, little woman." When they were out of the chauffeur's sight he put his arm around her waist and pressed her against him. All his affection and half his attention — it was what he granted her throughout their happy married life.

" But you haven't listened, Charles —"

" What's wrong?"

" I keep on telling you — Howards End. Miss Schlegel's got it."

" Got what?" asked Charles, unclasping her. " What the dickens are you talking about?"

"Now, Charles, you promised not to say those naughty —"

"Look here, I'm in no mood for foolery. It's no morning for it either."

"I tell you — I keep on telling you — Miss Schlegel — she's got it — your mother's left it to her — and you've all got to move out!"

"Howards End?"

"Howards End!" she screamed, mimicking him, and as she did so Evie came dashing out of the shrubbery.

"Dolly, go back at once! My father's much annoyed with you. Charles "— she hit herself wildly — "come in at once to father. He's had a letter that's too awful."

Charles began to run, but checked himself, and stepped heavily across the gravel path. There the house was — the nine windows, the unprolific vine. He exclaimed, "Schlegels again!" and as if to complete chaos, Dolly said, "Oh no, the matron of the nursing home has written instead of her."

"Come in, all three of you!" cried his father, no longer inert. "Dolly, why have you disobeyed me?"

"Oh, Mr. Wilcox —"

"I told you not to go out to the garage. I've heard you all shouting in the garden. I won't have it. Come in."

He stood in the porch, transformed, letters in his hand.

"Into the dining-room, every one of you. We can't discuss private matters in the middle of all the servants. Here, Charles, here; read these. See what you make."

Charles took two letters, and read them as he followed the procession. The first was a covering note from the matron. Mrs. Wilcox had desired her, when the funeral should be over, to forward the enclosed.

The enclosed — it was from his mother herself. She had written: " To my husband: I should like Miss Schlegel (Margaret) to have Howards End."

" I suppose we're going to have a talk about this? " he remarked, ominously calm.

" Certainly. I was coming out to you when Dolly —"

" Well, let's sit down."

" Come, Evie, don't waste time, sit down."

In silence they drew up to the breakfast-table. The events of yesterday — indeed, of this morning — suddenly receded into a past so remote that they seemed scarcely to have lived in it. Heavy breathings were heard. They were calming themselves. Charles, to steady them further, read the enclosure out loud: " A note in my mother's handwriting, in an envelope addressed to my father, sealed. Inside: ' I should like Miss Schlegel (Margaret) to have Howards End.' No date, no signature. Forwarded through the matron of that nursing home. Now, the question is —"

Dolly interrupted him. " But I say that note isn't legal. Houses ought to be done by a lawyer, Charles, surely."

Her husband worked his jaw severely. Little lumps appeared in front of either ear — a symptom that she had not yet learnt to respect, and she asked whether she might see the note. Charles looked at his father for permission, who said abstractedly, " Give it her." She seized it, and at once exclaimed: " Why, it's only in pencil! I said so. Pencil never counts."

" We know that it is not legally binding, Dolly," said Mr. Wilcox, speaking from out of his fortress. " We are aware of that. Legally, I should be justified in tearing it up and throwing it into the fire. Of course, my dear, we consider you as one of the family, but it will be better if you do not interfere with what you do not understand."

Charles, vexed both with his father and his wife, then repeated: "The question is —" He had cleared a space of the breakfast-table from plates and knives, so that he could draw patterns on the tablecloth. "The question is whether Miss Schlegel, during the fortnight we were all away, whether she unduly —" He stopped.

"I don't think that," said his father, whose nature was nobler than his son's.

"Don't think what?"

"That she would have — that it is a case of undue influence. No, to my mind the question is the — the invalid's condition at the time she wrote."

"My dear father, consult an expert if you like, but I don't admit it is my mother's writing."

"Why, you just said it was!" cried Dolly.

"Never mind if I did," he blazed out; "and hold your tongue."

The poor little wife coloured at this, and, drawing her handkerchief from her pocket, shed a few tears. No one noticed her. Evie was scowling like an angry boy. The two men were gradually assuming the manner of the committee-room. They were both at their best when serving on committees. They did not make the mistake of handling human affairs in the bulk, but disposed of them item by item, sharply. Calligraphy was the item before them now, and on it they turned their well-trained brains. Charles, after a little demur, accepted the writing as genuine, and they passed on to the next point. It is the best — perhaps the only — way of dodging emotion. They were the average human article, and had they considered the note as a whole it would have driven them miserable or mad. Considered item by item, the emotional content was minimized, and all went forward smoothly. The clock ticked, the coals blazed higher, and contended with the white radiance that poured in through the windows. Unnoticed, the sun occupied his sky, and the shadows of the tree stems, extraordinarily solid, fell like trenches of purple across the frosted lawn. It was a glorious winter morning. Evie's fox terrier, who had passed for white, was only a dirty grey dog now, so intense was the purity that surrounded him. He was discredited, but the blackbirds that he was chasing glowed with Arabian darkness, for all the conventional colouring of life had been altered. Inside, the clock struck ten with a rich and confident note. Other clocks confirmed it, and the discussion moved towards its close.

To follow it is unnecessary. It is rather a moment when the commentator should step forward. Ought the Wilcoxes to have offered their home to Margaret? I think not. The appeal was too flimsy. It was not legal; it had been written in illness, and under the spell of a sudden friendship; it was contrary to the dead woman's intentions in the past, contrary to her very nature, so far as that nature was understood by them. To them Howards End was a house: they could not know that to her it had been a spirit, for which she sought a spiritual heir. And — pushing one step farther in these mists — may they not have decided even better than they supposed? Is it credible that the possessions of the spirit can be bequeathed at all? Has the soul offspring? A wych-elm tree, a vine, a wisp of hay with dew on it — can passion for such things be transmitted where there is no bond of blood? No; the Wilcoxes are not to be blamed. The problem is too terrific, and they could not even perceive a problem. No; it is natural and fitting that after due debate they should tear the note up and throw it on to their dining-room fire. The practical moralist may acquit them absolutely. He who strives to look deeper may acquit them — almost. For one hard fact remains. They did neglect a personal appeal. The woman who had died did say to them, " Do this," and they answered, " We will not."

The incident made a most painful impression on them. Grief mounted into the brain and worked there disquietingly. Yesterday they had lamented : " She was a dear mother, a true wife : in our absence she neglected her health and died." Today they thought : " She was not as true, as dear, as we supposed." The desire for a more inward light had found expression at last, the unseen had impacted on the seen, and all that they could say was " Treachery." Mrs. Wilcox had been treacherous to the family, to the laws of property, to her own written word. How did she expect Howards End to be conveyed to Miss Schlegel ? Was her husband, to whom it legally belonged, to make it over to her as a free gift ? Was the said Miss Schlegel to have a life interest in it, or to own it absolutely ? Was there to be no compensation for the garage and other improvements that they had made under the assumption that all would be theirs some day ? Treacherous ! treacherous and absurd ! When we think the dead both treacherous and absurd, we have gone far towards reconciling ourselves to their departure. That note, scribbled in pencil, sent through the matron, was unbusinesslike as well as cruel, and decreased at once the value of the woman who had written it.

" Ah, well ! " said Mr. Wilcox, rising from the table. " I shouldn't have thought it possible."

" Mother couldn't have meant it," said Evie, still frowning.

" No, my girl, of course not."

" Mother believed so in ancestors too — it isn't like her to leave anything to an outsider, who'd never appreciate."

" The whole thing is unlike her," he announced. " If Miss Schlegel had been poor, if she had wanted a house, I could understand it a little. But she has a house of her own. Why should she want another? She wouldn't have any use for Howards End."

" That time may prove," murmured Charles.

" How? " asked his sister.

" Presumably she knows — mother will have told her. She got twice or three times into the nursing home. Presumably she is awaiting developments."

" What a horrid woman! " And Dolly, who had recovered, cried, " Why, she may be coming down to turn us out now! "

Charles put her right. " I wish she would," he said ominously. " I could then deal with her."

" So could I," echoed his father, who was feeling rather in the cold. Charles had been kind in undertaking the funeral arrangements and in telling him to eat his breakfast, but the boy as he grew up was a little dictatorial, and assumed the post of chairman too readily. " I could deal with her, if she comes, but she won't come. You're all a bit hard on Miss Schlegel."

" That Paul business was pretty scandalous, though."

" I want no more of the Paul business, Charles, as I said at the time, and besides, it is quite apart from this business. Margaret Schlegel has been officious and tiresome during this terrible week, and we have all suffered under her, but upon my soul she's honest. She's *not* in collusion with the matron. I'm absolutely certain of it. Nor was she with the doctor. I'm equally certain of that. She did not hide anything from us, for up to that very afternoon she was as ignorant as we are. She, like ourselves, was a dupe —" He stopped for a moment. " You see, Charles, in her terrible pain your poor mother put us all in false positions. Paul would not have left England, you would not have gone to Italy, nor Evie and

I into Yorkshire, if only we had known. Well, Miss Schlegel's position has been equally false. Take all in all, she has not come out of it badly."

Evie said: "But those chrysanthemums —"

"Or coming down to the funeral at all —" echoed Dolly.

"Why shouldn't she come down? She had the right to, and she stood far back among the Hilton women. The flowers — certainly we should not have sent such flowers, but they may have seemed the right thing to her, Evie, and for all you know they may be the custom in Germany."

"Oh, I forget she isn't really English," cried Evie. "That would explain a lot."

"She's a cosmopolitan," said Charles, looking at his watch. "I admit I'm rather down on cosmopolitans. My fault, doubtless. I cannot stand them, and a German cosmopolitan is the limit. I think that's about all, isn't it? I want to run down and see Chalkeley. A bicycle will do. And, by the way, I wish you'd speak to Crane some time. I'm certain he's had my new car out."

"Has he done it any harm?"

"No."

"In that case I shall let it pass. It's not worth while having a row."

Charles and his father sometimes disagreed. But they always parted with an increased regard for one another, and each desired no doughtier comrade when it was necessary to voyage for a little past the emotions. So the sailors of Ulysses voyaged past the Sirens, having first stopped one another's ears with wool.

Chapter XII

CHARLES need not have been anxious. Miss Schlegel had never heard of his mother's strange request. She was to hear of it in after years, when she had built up her life differently, and it was to fit into position as the headstone of the corner. Her mind was bent on other questions now, and by her also it would have been rejected as the fantasy of an invalid.

She was parting from these Wilcoxes for the second time. Paul and his mother, ripple and great wave, had flowed into her life and ebbed out of it for ever. The ripple had left no traces behind: the wave had strewn at her feet fragments torn from the unknown. A curious seeker, she stood for a while at the verge of the sea that tells so little, but tells a little, and watched the outgoing of this last tremendous tide. Her friend had vanished in agony, but not, she believed, in degradation. Her withdrawal had hinted at other things besides disease and pain. Some leave our life with tears, others with an insane frigidity; Mrs. Wilcox had taken the middle course, which only rarer natures can pursue. She had kept proportion. She had told a little of her grim secret to her friends, but not too much; she had shut up her heart — almost, but not entirely. It is thus, if there is any rule, that we ought to die — neither as victim nor as fanatic, but as the seafarer who can greet with an equal eye the deep that he is entering, and the shore that he must leave.

The last word — whatever it would be — had certainly not been said in Hilton churchyard. She had not died there. A funeral is not death, any more than baptism is birth or marriage union. All three are the clumsy devices, coming now too late, now too early, by which Society would register the quick motions of man. In Margaret's eyes Mrs. Wilcox had escaped registration. She had gone out of life vividly, her own way, and no dust was so truly dust as the contents of that heavy coffin, lowered with ceremonial until it rested on the dust of the earth, no flowers so utterly wasted as the chrysanthemums that the frost must have withered before morning. Margaret had once said she "loved superstition." It was not true. Few women had tried more earnestly to pierce the accretions in which body and soul are enwrapped. The death of Mrs. Wilcox had helped her in her work. She saw a little more clearly than hitherto what a human being is, and to what he may aspire. Truer relationships gleamed. Perhaps the last word would be hope — hope even on this side of the grave.

Meanwhile, she could take an interest in the survivors. In spite of her Christmas duties, in spite of her brother, the Wilcoxes continued to play a considerable part in her thoughts. She had seen so much of them in the final week. They were not "her sort," they were often suspicious and stupid, and deficient where she excelled; but collision with them stimulated her, and she felt an interest that verged into liking, even for Charles. She desired to protect them, and often felt that they could protect her, excelling where she was deficient. Once past the rocks of emotion, they knew so well what to do, whom to send for; their hands were on all the ropes, they had grit as well as grittiness, and she valued grit enormously. They led a life that she could not attain to — the outer life of "telegrams and anger," which had detonated when Helen and Paul had touched in June, and had detonated again the other week. To Margaret this life was to remain a real force. She could not despise it, as Helen and Tibby affected to do. It fostered such virtues as neatness, decision, and obedience, virtues of the second rank, no doubt, but they have formed our civilization. They form character, too; Margaret could not doubt it: they keep the soul from becoming sloppy. How dare Schlegels despise Wilcoxes, when it takes all sorts to make a world?

"Don't brood too much," she wrote to Helen, "on the superiority of the unseen to the seen. It's true, but to brood on it is mediaeval. Our business is not to contrast the two, but to reconcile them."

Helen replied that she had no intention of brooding on such a dull subject. What did her sister take her for? The weather was magnificent. She and the Mosebachs had gone tobogganing on the only hill that Pomerania boasted. It was fun, but overcrowded, for the rest of Pomerania had gone there too. Helen loved the country, and her letter glowed with physical exercise and poetry. She spoke of the scenery, quiet, yet august; of the snow-clad fields, with their scampering herds of deer; of the river and its quaint entrance into the Baltic Sea; of the Oderberge, only three hundred feet high, from which one slid all too quickly back into the Pomeranian plains, and yet these Oderberge were real mountains, with pine-forests, streams, and views complete. "It isn't size that counts so much as the way things are arranged." In another paragraph she referred to Mrs. Wilcox sympathetically, but the news had not bitten into her. She had not realized the accessories of death, which are in a sense more memorable than death itself. The atmosphere of precautions and recriminations, and in the midst a human body growing more vivid because it was in pain; the end of that body in Hilton churchyard; the survival of something that suggested hope, vivid in its turn against life's workaday cheerfulness; — all these were lost to Helen, who only felt that a pleasant lady could now be pleasant no longer. She returned to Wickham Place full of her own affairs — she had had another proposal — and Margaret, after a moment's hesitation, was content that this should be so.

The proposal had not been a serious matter. It was the work of Fräulein Mosebach, who had conceived the large and patriotic notion of winning back her cousins to the Fatherland by matrimony. England had played Paul Wilcox, and lost; Germany played Herr Förstmeister some one — Helen could not remember his name. Herr Förstmeister lived in a wood, and standing on the summit of the Oderberge, he had pointed out his house to Helen, or rather, had pointed out the wedge of pines in which it lay. She had exclaimed, " Oh, how lovely! That's the place for me! " and in the evening Frieda appeared in her bedroom. " I have a message, dear Helen," etc., and so she had, but had been very nice when Helen laughed; quite understood — a forest too solitary and damp — quite agreed, but Herr Förstmeister believed he had assurance to the contrary. Germany had lost, but with good-humour; holding the manhood of the world, she felt bound to win. " And there will even be some one for Tibby," concluded Helen. " There now, Tibby, think of that; Frieda is saving up a little girl for you, in pig-tails and white worsted stockings, but the feet of the stockings are pink, as if the little girl had trodden in strawberries. I've talked too much. My head aches. Now you talk."

Tibby consented to talk. He too was full of his own affairs, for he had just been up to try for a scholarship at Oxford. The men were down, and the candidates had been housed in various colleges, and had dined in hall. Tibby was sensitive to beauty, the experience was new, and he gave a description of his visit that was almost glowing. The august and mellow University, soaked with the richness of the western counties that it has served for a thousand years, appealed at once to the boy's taste: it was the kind of thing he could understand, and he understood it all the better because it was empty. Oxford is — Oxford: not a mere receptacle for youth, like Cambridge. Perhaps it wants its inmates to love it rather than to love one another: such at all events was to be its effect on Tibby. His sisters sent him there that he might make friends, for they knew that his education had been cranky, and had severed him from other boys and men. He made no friends. His Oxford remained Oxford empty, and he took into life with him, not the memory of a radiance, but the memory of a colour scheme.

It pleased Margaret to hear her brother and sister talking. They did not get on overwell as a rule. For a few moments she listened to them, feeling elderly and benign. Then something occurred to her, and she interrupted:

" Helen, I told you about poor Mrs. Wilcox; that sad business? "

" Yes."

" I have had a correspondence with her son. He was winding up the estate, and wrote to ask me whether his mother had wanted me to have anything. I thought it good of him, considering I knew her so little. I said that she had once spoken of giving me a Christmas present, but we both forgot about it afterwards."

" I hope Charles took the hint."

" Yes — that is to say, her husband wrote later on, and thanked me for being a little kind to her, and actually gave me her silver vinaigrette. Don't you think that is extraordinarily generous? It has made me like him very much. He hopes that this will not be the end of our acquaintance, but that you and I will go and stop with Evie some time in the future. I like Mr. Wilcox. He is taking up his work — rubber — it is a big business. I gather he is launching out rather. Charles is in it, too. Charles is married — a pretty little creature, but she doesn't seem wise. They took on the flat, but now they have gone off to a house of their own."

Helen, after a decent pause, continued her account of Stettin. How quickly a situation changes! In June she had been in a crisis; even in November she could blush and be unnatural; now it was January, and the whole affair lay forgotten. Looking back on the past six months, Margaret realized the chaotic nature of our daily life, and its difference from the orderly sequence that has been fabricated by historians. Actual life is full of false clues and sign-posts that lead nowhere. With infinite effort we nerve ourselves for a crisis that never comes. The most successful career must show a waste of strength that might have removed mountains, and the most unsuccessful is not that of the man who is taken unprepared, but of him who has prepared and is never taken. On a tragedy of that kind our national morality is duly silent. It assumes that preparation against danger is in itself a good, and that men, like nations, are the better for staggering through life fully armed. The tragedy of preparedness has scarcely been handled, save by the Greeks. Life is indeed dangerous, but not in the way morality would have us believe. It is indeed unmanageable, but the essence of it is not a battle. It is unmanageable because it is a romance, and its essence is romantic beauty.

Margaret hoped that for the future she would be less cautious, not more cautious, than she had been in the past.

Chapter XIII

OVER two years passed, and the Schlegel household continued to lead its life of cultured but not ignoble ease, still swimming gracefully on the grey tides of London. Concerts and plays swept past them, money had been spent and renewed, reputations won and lost, and the city herself, emblematic of their lives, rose and fell in a continual flux, while her shallows washed more widely against the hills of Surrey and over the fields of Hertfordshire. This famous building had arisen, that was doomed. Today Whitehall had been transformed: it would be the turn of Regent Street tomorrow. And month by month the roads smelt more strongly of petrol, and were more difficult to cross, and human beings heard each other speak with greater difficulty, breathed less of the air, and saw less of the sky. Nature withdrew: the leaves were falling by midsummer; the sun shone through dirt with an admired obscurity.

To speak against London is no longer fashionable. The Earth as an artistic cult has had its day, and the literature of the near future will probably ignore the country and seek inspiration from the town. One can understand the reaction. Of Pan and the elemental forces, the public has heard a little too much — they seem Victorian, while London is Georgian — and those who care for the earth with sincerity may wait long ere the pendulum swings back to her again. Certainly London fascinates. One visualizes it as a tract of quivering grey, intelligent without purpose, and excitable without love; as a spirit that has altered before it can be chronicled; as a heart that certainly beats, but with no pulsation of humanity. It lies beyond everything: Nature, with all her cruelty, comes nearer to us than do these crowds of men. A friend explains himself: the earth is explicable — from her we came, and we must return to her. But who can explain Westminster Bridge Road or Liverpool Street in the morning — the city inhaling — or the same thoroughfares in the evening — the city exhaling her exhausted air? We reach in desperation beyond the fog, beyond the very stars, the voids of the universe are ransacked to justify the monster, and stamped with a human face. London is religion's opportunity — not the decorous religion of theologians, but anthropomorphic, crude. Yes, the continuous flow would be tolerable if a man of our own sort — not any one pompous or tearful — were caring for us up in the sky.

The Londoner seldom understands his city until it sweeps him, too, away from his moorings, and Margaret's eyes were not opened until the lease of Wickham Place expired. She had always known that it must expire, but the knowledge only became vivid about nine months before the event. Then the house was suddenly ringed with pathos. It had seen so much happiness. Why had it to be swept away? In the streets of the city she noted for the first time the architecture of hurry, and heard the language of hurry on the mouths of its inhabitants — clipped words, formless sentences, potted expressions of approval or disgust. Month by month things were stepping livelier, but to what goal? The population still rose, but what was the quality of the men born? The particular millionaire who owned the freehold of Wickham Place, and desired to erect Babylonian flats upon it — what right had he to stir so large a portion of the quivering jelly? He was not a fool — she had heard him expose Socialism — but true insight began just where his intelligence ended, and one gathered that this was the case with most millionaires. What right had such men — But Margaret checked herself. That way lies madness. Thank goodness she, too, had some money, and could purchase a new home.

Tibby, now in his second year at Oxford, was down for the Easter vacation, and Margaret took the opportunity of having a serious talk with him. Did he at all know where he wanted to live? Tibby didn't know that he did know. Did he at all know what he wanted to do? He was equally uncertain, but when pressed remarked that he should prefer to be quite free of any profession. Margaret was not shocked, but went on sewing for a few minutes before she replied:

" I was thinking of Mr. Vyse. He never strikes me as particularly happy."

" Ye-es," said Tibby, and then held his mouth open in a curious quiver, as if he, too, had thought of Mr. Vyse, had seen round, through, over, and beyond Mr. Vyse, had weighed Mr. Vyse, grouped him, and finally dismissed him as having no possible bearing on the subject under discussion. That bleat of Tibby's infuriated Helen. But Helen was now down in the dining-room preparing a speech about political economy. At times her voice could be heard declaiming through the floor.

" But Mr. Vyse is rather a wretched, weedy man, don't you think? Then there's Guy. That was a pitiful business. Besides "— shifting to the general — " every one is the better for some regular work."

Groans.

" I shall stick to it," she continued, smiling. " I am not saying it to educate you; it is what I really think. I believe that in the last century men have developed the desire for work, and they must not starve it. It's a new desire. It goes with a great deal that's bad, but in itself it's good, and I hope that for women, too, 'not to work' will soon become as shocking as 'not to be married' was a hundred years ago."

"I have no experience of this profound desire to which you allude," enunciated Tibby.

"Then we'll leave the subject till you do. I'm not going to rattle you round. Take your time. Only do think over the lives of the men you like most, and see how they've arranged them."

"I like Guy and Mr. Vyse most," said Tibby faintly, and leant so far back in his chair that he extended in a horizontal line from knees to throat.

"And don't think I'm not serious because I don't use the traditional arguments — making money, a sphere awaiting you, and so on — all of which are, for various reasons, cant." She sewed on. "I'm only your sister. I haven't any authority over you, and I don't want to have any. Just to put before you what I think the truth. You see "— she shook off the pince-nez to which she had recently taken —" in a few years we shall be the same age practically, and I shall want you to help me. Men are so much nicer than women."

"Labouring under such a delusion, why do you not marry?"

"I sometimes jolly well think I would if I got the chance."

"Has nobody arst you?"

"Only ninnies."

"Do people ask Helen?"

"Plentifully."

"Tell me about them."

"No."

"Tell me about your ninnies, then."

"They were men who had nothing better to do," said his sister, feeling that she was entitled to score this point. "So take warning: you must work, or else you must pretend to work, which is what I do. Work, work, work if you'd save your soul and your body.

It is honestly a necessity, dear boy. Look at the Wilcoxes, look at Mr. Pembroke. With all their defects of temper and understanding, such men give me more pleasure than many who are better equipped and I think it is because they have worked regularly and honestly."

"Spare me the Wilcoxes," he moaned.

"I shall not. They are the right sort."

"Oh, goodness me, Meg!" he protested, suddenly sitting up, alert and angry. Tibby, for all his defects, had a genuine personality.

"Well, they're as near the right sort as you can imagine."

"No, no — oh, no!"

"I was thinking of the younger son, whom I once classed as a ninny, but who came back so ill from Nigeria. He's gone out there again, Evie Wilcox tells me — out to his duty."

"Duty" always elicited a groan.

"He doesn't want the money, it is work he wants, though it is beastly work — dull country, dishonest natives, an eternal fidget over fresh water and food. A nation who can produce men of that sort may well be proud. No wonder England has become an Empire."

"*Empire!*"

"I can't bother over results," said Margaret, a little sadly. "They are too difficult for me. I can only look at the men. An Empire bores me, so far, but I can appreciate the heroism that builds it up. London bores me, but what thousands of splendid people are labouring to make London —"

"What it is," he sneered.

"What it is, worse luck. I want activity without civilization. How paradoxical! Yet I expect that is what we shall find in heaven."

"And I," said Tibby, "want civilization without activity, which, I expect, is what we shall find in the other place."

"You needn't go as far as the other place, Tibbikins, if you want that. You can find it at Oxford."

"Stupid—"

"If I'm stupid, get me back to the house-hunting. I'll even live in Oxford if you like—North Oxford. I'll live anywhere except Bournemouth, Torquay, and Cheltenham. Oh yes, or Ilfracombe and Swanage and Tunbridge Wells and Surbiton and Bedford. There on no account."

"London, then."

"I agree, but Helen rather wants to get away from London. However, there's no reason we shouldn't have a house in the country and also a flat in town, provided we all stick together ∴ d contribute. Though of course— Oh, how one does maunder on, and to think, to think of the people who are really poor. How do they live? Not to move about the world would kill me."

As she spoke, the door was flung open, and Helen burst in in a state of extreme excitement.

"Oh, my dears, what do you think? You'll never guess. A woman's been here asking me for her husband. Her *what?*" (Helen was fond of supplying her own surprise.) "Yes, for her husband, and it really is so."

"Not anything to do with Bracknell?" cried Margaret, who had lately taken on an unemployed of that name to clean the knives and boots.

"I offered Bracknell, and he was rejected. So was Tibby. (Cheer up, Tibby!) It's no one we know. I said, 'Hunt, my good woman; have a good look round, hunt under the tables, poke up the chimney, shake out the antimacassars. Husband? husband?' Oh, and she so magnificently dressed and tinkling like a chandelier."

" Now, Helen, what did happen really? "

" What I say. I was, as it were, orating my speech. Annie opens the door like a fool, and shows a female straight in on me, with my mouth open. Then we began — very civilly. ' I want my husband, what I have reason to believe is here.' No — how unjust one is. She said ' whom,' not ' what.' She got it perfectly. So I said, ' Name, please? ' and she said, ' Lan, Miss,' and there we were."

" Lan? "

" Lan or Len. We were not nice about our vowels. Lanoline."

" But what an extraordinary —"

" I said, ' My good Mrs. Lanoline, we have some grave misunderstanding here. Beautiful as I am, my modesty is even more remarkable than my beauty, and never, never has Mr. Lanoline rested his eyes on mine.' "

" I hope you were pleased," said Tibby.

" Of course," Helen squeaked. " A perfectly delightful experience. Oh, Mrs. Lanoline's a dear — she asked for a husband as if he was an umbrella. She mislaid him Saturday afternoon — and for a long time suffered no inconvenience. But all night, and all this morning her apprehensions grew. Breakfast didn't seem the same — no, no more did lunch, and so she strolled up to 2, Wickham Place as being the most likely place for the missing article."

" But how on earth —"

" Don't begin how on earthing. ' I know what I know,' she kept repeating, not uncivilly, but with extreme gloom. In vain I asked her what she did know. Some knew what others knew, and others didn't, and if they didn't, then others again had better be careful. Oh dear, she was incompetent! She had a face like a silkworm, and the dining-room reeks of orris-root. We chatted pleasantly a little about husbands, and I wondered where hers was too, and advised her to go to the police. She thanked me. We agreed that Mr. Lanoline's a notty, notty man, and hasn't no business to go on the lardy-da. But I think she suspected me up to the last. Bags I writing to Aunt Juley about this. Now, Meg, remember — bags I."

"Bag it by all means," murmured Margaret, putting down her work. "I'm not sure that this is so funny, Helen. It means some horrible volcano smoking somewhere, doesn't it?"

"I don't think so — she doesn't really mind. The admirable creature isn't capable of tragedy."

"Her husband may be, though," said Margaret, moving to the window.

"Oh, no, not likely. No one capable of tragedy could have married Mrs. Lanoline."

"Was she pretty?"

"Her figure may have been good once."

The flats, their only outlook, hung like an ornate curtain between Margaret and the welter of London. Her thoughts turned sadly to house-hunting. Wickham Place had been so safe. She feared, fantastically, that her own little flock might be moving into turmoil and squalor, into nearer contact with such episodes as these.

"Tibby and I have again been wondering where we'll live next September," she said at last.

"Tibby had better first wonder what he'll do," retorted Helen; and that topic was resumed, but with acrimony. Then tea came, and after tea Helen went on preparing her speech, and Margaret prepared one, too, for they were going out to a discussion society on the morrow. But her thoughts were poisoned. Mrs. Lanoline had risen out of the abyss, like a faint smell, a goblin football, telling of a life where love and hatred had both decayed.

Chapter XIV

THE mystery, like so many mysteries, was explained. Next day, just as they were dressed to go out to dinner, a Mr. Bast called. He was a clerk in the employment of the Porphyrion Fire Insurance Company. Thus much from his card. He had come "about the lady yesterday." Thus much from Annie, who had shown him into the dining-room.

"Cheers, children!" cried Helen. "It's Mrs. Lanoline."

Tibby was interested. The three hurried downstairs, to find, not the gay dog they expected, but a young man, colourless, toneless, who had already the mournful eyes above a drooping moustache that are so common in London, and that haunt some streets of the city like accusing presences. One guessed him as the third generation, grandson to the shepherd or ploughboy whom civilization had sucked into the town; as one of the thousands who have lost the life of the body and failed to reach the life of the spirit. Hints of robustness survived in him, more than a hint of primitive good looks, and Margaret, noting the spine that might have been straight, and the chest that might have broadened, wondered whether it paid to give up the glory of the animal for a tail coat and a couple of ideas. Culture had worked in her own case, but during the last few weeks she had doubted whether it humanized the majority, so wide and so widening is the gulf that stretches between the natural and the philosophic man, so many the good chaps who are wrecked in trying to cross it. She knew this type very well — the vague aspirations, the mental dishonesty, the familiarity with the outsides of books. She knew the very tones in which he would address her. She was only unprepared for an example of her own visit-ing-card.

"You wouldn't remember giving me this, Miss Schlegel?" said he, uneasily familiar.

"No; I can't say I do."

"Well, that was how it happened, you see."

"Where did we meet, Mr. Bast? For the minute I don't remember."

"It was a concert at the Queen's Hall. I think you will recollect," he added pretentiously, "when I tell you that it included a performance of the Fifth Sym-phony of Beethoven."

"We hear the Fifth practically every time it's done, so I'm not sure — do you remember, Helen?"

"Was it the time the sandy cat walked round the balustrade?"

He thought not.

"Then I don't remember. That's the only Beethoven I ever remember specially."

"And you, if I may say so, took away my umbrella, inadvertently of course."

"Likely enough," Helen laughed, "for I steal um-brellas even oftener than I hear Beethoven. Did you get it back?"

"Yes, thank you, Miss Schlegel."

"The mistake arose out of my card, did it?" in-terposed Margaret.

"Yes, the mistake arose — it was a mistake."

"The lady who called here yesterday thought that you were calling too, and that she could find you?" she continued, pushing him forward, for, though he had promised an explanation, he seemed unable to give one.

"That's so, calling too — a mistake."

"Then why —?" began Helen, but Margaret laid a hand on her arm.

"I said to my wife," he continued more rapidly — "I said to Mrs. Bast, 'I have to pay a call on some friends,' and Mrs. Bast said to me, 'Do go.' While I was gone, however, she wanted me on important business, and thought I had come here, owing to the card, and so came after me, and I beg to tender my apologies, and hers as well, for any inconvenience we may have inadvertently caused you."

"No inconvenience," said Helen; "but I still don't understand."

An air of evasion characterized Mr. Bast. He explained again, but was obviously lying, and Helen didn't see why he should get off. She had the cruelty of youth. Neglecting her sister's pressure, she said, "I still don't understand. When did you say you paid this call?"

"Call? What call?" said he, staring as if her question had been a foolish one, a favourite device of those in mid-stream.

"This afternoon call."

"In the afternoon, of course!" he replied, and looked at Tibby to see how the repartee went. But Tibby, himself a repartee, was unsympathetic, and said, "Saturday afternoon or Sunday afternoon?"

"S — Saturday."

"Really!" said Helen; "and you were still calling on Sunday, when your wife came here. A long visit."

"I don't call that fair," said Mr. Bast, going scarlet and handsome. There was fight in his eyes. "I know what you mean, and it isn't so."

"Oh, don't let us mind," said Margaret, distressed again by odours from the abyss.

"It was something else," he asserted, his elaborate manner breaking down. "I was somewhere else to what you think, so there!"

"It was good of you to come and explain," she said.
"The rest is naturally no concern of ours."

"Yes, but I want — I wanted — have you ever read
'The Ordeal of Richard Feverel'?"

Margaret nodded.

"It's a beautiful book. I wanted to get back to the
Earth, don't you see, like Richard does in the end.
Or have you ever read Stevenson's 'Prince Otto'?"

Helen and Tibby groaned gently.

"That's another beautiful book. You get back to
the Earth in that. I wanted —" He mouthed affectedly. Then through the mists of his culture came
a hard fact, hard as a pebble. "I walked all the Saturday night," said Leonard. "I walked." A thrill
of approval ran through the sisters. But culture
closed in again. He asked whether they had ever read
E. V. Lucas's "Open Road."

Said Helen, "No doubt it's another beautiful book,
but I'd rather hear about your road."

"Oh, I walked."

"How far?"

"I don't know, nor for how long. It got too dark
to see my watch."

"Were you walking alone, may I ask?"

"Yes," he said, straightening himself; "but we'd
been talking it over at the office. There's been a lot
of talk at the office lately about these things. The fellows there said one steers by the Pole Star, and I looked
it up in the celestial atlas, but once out of doors everything gets so mixed —"

"Don't talk to me about the Pole Star," interrupted
Helen, who was becoming interested. "I know its little ways. It goes round and round, and you go round
after it."

"Well, I lost it entirely. First of all the street
lamps, then the trees, and towards morning it got
cloudy."

Tibby, who preferred his comedy undiluted, slipped from the room. He knew that this fellow would never attain to poetry, and did not want to hear him trying. Margaret and Helen remained. Their brother influenced them more than they knew: in his absence they were stirred to enthusiasm more easily.

"Where did you start from?" cried Margaret. "Do tell us more."

"I took the Underground to Wimbledon. As I came out of the office I said to myself, 'I must have a walk once in a way. If I don't take this walk now, I shall never take it.' I had a bit of dinner at Wimbledon, and then —"

"But not good country there, is it?"

"It was gas-lamps for hours. Still, I had all the night, and being out was the great thing. I did get into woods, too, presently."

"Yes, go on," said Helen.

"You've no idea how difficult uneven ground is when it's dark."

"Did you actually go off the roads?"

"Oh yes. I always meant to go off the roads, but the worst of it is that it's more difficult to find one's way."

"Mr. Bast, you're a born adventurer," laughed Margaret. "No professional athlete would have attempted what you've done. It's a wonder your walk didn't end in a broken neck. Whatever did your wife say?"

"Professional athletes never move without lanterns and compasses," said Helen. "Besides, they can't walk. It tires them. Go on."

"I felt like R. L. S. You probably remember how in 'Virginibus —'"

"Yes, but the wood. This 'ere wood. How did you get out of it?"

"I managed one wood, and found a road the other

side which went a good bit uphill. I rather fancy it was those North Downs, for the road went off into grass, and I got into another wood. That was awful, with gorse bushes. I did wish I'd never come, but suddenly it got light — just while I seemed going under one tree. Then I found a road down to a station, and took the first train I could back to London."

" But was the dawn wonderful? " asked Helen.

With unforgettable sincerity he replied, " No." The word flew again like a pebble from the sling. Down toppled all that had seemed ignoble or literary in his talk, down toppled tiresome R. L. S. and the " love of the earth " and his silk top-hat. In the presence of these women Leonard had arrived, and he spoke with a flow, an exultation, that he had seldom known.

" The dawn was only grey, it was nothing to mention —"

" Just a grey evening turned upside down. I know."

"— and I was too tired to lift up my head to look at it, and so cold too. I'm glad I did it, and yet at the time it bored me more than I can say. And besides — you can believe me or not as you choose — I was very hungry. That dinner at Wimbledon — I meant it to last me all night like other dinners. I never thought that walking would make such a difference. Why, when you're walking you want, as it were, a breakfast and luncheon and tea during the night as well, and I'd nothing but a packet of Woodbines. Lord, I did feel bad! Looking back, it wasn't what you may call enjoyment. It was more a case of sticking to it. I did stick. I — I was determined. Oh, hang it all! what's the good — I mean, the good of living in a room for ever? There one goes on day after day, same old game, same up and down to town, until you forget there is any other game. You ought to see once in a way what's going on outside, if it's only nothing particular after all."

" I should just think you ought," said Helen, sitting on the edge of the table.

The sound of a lady's voice recalled him from sincerity, and he said: " Curious it should all come about from reading something of Richard Jefferies."

" Excuse me, Mr. Bast, but you're wrong there. It didn't. It came from something far greater."

But she could not stop him. Borrow was imminent after Jefferies — Borrow, Thoreau, and sorrow. R. L. S. brought up the rear, and the outburst ended in a swamp of books. No disrespect to these great names. The fault is ours, not theirs. They mean us to use them for sign-posts, and are not to blame if, in our weakness, we mistake the sign-post for the destination. And Leonard had reached the destination. He had visited the county of Surrey when darkness covered its amenities, and its cosy villas had re-entered ancient night. Every twelve hours this miracle happens, but he had troubled to go and see for himself. Within his cramped little mind dwelt something that was greater than Jefferies' books — the spirit that led Jefferies to write them; and his dawn, though revealing nothing but monotones, was part of the eternal sunrise that shows George Borrow Stonehenge.

" Then you don't think I was foolish?" he asked, becoming again the naïve and sweet-tempered boy for whom Nature had intended him.

" Heavens, no!" replied Margaret.

" Heaven help us if we do!" replied Helen.

" I'm very glad you say that. Now, my wife would never understand — not if I explained for days."

" No, it wasn't foolish!" cried Helen, her eyes aflame. " You've pushed back the boundaries; I think it splendid of you."

" You've not been content to dream as we have —"

"Though we have walked, too —"

"I must show you a picture upstairs —"

Here the door-bell rang. The hansom had come to take them to their evening party.

"Oh, bother, not to say dash — I had forgotten we were dining out; but do, do, come round again and have a talk."

"Yes, you must — do," echoed Margaret.

Leonard, with extreme sentiment, replied: "No, I shall not. It's better like this."

"Why better?" asked Margaret.

"No, it is better not to risk a second interview. I shall always look back on this talk with you as one of the finest things in my life. Really. I mean this. We can never repeat. It has done me real good, and there we had better leave it."

"That's rather a sad view of life, surely."

"Things so often get spoiled."

"I know," flashed Helen, "but people don't."

He could not understand this. He continued in a vein which mingled true imagination and false. What he said wasn't wrong, but it wasn't right, and a false note jarred. One little twist, they felt, and the instrument might be in tune. One little strain, and it might be silent for ever. He thanked the ladies very much, but he would not call again. There was a moment's awkwardness, and then Helen said: "Go, then; perhaps you know best; but never forget you're better than Jefferies." And he went. Their hansom caught him up at the corner, passed with a waving of hands, and vanished with its accomplished load into the evening.

London was beginning to illuminate herself against the night. Electric lights sizzled and jagged in the main thoroughfares, gas-lamps in the side streets glimmered a canary gold or green. The sky was a crimson battlefield of spring, but London was not afraid. Her smoke mitigated the splendour, and the clouds down Oxford Street were a delicately painted ceiling, which adorned while it did not distract. She has never known the clear-cut armies of the purer air. Leonard hurried through her tinted wonders, very much part of the picture. His was a grey life, and to brighten it he had ruled off a few corners for romance. The Miss Schlegels — or, to speak more accurately, his interview with them — were to fill such a corner, nor was it by any means the first time that he had talked intimately to strangers. The habit was analogous to a debauch, an outlet, though the worst of outlets, for instincts that would not be denied. Terrifying him, it would beat down his suspicions and prudence until he was confiding secrets to people whom he had scarcely seen. It brought him many fears and some pleasant memories. Perhaps the keenest happiness he had ever known was during a railway journey to Cambridge, where a decent-mannered undergraduate had spoken to him. They had got into conversation, and gradually Leonard flung reticence aside, told some of his domestic troubles, and hinted at the rest. The undergraduate, supposing they could start a friendship, asked him to "coffee after hall," which he accepted, but afterwards grew shy, and took care not to stir from the commercial hotel where he lodged. He did not want Romance to collide with the Porphyrion, still less with Jacky, and people with fuller, happier lives are slow to understand this. To the Schlegels, as to the undergraduate, he was an interesting creature, of whom they wanted to see more. But they to him were denizens of Romance, who must keep to the corner he had assigned them, pictures that must not walk out of their frames.

His behaviour over Margaret's visiting-card had been typical. His had scarcely been a tragic marriage. Where there is no money and no inclination to violence tragedy cannot be generated. He could not leave his wife, and he did not want to hit her. Petulance and squalor were enough. Here "that card" had come in. Leonard, though furtive, was untidy, and left it lying about. Jacky found it, and then began, "What's that card, eh?" "Yes, don't you wish you knew what that card was?" "Len, who's Miss Schlegel?" etc. Months passed, and the card, now as a joke, now as a grievance, was handed about, getting dirtier and dirtier. It followed them when they moved from Camelia Road to Tulse Hill. It was submitted to third parties. A few inches of pasteboard, it became the battlefield on which the souls of Leonard and his wife contended. Why did he not say, "A lady took my umbrella, another gave me this that I might call for my umbrella"? Because Jacky would have disbelieved him? Partly, but chiefly because he was sentimental. No affection gathered round the card, but it symbolized the life of culture, that Jacky should never spoil. At night he would say to himself, "Well, at all events, she doesn't know about that card. Yah! done her there!"

Poor Jacky! she was not a bad sort, and had a great deal to bear. She drew her own conclusion — she was only capable of drawing one conclusion — and in the fulness of time she acted upon it. All the Friday Leonard had refused to speak to her, and had spent the evening observing the stars. On the Saturday he went up, as usual, to town, but he came not back Saturday night nor Sunday morning, nor Sunday afternoon. The inconvenience grew intolerable, and though she was now of a retiring habit, and shy of women, she went up to Wickham Place. Leonard returned in her absence. The card, the fatal card, was gone from the pages of Ruskin, and he guessed what had happened.

"Well?" he had exclaimed, greeting her with peals of laughter. "I know where you've been, but you don't know where I've been."

Jacky sighed, said, " Len, I do think you might explain," and resumed domesticity.

Explanations were difficult at this stage, and Leonard was too silly — or it is tempting to write, too sound a chap to attempt them. His reticence was not entirely the shoddy article that a business life promotes, the reticence that pretends that nothing is something, and hides behind the *Daily Telegraph*. The adventurer, also, is reticent, and it is an adventure for a clerk to walk for a few hours in darkness. You may laugh at him, you who have slept nights out on the veldt, with your rifle beside you and all the atmosphere of adventure pat. And you also may laugh who think adventures silly. But do not be surprised if Leonard is shy whenever he meets you, and if the Schlegels rather than Jacky hear about the dawn.

That the Schlegels had not thought him foolish became a permanent joy. He was at his best when he thought of them. It buoyed him as he journeyed home beneath fading heavens. Somehow the barriers of wealth had fallen, and there had been — he could not phrase it — a general assertion of the wonder of the world. " My conviction," says the mystic, " gains infinitely the moment another soul will believe in it," and they had agreed that there was something beyond life's daily grey. He took off his top-hat and smoothed it thoughtfully. He had hitherto supposed the unknown to be books, literature, clever conversation, culture. One raised oneself by study, and got upsides with the world. But in that quick interchange a new light dawned. Was that " something " walking in the dark among the surburban hills?

He discovered that he was going bareheaded down Regent Street. London came back with a rush. Few were about at this hour, but all whom he passed looked at him with a hostility that was the more impressive because it was unconscious. He put his hat on. It was too big; his head disappeared like a pudding into a basin, the ears bending outwards at the touch of the curly brim. He wore it a little backwards, and its effect was greatly to elongate the face and to bring out the distance between the eyes and the moustache. Thus equipped, he escaped criticism. No one felt uneasy as he titupped along the pavements, the heart of a man ticking fast in his chest.

Chapter XV

THE sisters went out to dinner full of their adventure, and when they were both full of the same subject, there were few dinner-parties that could stand up against them. This particular one, which was all ladies, had more kick in it than most, but succumbed after a struggle. Helen at one part of the table, Margaret at the other, would talk of Mr. Bast and of no one else, and somewhere about the entrée their monologues collided, fell ruining, and became common property. Nor was this all. The dinner-party was really an informal discussion club; there was a paper after it, read amid coffee-cups and laughter in the drawing-room, but dealing more or less thoughtfully with some topic of general interest. After the paper came a debate, and in this debate Mr. Bast also figured, appearing now as a bright spot in civilization, now as a dark spot, according to the temperament of the speaker. The subject of the paper had been, "How ought I to dispose of my money?" the reader professing to be a millionaire on the point of death, inclined to bequeath her fortune for the foundation of local art galleries, but open to conviction from other sources. The various parts had been assigned beforehand, and some of the speeches were amusing. The hostess assumed the ungrateful rôle of "the millionaire's eldest son," and implored her expiring parent not to dislocate Society by allowing such vast sums to pass out of the family. Money was the fruit of self-denial, and the second generation had a right to profit by the self-denial of the first. What right had 'Mr. Bast' to profit? The National Gallery was good enough for the likes of him. After property had had its say — a saying that is necessarily ungracious — the various philanthropists stepped forward. Something must be done for 'Mr. Bast': his conditions must be improved without impairing his independence; he must have a free library, or free tennis-courts; his rent must be paid in such a way that he did not know it was being paid; it must be made worth his while to join the Territorials; he must be forcibly parted from his uninspiring wife, the money going to her as compensation; he must be assigned a Twin Star, some member of the leisured classes who would watch over him ceaselessly (groans from Helen); he must be given food but no clothes, clothes but no food, a third-return ticket to Venice, without either food or clothes when he arrived there. In short, he might be given anything and everything so long as it was not the money itself.

And here Margaret interrupted.

"Order, order, Miss Schlegel!" said the reader of the paper. "You are here, I understand, to advise me in the interests of the Society for the Preservation of Places of Historic Interest or Natural Beauty. I cannot have you speaking out of your rôle. It makes my poor head go round, and I think you forget that I am very ill."

"Your head won't go round if only you'll listen to my argument," said Margaret. "Why not give him the money itself? You're supposed to have about thirty thousand a year."

"Have I? I thought I had a million."

"Wasn't a million your capital? Dear me! we ought to have settled that. Still, it doesn't matter. Whatever you've got, I order you to give as many poor men as you can three hundred a year each."

"But that would be pauperizing them," said an earnest girl, who liked the Schlegels, but thought them a little unspiritual at times.

"Not if you gave them so much. A big windfall would not pauperize a man. It is these little driblets, distributed among too many, that do the harm. Money's educational. It's far more educational than the things it buys." There was a protest. "In a sense," added Margaret, but the protest continued. "Well, isn't the most civilized thing going, the man who has learnt to wear his income properly?"

"Exactly what your Mr. Basts won't do."

"Give them a chance. Give them money. Don't dole them out poetry-books and railway-tickets like babies. Give them the wherewithal to buy these things. When your Socialism comes it may be different, and we may think in terms of commodities instead of cash. Till it comes give people cash, for it is the warp of civilization, whatever the woof may be. The imagination ought to play upon money and realize it vividly, for it's the — the second most important thing in the world. It is so slurred over and hushed up, there is so little clear thinking — oh, political economy, of course, but so few of us think clearly about our own private incomes, and admit that independent thoughts are in nine cases out of ten the result of independent means. Money: give Mr. Bast money, and don't bother about his ideals. He'll pick up those for himself."

She leant back while the more earnest members of the club began to misconstrue her. The female mind, though cruelly practical in daily life, cannot bear to hear ideals belittled in conversation, and Miss Schlegel was asked however she could say such dreadful things, and what it would profit Mr. Bast if he gained the whole world and lost his own soul. She answered, "Nothing, but he would not gain his soul until he had gained a little of the world." Then they said, "No, they did not believe it," and she admitted that an over-worked clerk may save his soul in the superterrestrial sense, where the effort will be taken for the deed, but she denied that he will ever explore the spiritual resources of this world, will ever know the rarer joys of the body, or attain to clear and passionate intercourse with his fellows. Others had attacked the fabric of Society — Property, Interest, etc.; she only fixed her eyes on a few human beings, to see how, under present conditions, they could be made happier. Doing good to humanity was useless: the many-coloured efforts thereto spreading over the vast area like films and resulting in an universal grey. To do good to one, or, as in this case, to a few, was the utmost she dare hope for.

Between the idealists, and the political economists, Margaret had a bad time. Disagreeing elsewhere, they agreed in disowning her, and in keeping the administration of the millionaire's money in their own hands. The earnest girl brought forward a scheme of "personal supervision and mutual help," the effect of which was to alter poor people until they became exactly like people who were not so poor. The hostess pertinently remarked that she, as eldest son, might surely rank among the millionaire's legatees. Margaret weakly admitted the claim, and another claim was at once set up by Helen, who declared that she had been the millionaire's housemaid for over forty years, overfed and underpaid; was nothing to be done for her, so corpulent and poor? The millionaire then read out her last will and testament, in which she left the whole of her fortune to the Chancellor of the Exchequer. Then she died. The serious parts of the discussion had been of higher merit than the playful — in a men's debate is the reverse more general? — but the meeting broke up hilariously enough, and a dozen happy ladies dispersed to their homes.

Helen and Margaret walked the earnest girl as far

as Battersea Bridge Station, arguing copiously all the
way. When she had gone they were conscious of an
alleviation, and of the great beauty of the evening.
They turned back towards Oakley Street. The lamps
and the plane-trees, following the line of the embankment, struck a note of dignity that is rare in English
cities. The seats, almost deserted, were here and there
occupied by gentlefolk in evening dress, who had
strolled out from the houses behind to enjoy fresh air
and the whisper of the rising tide. There is something
continental about Chelsea Embankment. It is an open
space used rightly, a blessing more frequent in Germany than here. As Margaret and Helen sat down,
the city behind them seemed to be a vast theatre, an
opera-house in which some endless trilogy was performing, and they themselves a pair of satisfied sub-
scribers, who did not mind losing a little of the second
act.

" Cold? "

" No."

" Tired? "

" Doesn't matter."

The earnest girl's train rumbled away over the
bridge.

" I say, Helen —"

" Well? "

" Are we really going to follow up Mr. Bast? "

" I don't know."

" I think we won't."

" As you like."

" It's no good, I think, unless you really mean to
know people. The discussion brought that home to
me. We got on well enough with him in a spirit of
excitement, but think of rational intercourse. We
mustn't play at friendship. No, it's no good."

" There's Mrs. Lanoline, too," Helen yawned. " So
dull."

" Just so, and possibly worse than dull."

" I should like to know how he got hold of your card."

" But he said — something about a concert and an umbrella —"

" Then did the card see the wife —"

" Helen, come to bed."

" No, just a little longer, it is so beautiful. Tell me; oh yes; did you say money is the warp of the world? "

" Yes."

" Then what's the woof? "

" Very much what one chooses," said Margaret. " It's something that isn't money — one can't say more."

" Walking at night? "

" Probably."

" For Tibby, Oxford? "

" It seems so."

" For you? "

" Now that we have to leave Wickham Place, I begin to think it's that. For Mrs. Wilcox it was certainly Howards End."

One's own name will carry immense distances. Mr. Wilcox, who was sitting with friends many seats away, heard his, rose to his feet, and strolled along towards the speakers.

" It is sad to suppose that places may ever be more important than people," continued Margaret.

" Why, Meg? They're so much nicer generally. I'd rather think of that forester's house in Pomerania than of the fat Herr Förstmeister who lived in it."

" I believe we shall come to care about people less and less, Helen. The more people one knows the easier it becomes to replace them. It's one of the curses of London. I quite expect to end my life caring most for a place."

Here Mr. Wilcox reached them. It was several weeks since they had met.

"How do you do?" he cried. "I thought I recognized your voices. Whatever are you both doing down here?"

His tones were protective. He implied that one ought not to sit out on Chelsea Embankment without a male escort. Helen resented this, but Margaret accepted it as part of the good man's equipment.

"What an age it is since I've seen you, Mr. Wilcox. I met Evie in the Tube, though, lately. I hope you have good news of your son."

"Paul?" said Mr. Wilcox, extinguishing his cigarette, and sitting down between them. "Oh, Paul's all right. We had a line from Madeira. He'll be at work again by now."

"Ugh —" said Helen, shuddering from complex causes.

"I beg your pardon?"

"Isn't the climate of Nigeria too horrible?"

"Some one's got to go," he said simply. "England will never keep her trade overseas unless she is prepared to make sacrifices. Unless we get firm in West Africa, Ger — untold complications may follow. Now tell me all your news."

"Oh, we've had a splendid evening," cried Helen, who always woke up at the advent of a visitor. "We belong to a kind of club that reads papers, Margaret and I — all women, but there is a discussion after. This evening it was on how one ought to leave one's money — whether to one's family, or to the poor, and if so how — oh, most interesting."

The man of business smiled. Since his wife's death he had almost doubled his income. He was an important figure at last, a reassuring name on company prospectuses, and life had treated him very well. The world seemed in his grasp as he listened to the

River Thames, which still flowed inland from the sea. So wonderful to the girls, it held no mysteries for him. He had helped to shorten its long tidal trough by taking shares in the lock at Teddington, and if he and other capitalists thought good, some day it could be shortened again. With a good dinner inside him and an amiable but academic woman on either flank, he felt that his hands were on all the ropes of life, and that what he did not know could not be worth knowing.

"Sounds a most original entertainment!" he exclaimed, and laughed in his pleasant way. "I wish Evie would go to that sort of thing. But she hasn't the time. She's taken to breed Aberdeen terriers — jolly little dogs."

"I expect we'd better be doing the same, really."

"We pretend we're improving ourselves, you see," said Helen a little sharply, for the Wilcox glamour is not of the kind that returns, and she had bitter memories of the days when a speech such as he had just made would have impressed her favourably. "We suppose it is a good thing to waste an evening once a fortnight over a debate, but, as my sister says, it may be better to breed dogs."

"Not at all. I don't agree with your sister. There's nothing like a debate to teach one quic' ness. I often wish I had gone in for them when I was a youngster. It would have helped me no end."

"Quickness — ?"

"Yes. Quickness in argument. Time after time I've missed scoring a point because the other man has had the gift of the gab and I haven't. Oh, I believe in these discussions."

The patronizing tone thought Margaret, came well enough from a man who was old enough to be their father. She had always maintained that Mr. Wilcox had a charm. In times of sorrow or emotion his inadequacy had pained her, but it was pleasant to listen to him now, and to watch his thick brown moustache and high forehead confronting the stars. But Helen was nettled. The aim of *their* debates she implied was Truth.

" Oh yes, it doesn't much matter what subject you take," said he.

Margaret laughed and said, " But this is going to be far better than the debate itself." Helen recovered herself and laughed too. " No, I won't go on," she declared. " I'll just put our special case to Mr. Wilcox."

" About Mr. Bast? Yes, do. He'll be more lenient to a special case."

" But, Mr. Wilcox, do first light another cigarette. It's this. We've just come across a young fellow, who's evidently very poor, and who seems interest —"

" What's his profession? "

" Clerk."

" What in? "

" Do you remember, Margaret? "

" Porphyrion Fire Insurance Company."

" Oh yes; the nice people who gave Aunt Juley a new hearth-rug. He seems interesting, in some ways very, and one wishes one could help him. He is married to a wife whom he doesn't seem to care for much. He likes books, and what one may roughly call adventure, and if he had a chance — But he is so poor. He lives a life where all the money is apt to go on nonsense and clothes. One is so afraid that circumstances will be too strong for him and that he will sink. Well, he got mixed up in our debate. He wasn't the subject of it, but it seemed to bear on his point. Suppose a millionaire died, and desired to leave money to help such a man. How should he be helped? Should he be given three hundred pounds a year direct, which was Margaret's plan? Most of them thought this would pauperize him. Should he and those like him be given free libraries? I said 'No!' He doesn't want more books to read, but to read books rightly. My suggestion was he should be given something every year towards a summer holiday, but then there is his wife, and they said she would have to go too. Nothing seemed quite right! Now what do you think? Imagine that you were a millionaire, and wanted to help the poor. What would you do?"

Mr. Wilcox, whose fortune was not so very far below the standard indicated, laughed exuberantly. "My dear Miss Schlegel, I will not rush in where your sex has been unable to tread. I will not add another plan to the numerous excellent ones that have been already suggested. My only contribution is this: let your young friend clear out of the Porphyrion Fire Insurance Company with all possible speed."

"Why?" said Margaret.

He lowered his voice. "This is between friends. It'll be in the Receiver's hands before Christmas. It'll smash," he added, thinking that she had not understood.

"Dear me, Helen, listen to that. And he'll have to get another place!"

"*Will* have? Let him leave the ship before it sinks. Let him get one now."

"Rather than wait, to make sure?"

"Decidedly."

"Why's that?"

Again the Olympian laugh, and the lowered voice. "Naturally the man who's in a situation when he applies stands a better chance, is in a stronger position, than the man who isn't. It looks as if he's worth something. I know by myself — (this is letting you into the State secrets) — it affects an employer greatly. Human nature, I'm afraid."

"I hadn't thought of that," murmured Margaret,

while Helen said, "Our human nature appears to be the other way round. We employ people because they're unemployed. The boot man, for instance."

"And how does he clean the boots?"

"Not well," confessed Margaret.

"There you are!"

"Then do you really advise us to tell this youth —"

"I advise nothing," he interrupted, glancing up and down the Embankment, in case his indiscretion had been overheard. "I oughtn't to have spoken — but I happen to know, being more or less behind the scenes. The Porphyrion's a bad, bad concern — Now, don't say I said so. It's outside the Tariff Ring."

"Certainly I won't say. In fact, I don't know what that means."

"I thought an insurance company never smashed," was Helen's contribution. "Don't the others always run in and save them?"

"You're thinking of reinsurance," said Mr. Wilcox mildly. "It is exactly there that the Porphyrion is weak. It has tried to undercut, has been badly hit by a long series of small fires, and it hasn't been able to reinsure. I'm afraid that public companies don't save one another for love."

"'Human nature,' I suppose," quoted Helen, and he laughed and agreed that it was. When Margaret said that she supposed that clerks, like every one else, found it extremely difficult to get situations in these days, he replied, "Yes, extremely," and rose to rejoin his friends. He knew by his own office — seldom a vacant post, and hundreds of applicants for it; at present no vacant post.

"And how's Howards End looking?" said Margaret, wishing to change the subject before they parted. Mr. Wilcox was a little apt to think one wanted to get something out of him.

"It's let."

" Really. And you wandering homeless in long-haired Chelsea? How strange are the ways of Fate! "

" No; it's let unfurnished. We've moved."

" Why, I thought of you both as anchored there for ever. Evie never told me."

" I dare say when you met Evie the thing wasn't settled. We only moved a week ago. Paul has rather a feeling for the old place, and we held on for him to have his holiday there; but, really, it is impossibly small. Endless drawbacks. I forget whether you've been up to it? "

" As far as the house, never."

" Well, Howards End is one of those converted farms. They don't really do, spend what you will on them. We messed away with a garage all among the wych-elm roots, and last year we enclosed a bit of the meadow and attempted a rockery. Evie got rather keen on Alpine plants. But it didn't do — no, it didn't do. You remember, or your sister will remember, the farm with those abominable guinea-fowls, and the hedge that the old woman never would cut properly, so that it all went thin at the bottom. And, inside the house, the beams — and the stair-case through a door — picturesque enough, but not a place to live in." He glanced over the parapet cheerfully. " Full tide. And the position wasn't right either. The neighbourhood's getting suburban. Either be in London or out of it, I say; so we've taken a house in Ducie Street, close to Sloane Street, and a place right down in Shropshire — Oniton Grange. Ever heard of Oniton? Do come and see us — right away from everywhere, up towards Wales."

" What a change! " said Margaret. But the change was in her own voice, which had become most sad. " I can't imagine Howards End or Hilton without you."

"Hilton isn't without us," he replied. "Charles is there still."

"Still?" said Margaret, who had not kept up with the Charles'. "But I thought he was still at Epsom. They were furnishing that Christmas — one Christmas. How everything alters! I used to admire Mrs. Charles from our windows very often. Wasn't it Epsom?"

"Yes, but they moved eighteen months ago. Charles, the good chap"—his voice dropped— "thought I should be lonely. I didn't want him to move, but he would, and took a house at the other end of Hilton, down by the Six Hills. He had a motor, too. There they all are, a very jolly party — he and she and the two grandchildren."

"I manage other people's affairs so much better than they manage them themselves," said Margaret as they shook hands. "When you moved out of Howards End, I should have moved Mr. Charles Wilcox into it. I should have kept so remarkable a place in the family."

"So it is," he replied. "I haven't sold it, and don't mean to."

"No; but none of you are there."

"Oh, we've got a splendid tenant — Hamar Bryce, an invalid. If Charles ever wanted it — but he won't. Dolly is so dependent on modern conveniences. No, we have all decided against Howards End. We like it in a way, but now we feel that it is neither one thing nor the other. One must have one thing or the other."

"And some people are lucky enough to have both. You're doing yourself proud, Mr. Wilcox. My congratulations."

"And mine," said Helen.

"Do remind Evie to come and see us — two, Wickham Place. We shan't be there very long, either."

"You, too, on the move?"

"Next September," Margaret sighed.

"Every one moving! Good-bye."

The tide had begun to ebb. Margaret leant over the parapet and watched it sadly. Mr. Wilcox had forgotten his wife, Helen her lover; she herself was probably forgetting. Every one moving. Is it worth while attempting the past when there is this continual flux even in the hearts of men?

Helen roused her by saying: "What a prosperous vulgarian Mr. Wilcox has grown! I have very little use for him in these days. However, he did tell us about the Porphyrion. Let us write to Mr. Bast as soon as ever we get home, and tell him to clear out of it at once."

"Do; yes, that's worth doing. Let us."

"Let's ask him to tea."

Chapter XVI

LEONARD accepted the invitation to tea next Saturday. But he was right; the visit proved a conspicuous failure.

"Sugar?" said Margaret.

"Cake?" said Helen. "The big cake or the little deadlies? I'm afraid you thought my letter rather odd, but we'll explain — we aren't odd, really — nor affected, really. We're over-expressive: that's all."

As a lady's lap-dog Leonard did not excel. He was not an Italian, still less a Frenchman, in whose blood there runs the very spirit of persiflage and of gracious repartee. His wit was the Cockney's; it opened no doors into imagination, and Helen was drawn up short by "The more a lady has to say, the better," administered waggishly.

"Oh, yes," she said.

"Ladies brighten —"

"Yes, I know. The darlings are regular sunbeams. Let me give you a plate."

"How do you like your work?" interposed Margaret.

He, too, was drawn up short. He would not have these women prying into his work. They were Romance, and so was the room to which he had at last penetrated, with the queer sketches of people bathing upon its walls, and so were the very tea-cups, with their delicate borders of wild strawberries. But he would not let Romance interfere with his life. There is the devil to pay then.

"Oh, well enough," he answered.

—158—

" Your company is the Porphyrion, isn't it? "

" Yes, that's so "— becoming rather offended. " It's funny how things get round."

" Why funny? " asked Helen, who did not follow the workings of his mind. " It was written as large as life on your card, and considering we wrote to you there, and that you replied on the stamped paper —"

" Would you call the Porphyrion one of the big Insurance Companies? " pursued Margaret.

" It depends what you call big."

" I mean by big, a solid, well-established concern, that offers a reasonably good career to its employés."

" I couldn't say — some would tell you one thing and others another," said the employé uneasily. " For my own part "— he shook his head —" I only believe half I hear. Not that even; it's safer. Those clever ones come to the worse grief, I've often noticed. Ah, you can't be too careful."

He drank, and wiped his moustache, which was going to be one of those moustaches that always droop into tea-cups — more bother than they're worth, surely, and not fashionable either.

" I quite agree, and that's why I was curious to know: is it a solid, well-established concern? "

Leonard had no idea. He understood his own corner of the machine, but nothing beyond it. He desired to confess neither knowledge nor ignorance, and under these circumstances, another motion of the head seemed safest. To him, as to the British public, the Porphyrion was the Porphyrion of the advertisement — a giant, in the classical style, but draped sufficiently, who held in one hand a burning torch, and pointed with the other to St. Paul's and Windsor Castle. A large sum of money was inscribed below, and you drew your own conclusions. This giant caused Leonard to do arithmetic and write letters, to explain the regulations to new clients, and re-explain them to old ones. A giant was of an impulsive morality — one knew that much. He would pay for Mrs. Munt's hearth-rug with ostentatious haste, a large claim he would repudiate quietly, and fight court by court. But his true fighting weight, his antecedents, his amours with other members of the commercial Pantheon — all these were as uncertain to ordinary mortals as were the escapades of Zeus. While the gods are powerful, we learn little about them. It is only in the days of their decadence that a strong light beats into heaven.

"We were told the Porphyrion's no go," blurted Helen. "We wanted to tell you; that's why we wrote."

"A friend of ours did think that it is unsufficiently reinsured," said Margaret.

Now Leonard had his clue. He must praise the Porphyrion. "You can tell your friend," he said, "that he's quite wrong."

"Oh, good!"

The young man coloured a little. In his circle to be wrong was fatal. The Miss Schlegels did not mind being wrong. They were genuinely glad that they had been misinformed. To them nothing was fatal but evil.

"Wrong, so to speak," he added.

"How 'so to speak'?"

"I mean I wouldn't say he's right altogether."

But this was a blunder. "Then he is right partly," said the elder woman, quick as lightning.

Leonard replied that every one was right partly, if it came to that.

"Mr. Bast, I don't understand business, and I dare say my questions are stupid, but can you tell me what makes a concern 'right' or 'wrong'?"

Leonard sat back with a sigh.

"Our friend, who is also a business man, was so positive. He said before Christmas —"

"And advised you to clear out of it," concluded Helen. "But I don't see why he should know better than you do."

Leonard rubbed his hands. He was tempted to say that he knew nothing about the thing at all. But a commercial training was too strong for him. Nor could he say it was a bad thing, for this would be giving it away; nor yet that it was good, for this would be giving it away equally. He attempted to suggest that it was something between the two, with vast possibilities in either direction, but broke down under the gaze of four sincere eyes. As yet he scarcely distinguished between the two sisters. One was more beautiful and more lively, but "the Miss Schlegels" still remained a composite Indian god, whose waving arms and contradictory speeches were the product of a single mind.

"One can but see," he remarked, adding, "as Ibsen says, 'things happen.'" He was itching to talk about books and make the most of his romantic hour. Minute after minute slipped away, while the ladies, with imperfect skill, discussed the subject of reinsurance or praised their anonymous friend. Leonard grew annoyed — perhaps rightly. He made vague remarks about not being one of those who minded their affairs being talked over by others, but they did not take the hint. Men might have shown more tact. Women, however tactful elsewhere, are heavy-handed here. They cannot see why we should shroud our incomes and our prospects in a veil. "How much exactly have you, and how much do you expect to have next June?" And these were women with a theory, who held that reticence about money matters is absurd, and that life would be truer if each would state the exact size of the golden island upon which he stands, the exact stretch of warp over which he throws the woof that is not money. How can we do justice to the pattern otherwise?

And the precious minutes slipped away, and Jacky and squalor came nearer. At last he could bear it no longer, and broke in, reciting the names of books feverishly. There was a moment of piercing joy when Margaret said, "So *you* like Carlyle," and then the door opened, and "Mr. Wilcox, Miss Wilcox" entered, preceded by two prancing puppies.

"Oh, the dears! Oh, Evie, how too impossibly sweet!" screamed Helen, falling on her hands and knees.

"We brought the little fellows round," said Mr. Wilcox.

"I bred 'em myself."

"Oh, really! Mr. Bast, come and play with puppies."

"I've got to be going now," said Leonard sourly.

"But play with puppies a little first."

"This is Ahab, that's Jezebel," said Evie, who was one of those who name animals after the less successful characters of Old Testament history.

"I've got to be going."

Helen was too much occupied with puppies to notice him.

"Mr. Wilcox, Mr. Ba— Must you be really? Good-bye!"

"Come again," said Helen from the floor.

Then Leonard's gorge arose. Why should he come again? What was the good of it? He said roundly: "No, I shan't; I knew it would be a failure."

Most people would have let him go. "A little mistake. We tried knowing another class — impossible." But the Schlegels had never played with life. They had attempted friendship, and they would take the consequences. Helen retorted, "I call that a very rude remark. What do you want to turn on me like that for?" and suddenly the drawing-room re-echoed to a vulgar row.

"You ask me why I turn on you?"

"Yes."

"What do you want to have me here for?"

"To help you, you silly boy!" cried Helen. "And don't shout."

"*I* don't want your patronage. *I* don't want your tea. I was quite happy. What do you want to unsettle me for?" He turned to Mr. Wilcox. "I put it to this gentleman. I ask you, sir, am to have my brain picked?"

Mr. Wilcox turned to Margaret with the air of humorous strength that he could so well command. "Are we intruding, Miss Schlegel? Can we be of any use or shall we go?"

But Margaret ignored him.

"I'm connected with a leading insurance company, sir. I receive what I take to be an invitation from these — ladies" (he drawled the word). "I come, and it's to have my brain picked. I ask you, is it fair?"

"Highly unfair," said Mr. Wilcox, drawing a gasp from Evie, who knew that her father was becoming dangerous.

"There, you hear that? Most unfair, the gentleman says. There! Not content with "— pointing at Margaret —" you can't deny it." His voice rose: he was falling into the rhythm of a scene with Jacky. "But as soon as I'm useful it's a very different thing. 'Oh yes, send for him. Cross-question him. Pick his brains.' Oh yes. Now, take me on the whole, I'm a quiet fellow: I'm law-abiding, I don't wish any unpleasantness; but I — I —"

"You," said Margaret —" you — you —"

Laughter from Evie, as at a repartee.

"You are the man who tried to walk by the Pole star."

More laughter.

"You saw the sunrise."

Laughter.

"You tried to get away from the fogs that are stifling us all — away past books and houses to the truth. You were looking for a real home."

"I fail to see the connection," said Leonard, hot with stupid anger.

"So do I." There was a pause. "You were that last Sunday — you are this today. Mr. Bast! I and my sister have talked you over. We wanted to help you; we also supposed you might help us. We did not have you here out of charity — which bores us — but because we hoped there would be a connection between last Sunday and other days. What is the good of your stars and trees, your sunrise and the wind, if they do not enter into our daily lives? They have never entered into mine, but into yours, we thought — Haven't we all to struggle against life's daily greyness, against pettiness, against mechanical cheerfulness, against suspicion? I struggle by remembering my friends; others I have known by remembering some place — some beloved place or tree — we thought you one of these."

"Of course, if there's been any misunderstanding," mumbled Leonard, "all I can do is to go. But I beg to state —" He paused. Ahab and Jezebel danced at his boots and made him look ridiculous. "You were picking my brain for official information — I can prove it — I —" He blew his nose and left them.

"Can I help you now?" said Mr. Wilcox, turning to Margaret. "May I have one quiet word with him in the hall?"

"Helen, go after him — do anything — *anything* — to make the noodle understand."

Helen hesitated.

" But really —" said their visitor. " Ought she to? "

At once she went.

He resumed. " I would have chimed in, but I felt that you could polish him off for yourselves — I didn't interfere. You were splendid, Miss Schlegel — absolutely splendid. You can take my word for it, but there are very few women who could have managed him."

" Oh yes," said Margaret distractedly.

" Bowling him over with those long sentences was what fetched me," cried Evie.

" Yes, indeed," chuckled her father; " all that part about ' mechanical cheerfulness '— oh, fine! "

" I'm very sorry," said Margaret, collecting herself. " He's a nice creature really. I cannot think what set him off. It has been most unpleasant for you."

" Oh, *I* didn't mind." Then he changed his mood. He asked if he might speak as an old friend, and, permission given, said: " Oughtn't you really to be more careful? "

Margaret laughed, though her thoughts still strayed after Helen. " Do you realize that it's all your fault? " she said. " You're responsible."

" I? "

" This is the young man whom we were to warn against the Porphyrion. We warn him, and — look! "

Mr. Wilcox was annoyed. " I hardly consider that a fair deduction," he said.

" Obviously unfair," said Margaret. " I was only thinking how tangled things are. It's our fault mostly — neither yours nor his."

" Not his? "

" No."

" Miss Schlegel, you are too kind."

" Yes, indeed," nodded Evie, a little contemptuously.

"You behave much too well to people, and then they impose on you. I know the world and that type of man, and as soon as I entered the room I saw you had not been treating him properly. You must keep that type at a distance. Otherwise they forget themselves. Sad, but true. They aren't our sort, and one must face the fact."

"Ye-es."

"Do admit that we should never have had the outburst if he was a gentleman."

"I admit it willingly," said Margaret, who was pacing up and down the room. "A gentleman would have kept his suspicions to himself."

Mr. Wilcox watched her with a vague uneasiness.

"What did he suspect you of?"

"Of wanting to make money out of him."

"Intolerable brute! But how were you to benefit?"

"Exactly. How indeed! Just horrible, corroding suspicion. One touch of thought or of goodwill would have brushed it away. Just the senseless fear that does make men intolerable brutes."

"I come back to my original point. You ought to be more careful, Miss Schlegel. Your servants ought to have orders not to let such people in."

She turned to him frankly. "Let me explain exactly why we like this man, and want to see him again."

"That's your clever way of thinking. I shall never believe you like him."

"I do. Firstly, because he cares for physical adventure, just as you do. Yes, you go motoring and shooting; he would like to go camping out. Secondly, he cares for something special *in* adventure. It is quickest to call that special something poetry—"

"Oh, he's one of that writer sort."

"No—oh no! I mean he may be, but it would be

loathsome stiff. His brain is filled with the husks of books, culture — horrible; we want him to wash out his brain and go to the real thing. We want to show him how he may get upsides with life. As I said, either friends or the country, some " — she hesitated — " either some very dear person or some very dear place seems necessary to relieve life's daily grey, and to show that it is grey. If possible, one should have both."

Some of her words ran past Mr. Wilcox. He let them run past. Others he caught and criticized with admirable lucidity.

" Your mistake is this, and it is a very common mistake. This young bounder has a life of his own. What right have you to conclude it is an unsuccessful life, or, as you call it, ' grey '? "

" Because — "

" One minute. You know nothing about him. He probably has his own joys and interests — wife, children, snug little home. That's where we practical fellows " — he smiled — " are more tolerant than you intellectuals. We live and let live, and assume that things are jogging on fairly well elsewhere, and that the ordinary plain man may be trusted to look after his own affairs. I quite grant — I look at the faces of the clerks in my own office, and observe them to be dull, but I don't know what's going on beneath. So, by the way, with London. I have heard you rail against London, Miss Schlegel, and it seems a funny thing to say but I was very angry with you. What do you know about London? You only see civilization from the outside. I don't say in your case, but in too many cases that attitude leads to morbidity, discontent, and Socialism."

She admitted the strength of his position, though it undermined imagination. As he spoke, some outposts of poetry and perhaps of sympathy fell ruining, and she retreated to what she called her " second line " — to the special facts of the case.

" His wife is an old bore," she said simply. " He never came home last Saturday night because he wanted to be alone, and she thought he was with us."

" With *you?* "

" Yes." Evie tittered. " He hasn't got the cosy home that you assumed. He needs outside interests."

" Naughty young man! " cried the girl.

" Naughty? " said Margaret, who hated naughtiness more than sin. " When you're married, Miss Wilcox, won't you want outside interests? "

" He has apparently got them," put in Mr. Wilcox slyly.

" Yes, indeed, father."

" He was tramping in Surrey, if you mean that," said Margaret, pacing away rather crossly.

" Oh, I dare say! "

" Miss Wilcox, he was! "

" M-m-m-m! " from Mr. Wilcox, who thought the episode amusing, if risqué. With most ladies he would not have discussed it, but he was trading on Margaret's reputation as an emancipated woman.

" He said so, and about such a thing he wouldn't lie."

They both began to laugh.

" That's where I differ from you. Men lie about their positions and prospects, but not about a thing of that sort."

He shook his head. " Miss Schlegel, excuse me, but I know the type."

" I said before — he isn't a type. He cares about adventures rightly. He's certain that our smug existence isn't all. He's vulgar and hysterical and bookish, but I don't think that sums him up. There's manhood in him as well. Yes, that's what I'm trying to say. He's a real man."

As she spoke their eyes met, and it was as if Mr. Wilcox's defences fell. She saw back to the real man in him. Unwittingly she had touched his emotions. A woman and two men — they had formed the magic triangle of sex, and the male was thrilled to jealousy, in case the female was attracted by another male. Love, say the ascetics, reveals our shameful kinship with the beasts. Be it so: one can bear that; jealousy is the real shame. It is jealousy, not love, that connects us with the farmyard intolerably, and calls up visions of two angry cocks and a complacent hen. Margaret crushed complacency down because she was civilized. Mr. Wilcox, uncivilized, continued to feel anger long after he had rebuilt his defences, and was again presenting a bastion to the world.

" Miss Schlegel, you're a pair of dear creatures, but you really *must* be careful in this uncharitable world. What does your brother say?"

" I forget."

" Surely he has some opinion?"

" He laughs, if I remember correctly."

" He's very clever, isn't he?" said Evie, who had met and detested Tibby at Oxford.

" Yes, pretty well — but I wonder what Helen's doing."

" She is very young to undertake this sort of thing," said Mr. Wilcox.

Margaret went out into the landing. She heard no sound, and Mr. Bast's topper was missing from the hall.

" Helen!" she called.

" Yes!" replied a voice from the library.

" You in there?"

" Yes — he's gone some time."

Margaret went to her. "Why, you're all alone," she said.

" Yes — it's all right, Meg. Poor, poor creature —"

"Come back to the Wilcoxes and tell me later — Mr. W. much concerned, and slightly titillated."

"Oh, I've no patience with him. I hate him. Poor dear Mr. Bast! he wanted to talk literature, and we would talk business. Such a muddle of a man, and yet so worth pulling through. I like him extraordinarily."

"Well done," said Margaret, kissing her, "but come into the drawing-room now, and don't talk about him to the Wilcoxes. Make light of the whole thing."

Helen came and behaved with a cheerfulness that reassured their visitor — this hen at all events was fancy-free.

"He's gone with my blessing," she cried, "and now for puppies."

As they drove away, Mr. Wilcox said to his daughter:

"I am really concerned at the way those girls go on. They are as clever as you make 'em, but unpractical — God bless me! One of these days they'll go too far. Girls like that oughtn't to live alone in London. Until they marry, they ought to have some one to look after them. We must look in more often — we're better than no one. You like them, don't you, Evie?"

Evie replied: "Helen's right enough, but I can't stand the toothy one. And I shouldn't have called either of them girls."

Evie had grown up handsome. Dark-eyed, with the glow of youth under sunburn, built firmly and firm-lipped, she was the best the Wilcoxes could do in the way of feminine beauty. For the present, puppies and her father were the only things she loved, but the net of matrimony was being prepared for her, and a few days later she was attracted to a Mr. Percy Cahill, an uncle of Mrs. Charles, and he was attracted to her.

Chapter XVII

THE Age of Property holds bitter moments even for a proprietor. When a move is imminent, furniture becomes ridiculous, and Margaret now lay awake at nights wondering where, where on earth they and all their belongings would be deposited in September next. Chairs, tables, pictures, books, that had rumbled down to them through the generations, must rumble forward again like a slide of rubbish to which she longed to give the final push, and send toppling into the sea. But there were all their father's books — they never read them, but they were their father's, and must be kept. There was the marble-topped chiffonier — their mother had set store by it, they could not remember why. Round every knob and cushion in the house sentiment gathered, a sentiment that was at times personal, but more often a faint piety to the dead, a prolongation of rites that might have ended at the grave.

It was absurd, if you came to think of it; Helen and Tibby came to think of it: Margaret was too busy with the house-agents. The feudal ownership of land did bring dignity, whereas the modern ownership of movables is reducing us again to a nomadic horde. We are reverting to the civilization of luggage, and historians of the future will note how the middle classes accreted possessions without taking root in the earth, and may find in this the secret of their imaginative poverty. The Schlegels were certainly the poorer for the loss of Wickham Place. It had helped to balance their lives, and almost to counsel them. Nor is their ground-landlord spiritually the richer. He has built flats on its site, his motor-cars grow swifter, his exposures of Socialism more trenchant. But he has spilt the precious distillation of the years, and no chemistry of his can give it back to society again.

Margaret grew depressed; she was anxious to settle on a house before they left town to pay their annual visit to Mrs. Munt. She enjoyed this visit, and wanted to have her mind at ease for it. Swanage, though dull, was stable, and this year she longed more than usual for its fresh air and for the magnificent downs that guard it on the north. But London thwarted her; in its atmosphere she could not concentrate. London only stimulates, it cannot sustain; and Margaret, hurrying over its surface for a house without knowing what sort of a house she wanted, was paying for many a thrilling sensation in the past. She could not even break loose from culture, and her time was wasted by concerts which it would be a sin to miss, and invitations which it would never do to refuse. At last she grew desperate; she resolved that she would go nowhere and be at home to no one until she found a house, and broke the resolution in half an hour.

Once she had humorously lamented that she had never been to Simpson's restaurant in the Strand. Now a note arrived from Miss Wilcox, asking her to lunch there. Mr. Cahill was coming, and the three would have such a jolly chat, and perhaps end up at the Hippodrome. Margaret had no strong regard for Evie, and no desire to meet her fiancé, and she was surprised that Helen, who had been far funnier about Simpson's, had not been asked instead. But the invitation touched her by its intimate tone. She must know Evie Wilcox better than she supposed, and declaring that she " simply must," she accepted.

But when she saw Evie at the entrance of the restaurant, staring fiercely at nothing after the fashion of athletic women, her heart failed her anew. Miss Wilcox had changed perceptibly since her engagement. Her voice was gruffer, her manner more downright, and she was inclined to patronize the more foolish virgin. Margaret was silly enough to be pained at this. Depressed at her isolation, she saw not only houses and furniture, but the vessel of life itself slipping past her, with people like Evie and Mr. Cahill on board.

There are moments when virtue and wisdom fail us, and one of them came to her at Simpson's in the Strand. As she trod the staircase, narrow, but carpeted thickly, as she entered the eating-room, where saddles of mutton were being trundled up to expectant clergymen, she had a strong, if erroneous, conviction of her own futility, and wished she had never come out of her backwater, where nothing happened except art and literature, and where no one ever got married or succeeded in remaining engaged. Then came a little surprise. 'Father might be of the party — yes, father was.' With a smile of pleasure she moved forward to greet him, and her feeling of loneliness vanished.

"I thought I'd get round if I could," said he. "Evie told me of her little plan, so I just slipped in and secured a table. Always secure a table first. Evie, don't pretend you want to sit by your old father, because you don't. Miss Schlegel, come in my side, out of pity. My goodness, but you look tired! Been worrying round after your young clerks?"

"No, after houses," said Margaret, edging past him into the box. "I'm hungry, not tired; I want to eat heaps."

"That's good. What'll you have?"

"Fish pie," said she, with a glance at the menu.

"Fish pie! Fancy coming for fish pie to Simpson's. It's not a bit the thing to go for here."

"Go for something for me, then," said Margaret, pulling off her gloves. Her spirits were rising, and his reference to Leonard Bast had warmed her curiously.

"Saddle of mutton," said he after profound reflection; "and cider to drink. That's the type of thing. I like this place, for a joke, once in a way. It is so thoroughly Old English. Don't you agree?"

"Yes," said Margaret, who didn't. The order was given, the joint rolled up, and the carver, under Mr. Wilcox's direction, cut the meat where it was succulent, and piled their plates high. Mr. Cahill insisted on sirloin, but admitted that he had made a mistake later on. He and Evie soon fell into a conversation of the "No, I didn't; yes, you did" type — conversation which, though fascinating to those who are engaged in it, neither desires nor deserves the attention of others.

"It's a golden rule to tip the carver. Tip everywhere's my motto."

"Perhaps it does make life more human."

"Then the fellows know one again. Especially in the East, if you tip, they remember you from year's end to year's end."

"Have you been in the East?"

"Oh, Greece and the Levant. I used to go out for sport and business to Cyprus; some military society of a sort there. A few piastres, properly distributed, help to keep one's memory green. But you, of course, think this shockingly cynical. How's your discussion society getting on? Any new Utopias lately?"

"No, I'm house-hunting, Mr. Wilcox, as I've already told you once. Do you know of any houses?"

"Afraid I don't."

"Well, what's the point of being practical if you can't find two distressed females a house? We merely want a small house with large rooms, and plenty of them."

"Evie, I like that! Miss Schlegel expects me to turn house agent for her!"

"What's that, father?"

"I want a new home in September, and some one must find it. I can't."

"Percy, do you know of anything?"

"I can't say I do," said Mr. Cahill.

"How like you! You're never any good."

"Never any good. Just listen to her! Never any good. Oh, come!"

"Well, you aren't. Miss Schlegel, is he?"

The torrent of their love, having splashed these drops at Margaret, swept away on its habitual course. She sympathized with it now, for a little comfort had restored her geniality. Speech and silence pleased her equally, and while Mr. Wilcox made some preliminary inquiries about cheese, her eyes surveyed the restaurant, and admired its well-calculated tributes to the solidity of our past. Though no more Old English than the works of Kipling, it had selected its reminiscences so adroitly that her criticism was lulled, and the guests whom it was nourishing for imperial purposes bore the outer semblance of Parson Adams or Tom Jones. Scraps of their talk jarred oddly on the ear. "Right you are! I'll cable out to Uganda this evening," came from the table behind. "Their Emperor wants war; well, let him have it," was the opinion of a clergyman. She smiled at such incongruities. "Next time," she said to Mr. Wilcox, "you shall come to lunch with me at Mr. Eustace Miles's."

"With pleasure."

"No, you'd hate it," she said, pushing her glass towards him for some more cider. "It's all proteids and body buildings, and people come up to you and beg your pardon, but you have such a beautiful aura."

"A what?"

"Never heard of an aura? Oh, happy, happy man!

I scrub at mine for hours. Nor of an astral plane?"

He had heard of astral planes, and censured them.

"Just so. Luckily it was Helen's aura, not mine, and she had to chaperone it and do the politenesses. I just sat with my handkerchief in my mouth till the man went."

"Funny experiences seem to come to you two girls. No one's ever asked me about my — what d'ye call it? Perhaps I've not got one."

"You're bound to have one, but it may be such a terrible colour that no one dares mention it."

"Tell me, though, Miss Schlegel, do you really believe in the supernatural and all that?"

"Too difficult a question."

"Why's that? Gruyère or Stilton?"

"Gruyère, please."

"Better have Stilton."

"Stilton. Because, though I don't believe in auras, and think Theosophy's only a halfway-house —"

"— Yet there may be something in it all the same," he concluded, with a frown.

"Not even that. It may be halfway in the wrong direction. I can't explain. I don't believe in all these fads, and yet I don't like saying that I don't believe in them."

He seemed unsatisfied, and said: "So you wouldn't give me your word that you *don't* hold with astral bodies and all the rest of it?"

"I could," said Margaret, surprised that the point was of any importance to him. "Indeed, I will. When I talked about scrubbing my aura, I was only trying to be funny. But why do you want this settled?"

"I don't know."

"Now, Mr. Wilcox, you do know."

"Yes, I am," "No, you're not," burst from the lovers opposite. Margaret was silent for a moment, and then changed the subject.

" How's your house? "

" Much the same as when you honoured it last week."

" I don't mean Ducie Street. Howards End, of course."

" Why ' of course '? "

" Can't you turn out your tenant and let it to us? We're nearly demented."

" Let me think. I wish I could help you. But I thought you wanted to be in town. One bit of advice: fix your district, then fix your price, and then don't budge. That's how I got both Ducie Street and Oniton. I said to myself, ' I mean to be exactly here,' and I was, and Oniton's a place in a thousand."

" But I do budge. Gentlemen seem to mesmerize houses — cow them with an eye, and up they come, trembling. Ladies can't. It's the houses that are mesmerizing me. I've no control over the saucy things. Houses are alive. No? "

" I'm out of my depth," he said, and added: " Didn't you talk rather like that to your office boy? "

" Did I? — I mean I did, more or less. I talk the same way to every one — or try to."

" Yes, I know. And how much do you suppose that he understood of it? "

" That's his lookout. I don't believe in suiting my conversation to my company. One can doubtless hit upon some medium of exchange that seems to do well enough, but it's no more like the real thing than money is like food. There's no nourishment in it. You pass it to the lower classes, and they pass it back to you, and this you call ' social intercourse ' or ' mutual endeavour,' when it's mutual priggishness if it's anything. Our friends at Chelsea don't see this. They say one ought to be at all costs intelligible, and sac-rifice —"

" Lower classes," interrupted Mr. Wilcox, as it were thrusting his hand into her speech. " Well, you do admit that there are rich and poor. That's some-thing."

Margaret could not reply. Was he incredibly stupid, or did he understand her better than she under-stood herself?

" You do admit that, if wealth was divided up equally, in a few years there would be rich and poor again just the same. The hard-working man would come to the top, the wastrel sink to the bottom."

" Every one admits that."

" Your Socialists don't."

" My Socialists do. Yours mayn't; but I strongly suspect yours of being not Socialists, but ninepins, which you have constructed for your own amusement. I can't imagine any living creature who would bowl over quite so easily."

He would have resented this had she not been a woman. But women may say anything — it was one of his holiest beliefs — and he only retorted, with a gay smile: " I don't care. You've made two damag-ing admissions, and I'm heartily with you in both."

In time they finished lunch, and Margaret, who had excused herself from the Hippodrome, took her leave. Evie had scarcely addressed her, and she suspected that the entertainment had been planned by the father. He and she were advancing out of their respective families towards a more intimate acquaintance. It had begun long ago. She had been his wife's friend, and, as such, he had given her that silver vinaigrette as a memento. It was pretty of him to have given that vinaigrette, and he had always preferred her to Helen — unlike most men. But the advance had been astonishing lately. They had done more in a week than in two years, and were really beginning to know each other.

She did not forget his promise to sample Eustace Miles, and asked him as soon as she could secure Tibby as his chaperon. He came, and partook of body-building dishes with humility.

Next morning the Schlegels left for Swanage. They had not succeeded in finding a new home.

Chapter XVIII

AS they were seated at Aunt Juley's breakfast-table at The Bays, parrying her excessive hospitality and enjoying the view of the bay, a letter came for Margaret and threw her into perturbation. It was from Mr. Wilcox. It announced an "important change" in his plans. Owing to Evie's marriage, he had decided to give up his house in Ducie Street, and was willing to let it on a yearly tenancy. It was a businesslike letter, and stated frankly what he would do for them and what he would not do. Also the rent. If they approved, Margaret was to come up *at once* — the words were underlined, as is necessary when dealing with women — and to go over the house with him. If they disapproved, a wire would oblige, as he should put it into the hands of an agent.

The letter perturbed, because she was not sure what it meant. If he liked her, if he had manœuvred to get her to Simpson's, might this be a manœuvre to get her to London, and result in an offer of marriage? She put it to herself as indelicately as possible, in the hope that her brain would cry, "Rubbish, you're a self-conscious fool!" But her brain only tingled a little and was silent, and for a time she sat gazing at the mincing waves, and wondering whether the news would seem strange to the others.

As soon as she began speaking, the sound of her own voice reassured her. There could be nothing in it. The replies also were typical, and in the burr of conversation her fears vanished.

"You needn't go though —" began her hostess.

"I needn't, but hadn't I better? It's really getting rather serious. We let chance after chance slip, and the end of it is we shall be bundled out bag and baggage into the street. We don't know what we *want*, that's the mischief with us —"

"No, we have no real ties," said Helen, helping herself to toast.

"Shan't I go up to town today, take the house if it's the least possible, and then come down by the afternoon train tomorrow, and start enjoying myself. I shall be no fun to myself or to others until this business is off my mind."

"But you won't do anything rash, Margaret?"

"There's nothing rash to do."

"Who *are* the Wilcoxes?" said Tibby, a question that sounds silly, but was really extremely subtle, as his aunt found to her cost when she tried to answer it. "I don't *manage* the Wilcoxes; I don't see where they come *in*."

"No more do I," agreed Helen. "It's funny that we just don't lose sight of them. Out of all our hotel acquaintances, Mr. Wilcox is the only one who has stuck. It is now over three years, and we have drifted away from far more interesting people in that time."

"Interesting people don't get one houses."

"Meg, if you start in your honest-English vein, I shall throw the treacle at you."

"It's a better vein than the cosmopolitan," said Margaret, getting up. "Now, children, which is it to be? You know the Ducie Street house. Shall I say yes or shall I say no? Tibby love — which? I'm specially anxious to pin you both."

"It all depends what meaning you attach to the word 'possi —'"

"It depends on nothing of the sort. Say 'yes.'"

"Say 'no.'"

Then Margaret spoke rather seriously. "I think,"

she said, "that our race is degenerating. We cannot settle even this little thing; what will it be like when we have to settle a big one?"

"It will be as easy as eating," returned Helen.

"I was thinking of father. How could he settle to leave Germany as he did, when he had fought for it as a young man, and all his feelings and friends were Prussian? How could he break loose with Patriotism and begin aiming at something else? It would have killed me. When he was nearly forty he could change countries and ideals — and we, at our age, can't change houses. It's humiliating."

"Your father may have been able to change countries," said Mrs. Munt with asperity, "and that may or may not be a good thing. But he could change houses no better than you can, in fact, much worse. Never shall I forget what poor Emily suffered in the move from Manchester."

"I knew it," cried Helen. "I told you so. It is the little things one bungles at. The big, real ones are nothing when they come."

"Bungle, my dear! You are too little to recollect — in fact, you weren't there. But the furniture was actually in the vans and on the move before the lease for Wickham Place was signed, and Emily took train with baby — who was Margaret then — and the smaller luggage for London, without so much as knowing where her new home would be. Getting away from that house may be hard, but it is nothing to the misery that we all went through getting you into it."

Helen, with her mouth full, cried:

"And that's the man who beat the Austrians, and the Danes, and the French, and who beat the Germans that were inside himself. And we're like him."

"Speak for yourself," said Tibby. "Remember that I am cosmopolitan, please."

"Helen may be right."

"Of course she's right," said Helen.

Helen might be right, but she did not go up to London. Margaret did that. An interrupted holiday is the worst of the minor worries, and one may be pardoned for feeling morbid when a business letter snatches one away from the sea and friends. She could not believe that her father had ever felt the same. Her eyes had been troubling her lately, so that she could not read in the train, and it bored her to look at the landscape, which she had seen but yesterday. At Southampton she "waved" to Frieda: Frieda was on her way down to join them at Swanage, and Mrs. Munt had calculated that their trains would cross. But Frieda was looking the other way, and Margaret travelled on to town feeling solitary and old-maidish. How like an old maid to fancy that Mr. Wilcox was courting her! She had once visited a spinster — poor, silly, and unattractive — whose mania it was that every man who approached her fell in love. How Margaret's heart had bled for the deluded thing! How she had lectured, reasoned, and in despair acquiesced! "I may have been deceived by the curate, my dear, but the young fellow who brings the midday post really is fond of me, and has, as a matter fact —" It had always seemed to her the most hideous corner of old age, yet she might be driven into it herself by the mere pressure of virginity.

Mr. Wilcox met her at Waterloo himself. She felt certain that he was not the same as usual; for one thing, he took offence at everything she said.

"This is awfully kind of you," she began, "but I'm afraid it's not going to do. The house has not been built that suits the Schlegel family."

"What! Have you come up determined not to deal?"

"Not exactly."

"Not exactly? In that case let's be starting."

She lingered to admire the motor, which was new, and a fairer creature than the vermilion giant that had borne Aunt Juley to her doom three years before.

"Presumably it's very beautiful," she said. "How do you like it, Crane?"

"Come, let's be starting," repeated her host. "How on earth did you know that my chauffeur was called Crane?"

"Why, I know Crane: I've been for a drive with Evie once. I know that you've got a parlourmaid called Milton. I know all sorts of things."

"Evie!" he echoed in injured tones. "You won't see her. She's gone out with Cahill. It's no fun, I can tell you, being left so much alone. I've got my work all day — indeed, a great deal too much of it — but when I come home in the evening, I tell you, I can't stand the house."

"In my absurd way, I'm lonely too," Margaret replied. "It's heart-breaking to leave one's old home. I scarcely remember anything before Wickham Place, and Helen and Tibby were born there. Helen says —"

"You, too, feel lonely?"

"Horribly. Hullo, Parliament's back!"

Mr. Wilcox glanced at Parliament contemptuously. The more important ropes of life lay elsewhere. "Yes, they are talking again," said he. "But you were going to say —"

"Only some rubbish about furniture. Helen says it alone endures while men and houses perish, and that in the end the world will be a desert of chairs and sofas — just imagine it! — rolling through infinity with no one to sit upon them."

"Your sister always likes her little joke."

"She says 'Yes,' my brother says 'No,' to Ducie Street. It's no fun helping us, Mr. Wilcox, I assure you."

" You are not as unpractical as you pretend. I shall never believe it."

Margaret laughed. But she was — quite as unpractical. She could not concentrate on details. Parliament, the Thames, the irresponsive chauffeur, would flash into the field of house-hunting, and all demand some comment or response. It is impossible to see modern life steadily and see it whole, and she had chosen to see it whole. Mr. Wilcox saw steadily. He never bothered over the mysterious or the private. The Thames might run inland from the sea, the chauffeur might conceal all passion and philosophy beneath his unhealthy skin. They knew their own business, and he knew his.

Yet she liked being with him. He was not a rebuke, but a stimulus, and banished morbidity. Some twenty years her senior, he preserved a gift that she supposed herself to have already lost — not youth's creative power, but its self-confidence and optimism. He was so sure that it was a very pleasant world. His complexion was robust, his hair had receded but not thinned, the thick moustache and the eyes that Helen had compared to brandy-balls had an agreeable menace in them, whether they were turned towards the slums or towards the stars. Some day — in the millennium — there may be no need for his type. At present, homage is due to it from those who think themselves superior, and who possibly are.

" At all events you responded to my telegram promptly," he remarked.

" Oh, even I know a good thing when I see it."

" I'm glad you don't despise the goods of this world."

" Heavens, no! Only idiots and prigs do that."

" I am glad, very glad," he repeated, suddenly softening and turning to her, as if the remark had pleased him. " There is so much cant talked in would-be intellectual circles. I am glad you don't share it. Self-denial is all very well as a means of strengthening the character. But I can't stand those people who run down comforts. They have usually some axe to grind. Can you?"

"Comforts are of two kinds," said Margaret, who was keeping herself in hand —"those we can share with others, like fire, weather, or music; and those we can't — food, for instance. It depends."

"I mean reasonable comforts, of course. I shouldn't like to think that you —" He bent nearer; the sentence died unfinished. Margaret's head turned very stupid, and the inside of it seemed to revolve like the beacon in a lighthouse. He did not kiss her, for the hour was half-past twelve, and the car was passing by the stables of Buckingham Palace. But the atmosphere was so charged with emotion that people only seemed to exist on her account, and she was surprised that Crane did not realize this, and turn round. Idiot though she might be, surely Mr. Wilcox was more — how should one put it? — more psychological than usual. Always a good judge of character for business purposes, he seemed this afternoon to enlarge his field, and to note qualities outside neatness, obedience, and decision.

"I want to go over the whole house," she announced when they arrived. "As soon as I get back to Swanage, which will be tomorrow afternoon, I'll talk it over once more with Helen and Tibby, and wire you 'yes' or 'no.'"

"Right. The dining-room." And they began their survey.

The dining-room was big, but over-furnished. Chelsea would have moaned aloud. Mr. Wilcox had eschewed those decorative schemes that wince, and relent, and refrain, and achieve beauty by sacrificing comfort and pluck. After so much self-colour and self-denial, Margaret viewed with relief the sumptuous dado, the frieze, the gilded wall-paper, amid whose foliage parrots sang. It would never do with her own furniture, but those heavy chairs, that immense sideboard loaded with presentation plate, stood up against its pressure like men. The room suggested men, and Margaret, keen to derive the modern capitalist from the warriors and hunters of the past, saw it as an ancient guest-hall, where the lord sat at meat among his thanes. Even the Bible — the Dutch Bible that Charles had brought back from the Boer War — fell into position. Such a room admitted loot.

" Now the entrance-hall."

The entrance-hall was paved.

" Here we fellows smoke."

We fellows smoked in chairs of maroon leather. It was as if a motor-car had spawned. " Oh, jolly!" said Margaret, sinking into one of them.

" You do like it?" he said, fixing his eyes on her upturned face, and surely betraying an almost intimate note. " It's all rubbish not making oneself comfortable. Isn't it?"

" Ye-es. Semi-rubbish. Are those Cruikshanks?"

" Gillrays. Shall we go on upstairs?"

" Does all this furniture come from Howards End?"

" The Howards End furniture has all gone to Oniton."

" Does — However, I'm concerned with the house, not the furniture. How big is this smoking-room?"

" Thirty by fifteen. No, wait a minute. Fifteen and a half."

" Ah, well. Mr. Wilcox, aren't you ever amused at the solemnity with which we middle classes approach the subject of houses?"

They proceeded to the drawing-room. Chelsea managed better here. It was sallow and ineffective.

One could visualize the ladies withdrawing to it, while their lords discussed life's realities below, to the accompaniment of cigars. Had Mrs. Wilcox's drawing-room looked thus at Howards End? Just as this thought entered Margaret's brain, Mr. Wilcox did ask her to be his wife, and the knowledge that she had been right so overcame her that she nearly fainted.

But the proposal was not to rank among the world's great love scenes.

"Miss Schlegel"—his voice was firm—"I have had you up on false pretences. I want to speak about a much more serious matter than a house."

Margaret almost answered: "I know—"

"Could you be induced to share my—is it probable—"

"Oh, Mr. Wilcox!" she interrupted, holding the piano and averting her eyes. "I see, I see. I will write to you afterwards if I may."

He began to stammer. "Miss Schlegel—Margaret—you don't understand."

"Oh yes! Indeed, yes!" said Margaret.

"I am asking you to be my wife."

So deep already was her sympathy, that when he said, "I am asking you to be my wife," she made herself give a little start. She must show surprise if he expected it. An immense joy came over her. It was indescribable. It had nothing to do with humanity, and most resembled the all-pervading happiness of fine weather. Fine weather is due to the sun, but Margaret could think of no central radiance here. She stood in his drawing-room happy, and longing to give happiness. On leaving him she realized that the central radiance had been love.

"You aren't offended, Miss Schlegel?"

"How could I be offended?"

There was a moment's pause. He was anxious to get rid of her, and she knew it. She had too much intuition to look at him as he struggled for possessions that money cannot buy. He desired comradeship and affection, but he feared them, and she, who had taught herself only to desire, and could have clothed the struggle with beauty, held back, and hesitated with him.

" Good-bye," she continued. " You will have a letter from me — I am going back to Swanage tomorrow."

" Thank you."

" Good-bye, and it's you I thank."

" I may order the motor round, mayn't I?"

" That would be most kind."

" I wish I had written instead. Ought I to have written?"

" Not at all."

" There's just one question —"

She shook her head. He looked a little bewildered, and they parted.

They parted without shaking hands: she had kept the interview, for his sake, in tints of the quietest grey. Yet she thrilled with happiness ere she reached her own house. Others had loved her in the past, if one may apply to their brief desires so grave a word, but those others had been " ninnies "— young men who had nothing to do, old men who could find nobody better. And she had often " loved," too, but only so far as the facts of sex demanded: mere yearnings for the masculine, to be dismissed for what they were worth, with a smile. Never before had her personality been touched. She was not young or very rich, and it amazed her that a man of any standing should take her seriously. As she sat trying to do accounts in her empty house, amidst beautiful pictures and noble books, waves of emotion broke, as if a tide of passion was flowing through the night air. She shook her head, tried to concentrate her attention, and failed. In vain did she repeat: "But I've been through this sort of thing before." She had never been through it; the big machinery, as opposed to the little, had been set in motion, and the idea that Mr. Wilcox loved, obsessed her before she came to love him in return.

She would come to no decision yet. "Oh, sir, this is so sudden "—that prudish phrase exactly expressed her when her time came. Premonitions are not preparation. She must examine more closely her own nature and his; she must talk it over judicially with Helen. It had been a strange love-scene — the central radiance unacknowledged from first to last. She, in his place, would have said "Ich liebe dich," but perhaps it was not his habit to open the heart. He might have done it if she had pressed him — as a matter of duty, perhaps; England expects every man to open his heart once; but the effort would have jarred him, and never, if she could avoid it, should he lose those defences that he had chosen to raise against the world. He must never be bothered with emotional talk, or with a display of sympathy. He was an elderly man now, and it would be futile and impudent to correct him.

Mrs. Wilcox strayed in and out, ever a welcome ghost; surveying the scene, thought Margaret, without one hint of bitterness.

Chapter XIX

IF one wanted to show a foreigner England, perhaps the wisest course would be to take him to the final section of the Purbeck Hills, and stand him on their summit, a few miles to the east of Corfe. Then system after system of our island would roll together under his feet. Beneath him is the valley of the Frome, and all the wild lands that come tossing down from Dorchester, black and gold, to mirror their gorse in the expanses of Poole. The valley of the Stour is beyond, unaccountable stream, dirty at Blandford, pure at Wimborne — the Stour, sliding out of fat fields, to marry the Avon beneath the tower of Christchurch. The valley of the Avon — invisible, but far to the north the trained eye may see Clearbury Ring that guards it, and the imagination may leap beyond that on to Salisbury Plain itself, and beyond the Plain to all the glorious downs of Central England. Nor is Suburbia absent. Bournemouth's ignoble coast cowers to the right, heralding the pine-trees that mean, for all their beauty, red houses, and the Stock Exchange, and extend to the gates of London itself. So tremendous is the City's trail! But the cliffs of Freshwater it shall never touch, and the island will guard the Island's purity till the end of time. Seen from the west, the Wight is beautiful beyond all laws of beauty. It is as if a fragment of England floated forward to greet the foreigner — chalk of our chalk, turf of our turf, epitome of what will follow. And behind the fragment lies Southampton, hostess to the nations, and Portsmouth, a latent fire, and all around it, with double and treble collision of tides, swirls the sea. How many villages appear in this view! How many castles! How many churches, vanished or triumphant! How many ships, railways, and roads! What incredible variety of men working beneath that lucent sky to what final end! The reason fails, like a wave on the Swanage beach; the imagination swells, spreads, and deepens, until it becomes geographic and encircles England.

So Frieda Mosebach, now Frau Architect Liesecke, and mother to her husband's baby, was brought up to these heights to be impressed, and, after a prolonged gaze, she said that the hills were more swelling here than in Pomerania, which was true, but did not seem to Mrs. Munt apposite. Poole Harbour was dry, which led her to praise the absence of muddy foreshore at Friedrich Wilhelms Bad, Rügen, where beech-trees hang over the tideless Baltic, and cows may contemplate the brine. Rather unhealthy Mrs. Munt thought this would be, water being safer when it moved about.

"And your English lakes — Vindermere, Grasmere — are they, then, unhealthy?"

"No, Frau Liesecke; but that is because they are fresh water, and different. Salt water ought to have tides, and go up and down a great deal, or else it smells. Look, for instance, at an aquarium."

"An aquarium! Oh, *Meesis* Munt, you mean to tell me that fresh aquariums stink less than salt? Why, when Victor, my brother-in-law, collected many tadpoles —"

"You are not to say 'stink,'" interrupted Helen; "at least, you may say it, but you must pretend you are being funny while you say it."

"Then 'smell.' And the mud of your Pool down there — does it not smell, or may I say 'stink, ha, ha'?"

"There always has been mud in Poole Harbour," said Mrs. Munt, with a slight frown. "The rivers bring it down, and a most valuable oyster-fishery depends upon it."

"Yes, that is so," conceded Frieda; and another international incident was closed.

"'Bournemouth is,'" resumed their hostess, quoting a local rhyme to which she was much attached — "'Bournemouth is, Poole was, and Swanage is to be the most important town of all and biggest of the three.' Now, Frau Liesecke, I have shown you Bournemouth, and I have shown you Poole, so let us walk backward a little, and look down again at Swanage."

"Aunt Juley, wouldn't that be Meg's train?"

A tiny puff of smoke had been circling the harbour, and now was bearing southwards towards them over the black and the gold.

"Oh, dearest Margaret, I do hope she won't be overtired."

"Oh, I do wonder — I do wonder whether she's taken the house."

"I hope she hasn't been hasty."

"So do I — oh, *so* do I."

"Will it be as beautiful as Wickham Place?" Frieda asked.

"I should think it would. Trust Mr. Wilcox for doing himself proud. All those Ducie Street houses are beautiful in their modern way, and I can't think why he doesn't keep on with it. But it's really for Evie that he went there, and now that Evie's going to be married —"

"Ah!"

"You've never seen Miss Wilcox, Frieda. How absurdly matrimonial you are!"

"But sister to that Paul?"

" Yes."

" And to that Charles," said Mrs. Munt with feeling. " Oh, Helen, Helen, what a time that was! "

Helen laughed. " Meg and I haven't got such tender hearts. If there's a chance of a cheap house, we go for it."

" Now look, Frau Liesecke, at my niece's train. You see, it is coming towards us — coming, coming; and, when it gets to Corfe, it will actually go *through* the downs, on which we are standing, so that, if we walk over, as I suggested, and look down on Swanage, we shall see it coming on the other side. Shall we? "

Frieda assented, and in a few minutes they had crossed the ridge and exchanged the greater view for the lesser. Rather a dull valley lay below, backed by the slope of the coastward downs. They were looking across the Isle of Purbeck and on to Swanage, soon to be the most important town of all, and ugliest of the three. Margaret's train reappeared as promised, and was greeted with approval by her aunt. It came to a standstill in the middle distance, and there it had been planned that Tibby should meet her, and drive her, and a tea-basket, up to join them.

" You see," continued Helen to her cousin, " the Wilcoxes collect houses as your Victor collects tadpoles. They have, one, Ducie Street; two, Howards End, where my great rumpus was; three, a country seat in Shropshire; four, Charles has a house in Hilton; and five, another near Epsom; and six, Evie will have a house when she marries, and probably a pied-à-terre in the country — which makes seven. Oh yes, and Paul a hut in Africa makes eight. I wish we could get Howards End. That was something like a dear little house! Didn't you think so, Aunt Juley? "

" I had too much to do, dear, to look at it," said Mrs. Munt, with a gracious dignity. " I had everything to settle and explain, and Charles Wilcox to keep in his place besides. It isn't likely I should remember much. I just remember having lunch in your bedroom."

"Yes, so do I. But, oh dear, dear, how dead it all seems! And in the autumn there began this anti-Pauline movement — you, and Frieda, and Meg, and Mrs. Wilcox, all obsessed with the idea that I might yet marry Paul."

"You yet may," said Frieda despondently.

Helen shook her head. "The Great Wilcox Peril will never return. If I'm certain of anything it's of that."

"One is certain of nothing but the truth of one's own emotions."

The remark fell damply on the conversation. But Helen slipped her arm round her cousin, somehow liking her the better for making it. It was not an original remark, nor had Frieda appropriated it passionately, for she had a patriotic rather than a philosophic mind. Yet it betrayed that interest in the universal which the average Teuton possesses and the average Englishman does not. It was, however illogically, the good, the beautiful, the true, as opposed to the respectable, the pretty, the adequate. It was a landscape of Böcklin's beside a landscape of Leader's, strident and ill-considered, but quivering into supernatural life. It sharpened idealism, stirred the soul. It may have been a bad preparation for what followed.

"Look!" cried Aunt Juley, hurrying away from generalities over the narrow summit of the down. "Stand where I stand, and you will see the pony-cart coming. I see the pony-cart coming."

They stood and saw the pony-cart coming. Margaret and Tibby were presently seen coming in it. Leaving the outskirts of Swanage, it drove for a little through the budding lanes, and then began the ascent.

"Have you got the house?" they shouted, long before she could possibly hear.

Helen ran down to meet her. The highroad passed over a saddle, and a track went thence at right angles along the ridge of the down.

"Have you got the house?"

Margaret shook her head.

"Oh, what a nuisance! So we're as we were?"

"Not exactly."

She got out, looking tired.

"Some mystery," said Tibby. "We are to be enlightened presently."

Margaret came close up to her and whispered that she had had a proposal of marriage from Mr. Wilcox.

Helen was amused. She opened the gate on to the downs so that her brother might lead the pony through. "It's just like a widower," she remarked. "They've cheek enough for anything, and invariably select one of their first wife's friends."

Margaret's face flashed despair.

"That type —" She broke off with a cry. "Meg, not anything wrong with you?"

"Wait one minute," said Margaret, whispering always.

"But you've never conceivably — you've never —" She pulled herself together. "Tibby, hurry up through; I can't hold this gate indefinitely. Aunt Juley! I say, Aunt Juley, make the tea, will you, and Frieda; we've got to talk houses, and'll come on afterwards." And then, turning her face to her sister's, she burst into tears.

Margaret was stupefied. She heard herself saying, "Oh, really —" She felt herself touched with a hand that trembled.

"Don't," sobbed Helen, "don't, don't, Meg, don't!" She seemed incapable of saying any other word. Margaret, trembling herself, led her forward up the road,

till they strayed through another gate on to the down.
"Don't, don't do such a thing! I tell you not to —
don't! I know — don't!"

"What do you know?"

"Panic and emptiness," sobbed Helen. "Don't!"

Then Margaret thought, "Helen is a little selfish.
I have never behaved like this when there has seemed
a chance of her marrying." She said: "But we
would still see each other very often, and —"

"It's not a thing like that," sobbed Helen. And she
broke right away and wandered distractedly upwards,
stretching her hands towards the view and crying.

"What's happened to you?" called Margaret, following through the wind that gathers at sundown on
the northern slopes of hills. "But it's stupid!" And
suddenly stupidity seized her, and the immense landscape was blurred. But Helen turned back.

"Meg —"

"I don't know what's happened to either of us,"
said Margaret, wiping her eyes. "We must both have
gone mad." Then Helen wiped hers, and they even
laughed a little.

"Look here, sit down."

"All right; I'll sit down if you'll sit down."

"There. (One kiss.) Now, whatever, whatever
is the matter?"

"I do mean what I said. Don't; it wouldn't do."

"Oh, Helen, stop saying 'don't'! It's ignorant.
It's as if your head wasn't out of the slime. 'Don't'
is probably what Mrs. Bast says all the day to Mr.
Bast."

Helen was silent.

"Well?"

"Tell me about it first, and meanwhile perhaps I'll
have got my head out of the slime."

"That's better. Well, where shall I begin? When
I arrived at Waterloo — no, I'll go back before that,

because I'm anxious you should know everything from the first. The 'first' was about ten days ago. It was the day Mr. Bast came to tea and lost his temper. I was defending him, and Mr. Wilcox became jealous about me, however slightly. I thought it was the involuntary thing, which men can't help any more than we can. You know — at least, I know in my own case — when a man has said to me, 'So-and-so's a pretty girl,' I am seized with a momentary sourness against So-and-so, and long to tweak her ear. It's a tiresome feeling, but not an important one, and one easily manages it. But it wasn't only this in Mr. Wilcox's case, I gather now."

"Then you love him?"

Margaret considered. "It is wonderful knowing that a real man cares for you," she said. "The mere fact of that grows more tremendous. Remember, I've known and liked him steadily for nearly three years."

"But loved him?"

Margaret peered into her past. It is pleasant to analyze feelings while they are still only feelings, and unembodied in the social fabric. With her arm round Helen, and her eyes shifting over the view, as if this county or that could reveal the secret of her own heart, she meditated honestly, and said, "No."

"But you will?"

"Yes," said Margaret, "of that I'm pretty sure. Indeed, I began the moment he spoke to me."

"And have settled to marry him?"

"I had, but am wanting a long talk about it now. What *is* it against him, Helen? You must try and say."

Helen, in her turn, looked outwards. "It is ever since Paul," she said finally.

"But what has Mr. Wilcox to do with Paul?"

"But he was there, they were all there that morning when I came down to breakfast, and saw that Paul was frightened — the man who loved me frightened and all his paraphernalia fallen, so that I knew it was impossible, because personal relations are the important thing for ever and ever, and not this outer life of telegrams and anger."

She poured the sentence forth in one breath, but her sister understood it, because it touched on thoughts that were familiar between them.

" That's foolish. In the first place, I disagree about the outer life. Well, we've often argued that. The real point is that there is the widest gulf between my love-making and yours. Yours was romance; mine will be prose. I'm not running it down — a very good kind of prose, but well considered, well thought out. For instance, I know all Mr. Wilcox's faults. He's afraid of emotion. He cares too much about success, too little about the past. His sympathy lacks poetry, and so isn't sympathy really. I'd even say "— she looked at the shining lagoons —" that, spiritually, he's not as honest as I am. Doesn't that satisfy you? "

" No, it doesn't," said Helen. " It makes me feel worse and worse. You must be mad."

Margaret made a movement of irritation.

" I don't intend him, or any man or any woman, to be all my life — good heavens, no! There are heaps of things in me that he doesn't, and shall never, understand."

Thus she spoke before the wedding ceremony and the physical union, before the astonishing glass shade had fallen that interposes between married couples and the world. She was to keep her independence more than do most women as yet. Marriage was to alter her fortunes rather than her character, and she was not far wrong in boasting that she understood her future husband. Yet he did alter her character — a little. There was an unforeseen surprise, a cessation of the winds and odours of life, a social pressure that would have her think conjugally.

"So with him," she continued. "There are heaps of things in him — more especially things that he does — that will always be hidden from me. He has all those public qualities which you so despise and enable all this —" She waved her hand at the landscape, which confirmed anything. "If Wilcoxes hadn't worked and died in England for thousands of years, you and I couldn't sit here without having our throats cut. There would be no trains, no ships to carry us literary people about in, no fields even. Just savagery. No — perhaps not even that. Without their spirit life might never have moved out of protoplasm. More and more do I refuse to draw my income and sneer at those who guarantee it. There are times when it seems to me —"

"And to me, and to all women. So one kissed Paul."

"That's brutal," said Margaret. "Mine is an absolutely different case. I've thought things out."

"It makes no difference thinking things out. They come to the same."

"Rubbish!"

There was a long silence, during which the tide returned into Poole Harbour. "One would lose something," murmured Helen, apparently to herself. The water crept over the mud-flats towards the gorse and the blackened heather. Branksea Island lost its immense foreshores, and became a sombre episode of trees. Frome was forced inward towards Dorchester, Stour against Wimborne, Avon towards Salisbury, and over the immense displacement the sun presided, leading it to triumph ere he sank to rest. England was alive, throbbing through all her estuaries, crying for joy through the mouths of all her gulls, and the north wind, with contrary motion, blew stronger against her rising seas. What did it mean? For what end are her fair complexities, her changes of soil, her sinuous coast? Does she belong to those who have moulded her and made her feared by other lands, or to those who have added nothing to her power, but have somehow seen her, seen the whole island at once, lying as a jewel in a silver sea, sailing as a ship of souls, with all the brave world's fleet accompanying her towards eternity?

Chapter XX

MARGARET had often wondered at the disturbance that takes place in the world's waters, when Love, who seems so tiny a pebble, slips in. Whom does Love concern beyond the beloved and the lover? Yet his impact deluges a hundred shores. No doubt the disturbance is really the spirit of the generations, welcoming the new generation, and chafing against the ultimate Fate, who holds all the seas in the palm of her hand. But Love cannot understand this. He cannot comprehend another's infinity; he is conscious only of his own — flying sunbeam, falling rose, pebble that asks for one quiet plunge below the fretting interplay of space and time. He knows that he will survive at the end of things, and be gathered by Fate as a jewel from the slime, and be handed with admiration round the assembly of the gods. "Men did produce this," they will say, and, saying, they will give men immortality. But meanwhile — what agitations meanwhile! The foundations of Property and Propriety are laid bare, twin rocks; Family Pride flounders to the surface, puffing and blowing, and refusing to be comforted; Theology, vaguely ascetic, gets up a nasty ground swell. Then the lawyers are aroused — cold brood — and creep out of their holes. They do what they can; they tidy up Property and Propriety, reassure Theology and Family Pride. Half-guineas are poured on the troubled waters, the lawyers creep back, and, if all has gone well, Love joins one man and woman together in Matrimony.

Margaret had expected the disturbance, and was not irritated by it. For a sensitive woman she had steady nerves, and could bear with the incongruous and the grotesque; and, besides, there was nothing excessive about her love-affair. Good-humour was the dominant note of her relations with Mr. Wilcox, or, as I must now call him, Henry. Henry did not encourage romance, and she was no girl to fidget for it. An acquaintance had become a lover, might become a husband, but would retain all that she had noted in the acquaintance; and love must confirm an old relation rather than reveal a new one.

In this spirit she promised to marry him.

He was in Swanage on the morrow, bearing the engagement-ring. They greeted one another with a hearty cordiality that impressed Aunt Juley. Henry dined at The Bays, but had engaged a bedroom in the principal hotel: he was one of those men who know the principal hotel by instinct. After dinner he asked Margaret if she wouldn't care for a turn on the Parade. She accepted, and could not repress a little tremor; it would be her first real love scene. But as she put on her hat she burst out laughing. Love was so unlike the article served up in books: the joy, though genuine, was different; the mystery an unexpected mystery. For one thing, Mr. Wilcox still seemed a stranger.

For a time they talked about the ring; then she said:
" Do you remember the Embankment at Chelsea? It can't be ten days ago."

" Yes," he said, laughing. " And you and your sister were head and ears deep in some Quixotic scheme. Ah well!"

" I little thought then, certainly. Did you?"

" I don't know about that; I shouldn't like to say."

" Why, was it earlier?" she cried. " Did you think of me this way earlier! How extraordinarily interesting, Henry! Tell me."

But Henry had no intention of telling. Perhaps he could not have told, for his mental states became obscure as soon as he had passed through them. He misliked the very word "interesting," connoting it with wasted energy and even with morbidity. Hard facts were enough for him.

"I didn't think of it," she pursued. "No; when you spoke to me in the drawing-room, that was practically the first. It was all so different from what it's supposed to be. On the stage, or in books, a proposal is — how shall I put it? — a full-blown affair, a kind of bouquet; it loses its literal meaning. But in life a proposal really is a proposal —"

"By the way —"

"— a suggestion, a seed," she concluded; and the thought flew away into darkness.

"I was thinking, if you didn't mind, that we ought to spend this evening in a business talk; there will be so much to settle."

"I think so too. Tell me, in the first place, how did you get on with Tibby?"

"With your brother?"

"Yes, during cigarettes."

"Oh, very well."

"I am so glad," she answered, a little surprised. "What did you talk about? Me, presumably."

"About Greece too."

"Greece was a very good card, Henry. Tibby's only a boy still, and one has to pick and choose subjects a little. Well done."

"I was telling him I have shares in a currant-farm near Calamata."

"What a delightful thing to have shares in! Can't we go there for our honeymoon?"

"What to do?"

"To eat the currants. And isn't there marvellous scenery?"

" Moderately, but it's not the kind of place one could possibly go to with a lady."

" Why not? "

" No hotels."

" Some ladies do without hotels. Are you aware that Helen and I have walked alone over the Apennines, with our luggage on our backs? "

" I wasn't aware, and, if I can manage it, you will never do such a thing again."

She said more gravely: " You haven't found time for a talk with Helen yet, I suppose? "

" No."

" Do, before you go. I am so anxious you two should be friends."

" Your sister and I have always hit it off," he said negligently. " But we're drifting away from our business. Let me begin at the beginning. You know that Evie is going to marry Percy Cahill."

" Dolly's uncle."

" Exactly. The girl's madly in love with him. A very good sort of fellow, but he demands — and rightly — a suitable provision with her. And in the second place, you will naturally understand, there is Charles. Before leaving town, I wrote Charles a very careful letter. You see, he has an increasing family and increasing expenses, and the I. and W. A. is nothing particular just now, though capable of development."

" Poor fellow! " murmured Margaret, looking out to sea, and not understanding.

" Charles being the elder son, some day Charles will have Howards End; but I am anxious, in my own happiness, not to be unjust to others."

" Of course not," she began, and then gave a little cry. " You mean money. How stupid I am! Of course not! "

Oddly enough, he winced a little at the word. " Yes.

Money, since you put it so frankly. I am determined to be just to all — just to you, just to them. I am determined that my children shall have no case against me."

" Be generous to them," she said sharply. " Bother justice ! "

" I am determined — and have already written to Charles to that effect —"

" But how much have you got ? "

" What ? "

" How much have you a year ? I've six hundred."

" My income ? "

" Yes. We must begin with how much you have, before we can settle how much you can give Charles. Justice, and even generosity, depend on that."

" I must say you're a downright young woman," he observed, patting her arm and laughing a little. " What a question to spring on a fellow ! "

" Don't you know your income ? Or don't you want to tell it me ? "

" I —"

" That's all right "— now she patted him —" don't tell me. I don't want to know. I can do the sum just as well by proportion. Divide your income into ten parts. How many parts would you give to Evie, how many to Charles, how many to Paul ? "

" The fact is, my dear, I hadn't any intention of bothering you with details. I only wanted to let you know that — well, that something must be done for the others, and you've understood me perfectly, so let's pass on to the next point."

" Yes, we've settled that," said Margaret, undisturbed by his strategic blunderings. " Go ahead ; give away all you can, bearing in mind I've a clear six hundred. What a mercy it is to have all this money about one ! "

"We've none too much, I assure you; you're marrying a poor man."

"Helen wouldn't agree with me here," she continued. "Helen daren't slang the rich, being rich herself, but she would like to. There's an odd notion, that I haven't yet got hold of, running about at the back of her brain, that poverty is somehow 'real.' She dislikes all organization, and probably confuses wealth with the technique of wealth. Sovereigns in a stocking wouldn't bother her; cheques do. Helen is too relentless. One can't deal in her high-handed manner with the world."

"There's this other point, and then I must go back to my hotel and write some letters. What's to be done now about the house in Ducie Street?"

"Keep it on — at least, it depends. When do you want to marry me?"

She raised her voice, as too often, and some youths, who were also taking the evening air, overheard her. "Getting a bit hot, eh?" said one. Mr. Wilcox turned on them, and said sharply, "I say!" There was silence. "Take care I don't report you to the police." They moved away quietly enough, but were only biding their time, and the rest of the conversation was punctuated by peals of ungovernable laughter.

Lowering his voice and infusing a hint of reproof into it, he said: "Evie will probably be married in September. We could scarcely think of anything before then."

"The earlier the nicer, Henry. Females are not supposed to say such things, but the earlier the nicer."

"How about September for us too?" he asked, rather dryly.

"Right. Shall we go into Ducie Street ourselves in September? Or shall we try to bounce Helen and Tibby into it? That's rather an idea. They are so unbusinesslike, we could make them do anything by judicious management. Look here — yes. We'll do that. And we ourselves could live at Howards End or Shropshire."

He blew out his cheeks. "Heavens! how you women do fly round! My head's in a whirl. Point by point, Margaret. Howards End's impossible. I let it to Hamar Bryce on a three years' agreement last March. Don't you remember? Oniton. Well, that is much, much too far away to rely on entirely. You will be able to be down there entertaining a certain amount, but we must have a house within easy reach of Town. Only Ducie Street has huge drawbacks. There's a mews behind."

Margaret could not help laughing. It was the first she had heard of the mews behind Ducie Street. When she was a possible tenant it had suppressed itself, not consciously, but automatically. The breezy Wilcox manner, though genuine, lacked the clearness of vision that is imperative for truth. When Henry lived in Ducie Street he remembered the mews; when he tried to let he forgot it; and if any one had remarked that the mews must be either there or not, he would have felt annoyed, and afterwards have found some opportunity of stigmatizing the speaker as academic. So does my grocer stigmatize me when I complain of the quality of his sultanas, and he answers in one breath that they are the best sultanas, and how can I expect the best sultanas at that price? It is a flaw inherent in the business mind, and Margaret may do well to be tender to it, considering all that the business mind has done for England.

" Yes, in summer especially, the mews is a serious nuisance. The smoking-room, too, is an abominable little den. The house opposite has been taken by operatic people. Ducie Street's going down, it's my private opinion."

"How sad! It's only a few years since they built those pretty houses."

"Shows things are moving. Good for trade."

"I hate this continual flux of London. It is an epitome of us at our worst — eternal formlessness; all the qualities, good, bad, and indifferent, streaming away — streaming, streaming for ever. That's why I dread it so. I mistrust rivers, even in scenery. Now, the sea —"

"High tide, yes."

"Hoy toid "— from the promenading youths.

"And these are the men to whom we give the vote," observed Mr. Wilcox, omitting to add that they were also the men to whom he gave work as clerks — work that scarcely encouraged them to grow into other men. "However, they have their own lives and interests. Let's get on."

He turned as he spoke, and prepared to see her back to The Bays. The business was over. His hotel was in the opposite direction, and if he accompanied her his letters would be late for the post. She implored him not to come, but he was obdurate.

"A nice beginning, if your aunt saw you slip in alone!"

"But I always do go about alone. Considering I've walked over the Apennines, it's common sense. You will make me so angry. I don't the least take it as a compliment."

He laughed, and lit a cigar. "It isn't meant as a compliment, my dear. I just won't have you going about in the dark. Such people about too! It's dangerous."

"Can't I look after myself? I do wish —"

"Come along, Margaret; no wheedling."

A younger woman might have resented his masterly ways, but Margaret had too firm a grip of life to make a fuss. She was, in her own way, as masterly. If he was a fortress she was a mountain peak, whom all might tread, but whom the snows made nightly virginal. Disdaining the heroic outfit, excitable in her methods, garrulous, episodical, shrill, she misled her lover much as she had misled her aunt. He mistook her fertility for weakness. He supposed her "as clever as they make 'em," but no more, not realizing that she was penetrating to the depths of his soul, and approving of what she found there.

And if insight were sufficient, if the inner life were the whole of life, their happiness has been assured.

They walked ahead briskly. The parade and the road after it were well lighted, but it was darker in Aunt Juley's garden. As they were going up by the side-paths, through some rhododendrons, Mr. Wilcox, who was in front, said "Margaret" rather huskily, turned, dropped his cigar, and took her in his arms.

She was startled, and nearly screamed, but recovered herself at once, and kissed with genuine love the lips that were pressed against her own. It was their first kiss, and when it was over he saw her safely to the door and rang the bell for her, but disappeared into the night before the maid answered it. On looking back, the incident displeased her. It was so isolated. Nothing in their previous conversation had heralded it, and, worse still, no tenderness had ensued. If a man cannot lead up to passion he can at all events lead down from it, and she had hoped, after her complaisance, for some interchange of gentle words. But he had hurried away as if ashamed, and for an instant she was reminded of Helen and Paul.

Chapter XXI

CHARLES had just been scolding his Dolly. She deserved the scolding, and had bent before it, but her head, though bloody, was unsubdued, and her chirrupings began to mingle with his retreating thunder.

"You've woken the baby. I knew you would. (Rum-ti-foo, Rackety-tackety-Tompkin!) I'm not responsible for what Uncle Percy does, nor for anybody else or anything, so there!"

"Who asked him while I was away? Who asked my sister down to meet him? Who sent them out in the motor day after day?"

"Charles, that reminds me of some poem."

"Does it indeed? We shall all be dancing to a very different music presently. Miss Schlegel has fairly got us on toast."

"I could simply scratch that woman's eyes out, and to say it's my fault is most unfair."

"It's your fault, and five months ago you admitted it."

"I didn't."

"You did."

"Tootle, tootle, playing on the pootle!" exclaimed Dolly, suddenly devoting herself to the child.

"It's all very well to turn the conversation, but father would never have dreamt of marrying as long as Evie was there to make him comfortable. But you must needs start match-making. Besides, Cahill's too old."

"Of course, if you're going to be rude to Uncle Percy —"

"Miss Schlegel always meant to get hold of Howards End, and, thanks to you, she's got it."

"I call the way you twist things round and make them hang together most unfair. You couldn't have been nastier if you'd caught me flirting. Could he, diddums?"

"We're in a bad hole, and must make the best of it. I shall answer the pater's letter civilly. He's evidently anxious to do the decent thing. But I do not intend to forget these Schlegels in a hurry. As long as they're on their best behaviour — Dolly, are you listening? — we'll behave, too. But if I find them giving themselves airs, or monopolizing my father, or at all ill-treating him, or worrying him with their artistic beastliness, I intend to put my foot down, yes, firmly. Taking my mother's place! Heaven knows what poor old Paul will say when the news reaches him."

The interlude closes. It has taken place in Charles's garden at Hilton. He and Dolly are sitting in deck-chairs, and their motor is regarding them placidly from its garage across the lawn. A short-frocked edition of Charles also regards them placidly; a perambulator edition is squeaking; a third edition is expected shortly. Nature is turning out Wilcoxes in this peaceful abode, so that they may inherit the earth.

Chapter XXII

MARGARET greeted her lord with peculiar tenderness on the morrow. Mature as he was, she might yet be able to help him to the building of the rainbow bridge that should connect the prose in us with the passion. Without it we are meaningless fragments, half monks, half beasts, unconnected arches that have never joined into a man. With it love is born, and alights on the highest curve, glowing against the grey, sober against the fire. Happy the man who sees from either aspect the glory of these outspread wings. The roads of his soul lie clear, and he and his friends shall find easy-going.

It was hard-going in the roads of Mr. Wilcox's soul. From boyhood he had neglected them. "I am not a fellow who bothers about my own inside." Outwardly he was cheerful, reliable, and brave; but within, all had reverted to chaos, ruled, so far as it was ruled at all, by an incomplete asceticism. Whether as boy, husband, or widower, he had always the sneaking belief that bodily passion is bad, a belief that is desirable only when held passionately. Religion had confirmed him. The words that were read aloud on Sunday to him and to other respectable men were the words that had once kindled the souls of St. Catharine and St. Francis into a white-hot hatred of the carnal. He could not be as the saints and love the Infinite with a seraphic ardour, but he could be a little ashamed of loving a wife. "Amabat, amare timebat." And it was here that Margaret hoped to help him.

It did not seem so difficult. She need trouble him

with no gift of her own. She would only point out the salvation that was latent in his own soul, and in the soul of every man. Only connect! That was the whole of her sermon. Only connect the prose and the passion, and both will be exalted, and human love will be seen at its height. Live in fragments no longer. Only connect, and the beast and the monk, robbed of the isolation that is life to either, will die.

Nor was the message difficult to give. It need not take the form of a good "talking." By quiet indications the bridge would be built and span their lives with beauty.

But she failed. For there was one quality in Henry for which she was never prepared, however much she reminded herself of it: his obtuseness. He simply did not notice things, and there was no more to be said. He never noticed that Helen and Frieda were hostile, or that Tibby was not interested in currant plantations; he never noticed the lights and shades that exist in the greyest conversation, the finger-posts, the milestones, the collisions, the illimitable views. Once — on another occasion — she scolded him about it. He was puzzled, but replied with a laugh: "My motto is Concentrate. I've no intention of frittering away my strength on that sort of thing." "It isn't frittering away the strength," she protested. "It's enlarging the space in which you may be strong." He answered: "You're a clever little woman, but my motto's Concentrate." And this morning he concentrated with a vengeance.

They met in the rhododendrons of yesterday. In the daylight the bushes were inconsiderable and the path was bright in the morning sun. She was with Helen, who had been ominously quiet since the affair was settled. "Here we all are!" she cried, and took him by one hand, retaining her sister's in the other.

"Here we are. Good-morning, Helen."

Helen replied, "Good-morning, Mr. Wilcox."

"Henry, she has had such a nice letter from the queer, cross boy. Do you remember him? He had a sad moustache, but the back of his head was young."

"I have had a letter too. Not a nice one — I want to talk it over with you:" for Leonard Bast was nothing to him now that she had given him her word; the triangle of sex was broken for ever.

"Thanks to your hint, he's clearing out of the Porphyrion."

"Not a bad business that Porphyrion," he said absently, as he took his own letter out of his pocket.

"Not a *bad* —" she exclaimed, dropping his hand. "Surely, on Chelsea Embankment —"

"Here's our hostess. Good-morning, Mrs. Munt. Fine rhododendrons. Good-morning, Frau Liesecke; we manage to grow flowers in England, don't we?"

"Not a *bad* business?"

"No. My letter's about Howards End. Bryce has been ordered abroad, and wants to sublet it. I am far from sure that I shall give him permission. There was no clause in the agreement. In my opinion, subletting is a mistake. If he can find me another tenant, whom I consider suitable, I may cancel the agreement. Morning, Schlegel. Don't you think that's better than subletting?"

Helen had dropped her hand now, and he had steered her past the whole party to the seaward side of the house. Beneath them was the bourgeois little bay, which must have yearned all through the centuries for just such a watering-place as Swanage to be built on its margin. The waves were colourless, and the Bournemouth steamer gave a further touch of insipidity, drawn up against the pier and hooting wildly for excursionists.

"When there is a sublet I find that damage —"

"Do excuse me, but about the Porphyrion. I don't feel easy — might I just bother you, Henry?"

Her manner was so serious that he stopped, and asked her a little sharply what she wanted.

"You said on Chelsea Embankment, surely, that it was a bad concern, so we advised this clerk to clear out. He writes this morning that he's taken our advice, and now you say it's not a bad concern."

"A clerk who clears out of any concern, good or bad, without securing a berth somewhere else first, is a fool, and I've no pity for him."

"He has not done that. He's going into a bank in Camden Town, he says. The salary's much lower, but he hopes to manage — a branch of Dempster's Bank. Is that all right?"

"Dempster! My goodness me, yes."

"More right than the Porphyrion?"

"Yes, yes, yes; safe as houses — safer."

"Very many thanks. I'm sorry — if you sublet — ?"

"If he sublets, I shan't have the same control. In theory there should be no more damage done at Howards End; in practice there will be. Things may be done for which no money can compensate. For instance, I shouldn't want that fine wych-elm spoilt. It hangs — Margaret, we must go and see the old place some time. It's pretty in its way. We'll motor down and have lunch with Charles."

"I should enjoy that," said Margaret bravely.

"What about next Wednesday?"

"Wednesday? No, I couldn't well do that. Aunt Juley expects us to stop here another week at least."

"But you can give that up now."

"Er — no," said Margaret, after a moment's thought.

"Oh, that'll be all right. I'll speak to her."

"This visit is a high solemnity. My aunt counts on

it year after year. She turns the house upside down for us; she invites our special friends — she scarcely knows Frieda, and we can't leave her on her hands. I missed one day, and she would be so hurt if I didn't stay the full ten."

" But I'll say a word to her. Don't you bother."

" Henry, I won't go. Don't bully me."

" You want to see the house, though?"

" Very much — I've heard so much about it, one way or the other. Aren't there pigs' teeth in the wych-elm?"

" *Pigs' teeth?*"

" And you chew the bark for toothache."

" What a rum notion! Of course not!"

" Perhaps I have confused it with some other tree. There are still a great number of sacred trees in England, it seems."

But he left her to intercept Mrs. Munt, whose voice could be heard in the distance: to be intercepted himself by Helen.

" Oh, Mr. Wilcox, about the Porphyrion —" she began, and went scarlet all over her face.

" It's all right," called Margaret, catching them up. " Dempster's Bank's better."

" But I think you told us the Porphyrion was bad, and would smash before Christmas."

" Did I? It was still outside the Tariff Ring, and had to take rotten policies. Lately it came in — safe as houses now."

" In other words, Mr. Bast need never have left it."

" No, the fellow needn't."

" — and needn't have started life elsewhere at a greatly reduced salary."

" He only says ' reduced,' " corrected Margaret, seeing trouble ahead.

" With a man so poor, every reduction must be great. I consider it a deplorable misfortune."

Mr. Wilcox, intent on his business with Mrs. Munt, was going steadily on, but the last remark made him say: "What? What's that? Do you mean that I'm responsible?"

"You're ridiculous, Helen."

"You seem to think —" He looked at his watch. "Let me explain the point to you. It is like this. You seem to assume, when a business concern is conducting a delicate negotiation, it ought to keep the public informed stage by stage. The Porphyrion, according to you, was bound to say, 'I am trying all I can to get into the Tariff Ring. I am not sure that I shall succeed, but it is the only thing that will save me from insolvency, and I am trying.' My dear Helen —"

"Is that your point? A man who had little money has less — that's mine."

"I am grieved for your clerk. But it is all in the day's work. It's part of the battle of life."

"A man who had little money," she repeated, "has less, owing to us. Under these circumstances I do not consider 'the battle of life' a happy expression."

"Oh come, come!" he protested pleasantly. "You're not to blame. No one's to blame."

"Is no one to blame for anything?"

"I wouldn't say that, but you're taking it far too seriously. Who is this fellow?"

"We have told you about the fellow twice already," said Helen. "You have even met the fellow. He is very poor and his wife is an extravagant imbecile. He is capable of better things. We — we, the upper classes — thought we would help him from the height of our superior knowledge — and here's the result!"

He raised his finger. "Now, a word of advice."

"I require no more advice."

"A word of advice. Don't take up that sentimental

attitude over the poor. See that she doesn't, Margaret. The poor are poor, and one's sorry for them, but there it is. As civilization moves forward, the shoe is bound to pinch in places, and it's absurd to pretend that any one is responsible personally. Neither you, nor I, nor my informant, nor the man who informed him, nor the directors of the Porphyrion, are to blame for this clerk's loss of salary. It's just the shoe pinching — no one can help it; and it might easily have been worse."

Helen quivered with indignation.

" By all means subscribe to charities — subscribe to them largely — but don't get carried away by absurd schemes of Social Reform. I see a good deal behind the scenes, and you can take it from me that there is no Social Question — except for a few journalists who try to get a living out of the phrase. There are just rich and poor, as there always have been and always will be. Point me out a time when men have been equal —"

" I didn't say —"

" Point me out a time when desire for equality has made them happier. No, no. You can't. There always have been rich and poor. I'm no fatalist. Heaven forbid! But our civilization is moulded by great impersonal forces " (his voice grew complacent; it always did when he eliminated the personal), " and there always will be rich and poor. You can't deny it " (and now it was a respectful voice)—" and you can't deny that, in spite of all, the tendency of civilization has on the whole been upward."

" Owing to God, I suppose," flashed Helen.

He stared at her.

" You grab the dollars. God does the rest."

It was no good instructing the girl if she was going to talk about God in that neurotic modern way. Fraternal to the last, he left her for the quieter company of Mrs. Munt. He thought, " She rather reminds me of Dolly."

Helen looked out at the sea.

" Don't even discuss political economy with Henry," advised her sister. " It'll only end in a cry."

" But he must be one of those men who have reconciled science with religion," said Helen slowly. " I don't like those men. They are scientific themselves, and talk of the survival of the fittest, and cut down the salaries of their clerks, and stunt the independence of all who may menace their comfort, but yet they believe that somehow good — it is always that sloppy ' somehow '— will be the outcome, and that in some mystical way the Mr. Basts of the future will benefit because the Mr. Basts of today are in pain."

" He is such a man in theory. But oh, Helen, in theory ! "

" But oh, Meg, what a theory ! "

" Why should you put things so bitterly, dearie ? "

" Because I'm an old maid," said Helen, biting her lip. " I can't think why I go on like this myself." She shook off her sister's hand and went into the house. Margaret, distressed at the day's beginning, followed the Bournemouth steamer with her eyes. She saw that Helen's nerves were exasperated by the unlucky Bast business beyond the bounds of politeness. There might at any minute be a real explosion, which even Henry would notice. Henry must be removed.

" Margaret ! " her aunt called. " Magsy ! It isn't true, surely, what Mr. Wilcox says, that you want to go away early next week ? "

" Not ' want,' " was Margaret's prompt reply; " but there is so much to be settled, and I do want to see the Charles'."

" But going away without taking the Weymouth trip, or even the Lulworth ? " said Mrs. Munt, coming nearer. "Without going once more up Nine Barrows Down?"

"I'm afraid so."

Mr. Wilcox rejoined her with, "Good! I did the breaking of the ice."

A wave of tenderness came over her. She put a hand on either shoulder, and looked deeply into the black, bright eyes. What was behind their competent stare? She knew, but was not disquieted.

Chapter XXIII

MARGARET had no intention of letting things slide, and the evening before she left Swanage she gave her sister a thorough scolding. She censured her, not for disapproving of the engagement, but for throwing over her disapproval a veil of mystery. Helen was equally frank. " Yes," she said, with the air of one looking inwards, " there is a mystery. I can't help it. It's not my fault. It's the way life has been made." Helen in those days was over-interested in the subconscious self. She exaggerated the Punch and Judy aspect of life, and spoke of mankind as puppets, whom an invisible showman twitches into love and war. Margaret pointed out that if she dwelt on this she, too, would eliminate the personal. Helen was silent for a minute, and then burst into a queer speech, which cleared the air. " Go on and marry him. I think you're splendid; and if any one can pull it off, you will." Margaret denied that there was anything to " pull off," but she continued: " Yes, there is, and I wasn't up to it with Paul. I can only do what's easy. I can only entice and be enticed. I can't, and won't, attempt difficult relations. If I marry, it will either be a man who's strong enough to boss me or whom I'm strong enough to boss. So I shan't ever marry, for there aren't such men. And Heaven help any one whom I do marry, for I shall certainly run away from him before you can say ' Jack Robinson.' There! Because I'm uneducated. But you, you're different; you're a heroine."

"Oh, Helen! Am I? Will it be as dreadful for poor Henry as all that?"

"You mean to keep proportion, and that's heroic, it's Greek, and I don't see why it shouldn't succeed with you. Go on and fight with him and help him. Don't ask *me* for help, or even for sympathy. Henceforward I'm going my own way. I mean to be thorough, because thoroughness is easy. I mean to dislike your husband, and to tell him so. I mean to make no concessions to Tibby. If Tibby wants to live with me, he must lump me. I mean to love *you* more than ever. Yes, I do. You and I have built up something real, because it is purely spiritual. There's no veil of mystery over us. Unreality and mystery begin as soon as one touches the body. The popular view is, as usual, exactly the wrong one. Our bothers are over tangible things — money, husbands, house-hunting. But Heaven will work of itself."

Margaret was grateful for this expression of affection, and answered, "Perhaps." All vistas close in the unseen — no one doubts it — but Helen closed them rather too quickly for her taste. At every turn of speech one was confronted with reality and the absolute. Perhaps Margaret grew too old for metaphysics, perhaps Henry was weaning her from them, but she felt that there was something a little unbalanced in the mind that so readily shreds the visible. The business man who assumes that this life is everything, and the mystic who asserts that it is nothing, fail, on this side and on that, to hit the truth. "Yes, I see, dear; it's about halfway between," Aunt Juley had hazarded in earlier years. No; truth, being alive, was not halfway between anything. It was only to be found by continuous excursions into either realm, and though proportion is the final secret, to espouse it at the outset is to insure sterility.

Helen, agreeing here, disagreeing there, would have

talked till midnight, but Margaret, with her packing to do, focussed the conversation on Henry. She might abuse Henry behind his back, but please would she always be civil to him in company? " I definitely dislike him, but I'll do what I can," promised Helen. " Do what you can with my friends in return."

This conversation made Margaret easier. Their inner life was so safe that they could bargain over externals in a way that would have been incredible to Aunt Juley, and impossible for Tibby or Charles. There are moments when the inner life actually pays," when years of self-scrutiny, conducted for no ulterior motive, are suddenly of practical use. Such moments are still rare in the West; that they come at all promises a fairer future. Margaret, though unable to understand her sister, was assured against estrangement, and returned to London with a more peaceful mind.

The following morning, at eleven o'clock, she presented herself at the offices of the Imperial and West African Rubber Company. She was glad to go there, for Henry had implied his business rather than described it, and the formlessness and vagueness that one associates with Africa itself had hitherto brooded over the main sources of his wealth. Not that a visit to the office cleared things up. There was just the ordinary surface scum of ledgers and polished counters and brass bars that began and stopped for no possible reason, of electric-light globes blossoming in triplets, of little rabbit-hutches faced with glass or wire, of little rabbits. And even when she penetrated to the inner depths, she found only the ordinary table and Turkey carpet, and though the map over the fireplace did depict a helping of West Africa, it was a very ordinary map. Another map hung opposite, on which the whole continent appeared, looking like a whale marked out for blubber, and by its side was a door, shut, but Henry's voice came through it, dictating a " strong " letter. She might have been at the Porphyrion, or Dempster's Bank, or her own wine-merchant's. Everything seems just alike in these days. But perhaps she was seeing the Imperial side of the company rather than its West African, and Imperialism always had been one of her difficulties.

" One minute! " called Mr. Wilcox on receiving her name. He touched a bell, the effect of which was to produce Charles.

Charles had written his father an adequate letter — more adequate than Evie's, through which a girlish indignation throbbed. And he greeted his future stepmother with propriety.

" I hope that my wife — how do you do? — will give you a decent lunch," was his opening. " I left instructions, but we live in a rough-and-ready way. She expects you back to tea, too, after you have had a look at Howards End. I wonder what you'll think of the place. I wouldn't touch it with tongs myself. Do sit down! It's a measly little place."

" I shall enjoy seeing it," said Margaret, feeling, for the first time, shy.

" You'll see it at its worst, for Bryce decamped abroad last Monday without even arranging for a charwoman to clear up after him. I never saw such a disgraceful mess. It's unbelievable. He wasn't in the house a month."

" I've more than a little bone to pick with Bryce," called Henry from the inner chamber.

" Why did he go so suddenly? "

" Invalid type; couldn't sleep."

" Poor fellow! "

" Poor fiddlesticks! " said Mr. Wilcox, joining them. " He had the impudence to put up notice-boards without as much as saying with your leave or by your leave. Charles flung them down."

"Yes, I flung them down," said Charles modestly.

"I've sent a telegram after him, and a pretty sharp one, too. He, and he in person is responsible for the upkeep of that house for the next three years."

"The keys are at the farm; we wouldn't have the keys."

"Quite right."

"Dolly would have taken them, but I was in, fortunately."

"What's Mr. Bryce like?" asked Margaret.

But nobody cared. Mr. Bryce was the tenant, who had no right to sublet; to have defined him further was a waste of time. On his misdeeds they descanted profusely, until the girl who had been typing the strong letter came out with it. Mr. Wilcox added his signature. "Now we'll be off," said he.

A motor-drive, a form of felicity detested by Margaret, awaited her. Charles saw them in, civil to the last, and in a moment the offices of the Imperial and West African Rubber Company faded away. But it was not an impressive drive. Perhaps the weather was to blame, being grey and banked high with weary clouds. Perhaps Hertfordshire is scarcely intended for motorists. Did not a gentleman once motor so quickly through Westmoreland that he missed it? and if Westmoreland can be missed, it will fare ill with a county whose delicate structure particularly needs the attentive eye. Hertfordshire is England at its quietest, with little emphasis of river and hill; it is England meditative. If Drayton were with us again to write a new edition of his incomparable poem, he would sing the nymphs of Hertfordshire as indeterminate of feature, with hair obfuscated by the London smoke. Their eyes would be sad, and averted from their fate towards the Northern flats, their leader not Isis or Sabrina, but the slowly flowing Lea. No glory of raiment would be theirs, no urgency of dance; but they would be real nymphs.

The chauffeur could not travel as quickly as he had hoped, for the Great North Road was full of Easter traffic. But he went quite quick enough for Margaret, a poor-spirited creature, who had chickens and children on the brain.

"They're all right," said Mr. Wilcox. "They'll learn — like the swallows and the telegraph-wires."

"Yes, but, while they're learning —"

"The motor's come to stay," he answered. "One must get about. There's a pretty church — oh, you aren't sharp enough. Well, look out, if the road worries you — right outward at the scenery."

She looked at the scenery. It heaved and merged like porridge. Presently it congealed. They had arrived.

Charles's house on the left; on the right the swelling forms of the Six Hills. Their appearance in such a neighbourhood surprised her. They interrupted the stream of residences that was thickening up towards Hilton. Beyond them she saw meadows and a wood, and beneath them she settled that soldiers of the best kind lay buried. She hated war and liked soldiers — it was one of her amiable inconsistencies.

But here was Dolly, dressed up to the nines, standing at the door to greet them, and here were the first drops of the rain. They ran in gaily, and after a long wait in the drawing-room sat down to the rough-and-ready lunch, every dish in which concealed or exuded cream. Mr. Bryce was the chief topic of conversation. Dolly described his visit with the key, while her father-in-law gave satisfaction by chaffing her and contradicting all she said. It was evidently the custom to laugh at Dolly. He chaffed Margaret, too, and Margaret, roused from a grave meditation, was pleased, and chaffed him back. Dolly seemed surprised, and eyed her curiously. After lunch the two children came down. Margaret disliked babies, but hit it off better with the two-year-old, and sent Dolly into fits of laughter by talking sense to him. "Kiss them now, and come away," said Mr. Wilcox. She came, but refused to kiss them: it was such hard luck on the little things, she said, and though Dolly proffered Chorly-worly and Porgly-woggles in turn, she was obdurate.

By this time it was raining steadily. The car came round with the hood up, and again she lost all sense of space. In a few minutes they stopped, and Crane opened the door of the car.

"What's happened?" asked Margaret.

"What do you suppose?" said Henry.

A little porch was close up against her face.

"Are we there already?"

"We are."

"Well, I never! In years ago it seemed so far away."

Smiling, but somehow disillusioned, she jumped out, and her impetus carried her to the front-door. She was about to open it, when Henry said: "That's no good; it's locked. Who's got the key?"

As he had himself forgotten to call for the key at the farm, no one replied. He also wanted to know who had left the front gate open, since a cow had strayed in from the road, and was spoiling the croquet lawn. Then he said rather crossly: "Margaret, you wait in the dry. I'll go down for the key. It isn't a hundred yards."

"Mayn't I come too?"

"No; I shall be back before I'm gone."

Then the car turned away, and it was as if a curtain had risen. For the second time that day she saw the appearance of the earth.

There were the greengage-trees that Helen had once

described, there the tennis lawn, there the hedge that would be glorious with dog-roses in June, but the vision now was of black and palest green. Down by the dell-hole more vivid colours were awakening, and Lent Lilies stood sentinel on its margin, or advanced in battalions over the grass. Tulips were a tray of jewels. She could not see the wych-elm tree, but a branch of the celebrated vine, studded with velvet knobs, had covered the porch. She was struck by the fertility of the soil; she had seldom been in a garden where the flowers looked so well, and even the weeds she was idly plucking out of the porch were intensely green. Why had poor Mr. Bryce fled from all this beauty? For she had already decided that the place was beautiful.

"Naughty cow! Go away!" cried Margaret to the cow, but without indignation.

Harder came the rain, pouring out of a windless sky, and spattering up from the notice-boards of the house-agents, which lay in a row on the lawn where Charles had hurled them. She must have interviewed Charles in another world — where one did have interviews. How Helen would revel in such a notion! Charles dead, all people dead, nothing alive but houses and gardens. The obvious dead, the intangible alive, and — no connection at all between them! Margaret smiled. Would that her own fancies were as clear-cut! Would that she could deal as high-handedly with the world! Smiling and sighing, she laid her hand upon the door. It opened. The house was not locked up at all.

She hesitated. Ought she to wait for Henry? He felt strongly about property, and might prefer to show her over himself. On the other hand, he had told her to keep in the dry, and the porch was beginning to drip. So she went in, and the draught from inside slammed the door behind.

Desolation greeted her. Dirty finger-prints were on the hall-windows, flue and rubbish on its unwashed boards. The civilization of luggage had been here for a month, and then decamped. Dining-room and drawing-room — right and left — were guessed only by their wall-papers. They were just rooms where one could shelter from the rain. Across the ceiling of each ran a great beam. The dining-room and hall revealed theirs openly, but the drawing-room's was match-boarded — because the facts of life must be concealed from ladies? Drawing-room, dining-room, and hall — how petty the names sounded! Here were simply three rooms where children could play and friends shelter from the rain. Yes, and they were beautiful.

Then she opened one of the doors opposite — there were two — and exchanged wall-papers for white-wash. It was the servants' part, though she scarcely realized that: just rooms again, where friends might shelter. The garden at the back was full of flowering cherries and plums. Farther on were hints of the meadow and a black cliff of pines. Yes, the meadow was beautiful.

Penned in by the desolate weather, she recaptured the sense of space which the motor had tried to rob from her. She remembered again that ten square miles are not ten times as wonderful as one square mile, that a thousand square miles are not practically the same as heaven. The phantom of bigness, which London encourages, was laid for ever when she paced from the hall at Howards End to its kitchen and heard the rains run this way and that where the watershed of the roof divided them.

Now Helen came to her mind, scrutinizing half Wessex from the ridge of the Purbeck Downs, and saying: "You will have to lose something." She was not so sure. For instance, she would double her kingdom by opening the door that concealed the stairs.

Now she thought of the map of Africa; of empires; of her father; of the two supreme nations, streams of whose life warmed her blood, but, mingling, had cooled her brain. She paced back into the hall, and as she did so the house reverberated.

"Is that you, Henry?" she called.

There was no answer, but the house reverberated again.

"Henry, have you got in?"

But it was the heart of the house beating, faintly at first, then loudly, martially. It dominated the rain.

It is the starved imagination, not the well-nourished, that is afraid. Margaret flung open the door to the stairs. A noise as of drums seemed to deafen her. A woman, an old woman, was descending, with figure erect, with face impassive, with lips that parted and said dryly:

"Oh! Well, I took you for Ruth Wilcox."

Margaret stammered: "I— Mrs. Wilcox— I?"

"In fancy, of course— in fancy. You had her way of walking. Good-day." And the old woman passed out into the rain.

Chapter XXIV

"I T gave her quite a turn," said Mr. Wilcox, when retailing the incident to Dolly at tea-time. "None of you girls have any nerves, really. Of course, a word from me put it all right, but silly old Miss Avery — she frightened you, didn't she, Margaret? There you stood clutching a bunch of weeds. She might have said something, instead of coming down the stairs with that alarming bonnet on. I passed her as I came in. Enough to make the car shy. I believe Miss Avery goes in for being a character; some old maids do." He lit a cigarette. "It is their last resource. Heaven knows what she was doing in the place; but that's Bryce's business, not mine."

"I wasn't as foolish as you suggest," said Margaret. "She only startled me, for the house had been silent so long."

"Did you take her for a spook?" asked Dolly, for whom "spooks" and "going to church" summarized the unseen.

"Not exactly."

"She really did frighten you," said Henry, who was far from discouraging timidity in females. "Poor Margaret! And very naturally. Uneducated classes are so stupid."

"Is Miss Avery uneducated classes?" Margaret asked, and found herself looking at the decoration scheme of Dolly's drawing-room.

"She's just one of the crew at the farm. People like that always assume things. She assumed you'd know who she was. She left all the Howards End

—232—

keys in the front lobby, and assumed that you'd seen
them as you came in, that you'd lock up the house
when you'd done, and would bring them on down to
her. And there was her niece hunting for them down
at the farm. Lack of education makes people very
casual. Hilton was full of women like Miss Avery
once."

" I shouldn't have disliked it, perhaps."

" Or Miss Avery giving me a wedding present," said
Dolly.

Which was illogical but interesting. Through Dolly,
Margaret was destined to learn a good deal.

" But Charles said I must try not to mind, because
she had known his grandmother."

" As usual, you've got the story wrong, my good
Dorothea."

" I meant great-grandmother — the one who left
Mrs. Wilcox the house. Weren't both of them and
Miss Avery friends when Howards End, too, was a
farm?"

Her father-in-law blew out a shaft of smoke. His
attitude to his dead wife was curious. He would allude to her, and hear her discussed, but never mentioned her by name. Nor was he interested in the dim,
bucolic past. Dolly was — for the following reason.

" Then hadn't Mrs. Wilcox a brother — or was it an
uncle? Anyhow, he popped the question, and Miss
Avery, she said ' No.' Just imagine, if she'd said
' Yes,' she would have been Charles's aunt. (Oh, I
say, that's rather good! ' Charlie's Aunt'! I must
chaff him about that this evening.) And the man went
out and was killed. Yes, I'm certain I've got it right
now. Tom Howard — he was the last of them."

" I believe so," said Mr. Wilcox negligently.

" I say! Howards End — Howard's Ended!" cried
Dolly. " I'm rather on the spot this evening, eh?"

" I wish you'd ask whether Crane's ended."

"Oh, Mr. Wilcox, how *can* you?"

"Because, if he has had enough tea, we ought to go.— Dolly's a good little woman," he continued, "but a little of her goes a long way. I couldn't live near her if you paid me."

Margaret smiled. Though presenting a firm front to outsiders, no Wilcox could live near, or near the possessions of, any other Wilcox. They had the colonial spirit, and were always making for some spot where the white man might carry his burden unobserved. Of course, Howards End was impossible, so long as the younger couple were established in Hilton. His objections to the house were plain as daylight now.

Crane had had enough tea, and was sent to the garage, where their car had been trickling muddy water over Charles's. The downpour had surely penetrated the Six Hills by now, bringing news of our restless civilization. "Curious mounds," said Henry, "but in with you now; another time." He had to be up in London by seven — if possible, by six-thirty. Once more she lost the sense of space; once more trees, houses, people, animals, hills, merged and heaved into one dirtiness, and she was at Wickham Place.

Her evening was pleasant. The sense of flux which had haunted her all the year disappeared for a time. She forgot the luggage and the motor-cars, and the hurrying men who know so much and connect so little. She recaptured the sense of space, which is the basis of all earthly beauty, and, starting from Howards End, she attempted to realize England. She failed — visions do not come when we try, though they may come through trying. But an unexpected love of the island awoke in her, connecting on this side with the joys of the flesh, on that with the inconceivable. Helen and her father had known this love, poor Leonard Bast was groping after it, but it had been hidden from Margaret till this afternoon. It had certainly come through the house and old Miss Avery. Through them: the notion of "through" persisted; her mind trembled towards a conclusion which only the unwise have put into words. Then, veering back into warmth, it dwelt on ruddy bricks, flowering plum-trees, and all the tangible joys of spring.

Henry, after allaying her agitation, had taken her over his property, and had explained to her the use and dimensions of the various rooms. He had sketched the history of the little estate. "It is so unlucky," ran the monologue, "that money wasn't put into it about fifty years ago. Then it had four — five — times the land — thirty acres at least. One could have made something out of it then — a small park, or at all events shrubberies, and rebuilt the house farther away from the road. What's the good of taking it in hand now? Nothing but the meadow left, and even that was heavily mortgaged when I first had to do with things — yes, and the house too. Oh, it was no joke." She saw two women as he spoke, one old, the other young, watching their inheritance melt away. She saw them greet him as a deliverer. "Mismanagement did it — besides, the days for small farms are over. It doesn't pay — except with intensive cultivation. Small holdings, back to the land — ah! philanthropic bunkum. Take it as a rule that nothing pays on a small scale. Most of the land you see (they were standing at an upper window, the only one which faced west) belongs to the people at the Park — they made their pile over copper — good chaps. Avery's Farm, Sishe's — what they call the Common, where you see that ruined oak — one after the other fell in, and so did this, as near as is no matter." But Henry had saved it; without fine feelings or deep insight, but he had saved it, and she loved him for the deed. "When I had more control I did what I could: sold off the two and a half animals, and the mangy pony, and the superannuated tools; pulled down the outhouses; drained; thinned out I don't know how many guelder-roses and elder-trees; and inside the house I turned the old kitchen into a hall, and made a kitchen behind where the dairy was. Garage and so on came later. But one could still tell it's been an old farm. And yet it isn't the place that would fetch one of your artistic crew." No, it wasn't; and if he did not quite understand it, the artistic crew would still less: it was English, and the wych-elm that she saw from the window was an English tree. No report had prepared her for its peculiar glory. It was neither warrior, nor lover, nor god; in none of these rôles do the English excel. It was a comrade, bending over the house, strength and adventure in its roots, but in its utmost fingers tenderness, and the girth, that a dozen men could not have spanned, became in the end evanescent, till pale bud clusters seemed to float in the air. It was a comrade. House and tree transcended any similes of sex. Margaret thought of them now, and was to think of them through many a windy night and London day, but to compare either to man, to woman, always dwarfed the vision. Yet they kept within limits of the human. Their message was not of eternity, but of hope on this side of the grave. As she stood in the one, gazing at the other, truer relationship had gleamed.

Another touch, and the account of her day is finished. They entered the garden for a minute, and to Mr. Wilcox's surprise she was right. Teeth, pigs' teeth, could be seen in the bark of the wych-elm tree — just the white tips of them showing. "Extraordinary!" he cried. "Who told you?"

"I heard of it one winter in London," was her answer, for she, too, avoided mentioning Mrs. Wilcox by name.

Chapter XXV

EVIE heard of her father's engagement when she was in for a tennis tournament, and her play went simply to pot. That she should marry and leave him had seemed natural enough; that he, left alone, should do the same was deceitful; and now Charles and Dolly said that it was all her fault. " But I never dreamt of such a thing," she grumbled. " Dad took me to call now and then, and made me ask her to Simpson's. Well, I'm altogether off dad." It was also an insult to their mother's memory; there they were agreed, and Evie had the idea of returning Mrs. Wilcox's lace and jewellery " as a protest." Against what it would protest she was not clear; but being only eighteen, the idea of renunciation appealed to her, the more as she did not care for jewellery or lace. Dolly then suggested that she and Uncle Percy should pretend to break off their engagement, and then perhaps Mr. Wilcox would quarrel with Miss Schlegel, and break off his; or Paul might be cabled for. But at this point Charles told them not to talk nonsense. So Evie settled to marry as soon as possible; it was no good hanging about with these Schlegels eyeing her. The date of her wedding was consequently put forward from September to August, and in the intoxication of presents she recovered much of her good-humour.

Margaret found that she was expected to figure at this function, and to figure largely; it would be such an opportunity, said Henry, for her to get to know his set. Sir James Bidder would be there, and all the Cahills and the Fussells, and his sister-in-law, Mrs. Warrington Wilcox, had fortunately got back from her tour round the world. Henry she loved, but his set promised to be another matter. He had not the knack of surrounding himself with nice people — indeed, for a man of ability and virtue his choice had been singularly unfortunate; he had no guiding principle beyond a certain preference for mediocrity; he was content to settle one of the greatest things in life haphazard, and so, while his investments went right, his friends generally went wrong. She would be told, " Oh, So-and-so's a good sort — a thundering good sort," and find, on meeting him, that he was a brute or a bore. If Henry had shown real affection, she would have understood, for affection explains everything. But he seemed without sentiment. The "thundering good sort " might at any moment become " a fellow for whom I never did have much use, and have less now," and be shaken off cheerily into oblivion. Margaret had done the same as a schoolgirl. Now she never forgot any one for whom she had once cared; she connected, though the connection might be bitter, and she hoped that some day Henry would do the same.

Evie was not to be married from Ducie Street. She had a fancy for something rural, and, besides, no one would be in London then, so she left her boxes for a few weeks at Oniton Grange, and her banns were duly published in the parish church, and for a couple of days the little town, dreaming between the ruddy hills, was roused by the clang of our civilization, and drew up by the roadside to let the motors pass. Oniton had been a discovery of Mr. Wilcox's — a discovery of which he was not altogether proud. It was up towards the Welsh border, and so difficult of access that he had concluded it must be something special. A ruined castle stood in the grounds. But having got there, what was one to do? The shooting was bad, the fishing indifferent, and women-folk reported the scenery as nothing much. The place turned out to be in the wrong part of Shropshire, damn it, and though he never damned his own property aloud, he was only waiting to get it off his hands, and then to let fly. Evie's marriage was its last appearance in public. As soon as a tenant was found, it became a house for which he never had had much use, and had less now, and, like Howards End, faded into Limbo.

But on Margaret Oniton was destined to make a lasting impression. She regarded it as her future home, and was anxious to start straight with the clergy, etc., and, if possible, to see something of the local life. It was a market-town — as tiny a one as England possesses — and had for ages served that lonely valley, and guarded our marches against the Kelt. In spite of the occasion, in spite of the numbing hilarity that greeted her as soon as she got into the reserved saloon at Paddington, her senses were awake and watching, and though Oniton was to prove one of her innumerable false starts, she never forgot it, nor the things that happened there.

The London party only numbered eight — the Fussells, father and son, two Anglo-Indian ladies named Mrs. Plynlimmon and Lady Edser, Mrs. Warrington Wilcox and her daughter, and lastly, the little girl, very smart and quiet, who figures at so many weddings, and who kept a watchful eye on Margaret, the bride-elect. Dolly was absent — a domestic event detained her at Hilton; Paul had cabled a humorous message; Charles was to meet them with a trio of motors at Shrewsbury. Helen had refused her invitation; Tibby had never answered his. The management was excellent, as was to be expected with anything that Henry undertook; one was conscious of his sensible and generous brain in the background. They were his guests as soon as they reached the train; a special label for their luggage; a courier; a special lunch; they had only to look pleasant and, where possible, pretty. Margaret thought with dismay of her own nuptials — presumably under the management of Tibby. " Mr. Theobald Schlegel and Miss Helen Schlegel request the pleasure of Mrs. Plynlimmon's company on the occasion of the marriage of their sister Margaret." The formula was incredible, but it must soon be printed and sent, and though Wickham Place need not compete with Oniton, it must feed its guests properly, and provide them with sufficient chairs. Her wedding would either be ramshackly or bourgeois — she hoped the latter. Such an affair as the present, staged with a deftness that was almost beautiful, lay beyond her powers and those of her friends.

The low rich purr of a Great Western express is not the worst background for conversation, and the journey passed pleasantly enough. Nothing could have exceeded the kindness of the two men. They raised windows for some ladies, and lowered them for others, they rang the bell for the servant, they identified the colleges as the train slipped past Oxford, they caught books or bag-purses in the act of tumbling on to the floor. Yet there was nothing finicky about their politeness: it had the Public School touch, and, though sedulous, was virile. More battles than Waterloo have been won on our playing-fields, and Margaret bowed to a charm of which she did not wholly approve, and said nothing when the Oxford colleges were identified wrongly. " Male and female created He them "; the journey to Shrewsbury confirmed this questionable statement, and the long glass saloon, that moved so easily and felt so comfortable, became a forcing-house for the idea of sex.

At Shrewsbury came fresh air. Margaret was all for sight-seeing, and while the others were finishing their tea at the Raven, she annexed a motor and hurried over the astonishing city. Her chauffeur was not the faithful Crane, but an Italian, who dearly loved making her late. Charles, watch in hand, though with a level brow, was standing in front of the hotel when they returned. It was perfectly all right, he told her; she was by no means the last. And then he dived into the coffee-room, and she heard him say, " For God's sake, hurry the women up; we shall never be off," and Albert Fussell reply, " Not I; I've done my share," and Colonel Fussell opine that the ladies were getting themselves up to kill. Presently Myra (Mrs. Warrington's daughter) appeared, and as she was his cousin, Charles blew her up a little: she had been changing her smart travelling hat for a smart motor hat. Then Mrs. Warrington herself, leading the quiet child; the two Anglo-Indian ladies were always last. Maids, courier, heavy luggage, had already gone on by a branch-line to a station nearer Oniton, but there were five hat-boxes and four dressing-bags to be packed, and five dust-cloaks to be put on, and to be put off at the last moment, because Charles declared them not necessary. The men presided over everything with unfailing good-humour. By half-past five the party was ready, and went out of Shrewsbury by the Welsh Bridge.

Shropshire had not the reticence of Hertfordshire. Though robbed of half its magic by swift movement, it still conveyed the sense of hills. They were nearing the buttresses that force the Severn eastern and make it an English stream, and the sun, sinking over the Sentinels of Wales, was straight in their eyes. Having picked up another guest, they turned southward, avoiding the greater mountains, but conscious of an occasional summit, rounded and mild, whose colouring differed in quality from that of the lower earth, and whose contours altered more slowly. Quiet mysteries were in progress behind those tossing horizons: the West, as ever, was retreating with some secret which may not be worth the discovery, but which no practical man will ever discover.

They spoke of Tariff Reform.

Mrs. Warrington was just back from the Colonies. Like many other critics of Empire, her mouth had been stopped with food, and she could only exclaim at the hospitality with which she had been received, and warn the Mother Country against trifling with young Titans. "They threaten to cut the painter," she cried, "and where shall we be then? Miss Schlegel, you'll undertake to keep Henry sound about Tariff Reform? It is our last hope."

Margaret playfully confessed herself on the other side, and they began to quote from their respective hand-books while the motor carried them deep into the hills. Curious these were, rather than impressive, for their outlines lacked beauty, and the pink fields on their summits suggested the handkerchiefs of a giant spread out to dry. An occasional outcrop of rock, an occasional wood, an occasional "forest," treeless and brown, all hinted at wildness to follow, but the main colour was an agricultural green. The air grew cooler; they had surmounted the last gradient, and Oniton lay below them with its church, its radiating houses, its castle, its river-girt peninsula. Close to the castle was a grey mansion, unintellectual but kindly, stretching with its grounds across the peninsula's neck — the sort of mansion that was built all over England in the beginning of the last century, while architecture was still an expression of the national character. That was the Grange, remarked Albert, over his shoulder, and then he jammed the brake on, and the motor slowed down and stopped. "I'm sorry," said he, turning round. "Do you mind getting out — by the door on the right? Steady on!"

"What's happened?" asked Mrs. Warrington.

Then the car behind them drew up, and the voice of Charles was heard saying: "Get out the women at once." There was a concourse of males, and Margaret and her companions were hustled out and received into the second car. What had happened? As it started off again, the door of a cottage opened, and a girl screamed wildly at them.

"What is it?" the ladies cried.

Charles drove them a hundred yards without speaking. Then he said: "It's all right. Your car just touched a dog."

"But stop!" cried Margaret, horrified.

"It didn't hurt him."

"Didn't really hurt him?" asked Myra.

"No."

"Do *please* stop!" said Margaret, leaning forward. She was standing up in the car, the other occupants holding her knees to steady her. "I want to go back, please."

Charles took no notice.

"We've left Mr. Fussell behind," said another; "and Angelo, and Crane."

"Yes, but no woman."

"I expect a little of "— Mrs. Warrington scratched her palm — "will be more to the point than one of us!"

"The insurance company sees to that," remarked Charles, "and Albert will do the talking."

"I want to go back, though, I say!" repeated Margaret, getting angry.

Charles took no notice. The motor, loaded with refugees, continued to travel very slowly down the hill. "The men are there," chorused the others. "Men will see to it."

"The men *can't* see to it. Oh, this is ridiculous! Charles, I ask you to stop."

"Stopping's no good," drawled Charles.

"Isn't it?" said Margaret, and jumped straight out of the car.

She fell on her knees, cut her gloves, shook her hat over her ear. Cries of alarm followed her. "You've hurt yourself," exclaimed Charles, jumping after her.

"Of course I've hurt myself!" she retorted.

"May I ask what—"

"There's nothing to ask," said Margaret.

"Your hand's bleeding."

"I know."

"I'm in for a frightful row from the pater."

"You should have thought of that sooner, Charles."

Charles had never been in such a position before. It was a woman in revolt who was hobbling away from him, and the sight was too strange to leave any room for anger. He recovered himself when the others caught them up: their sort he understood. He commanded them to go back.

Albert Fussell was seen walking towards them.

"It's all right!" he called. "It wasn't a dog, it was a cat."

"There!" exclaimed Charles triumphantly. "It's only a rotten cat."

"Got room in your car for a little un? I cut as soon as I saw it wasn't a dog; the chauffeurs are tackling the girl." But Margaret walked forward steadily. Why should the chauffeurs tackle the girl? Ladies sheltering behind men, men sheltering behind servants — the whole system's wrong, and she must challenge it.

"Miss Schlegel! 'Pon my word, you've hurt your hand."

"I'm just going to see," said Margaret. "Don't you wait, Mr. Fussell."

The second motor came round the corner. "It is

all right, madam," said Crane in his turn. He had
taken to call her madam.

"What's all right? The cat?"

"Yes, madam. The girl will receive compensation
for it."

"She was a very ruda girla," said Angelo from the
third motor thoughtfully.

"Wouldn't you have been rude?"

The Italian spread out his hands, implying that he
had not thought of rudeness, but would produce it if
it pleased her. The situation became absurd. The
gentlemen were again buzzing round Miss Schlegel
with offers of assistance, and Lady Edser began to
bind up her hand. She yielded, apologizing slightly,
and was led back to the car, and soon the landscape
resumed its motion, the lonely cottage disappeared, the
castle swelled on its cushion of turf, and they had arrived. No doubt she had disgraced herself. But she
felt their whole journey from London had been unreal. They had no part with the earth and its emotions. They were dust, and a stink, and cosmopolitan
chatter, and the girl whose cat had been killed had
lived more deeply than they.

"Oh, Henry," she exclaimed, "I have been so
naughty," for she had decided to take up this line.
"We ran over a cat. Charles told me not to jump
out, but I would, and look!" She held out her
bandaged hand. "Your poor Meg went such a
flop."

Mr. Wilcox looked bewildered. In evening dress,
he was standing to welcome his guests in the hall.

"Thinking it was a dog," added Mrs. Warrington.

"Ah, a dog's a companion!" said Colonel Fussell.
"A dog 'll remember you."

"Have you hurt yourself, Margaret?"

"Not to speak about; and it's my left hand."

"Well, hurry up and change."

She obeyed, as did the others. Mr. Wilcox then turned to his son.

"Now, Charles, what's happened?"

Charles was absolutely honest. He described what he believed to have happened. Albert had flattened out a cat, and Miss Schlegel had lost her nerve, as any woman might. She had been got safely into the other car, but when it was in motion had leapt out again, in spite of all that they could say. After walking a little on the road, she had calmed down and had said that she was sorry. His father accepted this explanation, and neither knew that Margaret had artfully prepared the way for it. It fitted in too well with their view of feminine nature. In the smoking-room, after dinner, the Colonel put forward the view that Miss Schlegel had jumped it out of devilry. Well he remembered as a young man, in the harbour of Gibraltar once, how a girl — a handome girl, too — had jumped overboard for a bet. He could see her now, and all the lads overboard after her. But Charles and Mr. Wilcox agreed it was much more probably nerves in Miss Schlegel's case. Charles was depressed. That woman had a tongue. She would bring worse disgrace on his father before she had done with them. He strolled out on to the castle mound to think the matter over. The evening was exquisite. On three sides of him a little river whispered, full of messages from the west; above his head the ruins made patterns against the sky. He carefully reviewed their dealings with this family, until he fitted Helen, and Margaret, and Aunt Juley into an orderly conspiracy. Paternity had made him suspicious. He had two children to look after, and more coming, and day by day they seemed less likely to grow up rich men. "It is all very well," he reflected, "the pater saying that he will be just to all, but one can't be just indefinitely. Money isn't elastic. What's to happen if Evie has a family? And, come to that, so may the pater. There'll not be enough to go round, for there's none coming in, either through Dolly or Percy. It's damnable!" He looked enviously at the Grange, whose windows poured light and laughter. First and last, this wedding would cost a pretty penny. Two ladies were strolling up and down the garden terrace, and as the syllables "Imperialism" were wafted to his ears, he guessed that one of them was his aunt. She might have helped him, if she too had not had a family to provide for. "Every one for himself," he repeated — a maxim which had cheered him in the past, but which rang grimly enough among the ruins of Oniton. He lacked his father's ability in business, and so had an ever higher regard for money; unless he could inherit plenty, he feared to leave his children poor.

As he sat thinking, one of the ladies left the terrace and walked into the meadow; he recognized her as Margaret by the white bandage that gleamed on her arm, and put out his cigar, lest the gleam should betray him. She climbed up the mound in zigzags, and at times stooped down, as if she was stroking the turf. It sounds absolutely incredible, but for a moment Charles thought that she was in love with him, and had come out to tempt him. Charles believed in temptresses, who are indeed the strong man's necessary complement, and having no sense of humour, he could not purge himself of the thought by a smile. Margaret, who was engaged to his father, and his sister's wedding-guest, kept on her way without noticing him, and he admitted that he had wronged her on this point. But what was she doing? Why was she stumbling about amongst the rubble and catching her dress in brambles and burrs? As she edged round the keep, she must have got to leeward and smelt his cigar-smoke, for she exclaimed, "Hullo! Who's that?"

Charles made no answer.

"Saxon or Kelt?" she continued, laughing in the darkness. "But it doesn't matter. Whichever you are, you will have to listen to me. I love this place. I love Shropshire. I hate London. I am glad that this will be my home. Ah, dear" — she was now moving back towards the house — "what a comfort to have arrived!"

"That woman means mischief," thought Charles, and compressed his lips. In a few minutes he followed her indoors, as the ground was getting damp. Mists were rising from the river, and presently it became invisible, though it whispered more loudly. There had been a heavy downpour in the Welsh hills.

Chapter XXVI

NEXT morning a fine mist covered the peninsula. The weather promised well, and the outline of the castle mound grew clearer each moment that Margaret watched it. Presently she saw the keep, and the sun painted the rubble gold, and charged the white sky with blue. The shadow of the house gathered itself together and fell over the garden. A cat looked up at her window and mewed. Lastly the river appeared, still holding the mists between its banks and its overhanging alders, and only visible as far as a hill, which cut off its upper reaches.

Margaret was fascinated by Oniton. She had said that she loved it, but it was rather its romantic tension that held her. The rounded Druids of whom she had caught glimpses in her drive, the rivers hurrying down from them to England, the carelessly modelled masses of the lower hills, thrilled her with poetry. The house was insignificant, but the prospect from it would be an eternal joy, and she thought of all the friends she would have to stop in it, and of the conversion of Henry himself to a rural life. Society, too, promised favourably. The rector of the parish had dined with them last night, and she found that he was a friend of her father's, and so knew what to find in her. She liked him. He would introduce her to the town. While, on her other side, Sir James Bidder sat, repeating that she only had to give the word, and he would whip up the county families for twenty miles round. Whether Sir James, who was Garden Seeds, had promised what he could perform, she doubted, but so long as Henry mistook them for the county families when they did call, she was content.

Charles and Albert Fussell now crossed the lawn. They were going for a morning dip, and a servant followed them with their bathing-dresses. She had meant to take a stroll herself before breakfast, but saw that the day was still sacred to men, and amused herself by watching their contretemps. In the first place the key of the bathing-shed could not be found. Charles stood by the riverside with folded hands, tragical, while the servant shouted, and was misunderstood by another servant in the garden. Then came a difficulty about a spring-board, and soon three people were running backwards and forwards over the meadow, with orders and counter orders and recriminations and apologies. If Margaret wanted to jump from a motor-car, she jumped; if Tibby thought paddling would benefit his ankles, he paddled; if a clerk desired adventure, he took a walk in the dark. But these athletes seemed paralysed. They could not bathe without their appliances, though the morning sun was calling and the last mists were rising from the dimpling stream. Had they found the life of the body after all? Could not the men whom they despised as milksops beat them, even on their own ground?

She thought of the bathing arrangements as they should be in her day — no worrying of servants, no appliances, beyond good sense. Her reflections were disturbed by the quiet child, who had come out to speak to the cat, but was now watching her watch the men. She called, " Good-morning, dear," a little sharply. Her voice spread consternation. Charles looked round, and though completely attired in indigo blue, vanished into the shed, and was seen no more.

" Miss Wilcox is up — " the child whispered, and then became unintelligible.

"What's that?"

It sounded like, "— cut-yoke — sack-back —"

"I can't hear."

"— On the bed — tissue-paper —"

Gathering that the wedding-dress was on view, and that a visit would be seemly, she went to Evie's room. All was hilarity here. Evie, in a petticoat, was dancing with one of the Anglo-Indian ladies, while the other was adoring yards of white satin. They screamed, they laughed, they sang, and the dog barked.

Margaret screamed a little too, but without conviction. She could not feel that a wedding was so funny. Perhaps something was missing in her equipment.

Evie gasped: "Dolly is a rotter not to be here! Oh, we would rag just then!" Then Margaret went down to breakfast.

Henry was already installed; he ate slowly and spoke little, and was, in Margaret's eyes, the only member of their party who dodged emotion successfully. She could not suppose him indifferent either to the loss of his daughter or to the presence of his future wife. Yet he dwelt intact, only issuing orders occasionally — orders that promoted the comfort of his guests. He inquired after her hand; he set her to pour out the coffee and Mrs. Warrington to pour out the tea. When Evie came down there was a moment's awkwardness, and both ladies rose to vacate their places. "Burton," called Henry, "serve tea and coffee from the sideboard!" It wasn't genuine tact, but it was tact, of a sort — the sort that is as useful as the genuine, and saves even more situations at Board meetings. Henry treated a marriage like a funeral, item by item, never raising his eyes to the whole, and "Death, where is thy sting? Love, where is thy victory?" one would exclaim at the close.

After breakfast she claimed a few words with him. It was always best to approach him formally. She asked for the interview, because he was going on to shoot grouse tomorrow, and she was returning to Helen in town.

"Certainly, dear," said he. "Of course, I have the time. What do you want?"

"Nothing."

"I was afraid something had gone wrong."

"No; I have nothing to say, but you may talk."

Glancing at his watch, he talked of the nasty curve at the lych-gate. She heard him with interest. Her surface could always respond to his without contempt, though all her deeper being might be yearning to help him. She had abandoned any plan of action. Love is the best, and the more she let herself love him, the more chance was there that he would set his soul in order. Such a moment as this, when they sat under fair weather by the walks of their future home, was so sweet to her that its sweetness would surely pierce to him. Each lift of his eyes, each parting of the thatched lip from the clean-shaven, must prelude the tenderness that kills the Monk and the Beast at a single blow. Disappointed a hundred times, she still hoped. She loved him with too clear a vision to fear his cloudiness. Whether he droned trivialities, as to-day, or sprang kisses on her in the twilight, she could pardon him, she could respond.

"If there is this nasty curve," she suggested, "couldn't we walk to the church? Not, of course, you and Evie; but the rest of us might very well go on first, and that would mean fewer carriages."

"One can't have ladies walking through the Market Square. The Fussells wouldn't like it; they were awfully particular at Charles's wedding. My — she — one of our party was anxious to walk, and certainly the church was just round the corner, and I shouldn't have minded; but the Colonel made a great point of it."

"You men shouldn't be so chivalrous," said Margaret thoughtfully.

"Why not?"

She knew why not, but said that she did not know.

He then announced that, unless she had anything special to say, he must visit the wine-cellar, and they went off together in search of Burton. Though clumsy and a little inconvenient, Oniton was a genuine country-house. They clattered down flagged passages, looking into room after room, and scaring unknown maids from the performance of obscure duties. The wedding-breakfast must be in readiness when they came back from church, and tea would be served in the garden. The sight of so many agitated and serious people made Margaret smile, but she reflected that they were paid to be serious, and enjoyed being agitated. Here were the lower wheels of the machine that was tossing Evie up into nuptial glory. A little boy blocked their way with pig-pails. His mind could not grasp their greatness, and he said: "By your leave; let me pass, please." Henry asked him where Burton was. But the servants were so new that they did not know one another's names. In the still-room sat the band, who had stipulated for champagne as part of their fee, and who were already drinking beer. Scents of Araby came from the kitchen, mingled with cries. Margaret knew what had happened there, for it happened at Wickham Place. One of the wedding dishes had boiled over, and the cook was throwing cedar-shavings to hide the smell. At last they came upon the butler. Henry gave him the keys, and handed Margaret down the cellar-stairs. Two doors were unlocked. She, who kept all her wine at the bottom of the linen-cupboard, was astonished at the sight. "We shall never get through it!" she cried, and the two men were suddenly drawn into brotherhood, and exchanged smiles. She felt as if she had again jumped out of the car while it was moving.

Certainly Oniton would take some digesting. It would be no small business to remain herself, and yet to assimilate such an establishment. She must remain herself, for his sake as well as her own, since a shadowy wife degrades the husband whom she accompanies; and she must assimilate for reasons of common honesty, since she had no right to marry a man and make him uncomfortable. Her only ally was the power of Home. The loss of Wickham Place had taught her more than its possession. Howards End had repeated the lesson. She was determined to create new sancties among these hills.

After visiting the wine-cellar, she dressed, and then came the wedding, which seemed a small affair when compared with the preparations for it. Everything went like one o'clock. Mr. Cahill materialized out of space, and was waiting for his bride at the church door. No one dropped the ring or mispronounced the responses, or trod on Evie's train, or cried. In a few minutes the clergymen performed their duty, the register was signed, and they were back in their carriages, negotiating the dangerous curve by the lych-gate. Margaret was convinced that they had not been married at all, and that the Norman church had been intent all the time on other business.

There were more documents to sign at the house, and the breakfast to eat, and then a few more people dropped in for the garden party. There had been a great many refusals, and after all it was not a very big affair — not as big as Margaret's would be. She noted the dishes and the strips of red carpet, that outwardly she might give Henry what was proper. But inwardly she hoped for something better than this blend of Sunday church and fox-hunting. If only some one had been upset! But this wedding had gone off so particularly well — " quite like a Durbar " in the opinion of Lady Edser, and she thoroughly agreed with her.

So the wasted day lumbered forward, the bride and bridegroom drove off, yelling with laughter, and for the second time the sun retreated towards the hills of Wales. Henry, who was more tired than he owned, came up to her in the castle meadow, and, in tones of unusual softness, said that he was pleased. Everything had gone off so well. She felt that he was praising her, too, and blushed; certainly she had done all she could with his intractable friends, and had made a special point of kow-towing to the men. They were breaking camp this evening: only the Warringtons and quiet child would stay the night, and the others were already moving towards the house to finish their packing. " I think it did go off well," she agreed. " Since I had to jump out of the motor, I'm thankful I lighted on my left hand. I am so very glad about it, Henry dear; I only hope that the guests at ours may be half as comfortable. You must all remember that we have no practical person among us, except my aunt, and she is not used to entertainments on a large scale."

" I know," he said gravely. " Under the circumstances, it would be better to put everything into the hands of Harrod's or Whiteley's, or even to go to some hotel."

" You desire a hotel?"

" Yes, because — well, I mustn't interfere with you. No doubt you want to be married from your old home."

" My old home's falling into pieces, Henry. I only want my new. Isn't it a perfect evening — "

" The Alexandrina isn't bad — "

" The Alexandrina," she echoed, more occupied with

the threads of smoke that were issuing from their chimneys, and ruling the sunlit slopes with parallels of grey.

" It's off Curzon Street."

" Is it? Let's be married from off Curzon Street."

Then she turned westward, to gaze at the swirling gold. Just where the river rounded the hill the sun caught it. Fairyland must lie above the bend, and its precious liquid was pouring towards them past Charles's bathing-shed. She gazed so long that her eyes were dazzled, and when they moved back to the house, she could not recognize the faces of people who were coming out of it. A parlour-maid was preceding them.

" Who are those people? " she asked.

" They're callers! " exclaimed Henry. " It's too late for callers."

" Perhaps they're town people who want to see the wedding presents."

" I'm not at home yet to townees."

" Well, hide among the ruins, and if I can stop them, I will."

He thanked her.

Margaret went forward, smiling socially. She supposed that these were unpunctual guests, who would have to be content with vicarious civility, since Evie and Charles were gone, Henry tired, and the others in their rooms. She assumed the airs of a hostess; not for long. For one of the group was Helen — Helen in her oldest clothes, and dominated by that tense, wounding excitement that had made her a terror in their nursery days.

" What is it? " she called. " Oh, what's wrong? Is Tibby ill? "

Helen spoke to her two companions, who fell back. Then she bore forward furiously.

"They're starving!" she shouted. "I found them starving!"

"Who? Why have you come?"

"The Basts."

"Oh, Helen!" moaned Margaret. "Whatever have you done now?"

"He has lost his place. He has been turned out of his bank. Yes, he's done for. We upper classes have ruined him, and I suppose you'll tell me it's the battle of life. Starving. His wife is ill. Starving. She fainted in the train."

"Helen, are you mad?"

"Perhaps. Yes. If you like, I'm mad. But I've brought them. I'll stand injustice no longer. I'll shov" ıp the wretchedness that lies under this luxury, this talk of impersonal forces, this cant about God doing what we're too slack to do ourselves."

"Have you actually brought two starving people from London to Shropshire, Helen?"

Helen was checked. She had not thought of this, and her hysteria abated. "There was a restaurant car on the train," she said.

"Don't be absurd. They aren't starving, and you know it. Now, begin from the beginning. I won't have such theatrical nonsense. How dare you! Yes, how dare you!" she repeated, as anger filled her, "bursting in to Evie's wedding in this heartless way. My goodness! but you've a perverted notion of philanthropy. Look"—she indicated the house—"servants, people out of the windows. They think it's some vulgar scandal, and I must explain, 'Oh no, it's only my sister screaming, and only two hangers-on of ours, whom she has brought here for no conceivable reason.'"

"Kindly take back that word 'hangers-on,'" said Helen, ominously calm.

" Very well," conceded Margaret, who for all her wrath was determined to avoid a real quarrel. " I, too, am sorry about them, but it beats me why you've brought them here, or why you're here yourself."

" It's our last chance of seeing Mr. Wilcox."

Margaret moved towards the house at this. She was determined not to worry Henry.

" He's going to Scotland. I know he is. I insist on seeing him."

" Yes, tomorrow."

" I knew it was our last chance."

" How do you do, Mr. Bast? " said Margaret, trying to control her voice. " This is an odd business. What view do you take of it? "

" There is Mrs. Bast, too," prompted Helen.

Jacky also shook hands. She, like her husband, was shy, and, furthermore, ill, and furthermore, so bestially stupid that she could not grasp what was happening. She only knew that the lady had swept down like a whirlwind last night, had paid the rent, redeemed the furniture, provided them with a dinner and breakfast, and ordered them to meet her at Paddington next morning. Leonard had feebly protested, and when the morning came, had suggested that they shouldn't go. But she, half mesmerized, had obeyed. The lady had told them to, and they must, and their bed-sitting-room had accordingly changed into Paddington, and Paddington into a railway carriage, that shook, and grew hot, and grew cold, and vanished entirely, and reappeared amid torrents of expensive scent. " You have fainted," said the lady in an awe-struck voice. " Perhaps the air will do you good." And perhaps it had, for here she was, feeling rather better among a lot of flowers.

" I'm sure I don't want to intrude," began Leonard, in answer to Margaret's question. " But you have been so kind to me in the past in warning me about the Porphyrion that I wondered — why, I wondered whether — "

" Whether we could get him back into the Porphyrion again," supplied Helen. " Meg, this has been a cheerful business. A bright evening's work that was on Chelsea Embankment."

Margaret shook her head and returned to Mr. Bast. " I don't understand. You left the Porphyrion because we suggested it was a bad concern, didn't you? "

" That's right."

" And went into a bank instead? "

" I told you all that," said Helen; " and they reduced their staff after he had been in a month, and now he's penniless, and I consider that we and our informant are directly to blame."

" I hate all this," Leonard muttered.

" I hope you do, Mr. Bast. But it's no good mincing matters. You have done yourself no good by coming here. If you intend to confront Mr. Wilcox, and to call him to account for a chance remark, you will make a very great mistake."

" I brought them. I did it all," cried Helen.

" I can only advise you to go at once. My sister has put you in a false position, and it is kindest to tell you so. It's too late to get to town, but you'll find a comfortable hotel in Oniton, where Mrs. Bast can rest, and I hope you'll be my guests there."

" That isn't what I want, Miss Schlegel," said Leonard. " You're very kind, and no doubt it's a false position, but you make me miserable. I seem no good at all."

" It's work he wants," interpreted Helen. " Can't you see? "

Then he said: " Jacky, let's go. We're more bother than we're worth. We're costing these ladies pounds and pounds already to get work for us, and they never will. There's nothing we're good enough to do."

"We would like to find you work," said Margaret rather conventionally. "We want to — I, like my sister. You're only down in your luck. Go to the hotel, have a good night's rest, and some day you shall pay me back the bill, if you prefer it."

But Leonard was near the abyss, and at such moments men see clearly. "You don't know what you're talking about," he said. "I shall never get work now. If rich people fail at one profession, they can try another. Not I. I had my groove, and I've got out of it. I could do one particular branch of insurance in one particular office well enough to command a salary, but that's all. Poetry's nothing, Miss Schlegel. One's thoughts about this and that are nothing. Your money, too, is nothing, if you'll understand me. I mean if a man over twenty once loses his own particular job, it's all over with him. I have seen it happen to others. Their friends gave them money for a little, but in the end they fall over the edge. It's no good. It's the whole world pulling. There always will be rich and poor."

He ceased. "Won't you have something to eat?" said Margaret. "I don't know what to do. It isn't my house, and though Mr. Wilcox would have been glad to see you at any other time — as I say, I don't know what to do, but I undertake to do what I can for you. Helen, offer them something. Do try a sandwich, Mrs. Bast."

They moved to a long table behind which a servant was still standing. Iced cakes, sandwiches innumerable, coffee, claret-cup, champagne, remained almost intact: their overfed guests could do no more. Leonard refused. Jacky thought she could manage a little. Margaret left them whispering together and had a few more words with Helen.

She said: "Helen, I like Mr. Bast. I agree that

he's worth helping. I agree that we are directly responsible."

" No, indirectly. Via Mr. Wilcox."

" Let me tell you once for all that if you take up that attitude, I'll do nothing. No doubt you're right logically, and are entitled to say a great many scathing things about Henry. Only, I won't have it. So choose."

Helen looked at the sunset.

" If you promise to take them quietly to the George, I will speak to Henry about them — in my own way, mind; there is to be none of this absurd screaming about justice. I have no use for justice. If it was only a question of money, we could do it ourselves. But he wants work, and that we can't give him, but possibly Henry can."

" It's his duty to," grumbled Helen.

" Nor am I concerned with duty. I'm concerned with the characters of various people whom we know, and how, things being as they are, things may be made a little better. Mr. Wilcox hates being asked favours: all business men do. But I am going to ask him, at the risk of a rebuff, because I want to make things a little better."

" Very well. I promise. You take it very calmly."

" Take them off to the George, then, and I'll try. Poor creatures! but they look tried." As they parted, she added: " I haven't nearly done with you, though, Helen. You have been most self-indulgent. I can't get over it. You have less restraint rather than more as you grow older. Think it over and alter yourself, or we shan't have happy lives."

She rejoined Henry. Fortunately he had been sitting down: these physical matters were important. " Was it townees?" he asked, greeting her with a pleasant smile.

"You'll never believe me," said Margaret, sitting down beside him. "It's all right now, but it was my sister."

"Helen here?" he cried, preparing to rise. "But she refused the invitation. I thought she despised weddings."

"Don't get up. She has not come to the wedding. I've bundled her off to the George."

Inherently hospitable, he protested.

"No; she has two of her protégés with her, and must keep with them."

"Let 'em all come."

"My dear Henry, did you see them?"

"I did catch sight of a brown bunch of a woman, certainly."

"The brown bunch was Helen, but did you catch sight of a sea-green and salmon bunch?"

"What! are they out beanfeasting?"

"No; business. They wanted to see me, and later on I want to talk to you about them."

She was ashamed of her own diplomacy. In dealing with a Wilcox, how tempting it was to lapse from comradeship, and to give him the kind of woman that he desired! Henry took the hint at once, and said: "Why later on? Tell me now. No time like the present."

"Shall I?"

"If it isn't a long story."

"Oh, not five minutes; but there's a sting at the end of it, for I want you to find the man some work in your office."

"What are his qualifications?"

"I don't know. He's a clerk."

"How old?"

"Twenty-five, perhaps."

"What's his name?"

"Bast," said Margaret, and was about to remind him that they had met at Wickham Place, but stopped herself. It had not been a successful meeting.

"Where was he before?"

"Dempster's Bank."

"Why did he leave?" he asked, still remembering nothing.

"They reduced their staff."

"All right; I'll see him."

It was the reward of her tact and devotion through the day. Now she understood why some women prefer influence to rights. Mrs. Plynlimmon, when condemning suffragettes, had said: "The woman who can't influence her husband to vote the way she wants ought to be ashamed of herself." Margaret had winced, but she was influencing Henry now, and though pleased at her little victory, she knew that she had won it by the methods of the harem.

"I should be glad if you took him," she said, "but I don't know whether he's qualified."

"I'll do what I can. But, Margaret, this mustn't be taken as a precedent."

"No, of course — of course —"

"I can't fit in your protégés every day. Business would suffer."

"I can promise you he's the last. He — he's rather a special case."

"Protégés always are."

She let it stand at that. He rose with a little extra touch of complacency, and held out his hand to help her up. How wide the gulf between Henry as he was and Henry as Helen thought he ought to be! And she herself — hovering as usual between the two, now accepting men as they are, now yearning with her sister for Truth. Love and Truth — their warfare seems eternal. Perhaps the whole visible world rests on it, and if they were one, life itself, like the spirits when Prospero was reconciled to his brother, might vanish into air, into thin air.

" Your protégé has made us late," said he. " The Fussells will just be starting."

On the whole she sided with men as they are. Henry would save the Basts as he had saved Howards End, while Helen and her friends were discussing the ethics of salvation. His was a slap-dash method, but the world has been built slap-dash, and the beauty of mountain and river and sunset may be but the varnish with which the unskilled artificer hides his joins. Oniton, like herself, was imperfect. Its apple-trees were stunted, its castle ruinous. It, too, had suffered in the border warfare between the Anglo-Saxon and the Kelt, between things as they are and as they ought to be. Once more the west was retreating, once again the orderly stars were dotting the eastern sky. There is certainly no rest for us on the earth. But there is happiness, and as Margaret descended the mound on her lover's arm, she felt that she was having her share.

To her annoyance, Mrs. Bast was still in the garden; the husband and Helen had left her there to finish her meal while they went to engage rooms. Margaret found this woman repellent. She had felt, when shaking her hand, an overpowering shame. She remembered the motive of her call at Wickham Place, and smelt again odours from the abyss — odours the more disturbing because they were involuntary. For there was no malice in Jacky. There she sat, a piece of cake in one hand, an empty champagne glass in the other, doing no harm to anybody.

" She's overtired," Margaret whispered.

" She's something else," said Henry. " This won't do. I can't have her in my garden in this state."

" Is she —" Margaret hesitated to add " drunk." Now that she was going to marry him, he had grown particular. He discountenanced risqué conversations now.

Henry went up to the woman. She raised her face, which gleamed in the twilight like a puff-ball.

"Madam, you will be more comfortable at the hotel," he said sharply.

Jacky replied: "If it isn't Hen!"

"Ne crois pas que le mari lui ressemble," apologized Margaret. "Il est tout à fait différent."

"Henry!" she repeated, quite distinctly.

Mr. Wilcox was much annoyed. "I can't congratulate you on your protégés," he remarked.

"Hen, don't go. You do love me, dear, don't you?"

"Bless us, what a person!" sighed Margaret, gathering up her skirts.

Jacky pointed with her cake. "You're a nice boy, you are." She yawned. "There now, I love you."

"Henry, I am awfully sorry."

"And pray why?" he asked, and looked at her so sternly that she feared he was ill. He seemed more scandalized than the facts demanded.

"To have brought this down on you."

"Pray don't apologize."

The voice continued.

"Why does she call you 'Hen'?" said Margaret innocently. "Has she ever seen you before?"

"Seen Hen before!" said Jacky. "Who hasn't seen Hen? He's serving you like me, my dear. These boys! You wait— Still we love 'em."

"Are you now satisfied?" Henry asked.

Margaret began to grow frightened. "I don't know what it is all about," she said. "Let's come in."

But he thought she was acting. He thought he was trapped. He saw his whole life crumbling. "Don't you indeed?" he said bitingly. "I do. Allow me to congratulate you on the success of your plan."

"This is Helen's plan, not mine."

" I now understand your interest in the Basts. Very well thought out. I am amused at your caution, Margaret. You are quite right — it was necessary. I am a man, and have lived a man's past. I have the honour to release you from your engagement."

Still she could not understand. She knew of life's seamy side as a theory; she could not grasp it as a fact. More words from Jacky were necessary — words unequivocal, undenied.

" So that —" burst from her, and she went indoors. She stopped herself from saying more.

" So what?" asked Colonel Fussell, who was getting ready to start in the hall.

" We were saying — Henry and I were just having the fiercest argument, my point being —" Seizing his fur coat from a footman, she offered to help him on. He protested, and there was a playful little scene.

" No, let me do that," said Henry, following.

" Thanks so much! You see — he has forgiven me!"

The Colonel said gallantly: " I don't expect there's much to forgive."

He got into the car. The ladies followed him after an interval. Maids, courier, and heavier luggage had been sent on earlier by the branch-line. Still chattering, still thanking their host and patronizing their future hostess, the guests were borne away.

Then Margaret continued: " So that woman has been your mistress?"

" You put it with your usual delicacy," he replied.

" When, please?"

" Why?"

" When, please?"

" Ten years ago."

She left him without a word. For it was not her tragedy: it was Mrs. Wilcox's.

Chapter XXVII

HELEN began to wonder why she had spent a matter of eight pounds in making some people ill and others angry. Now that the wave of excitement was ebbing, and had left her, Mr. Bast, and Mrs. Bast stranded for the night in a Shropshire hotel, she asked herself what forces had made the wave flow. At all events, no harm was done. Margaret would play the game properly now, and though Helen disapproved of her sister's methods, she knew that the Basts would benefit by them in the long-run.

"Mr. Wilcox is so illogical," she explained to Leonard, who had put his wife to bed, and was sitting with her in the empty coffee-room. "If we told him it was his duty to take you on, he might refuse to do it. The fact is, he isn't properly educated. I don't want to set you against him, but you'll find him a trial."

"I can never thank you sufficiently, Miss Schlegel," was all that Leonard felt equal to.

"I believe in personal responsibility. Don't you? And in personal everything. I hate — I suppose I oughtn't to say that — but the Wilcoxes are on the wrong tack surely. Or perhaps it isn't their fault. Perhaps the little thing that says ' I ' is missing out of the middle of their heads, and then it's a waste of time to blame them. There's a nightmare of a theory that says a special race is being born which will rule the rest of us in the future just because it lacks the little thing that says ' I.' Had you heard that?"

"I get no time for reading."

"Had you thought it, then? That there are two kinds of people — our kind, who live straight from the middle of their heads, and the other kind who can't, because their heads have no middle? They can't say 'I.' They *aren't* in fact, and so they're supermen. Pierpoint Morgan has never said 'I' in his life."

Leonard roused himself. If his benefactress wanted intellectual conversation, she must have it. She was more important than his ruined past. "I never got on to Nietzsche," he said. "But I always understood that those supermen were rather what you may call egoists."

"Oh, no, that's wrong," replied Helen. "No superman ever said 'I want,' because 'I want' must lead to the question, 'Who am I?' and so to Pity and to Justice. He only says 'want.' 'Want Europe,' if he's Napoleon; 'want wives,' if he's Bluebeard; 'want Botticelli,' if he's Pierpoint Morgan. Never the 'I'; and if you could pierce through him, you'd find panic and emptiness in the middle."

Leonard was silent for a moment. Then he said: "May I take it, Miss Schlegel, that you and I are both the sort that say 'I'?"

"Of course."

"And your sister too?"

"Of course," repeated Helen, a little sharply. She was annoyed with Margaret, but did not want her discussed. "All presentable people say 'I.'"

"But Mr. Wilcox — he is not perhaps —"

"I don't know that it's any good discussing Mr. Wilcox either."

"Quite so, quite so," he agreed. Helen asked herself why she had snubbed him. Once or twice during the day she had encouraged him to criticize, and then had pulled him up short. Was she afraid of him presuming? If so, it was disgusting of her.

But he was thinking the snub quite natural. Everything she did was natural, and incapable of causing offence. While the Miss Schlegels were together he had felt them scarcely human — a sort of admonitory whirligig. But a Miss Schlegel alone was different. She was in Helen's case unmarried, in Margaret's about to be married, in neither case an echo of her sister. A light had fallen at last into this rich upper world, and he saw that it was full of men and women, some of whom were more friendly to him than others. Helen had become " his " Miss Schlegel, who scolded him and corresponded with him, and had swept down yesterday with grateful vehemence. Margaret, though not unkind, was severe and remote. He would not presume to help her, for instance. He had never liked her, and began to think that his original impression was true, and that her sister did not like her either. Helen was certainly lonely. She, who gave away so much, was receiving too little. Leonard was pleased to think that he could spare her vexation by holding his tongue and concealing what he knew about Mr. Wilcox. Jacky had announced her discovery when he fetched her from the lawn. After the first shock, he did not mind for himself. By now he had no illusions about his wife, and this was only one new stain on the face of a love that had never been pure. To keep perfection perfect, that should be his ideal, if the future gave him time to have ideals. Helen, and Margaret for Helen's sake, must not know.

Helen disconcerted him by turning the conversation to his wife. " Mrs. Bast — does she ever say ' I '? " she asked, half mischievously, and then, " Is she very tired? "

" It's better she stops in her room," said Leonard.

" Shall I sit up with her? "

" No, thank you; she does not need company."

" Mr. Bast, what kind of woman is your wife? "

Leonard blushed up to his eyes.

"You ought to know my ways by now. Does that question offend you?"

"No, oh no, Miss Schlegel, no."

"Because I love honesty. Don't pretend your marriage has been a happy one. You and she can have nothing in common."

He did not deny it, but said shyly: "I suppose that's pretty obvious; but Jacky never meant to do anybody any harm. When things went wrong, or I heard things, I used to think it was her fault, but, looking back, it's more mine. I needn't have married her, but as I have I must stick to her and keep her."

"How long have you been married?"

"Nearly three years."

"What did your people say?"

"They will not have anything to do with us. They had a sort of family council when they heard I was married, and cut us off altogether."

Helen began to pace up and down the room. "My good boy, what a mess!" she said gently. "Who are your people?"

He could answer this. His parents, who were dead, had been in trade; his sisters had married commercial travellers; his brother was a lay-reader.

"And your grandparents?"

Leonard told her a secret that he had held shameful up to now. "They were just nothing at all," he said, "— agricultural labourers and that sort."

"So! From which part?"

"Lincolnshire mostly, but my mother's father — he, oddly enough, came from these parts round here."

"From this very Shropshire. Yes, that is odd. My mother's people were Lancashire. But why do your brother and your sisters object to Mrs. Bast?"

"Oh, I don't know."

"Excuse me, you do know. I am not a baby. I can bear anything you tell me, and the more you tell the more I shall be able to help. Have they heard anything against her?"

He was silent.

"I think I have guessed now," said Helen very gravely.

"I don't think so, Miss Schlegel; I hope not."

"We must be honest, even over these things. I have guessed. I am frightfully, dreadfully sorry, but it does not make the least difference to me. I shall feel just the same to both of you. I blame, not your wife for these things, but men."

Leonard left it at that — so long as she did not guess the man. She stood at the window and slowly pulled up the blinds. The hotel looked over a dark square. The mists had begun. When she turned back to him her eyes were shining.

"Don't you worry," he pleaded. "I can't bear that. We shall be all right if I get work. If I could only get work — something regular to do. Then it wouldn't be so bad again. I don't trouble after books as I used. I can imagine that with regular work we should settle down again. It stops one thinking."

"Settle down to what?"

"Oh, just settle down."

"And that's to be life!" said Helen, with a catch in her throat. "How can you, with all the beautiful things to see and do — with music — with walking at night —"

"Walking is well enough when a man's in work," he answered. "Oh, I did talk a lot of nonsense once, but there's nothing like a bailiff in the house to drive it out of you. When I saw him fingering my Ruskins and Stevensons, I seemed to see life straight real, and it isn't a pretty sight. My books are back again, thanks to you, but they'll never be the same to me again, and I shan't ever again think night in the woods is wonderful."

"Why not?" asked Helen, throwing up the window.

"Because I see one must have money."

"Well, you're wrong."

"I wish I was wrong, but — the clergyman — he has money of his own, or else he's paid; the poet or the musician — just the same; the tramp — he's no different. The tramp goes to the workhouse in the end, and is paid for with other people's money. Miss Schlegel, the real thing's money and all the rest is a dream."

"You're still wrong. You've forgotten Death."

Leonard could not understand.

"If we lived for ever what you say would be true. But we have to die, we have to leave life presently. Injustice and greed would be the real thing if we lived for ever. As it is, we must hold to other things, because Death is coming. I love Death — not morbidly, but because He explains. He shows me the emptiness of Money. Death and Money are the eternal foes. Not Death and Life. Never mind what lies behind Death, Mr. Bast, but be sure that the poet and the musician and the tramp will be happier in it than the man who has never learnt to say, 'I am I.'"

"I wonder."

"We are all in a mist — I know but I can help you this far — men like the Wilcoxes are deeper in the mist than any. Sane, sound Englishmen! building up empires, levelling all the world into what they call common sense. But mention Death to them and they're offended, because Death's really Imperial, and He cries out against them for ever."

"I am as afraid of Death as any one."

"But not of the idea of Death."

"But what is the difference?"

"Infinite difference," said Helen, more gravely than before.

Leonard looked at her wondering, and had the sense of great things sweeping out of the shrouded night. But he could not receive them, because his heart was still full of little things. As the lost umbrella had spoilt the concert at Queen's Hall, so the lost situation was obscuring the diviner harmonies now. Death, Life and Materialism were fine words, but would Mr. Wilcox take him on as a clerk? Talk as one would, Mr. Wilcox was king of this world, the superman, with his own morality, whose head remained in the clouds.

"I must be stupid," he said apologetically.

While to Helen the paradox became clearer and clearer. "Death destroys a man: the idea of Death saves him." Behind the coffins and the skeletons that stay the vulgar mind lies something so immense that all that is great in us responds to it. Men of the world may recoil from the charnel-house that they will one day enter, but Love knows better. Death is his foe, but his peer, and in their age-long struggle the thews of Love have been strengthened, and his vision cleared, until there is no one who can stand against him.

"So never give in," continued the girl, and restated again and again the vague yet convincing plea that the Invisible lodges against the Visible. Her excitement grew as she tried to cut the rope that fastened Leonard to the earth. Woven of bitter experience, it resisted her. Presently the waitress entered and gave her a letter from Margaret. Another note, addressed to Leonard, was inside. They read them, listening to the murmurings of the river.

Chapter XXVIII

FOR many hours Margaret did nothing; then she controlled herself, and wrote some letters. She was too bruised to speak to Henry; she could pity him, and even determine to marry him, but as yet all lay too deep in her heart for speech. On the surface the sense of his degradation was too strong. She could not command voice or look, and the gentle words that she forced out through her pen seemed to proceed from some other person.

" My dearest boy," she began, " this is not to part us. It is everything or nothing, and I mean it to be nothing. It happened long before we ever met, and even if it had happened since, I should be writing the same, I hope. I do understand."

But she crossed out " I do understand "; it struck a false note. Henry could not bear to be understood. She also crossed out, " It is everything or nothing." Henry would resent so strong a grasp of the situation. She must not comment; comment is unfeminine.

" I think that'll about do," she thought.

Then the sense of his degradation choked her. Was he worth all this bother? To have yielded to a woman of that sort was everything, yes, it was, and she could not be his wife. She tried to translate his temptation into her own language, and her brain reeled. Men must be different, even to want to yield to such a temptation. Her belief in comradeship was stifled, and she saw life as from that glass saloon on the Great Western, which sheltered male and female alike from the fresh air. Are the sexes really races, each with its own code of morality, and their mutual love a mere device of Nature to keep things going? Strip human intercourse of the proprieties, and is it reduced to this? Her judgment told her no. She knew that out of Nature's device we have built a magic that will win us immortality. Far more mysterious than the call of sex to sex is the tenderness that we throw into that call; far wider is the gulf between us and the farm-yard than between the farmyard and the garbage that nourishes it. We are evolving, in ways that Science cannot measure, to ends that Theology dares not con-template. "Men did produce one jewel," the gods will say, and, saying, will give us immortality. Mar-garet knew all this, but for the moment she could not feel it, and transformed the marriage of Evie and Mr. Cahill into a carnival of fools, and her own marriage — too miserable to think of that, she tore up the letter, and then wrote another:

"DEAR MR. BAST,
"I have spoken to Mr. Wilcox about you, as I prom-ised, and am sorry to say that he has no vacancy for you.
"Yours truly,
"M. J. SCHLEGEL."

She enclosed this in a note to Helen, over which she took less trouble than she might have done; but her head was aching, and she could not stop to pick her words:

"DEAR HELEN,
"Give him this. The Basts are no good. Henry found the woman drunk on the lawn. I am having a room got ready for you here, and will you please come round at once on getting this? The Basts are not at all the type we should trouble about. I may go round to them myself in the morn-ing, and do anything that is fair.
"M."

In writing this, Margaret felt that she was being practical. Something might be arranged for the

Basts later on, but they must be silenced for the moment. She hoped to avoid a conversation between the woman and Helen. She rang the bell for a servant, but no one answered it; Mr. Wilcox and the Warringtons were gone to bed, and the kitchen was abandoned to Saturnalia. Consequently she went over to the George herself. She did not enter the hotel, for discussion would have been perilous, and, saying that the letter was important, she gave it to the waitress. As she recrossed the square she saw Helen and Mr. Bast looking out of the window of the coffee-room, and feared she was already too late. Her task was not yet over; she ought to tell Henry what she had done.

This came easily, for she saw him in the hall. The night wind had been rattling the pictures against the wall, and the noise had disturbed him.

" Who's there? " he called, quite the householder.

Margaret walked in and past him.

" I have asked Helen to sleep," she said. " She is best here; so don't lock the front-door."

" I thought some one had got in," said Henry.

" At the same time I told the man that we could do nothing for him. I don't know about later, but now the Basts must clearly go."

" Did you say that your sister is sleeping here, after all? "

" Probably."

" Is she to be shown up to your room? "

" I have naturally nothing to say to her; I am going to bed. Will you tell the servants about Helen? Could some one go to carry her bag? "

He tapped a little gong, which had been bought to summon the servants.

" You must make more noise than that if you want them to hear."

Henry opened a door, and down the corridor came shouts of laughter. " Far too much screaming there," he said, and strode towards it. Margaret went up-stairs, uncertain whether to be glad that they had met, or sorry. They had behaved as if nothing had hap-pened, and her deepest instincts told her that this was wrong. For his own sake, some explanation was due.

And yet — what could an explanation tell her? A date, a place, a few details, which she could imagine all too clearly. Now that the first shock was over, she saw that there was every reason to premise a Mrs. Bast. Henry's inner life had long laid open to her — his intellectual confusion, his obtuseness to personal in-fluence, his strong but furtive passions. Should she refuse him because his outer life corresponded? Per-haps. Perhaps, if the dishonour had been done to her, but it was done long before her day. She strug-gled against the feeling. She told herself that Mrs. Wilcox's wrong was her own. But she was not a bar-ren theorist. As she undressed, her anger, her re-gard for the dead, her desire for a scene, all grew weak. Henry must have it as he liked, for she loved him, and some day she would use her love to make him a better man.

Pity was at the bottom of her actions all through this crisis. Pity, if one may generalize, is at the bot-tom of woman. When men like us, it is for our better qualities, and however tender their liking, we dare not be unworthy of it, or they will quietly let us go. But unworthiness stimulates woman. It brings out her deeper nature, for good or for evil.

Here was the core of the question. Henry must be forgiven, and made better by love; nothing else mat-tered. Mrs. Wilcox, that unquiet yet kindly ghost, must be left to her own wrong. To her everything was in proportion now, and she, too, would pity the man who was blundering up and down their lives. Had Mrs. Wilcox known of his trespass? An interest-ing question, but Margaret fell asleep, tethered by af-

fection, and lulled by the murmurs of the river that
descended all the night from Wales. She felt herself at one with her future home, colouring it and
coloured by it, and awoke to see, for the second time,
Oniton Castle conquering the morning mists.

Chapter XXIX

"HENRY dear ——" was her greeting. He had finished his breakfast, and was beginning the *Times*. His sister-in-law was packing. She knelt by him and took the paper from him, feeling that it was unusually heavy and thick. Then, putting her face where it had been, she looked up in his eyes.

"Henry dear, look at me. No, I won't have you shirking. Look at me. There. That's all."

"You're referring to last evening," he said huskily. "I have released you from your engagement. I could find excuses, but I won't. No, I won't. A thousand times no. I'm a bad lot, and must be left at that."

Expelled from his old fortress, Mr. Wilcox was building a new one. He could no longer appear respectable to her, so he defended himself instead in a lurid past. It was not true repentance.

"Leave it where you will, boy. It's not going to trouble us: I know what I'm talking about, and it will make no difference."

"No difference?" he inquired. "No difference, when you find that I am not the fellow you thought?" He was annoyed with Miss Schlegel here. He would have preferred her to be prostrated by the blow, or even to rage. Against the tide of his sin flowed the feeling that she was not altogether womanly. Her eyes gazed too straight; they had read books that are suitable for men only. And though he had dreaded a scene, and though she had determined against one, there was a scene, all the same. It was somehow imperative.

"I am unworthy of you," he began. "Had I been worthy, I should not have released you from your engagement. I know what I am talking about. I can't bear to talk of such things. We had better leave it."

She kissed his hand. He jerked it from her, and, rising to his feet, went on: "You, with your sheltered life, and refined pursuits, and friends, and books, you and your sister, and women like you — I say, how can you guess the temptations that lie round a man?"

"It is difficult for us," said Margaret; "but if we are worth marrying, we do guess."

"Cut off from decent society and family ties, what do you suppose happens to thousands of young fellows overseas? Isolated. No one near. I know by bitter experience, and yet you say it makes 'no difference.'"

"Not to me."

He laughed bitterly. Margaret went to the sideboard and helped herself to one of the breakfast dishes. Being the last down, she turned out the spirit-lamp that kept them warm. She was tender, but grave. She knew that Henry was not so much confessing his soul as pointing out the gulf between the male soul and the female, and she did not desire to hear him on this point.

"Did Helen come?" she asked.

He shook his head.

"But that won't do at all, at all! We don't want her gossiping with Mrs. Bast."

"Good God! no!" he exclaimed, suddenly natural. Then he caught himself up. "Let them gossip. My game's up, though I thank you for your unselfishness — little as my thanks are worth."

"Didn't she send me a message or anything?"

"I heard of none."

"Would you ring the bell, please?"

" What to do ? "

" Why, to inquire."

He swaggered up to it tragically, and sounded a peal. Margaret poured herself out some coffee. The butler came, and said that Miss Schlegel had slept at the George, so far as he had heard. Should he go round to the George?

" I'll go, thank you," said Margaret, and dismissed him.

" It is no good," said Henry. " Those things leak out; you cannot stop a story once it has started. I have known cases of other men — I despised them once, I thought that *I'm* different, *I* shall never be tempted. Oh, Margaret —" He came and sat down near her, improvising emotion. She could not bear to listen to him. " We fellows all come to grief once in our time. Will you believe that? There are moments when the strongest man — ' Let him who standeth, take heed lest he fall.' That's true, isn't it? If you knew all, you would excuse me. I was far from good influences — far even from England. I was very, very lonely, and longed for a woman's voice. That's enough. I have told you too much already for you to forgive me now."

" Yes, that's enough, dear."

" I have "— he lowered his voice —" I have been through hell."

Gravely she considered this claim. Had he? Had he suffered tortures of remorse, or had it been, " There! that's over. Now for respectable life again "? The latter, if she read him rightly. A man who has been through hell does not boast of his virility. He is humble and hides it, if, indeed, it still exists. Only in legend does the sinner come forth penitent, but terrible, to conquer pure woman by his resistless power. Henry was anxious to be terrible, but had not got it in him. He was a good average

Englishman, who had slipped. The really culpable point — his faithlessness to Mrs. Wilcox — never seemed to strike him. She longed to mention Mrs. Wilcox.

And bit by bit the story was told her. It was a very simple story. Ten years ago was the time, a garrison town in Cyprus the place. Now and then he asked her whether she could possibly forgive him, and she answered, "I have already forgiven you, Henry." She chose her words carefully, and so saved him from panic. She played the girl, until he could rebuild his fortress and hide his soul from the world. When the butler came to clear away, Henry was in a very different mood — asked the fellow what he was in such a hurry for, complained of the noise last night in the servants' hall. Margaret looked intently at the butler. He, as a handsome young man, was faintly attractive to her as a woman — an attraction so faint as scarcely to be perceptible, yet the skies would have fallen if she had mentioned it to Henry.

On her return from the George the building operations were complete, and the old Henry fronted her, competent, cynical, and kind. He had made a clean breast, had been forgiven, and the great thing now was to forget his failure, and to send it the way of other unsuccessful investments. Jacky rejoined Howards End and Ducie Street, and the vermilion motor-car, and the Argentine Hard Dollars, and all the things and people for whom he had never had much use and had less now. Their memory hampered him. He could scarcely attend to Margaret who brought back disquieting news from the George. Helen and her clients had gone.

"Well, let them go — the man and his wife, I mean, for the more we see of your sister the better."

"But they have gone separately — Helen very early, the Basts just before I arrived. They have left no message. They have answered neither of my notes. I don't like to think what it all means."

" What did you say in the notes? "

" I told you last night."

" Oh — ah — yes! Dear, would you like one turn in the garden? "

Margaret took his arm. The beautiful weather soothed her. But the wheels of Evie's wedding were still at work, tossing the guests outwards as deftly as they had drawn them in, and she could not be with him long. It had been arranged that they should motor to Shrewsbury, whence he would go north, and she back to London with the Warringtons. For a fraction of time she was happy. Then her brain recommenced.

" I am afraid there has been gossiping of some kind at the George. Helen would not have left unless she had heard something. I mismanaged that. It is wretched. I ought to have parted her from that woman at once."

" Margaret! " he exclaimed, loosing her arm impressively.

" Yes — yes, Henry? "

" I am far from a saint — in fact, the reverse — but you have taken me, for better or worse. Bygones must be bygones. You have promised to forgive me. Margaret, a promise is a promise. Never mention that woman again."

" Except for some practical reason — never."

" Practical! You practical! "

" Yes, I'm practical," she murmured, stooping over the mowing-machine and playing with the grass which trickled through her fingers like sand.

He had silenced her, but her fears made him uneasy. Not for the first time, he was threatened with blackmail. He was rich and supposed to be moral; the Basts knew that he was not, and might find it profitable to hint as much.

" At all events, you mustn't worry," he said. " This is a man's business." He thought intently. " On no account mention it to anybody."

Margaret flushed at advice so elementary, but he was really paving the way for a lie. If necessary he would deny that he had ever known Mrs. Bast, and prosecute her for libel. Perhaps he never had known her. Here was Margaret, who behaved as if he had not. There the house. Round them were half a dozen gardeners, clearing up after his daughter's wedding. All was so solid and spruce, that the past flew up out of sight like a spring-blind, leaving only the last five minutes unrolled.

Glancing at these, he saw that the car would be round during the next five, and plunged into action. Gongs were tapped, orders issued, Margaret was sent to dress, and the housemaid to sweep up the long trickle of grass that she had left across the hall. As is Man to the Universe, so was the mind of Mr. Wilcox to the minds of some men — a concentrated light upon a tiny spot, a little Ten Minutes moving self-contained through its appointed years. No Pagan he, who lives for the Now, and may be wiser than all philosophers. He lived for the five minutes that have past, and the five to come ; he had the business mind.

How did he stand now, as his motor slipped out of Oniton and breasted the great round hills? Margaret had heard a certain rumour, but was all right. She had forgiven him, God bless her, and he felt the manlier for it. Charles and Evie had not heard it, and never must hear. No more must Paul. Over his children he felt great tenderness, which he did not try to track to a cause : Mrs. Wilcox was too far back in his life. He did not connect her with the sudden aching love that he felt for Evie. Poor little Evie! he trusted that Cahill would make her a decent husband.

And Margaret? How did she stand?

She had several minor worries. Clearly her sister had heard something. She dreaded meeting her in town. And she was anxious about Leonard, for whom they certainly were responsible. Nor ought Mrs. Bast to starve. But the main situation had not altered. She still loved Henry. His actions, not his disposition, had disappointed her, and she could bear that. And she loved her future home. Standing up in the car, just where she had leapt from it two days before, she gazed back with deep emotion upon Oniton. Besides the Grange and the Castle keep, she could now pick out the church and the black-and-white gables of the George. There was the bridge, and the river nibbling its green peninsula. She could even see the bathing-shed, but while she was looking for Charles's new springboard, the forehead of the hill rose up and hid the whole scene.

She never saw it again. Day and night the river flows down into England, day after day the sun retreats into the Welsh mountains, and the tower chimes, "See the Conquering Hero." But the Wilcoxes have no part in the place, nor in any place. It is not their names that recur in the parish register. It is not their ghosts that sigh among the alders at evening. They have swept into the valley and swept out of it, leaving a little dust and a little money behind.

Chapter XXX

TIBBY was now approaching his last year at Oxford. He had moved out of college, and was contemplating the Universe, or such portions of it as concerned him, from his comfortable lodgings in Long Wall. He was not concerned with much. When a young man is untroubled by passions and sincerely indifferent to public opinion, his outlook is necessarily limited. Tibby neither wished to strengthen the position of the rich nor to improve that of the poor, and so was well content to watch the elms nodding behind the mildly embattled parapets of Magdalen. There are worse lives. Though selfish, he was never cruel; though affected in manner, he never posed. Like Margaret, he disdained the heroic equipment, and it was only after many visits that men discovered Schlegel to possess a character and a brain. He had done well in Mods, much to the surprise of those who attended lectures and took proper exercise, and was now glancing disdainfully at Chinese in case he should some day consent to qualify as a Student Interpreter. To him thus employed Helen entered. A telegram had preceded her.

He noticed, in a distant way, that his sister had altered. As a rule he found her too pronounced, and had never come across this look of appeal, pathetic yet dignified — the look of a sailor who has lost everything at sea.

"I have come from Oniton," she began. "There has been a great deal of trouble there."

" Who's for lunch? " said Tibby, picking up the claret, which was warming in the hearth. Helen sat down submissively at the table. " Why such an early start? " he asked.

" Sunrise or something — when I could get away."

" So I surmise. Why? "

" I don't know what's to be done, Tibby. I am very much upset at a piece of news that concerns Meg, and do not want to face her, and I am not going back to Wickham Place. I stopped here to tell you this."

The landlady came in with the cutlets. Tibby put a marker in the leaves of his Chinese Grammar and helped them. Oxford — the Oxford of the vacation — dreamed and rustled outside, and indoors the little fire was coated with grey where the sunshine touched it. Helen continued her odd story.

" Give Meg my love and say that I want to be alone. I mean to go to Munich or else Bonn."

" Such a message is easily given," said her brother.

" As regards Wickham Place and my share of the furniture, you and she are to do exactly as you like. My own feeling is that everything may just as well be sold. What does one want with dusty economic books, which have made the world no better, or with mother's hideous chiffoniers? I have also another commission for you. I want you to deliver a letter." She got up. " I haven't written it yet. Why shouldn't I post it, though? " She sat down again. " My head is rather wretched. I hope that none of your friends are likely to come in."

Tibby locked the door. His friends often found it in this condition. Then he asked whether anything had gone wrong at Evie's wedding.

" Not there," said Helen, and burst into tears.

He had known her hysterical — it was one of her aspects with which he had no concern — and yet these tears touched him as something unusual. They were nearer the things that did concern him, such as music. He laid down his knife and looked at her curiously. Then, as she continued to sob, he went on with his lunch.

The time came for the second course, and she was still crying. Apple Charlotte was to follow, which spoils by waiting. " Do you mind Mrs. Martlett coming in? " he asked, " or shall I take it from her at the door? "

" Could I bathe my eyes, Tibby? "

He took her to his bedroom, and introduced the pudding in her absence. Having helped himself, he put it down to warm in the hearth. His hand stretched towards the Grammar, and soon he was turning over the pages, raising his eyebrows scornfully, perhaps at human nature, perhaps at Chinese. To him thus employed Helen returned. She had pulled herself together, but the grave appeal had not vanished from her eyes.

" Now for the explanation," she said. " Why didn't I begin with it? I have found out something about Mr. Wilcox. He has behaved very wrongly indeed, and ruined two people's lives. It all came on me very suddenly last night; I am very much upset, and I do not know what to do. Mrs. Bast —"

" Oh, those people! "

Helen seemed silenced.

" Shall I lock the door again? "

" No, thanks, Tibbikins. You're being very good to me. I want to tell you the story before I go abroad. You must do exactly what you like — treat it as part of the furniture. Meg cannot have heard it yet, I think. But I cannot face her and tell her that the man she is going to marry has misconducted himself. I don't even know whether she ought to be told. Knowing as she does that I dislike him, she will suspect me, and think that I want to ruin her match. I simply don't know what to make of such a thing. I trust your judgment. What would you do?"

" I gather he has had a mistress," said Tibby.

Helen flushed with shame and anger. " And ruined two people's lives. And goes about saying that personal actions count for nothing, and there always will be rich and poor. He met her when he was trying to get rich out in Cyprus — I don't wish to make him worse than he is, and no doubt she was ready enough to meet him. But there it is. They met. He goes his way and she goes hers. What do you suppose is the end of such women?"

He conceded that it was a bad business.

" They end in two ways: Either they sink till the lunatic asylums and the workhouses are full of them, and cause Mr. Wilcox to write letters to the papers complaining of our national degeneracy, or else they entrap a boy into marriage before it is too late. She — I can't blame her.

" But this isn't all," she continued after a long pause, during which the landlady served them with coffee. " I come now to the business that took us to Oniton. We went all three. Acting on Mr. Wilcox's advice, the man throws up a secure situation and takes an insecure one, from which he is dismissed. There are certain excuses, but in the main Mr. Wilcox is to blame, as Meg herself admitted. It is only common justice that he should employ the man himself. But he meets the woman, and, like the cur that he is, he refuses, and tries to get rid of them. He makes Meg write. Two notes came from her late that evening — one for me, one for Leonard, dismissing him with barely a reason. I couldn't understand. Then it comes out that Mrs. Bast had spoken to Mr. Wilcox on the lawn while we left her to get rooms, and was still speaking about him when Leonard came back to her. This Leonard knew all along. He thought it natural he should be ruined twice. Natural! Could you have contained yourself?"

"It is certainly a very bad business," said Tibby.

His reply seemed to calm his sister. "I was afraid that I saw it out of proportion. But you are right outside it, and you must know. In a day or two — or perhaps a week — take whatever steps you think fit. I leave it in your hands."

She concluded her charge.

"The facts as they touch Meg are all before you," she added; and Tibby sighed and felt it rather hard that, because of his open mind, he should be empanelled to serve as a juror. He had never been interested in human beings, for which one must blame him, but he had had rather too much of them at Wickham Place. Just as some people cease to attend when books are mentioned, so Tibby's attention wandered when " personal relations " came under discussion. Ought Margaret to know what Helen knew the Basts to know? Similar questions had vexed him from infancy, and at Oxford he had learned to say that the importance of human beings has been vastly overrated by specialists. The epigram, with its faint whiff of the eighties, meant nothing. But he might have let it off now if his sister had not been ceaselessly beautiful.

"You see, Helen — have a cigarette — I don't see what I'm to do."

"Then there's nothing to be done. I dare say you are right. Let them marry. There remains the question of compensation."

"Do you want me to adjudicate that too? Had you not better consult an expert?"

"This part is in confidence," said Helen. "It has nothing to do with Meg, and do not mention it to her. The compensation — I do not see who is to pay it if I don't, and I have already decided on the minimum sum. As soon as possible I am placing it to your account, and when I am in Germany you will pay it over for me. I shall never forget your kindness, Tibbikins, if you do this."

" What is the sum? "

" Five thousand."

" Good God alive! " said Tibby, and went crimson.

" Now, what is the good of driblets? To go through life having done one thing — to have raised one person from the abyss: not these puny gifts of shillings and blankets — making the grey more grey. No doubt people will think me extraordinary."

" I don't care a damn what people think! " cried he, heated to unusual manliness of diction. " But it's half what you have."

" Not nearly half." She spread out her hands over her soiled skirt. " I have far too much, and we settled at Chelsea last spring that three hundred a year is necessary to set a man on his feet. What I give will bring in a hundred and fifty between two. It isn't enough."

He could not recover. He was not angry or even shocked, and he saw that Helen would still have plenty to live on. But it amazed him to think what haycocks people can make of their lives. His delicate intonations would not work, and he could only blurt out that the five thousand pounds would mean a great deal of bother for him personally.

" I didn't expect you to understand me."

" I? I understand nobody."

" But you'll do it? "

" Apparently."

" I leave you two commissions, then. The first concerns Mr. Wilcox, and you are to use your discretion. The second concerns the money, and is to be mentioned to no one, and carried out literally. You will send a hundred pounds on account tomorrow."

He walked with her to the station, passing through

those streets whose serried beauty never bewildered him and never fatigued. The lovely creature raised domes and spires into the cloudless blue, and only the ganglion of vulgarity round Carfax showed how evanescent was the phantom, how faint its claim to represent England. Helen, rehearsing her commission, noticed nothing: the Basts were in her brain, and she retold the crisis in a meditative way, which might have made other men curious. She was seeing whether it would hold. He asked her once why she had taken the Basts right into the heart of Evie's wedding. She stopped like a frightened animal and said, "Does that seem to you so odd?" Her eyes, the hand laid on the mouth, quite haunted him, until they were absorbed into the figure of St. Mary the Virgin, before whom he paused for a moment on the walk home.

It is convenient to follow him in the discharge of his duties. Margaret summoned him the next day. She was terrified at Helen's flight, and he had to say that she had called in at Oxford. Then she said: "Did she seem worried at any rumour about Henry?" He answered, "Yes." "I knew it was that!" she exclaimed. "I'll write to her." Tibby was relieved.

He then sent the cheque to the address that Helen gave him, and stated that later on he was instructed to forward five thousand pounds. An answer came back, very civil and quiet in tone — such an answer as Tibby himself would have given. The cheque was returned, the legacy refused, the writer being in no need of money. Tibby forwarded this to Helen, adding in the fulness of his heart that Leonard Bast seemed somewhat a monumental person after all. Helen's reply was frantic. He was to take no notice. He was to go down at once and say that she commanded acceptance. He went. A scurf of books and china ornaments awaited him. The Basts had just been evicted for not paying their rent, and had wandered no one knew whither. Helen had begun bungling with her money by this time, and had even sold out her shares in the Nottingham and Derby Railway. For some weeks she did nothing. Then she reinvested, and, owing to the good advice of her stockbrokers, became rather richer than she had been before.

Chapter XXXI

HOUSES have their own ways of dying, falling as variously as the generations of men, some with a tragic roar, some quietly, but to an after-life in the city of ghosts, while from others — and thus was the death of Wickham Place — the spirit slips before the body perishes. It had decayed in the spring, disintegrating the girls more than they knew, and causing either to accost unfamiliar regions. By September it was a corpse, void of emotion, and scarcely hallowed by the memories of thirty years of happiness. Through its round-topped doorway passed furniture, and pictures, and books, until the last room was gutted and the last van had rumbled away. It stood for a week or two longer, open-eyed, as if astonished at its own emptiness. Then it fell. Navvies came, and spilt it back into the grey. With their muscles and their beery good temper, they were not the worst of undertakers for a house which had always been human, and had not mistaken culture for an end.

The furniture, with a few exceptions, went down into Hertfordshire, Mr. Wilcox having most kindly offered Howards End as a warehouse. Mr. Bryce had died abroad — an unsatisfactory affair — and as there seemed little guarantee that the rent would be paid regularly, he cancelled the agreement, and resumed possession himself. Until he relet the house, the Schlegels were welcome to stack their furniture in the garage and lower rooms. Margaret demurred, but Tibby accepted the offer gladly; it saved him from coming to any decision about the future. The plate and the more valuable pictures found a safer home in London, but the bulk of the things went country-ways, and were entrusted to the guardianship of Miss Avery.

Shortly before the move, our hero and heroine were married. They have weathered the storm, and may reasonably expect peace. To have no illusions and yet to love — what stronger surety can a woman find? She had seen her husband's past as well as his heart. She knew her own heart with a thoroughness that commonplace people believe impossible. The heart of Mrs. Wilcox was alone hidden, and perhaps it is superstitious to speculate on the feelings of the dead. They were married quietly — really quietly, for as the day approached she refused to go through another Oniton. Her brother gave her away, her aunt, who was out of health, presided over a few colourless refreshments. The Wilcoxes were represented by Charles, who witnessed the marriage settlement, and by Mr. Cahill. Paul did send a cablegram. In a few minutes, and without the aid of music, the clergyman made them man and wife, and soon the glass shade had fallen that cuts off married couples from the world. She, a monogamist, regretted the cessation of some of life's innocent odours; he, whose instincts were polygamous, felt morally braced by the change, and less liable to the temptations that had assailed him in the past.

They spent their honeymoon near Innsbruck. Henry knew of a reliable hotel there, and Margaret hoped for a meeting with her sister. In this she was disappointed. As they came south, Helen retreated over the Brenner, and wrote an unsatisfactory postcard from the shores of the Lake of Garda, saying that her plans were uncertain and had better be ignored. Evidently she disliked meeting Henry. Two months are surely enough to accustom an outsider to a situation which a wife has accepted in two days, and Margaret had again to regret her sister's lack of self-control. In a long letter she pointed out the need of charity in sexual matters: so little is known about them; it is hard enough for those who are personally touched to judge; then how futile must be the verdict of Society. "I don't say there is no standard, for that would destroy morality; only that there can be no standard until our impulses are classified and better understood." Helen thanked her for her kind letter — rather a curious reply. She moved south again, and spoke of wintering in Naples.

Mr. Wilcox was not sorry that the meeting failed. Helen left him time to grow skin over his wound. There were still moments when it pained him. Had he only known that Margaret was awaiting him — Margaret, so lively and intelligent, and yet so submissive — he would have kept himself worthier of her. Incapable of grouping the past, he confused the episode of Jacky with another episode that had taken place in the days of his bachelorhood. The two made one crop of wild oats, for which he was heartily sorry, and he could not see that those oats are of a darker stock which are rooted in another's dishonour. Unchastity and infidelity were as confused to him as to the Middle Ages, his only moral teacher. Ruth (poor old Ruth!) did not enter into his calculations at all, for poor old Ruth had never found him out.

His affection for his present wife grew steadily. Her cleverness gave him no trouble, and, indeed, he liked to see her reading poetry or something about social questions; it distinguished her from the wives of other men. He had only to call, and she clapped the book up and was ready to do what he wished. Then they would argue so jollily, and once or twice she had him in quite a tight corner, but as soon as he grew really serious, she gave in. Man is for war, woman for the recreation of the warrior, but he does not dislike it if she makes a show of fight. She cannot win in a real battle, having no muscles, only nerves. Nerves make her jump out of a moving motor-car, or refuse to be married fashionably. The warrior may well allow her to triumph on such occasions; they move not the imperishable plinth of things that touch his peace.

Margaret had a bad attack of these nerves during the honeymoon. He told her — casually, as was his habit — that Oniton Grange was let. She showed her annoyance, and asked rather crossly why she had not been consulted.

"I didn't want to bother you," he replied. " Besides, I have only heard for certain this morning."

"Where are we to live?" said Margaret, trying to laugh. "I loved the place extraordinarily. Don't you believe in having a permanent home, Henry?"

He assured her that she misunderstood him. It is home life that distinguishes us from the foreigner. But he did not believe in a damp home.

"This is news. I never heard till this minute that Oniton was damp."

"My dear girl!"— he flung out his hand —"have you eyes? have you a skin? How could it be anything but damp in such a situation? In the first place, the Grange is on clay, and built where the castle moat must have been; then there's that detestable little river, steaming all night like a kettle. Feel the cellar walls; look up under the eaves. Ask Sir James or any one. Those Shropshire valleys are notorious. The only possible place for a house in Shropshire is on a hill; but, for my part, I think the country is too far from London, and the scenery nothing special."

Margaret could not resist saying, "Why did you go there, then?"

"I — because —" He drew his head back and

grew rather angry. "Why have we come to the Tyrol, if it comes to that? One might go on asking such questions indefinitely."

One might; but he was only gaining time for a plausible answer. Out it came, and he believed it as soon as it was spoken.

"The truth is, I took Oniton on account of Evie. Don't let this go any further."

"Certainly not."

"I shouldn't like her to know that she nearly let me in for a very bad bargain. No sooner did I sign the agreement than she got engaged. Poor little girl! She was so keen on it all, and wouldn't even wait to make proper inquiries about the shooting. Afraid it would get snapped up — just like all of your sex. Well, no harm's done. She has had her country wedding, and I've got rid of my house to some fellows who are starting a preparatory school."

"Where shall we live, then, Henry? I should enjoy living somewhere."

"I have not yet decided. What about Norfolk?"

Margaret was silent. Marriage had not saved her from the sense of flux. London was but a foretaste of this nomadic civilization which is altering human nature so profoundly, and throws upon personal relations a stress greater than they have ever borne before. Under cosmopolitanism, if it comes, we shall receive no help from the earth. Trees and meadows and mountains will only be a spectacle, and the binding force that they once exercised on character must be entrusted to Love alone. May Love be equal to the task!

"It is now what?" continued Henry. "Nearly October. Let us camp for the winter at Ducie Street, and look out for something in the spring."

"If possible, something permanent. I can't be as

young as I was, for these alterations don't suit me."

"But, my dear, which would you rather have — alterations or rheumatism?"

"I see your point," said Margaret, getting up. "If Oniton is really damp, it is impossible, and must be inhabited by little boys. Only, in the spring, let us look before we leap. I will take warning by Evie, and not hurry you. Remember that you have a free hand this time. These endless moves must be bad for the furniture, and are certainly expensive."

"What a practical little woman it is! What's it been reading? Theo — theo — how much?"

"Theosophy."

So Ducie Street was her first fate — a pleasant enough fate. The house, being only a little larger than Wickham Place, trained her for the immense establishment that was promised in the spring. They were frequently away, but at home life ran fairly regularly. In the morning Henry went to the business, and his sandwich — a relic this of some prehistoric craving — was always cut by her own hand. He did not rely upon the sandwich for lunch, but liked to have it by him in case he grew hungry at eleven. When he had gone, there was the house to look after, and the servants to humanize, and several kettles of Helen's to keep on the boil. Her conscience pricked her a little about the Basts; she was not sorry to have lost sight of them. No doubt Leonard was worth helping, but being Henry's wife, she preferred to help some one else. As for theatres and discussion societies, they attracted her less and less. She began to " miss " new movements, and to spend her spare time re-reading or thinking, rather to the concern of her Chelsea friends. They attributed the change to her marriage, and perhaps some deep instinct did warn her not to travel further from her husband than was inevitable. Yet the main cause lay deeper still; she had outgrown stimulants, and was passing from words to things. It was doubtless a pity not to keep up with Wedekind or John, but some closing of the gates is inevitable after thirty, if the mind itself is to become a creative power.

Chapter XXXII

SHE was looking at plans one day in the following spring — they had finally decided to go down into Sussex and build — when Mrs. Charles Wilcox was announced.

" Have you heard the news? " Dolly cried, as soon as she entered the room. " Charles is so ang — I mean he is sure you know about it, or rather, that you don't know."

" Why, Dolly! " said Margaret, placidly kissing her. " Here's a surprise! How are the boys and the baby? "

Boys and the baby were well, and in describing a great row that there had been at Hilton Tennis Club, Dolly forgot her news. The wrong people had tried to get in. The rector, as representing the older inhabitants, had said — Charles had said — the tax-collector had said — Charles had regretted not saying — and she closed the description with, "But lucky you, with four courts of your own at Midhurst."

" It will be very jolly," replied Margaret.

" Are those the plans? Does it matter me seeing them? "

" Of course not."

" Charles has never seen the plans."

" They have only just arrived. Here is the ground floor — no, that's rather difficult. Try the elevation. We are to have a good many gables and a picturesque sky-line."

" What makes it smell so funny? " said Dolly, after

a moment's inspection. She was incapable of understanding plans or maps.

" I suppose the paper."

" And *which* way up is it? "

" Just the ordinary way up. That's the sky-line,
and the part that smells strongest is the sky."

" Well, ask me another. Margaret — oh — what
was I going to say? How's Helen? "

" Quite well."

" Is she never coming back to England? Every one
thinks it's awfully odd she doesn't."

" So it is," said Margaret, trying to conceal her
vexation. She was getting rather sore on this point.
" Helen is odd, awfully. She has now been away
eight months."

" But hasn't she any address? "

" A poste restante somewhere in Bavaria is her address. Do write her a line. I will look it up for
you."

" No, don't bother. That's eight months she has
been away, surely? "

" Exactly. She left just after Evie's wedding. It
would be eight months."

" Just when baby was born, then? "

" Just so."

Dolly sighed, and stared enviously round the drawing-room. She was beginning to lose her brightness
and good looks. The Charles' were not well off, for
Mr. Wilcox, having brought up his children with expensive tastes, believed in letting them shift for themselves. After all, he had not treated them generously.
Yet another baby was expected, she told Margaret,
and they would have to give up the motor. Margaret sympathized, but in a formal fashion, and Dolly
little imagined that the step-mother was urging Mr.
Wilcox to make them a more liberal allowance. She
sighed again, and at last the particular grievance was

remembered. "Oh yes," she cried, "that is it: Miss Avery has been unpacking your packing-cases."

"Why has she done that? How unnecessary!"

"Ask another. I suppose you ordered her to."

"I gave no such orders. Perhaps she was airing the things. She did undertake to light an occasional fire."

"It was far more than an air," said Dolly solemnly. "The floor sounds covered with books. Charles sent me to know what is to be done, for he feels certain you don't know."

"Books!" cried Margaret, moved by the holy word. "Dolly, are you serious? Has she been touching our books?"

"Hasn't she, though! What used to be the hall's full of them. Charles thought for certain you knew of it."

"I am very much obliged to you, Dolly. What can have come over Miss Avery? I must go down about it at once. Some of the books are my brother's, and are quite valuable. She had no right to open any of the cases."

"I say she's dotty. She was the one that never got married, you know. Oh, I say, perhaps she thinks your books are wedding-presents to herself. Old maids are taken that way sometimes. Miss Avery hates us all like poison ever since her frightful dust-up with Evie."

"I hadn't heard of that," said Margaret. A visit from Dolly had its compensations.

"Didn't you know she gave Evie a present last August, and Evie returned it, and then — oh, goloshes! You never read such a letter as Miss Avery wrote."

"But it was wrong of Evie to return it. It wasn't like her to do such a heartless thing."

"But the present was so expensive."

"Why does that make any difference, Dolly?"

" Still, when it costs over five pounds — I didn't
see it, but it was a lovely enamel pendant from a Bond
Street shop. You can't very well accept that kind of
thing from a farm woman. Now, can you?"

" You accepted a present from Miss Avery when you
were married."

" Oh, mine was old earthenware stuff — not worth
a halfpenny. Evie's was quite different. You'd have
to ask any one to the wedding who gave you a pendant
like that. Uncle Percy and Albert and father and
Charles all said it was quite impossible, and when four
men agree, what is a girl to do? Evie didn't want to
upset the old thing, so thought a sort of joking letter
best, and returned the pendant straight to the shop to
save Miss Avery trouble."

" But Miss Avery said — "

Dolly's eyes grew round. " It was a perfectly awful letter. Charles said it was the letter of a madman.
In the end she had the pendant back again from the
shop and threw it into the duckpond."

" Did she give any reasons?"

" We think she meant to be invited to Oniton, and
so climb into society."

" She's rather old for that," said Margaret pensively. " May not she have given the present to Evie
in remembrance of her mother?"

" That's a notion. Give every one their due, eh?
Well, I suppose I ought to be toddling. Come along
Mr. Muff — you want a new coat, but I don't know
who'll give it you, I'm sure; " and addressing her apparel with mournful humour, Dolly moved from the
room.

Margaret followed her to ask whether Henry knew
about Miss Avery's rudeness.

" Oh yes."

" I wonder, then, why he let me ask her to look after
the house."

"But she's only a farm woman," said Dolly, and her explanation proved correct. Henry only censured the lower classes when it suited him. He bore with Miss Avery as with Crane — because he could get good value out of them. "I have patience with a man who knows his job," he would say, really having patience with the job, and not the man. Paradoxical as it may sound, he had something of the artist about him; he would pass over an insult to his daughter sooner than lose a good charwoman for his wife.

Margaret judged it better to settle the little trouble herself. Parties were evidently ruffled. With Henry's permission, she wrote a pleasant note to Miss Avery, asking her to leave the cases untouched. Then, at the first convenient opportunity, she went down herself, intending to repack her belongings and store them properly in the local warehouse: the plan had been amateurish and a failure. Tibby promised to accompany her, but at the last moment begged to be excused. So, for the second time in her life, she entered the house alone.

Chapter XXXIII

THE day of her visit was exquisite, and the last of unclouded happiness that she was to have for many months. Her anxiety about Helen's extraordinary absence was still dormant, and as for a possible brush with Miss Avery — that only gave zest to the expedition. She had also eluded Dolly's invitation to luncheon. Walking straight up from the station, she crossed the village green and entered the long chestnut avenue that connects it with the church. The church itself stood in the village once. But it there attracted so many worshippers that the devil, in a pet, snatched it from its foundations, and poised it on an inconvenient knoll, three-quarters of a mile away. If this story is true, the chestnut avenue must have been planted by the angels. No more tempting approach could be imagined for the lukewarm Christian, and if he still finds the walk too long, the devil is defeated all the same, Science having built Holy Trinity, a Chapel of Ease, near the Charles', and roofed it with tin.

Up the avenue Margaret strolled slowly, stopping to watch the sky that gleamed through the upper branches of the chestnuts, or to finger the little horseshoes on the lower branches. Why has not England a great mythology? Our folklore has never advanced beyond daintiness, and the greater melodies about our country-side have all issued through the pipes of Greece. Deep and true as the native imagination can be, it seems to have failed here. It has stopped with the witches and the fairies. It cannot vivify one fraction of a summer field, or give names to half a dozen stars. England still waits for the supreme moment of her literature — for the great poet who shall voice her, or, better still, for the thousand little poets whose voices shall pass into our common talk.

At the church the scenery changed. The chestnut avenue opened into a road, smooth but narrow, which led into the untouched country. She followed it for over a mile. Its little hesitations pleased her. Having no urgent destiny, it strolled downhill or up as it wished, taking no trouble about the gradients, nor about the view, which nevertheless expanded. The great estates that throttle the south of Hertfordshire were less obtrusive here, and the appearance of the land was neither aristocratic nor suburban. To define it was difficult, but Margaret knew what it was not: it was not snobbish. Though its contours were slight, there was a touch of freedom in their sweep to which Surrey will never attain, and the distant brow of the Chilterns towered like a mountain. "Left to itself," was Margaret's opinion, "this county would vote Liberal." The comradeship, not passionate, that is our highest gift as a nation, was promised by it, as by the low brick farm where she called for the key.

But the inside of the farm was disappointing. A most finished young person received her. "Yes, Mrs. Wilcox; no, Mrs. Wilcox; oh yes, Mrs. Wilcox, auntie received your letter quite duly. Auntie has gone up to your little place at the present moment. Shall I send the servant to direct you?" Followed by: "Of course, auntie does not generally look after your place; she only does it to oblige a neighbour as something exceptional. It gives her something to do. She spends quite a lot of her time there. My husband says to me sometimes, 'Where's auntie?' I say, 'Need you ask? She's at Howards End.' Yes, Mrs. Wilcox. Mrs.

Wilcox, could I prevail upon you to accept a piece of cake? Not if I cut it for you?"

Margaret refused the cake, but unfortunately this acquired her gentility in the eyes of Miss Avery's niece.

"I cannot let you go on alone. Now don't. You really mustn't. I will direct you myself if it comes to that. I must get my hat. Now" — roguishly — "Mrs. Wilcox, don't you move while I'm gone."

Stunned, Margaret did not move from the best parlour, over which the touch of art nouveau had fallen. But the other rooms looked in keeping, though they conveyed the peculiar sadness of a rural interior. Here had lived an elder race, to which we look back with disquietude. The country which we visit at week-ends was really a home to it, and the graver sides of life, the deaths, the partings, the yearnings for love, have their deepest expression in the heart of the fields. All was not sadness. The sun was shining without. The thrush sang his two syllables on the budding guelder-rose. Some children were playing uproariously in heaps of golden straw. It was the presence of sadness at all that surprised Margaret, and ended by giving her a feeling of completeness. In these English farms, if anywhere, one might see life steadily and see it whole, group in one vision its transitoriness and its eternal youth, connect — connect without bitterness until all men are brothers. But her thoughts were interrupted by the return of Miss Avery's niece, and were so tranquillizing that she suffered the interruption gladly.

It was quicker to go out by the back door, and, after due explanations, they went out by it. The niece was now mortified by innumerable chickens, who rushed up to her feet for food, and by a shameless and maternal sow. She did not know what animals were coming to. But her gentility withered at the touch of the sweet air. The wind was rising, scattering the straw and ruffling the tails of the ducks as they floated in families over Evie's pendant. One of those delicious gales of spring, in which leaves still in bud seem to rustle, swept over the land and then fell silent. "Georgie," sang the thrush. "Cuckoo," came furtively from the cliff of pine-trees. "Georgie, pretty Georgie," and the other birds joined in with nonsense. The hedge was a half-painted picture which would be finished in a few days. Celandines grew on its banks, lords and ladies and primroses in the defended hollows; the wild rose-bushes, still bearing their withered hips, showed also the promise of blossom. Spring had come, clad in no classical garb, yet fairer than all springs; fairer even than she who walks through the myrtles of Tuscany with the graces before her and the zephyr behind.

The two women walked up the lane full of outward civility. But Margaret was thinking how difficult it was to be earnest about furniture on such a day, and the niece was thinking about hats. Thus engaged, they reached Howards End. Petulant cries of "Auntie!" severed the air. There was no reply, and the front door was locked.

"Are you sure that Miss Avery is up here?" asked Margaret.

"Oh yes, Mrs. Wilcox, quite sure. She is here daily."

Margaret tried to look in through the dining-room window, but the curtain inside was drawn tightly. So with the drawing-room and the hall. The appearance of these curtains was familiar, yet she did not remember them being there on her other visit: her impression was that Mr. Bryce had taken everything away. They tried the back. Here again they received no answer, and could see nothing; the kitchen-window was fitted with a blind, while the pantry and scullery had pieces of wood propped up against them, which looked ominously like the lids of packing-cases. Margaret thought of her books, and she lifted up her voice also. At the first cry she succeeded.

"Well, well!" replied some one inside the house. "If it isn't Mrs. Wilcox come at last!"

"Have you got the key, auntie?"

"Madge, go away," said Miss Avery, still invisible.

"Auntie, it's Mrs. Wilcox —"

Margaret supported her. "Your niece and I have come together — "

"Madge, go away. This is no moment for your hat."

The poor woman went red. "Auntie gets more eccentric lately," she said nervously.

"Miss Avery!" called Margaret. "I have come about the furniture. Could you kindly let me in?"

"Yes, Mrs. Wilcox," said the voice, "of course." But after that came silence. They called again without response. They walked round the house disconsolately.

"I hope Miss Avery is not ill," hazarded Margaret.

"Well, if you'll excuse me," said Madge, "perhaps I ought to be leaving you now. The servants need seeing to at the farm. Auntie is so odd at times." Gathering up her elegancies, she retired defeated, and, as if her departure had loosed a spring, the front door opened at once.

Miss Avery said, "Well, come right in, Mrs. Wilcox!" quite pleasantly and calmly.

"Thank you so much," began Margaret, but broke off at the sight of an umbrella-stand. It was her own.

"Come right into the hall first," said Miss Avery. She drew the curtain, and Margaret uttered a cry of despair. For an appalling thing had happened. The hall was fitted up with the contents of the library from Wickham Place. The carpet had been laid, the big work-table drawn up near the window; the bookcases filled the wall opposite the fireplace, and her father's sword — this is what bewildered her particularly — had been drawn from its scabbard and hung naked amongst the sober volumes. Miss Avery must have worked for days.

"I'm afraid this isn't what we meant," she began. "Mr. Wilcox and I never intended the cases to be touched. For instance, these books are my brother's. We are storing them for him and for my sister, who is abroad. When you kindly undertook to look after things, we never expected you to do so much."

"The house has been empty long enough," said the old woman.

Margaret refused to argue. "I dare say we didn't explain," she said civilly. "It has been a mistake, and very likely our mistake."

"Mrs. Wilcox, it has been mistake upon mistake for fifty years. The house is Mrs. Wilcox's, and she would not desire it to stand empty any longer."

To help the poor decaying brain, Margaret said:

"Yes, Mrs. Wilcox's house, the mother of Mr. Charles."

"Mistake upon mistake," said Miss Avery. "Mistake upon mistake."

"Well, I don't know," said Margaret, sitting down in one of her own chairs. "I really don't know what's to be done." She could not help laughing.

The other said: "Yes, it should be a merry house enough."

"I don't know — I dare say. Well, thank you very much, Miss Avery. Yes, that's all right. Delightful."

"There is still the parlour." She went through the door opposite and drew a curtain. Light flooded the drawing-room and the drawing-room furniture from Wickham Place. "And the dining-room." More curtains were drawn, more windows were flung open to the spring. " Then through here — " Miss Avery continued passing and repassing through the hall. Her voice was lost, but Margaret heard her pulling up the kitchen blind. " I've not finished here yet," she announced, returning. " There's still a deal to do. The farm lads will carry your great wardrobes upstairs, for there is no need to go into expense at Hilton."

" It is all a mistake," repeated Margaret, feeling that she must put her foot down. " A misunderstanding. Mr. Wilcox and I are not going to live at Howards End."

" Oh, indeed. On account of his hay fever?"

" We have settled to build a new home for ourselves in Sussex, and part of this furniture — my part — will go down there presently." She looked at Miss Avery intently, trying to understand the kink in her brain. Here was no maundering old woman. Her wrinkles were shrewd and humorous. She looked capable of scathing wit and also of high but unostentatious nobility.

" You think that you won't come back to live here, Mrs. Wilcox, but you will."

" That remains to be seen," said Margaret, smiling. " We have no intention of doing so for the present. We happen to need a much larger house. Circumstances oblige us to give big parties. Of course, some day — one never knows, does one?"

Miss Avery retorted: " Some day! Tcha! tcha! Don't talk about some day. You are living here now."

" Am I?"

" You are living here, and have been for the last ten minutes, if you ask me."

It was a senseless remark, but with a queer feeling of disloyalty Margaret rose from her chair. She felt that Henry had been obscurely censured. They went into the dining-room, where the sunlight poured in upon her mother's chiffonier, and upstairs, where many an old god peeped from a new niche. The furniture fitted extraordinarily well. In the central room — over the hall, the room that Helen had slept in four years ago — Miss Avery had placed Tibby's old bassinette.

" The nursery," she said.

Margaret turned away without speaking.

At last everything was seen. The kitchen and lobby were still stacked with furniture and straw, but, as far as she could make out, nothing had been broken or scratched. A pathetic display of ingenuity! Then they took a friendly stroll in the garden. It had gone wild since her last visit. The gravel sweep was weedy, and grass had sprung up at the very jaws of the garage. And Evie's rockery was only bumps. Perhaps Evie was responsible for Miss Avery's oddness. But Margaret suspected that the cause lay deeper, and that the girl's silly letter had but loosed the irritation of years.

" It's a beautiful meadow," she remarked. It was one of those open-air drawing-rooms that have been formed, hundreds of years ago, out of the smaller fields. So the boundary hedge zigzagged down the hill at right angles, and at the bottom there was a little green annex — a sort of powder-closet for the cows.

" Yes, the maidy's well enough," said Miss Avery, " for those that is, who don't suffer from sneezing." And she cackled maliciously. " I've seen Charlie Wilcox go out to my lads in hay time — oh, they ought to do this — they mustn't do that — he'd learn them to be lads. And just then the tickling took him. He has it from his father, with other things. There's not one Wilcox that can stand up against a field in June — I laughed fit to burst while he was courting Ruth."

" My brother gets hay fever too," said Margaret.

" This house lies too much on the land for them. Naturally, they were glad enough to slip in at first.

But Wilcoxes are better than nothing, as I see you've found."

Margaret laughed.

"They keep a place going, don't they? Yes, it is just that."

"They keep England going, it is my opinion."

But Miss Avery upset her by replying: "Ay, they breed like rabbits. Well, well, it's a funny world. But He who made it knows what He wants in it, I suppose. If Mrs. Charlie is expecting her fourth, it isn't for us to repine."

"They breed and they also work," said Margaret, conscious of some invitation to disloyalty, which was echoed by the very breeze and by the songs of the birds. "It certainly is a funny world, but so long as men like my husband and his sons govern it, I think it'll never be a bad one — never really bad."

"No, better'n nothing," said Miss Avery, and turned to the wych-elm.

On their way back to the farm she spoke of her old friend much more clearly than before. In the house Margaret had wondered whether she quite distinguished the first wife from the second. Now she said: "I never saw much of Ruth after her grandmother died, but we stayed civil. It was a very civil family. Old Mrs. Howard never spoke against anybody, nor let any one be turned away without food. Then it was never 'Trespassers will be prosecuted' in their land, but would people please not come in. Mrs. Howard was never created to run a farm."

"Had they no men to help them?" Margaret asked.

Miss Avery replied: "Things went on until there were no men."

"Until Mr. Wilcox came along," corrected Margaret, anxious that her husband should receive his dues.

"I suppose so; but Ruth should have married a —

no disrespect to you to say this, for I take it you were intended to get Wilcox any way, whether she got him first or no."

"Whom should she have married?"

"A soldier!" exclaimed the old woman. "Some real soldier."

Margaret was silent. It was a criticism of Henry's character far more trenchant than any of her own. She felt dissatisfied.

"But that's all over," she went on. "A better time is coming now, though you've kept me long enough waiting. In a couple of weeks I'll see your lights shining through the hedge of an evening. Have you ordered in coals?"

"We are not coming," said Margaret firmly. She respected Miss Avery too much to humour her. "No. Not coming. Never coming. It has all been a mistake. The furniture must be repacked at once, and I am very sorry but I am making other arrangements, and must ask you to give me the keys."

"Certainly, Mrs. Wilcox," said Miss Avery, and resigned her duties with a smile.

Relieved at this conclusion, and having sent her compliments to Madge, Margaret walked back to the station. She had intended to go to the furniture warehouse and give directions for removal, but the muddle had turned out more extensive than she expected, so she decided to consult Henry. It was as well that she did this. He was strongly against employing the local man whom he had previously recommended, and advised her to store in London after all.

But before this could be done an unexpected trouble fell upon her.

Chapter XXXIV

IT was not unexpected entirely. Aunt Juley's health had been bad all the winter. She had had a long series of colds and coughs, and had been too busy to get rid of them. She had scarcely promised her niece " to really take my tiresome chest in hand," when she caught a chill and developed acute pneumonia. Margaret and Tibby went down to Swanage. Helen was telegraphed for, and that spring party that after all gathered in that hospitable house had all the pathos of fair memories. On a perfect day, when the sky seemed blue porcelain, and the waves of the discreet little bay beat gentlest of tattoos upon the sand, Margaret hurried up through the rhododendrons, confronted again by the senselessness of Death One death may explain itself, but it throws no light upon another: the groping inquiry must begin anew. Preachers or scientists may generalize, but we know that no generality is possible about those whom we love; not one heaven awaits them, not even one oblivion. Aunt Juley, incapable of tragedy, slipped out of life with odd little laughs and apologies for having stopped in it so long. She was very weak; she could not rise to the occasion, or realize the great mystery which all agree must await her; it only seemed to her that she was quite done up — more done up than ever before; that she saw and heard and felt less every moment; and that, unless something changed, she would soon feel nothing. Her spare strength she devoted to plans: could not Margaret take some steamer expeditions? were mackerel cooked as Tibby liked them? She worried herself about Helen's absence, and also that she could be the cause of Helen's return. The nurses seemed to think such interests quite natural, and perhaps hers was an average approach to the Great Gate. But Margaret saw Death stripped of any false romance; whatever the idea of Death may contain, the process can be trivial and hideous.

"Important — Margaret dear, take the Lulworth when Helen comes."

"Helen won't be able to stop, Aunt Juley. She has telegraphed that she can only get away just to see you. She must go back to Germany as soon as you are well."

"How very odd of Helen! Mr. Wilcox — "

"Yes, dear?"

"Can he spare you?"

Henry wished her to come, and had been very kind. Yet again Margaret said so.

Mrs. Munt did not die. Quite outside her will, a more dignified power took hold of her and checked her on the downward slope. She returned, without emotion, as fidgety as ever. On the fourth day she was out of danger.

"Margaret — important," it went on: "I should like you to have some companion to take walks with. Do try Miss Conder."

"I have been a little walk with Miss Conder."

"But she is not really interesting. If only you had Helen."

"I have Tibby, Aunt Juley."

"No, but he has to do his Chinese. Some real companion is what you need. Really, Helen is odd."

"Helen is odd, very," agreed Margaret.

"Not content with going abroad, why does she want to go back there at once?"

"No doubt she will change her mind when she sees us. She has not the least balance."

That was the stock criticism about Helen, but Margaret's voice trembled as she made it. By now she was deeply pained at her sister's behaviour. It may be unbalanced to fly out of England, but to stop away eight months argues that the heart is awry as well as the head. A sick-bed could recall Helen, but she was deaf to more human calls; after a glimpse at her aunt, she would retire into her nebulous life behind some poste restante. She scarcely existed; her letters had become dull and infrequent; she had no wants and no curiosity. And it was all put down to poor Henry's account! Henry, long pardoned by his wife, was still too infamous to be greeted by his sister-in-law. It was morbid, and, to her alarm, Margaret fancied that she could trace the growth of morbidity back in Helen's life for nearly four years. The flight from Oniton; the unbalanced patronage of the Basts; the explosion of grief up on the Downs — all connected with Paul, an insignificant boy whose lips had kissed hers for a fraction of time. Margaret and Mrs. Wilcox had feared that they might kiss again. Foolishly: the real danger was reaction. Reaction against the Wilcoxes had eaten into her life until she was scarcely sane. At twenty-five she had an idée fixe. What hope was there for her as an old woman?

The more Margaret thought about it the more alarmed she became. For many months she had put the subject away, but it was too big to be slighted now. There was almost a taint of madness. Were all Helen's actions to be governed by a tiny mishap, such as may happen to any young man or woman? Can human nature be constructed on lines so insignificant? The blundering little encounter at Howards End was vital. It propagated itself where graver intercourse lay barren; it was stronger than sisterly intimacy, stronger than reason or books. In one of her moods Helen had confessed that she still "enjoyed" it in a certain sense. Paul had faded, but the magic of his caress endured. And where there is enjoyment of the past there may also be reaction — propagation at both ends.

Well, it is odd and sad that our minds should be such seed-beds, and we without power to choose the seed. But man is an odd, sad creature as yet, intent on pilfering the earth, and heedless of the growths within himself. He cannot be bored about psychology. He leaves it to the specialist, which is as if he should leave his dinner to be eaten by a steam-engine. He cannot be bothered to digest his own soul. Margaret and Helen have been more patient, and it is suggested that Margaret has succeeded — so far as success is yet possible. She does understand herself, she has some rudimentary control over her own growth. Whether Helen has succeeded one cannot say.

The day that Mrs. Munt rallied Helen's letter arrived. She had posted it at Munich, and would be in London herself on the morrow. It was a disquieting letter, though the opening was affectionate and sane.

"DEAREST MEG,
    "Give Helen's love to Aunt Juley. Tell her that I love, and have loved, her ever since I can remember. I shall be in London Thursday.

"My address will be care of the bankers. I have not yet settled on a hotel, so write or wire to me there and give me detailed news. If Aunt Juley is much better, or if, for a terrible reason, it would be no good my coming down to Swanage, you must not think it odd if I do not come. I have all sorts of plans in my head. I am living abroad at present, and want to get back as quickly as possible. Will you please tell me where our furniture is. I should like to take out one or two books; the rest are for you.

"Forgive me, dearest Meg. This must read like rather a tiresome letter, but all letters are from your loving
                                                    "HELEN."

It was a tiresome letter, for it tempted Margaret to tell a lie. If she wrote that Aunt Juley was still in danger her sister would come. Unhealthiness is contagious. We cannot be in contact with those who are in a morbid state without ourselves deteriorating. To " act for the best " might do Helen good, but would do herself harm, and, at the risk of disaster, she kept her colours flying a little longer. She replied that their aunt was much better, and awaited developments.

Tibby approved of her reply. Mellowing rapidly, he was a pleasanter companion than before. Oxford had done much for him. He had lost his peevishness, and could hide his indifference to people and his interest in food. But he had not grown more human. The years between eighteen and twenty-two, so magical for most, were leading him gently from boyhood to middle age. He had never known young-manliness, that quality which warms the heart till death, and gives Mr. Wilcox an imperishable charm. He was frigid, through no fault of his own, and without cruelty. He thought Helen wrong and Margaret right, but the family trouble was for him what a scene behind footlights is for most people. He had only one sug-gestion to make, and that was characteristic.

" Why don't you tell Mr. Wilcox? "

" About Helen? "

" Perhaps he has come across that sort of thing."

" He would do all he could, but — "

" Oh, you know best. But he is practical."

It was the student's belief in experts. Margaret demurred for one or two reasons. Presently Helen's answer came. She sent a telegram requesting the address of the furniture, as she would now return at once. Margaret replied, " Certainly not; meet me at the bankers at four." She and Tibby went up to London. Helen was not at the bankers, and they were refused her address. Helen had passed into chaos.

Margaret put her arm round her brother. He was all that she had left, and never had he seemed more unsubstantial.

"Tibby love, what next?"

He replied: "It is extraordinary."

"Dear, your judgment's often clearer than mine. Have you any notion what's at the back?"

"None, unless it's something mental."

"Oh—that!" said Margaret. "Quite impossible." But the suggestion had been uttered, and in a few minutes she took it up herself. Nothing else explained. And London agreed with Tibby. The mask fell off the city, and she saw it for what it really is — a caricature of infinity. The familiar barriers, the streets along which she moved, the houses between which she had made her little journeys for so many years, became negligible suddenly. Helen seemed one with grimy trees and the traffic and the slowly-flowing slabs of mud. She had accomplished a hideous act of renunciation and returned to the One. Margaret's own faith held firm. She knew the human soul will be merged, if it be merged at all, with the stars and the sea. Yet she felt that her sister had been going amiss for many years. It was symbolic the catastrophe should come now, on a London afternoon, while rain fell slowly.

Henry was the only hope. Henry was definite. He might know of some paths in the chaos that were hidden from them, and she determined to take Tibby's advice and lay the whole matter in his hands. They must call at his office. He could not well make it worse. She went for a few moments into St. Paul's, whose dome stands out of the welter so bravely, as if preaching the gospel of form. But within, St. Paul's is as its surroundings—echoes and whispers, inaudible songs, invisible mosaics, wet footmarks crossing and recrossing the floor. Si monumentum requiris, circumspice: it points us back to London. There was no hope of Helen here.

Henry was unsatisfactory at first. That she had expected. He was overjoyed to see her back from Swanage, and slow to admit the growth of a new trouble. When they told him of their search, he only chaffed Tibby and the Schlegels generally, and declared that it was " just like Helen " to lead her relatives a dance.

" That is what we all say," replied Margaret. " But why should it be just like Helen? Why should she be allowed to be so queer, and to grow queerer? "

" Don't ask me. I'm a plain man of business. I live and let live. My advice to you both is, don't worry. Margaret, you've got black marks again under your eyes. You know that's strictly forbidden. First your aunt — then your sister. No, we aren't going to have it. Are we, Theobald? " He rang the bell. " I'll give you some tea, and then you go straight to Ducie Street. I can't have my girl looking as old as her husband."

" All the same, you have not quite seen our point," said Tibby.

Mr. Wilcox, who was in good spirits, retorted, " I don't suppose I ever shall." He leant back, laughing at the gifted but ridiculous family, while the fire flickered over the map of Africa. Margaret motioned to her brother to go on. Rather diffident, he obeyed her.

" Margaret's point is this," he said. " Our sister may be mad."

Charles, who was working in the inner room, looked round.

" Come in, Charles," said Margaret kindly. " Could you help us at all? We are again in trouble."

" I'm afraid I cannot. What are the facts? We are all mad more or less, you know, in these days."

"The facts are as follows," replied Tibby, who had at times a pedantic lucidity. "The facts are that she has been in England for three days and will not see us. She has forbidden the bankers to give us her address. She refuses to answer questions. Margaret finds her letters colourless. There are other facts, but these are the most striking."

"She has never behaved like this before, then?" asked Henry.

"Of course not!" said his wife, with a frown.

"Well, my dear, how am I to know?"

A senseless spasm of annoyance came over her. "You know quite well that Helen never sins against affection," she said. "You must have noticed that much in her, surely."

"Oh yes; she and I have always hit it off together."

"No, Henry — can't you see? — I don't mean that."

She recovered herself, but not before Charles had observed her. Stupid and attentive, he was watching the scene.

"I was meaning that when she was eccentric in the past, one could trace it back to the heart in the long-run. She behaved oddly because she cared for someone, or wanted to help them. There's no possible excuse for her now. She is grieving us deeply, and that is why I am sure that she is not well. 'Mad' is too terrible a word, but she is not well. I shall never believe it. I shouldn't discuss my sister with you if I thought she was well — trouble you about her, I mean."

Henry began to grow serious. Ill-health was to him something perfectly definite. Generally well himself, he could not realize that we sink to it by slow gradations. The sick had no rights; they were outside the pale; one could lie to them remorselessly. When his first wife was seized, he had promised to take her down into Hertfordshire, but meanwhile arranged with a nursing-home instead. Helen, too, was ill. And the plan that he sketched out for her capture, clever and well-meaning as it was, drew its ethics from the wolf-pack.

"You want to get hold of her?" he said. "That's the problem, isn't it? She has got to see a doctor."

"For all I know she has seen one already."

"Yes, yes; don't interrupt." He rose to his feet and thought intently. The genial, tentative host disappeared, and they saw instead the man who had carved money out of Greece and Africa, and bought forests from the natives for a few bottles of gin. "I've got it," he said at last. "It's perfectly easy. Leave it to me. We'll send her down to Howards End."

"How will you do that?"

"After her books. Tell her that she must unpack them herself. Then you can meet her there."

"But, Henry, that's just what she won't let me do. It's part of her — whatever it is — never to see me."

"Of course you won't tell her you're going. When she is there, looking at the cases, you'll just stroll in. If nothing is wrong with her, so much the better. But there'll be the motor round the corner, and we can run her up to a specialist in no time."

Margaret shook her head. "It's quite impossible."

"Why?"

"It doesn't seem impossible to me," said Tibby; "it is surely a very tippy plan."

"It is impossible, because — " She looked at her husband sadly. "It's not the particular language that Helen and I talk if you see my meaning. It would do splendidly for other people, whom I don't blame."

"But Helen doesn't talk," said Tibby. "That's our whole difficulty. She won't talk your particular language, and on that account you think she's ill."

"No, Henry; it's sweet of you, but I couldn't."

"I see," he said; "you have scruples."

"I suppose so."

"And sooner than go against them you would have your sister suffer. You could have got her down to Swanage by a word, but you had scruples. And scruples are all very well. I am as scrupulous as any man alive, I hope; but when it is a case like this, when there is a question of madness —"

"I deny it's madness."

"You said just now — "

"It's madness when I say it, but not when you say it."

Henry shrugged his shoulders. "Margaret! Margaret!" he groaned. "No education can teach a woman logic. Now, my dear, my time is valuable. Do you want me to help you or not?"

"Not in that way."

"Answer my question. Plain question, plain answer. Do — "

Charles surprised them by interrupting. "Pater, we may as well keep Howards End out of it," he said.

"Why, Charles?"

Charles could give no reason; but Margaret felt as if, over tremendous distance, a salutation had passed between them.

"The whole house is at sixes and sevens," he said crossly. "We don't want any more mess."

"Who's 'we'?" asked his father. "My boy, pray, who's 'we'?"

"I am sure I beg your pardon," said Charles. "I appear always to be intruding."

By now Margaret wished she had never mentioned her trouble to her husband. Retreat was impossible. He was determined to push the matter to a satisfactory conclusion, and Helen faded as he talked. Her fair, flying hair and eager eyes counted for nothing, for she was ill, without rights, and any of her friends might hunt her. Sick at heart, Margaret joined in the chase. She wrote her sister a lying letter, at her husband's dictation; she said the furniture was all at Howards End, but could be seen on Monday next at 3 p. m., when a charwoman would be in attendance. It was a cold letter, and the more plausible for that. Helen would think she was offended. And on Monday next she and Henry were to lunch with Dolly, and then ambush themselves in the garden.

After they had gone, Mr. Wilcox said to his son: "I can't have this sort of behaviour, my boy. Margaret's too sweet-natured to mind, but I mind for her."

Charles made no answer.

"Is anything wrong with you, Charles, this afternoon?"

"No, pater; but you may be taking on a bigger business than you reckon."

"How?"

"Don't ask me."

Chapter XXXV

ONE speaks of the moods of spring, but the days that are her true children have only one mood; they are all full of the rising and dropping of winds, and the whistling of birds. New flowers may come out, the green embroidery of the hedges increase, but the same heaven broods overhead, soft, thick, and blue, the same figures, seen and unseen, are wandering by coppice and meadow. The morning that Margaret had spent with Miss Avery, and the afternoon she set out to entrap Helen, were the scales of a single balance. Time might never have moved, rain never have fallen, and man alone, with his schemes and ailments, was troubling Nature until he saw her through a veil of tears.

She protested no more. Whether Henry was right or wrong, he was most kind, and she knew of no other standard by which to judge him. She must trust him absolutely. As soon as he had taken up a business, his obtuseness vanished. He profited by the slightest indications, and the capture of Helen promised to be staged as deftly as the marriage of Evie.

They went down in the morning as arranged, and he discovered that their victim was actually in Hilton. On his arrival he called at all the livery-stables in the village, and had a few minutes' serious conversation with the proprietors. What he said, Margaret did not know — perhaps not the truth; but news arrived after lunch that a lady had come by the London train, and had taken a fly to Howards End.

"She was bound to drive," said Henry. "There will be her books."

"I cannot make it out," said Margaret for the hundredth time.

"Finish your coffee, dear. We must be off."

"Yes, Margaret, you know you must take plenty," said Dolly.

Margaret tried, but suddenly lifted her hand to her eyes. Dolly stole glances at her father-in-law which he did not answer. In the silence the motor came round to the door.

"You're not fit for it," he said anxiously. "Let me go alone. I know exactly what to do."

"Oh yes, I am fit," said Margaret, uncovering her face. "Only most frightfully worried. I cannot feel that Helen is really alive. Her letters and telegrams seem to have come from some one else. Her voice isn't in them. I don't believe your driver really saw her at the station. I wish I'd never mentioned it. I know that Charles is vexed. Yes, he is —" She seized Dolly's hand and kissed it. "There, Dolly will forgive me. There. Now we'll be off."

Henry had been looking at her closely. He did not like this breakdown.

"Don't you want to tidy yourself?" he asked.

"Have I time?"

"Yes, plenty."

She went to the lavatory by the front door, and as soon as the bolt slipped, Mr. Wilcox said quietly:

"Dolly, I'm going without her."

Dolly's eyes lit up with vulgar excitement. She followed him on tip-toe out to the car.

"Tell her I thought it best."

"Yes, Mr. Wilcox, I see."

"Say anything you like. All right."

The car started well, and with ordinary luck would have got away. But Porgly-woggles, who was playing in the garden, chose this moment to sit down in the middle of the path. Crane, in trying to pass him, ran one wheel over a bed of wallflowers. Dolly screamed. Margaret, hearing the noise, rushed out hatless, and was in time to jump on the footboard. She said not a single word: he was only treating her as she had treated Helen, and her rage at his dishonesty only helped to indicate what Helen would feel against them. She thought, " I deserve it: I am punished for lowering my colours." And she accepted his apologies with a calmness that astonished him.

" I still consider you are not fit for it," he kept saying.

" Perhaps I was not at lunch. But the whole thing is spread clearly before me now."

" I was meaning to act for the best."

" Just lend me your scarf, will you? This wind takes one's hair so."

" Certainly, dear girl. Are you all right now? "

" Look! My hands have stopped trembling."

" And have quite forgiven me? Then listen. Her cab should already have arrived at Howards End. (We're a little late, but no matter.) Our first move will be to send it down to wait at the farm, as, if possible, one doesn't want a scene before servants. A certain gentleman "— he pointed at Crane's back — " won't drive in, but will wait a little short of the front gate, behind the laurels. Have you still the keys of the house? "

" Yes. "

" Well, they aren't wanted. Do you remember how the house stands? "

" Yes."

" If we don't find her in the porch, we can stroll round into the garden. Our object —"

Here they stopped to pick up the doctor.

" I was just saying to my wife, Mansbridge, that our

main object is not to frighten Miss Schlegel. The house, as you know, is my property, so it should seem quite natural for us to be there. The trouble is evidently nervous — wouldn't you say so, Margaret?"

The doctor, a very young man, began to ask questions about Helen. Was she normal? Was there anything congenital or hereditary? Had anything occurred that was likely to alienate her from her family?

"Nothing," answered Margaret, wondering what would have happened if she had added: "Though she did resent my husband's immorality."

"She always was highly strung," pursued Henry, leaning back in the car as it shot past the church. "A tendency to spiritualism and those things, though nothing serious. Musical, literary, artistic, but I should say normal — a very charming girl."

Margaret's anger and terror increased every moment. How dare these men label her sister! What horrors lay ahead! What impertinences that shelter under the name of science! The pack was turning on Helen, to deny her human rights, and it seemed to Margaret that all Schlegels were threatened with her. "Were they normal?" What a question to ask! And it is always those who know nothing about human nature, who are bored by psychology and shocked by physiology, who ask it. However piteous her sister's state, she knew that she must be on her side. They would be mad together if the world chose to consider them so.

It was now five minutes past three. The car slowed down by the farm, in the yard of which Miss Avery was standing. Henry asked her whether a cab had gone past. She nodded, and the next moment they caught sight of it, at the end of the lane. The car ran silently like a beast of prey. So unsuspicious was Helen that she was sitting on the porch, with her back to the road. She had come. Only her head and shoulders were visible. She sat framed in the vine, and one of her hands played with the buds. The wind ruffled her hair, the sun glorified it; she was as she had always been.

Margaret was seated next to the door. Before her husband could prevent her, she slipped out. She ran to the garden gate, which was shut, passed through it, and deliberately pushed it in his face. The noise alarmed Helen. Margaret saw her rise with an unfamiliar movement, and, rushing into the porch, learnt the simple explanation of all their fears — her sister was with child.

" Is the truant all right ? " called Henry.

She had time to whisper: " Oh, my darling —" The keys of the house were in her hand. She unlocked Howards End and thrust Helen into it. " Yes, all right," she said, and stood with her back to the door.

Chapter XXXVI

"MARGARET, you look upset!" said Henry. Mansbridge had followed. Crane was at the gate, and the flyman had stood up on the box. Margaret shook her head at them; she could not speak any more. She remained clutching the keys, as if all their future depended on them. Henry was asking more questions. She shook her head again. His words had no sense. She heard him wonder why she had let Helen in. "You might have given me a knock with the gate," was another of his remarks. Presently she heard herself speaking. She, or some one for her, said "Go away." Henry came nearer. He repeated, "Margaret, you look upset again. My dear, give me the keys. What are you doing with Helen?"

"Oh, dearest, do go away, and I will manage it all."

"Manage what?"

He stretched out his hand for the keys. She might have obeyed if it had not been for the doctor.

"Stop that at least," she said piteously; the doctor had turned back, and was questioning the driver of Helen's cab. A new feeling came over her; she was fighting for women against men. She did not care about rights, but if men came into Howards End, it should be over her body.

"Come, this is an odd beginning," said her husband.

The doctor came forward now, and whispered two words to Mr. Wilcox — the scandal was out. Sincerely horrified, Henry stood gazing at the earth.

"I cannot help it," said Margaret. "Do wait. It's

not my fault. Please all four of you to go away now."

Now the flyman was whispering to Crane.

"We are relying on you to help us, Mrs. Wilcox," said the young doctor. "Could you go in and persuade your sister to come out?"

"On what grounds?" said Margaret, suddenly looking him straight in the eyes.

Thinking it professional to prevaricate, he murmured something about a nervous breakdown.

"I beg your pardon, but it is nothing of the sort. You are not qualified to attend my sister, Mr. Mansbridge. If we require your services, we will let you know."

"I can diagnose the case more bluntly if you wish," he retorted.

"You could, but you have not. You are, therefore, not qualified to attend my sister."

"Come, come, Margaret!" said Henry, never raising his eyes. "This is a terrible business, an appalling business. It's doctor's orders. Open the door."

"Forgive me, but I will not."

"I don't agree."

Margaret was silent.

"This business is as broad as it's long," contributed the doctor. "We had better all work together. You need us, Mrs. Wilcox, and we need you."

"Quite so," said Henry.

"I do not need you in the least," said Margaret.

The two men looked at each other anxiously.

"No more does my sister, who is still many weeks from her confinement."

"Margaret, Margaret!"

"Well, Henry, send your doctor away. What possible use is he now?"

Mr. Wilcox ran his eye over the house. He had a vague feeling that he must stand firm and support the doctor. He himself might need support, for there was trouble ahead.

"It all turns on affection now," said Margaret. "Affection. Don't you see?" Resuming her usual methods, she wrote the word on the house with her finger. "Surely you see. I like Helen very much, you not so much. Mr. Mansbridge doesn't know her. That's all. And affection, when reciprocated, gives rights. Put that down in your note-book, Mr. Mansbridge. It's a useful formula."

Henry told her to be calm.

"You don't know what you want yourselves," said Margaret, folding her arms. "For one sensible remark I will let you in. But you cannot make it. You would trouble my sister for no reason. I will not permit it. I'll stand here all the day sooner."

"Mansbridge," said Henry in a low voice, "perhaps not now."

The pack was breaking up. At a sign from his master, Crane also went back into the car.

"Now, Henry, you," she said gently. None of her bitterness had been directed at him. "Go away now, dear. I shall want your advice later, no doubt. Forgive me if I have been cross. But, seriously, you must go."

He was too stupid to leave her. Now it was Mr. Mansbridge who called in a low voice to him.

"I shall soon find you down at Dolly's," she called, as the gate at last clanged between them. The fly moved out of the way, the motor backed, turned a little, backed again, and turned in the narrow road. A string of farm carts came up in the middle; but she waited through all, for there was no hurry. When all was over and the car had started, she opened the door. "Oh, my darling!" she said. "My darling, forgive me." Helen was standing in the hall.

Chapter XXXVII

MARGARET bolted the door on the inside. Then she would have kissed her sister, but Helen, in a dignified voice, that came strangely from her, said:

"Convenient! You did not tell me that the books were unpacked. I have found nearly everything that I want."

"I told you nothing that was true."

"It has been a great surprise, certainly. Has Aunt Juley been ill?"

"Helen, you wouldn't think I'd invent that?"

"I suppose not," said Helen, turning away, and crying a very little. "But one loses faith in everything after this."

"We thought it was illness, but even then— I haven't behaved worthily."

Helen selected another book.

"I ought not to have consulted any one. What would our father have thought of me?"

She did not think of questioning her sister, nor of rebuking her. Both might be necessary in the future, but she had first to purge a greater crime than any that Helen could have committed — that want of confidence that is the work of the devil.

"Yes, I am annoyed," replied Helen. "My wishes should have been respected. I would have gone through this meeting if it was necessary, but after Aunt Juley recovered, it was not necessary. Planning my life, as I now have to do —"

"Come away from those books," called Margaret. "Helen, do talk to me."

"I was just saying that I have stopped living haphazard. One can't go through a great deal of —" she missed out the noun —" without planning one's actions in advance. I am going to have a child in June, and in the first place conversations, discussions, excitement, are not good for me. I will go through them if necessary, but only then. In the second place I have no right to trouble people. I cannot fit in with England as I know it. I have done something that the English never pardon. It would not be right for them to pardon it. So I must live where I am not known."

"But why didn't you tell me, dearest?"

"Yes," replied Helen judicially. "I might have, but decided to wait."

"I believe you would never have told me."

"Oh yes, I should. We have taken a flat in Munich."

Margaret glanced out of window.

"By 'we' I mean myself and Monica. But for her, I am and have been and always wish to be alone."

"I have not heard of Monica."

"You wouldn't have. She's an Italian — by birth at least. She makes her living by journalism. I met her originally on Garda. Monica is much the best person to see me through."

"You are very fond of her, then."

"She has been extraordinarily sensible with me."

Margaret guessed at Monica's type —"Italiano Inglesiato " they had named it: the crude feminist of the South, whom one respects but avoids. And Helen had turned to it in her need!

"You must not think that we shall never meet," said Helen, with a measured kindness. "I shall always have a room for you when you can be spared, and the longer you can be with me the better. But you haven't understood yet, Meg, and of course it is very difficult for you. This is a shock to you. It isn't to me, who have been thinking over our futures for many months, and they won't be changed by a slight contretemps, such as this. I cannot live in England."

"Helen, you've not forgiven me for my treachery. You *couldn't* talk like this to me if you had."

"Oh, Meg dear, why do we talk at all?" She dropped a book and sighed wearily. Then, recovering herself, she said: "Tell me, how is it that all the books are down here?"

"Series of mistakes."

"And a great deal of the furniture has been unpacked."

"All."

"Who lives here, then?"

"No one."

"I suppose you are letting it though."

"The house is dead," said Margaret with a frown. "Why worry on about it?"

"But I am interested. You talk as if I had lost all my interest in life. I am still Helen, I hope. Now this hasn't the feel of a dead house. The hall seems more alive even than in the old days, when it held the Wilcoxes' own things."

"Interested, are you? Very well, I must tell you, I suppose. My husband lent it on condition we — but by a mistake all our things were unpacked, and Miss Avery, instead of —" She stopped. "Look here, I can't go on like this. I warn you I won't. Helen, why should you be so miserably unkind to me, simply because you hate Henry?"

"I don't hate him now," said Helen. "I have stopped being a schoolgirl, and, Meg, once again, I'm not being unkind. But as for fitting in with your

English life — no, put it out of your head at once.
Imagine a visit from me at Ducie Street! It's unthinkable."

Margaret could not contradict her. It was appalling to see her quietly moving forward with her plans,
not bitter or excitable, neither asserting innocence nor
confessing guilt, merely desiring freedom and the company of those who would not blame her. She had
been through — how much? Margaret did not know.
But it was enough to part her from old habits as well
as old friends.

" Tell me about yourself," said Helen, who had
chosen her books, and was lingering over the furniture.

" There's nothing to tell."

" But your marriage has been happy, Meg? "

" Yes, but I don't feel inclined to talk."

" You feel as I do."

" Not that, but I can't."

" No more can I. It is a nuisance, but no good
trying."

Something had come between them. Perhaps it was
Society, which henceforward would exclude Helen.
Perhaps it was a third life, already potent as a spirit.
They could find no meeting-place. Both suffered
acutely, and were not comforted by the knowledge that
affection survived.

" Look here, Meg, is the coast clear? "

" You mean that you want to go away from me? "

" I suppose so — dear old lady! it isn't any use. I
knew we should have nothing to say. Give my love to
Aunt Juley and Tibby, and take more yourself than
I can say. Promise to come and see me in Munich
later."

" Certainly, dearest."

" For that is all we can do."

It seemed so. Most ghastly of all was Helen's common sense: Monica had been extraordinarily good for her.

" I am glad to have seen you and the things." She looked at the bookcase lovingly, as if she was saying farewell to the past.

Margaret unbolted the door. She remarked: " The car has gone, and here's your cab."

She led the way to it, glancing at the leaves and the sky. The spring had never seemed more beautiful. The driver, who was leaning on the gate, called out, " Please, lady, a message," and handed her Henry's visiting-card through the bars.

" How did this come?" she asked.

Crane had returned with it almost at once.

She read the card with annoyance. It was covered with instructions in domestic French. When she and her sister had talked she was to come back for the night to Dolly's. " Il faut dormir sur ce sujet." While Helen was to be found " une confortable chambre à l'hôtel." The final sentence displeased her greatly until she remembered that the Charles' had only one spare room, and so could not invite a third guest.

" Henry would have done what he could," she interpreted.

Helen had not followed her into the garden. The door once open, she lost her inclination to fly. She remained in the hall, going from bookcase to table. She grew more like the old Helen, irresponsible and charming.

" This *is* Mr. Wilcox's house?" she inquired.

" Surely you remember Howards End?"

" Remember? I who remember everything! But it looks to be ours now."

" Miss Avery was extraordinary," said Margaret, her own spirits lightening a little. Again she was invaded by a slight feeling of disloyalty. But it brought her relief, and she yielded to it. " She loved Mrs. Wilcox, and would rather furnish her house with our things than think of it empty. In consequence here are all the library books."

" Not all the books. She hasn't unpacked the Art Books, in which she may show her sense. And we never used to have the sword here."

" The sword looks well, though."

" Magnificent."

" Yes, doesn't it?"

" Where's the piano, Meg?"

" I warehoused that in London. Why?"

" Nothing."

" Curious, too, that the carpet fits."

" The carpet's a mistake," announced Helen. " I know that we had it in London, but this floor ought to be bare It is far too beautiful."

" You still have a mania for under-furnishing. Would you care to come into the dining-room before you start? There's no carpet there."

They went in, and each minute their talk became more natural.

" Oh, *what* a place for mother's chiffonier!" cried Helen.

" Look at the chairs, though."

" Oh, look at them! Wickham Place faced north, didn't it?"

" North-west."

" Anyhow, it is thirty years since any of those chairs have felt the sun. Feel. Their little backs are quite warm."

" But why has Miss Avery made them set to partners? I shall just —"

" Over here, Meg. Put it so that any one sitting will see the lawn."

Margaret moved a chair. Helen sat down in it.

" Ye-es. The window's too high."

" Try a drawing-room chair."

" No, I don't like the drawing-room so much. The beam has been match-boarded. It would have been so beautiful otherwise."

" Helen, what a memory you have for some things! You're perfectly right. It's a room that men have spoilt through trying to make it nice for women. Men don't know what we want —"

" And never will."

" I don't agree. In two thousand years they'll know."

" But the chairs show up wonderfully. Look where Tibby spilt the soup."

" Coffee. It was coffee surely."

Helen shook her head. " Impossible. Tibby was far too young to be given coffee at that time."

" Was father alive? "

" Yes."

" Then you're right and it must have been soup. I was thinking of much later — that unsuccessful visit of Aunt Juley's, when she didn't realize that Tibby had grown up. It was coffee then, for he threw it down on purpose. There was some rhyme, ' Tea, coffee — coffee, tea,' that she said to him every morning at breakfast. Wait a minute — how did it go? "

" I know — no, I don't. What a detestable boy Tibby was! "

" But the rhyme was simply awful. No decent person could have put up with it."

" Ah, that greengage tree," cried Helen, as if the garden was also part of their childhood. " Why do I connect it with dumbbells? And there come the chickens. The grass wants cutting. I love yellow-hammers —"

Margaret interrupted her. " I have got it," she announced.

"'Tea, tea, coffee, tea,
Or chocolaritee.'

"That every morning for three weeks. No wonder Tibby was wild."

"Tibby is moderately a dear now," said Helen.

"There! I knew you'd say that in the end. Of course he's a dear."

A bell rang.

"Listen! what's that?"

Helen said, "Perhaps the Wilcoxes are beginning the siege."

"What nonsense — listen!"

And the triviality faded from their faces, though it left something behind — the knowledge that they never could be parted because their love was rooted in common things. Explanations and appeals had failed; they had tried for a common meeting-ground, and had only made each other unhappy. And all the time their salvation was lying round them — the past sanctifying the present; the present, with wild heart-throb, declaring that there would after all be a future, with laughter and the voices of children. Helen, still smiling, came up to her sister. She said, "It is always Meg." They looked into each other's eyes. The inner life had paid.

Solemnly the clapper tolled. No one was in the front. Margaret went to the kitchen, and struggled between packing-cases to the window. Their visitor was only a little boy with a tin can. And triviality returned.

"Little boy, what do you want?"

"Please, I am the milk."

"Did Miss Avery send you?" said Margaret, rather sharply.

"Yes, please."

"Then take it back and say we require no milk." While she called to Helen, "No, it's not the siege, but possibly an attempt to provision us against one."

" But I like milk," cried Helen. " Why send it away?"

" Do you? Oh, very well. But we've nothing to put it in, and he wants the can."

" Please, I'm to call in the morning for the can," said the boy.

" The house will be locked up then."

" In the morning would I bring eggs, too?"

" Are you the boy whom I saw playing in the stacks last week?"

The child hung his head.

" Well, run away and do it again."

" Nice little boy," whispered Helen. " I say, what's your name? Mine's Helen."

" Tom."

That was Helen all over. The Wilcoxes, too, would ask a child its name, but they never told their names in return.

" Tom, this one here is Margaret. And at home we've another called Tibby."

" Mine are lop-eared," replied Tom, supposing Tibby to be a rabbit.

" You're a very good and rather a clever little boy. Mind you come again.— Isn't he charming?"

" Undoubtedly," said Margaret. " He is probably the son of Madge, and Madge is dreadful. But this place has wonderful powers."

" What do you mean?"

" I don't know."

" Because I probably agree with you."

" It kills what is dreadful and makes what is beautiful live."

" I do agree," said Helen, as she sipped the milk. " But you said that the house was dead not half an hour ago."

" Meaning that I was dead. I felt it."

" Yes, the house has a surer life than we, even if it was empty, and, as it is, I can't get over that for thirty years the sun has never shone full on our furniture. After all, Wickham Place was a grave. Meg, I've a startling idea."

" What is it?"

" Drink some milk to steady you."

Margaret obeyed.

" No, I won't tell you yet," said Helen, " because you may laugh or be angry. Let's go upstairs first and give the rooms an airing."

They opened window after window, till the inside, too, was rustling to the spring. Curtains blew, picture-frames tapped cheerfully. Helen uttered cries of excitement as she found this bed obviously in its right place, that in its wrong one. She was angry with Miss Avery for not having moved the wardrobes up. " Then one would see really." She admired the view. She was the Helen who had written the memorable letters four years ago. As they leant out, looking westward, she said: " About my idea. Couldn't you and I camp out in this house for the night?"

" I don't think we could well do that," said Margaret.

" Here are beds, tables, towels —"

" I know; but the house isn't supposed to be slept in, and Henry's suggestion was —"

" I require no suggestions. I shall not alter anything in my plans. But it would give me so much pleasure to have one night here with you. It will be something to look back on. Oh, Meg lovey, do let's!"

" But, Helen, my pet," said Margaret, " we can't without getting Henry's leave. Of course, he would give it, but you said yourself that you couldn't visit at Ducie Street now, and this is equally intimate."

" Ducie Street is his house. This is ours. Our furniture, our sort of people coming to the door. Do let us camp out, just one night, and Tom shall feed us on eggs and milk. Why not? It's a moon."

Margaret hesitated. " I feel Charles wouldn't like it," she said at last. " Even our furniture annoyed him, and I was going to clear it out when Aunt Juley's illness prevented me. I sympathize with Charles. He feels it's his mother's house. He loves it in rather an untaking way. Henry I could answer for — not Charles."

" I know he won't like it," said Helen. " But I am going to pass out of their lives. What difference will it make in the long run if they say, ' And she even spent the night at Howards End'?"

" How do you know you'll pass out of their lives? We have thought that twice before."

" Because my plans —"

"— which you change in a moment."

" Then because my life is great and theirs are little," said Helen, taking fire. " I know of things they can't know of, and so do you. We *know* that there's poetry. We *know* that there's death. They can only take them on hearsay. We know this is our house, because it feels ours. Oh, they may take the title-deeds and the doorkeys, but for this one night we are at home."

" It would be lovely to have you once more alone," said Margaret. " It may be a chance in a thousand."

" Yes, and we could talk." She dropped her voice. " It won't be a very glorious story. But under that wych-elm — honestly, I see little happiness ahead. Cannot I have this one night with you?"

" I needn't say how much it would mean to me."

" Then let us."

" It is no good hesitating. Shall I drive down to Hilton now and get leave?"

" Oh, we don't want leave."

But Margaret was a loyal wife. In spite of imagination and poetry — perhaps on account of them — she could sympathize with the technical attitude that Henry would adopt. If possible, she would be technical, too. A night's lodging — and they demanded no more — need not involve the discussion of general principles.

"Charles may say no," grumbled Helen.

"We shan't consult him."

"Go if you like; I should have stopped without leave."

It was the touch of selfishness, which was not enough to mar Helen's character, and even added to its beauty. She would have stopped without leave, and escaped to Germany the next morning. Margaret kissed her.

"Expect me back before dark. I am looking forward to it so much. It is like you to have thought of such a beautiful thing."

"Not a thing, only an ending," said Helen rather sadly; and the sense of tragedy closed in on Margaret again as soon as she left the house.

She was afraid of Miss Avery. It is disquieting to fulfil a prophecy, however superficially. She was glad to see no watching figure as she drove past the farm, but only little Tom, turning somersaults in the straw.

Chapter XXXVIII

THE tragedy began quietly enough, and like many another talk, by the man's deft assertion of his superiority. Henry heard her arguing with the driver, stepped out and settled the fellow, who was inclined to be rude, and then led the way to some chairs on the lawn. Dolly, who had not been "told," ran out with offers of tea. He refused them, and ordered her to wheel baby's perambulator away, as they desired to be alone.

"But the diddums can't listen; he isn't nine months old," she pleaded.

"That's not what I was saying," retorted her father-in-law.

Baby was wheeled out of earshot, and did not hear about the crisis till later years. It was now the turn of Margaret.

"Is it what we feared?" he asked.

"It is."

"Dear girl," he began, "there is a troublesome business ahead of us, and nothing but the most absolute honesty and plain speech will see us through." Margaret bent her head. "I am obliged to question you on subjects we'd both prefer to leave untouched. As you know, I am not one of your Bernard Shaws who consider nothing sacred. To speak as I must will pain me, but there are occasions — We are husband and wife, not children. I am a man of the world, and you are a most exceptional woman."

All Margaret's senses forsook her. She blushed, and looked past him at the Six Hills, covered with spring herbage. Noting her colour, he grew still more kind.

"I see that you feel as I felt when — My poor little wife! Oh, be brave! Just one or two questions, and I have done with you. Was your sister wearing a wedding-ring?"

Margaret stammered a " No."

There was an appalling silence.

"Henry, I really came to ask a favour about Howards End."

"One point at a time. I am now obliged to ask for the name of her seducer."

She rose to her feet and held the chair between them. Her colour had ebbed, and she was grey. It did not displease him that she should receive his question thus.

"Take your time," he counselled her. "Remember that this is far worse for me than for you."

She swayed; he feared she was going to faint. Then speech came, and she said slowly: "Seducer? No; I do not know her seducer's name."

"Would she not tell you?"

"I never even asked her who seduced her," said Margaret, dwelling on the hateful word thoughtfully.

"That is singular." Then he changed his mind. "Natural perhaps, dear girl, that you shouldn't ask. But until his name is known, nothing can be done. Sit down. How terrible it is to see you so upset! I knew you weren't fit for it. I wish I hadn't taken you."

Margaret answered, "I like to stand, if you don't mind, for it gives me a pleasant view of the Six Hills."

"As you like."

"Have you anything else to ask me, Henry?"

"Next you must tell me whether you have gathered anything. I have often noticed your insight, dear. I only wish my own was as good. You may have guessed something, even though your sister said nothing. The slightest hint would help us."

"Who is 'we'?"

" I thought it best to ring up Charles."

" That was unnecessary," said Margaret, growing warmer. " This news will give Charles disproportionate pain."

" He has at once gone to call on your brother."

" That too was unnecessary."

" Let me explain, dear, how the matter stands. You don't think that I and my son are other than gentlemen? It is in Helen's interests that we are acting. It is still not too late to save her name."

Then Margaret hit out for the first time. " Are we to make her seducer marry her?" she asked.

"If possible. Yes."

" But, Henry, suppose he turned out to be married already? One has heard of such cases."

" In that case he must pay heavily for his misconduct, and be thrashed within an inch of his life."

So her first blow missed. She was thankful of it. What had tempted her to imperil both of their lives? Henry's obtuseness had saved her as well as himself. Exhausted with anger, she sat down again, blinking at him as he told her as much as he thought fit. At last she said: " May I ask you my question now?"

" Certainly, my dear."

" Tomorrow Helen goes to Munich —"

" Well, possibly she is right."

" Henry, let a lady finish. Tomorrow she goes; tonight, with your permission, she would like to sleep at Howards End."

It was the crisis of his life. Again she would have recalled the words as soon as they were uttered. She had not led up to them with sufficient care. She longed to warn him that they were far more important than he supposed. She saw him weighing them, as if they were a business proposition.

" Why Howards End? " he said at last. " Would she not be more comfortable, as I suggested, at the hotel? "

Margaret hastened to give him reasons. " It is an odd request, but you know what Helen is and what women in her state are." He frowned, and moved irritably. " She has the idea that one night in your house would give her pleasure and do her good. I think she's right. Being one of those imaginative girls, the presence of all our books and furniture soothes her. This is a fact. It is the end of her girlhood. Her last words to me were, ' A beautiful ending.' "

" She values the old furniture for sentimental reasons, in fact."

" Exactly. You have quite understood. It is her last hope of being with it."

" I don't agree there, my dear! Helen will have her share of the goods wherever she goes — possibly more than her share, for you are so fond of her that you'd give her anything of yours that she fancies, wouldn't you? and I'd raise no objection. I could understand it if it was her old home, because a home, or a house " — he changed the word, designedly; he had thought of a telling point — " because a house in which one has once lived becomes in a sort of way sacred, I don't know why. Associations and so on. Now Helen has no associations with Howards End, though I and Charles and Evie have. I do not see why she wants to stay the night there. She will only catch cold."

" Leave it that you don't see," cried Margaret. " Call it fancy. But realize that fancy is a scientific fact. Helen is fanciful, and wants to."

Then he surprised her — a rare occurrence. He shot an unexpected bolt. " If she wants to sleep one night, she may want to sleep two. We shall never get her out of the house, perhaps."

"Well?" said Margaret, with the precipice in sight. "And suppose we don't get her out of the house? Would it matter? She would do no one any harm."

Again the irritated gesture.

"No, Henry," she panted, receding. "I didn't mean that. We will only trouble Howards End for this one night. I take her to London tomorrow—"

"Do you intend to sleep in a damp house, too?"

"She cannot be left alone."

"That's quite impossible! Madness. You must be here to meet Charles."

"I have already told you that your message to Charles was unnecessary, and I have no desire to meet him."

"Margaret—my Margaret—"

"What has this business to do with Charles? If it concerns me little, it concerns you less, and Charles not at all."

"As the future owner of Howards End," said Mr. Wilcox, arching his fingers, "I should say that it did concern Charles."

"In what way? Will Helen's condition depreciate the property?"

"My dear, you are forgetting yourself."

"I think you yourself recommended plain speaking."

They looked at each other in amazement. The precipice was at their feet now.

"Helen commands my sympathy," said Henry. "As your husband, I shall do all for her that I can, and I have no doubt that she will prove more sinned against than sinning. But I cannot treat her as if nothing has happened. I should be false to my position in society if I did."

She controlled herself for the last time. "No, let

us go back to Helen's request," she said. "It is unreasonable, but the request of an unhappy girl. Tomorrow she will go to Germany, and trouble society no longer. Tonight she asks to sleep in your empty house — a house which you do not care about, and which you have not occupied for over a year. May she? Will you give my sister leave? Will you forgive her — as you hope to be forgiven, and as you have actually been forgiven? Forgive her for one night only. That will be enough."

"As I have actually been forgiven —?"

"Never mind for the moment what I mean by that," said Margaret. "Answer my question."

Perhaps some hint of her meaning did dawn on him. If so, he blotted it out. Straight from his fortress he answered: "I seem rather unaccommodating, but I have some experience of life, and know how one thing leads to another. I am afraid that your sister had better sleep at the hotel. I have my children and the memory of my dear wife to consider. I am sorry, but see that she leaves my house at once."

"You mentioned Mrs. Wilcox."

"I beg your pardon?"

"A rare occurrence. In reply, may I mention Mrs. Bast?"

"You have not been yourself all day," said Henry, and rose from his seat with face unmoved. Margaret rushed at him and seized both his hands. She was transfigured.

"Not any more of this!" she cried "You shall see the connection if it kills you, Henry! You have had a mistress — I forgave you. My sister has a lover — you drive her from the house. Do you see the connection? Stupid, hypocritical, cruel — oh, contemptible! — a man who insults his wife when she's alive and cants with her memory when she's dead. A man who ruins a woman for his pleasure, and casts her off to ruin other men. And gives bad financial advice, and then says he is not responsible. These, man, are you. You can't recognize them, because you cannot connect. I've had enough of your unweeded kindness. I've spoilt you long enough. All your life you have been spoiled. Mrs. Wilcox spoiled you. No one has ever told what you are — muddled, criminally muddled. Men like you use repentance as a blind, so don't repent. Only say to yourself, ' What Helen has done, I've done.' "

" The two cases are different," Henry stammered. His real retort was not quite ready. His brain was still in a whirl, and he wanted a little longer.

" In what way different? You have betrayed Mrs. Wilcox, Helen only herself. You remain in society, Helen can't. You have had only pleasure, she may die. You have the insolence to talk to me of differences, Henry? "

Oh, the uselessness of it! Henry's retort came.

" I perceive you are attempting blackmail. It is scarcely a pretty weapon for a wife to use against her husband. My rule through life has been never to pay the least attention to threats, and I can only repeat what I said before : I do not give you and your sister leave to sleep at Howards End."

Margaret loosed his hands. He went into the house, wiping first one and then the other on his handkerchief. For a little she stood looking at the Six Hills, tombs of warriors, breasts of the spring. Then she passed out into what was now the evening.

Chapter XXXIX

CHARLES and Tibby met at Ducie Street, where the latter was staying. Their interview was short and absurd. They had nothing in common but the English language, and tried by its help to express what neither of them understood. Charles saw in Helen the family foe. He had singled her out as the most dangerous of the Schlegels, and, angry as he was, looked forward to telling his wife how right he had been. His mind was made up at once: the girl must be got out of the way before she disgraced them farther. If occasion offered she might be married to a villain or, possibly, to a fool. But this was a concession to morality, it formed no part of his main scheme. Honest and hearty was Charles's dislike, and the past spread itself out very clearly before him; hatred is a skilful compositor. As if they were heads in a note-book, he ran through all the incidents of the Schlegels' campaign: the attempt to compromise his brother, his mother's legacy, his father's marriage, the introduction of the furniture, the unpacking of the same. He had not yet heard of the request to sleep at Howards End; that was to be their master-stroke and the opportunity for his. But he already felt that Howards End was the objective, and, though he disliked the house, was determined to defend it.

Tibby, on the other hand, had no opinions. He stood above the conventions: his sister had a right to do what she thought right. It is not difficult to stand above the conventions when we leave no hostages among them; men can always be more unconventional than women, and a bachelor of independent means need encounter no difficulties at all. Unlike Charles, Tibby had money enough; his ancestors had earned it for him, and if he shocked the people in one set of lodgings he had only to move into another. His was the Leisure without sympathy — an attitude as fatal as the strenuous: a little cold culture may be raised on it, but no art. His sisters had seen the family danger, and had never forgotten to discount the gold islets that raised them from the sea. Tibby gave all the praise to himself, and so despised the struggling and the submerged.

Hence the absurdity of the interview; the gulf between them was economic as well as spiritual. But several facts passed: Charles pressed for them with an impertinence that the undergraduate could not withstand. On what date had Helen gone abroad? To whom? (Charles was anxious to fasten the scandal on Germany.) Then, changing his tactics, he said roughly: "I suppose you realize that you are your sister's protector?"

"In what sense?"

"If a man played about with my sister, I'd send a bullet through him, but perhaps you don't mind."

"I mind very much," protested Tibby.

"Who d'ye suspect, then? Speak out, man. One always suspects some one."

"No one. I don't think so." Involuntarily he blushed. He had remembered the scene in his Oxford rooms.

"You are hiding something," said Charles. As interviews go, he got the best of this one. "When you saw her last, did she mention any one's name? Yes, or no!" he thundered, so that Tibby started.

"In my rooms she mentioned some friends, called the Basts —"

"Who are the Basts?"

" People — friends of hers at Evie's wedding."

" I don't remember. But, by great Scott! I do. My aunt told me about some tag-rag. Was she full of them when you saw her? Is there a man? Did she speak of the man? Or — look here — have you had any dealings with him? "

Tibby was silent. Without intending it, he had betrayed his sister's confidence; he was not enough interested in human life to see where things will lead to. He had a strong regard for honesty, and his word, once given, had always been kept up to now. He was deeply vexed, not only for the harm he had done Helen, but for the flaw he had discovered in his own equipment.

" I see — you are in his confidence. They met at your rooms. Oh, what a family, what a family! God help the poor pater —"

And Tibby found himself alone.

Chapter XL

LEONARD — he would figure at length in a newspaper report, but that evening he did not count for much. The foot of the tree was in shadow, since the moon was still hidden behind the house. But above, to right, to left, down the long meadow the moonlight was streaming. Leonard seemed not a man, but a cause.

Perhaps it was Helen's way of falling in love — a curious way to Margaret, whose agony and whose contempt of Henry were yet imprinted with his image. Helen forgot people. They were husks that had enclosed her emotion. She could pity, or sacrifice herself, or have instincts, but had she ever loved in the noblest way, where man and woman, having lost themselves in sex, desire to lose sex itself in comradeship?

Margaret wondered, but said no word of blame. This was Helen's evening. Troubles enough lay ahead of her — the loss of friends and of social advantages, the agony, the supreme agony, of motherhood, which is even yet not a matter of common knowledge. For the present let the moon shine brightly and the breezes of the spring blow gently, dying away from the gale of the day, and let the earth, who brings increase, bring peace. Not even to herself dare she blame Helen. She could not assess her trespass by any moral code; it was everything or nothing. Morality can tell us that murder is worse than stealing, and group most sins in an order all must approve, but it cannot group Helen. The surer its pronouncements on this point, the surer may we be that morality is not speaking. Christ was evasive when they questioned Him. It is those that cannot connect who hasten to cast the first stone.

This was Helen's evening — won at what cost, and not to be marred by the sorrows of others. Of her own tragedy Margaret never uttered a word.

" One isolates," said Helen slowly. " I isolated Mr. Wilcox from the other forces that were pulling Leonard downhill. Consequently, I was full of pity, and almost of revenge. For weeks I had blamed Mr. Wilcox only, and so, when your letters came —"

" I need never have written them," sighed Margaret. " They never shielded Henry. How hopeless it is to tidy away the past, even for others ! "

" I did not know that it was your own idea to dismiss the Basts."

" Looking back, that was wrong of me."

" Looking back, darling, I know that it was right. It is right to save the man whom one loves. I am less enthusiastic about justice now. But we both thought you wrote at his dictation. It seemed the last touch of his callousness. Being very much wrought up by this time — and Mrs. Bast was upstairs. I had not seen her, and had talked for a long time to Leonard — I had snubbed him for no reason, and that should have warned me I was in danger. So when the notes came I wanted us to go to you for an explanation. He said that he guessed the explanation — he knew of it, and you mustn't know. I pressed him to tell me. He said no one must know ; it was something to do with his wife. Right up to the end we were Mr. Bast and Miss Schlegel. I was going to tell him that he must be frank with me when I saw his eyes, and guessed that Mr. Wilcox had ruined him in two ways, not one. I drew him to me. I made him tell me. I felt very lonely myself. He is not to blame.

He would have gone on worshipping me. I want never to see him again, though it sounds appalling. I wanted to give him money and feel finished. Oh, Meg, the little that is known about these things!"

She laid her face against the tree.

"The little, too, that is known about growth! Both times it was loneliness, and the night, and panic afterwards. Did Leonard grow out of Paul?"

Margaret did not speak for a moment. So tired was she that her attention had actually wandered to the teeth — the teeth that had been thrust into the tree's bark to medicate it. From where she sat she could see them gleam. She had been trying to count them. "Leonard is a better growth than madness," she said. "I was afraid that you would react against Paul until you went over the verge."

"I did react until I found poor Leonard. I am steady now. I shan't ever *like* your Henry, dearest Meg, or even speak kindly about him, but all that blinding hate is over. I shall never rave against Wilcoxes any more. I understand how you married him, and you will now be very happy."

Margaret did not reply.

"Yes," repeated Helen, her voice growing more tender, "I do at last understand."

"Except Mrs. Wilcox, dearest, no one understands our little movements."

"Because in death — I agree."

"Not quite. I feel that you and I and Henry are only fragments of that woman's mind. She knows everything. She is everything. She is the house, and the tree that leans over it. People have their own deaths as well as their own lives, and even if there is nothing beyond death, we shall differ in our nothingness. I cannot believe that knowledge such as hers will perish with knowledge such as mine. She knew about realities. She knew when people were in love, though she was not in the room. I don't doubt that she knew when Henry deceived her."

"Good-night, Mrs. Wilcox," called a voice.

"Oh, good-night, Miss Avery."

"Why should Miss Avery work for us?" Helen murmured.

"Why, indeed?"

Miss Avery crossed the lawn and merged into the hedge that divided it from the farm. An old gap, which Mr. Wilcox had filled up, had reappeared, and her track through the dew followed the path that he had turfed over, when he improved the garden and made it possible for games.

"This is not quite our house yet," said Helen. "When Miss Avery called, I felt we are only a couple of tourists."

"We shall be that everywhere, and for ever."

"But affectionate tourists —"

"But tourists who pretend each hotel is their home."

"I can't pretend very long," said Helen. "Sitting under this tree one forgets, but I know that tomorrow I shall see the moon rise out of Germany. Not all your goodness can alter the facts of the case. Unless you will come with me."

Margaret thought for a moment. In the past year she had grown so fond of England that to leave it was a real grief. Yet what detained her? No doubt Henry would pardon her outburst, and go on blustering and muddling into a ripe old age. But what was the good? She had just as soon vanish from his mind.

"Are you serious in asking me, Helen? Should I get on with your Monica?"

"You would not, but I am serious in asking you."

"Still, no more plans now. And no more reminiscences."

They were silent for a little. It was Helen's evening.

The present flowed by them like a stream. The tree rustled. It had made music before they were born, and would continue after their deaths, but its song was of the moment. The moment had passed. The tree rustled again. Their senses were sharpened, and they seemed to apprehend life. Life passed. The tree rustled again.

"Sleep now," said Margaret.

The peace of the country was entering into her. It has no commerce with memory, and little with hope. Least of all is it concerned with the hopes of the next five minutes. It is the peace of the present, which passes understanding. Its murmur came "now," and "now" once more as they trod the gravel, and "now," as the moonlight fell upon their father's sword. They passed upstairs, kissed, and amidst the endless iterations fell asleep. The house had enshadowed the tree at first, but as the moon rose higher the two disentangled, and were clear for a few moments at midnight. Margaret awoke and looked into the garden. How incomprehensible that Leonard Bast should have won her this night of peace! Was he also part of Mrs. Wilcox's mind?

Chapter XLI

FAR different was Leonard's development. The months after Oniton, whatever minor troubles they might bring him, were all overshadowed by Remorse. When Helen looked back she could philosophize, or she could look into the future and plan for her child. But the father saw nothing beyond his own sin. Weeks afterwards, in the midst of other occupations, he would suddenly cry out, "Brute — you brute, I couldn't have —" and be rent into two people who held dialogues. Or brown rain would descend, blotting out faces and the sky. Even Jacky noticed the change in him. Most terrible were his sufferings when he awoke from sleep. Sometimes he was happy at first, but grew conscious of a burden hanging to him and weighing down his thoughts when they would move. Or little irons scorched his body. Or a sword stabbed him. He would sit at the edge of his bed, holding his heart and moaning, "Oh what *shall* I do, whatever *shall* I do?" Nothing brought ease. He could put distance between him and the trespass, but it grew in his soul.

Remorse is not among the eternal verities. The Greeks were right to dethrone her. Her action is too capricious, as though the Erinyes selected for punishment only certain men and certain sins. And of all means to regeneration Remorse is surely the most wasteful. It cuts away healthy tissues with the poisoned. It is a knife that probes far deeper than the evil. Leonard was driven straight through its torments and emerged pure, but enfeebled — a better man, who would never lose control of himself again, but also a smaller man, who had less to control. Nor did purity mean peace. The use of the knife can become a habit as hard to shake off as passion itself, and Leonard continued to start with a cry out of dreams.

He built up a situation that was far enough from the truth. It never occurred to him that Helen was to blame. He forgot the intensity of their talk, the charm that had been lent him by sincerity, the magic of Oniton under darkness and of the whispering river. Helen loved the absolute. Leonard had been ruined absolutely, and had appeared to her as a man apart, isolated from the world. A real man, who cared for adventure and beauty, who desired to live decently and pay his way, who could have travelled more gloriously through life than the Juggernaut car that was crushing him. Memories of Evie's wedding had warped her, the starched servants, the yards of uneaten food, the rustle of overdressed women, motor-cars oozing grease on the gravel, rubbish on a pretentious band. She had tasted the lees of this on her arrival: in the darkness, after failure, they intoxicated her. She and the victim seemed alone in a world of unreality, and she loved him absolutely, perhaps for half an hour.

In the morning she was gone. The note that she left, tender and hysterical in tone, and intended to be most kind, hurt her lover terribly. It was as if some work of art had been broken by him, some picture in the National Gallery slashed out of its frame. When he recalled her talents and her social position, he felt that the first passer-by had a right to shoot him down. He was afraid of the waitress and the porters at the railway-station. He was afraid at first of his wife, though later he was to regard her with a strange new tenderness, and to think, " There is nothing to choose between us, after all."

The expedition to Shropshire crippled the Basts per-

manently. Helen in her flight forgot to settle the hotel
bill, and took their return tickets away with her; they
had to pawn Jacky's bangles to get home, and the
smash came a few days afterwards. It is true that
Helen offered him five thousand pounds, but such a
sum meant nothing to him. He could not see that the
girl was desperately righting herself, and trying to
save something out of the disaster, if it was only five
thousand pounds. But he had to live somehow. He
turned to his family, and degraded himself to a professional beggar. There was nothing else for him to do.

"A letter from Leonard," thought Blanche, his sister; "and after all this time." She hid it, so that her
husband should not see, and when he had gone to his
work read it with some emotion, and sent the prodigal
a little money out of her dress allowance.

"A letter from Leonard!" said the other sister,
Laura, a few days later. She showed it to her husband. He wrote a cruel insolent reply, but sent more
money than Blanche, so Leonard soon wrote to him
again.

And during the winter the system was developed.
Leonard realized that they need never starve, because
it would be too painful for his relatives. Society is
based on the family, and the clever wastrel can exploit this indefinitely. Without a generous thought on
either side, pounds and pounds passed. The donors
disliked Leonard, and he grew to hate them intensely.
When Laura censured his immoral marriage, he
thought bitterly, " She minds that! What would she
say if she knew the truth?" When Blanche's husband offered him work, he found some pretext for
avoiding it. He had wanted work keenly at Oniton,
but too much anxiety had shattered him; he was joining the unemployable. When his brother, the lay-
reader, did not reply to a letter, he wrote again, saying
that he and Jacky would come down to his village on

foot. He did not intend this as blackmail. Still, the brother sent a postal order, and it became part of the system. And so passed his winter and his spring.

In the horror there are two bright spots. He never confused the past. He remained alive, and blessed are those who live, if it is only to a sense of sinfulness. The anodyne of muddledom, by which most men blur and blend their mistakes, never passed Leonard's lips —

> "And if I drink oblivion of a day,
> So shorten I the stature of my soul."

It is a hard saying, and a hard man wrote it, but it lies at the foot of all character.

And the other bright spot was his tenderness for Jacky. He pitied her with nobility now — not the contemptuous pity of a man who sticks to a woman through thick and thin. He tried to be less irritable. He wondered what her hungry eyes desired — nothing that she could express, or that he or any man could give her. Would she ever receive the justice that is mercy — the justice for by-products that the world is too busy to bestow? She was fond of flowers, generous with money, and not revengeful. If she had borne him a child he might have cared for her. Unmarried, Leonard would never have begged; he would have flickered out and died. But the whole of life is mixed. He had to provide for Jacky, and went down dirty paths that she might have a few feathers and dishes of food that suited her.

One day he caught sight of Margaret and her brother. He was in St. Paul's. He had entered the cathedral partly to avoid the rain and partly to see a picture that had educated him in former years. But the light was bad, the picture ill placed, and Time and Judgment were inside him now. Death alone still charmed him, with her lap of poppies, on which all men shall sleep. He took one glance, and turned aimlessly away towards a chair. Then down the nave he saw Miss Schlegel and her brother. They stood in the fairway of passengers, and their faces were extremely grave. He was perfectly certain that they were in trouble about their sister.

Once outside — and he fled immediately — he wished that he had spoken to them. What was his life? What were a few angry words, or even imprisonment? He had done wrong — that was the true terror. Whatever they might know, he would tell them everything he knew. He re-entered St. Paul's. But they had moved in his absence, and had gone to lay their difficulties before Mr. Wilcox and Charles.

The sight of Margaret turned remorse into new channels. He desired to confess, and though the desire is proof of a weakened nature, which is about to lose the essence of human intercourse, it did not take an ignoble form. He did not suppose that confession would bring him happiness. It was rather that he yearned to get clear of the tangle. So does the suicide yearn. The impulses are akin, and the crime of suicide lies rather in its disregard for the feelings of those whom we leave behind. Confession need harm no one — it can satisfy that test — and though it was unEnglish, and ignored by our Anglican cathedral, Leonard had a right to decide upon it.

Moreover, he trusted Margaret. He wanted her hardness now. That cold, intellectual nature of hers would be just, if unkind. He would do whatever she told him, even if he had to see Helen. That was the supreme punishment she would exact. And perhaps she would tell him how Helen was. That was the supreme reward.

He knew nothing about Margaret, not even whether she was married to Mr. Wilcox, and tracking her out took several days. That evening he toiled through the wet to Wickham Place, where the new flats were now appearing. Was he also the cause of their move? Were they expelled from society on his account? Thence to a public library, but could find no satisfactory Schlegel in the directory. On the morrow he searched again. He hung about outside Mr. Wilcox's office at lunch time, and, as the clerks came out said: "Excuse me, sir, but is your boss married?" Most of them stared, some said, "What's that to you?" but one, who had not yet acquired reticence, told him what he wished. Leonard could not learn the private address. That necessitated more trouble with directories and tubes. Ducie Street was not discovered till the Monday, the day that Margaret and her husband went down on their hunting expedition to Howards End.

He called at about four o'clock. The weather had changed, and the sun shone gaily on the ornamental steps — black and white marble in triangles. Leonard lowered his eyes to them after ringing the bell. He felt in curious health: doors seemed to be opening and shutting inside his body, and he had been obliged to sleep sitting up in bed, with his back propped against the wall. When the parlourmaid came he could not see her face; the brown rain had descended suddenly.

"Does Mrs. Wilcox live here?" he asked.

"She's out," was the answer.

"When will she be back?"

"I'll ask," said the parlourmaid.

Margaret had given instructions that no one who mentioned her name should ever be rebuffed. Putting the door on the chain — for Leonard's appearance demanded this — she went through to the smoking-room, which was occupied by Tibby. Tibby was asleep. He had had a good lunch. Charles Wilcox had not yet rung him up for the distracting interview. He said drowsily: "I don't know. Hilton. Howards End. Who is it?"

" I'll ask, sir."

" No, don't bother."

" They have taken the car to Howards End," said the parlourmaid to Leonard.

He thanked her, and asked whereabouts that place was.

" You appear to want to know a good deal," she remarked. But Margaret had forbidden her to be mysterious. She told him against her better judgment that Howards End was in Hertfordshire.

" Is it a village, please? "

" Village! It's Mr. Wilcox's private house — at least, it's one of them. Mrs. Wilcox keeps her furniture there. Hilton is the village."

" Yes. And when will they be back? "

" Mr. Schlegel doesn't know. We can't know everything, can we? " She shut him out, and went to attend to the telephone, which was ringing furiously.

He loitered away another night of agony. Confession grew more difficult. As soon as possible he went to bed. He watched a patch of moonlight cross the floor of their lodging, and, as sometimes happens when the mind is overtaxed, he fell asleep for the rest of the room, but kept awake for the patch of moonlight. Horrible! Then began one of those disintegrating dialogues. Part of him said: " Why horrible? It's ordinary light from the room." " But it moves." " So does the moon." " But it is a clenched fist." " Why not? " " But it is going to touch me." " Let it." And, seeming to gather motion, the patch ran up his blanket. Presently a blue snake appeared; then another, parallel to it. " Is there life in the moon? " " Of course." " But I thought it was uninhabited." " Not by Time, Death, Judgment, and the smaller snakes." " Smaller snakes! " said Leonard indignantly and aloud. " What a notion! " By a rending effort of the will he woke the rest of the room up.

Jacky, the bed, their food, their clothes on the chair, gradually entered his consciousness, and the horror vanished outwards, like a ring that is spreading through water.

"I say, Jacky, I'm going out for a bit."

She was breathing regularly. The patch of light fell clear of the striped blanket, and began to cover the shawl that lay over her feet. Why had he been afraid? He went to the window, and saw that the moon was descending through a clear sky. He saw her volcanoes, and the bright expanses that a gracious error has named seas. They paled, for the sun, who had lit them up, was coming to light the earth. Sea of Serenity, Sea of Tranquillity, Ocean of the Lunar Storms, merged into one lucent drop, itself to slip into the sempiternal dawn. And he had been afraid of the moon!

He dressed among the contending lights, and went through his money. It was running low again, but enough for a return ticket to Hilton. As it clinked Jacky opened her eyes.

"Hullo, Len! What ho, Len!"

"What ho, Jacky! see you again later."

She turned over and slept.

The house was unlocked, their landlord being a salesman at Covent Garden. Leonard passed out and made his way down to the station. The train, though it did not start for an hour, was already drawn up at the end of the platform, and he lay down in it and slept. With the first jolt he was in daylight; they had left the gateways of King's Cross, and were under blue sky. Tunnels followed, and after each the sky grew bluer, and from the embankment at Finsbury Park he had his first sight of the sun. It rolled along behind the eastern smokes — a wheel, whose fellow was the descending moon — and as yet it seemed the servant of the blue sky, not its lord. He dozed again.

Over Tewin Water it was day. To the left fell the shadow of the embankment and its arches; to the right Leonard saw up into the Tewin Woods and towards the church, with its wild legend of immortality. Six forest trees — that is a fact — grow out of one of the graves in Tewin churchyard. The grave's occupant — that is the legend — is an atheist, who declared that if God existed, six forest trees would grow out of her grave. These things in Hertfordshire; and farther afield lay the house of a hermit — Mrs. Wilcox had known him — who barred himself up, and wrote prophecies, and gave all he had to the poor. While, powdered in between, were the villas of business men, who saw life more steadily, though with the steadiness of the half-closed eye. Over all the sun was streaming, to all the birds were singing, to all the primroses were yellow, and the speedwell blue, and the country, however they interpreted her, was uttering her cry of "now." She did not free Leonard yet, and the knife plunged deeper into his heart as the train drew up at Hilton. But remorse had become beautiful.

Hilton was asleep, or at the earliest, breakfasting. Leonard noticed the contrast when he stepped out of it into the country. Here men had been up since dawn. Their hours were ruled, not by a London office, but by the movements of the crops and the sun. That they were men of the finest type only the sentimentalist can declare. But they kept to the life of daylight. They are England's hope. Clumsily they carry forward the torch of the sun, until such time as the nation sees fit to take it up. Half clodhopper, half board-school prig, they can still throw back to a nobler stock, and breed yeomen.

At the chalk pit a motor passed him. In it was another type, whom Nature favours — the Imperial. Healthy, ever in motion, it hopes to inherit the earth. It breeds as quickly as the yeoman, and as soundly;

strong is the temptation to acclaim it as a super-yeoman, who carries his country's virtue overseas. But the Imperialist is not what he thinks or seems. He is a destroyer. He prepares the way for cosmopolitanism, and though his ambitions may be fulfilled, the earth that he inherits will be grey.

To Leonard, intent on his private sin, there came the conviction of innate goodness elsewhere. It was not the optimism which he had been taught at school. Again and again must the drums tap, and the goblins stalk over the universe before joy can be purged of the superficial. It was rather paradoxical, and arose from his sorrow. Death destroys a man, but the idea of death saves him — that is the best account of it that has yet been given. Squalor and tragedy can beckon to all that is great in us, and strengthen the wings of love. They can beckon; it is not certain that they will, for they are not love's servants. But they can beckon, and the knowledge of this incredible truth comforted him.

As he approached the house all thought stopped. Contradictory notions stood side by side in his mind. He was terrified but happy, ashamed, but had done no sin. He knew the confession: "Mrs. Wilcox, I have done wrong," but sunrise had robbed its meaning, and he felt rather on a supreme adventure.

He entered a garden, steadied himself against a motor-car that he found in it, found a door open and entered a house. Yes, it would be very easy. From a room to the left he heard voices, Margaret's amongst them. His own name was called aloud, and a man whom he had never seen said, "Oh, is he there? I am not surprised. I now thrash him within an inch of his life."

"Mrs. Wilcox," said Leonard, "I have done wrong."

The man took him by the collar and cried, "Bring

me a stick." Women were screaming. A stick, very bright, descended. It hurt him, not where it descended, but in the heart. Books fell over him in a shower. Nothing had sense.

" Get some water," commanded Charles, who had all through kept very calm. " He's shamming. Of course I only used the blade. Here, carry him out into the air."

Thinking that he understood these things, Margaret obeyed him. They laid Leonard, who was dead, on the gravel; Helen poured water over him.

" That's enough," said Charles.

" Yes, murder's enough," said Miss Avery, coming out of the house with the sword.

Chapter XLII

WHEN Charles left Ducie Street he had caught the first train home, but had no inkling of the newest development until late at night. Then his father, who had dined alone, sent for him, and in very grave tones inquired for Margaret.

"I don't know where she is, pater," said Charles. "Dolly kept back dinner nearly an hour for her."

"Tell me when she comes in."

Another hour passed. The servants went to bed, and Charles visited his father again, to receive further instructions. Mrs. Wilcox had still not returned.

"I'll sit up for her as late as you like, but she can hardly be coming. Isn't she stopping with her sister at the hotel?"

"Perhaps," said Mr. Wilcox thoughtfully—"perhaps."

"Can I do anything for you, sir?"

"Not tonight, my boy."

Mr. Wilcox liked being called sir. He raised his eyes and gave his son more open a look of tenderness than he usually ventured. He saw Charles as little boy and strong man in one. Though his wife had proved unstable his children were left to him.

After midnight he tapped on Charles's door. "I can't sleep," he said. "I had better have a talk with you and get it over."

He complained of the heat. Charles took him out into the garden, and they paced up and down in their dressing-gowns. Charles became very quiet as the story unrolled; he had known all along that Margaret was as bad as her sister.

" She will feel differently in the morning," said Mr. Wilcox, who had of course said nothing about Mrs. Bast. " But I cannot let this kind of thing continue without comment. I am morally certain that she is with her sister at Howards End. The house is mine — and, Charles, it will be yours — and when I say that no one is to live there, I mean that no one is to live there. I won't have it." He looked angrily at the moon. " To my mind this question is connected with something far greater, the rights of property itself."

" Undoubtedly," said Charles.

Mr. Wilcox linked his arm in his son's, but somehow liked him less as he told him more. " I don't want you to conclude that my wife and I had anything of the nature of a quarrel. She was only overwrought, as who would not be? I shall do what I can for Helen, but on the understanding that they clear out of the house at once. Do you see? That is a sine qua non."

" Then at eight tomorrow I may go up in the car? "

" Eight or earlier. Say that you are acting as my representative, and, of course, use no violence, Charles."

On the morrow, as Charles returned, leaving Leonard dead upon the gravel, it did not seem to him that he had used violence. Death was due to heart disease. His stepmother herself had said so, and even Miss Avery had acknowledged that he only used the flat of the sword. On his way through the village he informed the police, who thanked him, and said there must be an inquest. He found his father in the garden shading his eyes from the sun.

" It has been pretty horrible," said Charles gravely. " They were there, and they had the man up there with them too."

" What — what man? "

" I told you last night. His name was Bast."

" My God, is it possible? " said Mr. Wilcox. " In your mother's house! Charles, in your mother's house! "

" I know, pater. That was what I felt. As a matter of fact, there is no need to trouble about the man. He was in the last stages of heart disease, and just before I could show him what I thought of him he went off. The police are seeing about it at this moment."

Mr. Wilcox listened attentively.

" I got up there — oh, it couldn't have been more than half-past seven. The Avery woman was lighting a fire for them. They were still upstairs. I waited in the drawing-room. We were all moderately civil and collected, though I had my suspicions. I gave them your message, and Mrs. Wilcox said, ' Oh yes, I see; yes,' in that way of hers."

" Nothing else? "

" I promised to tell you, ' with her love,' that she was going to Germany with her sister this evening. That was all we had time for."

Mr. Wilcox seemed relieved.

" Because by then I suppose the man got tired of hiding, for suddenly Mrs. Wilcox screamed out his name. I recognized it, and I went for him in the hall. Was I right, pater? I thought things were going a little too far."

" Right, my dear boy? I don't know. But you would have been no son of mine if you hadn't. Then did he just — just — crumple up as you said? " He shrunk from the simple word.

" He caught hold of the bookcase, which came down over him. So I merely put the sword down and carried him into the garden. We all thought he was shamming. However, he's dead right enough. Awful business!"

"Sword?" cried his father, with anxiety in his voice. "What sword? Whose sword?"

"A sword of theirs."

"What were you doing with it?"

"Well, didn't you see, pater, I had to snatch up the first thing handy. I hadn't a riding-whip or stick. I caught him once or twice over the shoulders with the flat of their old German sword."

"Then what?"

"He pulled over the bookcase, as I said, and fell," said Charles, with a sigh. It was no fun doing errands for his father, who was never quite satisfied.

"But the real cause was heart disease? Of that you're sure?"

"That or a fit. However, we shall hear more than enough at the inquest on such unsavoury topics."

They went into breakfast. Charles had a racking headache, consequent on motoring before food. He was also anxious about the future, reflecting that the police must detain Helen and Margaret for the inquest and ferret the whole thing out. He saw himself obliged to leave Hilton. One could not afford to live near the scene of a scandal — it was not fair on one's wife. His comfort was that the pater's eyes were opened at last. There would be a horrible smash up, and probably a separation from Margaret; then they would all start again, more as they had been in his mother's time.

"I think I'll go round to the police-station," said his father when breakfast was over.

"What for?" cried Dolly, who had still not been "told."

"Very well, sir. Which car will you have?"

"I think I'll walk."

"It's a good half-mile," asid Charles, stepping into

the garden. " The sun's very hot for April. Shan't
I take you up, and then, perhaps, a little spin round by
Tewin? "

" You go on as if I didn't know my own mind,"
said Mr. Wilcox fretfully. Charles hardened his
mouth. " You young fellows' one idea is to get into
a motor. I tell you, I want to walk: I'm very fond
of walking."

" Oh, all right; I'm about the house if you want me
for anything. I thought of not going up to the office
today, if that is your wish."

" It is, indeed, my boy," said Mr. Wilcox, and laid
a hand on his sleeve.

Charles did not like it; he was uneasy about his father, who did not seem himself this morning. There
was a petulant touch about him — more like a woman.
Could it be that he was growing old? The Wilcoxes
were not lacking in affection; they had it royally, but
they did not know how to use it. It was the talent in
the napkin, and, for a warm-hearted man, Charles had
conveyed very little joy. As he watched his father
shuffling up the road, he had a vague regret — a wish
that something had been different somewhere — a wish
(though he did not express it thus) that he had been
taught to say " I " in his youth. He meant to make up
for Margaret's defection, but knew that his father had
been very happy with her until yesterday. How had
she done it? By some dishonest trick, no doubt —
but how?

Mr. Wilcox reappeared at eleven, looking very tired.
There was to be an inquest on Leonard's body tomorrow, and the police required his son to attend.

" I expected that," said Charles. " I shall naturally
be the most important witness there."

Chapter XLIII

OUT of the turmoil and horror that had begun with Aunt Juley's illness and was not even to end with Leonard's death, it seemed impossible to Margaret that healthy life should re-emerge. Events succeeded in a logical, yet senseless, train. People lost their humanity, and took values as arbitrary as those in a pack of playing-cards. It was natural that Henry should do this and cause Helen to do that, and then think her wrong for doing it; natural that she herself should think him wrong; natural that Leonard should want to know how Helen was, and come, and Charles be angry with him for coming — natural, but unreal. In this jangle of causes and effects what had become of their true selves? Here Leonard lay dead in the garden, from natural causes; yet life was a deep, deep river, death a blue sky, life was a house, death a wisp of hay, a flower, a tower, life and death were anything and everything, except this ordered insanity, where the king takes the queen, and the ace the king. Ah, no; there was beauty and adventure behind, such as the man at her feet had yearned for; there was hope this side of the grave; there were truer relationships beyond the limits that fetter us now. As a prisoner looks up and sees stars beckoning, so she, from the turmoil and horror of those days, caught glimpses of the diviner wheels.

And Helen, dumb with fright, but trying to keep calm for the child's sake, and Miss Avery, calm, but murmuring tenderly, " No one ever told the lad he'll have a child "—they also reminded her that horror is not the end. To what ultimate harmony we tend she did not know, but there seemed great chance that a child would be born into the world, to take the great chances of beauty and adventure that the world offers. She moved through the sunlit garden, gathering narcissi, crimson-eyed and white. There was nothing else to be done; the time for telegrams and anger was over, and it seemed wisest that the hands of Leonard should be folded on his breast and be filled with flowers. Here was the father; leave it at that. Let Squalor be turned into Tragedy, whose eyes are the stars, and whose hands hold the sunset and the dawn.

A..d even the influx of officials, even the return of the doctor, vulgar and acute, could not shake her belief in the eternity of beauty. Science explained people, but could not understand them. After long centuries among the bones and muscles it might be advancing to knowledge of the nerves, but this would never give understanding. One could open the heart to Mr. Mansbridge and his sort without discovering its secrets to them, for they wanted everything down in black and white, and black and white was exactly what they were left with.

They questioned her closely about Charles. She never suspected why. Death had come, and the doctor agreed that it was due to heart disease. They asked to see her father's sword. She explained that Charles's anger was natural, but mistaken. Miserable questions about Leonard followed, all of which she answered unfalteringly. Then back to Charles again. " No doubt Mr. Wilcox may have induced death," she said; " but if it wasn't one thing it would have been another, as you yourselves know." At last they thanked her, and took the sword and the body down to Hilton. She began to pick up the books from the floor.

Helen had gone to the farm. It was the best place

for her, since she had to wait for the inquest. Though, as if things were not hard enough, Madge and her husband had raised trouble; they did not see why they should receive the offscourings of Howards End. And, of course, they were right. The whole world was going to be right, and amply avenge any brave talk against the conventions. " Nothing matters," the Schlegels had said in the past, " except one's self-respect and that of one's friends." When the time came, other things mattered terribly. However, Madge had yielded, and Helen was assured of peace for one day and night, and tomorrow she would return to Germany.

As for herself, she determined to go too. No message came from Henry; perhaps he expected her to apologize. Now that she had time to think over her own tragedy, she was unrepentant. She neither forgave him for his behaviour nor wished to forgive him. Her speech to him seemed perfect. She would not have altered a word. It had to be uttered once in a life, to adjust the lopsidedness of the world. It was spoken not only to her husband, but to thousands of men like him — a protest against the inner darkness in high places that comes with a commercial age. Though he would build up his life without hers, she could not apologize. He had refused to connect, on the clearest issue that can be laid before a man, and their love must take the consequences.

No, there was nothing more to be done. They had tried not to go over the precipice but perhaps the fall was inevitable. And it comforted her to think that the future was certainly inevitable: cause and effect would go jangling forward to some goal doubtless, but to none that she could imagine. At such moments the soul retires within, to float upon the bosom of a deeper stream, and has communion with the dead, and sees the world's glory not diminished, but different in kind to what she has supposed. She alters her focus until trivial things are blurred. Margaret had been tending this way all the winter. Leonard's death brought her to the goal. Alas! that Henry should fade away as reality emerged, and only her love for him should remain clear, stamped with his image like the cameos we rescue out of dreams.

With unfaltering eye she traced his future. He would soon present a healthy mind to the world again, and what did he or the world care if he was rotten at the core? He would grow into a rich, jolly old man, at times a little sentimental about women, but emptying his glass with any one. Tenacious of power, he would keep Charles and the rest dependent, and retire from business reluctantly and at an advanced age. He would settle down — though she could not realize this. In her eyes Henry was always moving and causing others to move, until the ends of the earth met. But in time he must get too tired to move, and settle down. What next? The inevitable word. The release of the soul to its appropriate Heaven.

Would they meet in it? Margaret believed in immortality for herself. An eternal future had always seemed natural to her. And Henry believed in it for himself. Yet, would they meet again? Are there not rather endless levels beyond the grave, as the theory that he had censured teaches? And his level, whether higher or lower, could it possibly be the same as hers?

Thus gravely meditating, she was summoned by him. He sent up Crane in the motor. Other servants passed like water, but the chauffeur remained, though impertinent and disloyal. Margaret disliked Crane, and he knew it.

" Is it the keys that Mr. Wilcox wants? " she asked.

" He didn't say, madam."

" You haven't any note for me? "

"He didn't say, madam."

After a moment's thought she locked up Howards End. It was pitiable to see in it the stirrings of warmth that would be quenched for ever. She raked out the fire that was blazing in the kitchen, and spread the coals in the gravelled yard. She closed the windows and drew the curtains. Henry would probably sell the place now.

She was determined not to spare him, for nothing new had happened as far as they were concerned. Her mood might never have altered from yesterday evening. He was standing a little outside Charles's gate, and motioned the car to stop. When his wife got out he said hoarsely: "I prefer to discuss things with you outside."

"It will be more appropriate in the road, I am afraid," said Margaret. "Did you get my message?"

"What about?"

"I am going to Germany with my sister. I must tell you now that I shall make it my permanent home. Our talk last night was more important than you have realized. I am unable to forgive you and am leaving you."

"I am extremely tired," said Henry, in injured tones. "I have been walking about all the morning, and wish to sit down."

"Certainly, if you will consent to sit on the grass."

The Great North Road should have been bordered all its length with glebe. Henry's kind had filched most of it. She moved to the scrap opposite, wherein were the Six Hills. They sat down on the farther side, so that they could not be seen by Charles or Dolly.

"Here are your keys," said Margaret. She tossed them towards him. They fell on the sunlit slope of grass, and he did not pick them up.

"I have something to tell you," he said gently.

She knew this superficial gentleness, this confession of hastiness, that was only intended to enhance her admiration of the male.

" I don't want to hear it," she replied. " My sister is going to be ill. My life is going to be with her now. We must manage to build up something, she and I and her child."

" Where are you going? "

" Munich. We start after the inquest, if she is not too ill."

" After the inquest? "

" Yes."

" Have you realized what the verdict at the inquest will be? "

" Yes, heart disease."

" No, my dear; manslaughter."

Margaret drove her fingers through the grass. The hill beneath her moved as if it was alive.

" Manslaughter," repeated Mr. Wilcox. " Charles may go to prison. I dare not tell him. I don't know what to do — what to do. I'm broken — I'm ended."

No sudden warmth arose in her. She did not see that to break him was her only hope. She did not enfold the sufferer in her arms. But all through that day and the next a new life began to move. The verdict was brought in. Charles was committed for trial. It was against all reason that he should be punished, but the law, being made in his image, sentenced him to three years' imprisonment. Then Henry's fortress gave way. He could bear no one but his wife, he shambled up to Margaret afterwards and asked her to do what she could with him. She did what seemed easiest — she took him down to recruit at Howards End.

Chapter XLIV

TOM'S father was cutting the big meadow. He passed again and again amid whirring blades and sweet odours of grass, encompassing with narrowing circles the sacred centre of the field. Tom was negotiating with Helen.

"I haven't any idea," she replied. "Do you suppose baby may, Meg?"

Margaret put down her work and regarded them absently. "What was that?" she asked.

"Tom wants to know whether baby is old enough to play with hay?"

"I haven't the least notion," answered Margaret, and took up her work again.

"Now, Tom, baby is not to stand; he is not to lie on his face; he is not to lie so that his head wags; he is not to be teased or tickled; and he is not to be cut into two or more pieces by the cutter. Will you be as careful as all that?"

Tom held out his arms.

"That child is a wonderful nursemaid," remarked Margaret.

"He is fond of baby. That's why he does it!" was Helen's answer. "They're going to be lifelong friends."

"Starting at the ages of six and one?"

"Of course. It will be a great thing for Tom."

"It may be a greater thing for baby."

Fourteen months had passed, but Margaret still stopped at Howards End. No better plan had occurred to her. The meadow was being recut, the

great red poppies were reopening in the garden. July
would follow with the little red poppies among the
wheat, August with the cutting of the wheat. These
little events would become part of her year after
year. Every summer she would fear lest the well
should give out, every winter lest the pipes should
freeze; every westerly gale might blow the wych-elm
down and bring the end of all things, and so she could
not read or talk during a westerly gale. The air was
tranquil now. She and her sister were sitting on the
remains of Evie's rockery, where the lawn merged into
the field.

"What a time they all are!" said Helen. "What
can they be doing inside?" Margaret, who was growing less talkative, made no answer. The noise of the
cutter came intermittently, like the breaking of waves.
Close by them a man was preparing to scythe out one
of the dell-holes.

"I wish Henry was out to enjoy this," said Helen.
"This lovely weather and to be shut up in the house!
It's very hard."

"It has to be," said Margaret. "The hay-fever is
his chief objection against living here, but he thinks
it worth while."

"Meg, is or isn't he ill? I can't make out."

"Not ill. Eternally tired. He has worked very
hard all his life, and noticed nothing. Those are the
people who collapse when they do notice a thing."

"I suppose he worries dreadfully about his part of
the tangle."

"Dreadfully. That is why I wish Dolly had not
come, too, today. Still, he wanted them all to come.
It has to be."

"Why does he want them?"

Margaret did not answer.

"Meg, may I tell you something? I like Henry."

"You'd be odd if you didn't," said Margaret.

"I usen't to."

"Usen't!" She lowered her eyes a moment to the black abyss of the past. They had crossed it, always excepting Leonard and Charles. They were building up a new life, obscure, yet gilded with tranquillity. Leonard was dead; Charles had two years more in prison. One usen't always to see clearly before that time. It was different now.

"I like Henry because he does worry."

"And he likes you because you don't."

Helen sighed. She seemed humiliated, and buried her face in her hands. After a time she said: "Above love," a transition less abrupt than it appeared.

Margaret never stopped working.

"I mean a woman's love for a man. I supposed I should hang my life on to that once, and was driven up and down and about as if something was worrying through me. But everything is peaceful now; I seem cured. That Herr Förstmeister, whom Frieda keeps writing about, must be a noble character, but he doesn't see that I shall never marry him or any one. It isn't shame or mistrust of myself. I simply couldn't. I'm ended. I used to be so dreamy about a man's love as a girl, and think that for good or evil love must be the great thing. But it hasn't been; it has been itself a dream. Do you agree?"

"I do not agree. I do not."

"I ought to remember Leonard as my lover," said Helen, stepping down into the field. "I tempted him, and killed him and it is surely the least I can do. I would like to throw out all my heart to Leonard on such an afternoon as this. But I cannot. It is no good pretending. I am forgetting him." Her eyes filled with tears. "How nothing seems to match — how, my darling, my precious —" She broke off. "Tommy!"

" Yes, please? "

" Baby's not to try and stand.— There's something wanting in me. I see you loving Henry, and understanding him better daily, and I know that death wouldn't part you in the least. But I— Is it some awful appalling, criminal defect? "

Margaret silenced her. She said: " It is only that people are far more different than is pretended. All over the world men and women are worrying because they cannot develop as they are supposed to develop. Here and there they have the matter out, and it comforts them. Don't fret yourself, Helen. Develop what you have; love your child. I do not love children. I am thankful to have none. I can play with their beauty and charm, but that is all — nothing real, not one scrap of what there ought to be. And others — others go farther still, and move outside humanity altogether. A place, as well as a person, may catch the glow. Don't you see that all this leads to comfort in the end? It is part of the battle against sameness. Differences — eternal differences, planted by God in a single family, so that there may always be colour; sorrow perhaps, but colour in the daily grey. Then I can't have you worrying about Leonard. Don't drag in the personal when it will not come. Forget him."

" Yes, yes, but what has Leonard got out of life? "

" Perhaps an adventure."

" Is that enough? "

" Not for us. But for him."

Helen took up a bunch of grass. She looked at the sorrel, and the red and white and yellow clover, and the quaker grass, and the daisies, and the bents that composed it. She raised it to her face.

" Is it sweetening yet? " asked Margaret.

" No, only withered."

" It will sweeten tomorrow."

Helen smiled. "Oh, Meg, you are a person," she said. "Think of the racket and torture this time last year. But now I couldn't stop unhappy if I tried. What a change — and all through you!"

"Oh, we merely settled down. You and Henry learnt to understand one another and to forgive, all through the autumn and the winter."

"Yes, but who settled us down?"

Margaret did not reply. The scything had begun, and she took off her pince-nez to watch it.

"You!" cried Helen. "You did it all, sweetest, though you're too stupid to see. Living here was your plan — I wanted you; he wanted you; and every one said it was impossible, but you knew. Just think of our lives without you, Meg — I and baby with Monica, revolting by theory, he handed about from Dolly to Evie. But you picked up the pieces, and made us a home. Can't it strike you — even for a moment — that your life has been heroic? Can't you remember the two months after Charles's arrest, when you began to act, and did all?"

"You were both ill at the time," said Margaret. "I did the obvious things. I had two invalids to nurse. Here was a house, ready furnished and empty. It was obvious. I didn't know myself it would turn into a permanent home. No doubt I have done a little towards straightening the tangle, but things that I can't phrase have helped me."

"I hope it will be permanent," said Helen, drifting away to other thoughts.

"I think so. There are moments when I feel Howards End peculiarly our own."

"All the same, London's creeping."

She pointed over the meadow — over eight or nine meadows, but at the end of them was a red rust.

"You see that in Surrey and even Hampshire now,"

she continued. "I can see it from the Purbeck Downs. And London is only part of something else, I'm afraid. Life's going to be melted down, all over the world."

Margaret knew that her sister spoke truly. Howards End, Oniton, the Purbeck Downs, the Oderberge, were all survivals, and the melting-pot was being prepared for them. Logically, they had no right to be alive. One's hope was in the weakness of logic. Were they possibly the earth beating time?

"Because a thing is going strong now, it need not go strong for ever," she said. "This craze for motion has only set in during the last hundred years. It may be followed by a civilization that won't be a movement, because it will rest on the earth. All the signs are against it now, but I can't help hoping, and very early in the morning in the garden I feel that our house is the future as well as the past."

They turned and looked at it. Their own memories coloured it now, for Helen's child had been born in the central room of the nine. Then Margaret said, "Oh, take care—!" for something moved behind the window of the hall, and the door opened.

"The conclave's breaking at last. I'll go."

It was Paul.

Helen retreated with the children far into the field. Friendly voices greeted her. Margaret rose, to encounter a man with a heavy black moustache.

"My father has asked for you," he said with hostility. She took her work and followed him.

"We have been talking business," he continued, "but I dare say you knew all about it beforehand."

"Yes, I did."

Clumsy of movement — for he had spent all his life in the saddle — Paul drove his foot against the paint of the front door. Mrs. Wilcox gave a little cry of annoyance. She did not like anything scratched; she stopped in the hall to take Dolly's boa and gloves out of a vase.

Her husband was lying in a great leather chair in the dining-room, and by his side, holding his hand rather ostentatiously, was Evie. Dolly, dressed in purple, sat near the window. The room was a little dark and airless; they were obliged to keep it like this until the carting of the hay. Margaret joined the family without speaking; the five of them had met already at tea, and she knew quite well what was going to be said. Averse to wasting her time, she went on sewing. The clock struck six.

"Is this going to suit every one?" said Henry in a weary voice. He used the old phrases, but their effect was unexpected and shadowy. "Because I don't want you all coming here later on and complaining that I have been unfair."

"It's apparently got to suit us," said Paul.

"I beg your pardon, my boy. You have only to speak, and I will leave the house to you instead."

Paul frowned ill-temperedly, and began scratching at his arm. "As I've given up the outdoor life that suited me, and I have come home to look after the business, it's no good my settling down here," he said at last. "It's not really the country, and it's not the town."

"Very well. Does my arrangement suit you, Evie?"

"Of course, father."

"And you, Dolly?"

Dolly raised her faded little face, which sorrow could wither but not steady. "Perfectly splendidly," she said. "I thought Charles wanted it for the boys, but last time I saw him he said no, because we cannot possibly live in this part of England again. Charles says we ought to change our name, but I cannot think what to, for Wilcox just suits Charles and me, and I can't think of any other name."

There was a general silence. Dolly looked nervously round, fearing that she had been inappropriate. Paul continued to scratch his arm.

"Then I leave Howards End to my wife absolutely," said Henry. "And let every one understand that; and after I am dead let there be no jealousy and no surprise."

Margaret did not answer. There was something uncanny in her triumph. She, who had never expected to conquer any one, had charged straight through these Wilcoxes and broken up their lives.

"In consequence, I leave my wife no money," said Henry. "That is her own wish. All that she would have had will be divided among you. I am also giving you a great deal in my lifetime, so that you may be independent of me. That is her wish, too. She also is giving away a great deal of money. She intends to diminish her income by half during the next ten years; she intends when she dies to leave the house to her — to her nephew, down in the field. Is all that clear? Does every one understand?"

Paul rose to his feet. He was accustomed to natives, and a very little shook him out of the Englishman. Feeling manly and cynical, he said: "Down in the field? Oh, come! I think we might have had the whole establishment, piccaninnies included."

Mrs. Cahill whispered: "Don't, Paul. You promised you'd take care." Feeling a woman of the world, she rose and prepared to take her leave.

Her father kissed her. "Good-bye, old girl," he said; "don't you worry about me."

"Good-bye, dad."

Then it was Dolly's turn. Anxious to contribute, she laughed nervously, and said: "Good-bye, Mr. Wilcox. It does seem curious that Mrs. Wilcox

should have left Margaret Howards End, and yet
she get it, after all."

From Evie came a sharply-drawn breath. "Good-
bye," she said to Margaret, and kissed her.

And again and again fell the word, like the ebb of
a dying sea.

"Good-bye."

"Good-bye, Dolly."

"So long, father."

"Good-bye, my boy; always take care of yourself."

"Good-bye, Mrs. Wilcox."

"Good-bye."

Margaret saw their visitors to the gate. Then she
returned to her husband and laid her head in his
hands. He was pitiably tired. But Dolly's remark
had interested her. At last she said: "Could you
tell me, Henry, what was that about Mrs. Wilcox
having left me Howards End?"

Tranquilly he replied: "Yes, she did. But that is
a very old story. When she was ill and you were so
kind to her she wanted to make you some return, and,
not being herself at the time, scribbled 'Howards End'
on a piece of paper. I went into it thoroughly, and,
as it was clearly fanciful, I set it aside, little knowing what my Margaret would be to me in the future."

Margaret was silent. Something shook her life in
its inmost recesses, and she shivered.

"I didn't do wrong, did I?" he asked, bending
down.

"You didn't, darling. Nothing has been done
wrong."

From the garden came laughter. "Here they are at
last!" exclaimed Henry, disengaging himself with a
smile. Helen rushed into the gloom, holding Tom by
one hand and carrying her baby on the other. There
were shouts of infectious joy.

" The field's cut!" Helen cried excitedly —"the big meadow! We've seen to the very end, and it'll be such a crop of hay as never!"

Weybridge, 1908-1910.

MAURICE

BEGUN 1913
FINISHED 1914

Dedicated to a Happier Year

PART
One

1 Once a term the whole school went for a walk—that is to say the three masters took part as well as all the boys. It was usually a pleasant outing, and everyone looked forward to it, forgot old scores, and behaved with freedom. Lest discipline should suffer, it took place just before the holidays, when leniency does no harm, and indeed it seemed more like a treat at home than school, for Mrs Abrahams, the Principal's wife, would meet them at the tea place with some lady friends, and be hospitable and motherly.

Mr Abrahams was a preparatory schoolmaster of the old-fashioned sort. He cared neither for work nor games, but fed his boys well and saw that they did not misbehave. The rest he left to the parents, and did not speculate how much the parents were leaving to him. Amid mutual compliments the boys passed out into a public school, healthy but backward, to receive upon undefended flesh the first blows of the world. There is much to be said for apathy in education, and Mr Abrahams's pupils did not do badly in the long run, became parents in their turn, and in some cases sent him their sons. Mr Read, the junior assistant, was a master of the same type, only stupider, while Mr Ducie, the senior, acted as a stimulant, and prevented the whole concern from going to sleep. They did not like him much, but knew that he was necessary. Mr Ducie was an able man, orthodox, but not out of touch with the world, nor incapable of seeing both sides of a question. He was unsuitable for parents and the denser boys, but good for the first form, and had even coached pupils into a scholarship. Nor was he a bad organizer. While affecting to hold the reins and to prefer Mr Read, Mr Abrahams really allowed Mr Ducie a free hand and ended by taking him into partnership.

Mr Ducie always had something on his mind. On this occasion it was Hall, one of the older boys, who was leaving them to go to a public school. He wanted to have a "good talk" with Hall, during the outing. His colleagues objected, since it would leave them more to do, and the Principal remarked that he had already talked to Hall, and that the boy would prefer to take his last walk with his school-fellows. This was probable, but Mr Ducie was never deterred from doing what is right. He smiled and was silent. Mr Read knew what the "good talk" would be, for early in their acquaintance they had touched on a certain theme professionally. Mr Read had disapproved. "Thin ice," he had said. The Principal neither knew nor would have wished to know. Parting from his pupils when they were fourteen, he forgot they had developed into men. They seemed to him a race small but complete, like the New Guinea pygmies, "my boys". And they were even easier to understand than pygmies, because they never married and seldom died. Celibate and immortal, the long procession passed before him, its thickness varying from twenty-five to forty at a time. "I see no use in books on education. Boys began before education was thought of." Mr Ducie would smile, for he was soaked in evolution.

From this to the boys.

"Sir, may I hold your hand. . . . Sir, you promised me. . . . Both Mr. Abrahams's hands were bagged and all Mr Read's. . . . Oh sir, did you hear that? He thinks Mr Read has three hands! . . . I didn't, I said 'fingers'. Green eye! Green eye!"

"When you have quite finished—!"

"Sir!"

"I'm going to walk with Hall alone."

There were cries of disappointment. The other masters, seeing that it was no good, called the pack off, and marshalled them along the cliff towards the downs. Hall, triumphant, sprang to Mr Ducie's side, and felt too old to take his hand. He was a plump, pretty lad, not in any way remarkable. In this he resembled his father, who had passed in the procession twenty-five years before, vanished into a public school, married, begotten a son and two daughters, and recently died of pneumonia. Mr Hall had been a good citizen, but lethargic. Mr Ducie had informed himself about him before they began the walk.

"Well, Hall, expecting a pi-jaw, eh?"

"I don't know, sir—Mr Abrahams' given me one with 'Those Holy Fields'. Mrs Abrahams' given me sleeve links. The fellows have given me a set of Guatemalas up to two dollars. Look, sir! The ones with the parrot on the pillar on."

"Splendid, splendid! What did Mr Abrahams say? Told you you were a miserable sinner, I hope."

The boy laughed. He did not understand Mr Ducie, but knew that he was meaning to be funny. He felt at ease because it was his last day at school, and even if he did wrong he would not get into a row. Besides, Mr Abrahams had declared him a success. "We are proud of him; he will do us honour at Sunnington": he had seen the beginning of the letter to his mother. And the boys had showered presents on him, declaring he was brave. A great mistake—he wasn't brave: he was afraid of the dark. But no one knew this.

"Well, what did Mr Abrahams say?" repeated Mr Ducie, when they reached the sands. A long talk threatened, and the boy wished he was up on the cliff with his friends, but he knew that wishing is useless when boy meets man.

"Mr Abrahams told me to copy my father, sir."

"Anything else?"

"I am never to do anything I should be ashamed to have mother see me do. No one can go wrong then, and the public school will be very different from this."

"Did Mr Abrahams say how?"

"All kinds of difficulties—more like the world."

"Did he tell you what the world is like?"

"No."

"Did you ask him?"

"No, sir."

"That wasn't very sensible of you, Hall. Clear things up. Mr Abrahams and I are here to answer your questions. What do you suppose the world—the world of grown-up people is like?"

"I can't tell. I'm a boy," he said, very sincerely. "Are they very treacherous, sir?"

Mr Ducie was amused and asked him what examples of treachery he had seen. He replied that grown-up people would not be unkind to boys, but were they not always cheating one another? Losing his schoolboy manner, he began to talk like a child, and became fanciful and amusing. Mr Ducie lay down on the sand to listen to him, lit his pipe, and looked up to the sky. The little watering-place where they lived was now far behind, the rest of the school away in front. The day was gray and windless, with little distinction between clouds and sun.

"You live with your mother, don't you?" he interrupted, seeing that the boy had gained confidence.

"Yes, sir."

"Have you any elder brothers?"

"No, sir—only Ada and Kitty."

"Any uncles?"

"No."

"So you don't know many men?"

"Mother keeps a coachman and George in the garden, but of course you mean gentlemen. Mother has three maid-servants to look after the house, but they are so idle that they will not mend Ada's stockings. Ada is my eldest little sister."

"How old are you?"

"Fourteen and three quarters."

"Well, you're an ignorant little beggar." They laughed. After a pause he said, "When I was your age, my father told me something that proved very useful and helped me a good deal." This was untrue: his father had never told him anything. But he needed a prelude to what he was going to say.

"Did he, sir?"

"Shall I tell you what it was?"

"Please, sir."

"I am going to talk to you for a few moments as if I were your father, Maurice! I shall call you by your real name." Then, very simply and kindly, he approached the mystery of sex. He spoke of male and female, created by God in the beginning in order that the earth might be peopled, and of the period when the male and female receive their powers. "You are just becoming a man now, Maurice; that is why I am telling you about this. It is not a thing that your mother can tell you, and you should not mention it to her nor to any lady, and if at your next school boys mention it to you, just shut them up; tell them you know. Have you heard about it before?"

"No, sir."

"Not a word?"

"No, sir."

Still smoking his pipe, Mr Ducie got up, and choosing a smooth piece of sand drew diagrams upon it with his walking-stick. "This will make it easier," he said to the boy, who watched dully: it bore no relation to his experiences. He was attentive, as was natural when he was the only one in the class, and he knew that the subject was serious and related to his own body. But he could not himself relate it; it fell to pieces as soon as Mr Ducie put it together, like an impossible sum. In vain he tried. His torpid brain would not awake. Puberty was there, but not intelligence, and manhood was stealing on him, as it always must, in a trance. Useless to break in upon that trance. Useless to describe it, however scientifically and sympathetically. The boy assents and is dragged back into sleep, not to be enticed there before his hour.

Mr Ducie, whatever his science, was sympathetic. Indeed he was too sympathetic; he attributed cultivated feelings to Maurice, and did not realize that he must either understand nothing or be overwhelmed. "All this is rather a bother," he said, "but one must get it over, one mustn't make a mystery of it. Then come the great things—Love, Life." He was fluent, having talked to boys in this way before, and he knew the kind of question they would ask. Maurice would not ask: he only said, "I see, I see, I see," and at first Mr Ducie feared he did not see. He examined him. The replies were satisfactory. They boy's memory was good and—so curious a fabric is the human—he even developed a spurious intelligence, a surface flicker to respond to the beaconing glow of the man's. In the end he did ask one or two questions about sex, and they were to the point. Mr Ducie was much pleased. "That's right," he said. "You need never be puzzled or bothered now."

Love and life still remained, and he touched on them as they strolled forward by the colourless sea. He spoke of the ideal man —chaste with asceticism. He sketched the glory of Woman. Engaged to be married himself, he grew more human, and his eyes coloured up behind the strong spectacles; his cheek flushed. To love a noble woman, to protect and serve her—this, he told the little boy, was the crown of life. "You can't understand now, you will some day, and when you do understand it, remember the poor old pedagogue who put you on the track. It all hangs together—all—and God's in his heaven, All's right with the world. Male and female! Ah wonderful!"

"I think I shall not marry," remarked Maurice.

"This day ten years hence—I invite you and your wife to dinner with my wife and me. Will you accept?"

"Oh sir!" He smiled with pleasure.

"It's a bargain, then!" It was at all events a good joke to end with. Maurice was flattered and began to contemplate marriage. But while they were easing off Mr Ducie stopped, and held his cheek as though every tooth ached. He turned and looked at the long expanse of sand behind.

"I never scratched out those infernal diagrams," he said slowly.

At the further end of the bay some people were following them, also by the edge of the sea. Their course would take them by the very spot where Mr Ducie had illustrated sex, and one of them was a lady. He ran back sweating with fear.

"Sir, won't it be all right?" Maurice cried. "The tide'll have covered them by now."

"Good Heavens . . . thank God . . . the tide's rising."

And suddenly for an instant of time, the boy despised him. "Liar," he thought. "Liar, coward, he's told me nothing." . . . Then darkness rolled up again, the darkness that is primeval but not eternal, and yields to its own painful dawn.

2 Maurice's mother lived near London, in a comfortable villa among some pines. There he and his sisters had been born, and thence his father had gone up to business every day, thither returning. They nearly left when the church was built, but they became accustomed to it, as to everything, and even found it a convenience. Church was the only place Mrs Hall had to go to—the shops delivered. The station was not far either, nor was a tolerable day school for the girls. It was a land of facilities, where nothing had to be striven for, and success was indistinguishable from failure.

Maurice liked his home, and recognized his mother as its presiding genius. Without her there would be no soft chairs or food or easy games, and he was grateful to her for providing so much, and loved her. He liked his sisters also. When he arrived they ran out with cries of joy, took off his greatcoat, and dropped it for the servants on the floor of the hall. It was nice to be the centre of attraction and show off about school. His Guatemala stamps were admired—so were "Those Holy Fields" and a Holbein photograph that Mr Ducie had given him. After tea the weather cleared, and Mrs Hall put on her goloshes and walked with him round the grounds. They went kissing one another and conversing aimlessly.

"Morrie . . ."

"Mummie . . ."

"Now I must give my Morrie a lovely time."

"Where's George?"

"Such a splendid report from Mr Abrahams. He says you remind him of your poor father. . . . Now what shall we do these holidays?"

"I like here best."

"Darling boy . . ." She embraced him, more affectionately than ever.

"There is nothing like home, as everyone finds. Yes, tomatoes—" she liked reciting the names of vegetables. "Tomatoes, radishes, broccoli, onions—"

"Tomatoes, broccoli, onions, purple potatoes, white potatoes," droned the little boy.

"Turnip tops—"

"Mother, where's George?"

"He left last week."

"Why did George leave?" he asked.

"He was getting too old. Howell always changes the boy every two years."

"Oh."

"Turnip tops," she continued, "potatoes again, beetroot— Morrie, how would you like to pay a little visit to grandpapa and Aunt Ida if they ask us? I want you to have a very nice time this holiday, dear—you have been so good, but then Mr Abrahams is such a good man; you see, your father was at his school too, and we are sending you to your father's old public school too— Sunnington—in order that you may grow up like your dear father in every way."

A sob interrupted her.

"Morrie, *darling*—"

The little boy was in tears.

"My pet, what is it?"

"I don't know . . . I don't know . . ."

"Why, Maurice . . ."

He shook his head. She was grieved at her failure to make him happy, and began to cry too. The girls ran out, exclaiming, "Mother, what's wrong with Maurice?"

"Oh, don't," he wailed. "Kitty, get out—"

"He's overtired," said Mrs Hall—her explanation for everything.

"I'm overtired."

"Come to your room, Morrie—Oh my sweet, this is really too dreadful."

"No—I'm all right." He clenched his teeth, and a great mass of sorrow that had overwhelmed him by rising to the surface began to sink. He could feel it going down into his heart until he was conscious of it no longer. "I'm all right." He looked around him fiercely and dried his eyes. "I'll play Halma, I think." Before the pieces were set, he was talking as before; the childish collapse was over.

He beat Ada, who worshipped him, and Kitty, who did not, and then ran into the garden again to see the coachman. "How d'ye do, Howell. How's Mrs Howell? How d'ye do, Mrs Howell," and so on, speaking in a patronizing voice, different from that he used to gentlefolks. Then altering back, "Isn't it a new garden boy?"

"Yes, Master Maurice."

"Was George too old?"

"No, Master Maurice. He wanted to better himself."

"Oh, you mean he gave notice."

"That's right."

"Mother said he was too old and you gave him notice."

"No, Master Maurice."

"My poor woodstacks'll be glad," said Mrs Howell. Maurice

(18)

and the late garden boy had been used to play about in them. "They are Mother's woodstacks, not yours," said Maurice and went indoors. The Howells were not offended, though they pretended to be so to one another. They had been servants all their lives, and liked a gentleman to be a snob. "He has quite a way with him already," they told the cook. "More like his father."

The Barrys, who came to dinner, were of the same opinion. Dr Barry was an old friend, or rather neighbour, of the family, and took a moderate interest in them. No one could be deeply interested in the Halls. Kitty he liked—she had hints of grit in her— but the girls were in bed, and he told his wife afterwards that Maurice ought to have been there too. "And stop there all his life. As he will. Like his father. What is the use of such people?"

When Maurice did go to bed, it was reluctantly. That room always frightened him. He had been such a man all the evening, but the old feeling came over him as soon as his mother had kissed him good night. The trouble was the looking-glass. He did not mind seeing his face in it, nor casting a shadow on the ceiling, but he did mind seeing his shadow on the ceiling reflected in the glass. He would arrange the candle so as to avoid the combination, and then dare himself to put it back and be gripped with fear. He knew what it was, it reminded him of nothing horrible. But he was afraid. In the end he would dash out the candle and leap into bed. Total darkness he could bear, but this room had the further defect of being opposite a street lamp. On good nights the light would penetrate the curtains unalarmingly, but sometimes blots like skulls fell over the furniture. His heart beat violently, and he lay in terror, with all his household close at hand.

As he opened his eyes to look whether the blots had grown smaller, he remembered George. Something stirred in the unfathomable depths of his heart. He whispered, "George,

George." Who was George? Nobody—just a common servant. Mother and Ada and Kitty were far more important. But he was too little to argue this. He did not even know that when he yielded to this sorrow he overcame the spectral and fell asleep.

3 Sunnington was the next stage in Maurice's career. He traversed it without attracting attention. He was not good at work, though better than he pretended, nor colossally good at games. If people noticed him they liked him, for he had a bright friendly face and responded to attention; but there were so many boys of his type—they formed the backbone of the school and we cannot notice each vertebra. He did the usual things—was kept in, once caned, rose from form to form on the classical side till he clung precariously to the sixth, and he became a house prefect, and later a school prefect and member of the first fifteen. Though clumsy, he had strength and physical pluck: at cricket he did not do so well. Having been bullied as a new boy, he bullied others when they seemed unhappy or weak, not because he was cruel but because it was the proper thing to do. In a word, he was a mediocre member of a mediocre school, and left a faint and favourable impression behind. "Hall? Wait a minute, which was Hall? Oh yes, I remember; clean run enough."

Beneath it all, he was bewildered. He had lost the precocious clearness of the child which transfigures and explains the universe, offering answers of miraculous insight and beauty. "Out of the mouths of babes and sucklings . . ." But not out of the mouth of the boy of sixteen. Maurice forgot he had ever been sexless, and only realized in maturity how just and clear the sensations of his earliest days must have been. He sank far below them now, for he was descending the Valley of the Shadow of Life. It lies between the lesser mountains and the greater, and without breathing its fogs no one can come through. He groped about in it longer than most boys.

Where all is obscure and unrealized the best similitude is a dream. Maurice had two dreams at school; they will interpret him.

In the first dream he felt very cross. He was playing football against a nondescript whose existence he resented. He made an effort and the nondescript turned into George, that garden boy. But he had to be careful or it would reappear. George headed down the field towards him, naked and jumping over the wood-stacks. "I shall go mad if he turns wrong now," said Maurice, and just as they collared this happened, and a brutal disappoint-ment woke him up. He did not connect it with Mr Ducie's homily, still less with his second dream, but he thought he was going to be ill, and afterwards that it was somehow a punish-ment for something.

The second dream is more difficult to convey. Nothing hap-pened. He scarcely saw a face, scarcely heard a voice say, "That is your friend," and then it was over, having filled him with beauty and taught him tenderness. He could die for such a friend, he would allow such a friend to die for him; they would make any sacrifice for each other, and count the world nothing, neither death nor distance nor crossness could part them, be-cause "this is my friend." Soon afterwards he was confirmed and tried to persuade himself that the friend must be Christ. But Christ has a mangy beard. Was he a Greek god, such as illus-trates the classical dictionary? More probable, but most prob-ably he was just a man. Maurice forbore to define his dream further. He had dragged it as far into life as it would come. He would never meet that man nor hear that voice again, yet they became more real than anything he knew, and would actually—

"Hall! Dreaming again! A hundred lines!"

"Sir—oh! Dative absolute."

"Dreaming again. Too late."

—would actually pull him back to them in broad daylight and drop a curtain. Then he would reimbibe the face and the four words, and would emerge yearning with tenderness and longing to be kind to everyone, because his friend wished it, and to be good that his friend might become more fond of him. Misery was somehow mixed up with all this happiness. It seemed as certain that he hadn't a friend as that he had one, and he would find a lonely place for tears, attributing them to the hundred lines.

Maurice's secret life can be understood now; it was part brutal, part ideal, like his dreams.

As soon as his body developed he became obscene. He supposed some special curse had descended on him, but he could not help it, for even when receiving the Holy Communion filthy thoughts would arise in his mind. The tone of the school was pure—that is to say, just before his arrival there had been a terrific scandal. The black sheep had been expelled, the remainder were drilled hard all day and policed at night, so it was his fortune or misfortune to have little opportunity of exchanging experiences with his school-fellows. He longed for smut, but heard little and contributed less, and his chief indecencies were solitary. Books: the school library was immaculate, but while at his grandfather's he came across an unexpurgated Martial, and stumbled about in it with burning ears. Thoughts: he had a dirty little collection. Acts: he desisted from these after the novelty was over, finding that they brought him more fatigue than pleasure.

All which, if it can be understood, took place in a trance. Maurice had fallen asleep in the Valley of the Shadow, far beneath the peaks of either range, and knew neither this nor that his school-fellows were sleeping likewise.

The other half of his life seemed infinitely remote from obscenity. As he rose in the school he began to make a religion of some other boy. When this boy, whether older or younger than himself, was present, he would laugh loudly, talk absurdly, and be unable to work. He dared not be kind—it was not the thing —still less to express his admiration in words. And the adored one would shake him off before long, and reduce him to sulks. However, he had his revenges. Other boys sometimes worshipped him, and when he realized this he would shake off them. The adoration was mutual on one occasion, both yearning for they knew not what, but the result was the same. They quarrelled in a few days. All that came out of the chaos were the two feelings of beauty and tenderness that he had first felt in a dream. They grew yearly, flourishing like plants that are all leaves and show no sign of flower. Towards the close of his education at Sunnington the growth stopped. A check, a silence, fell upon the complex processes, and very timidly the youth began to look around him.

4 He was nearly nineteen.

He stood on the platform on Prize Day, reciting a Greek Oration of his own composition. The hall was full of schoolboys and their parents, but Maurice affected to be addressing the Hague Conference, and to be pointing out to it the folly of its ways. "What stupidity is this, O andres Europenaici, to talk of abolishing war? What? Is not Ares the son of Zeus himself? Moreover, war renders you robust by exercising your limbs, not forsooth like those of my opponent." The Greek was vile: Maurice had got the prize on account of the Thought, and barely thus. The examining master had stretched a point in his favour since he was leaving and a respectable chap, and moreover leaving for Cambridge, where prize books on his shelves would help to advertise the school. So he received Grote's *History of Greece* amid tremendous applause. As he returned to his seat, which was next to his mother, he realized that he had again become popular, and wondered how. The clapping continued —it grew to an ovation; Ada and Kitty were pounding away with scarlet faces on the further side. Some of his friends, also leaving, cried "speech". This was irregular and quelled by the authorities, but the Headmaster himself rose and said a few words. Hall was one of them, and they would never cease to feel him so. The words were just. The school clapped not because Maurice was eminent but because he was average. It could celebrate itself in his image. People ran up to him afterwards saying "jolly good, old man", quite sentimentally, and even "it will be bilge in this hole without you." His relations shared in the triumph. On previous visits he had been hateful to them. "Sorry, mater, but you and the kids will have to walk alone" had been his remark after a football match when they had tried to join on to him in his mud and glory: Ada had cried. Now Ada was chatting quite ably to the Captain of the School, and Kitty was being handed cakes, and his mother was listening to his housemaster's wife, on the disappointments of installing hot air. Everyone and everything had suddenly harmonized. Was this the world?

A few yards off he saw Dr Barry, their neighbour from home, who caught his eye and called out in his alarming way, "Congratulations, Maurice, on your triumph. Overwhelming! I drink to it in this cup"—he drained it—"of extremely nasty tea."

Maurice laughed and went up to him, rather guiltily; for his conscience was bad. Dr Barry had asked him to befriend a little nephew, who had entered the school that term, but he had done nothing—it was not the thing. He wished that he had had more courage now that it was too late and he felt a man.

"And what's the next stage in your triumphal career? Cambridge?"

"So they say."

"So they say, do they? And what do you say?"

"I don't know," said the hero good-temperedly.

"And after Cambridge, what? Stock Exchange?"

"I suppose so—my father's old partner talks of letting me in if all goes well."

"And after you're let in by your father's old partner, what? A pretty wife?"

Maurice laughed again.

"Who will present the expectant world with a Maurice the third? After which old age, grandchildren, and finally the daisies. So that's your notion of a career. Well, it isn't mine."

"What's your notion, Doctor?" called Kitty.

"To help the weak and right the wrong, my dear," he replied, looking across at her.

"I'm sure it is all our notions," said the housemaster's wife, and Mrs Hall agreed.

"Oh no, it's not. It isn't consistently mine, or I should be looking after my Dickie instead of lingering on this scene of splendour."

"Do bring dear Dickie to say how d'ye do to me," asked Mrs Hall. "Is his father down here too?"

"Mother!" Kitty whispered.

"Yes. My brother died last year," said Dr Barry. "The incident slipped your memory. War did not render him robust by exercising his limbs, as Maurice supposes. He got a shell in the stomach."

He left them.

"I think Dr Barry gets cynical," remarked Ada. "I think he's jealous." She was right: Dr Barry, who had been a lady killer in his time, did resent the continuance of young men. Poor Maurice encountered him again. He had been saying goodbye to his housemaster's wife, who was a handsome woman, very civil to the older boys. They shook hands warmly. On turning away he heard Dr Barry's "Well, Maurice; a youth irresistible in love as in war," and caught his cynical glance.

"I don't know what you mean, Dr Barry."

"Oh, you young fellows! Butter wouldn't melt in your mouth these days. Don't know what I mean! Prudish of a petticoat! Be frank, man, be frank. You don't take anyone in. The frank mind's the pure mind. I'm a medical man and an old man and I tell you

that. Man that is born of woman must go with woman if the
human race is to continue."

Maurice stared after the housemaster's wife, underwent a
violent repulsion from her, and blushed crimson: he had remembered Mr Ducie's diagrams. A trouble—nothing as beautiful as a sorrow—rose to the surface of his mind, displayed its
ungainliness, and sank. Its precise nature he did not ask himself,
for his hour was not yet, but the hint was appalling, and, hero
though he was, he longed to be a little boy again, and to stroll
half awake for ever by the colourless sea. Dr Barry went on
lecturing him, and under the cover of a friendly manner said
much that gave pain.

5 He chose a college patronized by his chief school friend Chapman and by other old Sunningtonians, and during his first year managed to experience little in University life that was unfamiliar. He belonged to an Old Boys' Club, and they played games together, tea'd and lunched together, kept up their provincialisms and slang, sat elbow to elbow in hall, and walked arm in arm about the streets. Now and then they got drunk and boasted mysteriously about women, but their outlook remained that of the upper fifth, and some of them kept it through life. There was no feud between them and the other undergraduates, but they were too compact to be popular, too mediocre to lead, and they did not care to risk knowing men who had come from other public schools. All this suited Maurice. He was constitutionally lazy. Though none of his difficulties had been solved, none were added, which is something. The hush continued. He was less troubled by carnal thoughts. He stood still in the darkness instead of groping about in it, as if this was the end for which body and soul had been so painfully prepared.

During his second year he underwent a change. He had moved into college and it began to digest him. His days he might spend as before, but when the gates closed on him at night a new process began. Even as a freshman he made the important discovery that grown-up men behave politely to one another unless there is a reason for the contrary. Some third-year people had called on him in his digs. He had expected them to break his plates and insult the photograph of his mother, and when they did not he ceased planning how some day he should break theirs, thus saving time. And the manners of the dons were even more remarkable. Maurice was only waiting for such an atmosphere himself to soften. He did not enjoy being cruel and rude. It was against his nature. But it was necessary at school, or he might have gone under, and he had supposed it would have been even more necessary on the larger battlefield of the University.

Once inside college, his discoveries multiplied. People turned out to be alive. Hitherto he had supposed that they *were* what he *pretended* to be—flat pieces of cardboard stamped with a conventional design—but as he strolled about the courts at night and saw through the windows some men singing and others arguing and others at their books, there came by no process of reason a conviction that they were human beings with feelings akin to his own. He had never lived frankly since Mr Abrahams's school, and despite Dr Barry did not mean to begin; but he saw that while deceiving others he had been deceived, and mistaken them for the empty creatures he wanted them to think he was. No, they too had insides. "But, O Lord, not such an inside as mine." As soon as he thought about other people as real, Maurice became modest and conscious of sin: in all creation there could be no one as vile as himself: no wonder he pretended to be a piece of cardboard; if known as he was, he would be hounded out of the world. God, being altogether too large an order, did not worry him: he could not conceive of any censure being more terrific than, say, Joey Fetherstonhaugh's, who kept in the rooms below, or of any Hell as bitter as Coventry.

Shortly after this discovery he went to lunch with Mr Cornwallis, the Dean.

There were two other guests, Chapman and a B.A. from Trinity, a relative of the Dean's, by name Risley. Risley was dark,

tall and affected. He made an exaggerated gesture when introduced, and when he spoke, which was continually, he used
strong yet unmanly superlatives. Chapman caught Maurice's
eye and distended his nostrils, inviting him to side against the
newcomer. Maurice thought he would wait a bit first. His dis-
inclination to give pain was increasing, and besides he was not
sure that he loathed Risley, though no doubt he ought to, and in
a minute should. So Chapman ventured alone. Finding Risley
adored music, he began to run it down, saying, "I don't go in for
being superior," and so on.

"I do!"

"Oh, do you! In that case I beg your pardon."

"Come along, Chapman, you are in need of food," called Mr
Cornwallis, and promised himself some amusement at lunch.

" 'Spect Mr Risley isn't. I've put him off with my low talk."

They sat down, and Risley turned with a titter to Maurice
and said, "I simply *can't* think of any reply to that"; in each of
his sentences he accented one word violently. "It is so humiliating. 'No' won't do. 'Yes' won't do. What *is* to be done?"

"What about saying nothing?" said the Dean.

"To say nothing? Horrible. You must be mad."

"Are you always talking, may one ask?" inquired Chapman.
Risley said he was.

"Never get tired of it?"

"*Never.*"

"Ever tire other people?"

"*Never.*"

"Odd that."

"Do not suggest I've tired you. Untrue, untrue, you're beam-
ing."

"It's not at you if I am," said Chapman, who was hot-temp-
ered.

Maurice and the Dean laughed.

"I come to a standstill again. How amazing are the difficulties of conversation."

"You seem to carry on better than most of us can," remarked Maurice. He had not spoken before, and his voice, which was low but very gruff, made Risley shiver.

"Naturally. It is my forte. It is the only thing I care about, conversation."

"Is that serious?"

"Everything I say is serious." And somehow Maurice knew this was true. It had struck him at once that Risley was serious. "And are you serious?"

"Don't ask me."

"Then talk until you become so."

"Rubbish," growled the Dean.

Chapman laughed tempestuously.

"Rubbish?" He questioned Maurice, who, when he grasped the point, was understood to reply that deeds are more important than words.

"What is the difference? Words *are* deeds. Do you mean to say that these five minutes in Cornwallis's rooms have done nothing for you? Will you *ever* forget you have met me, for instance?"

Chapman grunted.

"But he will not, nor will you. And then I am told we ought to be doing something."

The Dean came to the rescue of the two Sunningtonians. He said to his young cousin, "You're unsound about memory. You confuse what's important with what's impressive. No doubt Chapman and Hall always will remember they've met you—"

"And forget this is a cutlet. Quite so."

"But the cutlet does some good to them, and you none."

"Obscurantist!"

"This is just like a book," said Chapman. "Eh, Hall?"

"I mean," said Risley, "oh how clearly I mean that the cutlet influences your subconscious lives, and I your conscious, and so I am not only more impressive than the cutlet but more important. Your Dean here, who dwells in Medieval Darkness and wishes you to do the same, pretends that only the subconscious, only the part of you that can be touched without your knowledge is important, and daily he drops soporific—"

"Oh, shut up," said the Dean.

"But I am a child of light—"

"Oh, shut up." And he turned the conversation on to normal lines. Risley was not egotistic, though he always talked about himself. He did not interrupt. Nor did he feign indifference. Gambolling like a dolphin, he accompanied them whithersoever they went, without hindering their course. He was at play, but seriously. It was as important to him to go to and fro as to them to go forward, and he loved keeping near them. A few months earlier Maurice would have agreed with Chapman, but now he was sure the man had an inside, and he wondered whether he should see more of him. He was pleased when, after lunch was over, Risley waited for him at the bottom of the stairs and said, "You didn't see. My cousin wasn't being human."

"He's good enough for us; that's all I know," exploded Chapman. "He's absolutely delightful."

"Exactly. Eunuchs are." And he was gone.

"Well, I'm—" exclaimed the other, but with British self-control suppressed the verb. He was deeply shocked. He didn't mind hot stuff in moderation, he told Maurice, but this was too much, it was bad form, ungentlemanly, the fellow could not have been through a public school. Maurice agreed. You could call your cousin a shit if you liked, but not a eunuch. Rotten style! All the same he was amused, and whenever he was hauled in in the future, mischievous and incongruous thoughts would occur to him about the Dean.

6 All that day and the next Maurice was planning how he could see this queer fish again. The chances were bad. He did not like to call on a senior-year man, and they were at different colleges. Risley, he gathered, was well known at the Union, and he went to the Tuesday debate in the hope of hearing him: perhaps he would be easier to understand in public. He was not attracted to the man in the sense that he wanted him for a friend, but he did feel he might help him—how, he didn't formulate. It was all very obscure, for the mountains still overshadowed Maurice. Risley, surely capering on the summit, might stretch him a helping hand.

Having failed at the Union, he had a reaction. He didn't want anyone's help; he was all right. Besides, none of his friends would stand Risley, and he must stick to his friends. But the reaction soon passed, and he longed to see him more than ever. Since Risley was so odd, might he not be odd too, and break all the undergraduate conventions by calling? One "ought to be human", and it was a human sort of thing to call. Much struck by the discovery, Maurice decided to be Bohemian also, and to enter the room making a witty speech in Risley's own style. "You've bargained for more than you've gained" occurred to him. It didn't sound very good, but Risley had been clever at not letting him feel a fool, so he would fire it off if inspired to nothing better, and leave the rest to luck.

For it had become an adventure. This man who said one ought to "talk, talk" had stirred Maurice incomprehensibly. One night, just before ten o'clock, he slipped into Trinity and waited in the Great Court until the gates were shut behind him. Looking up, he noticed the night. He was indifferent to beauty as a rule, but "what a show of stars!" he thought. And how the fountain splashed when the chimes died away, and the gates and doors all over Cambridge had been fastened up. Trinity men were around him—all of enormous intellect and culture. Maurice's set had laughed at Trinity, but they could not ignore its disdainful radiance, or deny the superiority it scarcely troubles to affirm. He had come to it without their knowledge, humbly, to ask its help. His witty speech faded in its atmosphere; and his heart beat violently. He was ashamed and afraid.

Risley's rooms were at the end of a short passage; which since it contained no obstacle was unlighted, and visitors slid along the wall until they hit the door. Maurice hit it sooner than he expected—a most awful whack—and exclaimed "Oh damnation" loudly, while the panels quivered.

"Come in," said a voice. Disappointment awaited him. The speaker was a man of his own college, by name Durham. Risley was out.

"Do you want Mr Risley? Hullo, Hall!"

"Hullo! Where's Risley?"

"I don't know."

"Oh, it's nothing. I'll go."

"Are you going back into college?" asked Durham without looking up: he was kneeling over a castle of pianola records on the floor.

"I suppose so, as he isn't here. It wasn't anything particular."

"Wait a sec, and I'll come too. I'm sorting out the Pathetic Symphony."

(35)

Maurice examined Risley's room and wondered what would have been said in it, and then sat on the table and looked at Durham. He was a small man—very small—with simple manners and a fair face, which had flushed when Maurice blundered in. In the college he had a reputation for brains and also for exclusiveness. Almost the only thing Maurice had heard about him was that he "went out too much", and this meeting in Trinity confirmed it.

"I can't find the March," he said. "Sorry."

"All right."

"I'm borrowing them to play on Fetherstonhaugh's pianola."

"Under me."

"Have you come into college, Hall?"

"Yes, I'm beginning my second year."

"Oh yes, of course, I'm third."

He spoke without arrogance, and Maurice, forgetting due honour to seniority, said, "You look more like a fresher than a third-year man, I must say."

"I may do, but I feel like an M.A."

Maurice regarded him attentively.

"Risley's an amazing chap," he continued.

Maurice did not reply.

"But all the same a little of him goes a long way."

"Still you don't mind borrowing his things."

He looked up again. "Oughtn't I to?" he asked.

"I'm only ragging, of course," said Maurice, slipping off the table. "Have you found that music yet?"

"No."

"Because I must be going"; he was in no hurry, but his heart, which had never stopped beating quickly, impelled him to say this.

"Oh. All right."

This was not what Maurice had intended. "What is it you want?" he asked, advancing.

"The March out of the Pathétique—"

"That means nothing to me. So you like this style of music."

"I do."

"A good waltz is more my style."

"Mine too," said Durham, meeting his eye. As a rule Maurice shifted, but he held firm on this occasion. Then Durham said, "The other movement may be in that pile over by the window. I must look. I shan't be long." Maurice said resolutely, "I must go now."

"All right, I'll stop."

Beaten and lonely, Maurice went. The stars blurred, the night had turned towards rain. But while the porter was getting the keys at the gate he heard quick footsteps behind him.

"Got your March?"

"No, I thought I'd come along with you instead."

Maurice walked a few steps in silence, then said, "Here, give me some of those things to carry."

"I've got them safe."

"Give," he said roughly, and jerked the records from under Durham's arm. No other conversation passed. On reaching their own college they went straight to Fetherstonhaugh's room, for there was time to try a little music over before eleven o'clock. Durham sat down at the pianola. Maurice knelt beside him.

"Didn't know you were in the aesthetic push, Hall," said the host.

"I'm not—I want to hear what they're up to."

Durham began, then desisted, saying he would start with the 5/4 instead.

"Why?"

"It's nearer waltzes."

"Oh, never mind that. Play what you like. Don't go shifting—it wastes time."

But he could not get his way this time. When he put his hand on the roller Durham said, "You'll tear it, let go," and fixed the 5/4 instead.

Maurice listened carefully to the music. He rather liked it.

"You ought to be this end," said Fetherstonhaugh, who was working by the fire. "You should get away from the machine as far as you can."

"I think so—Would you mind playing it again if Fetherstonhaugh doesn't mind?"

"Yes, do, Durham. It is a jolly thing."

Durham refused. Maurice saw that he was not pliable. He said, "A movement isn't like a separate piece—you can't repeat it"—an unintelligible excuse, but apparently valid. He played the Largo, which was far from jolly, and then eleven struck and Fetherstonhaugh made them tea. He and Durham were in for the same Tripos, and talked shop, while Maurice listened. His excitement had never ceased. He saw that Durham was not only clever, but had a tranquil and orderly brain. He knew what he wanted to read, where he was weak, and how far the officials could help him. He had neither the blind faith in tutors and lectures that was held by Maurice and his set nor the contempt professed by Fetherstonhaugh. "You can always learn something from an older man, even if he hasn't read the latest Germans." They argued a little about Sophocles, then in low water Durham said it was a pose in "us undergraduates" to ignore him and advised Fetherstonhaugh to re-read the *Ajax* with his eye on the characters rather than the author; he would learn more that way, both about Greek grammar and life.

Maurice regretted all this. He had somehow hoped to find the man unbalanced. Fetherstonhaugh was a great person, both in brain and brawn, and had a trenchant and copious manner. But Durham listened unmoved, shook out the falsities and approved the rest. What hope for Maurice who was nothing but falsities? A stab of anger went through him. Jumping up, he said good night, to regret his haste as soon as he was outside the door. He settled to wait, not on the staircase itself, for this struck him as absurd, but somewhere between its foot and Durham's own room. Going out into the court, he located the latter, even knocking at the door, though he knew the owner was absent, and looking in he studied furniture and pictures in the firelight. Then he took his stand on a sort of bridge in the courtyard. Unfortunately it was not a real bridge: it only spanned a slight depression in the ground, which the architect had tried to utilize in his effect. To stand on it was to feel in a photographic studio, and the parapet was too low to lean upon. Still, with a pipe in his mouth, Maurice looked fairly natural, and hoped it wouldn't rain.

The lights were out, except in Fetherstonhaugh's room. Twelve struck, then a quarter past. For a whole hour he might have been watching for Durham. Presently there was a noise on the staircase and the neat little figure ran out with a gown round its throat and books in its hand. It was the moment for which he had waited, but he found himself strolling away. Durham went to his rooms behind him. The opportunity was passing.

"Good night," he screamed; his voice was going out of gear, and startling them both.

"Who's that? Good night, Hall. Taking a stroll before bed?"

"I generally do. You don't want any more tea, I suppose?"

"Do I? No, perhaps it's a bit late for tea." Rather tepidly he added, "Like some whisky though?"

"Have you a drop?" leaped from Maurice.

"Yes—come in. Here I keep: ground floor."

"Oh, here!" Durham turned on the light. The fire was nearly out now. He told Maurice to sit down and brought up a table with glasses.

"Say when?"

"Thanks—most awfully, most awfully."

"Soda or plain?" he asked, yawning.

"Soda," said Maurice. But it was impossible to stop, for the man was tired and had only invited him out of civility. He drank and returned to his own room, where he provided himself with plenty of tobacco and went into the court again.

It was absolutely quiet now, and absolutely dark. Maurice walked to and fro on the hallowed grass, himself noiseless, his heart glowing. The rest of him fell asleep, bit by bit, and first of all his brain, his weakest organ. His body followed, then his feet carried him upstairs to escape the dawn. But his heart had lit never to be quenched again, and one thing in him at last was real.

Next morning he was calmer. He had a cold for one thing, the rain having soaked him unnoticed, and for another he had overslept to the extent of missing a chapel and two lectures. It was impossible to get his life straight. After lunch he changed for football, and being in good time flung himself on his sofa to sleep till tea. But he was not hungry. Refusing an invitation, he strolled out into the town and, meeting a Turkish bath, had one. It cured his cold, but made him late for another lecture. When hall came, he felt he could not face the mass of Old Sunningtonians, and, though he had not signed off, absented himself, and dined alone at the Union. He saw Risley there, but with indifference. Then the evening began again, and he found to his surprise that he was very clear-headed, and could do six hours' work in three. He went to bed at his usual time, and woke up healthy and very happy. Some instinct, deep below his consciousness, had advised him to let Durham and his thoughts about Durham have a twenty-four-hours' rest.

They began to see a little of one another. Durham asked him to lunch, and Maurice asked him back, but not too soon. A caution alien to his nature was at work. He had always been cautious pettily, but this was on a large scale. He became alert, and all his actions that October term might be described in the language of battle. He would not venture on to difficult ground. He spied out Durham's weaknesses as well as his strength. And above all he exercised and cleaned his powers.

If obliged to ask himself, "What's all this?" he would have replied, "Durham is another of those boys in whom I was interested at school," but he was obliged to ask nothing, and merely went ahead with his mouth and his mind shut. Each day with its contradictions slipped into the abyss, and he knew that he was gaining ground. Nothing else mattered. If he worked well and was nice socially, it was only a by-product, to which he had devoted no care. To ascend, to stretch a hand up the mountainside until a hand catches it, was the end for which he had been born. He forgot the hysteria of his first night and his stranger recovery. They were steps which he kicked behind him. He never even thought of tenderness and emotion; his considerations about Durham remained cold. Durham didn't dislike him, he was sure. That was all he wanted. One thing at a time. He didn't so much as have hopes, for hope distracts, and he had a great deal to see to.

7 Next term they were intimate at once.

"Hall, I nearly wrote a letter to you in the vac," said Durham, plunging into a conversation.

"That so?"

"But an awful screed. I'd been having a rotten time."

His voice was not very serious, and Maurice said, "What went wrong? Couldn't you keep down the Christmas pudding?"

It presently appeared that the pudding was allegorical; there had been a big family row.

"I don't know what you'll say—I'd rather like your opinion on what happened if it doesn't bore you."

"Not a bit," said Maurice.

"We've had a bust up on the religious question."

At that moment they were interrupted by Chapman.

"I'm sorry, we're fixing something," Maurice told him.

Chapman withdrew.

"You needn't have done that, any time would do for my rot," Durham protested. He went on more earnestly.

"Hall, I don't want to worry you with my beliefs, or rather with their absence, but to explain the situation I must just tell you that I'm unorthodox. I'm not a Christian."

Maurice held unorthodoxy to be bad form and had remarked last term in a college debate that if a man had doubts he might have the grace to keep them to himself. But he only said to Durham that it was a difficult question and a wide one.

"I know—it isn't about that. Leave it aside." He looked for a little into the fire. "It is about the way my mother took it. I told her six months ago—in the summer—and she didn't mind. She made some foolish joke, as she does, but that was all. It just passed over. I was thankful, for it had been on my mind for years. I had never believed since I found something that did me better, quite as a kid, and when I came to know Risley and his crew it seemed imperative to speak out. You know what a point they make of that—it's really their main point. So I spoke out. She said, 'Oh yes, you'll be wiser when you are as old as me': the mildest form of the thing conceivable, and I went away rejoicing. Now it's all come up again."

"Why?"

"Why? On account of Christmas. I didn't want to communicate. You're supposed to receive it three times a year—"

"Yes, I know. Holy Communion."

"—and at Christmas it came round. I said I wouldn't. Mother wheedled me in a way quite unlike her, asked me to do it this once to please her—then got cross, said I would damage her reputation as well as my own—we're the local squires and the neighbourhood's uncivilized. But what I couldn't stand was the end. She said I was wicked. I could have honoured her if she had said that six months before, but now! now to drag in holy words like wickedness and goodness in order to make me do what I disbelieved. I told her I have my own communions. 'If I went to them as you and the girls are doing to yours my gods would kill me!' I suppose that was too strong."

Maurice, not well understanding, said, "So did you go?"

"Where?"

"To the church."

Durham sprang up. His face was disgusted. Then he bit his lip and began to smile.

(43)

"No, I didn't go to church, Hall. I thought that was plain."

"I'm sorry—I wish you'd sit down. I didn't mean to offend you. I'm rather slow at catching."

Durham squatted on the rug close to Maurice's chair. "Have you known Chapman long?" he asked after a pause.

"Here and at school, five years."

"Oh." He seemed to reflect. "Give me a cigarette. Put it in my mouth. Thanks." Maurice supposed the talk was over, but after the swirl he went on. "You see—you mentioned you had a mother and two sisters, which is exactly my own allowance, and all through the row I was wondering what you would have done in my position."

"Your mother must be very different to mine."

"What is yours like?"

"She never makes a row about anything."

"Because you've never yet done anything she wouldn't approve, I expect—and never will."

"Oh no, she wouldn't fag herself."

"You can't tell, Hall, especially with women. I'm sick with her. That's my real trouble that I want your help about."

"She'll come round."

"Exactly, my dear chap, but shall I? I must have been pretending to like her. This row has shattered my lie. I did think I had stopped building lies. I despise her character, I am disgusted with her. There, I have told you what no one else in the world knows."

Maurice clenched his fist and hit Durham lightly on the head with it. "Hard luck," he breathed.

"Tell me about your home life."

"There's nothing to tell. We just go on."

"Lucky devils."

"Oh, I don't know. Are you ragging, or was your vac really beastly, Durham?"

"Absolute Hell, misery and Hell."

Maurice's fist unclenched to reform with a handful of hair in its grasp.

"Waou, that hurts!" cried the other joyously.

"What did your sisters say about Holy Communion?"

"One's married a clerg—No, that hurts."

"Absolute Hell, eh?"

"Hall, I never knew you were a fool—" he possessed himself of Maurice's hand— "and the other's engaged to Archibald London, Esquire, of the—Waou! Ee! Shut up, I'm going." He fell between Maurice's knees.

"Well, why don't you go if you're going?"

"Because I can't go."

It was the first time he had dared to play with Durham. Religion and relatives faded into the background, as he rolled him up in the hearth rug and fitted his head into the waste-paper basket. Hearing the noise, Fetherstonhaugh ran up and helped. There was nothing but ragging for many days after that, Durham becoming quite as silly as himself. Wherever they met, which was everywhere, they would butt and spar and embroil their friends. At last Durham got tired. Being the weaker he was hurt sometimes, and his chairs had been broken. Maurice felt the change at once. His coltishness passed, but they had become demonstrative during it. They walked arm in arm or arm around shoulder now. When they sat it was nearly always in the same position—Maurice in a chair, and Durham at his feet, leaning against him. In the world of their friends this attracted no notice. Maurice would stroke Durham's hair.

And their range increased elsewhere. During this Lent term Maurice came out as a theologian. It was not humbug entirely. He believed that he believed, and felt genuine pain when anything he was accustomed to met criticism—the pain that masquerades among the middle classes as Faith. It was not Faith, being inactive. It gave him no support, no wider outlook. It didn't exist till opposition touched it, when it ached like a useless nerve. They all had these nerves at home, and regarded them as divine, though neither the Bible nor the Prayer Book nor the Sacraments nor Christian ethics nor anything spiritual were alive to them. "But how can people?" they exclaimed, when anything was attacked, and subscribed to Defence Societies. Maurice's father was becoming a pillar of Church and Society when he died, and other things being alike Maurice would have stiffened too.

But other things were not to be alike. He had this overwhelming desire to impress Durham. He wanted to show his friend that he had something besides brute strength, and where his father would have kept canny silence he began to talk, talk. "You think I don't think, but I can tell you I do." Very often Durham made no reply and Maurice would be terrified lest he was losing him. He had heard it said, "Durham's all right as long as you amuse him, then he drops you," and feared lest by exhibiting his orthodoxy he was bringing on what he tried to avoid. But he could not stop. The craving for notice grew overwhelming, so he talked, talked.

One day Durham said, "Hall, why this thusness?"

"Religion means a lot to me," bluffed Maurice. "Because I say so little you think I don't feel. I care a lot."

"In that case come to coffee after hall."

They were just going in. Durham, being a scholar, had to read grace, and there was cynicism in his accent. During the meal they looked at each other. They sat at different tables, but Maurice had contrived to move his seat so that he could glance at his friend. The phase of bread pellets was over. Durham looked severe this evening and was not speaking to his neighbours. Maurice knew that he was thoughtful and wondered what about.

"You wanted to get it and you're going to," said Durham, sporting the door.

Maurice went cold and then crimson. But Durham's voice, when he next heard it, was attacking his opinions on the Trinity. He thought he minded about the Trinity, yet it seemed unimportant beside the fires of his terror. He sprawled in an armchair, all the strength out of him, with sweat on his forehead and hands. Durham moved about getting the coffee ready and saying, "I knew you wouldn't like this, but you have brought it on yourself. You can't expect me to bottle myself up indefinitely. I must let out sometimes."

"Go on," said Maurice, clearing his throat.

"I never meant to talk, for I respect people's opinions too much to laugh at them, but it doesn't seem to me that you have any opinions to respect. They're all second-hand tags—no, tenth-hand."

Maurice, who was recovering, remarked that this was pretty strong.

"You're always saying, 'I care a lot.'"

"And what right have you to assume that I don't?"

"You do care a lot about something, Hall, but it obviously isn't the Trinity."

"What is it then?"

"Rugger."

Maurice had another attack. His hand shook and he spilt the coffee on the arm of the chair. "You're a bit unfair," he heard himself saying. "You might at least have the grace to suggest that I care about people."

Durham looked surprised, but said, "You care nothing about the Trinity, any way."

"Oh, damn the Trinity."

He burst with laughter. "Exactly, exactly. We will now pass on to my next point."

"I don't see the use, and I've a rotten head any way—I mean a headache. Nothing's gained by—all this. No doubt I can't prove the thing—I mean the arrangement of Three Gods in One and One in Three. But it means a lot to millions of people, whatever you may say, and we aren't going to give it up. We feel about it very deeply. God is good. That is the main point. Why go off on a side track?"

"Why feel so deeply about a side track?"

"What?"

Durham tidied up his remarks for him.

"Well, the whole show all hangs together."

"So that if the Trinity went wrong it would invalidate the whole show?"

"I don't see that. Not at all."

He was doing badly, but his head really did ache, and when he wiped the sweat off it re-formed.

"No doubt I can't explain well, as I care for nothing but rugger."

Durham came and sat humorously on the edge of his chair.

"Look out—you've gone into the coffee now."

"Blast—so I have."

While he cleaned himself, Maurice unsported and looked out into the court. It seemed years since he had left it. He felt disinclined to be longer alone with Durham and called to some men to join them. A coffee of the usual type ensued, but when they left Maurice felt equally disinclined to leave with them. He flourished the Trinity again. "It's a mystery," he argued.

"It isn't a mystery to me. But I honour anyone to whom it really is."

Maurice felt uncomfortable and looked at his own thick brown hands. Was the Trinity really a mystery to him? Except at his confirmation had he given the institution five minutes' thought? The arrival of the other men had cleared his head, and, no longer emotional, he glanced at his mind. It appeared like his hands—serviceable, no doubt, and healthy, and capable of development. But it lacked refinement, it had never touched mysteries, nor a good deal else. It was thick and brown.

"My position's this," he announced after a pause. "I don't believe in the Trinity, I give in there, but on the other hand I was wrong when I said everything hangs together. It doesn't, and because I don't believe in the Trinity it doesn't mean I am not a Christian."

"What do you believe in?" said Durham, unchecked.

"The—the essentials."

"As?"

In a low voice Maurice said, "The Redemption." He had never spoken the words out of church before and thrilled with emotion. But he did not believe in them any more than in the Trinity, and knew that Durham would detect this. The Redemption was the highest card in the suit, but that suit wasn't trumps, and his friend could capture it with some miserable two.

All that Durham said at the time was, "Dante did believe in the Trinity," and going to the shelf found the concluding passage of the *Paradiso*. He read to Maurice about the three rainbow circles that intersect, and between their junctions is enshadowed a human face. Poetry bored Maurice, but towards the close he cried, "Whose face was it?"

"God's, don't you see?"

"But isn't that poem supposed to be a dream?"

Hall was a muddle-headed fellow, and Durham did not try to make sense of this, nor knew that Maurice was thinking of a dream of his own at school, and of the voice that had said, "That is your friend."

"Dante would have called it an awakening, not a dream."

"Then you think that sort of stuff's all right?"

"Belief's always right," replied Durham, putting back the book. "It's all right and it's also unmistakable. Every man has somewhere about him some belief for which he'd die. Only isn't it improbable that your parents and guardians told it to you? If there is one won't it be part of your own flesh and spirit? Show me that. Don't go hawking out tags like 'The Redemption' or 'The Trinity'."

"I've given up the Trinity."

"The Redemption, then."

"You're beastly hard," said Maurice. "I always knew I was stupid, it's no news. The Risley set are more your sort and you had better talk to them."

Durham looked awkward. He was nonplussed for a reply at last, and let Maurice slouch off without protest. Next day they met as usual. It had not been a tiff but a sudden gradient, and they travelled all the quicker after the rise. They talked theology again, Maurice defending the Redemption. He lost. He realized that he had no sense of Christ's existence or of his goodness, and should be positively sorry if there was such a person. His dislike of Christianity grew and became profound. In ten days he gave up communicating, in three weeks he cut out all the chapels he dared. Durham was puzzled by the rapidity. They were both puzzled, and Maurice, although he had lost and yielded all his opinions, had a queer feeling that he was really winning and carrying on a campaign that he had begun last term.

For Durham wasn't bored with him now. Durham couldn't do without him, and would be found at all hours curled up in his room and spoiling to argue. It was so unlike the man, who was reserved and no great dialectician. He gave as his reason for attacking Maurice's opinions that "They are so rotten, Hall, every-one else up here believes respectably." Was this the whole truth? Was there not something else behind his new manner and furious iconoclasm? Maurice thought there was. Outwardly in retreat, he thought that his Faith was a pawn well lost; for in capturing it Durham had exposed his heart.

Towards the end of term they touched upon a yet more delicate subject. They attended the Dean's translation class, and when one of the men was forging quietly ahead Mr Cornwallis observed in a flat toneless voice: "Omit: a reference to the unspeakable vice of the Greeks." Durham observed afterwards that he ought to lose his fellowship for such hypocrisy.

Maurice laughed.

"I regard it as a point of pure scholarship. The Greeks, or most of them, were that way inclined, and to omit it is to omit the mainstay of Athenian society."

"Is that so?"

"You've read the *Symposium*?"

Maurice had not, and did not add that he had explored Martial.

"It's all in there—not meat for babes, of course, but you ought to read it. Read it this vac."

No more was said at the time, but he was free of another subject, and one that he had never mentioned to any living soul. He hadn't known it could be mentioned, and when Durham did so in the middle of the sunlit court a breath of liberty touched him.

8 On reaching home he talked about Durham until the fact that he had a friend penetrated into the minds of his family. Ada wondered whether it was brother to a certain Miss Durham—not but what she was an only child—while Mrs Hall confused it with a don named Cumberland. Maurice was deeply wounded. One strong feeling arouses another, and a profound irritation against his womenkind set in. His relations with them hitherto had been trivial but stable, but it seemed iniquitous that anyone should mispronounce the name of the man who was more to him than all the world. Home emasculated everything.

It was the same with his atheism. No one felt as deeply as he expected. With the crudity of youth he drew his mother apart and said that he should always respect her religious prejudices and those of the girls, but that his own conscience permitted him to attend church no longer. She said it was a great misfortune.

"I knew you would be upset. I cannot help it, mother dearest. I am made that way and it is no good arguing."

"Your poor father always went to church."

"I'm not my father."

"Morrie, Morrie, what a thing to say."

"Well, he isn't," said Kitty in her perky way. "Really, mother, come."

"Kitty, dear, you here," cried Mrs Hall, feeling that disapproval was due and unwilling to bestow it on her son. "We were talking about things not suited, and you are perfectly wrong besides, for Maurice is the image of his father—Dr Barry said so."

"Well, Dr Barry doesn't go to church himself," said Maurice, falling into the family habit of talking all over the shop.

"He is a most clever man," said Mrs Hall with finality, "and Mrs Barry's the same."

This slip of their mother's convulsed Ada and Kitty. They would not stop laughing at the idea of Mrs Barry's being a man, and Maurice's atheism was forgotten. He did not communicate on Easter Sunday, and supposed the row would come then, as in Durham's case. But no one took any notice, for the suburbs no longer exact Christianity. This disgusted him; it made him look at society with new eyes. Did society, while professing to be so moral and sensitive, really mind anything?

He wrote often to Durham—long letters trying carefully to express shades of feeling. Durham made little of them and said so. His replies were equally long. Maurice never let them out of his pocket, changing them from suit to suit and even pinning them in his pyjamas when he went to bed. He would wake up and touch them and, watching the reflections from the street lamp, remember how he used to feel afraid as a little boy.

Episode of Gladys Olcott.

Miss Olcott was one of their infrequent guests. She had been good to Mrs Hall and Ada in some hydro, and, receiving an invitation, had followed it up. She was charming—at least the women said so, and male callers told the son of the house he was a lucky dog. He laughed, they laughed, and having ignored her at first he took to paying her attentions.

Now Maurice, though he did not know it, had become an attractive young man. Much exercise had tamed his clumsiness. He was heavy but alert, and his face seemed following the example of his body. Mrs Hall put it down to his moustache— "Maurice's moustache will be the making of him"—a remark more profound than she realized. Certainly the little black line of it did pull his face together, and show up his teeth when he smiled, and his clothes suited him also: by Durham's advice he kept to flannel trousers, even on Sunday.

He turned his smile on Miss Olcott—it seemed the proper thing to do. She responded. He put his muscles at her service by taking her out in his new side-car. He sprawled at her feet. Finding she smoked, he persuaded her to stop behind with him in the dining-room and to look between his eyes. Blue vapour quivered and shredded and built dissolving walls, and Maurice's thoughts voyaged with it, to vanish as soon as a window was opened for fresh air. He saw that she was pleased, and his family, servants and all, intrigued; he determined to go further.

Something went wrong at once. Maurice paid her compliments, said that her hair etc. was ripping. She tried to stop him, but he was insensitive, and did not know that he had annoyed her. He had read that girls always pretended to stop men who complimented them. He haunted her. When she excused herself from riding with him on the last day he played the domineering male. She was his guest, she came, and having taken her to some scenery that he considered romantic he pressed her little hand between his own.

It was not that Miss Olcott objected to having her hand pressed. Others had done it and Maurice could have done it had he guessed how. But she knew something was wrong. His touch revolted her. It was a corpse's. Springing up she cried, "Mr Hall, don't be silly. I mean *don't* be silly. I am not saying it to make you sillier."

"Miss Olcott—Gladys—I'd rather die than offend—" growled the boy, trying to keep it up.

"I must go back by train," she said, crying a little. "I must, I'm awfully sorry." She arrived home before him with a sensible little story about a headache and dust in her eyes, but his family also knew that something had gone wrong.

Except for this episode the vac passed pleasantly. Maurice did some reading, following his friend's advice rather than his tutor's, and he asserted in one or two ways his belief that he was grown up. At his instigation his mother dismissed the Howells who had long paralyzed the outdoor department, and set up a motor-car instead of a carriage. Everyone was impressed, including the Howells. He also called upon his father's old partner. He had inherited some business aptitude and some money, and it was settled that when he left Cambridge he should enter the firm as an unauthorized clerk; Hill and Hall, Stock Brokers. Maurice was stepping into the niche that England had prepared for him.

9 During the previous term he had reached an unusual level mentally, but the vac pulled him back towards public-schoolishness. He was less alert, he again behaved as he supposed he was supposed to behave—a perilous feat for one who is not dowered with imagination. His mind, not obscured totally, was often crossed by clouds, and though Miss Olcott had passed, the insincerity that led him to her remained. His family were the main cause of this. He had yet to realize that they were stronger than he and influenced him incalculably. Three weeks in their company left him untidy, sloppy, victorious in every item, yet defeated on the whole. He came back thinking, and even speaking, like his mother or Ada.

Till Durham arrived he had not noticed the deterioration. Durham had not been well, and came up a few days late. When his face, paler than usual, peered round the door, Maurice had a spasm of despair, and tried to recollect where they stood last term, and to gather up the threads of the campaign. He felt himself slack, and afraid of action. The worst part of him rose to the surface, and urged him to prefer comfort to joy.

"Hullo, old man," he said awkwardly.

Durham slipped in without speaking.

"What's wrong?"

"Nothing"; and Maurice knew that he had lost touch. Last term he would have understood this silent entrance.

"Anyhow, take a pew."

Durham sat upon the floor beyond his reach. It was late afternoon. The sounds of the May term, the scents of the Cambridge year in flower, floated in through the window and said to Maurice, "You are unworthy of us." He knew that he was three parts dead, an alien, a yokel in Athens. He had no business here, nor with such a friend.

"I say, Durham—"

Durham came nearer. Maurice stretched out a hand and felt the head nestle against it. He forgot what he was going to say. The sounds and scents whispered, "You are we, we are youth." Very gently he stroked the hair and ran his fingers down into it as if to caress the brain.

"I say, Durham, have you been all right?"

"Have you?"

"No."

"You wrote you were."

"I wasn't."

The truth in his own voice made him tremble. "A rotten vac and I never knew it," and wondered how long he should know it. The mist would lower again, he felt sure, and with an unhappy sigh he pulled Durham's head against his knee, as though it was a talisman for clear living. It lay there, and he had accomplished a new tenderness—stroked it steadily from temple to throat. Then, removing both hands, he dropped them on either side of him and sat sighing.

"Hall."

Maurice looked.

"Is there some trouble?"

He caressed and again withdrew. It seemed as certain that he hadn't as that he had a friend.

"Anything to do with that girl?"

"No."

"You wrote you liked her."

"I didn't—don't."

Deeper sighs broke from him. They rattled in his throat, turning to groans. His head fell back, and he forgot the pressure of Durham on his knee, forgot that Durham was watching his turbid agony. He stared at the ceiling with wrinkled mouth and eyes, understanding nothing except that man has been created to feel pain and loneliness without help from heaven.

Now Durham stretched up to him, stroked his hair. They clasped one another. They were lying breast against breast soon, head was on shoulder, but just as their cheeks met someone called "Hall" from the court, and he answered: he always had answered when people called. Both started violently, and Durham sprang to the mantelpiece where he leant his head on his arm. Absurd people came thundering up the stairs. They wanted tea. Maurice pointed to it, then was drawn into their conversation, and scarcely noticed his friend's departure. It had been an ordinary talk, he told himself, but too sentimental, and he cultivated a breeziness against their next meeting.

This took place soon enough. With half a dozen others he was starting for the theatre after hall when Durham called him.

"I knew you read the *Symposium* in the vac," he said in a low voice.

Maurice felt uneasy.

"Then you understand—without me saying more—"

"How do you mean?"

Durham could not wait. People were all around them, but with eyes that had gone intensely blue he whispered, "I love you."

Maurice was scandalized, horrified. He was shocked to the bottom of his suburban soul, and exclaimed, "Oh, rot!" The words, the manner, were out of him before he could recall them.

"Durham, you're an Englishman. I'm another. Don't talk nonsense. I'm not offended, because I know you don't mean it, but it's the only subject absolutely beyond the limit as you know, it's the worst crime in the calendar, and you must never mention it again. Durham! a rotten notion really—"

But his friend was gone, gone without a word, flying across the court, the bang of his door heard through the sounds of spring.

10 A slow nature such as Maurice's appears insensitive,
for it needs time even to feel. Its instinct is to assume
that nothing either for good or evil has happened, and to resist
the invader. Once gripped, it feels acutely, and its sensations in
love are particularly profound. Given time, it can know and impart ecstasy; given time, it can sink to the heart of Hell. Thus it
was that his agony began as a slight regret; sleepless nights and
lonely days must intensify it into a frenzy that consumed him. It
worked inwards, till it touched the root whence body and soul
both spring, the "I" that he had been trained to obscure, and,
realized at last, doubled its power and grew superhuman. For
it might have been joy. New worlds broke loose in him at this,
and he saw from the vastness of the ruin what ecstasy he had
lost, what a communion.

They did not speak again for two days. Durham would have
made it longer, but most of their friends were now in common,
and they were bound to meet. Realizing this, he wrote Maurice
an icy note suggesting that it would be a public convenience if
they behaved as if nothing had happened. He added, "I shall be
obliged if you will not mention my criminal morbidity to anyone. I am sure you will do this from the sensible way in which
you took the news." Maurice did not reply, but first put the note
with the letters he had received during the vac and afterwards
burnt them all.

He supposed the climax of agony had come. But he was fresh to real suffering as to reality of any kind. They had yet to meet. On the second afternoon they found themselves in the same four at tennis and the pain grew excruciating. He could scarcely stand or see; if he returned Durham's service the ball sent a throb up his arm. Then they were made to be partners; once they jostled, Durham winced, but managed to laugh in the old fashion.

Moreover, it proved convenient that he should come back to college in Maurice's side-car. He got in without demur. Maurice, who had not been to bed for two nights, went light-headed, turned the machine into a by-lane, and travelled top speed. There was a wagon in front, full of women. He drove straight at them, but when they screamed stuck on his brakes, and just avoided disaster. Durham made no comment. As he indicated in his note, he only spoke when others were present. All other intercourse was to end.

That evening Maurice went to bed as usual. But as he laid his head on the pillows a flood of tears oozed from it. He was horrified. A man crying! Fetherstonhaugh might hear him. He wept stifled in the sheets, he sprang about kicking, then struck his head against the wall and smashed the crockery. Someone did come up the stairs. He grew quiet at once and did not recommence when the footsteps died away. Lighting a candle, he looked with surprise at his torn pyjamas and trembling limbs. He continued to cry, for he could not stop, but the suicidal point had been passed, and, remaking the bed, he lay down. His gyp was clearing away the ruins when he opened his eyes. It seemed queer to Maurice that a gyp should have been dragged in. He wondered whether the man suspected anything, then slept again. On waking the second time he found letters on the floor—one from old Mr Grace, his grandfather, about the party that was to be given when he came of age, another from a don's wife asking him to lunch ("Mr Durham is coming too, so you won't be shy"), another from Ada with mention of Gladys Olcott. Yet again he fell asleep.

Madness is not for everyone, but Maurice's proved the thunderbolt that dispels the clouds. The storm had been working up not for three days as he supposed, but for six years. It had brewed in the obscurities of being where no eye pierces, his surroundings had thickened it. It had burst and he had not died. The brilliancy of day was around him, he stood upon the mountain range that overshadows youth, he saw.

Most of the day he sat with open eyes, as if looking into the Valley he had left. It was all so plain now. He had lied. He phrased it "been fed upon lies," but lies are the natural food of boyhood, and he had eaten greedily. His first resolve was to be more careful in the future. He would live straight, not because it mattered to anyone now, but for the sake of the game. He would not deceive himself so much. He would not—and this was the test—pretend to care about women when the only sex that attracted him was his own. He loved men and always had loved them. He longed to embrace them and mingle his being with theirs. Now that the man who returned his love had been lost, he admitted this.

11 After this crisis Maurice became a man. Hitherto—if human beings can be estimated—he had not been worth anyone's affection, but conventional, petty, treacherous to others, because to himself. Now he had the highest gift to offer. The idealism and the brutality that ran through boyhood had joined at last, and twined into love. No one might want such love, but he could not feel ashamed of it, because it was "he," neither body or soul, nor body and soul, but "he" working through both. He still suffered, yet a sense of triumph had come elsewhere. Pain had shown him a niche behind the world's judgements, whither he could withdraw.

There was still much to learn, and years passed before he explored certain abysses in his being—horrible enough they were. But he discovered the method and looked no more at scratches in the sand. He had awoken too late for happiness, but not for strength, and could feel an austere joy, as of a warrior who is homeless but stands fully armed.

As the term went on he decided to speak to Durham. He valued words highly, having so lately discovered them. Why should he suffer and cause his friend suffering, when words might put all right? He heard himself saying, "I really love you as you love me," and Durham replying, "Is that so? Then I forgive you," and to the ardour of youth such a conversation seemed possible, though somehow he did not conceive it as leading to joy. He made several attempts, but partly through his own shyness, partly through Durham's, they failed. If he went round, the door was sported, or else there were people inside; should he enter, Durham left when the other guests did. He invited him to meals—he could never come; he offered to lift him again for tennis, but an excuse was made. Even if they met in the court, Durham would affect to have forgotten something and run past him or away. He was surprised their friends did not notice the change, but few undergraduates are observant—they have too much to discover within themselves and it was a don who remarked that Durham had stopped honeymooning with that Hall person.

He found his opportunity after a debating society to which both belonged. Durham—pleading his Tripos—had sent in his resignation, but had begged that the society might meet in his rooms first, as he wished to take his share of hospitality. This was like him; he hated to be under an obligation to anyone. Maurice went and sat through a tedious evening. When everyone, including the host, surged out into the fresh air, he remained, thinking of the first night he had visited that room, and wondering whether the past cannot return.

Durham entered, and did not at once see who it was. Ignoring him utterly, he proceeded to tidy up for the night.

"You're beastly hard," blurted Maurice, "you don't know what it is to have a mind in a mess, and it makes you very hard."

Durham shook his head as one who refuses to listen. He looked so ill that Maurice had a wild desire to catch hold of him.

"You might give me a chance instead of avoiding me—I only want to discuss."

"We've discussed the whole evening."

"I mean the *Symposium,* like the ancient Greeks."

"Oh Hall, don't be so stupid—you ought to know that to be alone with you hurts me. No, please don't reopen. It's over. It's over." He went into the other room and began to undress. "Forgive this discourtesy, but I simply can't—my nerves are all nohow after three weeks of this."

"So are mine," cried Maurice.

"Poor, poor chap!"

"Durham, I'm in Hell."

"Oh, you'll get out. It's only the Hell of disgust. You've never done anything to be ashamed of, so you don't know what's really Hell."

Maurice gave a cry of pain. It was so unmistakable that Durham, who was about to close the door between them, said, "Very well, I'll discuss if you like. What's the matter? You appear to want to apologize about something. Why? You behave as if I'm annoyed with you. What have you done wrong? You've been thoroughly decent from first to last."

In vain he protested.

"So decent that I mistook your ordinary friendliness. When you were so good to me, above all the afternoon I came up—I thought it was something else. I am more sorry than I can ever say. I had no right to move out of my books and music, which was what I did when I met you. You won't want my apology any more than anything else I could give, but, Hall, I do make it most sincerely. It is a lasting grief to have insulted you."

His voice was feeble but clear, and his face like a sword. Maurice flung useless words about love.

"That's all, I think. Get married quickly and forget."

"Durham, I love you."

He laughed bitterly.

"I do—I have always—"

"Good night, good night."

"I tell you, I do—I came to say it—in your very own way—I have always been like the Greeks and didn't know."

"Expand the statement."

Words deserted him immediately. He could only speak when he was not asked to.

"Hall, don't be grotesque." He raised his hand, for Maurice had exclaimed. "It's like the very decent fellow you are to comfort me, but there are limits; one or two things I can't swallow."

"I'm not grotesque—"

"I shouldn't have said that. So do leave me. I'm thankful it's into your hands I fell. Most men would have reported me to the Dean or the Police."

"Oh, go to Hell, it's all you're fit for," cried Maurice, rushed into the court and heard once more the bang of the outer door. Furious he stood on the bridge in a night that resembled the first —drizzly with faint stars. He made no allowance for three weeks of torture unlike his own or for the poison which, secreted by one man, acts differently on another. He was enraged not to find his friend as he had left him. Twelve o'clock struck, one, two, and he was still planning what to say when there is nothing to say and the resources of speech are ended.

Then savage, reckless, drenched with the rain, he saw in the first glimmer of dawn the window of Durham's room, and his heart leapt alive and shook him to pieces. It cried "You love and are loved." He looked round the court. It cried "You are strong, he weak and alone," won over his will. Terrified at what he must do, he caught hold of the mullion and sprang.

"Maurice—"

As he alighted his name had been called out of dreams. The violence went out of his heart, and a purity that he had never imagined dwelt there instead. His friend had called him. He stood for a moment entranced, then the new emotion found him words, and laying his hand very gently upon the pillows he answered, "Clive!"

PART

Two

12 Clive had suffered little from bewilderment as a boy. His sincere mind, with its keen sense of right and wrong, had brought him the belief that he was damned instead. Deeply religious, with a living desire to reach God and to please Him, he found himself crossed at an early age by this other desire, obviously from Sodom. He had no doubt as to what it was: his emotion, more compact than Maurice's, was not split into the brutal and the ideal, nor did he waste years in bridging the gulf. He had in him the impulse that destroyed the City of the Plain. It should not ever become carnal, but why had he out of all Christians been punished with it?

At first he thought God must be trying him, and if he did not blaspheme would recompense him like Job. He therefore bowed his head, fasted, and kept away from anyone whom he found himself inclined to like. His sixteenth year was ceaseless torture. He told no one, and finally broke down and had to be removed from school. During the convalescence he found himself falling in love with a cousin who walked by his bath chair, a young married man. It was hopeless, he was damned.

These terrors had visited Maurice, but dimly: to Clive they were definite, continuous, and not more insistent at the Eucharist than elsewhere. He never mistook them, in spite of the rein he kept on grossness. He could control the body; it was the tainted soul that mocked his prayers.

The boy had always been a scholar, awake to the printed word, and the horrors the Bible had evoked for him were to be laid by Plato. Never could he forget his emotion at first reading the *Phaedrus*. He saw there his malady described exquisitely, calmly, as a passion which we can direct, like any other, towards good or bad. Here was no invitation to licence. He could not believe his good fortune at first—thought there must be some misunderstanding and that he and Plato were thinking of different things. Then he saw that the temperate pagan really did comprehend him, and, slipping past the Bible rather than opposing it, was offering a new guide for life. "To make the most of what I have." Not to crush it down, not vainly to wish that it was something else, but to cultivate it in such ways as will not vex either God or Man.

He was obliged however to throw over Christianity. Those who base their conduct upon what they are rather than upon what they ought to be, always must throw it over in the end, and besides, between Clive's temperament and that religion there is a secular feud. No clear-headed man can combine them. The temperament, to quote the legal formula, is "not to be mentioned among Christians", and a legend tells that all who shared it died on the morning of the Nativity. Clive regretted this. He came of a family of lawyers and squires, good and able men for the most part, and he did not wish to depart from their tradition. He wished Christianity would compromise with him a little and searched the Scriptures for support. There was David and Jonathan; there was even the "disciple that Jesus loved." But the Church's interpretation was against him; he could not find any rest for his soul in her without crippling it, and withdrew higher into the classics yearly.

By eighteen he was unusually mature, and so well under control that he could allow himself to be friendly with anyone who attracted him. Harmony had succeeded asceticism. At Cambridge he cultivated tender emotions for other under-graduates, and his life, hitherto gray, became slightly tinged with delicate hues. Cautious and sane, he advanced, nor was there anything petty in his caution. He was ready to go further should he consider it right.

In his second year he met Risley, himself "that way." Clive did not return the confidence which was given rather freely, nor did he like Risley and his set. But he was stimulated. He was glad to know that there were more of his sort about, and their frankness braced him into telling his mother about his agnosticism; it was all he could tell her. Mrs Durham, a worldly woman, made little protest. It was at Christmas the trouble came. Being the only gentry in the parish, the Durhams communicated separately, and to have the whole village looking on while she and her daughters knelt without Clive in the middle of that long footstool cut her with shame and stung her into anger. They quarrelled. He saw her for what she really was—withered, unsympathetic, empty—and in his disillusion found himself thinking vividly of Hall.

Hall: he was only one of several men whom he rather liked. True he, also, had a mother and two sisters, but Clive was too level-headed to pretend this was the only bond between them. He must like Hall more than he realized—must be a little in love with him. And as soon as they met he had a rush of emotion that carried him into intimacy.

The man was bourgeois, unfinished and stupid—the worst of confidants. Yet he told about his home troubles, touched out of all proportion by his dismissal of Chapman. When Hall started teasing he was charmed. Others held off, regarding him as sedate, and he liked being thrown about by a powerful and handsome boy. It was delightful too when Hall stroked his hair: the faces of the two people in the room would fade: he leant back till his cheek brushed the flannel of the trousers and felt the warmth strike through. He was under no illusion on these occasions. He knew what kind of pleasure he was receiving, and received it honestly, certain that it brought no harm to either of them. Hall was a man who only liked women—one could tell that at a glance.

Towards the end of the term he noticed that Hall had acquired a peculiar and beautiful expression. It came only now and then, was subtle and lay far down; he noticed it first when they were squabbling about theology. It was affectionate, kindly, and to that extent a natural expression, but there was mixed in it something that he had not observed in the man, a touch of—impudence? He was not sure, but liked it. It recurred when they met suddenly or had been silent. It beckoned to him across intellect, saying, "This is all very well, you're clever, we know—but come!" It haunted him so that he watched for it while his brain and tongue were busy, and when it came he felt himself replying, "I'll come—I didn't know."

"You can't help yourself now. You must come."

"I don't want to help myself."

"Come then."

He did come. He flung down all the barriers—not at once, for he did not live in a house that can be destroyed in a day. All that term and through letters afterwards he made the path clear. Once certain that Hall loved him, he unloosed his own love. Hitherto it had been dalliance, a passing pleasure for body and mind. How he despised that now. Love was harmonious, immense. He poured into it the dignity as well as the richness of his being, and indeed in that well-tempered soul the two were one. There was nothing humble about Clive. He knew his own worth, and, when he had expected to go through life without love, he had blamed circumstances rather than himself. Hall, though attractive and beautiful, had not condescended. They would meet on an equality next term.

But books meant so much for him he forgot that they were a bewilderment to others. Had he trusted the body there would have been no disaster, but by linking their love to the past he linked it to the present, and roused in his friend's mind the conventions and the fear of the law. He realized nothing of this. What Hall said he must mean. Otherwise why should he say it? Hall loathed him—had said so, "Oh, rot"—the words hurt more than any abuse, and rang in his ears for days. Hall was the healthy normal Englishman, who had never had a glimmer of what was up.

Great was the pain, great the mortification, but worse followed. So deeply had Clive become one with the beloved that he began to loathe himself. His whole philosophy of life broke down, and the sense of sin was reborn in its ruins, and crawled along corridors. Hall had said he was a criminal, and must know. He was damned. He dare never be friends with a young man again, for fear of corrupting him. Had he not lost Hall his faith in Christianity and attempted his purity besides?

During those three weeks Clive altered immensely, and was beyond the reach of argument when Hall—good, blundering creature—came to his room to comfort him, tried this and that without success, and vanished in a gust of temper. "Oh, go to Hell, it's all you're fit for." Never a truer word but hard to accept from the beloved. Clive's defeat increased: his life had been blown to pieces, and he felt no inward strength to rebuild it and clear out evil. His conclusion was "Ridiculous boy! I never loved him. I only had an image I made up in my polluted mind, and may God help me to get rid of it."

But it was this image that visited his sleep, and caused him to whisper its name.

"Maurice . . ."

"Clive . . ."

"Hall!" he gasped, fully awake. Warmth was upon him. "Maurice, Maurice, Maurice. . . . Oh *Maurice*—"

"I know."

"Maurice, I love you."

"I you."

They kissed, scarcely wishing it. Then Maurice vanished as he had come, through the window.

13 "I've missed two lectures already," remarked Maurice, who was breakfasting in his pyjamas.

"Cut them all—he'll only gate you."

"Will you come out in the side-car?"

"Yes, but a long way," said Clive, lighting a cigarette. "I can't stick Cambridge in this weather. Let's get right outside it ever so far and bathe. I can work as we go along—Oh damnation!"— for there were steps on the stairs. Joey Fetherstonhaugh looked in and asked one or other of them to play tennis with him that afternoon. Maurice accepted.

"Maurice! What did you do that for, you fool?"

"Cleared him out quickest. Clive, meet me at the garage in twenty minutes, bring your putrid books, and borrow Joey's goggles. I must dress. Bring some lunch too."

"What about horses instead?"

"Too slow."

They met as arranged. Joey's goggles had offered no difficulty, as he had been out. But as they threaded Jesus Lane they were hailed by the Dean.

"Hall, haven't you a lecture?"

"I overslept," called Maurice contemptuously.

"Hall! Hall! Stop when I speak."

Maurice went on. "No good arguing," he observed.

"Not the least."

They swirled across the bridge and into the Ely road. Maurice said, "Now we'll go to Hell." The machine was powerful, he reckless naturally. It leapt forward into the fens and the receding dome of the sky. They became a cloud of dust, a stench, and a roar to the world, but the air they breathed was pure, and all the noise they heard was the long drawn cheer of the wind. They cared for no one, they were outside humanity, and death, had it come, would only have continued their pursuit of a retreating horizon. A tower, a town—it had been Ely—were behind them, in front the same sky, paling at last as though heralding the sea. "Right turn," again, then "left," "right," until all sense of direction was gone. There was a rip, a grate. Maurice took no notice. A noise arose as of a thousand pebbles being shaken together between his legs. No accident occurred, but the machine came to a standstill among the dark black fields. The song of the lark was heard, the trail of dust began to settle behind them. They were alone.

"Let's eat," said Clive.

They ate on a grassy embankment. Above them the waters of a dyke moved imperceptibly, and reflected interminable willow trees. Man, who had created the whole landscape, was nowhere to be seen. After lunch Clive thought he ought to work. He spread out his books and was asleep in ten minutes. Maurice lay up by the water, smoking. A farmer's cart appeared, and it did occur to him to ask which county they were in. But he said nothing, nor did the farmer appear to notice him. When Clive awoke it was past three. "We shall want some tea soon," was his contribution.

"All right. Can you mend that bloody bike?"

"Oh yes, didn't something jam?" He yawned and walked down to the machine. "No, I can't, Maurice, can you?"

"Rather not."

They laid their cheeks together and began laughing. The smash struck them as extraordinarily funny. Grandpapa's present too! He had given it to Maurice against his coming of age in August. Clive said, "How if we left it and walked?"

"Yes, who'd do it any harm? Leave the coats and things inside it. Likewise Joey's goggles."

"What about my books?"

"Leave 'em too."

"I shan't want them after hall?"

"Oh, I don't know. Tea's more important than hall. It stands to reason—well what are you giggling at?—that if we follow a dyke long enough we must come to a pub."

"Why, they use it to water their beer!"

Maurice smote him on the ribs, and for ten minutes they played up amongst the trees, too silly for speech. Pensive again, they stood close together, then hid the bicycle behind dog roses, and started. Clive took his notebook away with him, but it did not survive in any useful form, for the dyke they were following branched.

"We must wade this," he said. "We can't go round or we shall never get anywhere. Maurice, look—we must keep in a bee line south."

"All right."

It did not matter which of them suggested what that day; the other always agreed. Clive took off his shoes and socks and rolled his trousers up. Then he stepped upon the brown surface of the dyke and vanished. He reappeared swimming.

"All that deep!" he spluttered, climbing out. "Maurice, no idea! Had you?"

Maurice cried, "I say, I must bathe properly." He did so, while Clive carried his clothes. The light grew radiant. Presently they came to a farm.

The farmer's wife was inhospitable and ungracious, but they spoke of her afterwards as "absolutely ripping." She did in the end give them tea and allow Clive to dry near her kitchen fire. She "left payment to them," and, when they overpaid her, grumbled. Nothing checked their spirits. They transmuted everything.

"Goodbye, we're greatly obliged," said Clive. "And if any of your men come across the bike: I wish we could describe where we left it better. Anyhow I'll give you my friend's card. Tie it on the bike if they will be so kind, and bring it down to the nearest station. Something of the sort, I don't know. The station master will wire to us."

The station was five miles on. When they reached it the sun was low, and they were not back in Cambridge till after hall. All this last part of the day was perfect. The train, for some unknown reason, was full, and they sat close together, talking quietly under the hubbub, and smiling. When they parted it was in the ordinary way: neither had an impulse to say anything special. The whole day had been ordinary. Yet it had never come before to either of them, nor was it to be repeated.

14 The Dean sent Maurice down.

Mr Cornwallis was not a severe official, and the boy had a tolerable record, but he could not overlook so gross a breach of discipline. "And why did you not stop when I called you, Hall?" Hall made no answer, did not even look sorry. He had a smouldering eye, and Mr Cornwallis, though much annoyed, realized that he was confronted with a man. In a dead, bloodless way, he even guessed what had happened.

"Yesterday you cut chapel, four lectures, including my own translation class, and hall. You have done this sort of thing before. It's unnecessary to add impertinence, don't you think? Well? No reply? You will go down and inform your mother of the reason. I shall inform her too. Until you write me a letter of apology, I shall not recommend your readmission to the college in October. Catch the twelve o'clock."

"All right."

Mr Cornwallis motioned him out.

No punishment was inflicted on Durham. He had been let off all lectures in view of his Tripos, and even if he had been remiss the Dean would not have worried him; the best classical scholar of his year, he had won special treatment. A good thing he would no longer be distracted by Hall. Mr Cornwallis always suspected such friendships. It was not natural that men of different characters and tastes should be intimate, and although undergraduates, unlike schoolboys, are officially normal, the dons exercised a certain amount of watchfulness, and felt it right to spoil a love affair when they could.

Clive helped him pack, and saw him off. He said little, lest he depressed his friend, who was still in the heroics, but his heart sank. It was his last term, for his mother would not let him stay up a fourth year, which meant that he and Maurice would never meet in Cambridge again. Their love belonged to it, and particularly to their rooms, so that he could not conceive of their meeting anywhere else. He wished that Maurice had not taken up a strong line with the Dean, but it was too late now, and that the side-car had not been lost. He connected that side-car with intensities—the agony of the tennis court, the joy of yesterday. Bound in a single motion, they seemed there closer to one another than elsewhere; the machine took on a life of its own, in which they met and realized the unity preached by Plato. It had gone, and when Maurice's train went also, actually tearing hand from hand, he broke down, and returning to his room wrote passionate sheets of despair.

Maurice received the letter the next morning. It completed what his family had begun, and he had his first explosion of rage against the world.

15 "I can't apologize, mother—I explained last night there's nothing to apologize about. They had no right to send me down when everyone cuts lectures. It's pure spite, and you can ask anyone—Ada, do try turning on the coffee instead of the salt water."

She sobbed, "Maurice, you've upset mother: how can you be so unkind and brutal?"

"I'm sure I don't mean to be. I don't see I've been unkind. I shall go straight into the business now, like father did, without taking one of their rotten degrees. I see no harm in that."

"You might have kept your poor father out, he never had any unpleasantness," said Mrs Hall. "Oh Morrie, my darling—and we did so look forward to Cambridge."

"All this crying's a mistake," announced Kitty, who aspired to the functions of a tonic. "It only makes Maurice think he's important, which he isn't: he'll write to the Dean as soon as no one wants him to."

"I shan't. It's unsuitable," replied her brother, hard as iron.

"I don't see that."

"Little girls don't see a good deal."

"I'm not so sure!"

He glanced at her. But she only said that she saw a good deal more than some little boys who thought themselves little men. She was merely maundering, and the fear, tinged with respect, that had arisen in him died down. No, he couldn't apologize. He had done nothing wrong and wouldn't say he had, it was the first taste of honesty he had known for years, and honesty is like blood. In his unbending mood the boy thought it would be possible to live without compromise, and ignore all that didn't yield to himself and Clive! Clive's letter had maddened him. No doubt he is stupid—the sensible lover would apologize and get back to comfort his friend—but it was the stupidity of passion, which would rather have nothing than a little.

They continued talking and weeping. At last he rose, said, "I can't eat to this accompaniment," and went into the garden. His mother followed with a tray. Her very softness enraged him, for love develops the athlete. It cost her nothing to muck about with tender words and toast: she only wanted to make him soft too.

She wanted to know whether she had heard rightly, was he refusing to apologize? She wondered what her father would say, and incidentally learnt that the birthday gift was lying beside some East Anglian drove. She grew seriously concerned, for its loss was more intelligible to her than the loss of a degree. The girls minded too. They mourned the bicycle for the rest of the morning, and, though Maurice could always silence them or send them out of earshot, he felt that their pliancy might sap his strength again, as in the Easter vacation.

In the afternoon he had a collapse. He remembered that Clive and he had only been together one day! And they had spent it careering about like fools—instead of in one another's arms! Maurice did not know that they had thus spent it perfectly—he was too young to detect the triviality of contact for contact's sake. Though restrained by his friend, he would have surfeited passion. Later on, when his love took second strength, he realized how well Fate had served him. The one embrace in the darkness, the one long day in the light and the wind, were twin columns, each useless without the other. And all the agony of separation that he went through now, instead of destroying, was to fulfil.

He tried to answer Clive's letter. Already he feared to ring false. In the evening he received another, composed of the words "Maurice! I love you." He answered, "Clive, I love you." Then they wrote every day and for all their care created new images in each other's hearts. Letters distort even more quickly than silence. A terror seized Clive that something was going wrong, and just before his exam he got leave to run down to town. Maurice lunched with him. It was horrible. Both were tired, and they had chosen a restaurant where they could not hear themselves speak. "I haven't enjoyed it," said Clive when he wished goodbye. Maurice felt relieved. He had pretended to himself that he had enjoyed it, and thus increased his misery. They agreed that they would confine themselves to facts in their letters, and only write when anything was urgent. The emotional strain relaxed, and Maurice, nearer to brain fever than he supposed, had several dreamless nights that healed him. But daily life remained a poor business.

His position at home was anomalous: Mrs Hall wished that someone would decide it for her. He looked like a man and had turned out the Howells last Easter; but on the other hand he had been sent down from Cambridge and was not yet twenty-one. What was his place in her house? Instigated by Kitty, she tried to assert herself, but Maurice, after a genuine look of surprise, laid back his ears. Mrs Hall wavered, and, though fond of her son, took the unwise step of appealing to Dr Barry. Maurice was asked to go round one evening to be talked to.

"Well, Maurice, and how goes the career? Not quite as you expected, eh?"

Maurice was still afraid of their neighbour.

"Not quite as your mother expected, which is more to the point."

"Not quite as anyone expected," said Maurice, looking at his hands.

Dr Barry then said, "Oh, it's all for the best. What do you want with a University Degree? It was never intended for the suburban classes. You're not going to be either a parson or a barrister or a pedagogue. And you are not a county gentleman. Sheer waste of time. Get into harness at once. Quite right to insult the Dean. The city's your place. Your mother—" He paused and lit a cigar, the boy had been offered nothing. "Your mother doesn't understand this. Worrying because you don't apologize. For my own part I think these things right themselves. You got into an atmosphere for which you are not suited, and you've very properly taken the first opportunity to get out of it."

"How do you mean, sir?"

"Oh. Not sufficiently clear? I mean that the county gentleman would apologize by instinct if he found he had behaved like a cad. You've a different tradition."

"I think I must be getting home now," said Maurice, not without dignity.

"Yes, I think you must. I didn't invite you to have a pleasant evening, as I hope you have realized."

"You've spoken straight—perhaps some day I shall too. I know I'd like to."

This set the Doctor off, and he cried:

"How dare you bully your mother, Maurice. You ought to be horsewhipped. You young puppy! Swaggering about instead of asking her to forgive you! I know all about it. She came here with tears in her eyes and asked me to speak. She and your sisters are my respected neighbours, and as long as a woman calls me I'm at her service. Don't answer me, sir, don't answer, I want none of your speech, straight or otherwise. You are a disgrace to chivalry. I don't know what the world is coming to. I don t know what the world—I'm disappointed and disgusted with you."

Maurice, outside at last, mopped his forehead. He was ashamed in a way. He knew he had behaved badly to his mother, and all the snob in him had been touched to the raw. But somehow he could not retract, could not alter. Once out of the rut, he seemed out of it for ever. "A disgrace to chivalry." He considered the accusation. If a woman had been in that side-car, if then he had refused to stop at the Dean's bidding, would Dr Barry have required an apology from him? Surely not. He followed out this train of thought with difficulty. His brain was still feeble. But he was obliged to use it, for so much in current speech and ideas needed translation before he could understand them.

His mother met him, looking ashamed herself; she felt, as he did, that she ought to have done her own scolding. Maurice had grown up, she complained to Kitty; the children went from one; it was all very sad. Kitty asserted her brother was still nothing but a boy, but all these women had a sense of some change in his mouth and eyes and voice since he had faced Dr Barry.

16 The Durhams lived in a remote part of England on the Wilts and Somerset border. Though not an old family they had held land for four generations, and its influence had passed into them. Clive's great-great-uncle had been Lord Chief Justice in the reign of George IV, and the nest he had feathered was Penge. The feathers were inclined to blow about now. A hundred years had nibbled into the fortune, which no wealthy bride had replenished, and both house and estate were marked, not indeed with decay, but with the immobility that precedes it.

The house lay among woods. A park, still ridged with the lines of vanished hedges, stretched around, giving light and air and pasture to horses and Alderney cows. Beyond it the trees began, most planted by old Sir Edwin, who had annexed the common lands. There were two entrances to the park, one up by the village, the other on the clayey road that went to the station. There had been no station in the old days, and the approach from it, which was undignified and led by the back premises, typified an afterthought of England's.

Maurice arrived in the evening. He had travelled straight from his grandfather's at Birmingham, where, rather tepidly, he had come of age. Though in disgrace, he had not been mulcted of his presents, but they were given and received without enthusiasm. He had looked forward so much to being twenty-one. Kitty implied that he did not enjoy it because he had gone to the bad. Quite nicely he pinched her ear for this and kissed her, which annoyed her a good deal. "You have no *sense* of things," she said crossly. He smiled.

From Alfriston Gardens, with its cousins and meat teas, the change to Penge was immense. County families, even when intelligent, have something alarming about them, and Maurice approached any seat with awe. True, Clive had met him and was with him in the brougham, but then so was a Mrs Sheepshanks, who had arrived by his train. Mrs Sheepshanks had a maid, following behind with her luggage and his in a cab, and he wondered whether he ought to have brought a servant too. The lodge gate was held by a little girl. Mrs Sheepshanks wished *everyone* curtsied. Clive trod on his foot when she said this, but he wasn't sure whether accidentally. He was sure of nothing. When they approached he mistook the back for the front, and prepared to open the door. Mrs Sheepshanks said, "Oh, but that's complimentary." Besides, there was a butler to open the door.

Tea, very bitter, was awaiting them, and Mrs Durham looked one way while she poured out the other. People stood about, all looking distinguished or there for some distinguished reason. They were doing things or causing others to do them: Miss Durham booked him to canvass tomorrow for Tariff Reform. They agreed politically; but the cry with which she greeted his alliance did not please him. "Mother, Mr Hall *is* sound." Major Western, a cousin also stopping in the house, would ask him about Cambridge. Did Army men mind one being sent down? . . . No, it was worse than the restaurant, for there Clive had been out of his element too.

"Pippa, does Mr Hall know his room?"

"The Blue Room, mama."

"The one with no fireplace," called Clive. "Show him up." He was seeing off some callers.

Miss Durham passed Maurice on to the butler. They went up a side staircase. Maurice saw the main flight to the right, and wondered whether he was being slighted. His room was small, furnished cheaply. It had no outlook. As he knelt down to unpack, a feeling of Sunnington came over him, and he determined, while he was at Penge, to work through all his clothes. They shouldn't suppose he was unfashionable; he was as good as anyone. But he had scarcely reached this conclusion when Clive rushed in with the sunlight behind him. "Maurice, I shall kiss you," he said, and did so.

"Where—what's through there?"

"Our study—" He was laughing, his expression wild and radiant.

"Oh, so that's why—"

"Maurice! Maurice! you've actually come. You're here. This place'll never seem the same again, I shall love it at last."

"It's jolly for me coming," said Maurice chokily: the sudden rush of joy made his head swim.

"Go on unpacking. So I arranged it on purpose. We're up this staircase by ourselves. It's as like college as I could manage."

"It's better."

"I really feel it will be."

There was a knock on the passage door. Maurice started, but Clive though still sitting on his shoulder said, "Come in!" indifferently. A housemaid entered with hot water.

"Except for meals we need never be in the other part of the house," he continued. "Either here or out of doors. Jolly, eh? I've a piano." He drew him into the study. "Look at the view. You may shoot rabbits out of this window. By the way, if my mother or Pippa tells you at dinner that they want you to do this or that tomorrow, you needn't worry. Say 'yes' to them if you like. You're actually going to ride with me, and they know it. It's only their ritual. On Sunday, when you haven't been to church they'll pretend afterwards you were there."

"But I've no proper riding breeches."

"I can't associate with you in that case," said Clive and bounded off.

When Maurice returned to the drawing-room he felt he had a greater right to be there than anyone. He walked up to Mrs Sheepshanks, opened his mouth before she could open hers, and was encouraging to her. He took his place in the absurd octet that was forming to go in—Clive and Mrs Sheepshanks, Major Western and another woman, another man and Pippa, himself and his hostess. She apologized for the smallness of the party.

"Not at all," said Maurice, and saw Clive glance at him maliciously: he had used the wrong tag. Mrs Durham then put him through his paces, but he did not care a damn whether he satisfied her or not. She had her son's features and seemed equally able, though not equally sincere. He understood why Clive should have come to despise her.

After dinner the men smoked, then joined the ladies. It was a suburban evening, but with a difference; these people had the air of settling something: they either just had arranged or soon would rearrange England. Yet the gate posts, the roads—he had noticed them on the way up—were in bad repair, and the timber wasn't kept properly, the windows stuck, the boards creaked. He was less impressed than he had expected by Penge.

When the ladies retired Clive said, "Maurice, you look sleepy too." Maurice took the hint, and five minutes afterwards they met again in the study, with all the night to talk into. They lit their pipes. It was the first time they had experienced full tranquillity together, and exquisite words would be spoken. They knew this, yet scarcely wanted to begin.

"I'll tell you my latest now," said Clive. "As soon as I got home I had a row with mother and told her I should stop up a fourth year."

Maurice gave a cry.

"What's wrong?"

"I've been sent down."

"But you're coming back in October."

"I'm not. Cornwallis said I must apologize, and I wouldn't— I thought you wouldn't be up, so I didn't care."

"And I settled to stop because I thought you would be up. Comedy of Errors."

Maurice stared gloomily before him.

"Comedy of Errors, not Tragedy. You can apologize now."

"It's too late."

Clive laughed. "Why too late? It makes it simpler. You didn't like to apologize until the term in which your offence was committed had come to an end. 'Dear Mr Cornwallis: Now that the term is over, I venture to write to you.' I'll draft the letter tomorrow."

Maurice pondered and finally exclaimed, "Clive, you're a devil."

"I'm a bit of an outlaw, I grant, but it serves these people right. As long as they talk of the unspeakable vice of the Greeks they can't expect fair play. It served my mother right when I slipped up to kiss you before dinner. She would have no mercy if she knew, she wouldn't attempt, wouldn't want to attempt to understand that I feel to you as Pippa to her fiancé, only far more nobly, far more deeply, body and soul, no starved medievalism of course, only a—a particular harmony of body and soul that I don't think women have even guessed. But you know."

"Yes. I'll apologize."

There was a long interval: they discussed the motor bicycle, which had never been heard of again. Clive made coffee.

"Tell me, what made you wake me that night after the Debating Society. Describe."

"I kept on thinking of something to say, and couldn't, so at last I couldn't even think, so I just came."

"Sort of thing you would do."

"Are you ragging?" asked Maurice shyly.

"My God!" There was a silence. "Tell me now about the night I first came up. Why did you make us both so unhappy?"

"I don't know, I say. I can't explain anything. Why did you mislead me with that rotten Plato? I was still in a muddle. A lot of things hadn't joined up in me that since have."

"But hadn't you been getting hold of me for months? Since first you saw me at Risley's, in fact."

"Don't ask me."

"It's a queer business, any way."

"It's that."

Clive laughed delightedly, and wriggled in his chair. "Maurice, the more I think it over the more certain I am that it's you who are the devil."

"Oh, all right."

"I should have gone through life half awake if you'd had the decency to leave me alone. Awake intellectually, yes, and emotionally in a way; but here—" He pointed with his pipe stem to his heart; and both smiled. "Perhaps we woke up one another. I like to think that any way."

"When did you first care about me?"

"Don't ask me," echoed Clive.

"Oh, be a bit serious—well—what was it in me you first cared about?"

"Like really to know?" asked Clive, who was in the mood Maurice adored—half mischievous, half passionate; a mood of supreme affection.

"Yes."

"Well, it was your beauty."

"My what?"

"Beauty. . . . I used to admire that man over the bookcase most."

"I can give points to a picture, I dare say," said Maurice, having glanced at the Michelangelo. "Clive, you're a silly little fool, and since you've brought it up I think you're beautiful, the only beautiful person I've ever seen. I love your voice and everything to do with you, down to your clothes or the room you are sitting in. I adore you."

Clive went crimson. "Sit up straight and let's change the subject," he said, all the folly out of him.

"I didn't mean to annoy you at all—"

"Those things must be said once, or we should never know they were in each other's hearts. I hadn't guessed, not so much at least. You've done all right, Maurice." He did not change the subject but developed it into another that had interested him recently, the precise influence of Desire upon our aesthetic judgements. "Look at that picture, for instance. I love it because, like the painter himself, I love the subject. I don't judge it with eyes of the normal man. There seem two roads for arriving at Beauty—one is in common, and all the world has reached Michelangelo by it, but the other is private to me and a few more. We come to him by both roads. On the other hand Greuze —his subject matter repels me. I can only get to him down one road. The rest of the world finds two."

Maurice did not interrupt: it was all charming nonsense to him.

"These private roads are perhaps a mistake," concluded Clive. "But as long as the human figure is painted they will be taken. Landscape is the only safe subject—or perhaps something geometric, rhythmical, inhuman absolutely. I wonder whether that is what the Mohammedans were up to and old Moses—I've just thought of this. If you introduce the human figure you at once arouse either disgust or desire. Very faintly sometimes, but it's there. 'Thou shalt not make for thyself any graven image—' because one couldn't possibly make it for all other people too. Maurice, shall we rewrite history? 'The Aesthetic Philosophy of the Decalogue.' I've always thought it remarkable of God not to have damned you or me in it. I used to put it down to him for righteousness, though now I suspect he was merely ill-informed. Still I might make out a case. Shall I choose it for a Fellowship Dissertation?"

"I can't follow, you know," said Maurice, a little ashamed.

And their love scene drew out, having the inestimable gain of a new language. No tradition overawed the boys. No convention settled what was poetic, what absurd. They were concerned with a passion that few English minds have admitted, and so created untrammelled. Something of exquisite beauty arose in the mind of each at last, something unforgettable and eternal, but built of the humblest scraps of speech and from the simplest emotions.

"I say, will you kiss me?" asked Maurice, when the sparrows woke in the eaves above them, and far out in the woods the ringdoves began to coo.

Clive shook his head, and smiling they parted, having established perfection in their lives, at all events for a time.

17 It seems strange that Maurice should have won any respect from the Durham family, but they did not dislike him. They only disliked people who wanted to know them well—it was a positive mania—and the rumour that a man wished to enter county society was a sufficient reason for excluding him from it. Inside (region of high interchange and dignified movements that meant nothing) were to be found several who, like Mr Hall, neither loved their fate nor feared it, and would depart without a sigh if necessary. The Durhams felt they were conferring a favour on him by treating him as one of themselves, yet were pleased he should take it as a matter of course, gratitude being mysteriously connected in their minds with ill breeding.

Wanting only his food and his friend, Maurice did not observe he was a success, and was surprised when the old lady claimed him for a talk towards the end of his visit. She had questioned him about his family and discovered the nakedness thereof, but this time her manner was deferential: she wanted his opinion of Clive.

"Mr Hall, we wish you to help us: Clive thinks so much of you. Do you consider it wise for him to stop up a fourth year at Cambridge?"

Maurice was wanting to wonder which horse he should ride in the afternoon: he only half attended, which gave an appearance of profundity.

"After the deplorable exhibition he has made of himself in the Tripos—is it wise?"

"He means to," said Maurice.

Mrs Durham nodded. "There you have gone to the root of the matter. Clive means to. Well, he is his own master. This place is his. Did he tell you?"

"No."

"Oh, Penge is his absolutely, under my husband's will. I must move to the dower house as soon as he marries—"

Maurice started; she looked at him and saw that he had coloured. "So there *is* some girl," she thought. Neglecting the point for a moment, she returned to Cambridge, and observed how little a fourth year would profit a "yokel"—she used the word with gay assurance—and how desirable it was that Clive should take his place in the countryside. There was the game, there were his tenants, there were finally politics. "His father represented the division, as you doubtless know."

"No."

"What does he talk to you about?" she laughed. "Anyhow, my husband was a member for seven years, and though a Lib is in now, one knows that cannot last. All our old friends are looking to him. But he must take his place, he must fit himself, and what on earth is the good of all this—I forget what—advanced work. He ought to spend the year travelling instead. He must go to America and if possible the Colonies. It has become absolutely indispensable."

"He speaks of travelling after Cambridge. He wants me to go."

"I trust you will—but not Greece, Mr Hall. That is travelling for play. Do dissuade him from Italy and Greece."

"I'd prefer America myself."

"Naturally—anyone sensible would; but he's a student—a dreamer—Pippa says he writes verse. Have you seen any?"

Maurice had seen a poem to himself. Conscious that life grew daily more amazing, he said nothing. Was he the same man who eight months back had been puzzled by Risley? What had deepened his vision? Section after section the armies of humanity were coming alive. Alive, but slightly absurd; they misunderstood *him* so utterly: they exposed their weakness when they thought themselves most acute. He could not help smiling.

"You evidently have . . ." Then suddenly: "Mr Hall, is there anyone? Some Newnham girl? Pippa declares there is."

"Pippa had better ask then," Maurice replied.

Mrs Durham was impressed. He had met one impertinence with another. Who would have expected such skill in a young man? He seemed even indifferent to his victory, and was smiling to one of the other guests, who approached over the lawn to tea. In the tones that she reserved for an equal she said, "Impress on him about America anyhow. He needs reality. I noticed that last year."

Maurice duly impressed, when they were riding through the glades alone.

"I thought you were going down," was Clive's comment. "Like them. They wouldn't look at Joey." Clive was in full reaction against his family, he hated the worldliness that they combined with complete ignorance of the World. "These children will be a nuisance," he remarked during a canter.

"What children?"

"Mine! The need of an heir for Penge. My mother calls it marriage, but that was all she was thinking of."

Maurice was silent. It had not occurred to him before that neither he nor his friend would leave life behind them.

"I shall be worried eternally. They've always some girl staying in the house as it is."

"Just go on growing old—"

"Eh, boy?"

"Nothing," said Maurice, and reined up. An immense sadness —he believed himself beyond such irritants—had risen up in his soul. He and the beloved would vanish utterly—would continue neither in Heaven nor on Earth. They had won past the conventions, but Nature still faced them, saying with even voice, "Very well, you are thus; I blame none of my children. But you must go the way of all sterility." The thought that he was sterile weighed on the young man with a sudden shame. His mother or Mrs Durham might lack mind or heart, but they had done visible work; they had handed on the torch their sons would tread out.

He had meant not to trouble Clive, but out it all came as soon as they lay down in the fern. Clive did not agree. "Why children?" he asked. "Why always children? For love to end where it begins is far more beautiful, and Nature knows it."

"Yes, but if everyone—"

Clive pulled him back into themselves. He murmured something about Eternity in an hour: Maurice did not understand, but the voice soothed him.

18 During the next two years Maurice and Clive had as much happiness as men under that star can expect. They were affectionate and consistent by nature, and, thanks to Clive, extremely sensible. Clive knew that ecstasy cannot last, but can carve a channel for something lasting, and he contrived a relation that proved permanent. If Maurice made love it was Clive who preserved it, and caused its rivers to water the garden. He could not bear that one drop should be wasted, either in bitterness or in sentimentality, and as time went on they abstained from avowals ("we have said everything") and almost from caresses. Their happiness was to be together; they radiated something of their calm amongst others, and could take their place in society.

Clive had expanded in this direction ever since he had understood Greek. The love that Socrates bore Phaedo now lay within his reach, love passionate but temperate, such as only finer natures can understand, and he found in Maurice a nature that was not indeed fine, but charmingly willing. He led the beloved up a narrow and beautiful path, high above either abyss. It went on until the final darkness—he could see no other terror—and when that descended they would at all events have lived more fully than either saint or sensualist, and would have extracted to their utmost the nobility and sweetness of the world. He educated Maurice, or rather his spirit educated Maurice's spirit, for they themselves became equal. Neither thought "Am I led; am I leading?" Love had caught him out of triviality and Maurice out of bewilderment in order that two imperfect souls might touch perfection.

So they proceeded outwardly like other men. Society received them, as she receives thousands like them. Behind Society slumbered the Law. They had their last year at Cambridge together, they travelled in Italy. Then the prison house closed, but on both of them. Clive was working for the bar, Maurice harnessed to an office. They were together still.

19 By this time their families had become acquainted. "They will never get on," they had agreed. "They belong to different sections of society." But, perhaps out of perversity, the families did get on, and Clive and Maurice found amusement in seeing them together. Both were misogynists, Clive especially. In the grip of their temperaments, they had not developed the imagination to do duty instead, and during their love women had become as remote as horses or cats; all that the creatures did seemed silly. When Kitty asked to hold Pippa's baby, when Mrs Durham and Mrs Hall visited the Royal Academy in unison, they saw a misfit in nature rather than in society, and gave wild explanations. There was nothing strange really: they themselves were sufficient cause. Their passion for each other was the strongest force in either family, and drew everything after it as a hidden current draws a boat. Mrs Hall and Mrs Durham came together because their sons were friends; "and now," said Mrs Hall, "we are friends too."

Maurice was present the day their "friendship" began. The matrons met in Pippa's London house. Pippa had married a Mr London, a coincidence that made a great impression on Kitty, who hoped she would not think of it and laugh during tea. Ada, as too silly for a first visit, had been left at home by Maurice's advice. Nothing happened. Then Pippa and her mother motored out to return the civility. He was in town but again nothing seemed to have happened, except that Pippa had praised Kitty's brains to Ada and Ada's beauty to Kitty, thus offending both girls, and Mrs Hall had warned Mrs Durham against installing hot air at Penge. Then they met again, and as far as he could see it was always like this; nothing, nothing, and still nothing.

Mrs Durham had of course her motives. She was looking out wives for Clive, and put down the Hall girls on her list. She had a theory one ought to cross breeds a bit, and Ada, though suburban, was healthy. No doubt the girl was a fool, but Mrs Durham did not propose to retire to the dower house in practice, whatever she might do in theory, and believed she could best manage Clive through his wife. Kitty had fewer qualifications. She was less foolish, less beautiful, and less rich. Ada would inherit the whole of her grandfather's fortune, which was considerable, and had always inherited his good humour. Mrs Durham met old Mr Grace once, and rather liked him.

Had she supposed the Halls were also planning she would have drawn back. Like Maurice they held her by their indifference. Mrs Hall was too idle to scheme, the girls too innocent. Mrs Durham regarded Ada as a favourable line and invited her to Penge. Only Pippa, into whose mind a breath of modernity had blown, began to think her brother's coldness odd. "Clive, *are* you going to marry?" she asked suddenly. But his reply, "No, do tell mother," dispelled her suspicions: it is the sort of reply a man who is going to marry would make.

No one worried Maurice. He had established his power at home, and his mother began to speak of him in the tones she had reserved for her husband. He was not only the son of the house, but more of a personage than had been expected. He kept the servants in order, understood the car, subscribed to this and not to that, tabooed certain of the girls' acquaintances. By twenty-three he was a promising suburban tyrant, whose rule was the stronger because it was fairly just and mild. Kitty protested, but she had no backing and no experience. In the end she had to say she was sorry and to receive a kiss. She was no match for this good-humoured and slightly hostile young man, and she failed to establish the advantage that his escapade at Cambridge had given her.

Maurice's habits became regular. He ate a large breakfast and caught the 8.36 to town. In the train he read the *Daily Telegraph*. He worked till 1.0, lunched lightly, and worked again through the afternoon. Returning home, he had some exercise and a large dinner, and in the evening he read the evening paper, or laid down the law, or played billiards or bridge.

But every Wednesday he slept at Clive's little flat in town. Weekends were also inviolable. They said at home, "You must never interfere with Maurice's Wednesdays or with his weekends. He would be most annoyed."

20 Clive got through his bar exams successfully, but just before he was called he had a slight touch of influenza with fever. Maurice came to see him as he was recovering, caught it, and went to bed himself. Thus they saw little of one another for several weeks, and when they did meet Clive was still white and nervy. He came down to the Halls', preferring their house to Pippa's, and hoping that the good food and quiet would set him up. He ate little, and when he spoke his theme was the futility of all things.

"I'm a barrister because I may enter public life," he said in reply to a question of Ada's. "But why should I enter public life? Who wants me?"

"Your mother says the county does."

"If the county wants anyone it wants a Radical. But I've talked to more people than my mother, and they're weary of us leisured classes coasting round in motor-cars and asking for something to do. All this solemn to and fro between great houses —it's a game without gaiety. You don't find it played outside England. (Maurice, I'm going to Greece.) No one wants us, or anything except a comfortable home."

"But to give a comfortable home's what public life is," shrilled Kitty.

"Is, or ought to be?"

"Well, it's all the same."

"Is and ought to be are not the same," said her mother, proud of grasping the distinction. "You ought to be not interrupting Mr Durham, whereas you—"

"—is," supplied Ada, and the family laugh made Clive jump.

"We are and we ought to be," concluded Mrs Hall. "Very different."

"Not always," contradicted Clive.

"Not always, remember that, Kitty," she echoed, vaguely admonitory: on other occasions he had not minded her. Kitty cried back to her first assertion. Ada was saying anything, Maurice nothing. He was eating away placidly, too used to such table talk to see that it worried his friend. Between the courses he told an anecdote. All were silent to listen to him. He spoke slowly, stupidly, without attending to his words or taking the trouble to be interesting. Suddenly Clive cut in with "I say— I'm going to faint," and fell off his chair.

"Get a pillow, Kitty: Ada, eau de cologne," said their brother. He loosened Clive's collar. "Mother, fan him; no; fan him . . ."

"Silly it is," murmured Clive.

As he spoke, Maurice kissed him.

"I'm all right now."

The girls and a servant came running in.

"I can walk," he said, the colour returning to his face.

"Certainly not," cried Mrs Hall. "Maurice'll carry you—Mr Durham, put your arms round Maurice."

"Come along, old man. The doctor: somebody telephone." He picked up his friend, who was so weak that he began to cry.

"Maurice—I'm a fool."

"Be a fool," said Maurice, and carried him upstairs, undressed him, and put him to bed. Mrs Hall knocked, and going out to her he said quickly, "Mother, you needn't tell the others I kissed Durham."

"Oh, certainly not."

"He wouldn't like it. I was rather upset and did it without thinking. As you know, we are great friends, relations almost."

It sufficed. She liked to have little secrets with her son; it reminded her of the time when she had been so much to him. Ada joined them with a hot water bottle, which he took in to the patient.

"The doctor'll see me like this," Clive sobbed.

"I hope he will."

"Why?"

Maurice lit a cigarette, and sat on the edge of the bed. "We want him to see you at your worst. Why did Pippa let you travel?"

"I was supposed to be well."

"Hell take you."

"Can we come in?" called Ada through the door.

"No. Send the doctor alone."

"He's here," cried Kitty in the distance. A man, little older than themselves, was announced.

"Hullo, Jowitt," said Maurice, rising. "Just cure me this chap. He's had influenza, and is supposed to be well. Result he's fainted, and can't stop crying."

"We know all about that," remarked Mr Jowitt, and stuck a thermometer into Clive's mouth. "Been working hard?"

"Yes, and now wants to go to Greece."

"So he shall. You clear out now. I'll see you downstairs."

Maurice obeyed, convinced that Clive was seriously ill. Jowitt followed in about ten minutes, and told Mrs Hall it was nothing much—a bad relapse. He wrote prescriptions, and said he would send in a nurse. Maurice followed him into the garden, and, laying a hand on his arm, said, "Now tell me how ill he is. This isn't a relapse. It's something more. Please tell me the truth."

"*He's* all right," said the other; somewhat annoyed, for he piqued himself on telling the truth. "I thought you realized that. He's stopped the hysteria and is getting off to sleep. It's just an ordinary relapse. He will have to be more careful this time than the other, that's all."

"And how long will these ordinary relapses, as you call them, go on? At any moment may he have this appalling pain?"

"He's only a bit uncomfortable—caught a chill in the car, he thinks."

"Jowitt, you don't tell me. A grown man doesn't cry, unless he's gone pretty far."

"That is only the weakness."

"Oh, give it your own name," said Maurice, removing his hand. "Besides, I'm keeping you."

"Not a bit, my young friend, I'm here to answer any difficulties."

"Well, if it's so slight, why are you sending in a nurse?"

"To amuse him. I understand he's well off."

"And can't we amuse him?"

"No, because of the infection. You were there when I told your mother none of you ought to go into the room."

"I thought you meant my sisters."

"You equally—more, for you've already caught it from him once."

"I won't have a nurse."

"Mrs Hall has telephoned to the Institute."

"Why is everything done in such a damned hurry?" said Maurice, raising his voice. "I shall nurse him myself."

"Have you wheeling the baby next."

"I beg your pardon?"

Jowitt went off laughing.

In tones that admitted no argument Maurice told his mother he should sleep in the patient's room. He would not have a bed

taken in, lest Clive woke up, but lay down on the floor with his
head on a foot-stool, and read by the rays of a candle lamp.
Before long Clive stirred and said feebly, "Oh damnation, oh
damnation."

"Want anything?" Maurice called.

"My inside's all wrong."

Maurice lifted him out of bed and put him on the night stool.
When relief had come he lifted him back.

"I can walk: you mustn't do this sort of thing."

"You'd do it for me."

He carried the stool down the passage and cleaned it. Now
that Clive was undignified and weak, he loved him as never
before.

"You mustn't," repeated Clive, when he came back. "It's too
filthy."

"Doesn't worry me," said Maurice, lying down. "Get off to
sleep again."

"The doctor told me he'd send a nurse."

"What do you want with a nurse? It's only a touch of diar-
rhoea. You can keep on all night as far as I'm concerned. Honestly it doesn't worry me—I don't say this to please you. It just
doesn't."

"I can't possibly—your office—"

"Look here, Clive, would you rather have a trained nurse or
me? One's coming tonight, but I left word she was to be sent
away again, because I'd rather chuck the office and look after
you myself, and thought you'd rather."

Clive was silent so long that Maurice thought him asleep. At
last he sighed, "I suppose I'd better have the nurse."

"Right: she will make you more comfortable than I can. Perhaps you're right."

Clive made no reply.

Ada had volunteered to sit up in the room below, and, according to arrangement, Maurice tapped three times, and while waiting for her studied Clive's blurred and sweaty face. It was useless the doctor talking: his friend was in agony. He longed to embrace him, but remembered this had brought on the hysteria, and besides, Clive was restrained, fastidious almost. As Ada did not come he went downstairs, and found that she had fallen asleep. She lay, the picture of health, in a big leather chair, with her hands dropped on either side and her feet stretched out. Her bosom rose and fell, her heavy black hair served as a cushion to her face, and between her lips he saw teeth and a scarlet tongue. "Wake up," he cried irritably.

Ada woke.

"How do you expect to hear the front door when the nurse comes?"

"How is poor Mr Durham?"

"Very ill; dangerously ill."

"Oh Maurice! Maurice!"

"The nurse is to stop. I called you, but you never came. Go off to bed now, as you can't even help that much."

"Mother said I must sit up, because the nurse mustn't be let in by a man—it wouldn't look well."

"I can't think how you have time to think of such rubbish," said Maurice.

"We must keep the house a good name."

He was silent, then laughed in the way the girls disliked. At the bottom of their hearts they disliked him entirely, but were too confused mentally to know this. His laugh was the only grievance they avowed.

"Nurses are not nice. No nice girl would be a nurse. If they are you may be sure they do not come from nice homes, or they would stop at home."

"Ada, how long were you at school?" asked her brother, as he helped himself to a drink.

"I call going to school stopping at home."

He set down his glass with a clank, and left her. Clive's eyes were open, but he did not speak or seem to know that Maurice had returned, nor did the coming of the nurse arouse him.

21 It was plain in a few days that nothing serious was amiss with the visitor. The attack, despite its dramatic start, was less serious than its predecessor, and soon allowed his removal to Penge. His appearance and spirits remained poor, but that must be expected after influenza, and no one except Maurice felt the least uneasiness.

Maurice thought seldom about disease and death, but when he did it was with strong disapproval. They could not be allowed to spoil his life or his friend's, and he brought all his youth and health to bear on Clive. He was with him constantly, going down uninvited to Penge for weekends or for a few days' holiday, and trying by example rather than precept to cheer him up. Clive did not respond. He could rouse himself in company, and even affect interest in a right of way question that had arisen between the Durhams and the British Public, but when they were alone he relapsed into gloom, would not speak, or spoke in a half serious, half joking way that tells of mental exhaustion. He determined to go to Greece. That was the only point on which he held firm. He would go, though the month would be September, and he alone. "It must be done," he said. "It is a vow. Every barbarian must give the Acropolis its chance once."

Maurice had no use for Greece. His interest in the classics had been slight and obscene, and had vanished when he loved

Clive. The stories of Harmodius and Aristogeiton, of Phaedrus. of the Theban Band were well enough for those whose hearts were empty, but no substitute for life. That Clive should occasionally prefer them puzzled him. In Italy, which he liked well enough in spite of the food and the frescoes, he had refused to cross to the yet holier land beyond the Adriatic. "It sounds out of repair" was his argument. "A heap of old stones without any paint on. At all events this"—he indicated the library of Siena Cathedral—"you may say what you like, but it is in working order." Clive, in his amusement, jumped up and down upon the Piccolomini tiles, and the custodian laughed too instead of scolding them. Italy had been very jolly—as much as one wants in the way of sight-seeing surely—but in these latter days Greece had cropped up again. Maurice hated the very word, and by a curious inversion connected it with morbidity and death. Whenever he wanted to plan, to play tennis, to talk nonsense, Greece intervened. Clive saw his antipathy, and took to teasing him about it, not very kindly.

For Clive wasn't kind: it was to Maurice the most serious of all the symptoms. He would make slightly malicious remarks, and use his intimate knowledge to wound. He failed: i.e., his knowledge was incomplete, or he would have known the impossibility of vexing athletic love. If Maurice sometimes parried outwardly it was because he felt it human to respond: he always had been put off Christ turning the other cheek. Inwardly nothing vexed him. The desire for union was too strong to admit resentment. And sometimes, quite cheerfully, he would conduct a parallel conversation, hitting out at Clive at times in acknowledgement of his presence, but going his own way towards light, in hope that the beloved would follow.

Their last conversation took place on these lines. It was the evening before Clive's departure, and he had the whole of the

Hall family to dine with him at the Savoy, as a return for their kindness to him, and had sandwiched them out between some other friends. "We shall know what it is if you fall *this* time," cried Ada, nodding at the champagne. "Your health!" he replied. "And the health of all ladies. Come, Maurice!" It pleased him to be slightly old-fashioned. Healths were drunk, and only Maurice detected the underlying bitterness.

After the banquet he said to Maurice, "Are you sleeping at home?"

"No."

"I thought you might want to see your people home."

"Not he, Mr Durham," said his mother. "Nothing I can do or say can make him miss a Wednesday. Maurice is a regular old bachelor."

"My flat's upside down with packing," remarked Clive. "I leave by the morning train, and go straight through to Marseilles."

Maurice took no notice, and came. They stood yawning at each other, while the lift descended for them, then sped upwards, climbed another stage on their feet, and went down a passage that recalled the approach to Risley's rooms at Trinity. The flat, small, dark, and silent, lay at the end. It was, as Clive said, littered with rubbish, but his housekeeper, who slept out, had made up Maurice's bed as usual, and had arranged drinks.

"Yet again," remarked Clive.

Maurice liked alcohol, and had a good head.

"I'm going to bed. I see you've found what you wanted."

"Take care of yourself. Don't overdo the ruins. By the way—" He took a phial out of his pocket. "I knew you'd forget this. Chlorodyne."

"Chlorodyne! Your contribution!"

He nodded.

"Chlorodyne for Greece. . . . Ada has been telling me that

you thought I was going to die. Why on earth do you worry about my health? There's no fear. I shan't ever have so clean and clear an experience as death."

"I know I shall die some time and I don't want to, nor you to. If either of us goes, nothing's left for both. I don't know if you call that clean and clear?"

"Yes, I do."

"Then I'd rather be dirty," said Maurice, after a pause. Clive shivered.

"Don't you agree?"

"Oh, you're getting like everyone else. You will have a theory. We can't go quietly ahead, we must always be formulating, though every formula breaks down. 'Dirt at all costs' is to be yours. I say there are cases when one gets too dirty. Then Lethe, if there is such a river, will wash it away. But there may not be such a river. The Greeks assumed little enough, yet too much perhaps. There may be no forgetfulness beyond the grave. This wretched equipment may continue. In other words, beyond the grave there may be Hell."

"Oh, balls."

Clive generally enjoyed his metaphysics. But this time he went on. "To forget everything—even happiness. Happiness! A casual tickling of someone or something against oneself— that's all. Would that we had never been lovers! For then, Maurice, you and I should have lain still and been quiet. We should have slept, then had we been at rest with kings and counsellors of the earth, which built desolate places for themselves—"

"What on earth are you talking about?"

"—or as an hidden untimely birth, we had not been: as infants which never saw light. But as it is—Well, don't look so serious."

"Don't try to be funny then," said Maurice. "I never did think anything of your speeches."

"Words conceal thought. That theory?"

"They make a silly noise. I don't care about your thoughts either."

"Then what do you care about in me?"

Maurice smiled: as soon as this question was asked, he felt happy, and refused to answer it.

"My beauty?" said Clive cynically. "These somewhat faded charms. My hair is falling out. Are you aware?"

"Bald as an egg by thirty."

"As an addled egg. Perhaps you like me for my mind. During and after my illness I must have been a delightful companion."

Maurice looked at him with tenderness. He was studying him, as in the earliest days of their acquaintance. Only then it was to find out what he was like, now what had gone wrong with him. Something was wrong. The diseases still simmered, vexing the brain, and causing it to be gloomy and perverse, and Maurice did not resent this: he hoped to succeed where the doctor had failed. He knew his own strength. Presently he would put it forth as love, and heal his friend, but for the moment he investigated.

"I expect you do like me for my mind—for its feebleness. You always knew I was inferior. You're wonderfully considerate—give me plenty of rope and never snub me as you did your family at dinner."

It was as if he wanted to pick a quarrel.

"Now and then you call me to heel—" He pinched him, pretending to be playful. Maurice started. "What is wrong now? Tired?"

"I'm off to bed."

"I.e., you're tired. Why can't you answer a question? I didn't say 'tired of me', though I might have."

"Have you ordered your taxi for the nine o'clock?"

"No, nor got my ticket. I shan't go to Greece at all. Perhaps it'll be as intolerable as England."

"Well, good night, old man." He went, deeply concerned, to his room. Why would everyone declare Clive was fit to travel? Clive even knew he wasn't himself. So methodical as a rule, he had put off taking his ticket till the last moment. He might still not go, but to express the hope was to defeat it. Maurice undressed, and catching sight of himself in the glass, thought, "A mercy I'm fit." He saw a well-trained serviceable body and a face that contradicted it no longer. Virility had harmonized them and shaded either with dark hair. Slipping on his pyjamas, he sprang into bed, concerned, yet profoundly happy, because he was strong enough to live for two. Clive had helped him. Clive would help him again when the pendulum swung, meanwhile he must help Clive, and all through life they would alternate thus: as he dozed off he had a further vision of love, that was not far from the ultimate.

There was a knock at the wall that divided their rooms.

"What is it?" he called; then, "Come in!" for Clive was now at the door.

"Can I come into your bed?"

"Come along," said Maurice, making room.

"I'm cold and miserable generally. I can't sleep. I don't know why."

Maurice did not misunderstand him. He knew and shared his opinions on this point. They lay side by side without touching. Presently Clive said, "It's no better here. I shall go." Maurice was not sorry, for he could not get to sleep either, though for a different reason, and he was afraid Clive might hear the drumming of his heart, and guess what it was.

22 Clive sat in the theatre of Dionysus. The stage was empty, as it had been for many centuries, the auditorium empty; the sun had set though the Acropolis behind still radiated heat. He saw barren plains running down to the sea, Salamis, Aegina, mountains, all blended in a violet evening. Here dwelt his gods—Pallas Athene in the first place: he might if he chose imagine her shrine untouched, and her statue catching the last of the glow. She understood all men, though motherless and a virgin. He had been coming to thank her for years because she had lifted him out of the mire.

But he saw only dying light and a dead land. He uttered no prayer, believed in no deity, and knew that the past was devoid of meaning like the present, and a refuge for cowards.

Well, he had written to Maurice at last. His letter was journeying down to the sea. Where one sterility touched another, it would embark and voyage past Sunium and Cythera, would land and embark, would land again. Maurice would get it as he was starting for his work. "Against my will I have become normal. I cannot help it." The words had been written.

He descended the theatre wearily. Who could help anything? Not only in sex, but in all things men have moved blindly, have evolved out of slime to dissolve into it when this accident of consequences is over. μὴ φῦναι τὸν ἅπαντα νικᾷ λόγον, sighed the actors in this very place two thousand years before. Even that remark, though further from vanity than most, was vain.

(116)

23 Dear Clive,

Please come back on receiving this. I have looked out your connections, and you can reach England on Tuesday week if you start at once. I am very anxious about you on account of your letter, as it shows how ill you are. I have waited to hear from you for a fortnight and now come two sentences, which I suppose mean that you cannot love anyone of your own sex any longer. We will see whether this is so as soon as you arrive!

I called upon Pippa yesterday. She was full of the lawsuit, and thinks your mother made a mistake in closing the path. Your mother has told the village she is not closing it against them. I called to get news of you, but Pippa had not heard either. You will be amused to hear that I have been learning some classical music lately—also golf. I get on as well as can be expected at Hill and Hall's. My mother has gone to Birmingham after changing backwards and forwards for a week. Now you have all the news. Wire on getting this, and again on reaching Dover.

Maurice.

Clive received this letter and shook his head. He was going with some hotel acquaintances up Pentelicus, and tore it to pieces on the top of the mountain. He had stopped loving Maurice and should have to say so plainly.

24 He stopped a week more at Athens, lest by any possibility he was wrong. The change had been so shocking that sometimes he thought Maurice was right, and that it was the finish of his illness. It humiliated him, for he had understood his soul, or, as he said, himself, ever since he was fifteen. But the body is deeper than the soul and its secrets inscrutable. There had been no warning—just a blind alteration of the life spirit, just an announcement, "You who loved men, will henceforward love women. Understand or not, it's the same to me." Whereupon he collapsed. He tried to clothe the change with reason, and understand it, in order that he might feel less humiliated: but it was of the nature of death or birth, and he failed.

It came during illness—possibly through illness. During the first attack, when he was severed from ordinary life and feverish, it seized an opportunity that it would have taken some time or other. He noticed how charming his nurse was and enjoyed obeying her. When he went a drive his eye rested on women. Little details, a hat, the way a skirt is held, scent, laughter, the delicate walk across mud—blended into a charming whole, and it pleased him to find that the women often answered his eye with equal pleasure. Men had never responded—they did not assume he admired them, and were either unconscious or puzzled. But women took admiration for granted. They might be offended or coy, but they understood, and welcomed him into a world of delicious interchange. All through the drive Clive was radiant. How happy normal people made their lives! On how little had he existed for twenty-four years! He chatted to his nurse, and felt her his for ever. He noticed the statues, the advertisements, the daily papers. Passing a cinema palace, he went in. The film was unbearable artistically, but the man who made it, the men and the women who looked on—they knew, and he was one of the them.

In no case could the exaltation have lasted. He was like one whose ears have been syringed; for the first few hours he hears super-normal sounds, which vanish when he adjusts himself to the human tradition. He had not gained a sense, but rearranged one, and life would not have appeared as a holiday for long. It saddened at once, for on his return Maurice was waiting for him, and a seizure resulted: like a fit, it struck at him from behind the brain. He murmured that he was too tired to talk, and escaped, and Maurice's illness gave him a further reprieve, during which he persuaded himself that their relations had not altered, and that he might without disloyalty contemplate women. He wrote affectionately and accepted the invitation to recruit, without misgivings.

He said he caught cold in the car; but in his heart he believed that the cause of his relapse was spiritual: to be with Maurice or anyone connected with him was suddenly revolting. The heat at dinner! The voices of the Halls! Their laughter! Maurice's anecdote! It mixed with the food—was the food. Unable to distinguish matter from spirit, he fainted.

But when he opened his eyes it was to the knowledge that love had died, so that he wept when his friend kissed him. Each kindness increased his suffering, until he asked the nurse to forbid Mr Hall to enter the room. Then he recovered and could fly to Penge, where he loved him as much as ever until he turned up.

He noticed the devotion, the heroism even, but his friend bored him. He longed for him to go back to town, and actually said so, so near the surface had the rock risen. Maurice shook his head and stopped.

Clive did not give in to the life spirit without a struggle. He believed in the intellect and tried to think himself back into the old state. He averted his eyes from women, and when that failed adopted childish and violent expedients. The one was this visit to Greece, the other—he could not recall it without disgust. Not until all emotion had ebbed would it have been possible. He regretted it deeply, for Maurice now inspired him with a physical dislike that made the future more difficult, and he wished to keep friends with his old lover, and to help him through the approaching catastrophe. It was all so complicated. When love flies it is remembered not as love but as something else. Blessed are the uneducated, who forget it entirely, and are never conscious of folly or pruriency in the past, of long aimless conversations.

25 Clive did not wire, nor start at once. Though desirous to be kind and training himself to think reasonably of Maurice, he refused to obey orders as of old. He returned to England at his leisure. He did wire from Folkestone to Maurice's office, and expected to be met at Charing Cross, and when he was not he took a train on to the suburbs, in order to explain as quickly as possible. His attitude was sympathetic and calm.

It was an October evening; the falling leaves, the mist, the hoot of an owl, filled him with pleasing melancholy. Greece had been clear but dead. He liked the atmosphere of the North, whose gospel is not truth, but compromise. He and his friend would arrange something that should include women. Sadder and older, but without a crisis, they would slip into a relation, as evening into night. He liked the night also. It had graciousness and repose. It was not absolutely dark. Just as he was about to lose his way up from the station, he saw another street lamp, and then past that another. There were chains in every direction, one of which he followed to his goal.

Kitty heard his voice, and came from the drawing-room to welcome him. He had always cared for Kitty least of the family —she was not a true woman, as he called it now—and she brought the news that Maurice was away for the night on business. "Mother and Ada are in church," she added. "They have had to walk because Maurice would take the car."

"Where has he gone?"

"Don't ask me. He leaves his address with the servants. We know even less about Maurice than when you were last here, if you think that possible. He has become a most mysterious person." She gave him tea, humming a tune.

Her lack of sense and of charm produced a not unwelcome reaction in her brother's favour. She continued to complain of him in the cowed fashion that she had inherited from Mrs Hall.

"It's only five minutes to church," remarked Clive.

"Yes, they would have been in to receive you if he had let us know. He keeps everything so secret, and then laughs at girls."

"It was I who did not let him know."

"What's Greece like?"

He told her. She was as bored as her brother would have been, and had not his gift of listening beneath words. Clive remembered how often he had held forth to Maurice and felt at the end an access of intimacy. There was a good deal to be saved out of the wreck of that passion. Maurice was big, and so sensible when once he understood.

Kitty proceeded, sketching her own affairs in a slightly clever way. She had asked to go to an Institute to acquire Domestic Economy, and her mother would have allowed her, but Maurice had put his foot down when he heard that the fees were three guineas a week. Kitty's grievances were mainly financial: she wanted an allowance. Ada had one. Ada, as heiress-apparent, had to "learn the value of money. But I am not to learn anything." Clive decided that he would tell his friend to treat the girl better; once before he had interfered, and Maurice, charming to the core, had made him feel he could say anything.

A deep voice interrupted them; the churchgoers were back. Ada came in, dressed in a jersey, tam o'shanter, and gray skirt; the autumn mist had left a delicate bloom upon her hair. Her cheeks were rosy, her eyes bright; she greeted him with obvious pleasure, and though her exclamations were the same as Kitty's they produced a different effect. "Why didn't you let us know?" she cried. "There will be nothing but the pie. We would have given you a real English dinner."

He said he must return to town in a few minutes but Mrs Hall insisted he should sleep. He was glad to do this. The house now filled with tender memories, especially when Ada spoke. He had forgotten she was so different from Kitty.

"I thought you were Maurice," he said to her. "Your voices are wonderfully alike."

"It's because I have a cold," she said, laughing.

"No, they are alike," said Mrs Hall. "Ada has Maurice's voice, his nose, by which of course I mean the mouth too, and his good spirits and good health. Three things, I often think of it. Kitty on the other hand has his brain."

All laughed. The three women were evidently fond of one another. Clive saw relations that he had not guessed, for they were expanding in the absence of their man. Plants live by the sun, yet a few of them flower at night-fall, and the Halls reminded him of the evening primroses that starred a deserted alley at Penge. When talking to her mother and sister, even Kitty had beauty, and he determined to rebuke Maurice about her; not unkindly, for Maurice was beautiful too, and bulked largely in this new vision.

The girls had been incited by Dr Barry to join an ambulance class, and after dinner Clive submitted his body to be bound. Ada tied up his scalp, Kitty his ankle, while Mrs Hall, happy and careless, repeated "Well, Mr Durham, this is a better illness than the last anyhow."

"Mrs Hall, I wish you would call me by my Christian name."

"Indeed I will. But Ada and Kitty—not you."

"I wish Ada and Kitty would too."

"Clive, then!" said Kitty.

"Kitty, then!"

"Clive."

"Ada—that's better." But he was blushing. "I hate formalities."

"So do I," came the chorus. "I care nothing for anyone's opinion—never did," and fixed him with candid eyes.

"Maurice on the other hand," from Mrs Hall, "is very particular."

"Maurice is a rip really—Waow, you're hurting my head."

"Waow, waow," Ada imitated.

There was a ring at the telephone.

"He has had your wire from the office," announced Kitty. "He wants to know whether you're here."

"Say I am."

"He's coming back tonight, then. Now he wants to talk to you."

Clive took the receiver, but only a burr arrived. They had been disconnected. They could not ring Maurice up as they did not know where he was, and Clive felt relieved, for the approach of reality alarmed him. He was so happy being bandaged: his friend would arrive soon enough. Now Ada bent over him. He saw features that he knew, with a light behind that glorified them. He turned from the dark hair and eyes to the unshadowed mouth or to the curves of the body, and found in her the exact need of his transition. He had seen more seductive women, but none that promised such peace. She was the compromise between memory and desire, she was the quiet evening that Greece had never known. No argument touched her, because she was tenderness, who reconciles present with past. He had not supposed there was such a creature except in Heaven, and he did not believe in Heaven. Now much had become possible suddenly. He lay looking into her eyes, where some of his hope lay reflected. He knew that he might make her love him, and the knowledge lit him with temperate fire. It was charming—he desired no more yet, and his only anxiety was lest Maurice should arrive, for a memory should remain a memory. Whenever the others ran out of the room to see whether that noise was the car, he kept her with him, and soon she understood that he wished this, and stopped without his command.

"If you knew what it is to be in England!" he said suddenly.

"Is Greece not nice?"

"Horrible."

She was distressed and Clive also sighed. Their eyes met.

"I'm so sorry, Clive."

"Oh, it's all over."

"What exactly was it—"

"Ada, it was this. While in Greece I had to reconstruct my life from the bottom. Not an easy task, but I think I've done it."

"We often talked of you. Maurice said you would like Greece."

"Maurice doesn't know—no one knows as much as you! I've told you more than anyone. Can you keep a secret?"

"Of course."

Clive was nonplussed. The conversation had become impossible. But Ada never expected continuity. To be alone with Clive, whom she innocently admired, was enough. She told him how thankful she was he had returned. He agreed, with vehemence. "Especially to return here."

"The car!" Kitty shrieked.

"Don't go!" he repeated, catching her hand.

"I must—Maurice—"

"Bother Maurice." He held her. There was a tumult in the hall. "Where's he gone?" his friend was roaring. "Where've you put him?"

"Ada, take me a walk tomorrow. See more of me. . . . That's settled."

Her brother burst in. Seeing the bandages, he thought there

had been an accident, then laughed at his mistake. "Come out of that, Clive. Why did you let them? I say, he looks well. You look well. Good man. Come and have a drink. I'll unpick you. No, girls, not you." Clive followed him, but, turning, had an imperceptible nod from Ada.

Maurice looked like an immense animal in his fur coat. He slipped it off as soon as they were alone, and came up smiling. "So you don't love me?" he challenged.

"All that must be tomorrow," said Clive, averting his eyes.

"Quite so. Have a drink."

"Maurice, I don't want a row."

"I do."

He waved the glass aside. The storm must burst. "But you mustn't talk to me like this," he continued. "It increases my difficulties."

"I want a row and I'll have it." He came in his oldest manner and thrust a hand into Clive's hair. "Sit down. Now why did you write me that letter?"

Clive did not reply. He was looking with growing dismay into the face he had once loved. The horror of masculinity had returned, and he wondered what would happen if Maurice tried to embrace him.

"Why? Eh? Now you're fit again, tell me."

"Go off my chair, and I will." Then he began one of the speeches he had prepared. It was scientific and impersonal, as this would wound Maurice least. "I have become normal—like other men, I don't know how, any more than I know how I was born. It is outside reason, it is against my wish. Ask any questions you like. I have come down here to answer them, for I couldn't go into details in my letter. But I wrote the letter because it was true."

"True, you say?"

"Was and is the truth."

"You say that you care for women only, not men?"

"I care for men, in the real sense, Maurice, and always shall."

"All that presently."

He too was impersonal, but he had not got off the chair. His fingers remained on Clive's head, touching the bandages, his mood had changed from gaiety to quiet concern. He was neither angry nor afraid, he only wanted to heal, and Clive, in the midst of repulsion, realized what a triumph of love was ruining, and how feeble or how ironical must be the power that governs Man.

"Who made you change?"

He disliked the form of the question. "No one. It was a change in me merely physical." He began to relate his experiences.

"Evidently the nurse," said Maurice thoughtfully. "I wish you had told me before. . . . I knew something had gone wrong and thought of several things, but not this. One oughtn't to keep secrets, or they get worse. One ought to talk, talk, talk—provided one has someone to talk to, as you and I have. If you'd have told me, you would have been right by now."

"Why?"

"Because I should have made you right."

"How?"

"You'll see," he said smiling.

"It's not the least good—I've changed."

"Can the leopard change his spots? Clive, you're in a muddle. It's part of your general health. I'm not anxious now, because you're well otherwise, you even look happy, and the rest must follow. I see you were afraid to tell me, lest it gave me pain, but we've got past sparing each other. You ought to have told me. What else am I here for? You can't trust anyone else. You and I are outlaws. All this"—he pointed to the middle-class comfort of the room—"would be taken from us if people knew."

He groaned. "But I've changed, I've changed."

We can only interpret by our experiences. Maurice could understand muddle, not change. "You only think you've changed," he said, smiling. "I used to think I had when Miss Olcott was here, but it all went when I returned to you."

"I know my own mind," said Clive, getting warm and freeing himself from the chair. "I was never like you."

"You are now. Do you remember how I pretended—"

"Of course I remember. Don't be childish."

"We love each other, and know it. Then what else—"

"Oh, for God's sake, Maurice, hold your tongue. If I love anyone it's Ada." He added, "I take her at random as an example."

But an example was the one thing Maurice could realize. "Ada?" he said, with a change of tone.

"Only to prove to you the sort of thing."

"You scarcely know Ada."

"Nor did I know my nurse or the other women I've mentioned. As I said before, it's no special person, only a tendency."

"Who was in when you arrived?"

"Kitty."

"But it's Ada, not Kitty."

"Yes, but I don't mean—Oh, don't be stupid!"

"What do you mean?"

"Anyhow, you understand, now," said Clive, trying to keep impersonal, and turning to the comforting words with which his discourse should have concluded. "I've changed. Now I want you to understand too that the change won't spoil anything in our friendship that is real. I like you enormously—more than any man I've ever met" (he did not feel this as he said it) "I most enormously respect and admire you. It's character, not passion, that is the real bond."

"Did you say something to Ada just before I came in? Didn't you hear my car come up? Why did Kitty and my mother come

out and not you? You must have heard my noise. You knew I
flung up my work for you. You never talked to me down the telephone. You didn't write or come back from Greece. How much
did you see of her when you were here before?"

"Look here, old man, I can't be cross-questioned."

"You said you could."

"Not about your sister."

"Why not?"

"You must shut up, I say. Come back to what I was saying
about character—the real tie between human beings. You can't
build a house on the sand, and passion's sand. We want bed
rock . . ."

"Ada!" he called, suddenly deliberate.

Clive shouted in horror. "What for?"

"Ada! Ada!"

He rushed at the door and locked it. "Maurice, it mustn't end
like this—not a row," he implored. But as Maurice approached
he pulled out the key and clenched it, for chivalry had awoken
at last. "You can't drag in a woman," he breathed; "I won't have
it."

"Give that up."

"I mustn't. Don't make it worse. No—no."

Maurice bore down on him. He escaped: they dodged round
the big chair, arguing for the key in whispers.

They touched with hostility, then parted for ever, the key
falling between them.

"Clive, did I hurt you?"

"No."

"My darling, I didn't mean to."

"I'm all right."

They looked at one another for a moment before beginning
new lives. "What an ending," he sobbed, "what an ending."

"I do rather love her," said Clive, very pale.

"What's going to happen?" said Maurice, sitting down and wiping his mouth. "Arrange . . . I'm done for."

Since Ada was in the passage Clive went out to her: to Woman was his first duty. Having appeased her with vague words, he returned to the smoking-room, but the door was now locked between them. He heard Maurice turn out the electric light and sit down with a thud.

"Don't be an ass anyway," he called nervously. There was no reply. Clive scarcely knew what to do. At any rate he could not stop in the house. Asserting a man's prerogative, he announced that he must sleep in town after all, in which the women acquiesced. He left the darkness within for that without: the leaves fell as he went to the station, the owls hooted, the mist enveloped him. It was so late that the lamps had been extinguished in the suburban roads, and total night without compromise weighed on him, as on his friend. He too suffered and exclaimed, "What an ending!" but he was promised a dawn. The love of women would rise as certainly as the sun, scorching up immaturity and ushering the full human day, and even in his pain he knew this. He would not marry Ada—she had been transitional—but some goddess of the new universe that had opened to him in London, someone utterly unlike Maurice Hall.

PART

Three

26 For three years Maurice had been so fit and happy that he went on automatically for a day longer. He woke with the feeling that it must be all right soon. Clive would come back, apologizing or not as he chose, and he would apologize to Clive. Clive must love him, because his whole life was dependent on love and here it was going on as usual. How could he sleep and rest if he had no friend? When he returned from town to find no news, he remained for a little calm, and allowed his family to speculate on Clive's departure. But he began to watch Ada. She looked sad—even their mother noticed it. Shading his eyes, he watched her. Save for her, he would have dismissed the scene as "one of Clive's long speeches", but she came into that speech as an example. He wondered why she was sad.

"I say—" he called when they were alone; he had no idea what he was going to say, though a sudden blackness should have warned him. She replied, but he could not hear her voice. "What's wrong with you?" he asked, trembling.

"Nothing."

"There is—I can see it. You can't take me in."

"Oh no—really, Maurice, nothing."

"Why did—what did he say?"

"Nothing."

"Who said nothing?" he yelled, crashing both fists on the table. He had caught her.

"Nothing—only Clive."

The name on her lips opened Hell. He suffered hideously and before he could stop himself had spoken words that neither ever forgot. He accused his sister of corrupting his friend. He let her suppose that Clive had complained of her conduct and gone back to town on that account. Her gentle nature was so outraged that she could not defend herself, but sobbed and sobbed, and implored him not to speak to her mother, just as if she were guilty. He assented: jealousy had maddened him.

"But when you see him—Mr Durham—tell him I didn't mean —say there's no one whom I'd rather—"

"—go wrong with," he supplied: not till later did he understand his own blackguardism.

Hiding her face, Ada collapsed.

"I shall not tell him. I shall never see Durham again to tell. You've the satisfaction of breaking up that friendship."

She sobbed, "I don't mind that—you've always been so unkind to us, always." He drew up at last. Kitty had said that sort of thing to him, but never Ada. He saw that beneath their obsequious surface his sisters disliked him: he had not even succeeded at home. Muttering "It's not my fault," he left her.

A refined nature would have behaved better and perhaps have suffered less. Maurice was not intellectual, nor religious, nor had he that strange solace of self-pity that is granted to some. Except on one point his temperament was normal, and he behaved as would the average man who after two years of happiness had been betrayed by his wife. It was nothing to him that Nature had caught up this dropped stitch in order to continue her pattern. While he had love he had kept reason. Now he saw Clive's change as treachery and Ada as its cause, and returned in a few hours to the abyss where he had wandered as a boy.

After this explosion his career went forward. He caught the

usual train to town, to earn and spend money in the old manner; he read the old papers and discussed strikes and the divorce
laws with his friends. At first he was proud of his self-control:
did not he hold Clive's reputation in the hollow of his hand?
But he grew more bitter, he wished that he had shouted while
he had the strength and smashed down this front of lies. What if
he too were involved? His family, his position in society—they
had been nothing to him for years. He was an outlaw in disguise.
Perhaps among those who took to the greenwood in old time
there had been two men like himself—two. At times he entertained the dream. Two men can defy the world.

Yes: the heart of his agony would be loneliness. He took time
to realize this, being slow. The incestuous jealousy, the mortification, the rage at his past obtuseness—these might pass, and
having done much harm they did pass. Memories of Clive might
pass. But the loneliness remained. He would wake and gasp
"I've no one!" or "Oh Christ, what a world!" Clive took to visiting
him in dreams. He knew there was no one, but Clive, smiling in
his sweet way, said "I'm genuine this time," to torture him. Once
he had a dream about the dream of the face and the voice, a
dream about it, no nearer. Also old dreams of the other sort, that
tried to disintegrate him. Days followed nights. An immense
silence, as of death, encircled the young man, and as he was going up to town one morning it struck him that he really was
dead. What was the use of money-grubbing, eating, and playing
games? That was all he did or had ever done.

"Life's a damn poor show," he exclaimed, crumpling up the
Daily Telegraph.

The other occupants of the carriage who liked him began to
laugh.

"I'd jump out of the window for twopence."

Having spoken, he began to contemplate suicide. There was

nothing to deter him. He had no initial fear of death, and no sense of a world beyond it, nor did he mind disgracing his family. He knew that loneliness was poisoning him, so that he grew viler as well as more unhappy. Under these circumstances might he not cease? He began to compare ways and means, and would have shot himself but for an unexpected event. This event was the illness and death of his grandfather, which induced a new state of mind.

Meanwhile, he had received letters from Clive, but they always contained the sentence, "We had better not meet just yet." He grasped the situation now—his friend would do anything for him except be with him; it had been thus ever since the first illness, and on these lines he was offered friendship in the future. Maurice did not cease to love, but his heart had been broken; he never had wild thoughts of winning Clive back. What he grasped he grasped with a firmness that the refined might envy, and suffered up to the hilt.

He answered these letters, oddly sincere. He still wrote what was true, and confided that he was unbearably lonely and should blow out his brains before the year ended. But he wrote without emotion. It was more a tribute to their heroic past, and accepted by Durham as such. His replies were unemotional also, and it was plain that, however much help he was given and however hard he tried, he could no longer penetrate into Maurice's mind.

27 Maurice's grandfather was an example of the growth that may come with old age. Throughout life he had been the ordinary business man—hard and touchy—but he retired not too late, and with surprising results. He took to "reading", and though the direct effects were grotesque, a softness was generated that transformed his character. The opinions of others—once to be contradicted or ignored—appeared worthy of note, and their desires worth humouring. Ida, his unmarried daughter, who kept house for him, had dreaded the time "when my father will have nothing to do", and herself impervious, did not realize that he had changed until he was about to leave her.

The old gentleman employed his leisure in evolving a new religion—or rather a new cosmogony, for it did not contradict chapel. The chief point was that God lives inside the sun, whose bright envelope consists of the spirits of the blessed. Sunspots reveal God to men, so that when they occurred Mr Grace spent hours at his telescope, noting the interior darkness. The incarnation was a sort of sunspot.

He was glad to discuss his discovery with anyone, but did not proselytize, remarking that each must settle for himself: Clive Durham, with whom he had once had a long talk, knew as much about his opinions as anyone. They were those of the practical man who tries to think spiritually—absurd and materialistic, but first hand. Mr Grace had rejected the tasteful accounts of the unseen that are handed out by the churches, and for that reason the hellenist had got on with him.

Now he was dying. A past of questionable honesty had faded, and he looked forward to joining those he loved and to be joined in due season by those whom he left behind. He summoned his late employees—men without illusions, but they "humoured the old hypocrite". He summoned his family, whom he had always treated well. His last days were very beautiful. To inquire into the causes of beauty were to inquire too closely, and only a cynic would dispel the blended Sorrow and Peace that perfumed Alfriston Gardens while a dear old man lay dying.

The relations came separately, in parties of two and three. All, except Maurice, were impressed. There was no intrigue, as Mr Grace had been open about his will, and each knew what to expect. Ada, as the favourite grandchild, shared the fortune with her aunt. The rest had legacies. Maurice did not propose to receive his. He did nothing to force Death on, but it waited to meet him at the right moment, probably when he returned.

But the sight of a fellow-traveller disconcerted him. His grandfather was getting ready for a journey to the sun, and, garrulous with illness, poured out to him one December afternoon. "Maurice, you read the papers. You've seen the new theory —" It was that a meteor swarm impinged on the rings of Saturn, and chipped pieces off them that fell into the sun. Now Mr Grace located the wicked in the outer planets of our system, and since he disbelieved in eternal damnation had been troubled how to extricate them. The new theory explained this. They were chipped off and reabsorbed into the good! Courteous and grave, the young man listened until a fear seized him that this tosh might be true. The fear was momentary, yet started one of those rearrangements that affect the whole character. It left him with the conviction that his grandfather was convinced. One more human being had come alive. He had accomplished an act of creation, and as he did so Death turned her head away. "It's a great thing to believe as you do," he said very sadly. "Since Cambridge I believe in nothing—except in a sort of darkness."

"Ah, when I was your age—and now I see a bright light—no electric light can compare to it."

"When you were my age, grandfather, what?"

But Mr Grace did not answer questions. He said, "Brighter than magnesium wire—the light within," then drew a stupid parallel between God, dark inside the glowing sun, and the soul, invisible inside the visible body. "The power within—the soul: let it out, but not yet, not till the evening." He paused. "Maurice, be good to your mother; to your sisters; to your wife and children; to your clerks, as I have." He paused again and Maurice grunted, but not disrespectfully. He was caught by the phrase "not till the evening, do not let it out till the evening." The old man rambled ahead. One ought to be good—kind—brave: all the old advice. Yet it was sincere. It came from a living heart.

"Why?" he interrupted. "Grandpapa, why?"

"The light within—"

"I haven't one." He laughed lest emotion should master him. "Such light as I had went out six weeks ago. I don't want to be good or kind or brave. If I go on living I shall be—not those things: the reverse of them. I don't want that either; I don't want anything."

"The light within—"

Maurice had neared confidences, but they would not have been listened to. His grandfather didn't, couldn't understand. He was only to get "the light within—be kind", yet the phrase continued the rearrangement that had begun inside him. Why *should* one be kind and good? For someone's sake—for the sake of Clive or God or the sun? But he had no one. No one except his mother mattered and she only a little. He was practically alone, and why should he go on living? There was really no reason, yet he had a dreary feeling he should, because he had not got Death either; she, like Love, had glanced at him for a minute, then turned away, and left him to "play the game". And he might have to play as long as his grandfather, and retire as absurdly.

28 His change, then, cannot be described as a conversion. There was nothing edifying about it. When he came home and examined the pistol he would never use, he was seized with disgust; when he greeted his mother no unfathomable love for her welled up. He lived on, miserable and misunderstood, as before, and increasingly lonely. One cannot write those words too often: Maurice's loneliness: it increased.

But a change there had been. He set himself to acquire new habits, and in particular those minor arts of life that he had neglected when with Clive. Punctuality, courtesy, patriotism, chivalry even—here were a few. He practised a severe self-discipline. It was necessary not only to acquire the art, but to know when to apply it, and gently to modify his behaviour. At first he could do little. He had taken up a line to which his family and the world were accustomed, and any deviation worried them. This came out very strongly in a conversation with Ada.

Ada had become engaged to his old chum Chapman, and his hideous rivalry with her could end. Even after his grandfather's death he had feared she might marry Clive, and gone hot with jealousy. Clive would marry someone. But the thought of him with Ada remained maddening, and he could scarcely have behaved properly unless it had been removed.

The match was excellent, and having approved of it publicly he took her aside, and said, "Ada, I behaved so badly to you,

dear, after Clive's visit. I want to say so now and ask you to forgive me. It's given a lot of pain since. I'm very sorry."

She looked surprised and not quite pleased; he saw that she
still disliked him. She muttered, "That's all over—I love Arthur
now."

"I wish I had not gone mad that evening, but I happened to be
very much worried about something. Clive never said what I let
you think he said either. He never blamed you."

"I don't care whether he did. It doesn't signify."

Her brother's apologies were so rare that she seized the opportunity to trample on him. "When did you last see him?"—
Kitty had suggested they had quarrelled.

"Not for some time."

"Those weekends and Wednesdays seem to have quite
stopped."

"I wish you happiness. Old Chappie's a good fellow. For two
people who are in love to marry strikes me as very jolly."

"It's very kind of you to wish me happiness, Maurice, I'm sure.
I hope I shall have it whether I am wished it or not." (This was
described to Chapman afterwards as a "repartee.") "I'm sure I
wish you the same sort of thing you've been wishing me all along
equally." Her face reddened. She had suffered a good deal, and
was by no means indifferent to Clive, whose withdrawal had
hurt her.

Maurice guessed as much and looked gloomily at her. Then
he changed the subject, and, being without memory, she recovered her temper. But she could not forgive her brother: indeed
it was not right that one of her temperament should, since he
had insulted her centrally, and marred the dawning of a love.

Similar difficulties arose with Kitty. She also was on his conscience, but was displeased when he made amends. He offered
to pay her fees at the Domestic Institute whereon her soul had

(142)

been so long set, and, though she accepted, it was ungraciously, and with the remark, "I expect I'm too old now to properly learn anything." She and Ada incited each other to thwart him in little things. Mrs Hall was shocked at first and rebuked them, but finding her son too indifferent to protect himself, she grew indifferent too. She was fond of him, but would not fight for him any more than she would fight against him when he was rude to the Dean. And so it happened that he was considered less in the house, and during the winter rather lost the position he had won at Cambridge. It began to be "Oh, Maurice won't mind—he can walk—sleep on the camp bed—smoke without a fire." He raised no objection—this was the sort of thing he now lived for—but he noted the subtle change and how it coincided with the coming of loneliness.

The world was likewise puzzled. He joined the Territorials—hitherto he had held off on the ground that the country can only be saved by conscription. He supported the social work even of the Church. He gave up Saturday golf in order to play football with the youths of the College Settlement in South London, and his Wednesday evenings in order to teach arithmetic and boxing to them. The railway carriage felt a little suspicious. Hall had turned serious, what! He cut down his expenses that he might subscribe more largely to charities—to preventive charities: he would not give a halfpenny to rescue work. What with all this and what with his stockbroking, he managed to keep on the go.

Yet he was doing a fine thing—proving on how little the soul can exist. Fed neither by Heaven nor by Earth he was going forward, a lamp that would have blown out, were materialism true. He hadn't a God, he hadn't a lover—the two usual incentives to virtue. But on he struggled with his back to ease, because dignity demanded it. There was no one to watch him, nor did he watch himself, but struggles like his are the supreme achievements of humanity, and surpass any legends about Heaven.

No reward awaited him. This work, like much that had gone before, was to fall ruining. But he did not fall with it, and the muscles it had developed remained for another use.

29 The crash came on a Sunday in spring—exquisite weather. They sat round the breakfast table, in mourning because of Grandpa, but otherwise worldly. Besides his mother and sisters, there was impossible Aunt Ida, who lived with them now, and a Miss Tonks, a friend whom Kitty had made at the Domestic Institute, and who indeed seemed its only tangible product. Between Ada and himself stood an empty chair.

"Oh, Mr Durham's engaged to be married," cried Mrs Hall, who was reading a letter. "How friendly of his mother to tell me. Penge, a county estate," she explained to Miss Tonks.

"That won't impress Violet, mother. She's a socialist."

"Am I, Kitty? Good news."

"You mean bad news, Miss Tonks," said Aunt Ida.

"Mother, who toom?"

"You will say 'Who toom' as a joke too often."

"Oh mother, get on, who is she?" asked Ada, having stifled a regret.

"Lady Anne Woods. You can read the letter for yourselves. He met her in Greece. Lady Anne Woods. Daughter of Sir H. Woods."

There was an outcry amongst the well-informed. It was subsequently found that Mrs Durham's sentence ran, "I will now tell you the name of the lady: Anne Woods: daughter of Sir H.

(145)

Woods." But even then it was remarkable, and owing to Greece romantic.

"Maurice!" said his aunt across the hubbub.

"Hullo!"

"That boy's late."

Leaning back in his chair he shouted "Dickie!" at the ceiling: they were putting up Dr Barry's young nephew for the week-end, to oblige.

"He doesn't even sleep above, so that's no good," said Kitty.

"I'll go up."

He smoked half a cigarette in the garden and returned. The news had nearly upset him after all. It had come so brutally, and —what hurt him as much—no one behaved as if it were his concern. Nor was it. Mrs Durham and his mother were the principals now. Their friendship had survived the heroic.

He was thinking, "Clive might have written: for the sake of the past he might", when his aunt interrupted him. "That boy's never come," she complained.

He rose with a smile. "My fault. I forgot."

"Forgot!" Everyone concentrated on him. "Forgot when you went out specially? Oh Morrie, you are a funny boy." He left the room, pursued by humorous scorn, and almost forgot again. "In there's my work," he thought, and a deadly lassitude fell on him.

He went upstairs with the tread of an older man, and drew breath at the top. He stretched his arms wide. The morning was exquisite—made for others: for them the leaves rustled and the sun poured into the house. He banged at Dickie Barry's door, and, as that seemed no use, opened it.

The boy, who had been to a dance the night before, remained asleep. He lay with his limbs uncovered. He lay unashamed, embraced and penetrated by the sun. The lips were parted, the down on the upper was touched with gold, the hair broken into countless glories, the body was a delicate amber. To anyone he would have seemed beautiful, and to Maurice who reached him by two paths he became the World's desire.

"It's past nine," he said as soon as he could speak.

Dickie groaned and pulled up the bedclothes to his chin.

"Breakfast—wake up."

"How long have you been here?" he asked, opening his eyes, which were all of him that was now visible, and gazing into Maurice's.

"A little," he said, after a pause.

"I'm awfully sorry."

"You can be as late as you like—it's only I didn't want you to miss the jolly day."

Downstairs they were revelling in snobbery. Kitty asked him whether he had known about Miss Woods. He answered "Yes" —a lie that marked an epoch. Then his aunt's voice arrived, was that boy never coming?

"I told him not to hurry," said Maurice, trembling all over.

"Maurice, you're not very practical, dear," said Mrs Hall.

"He's on a visit."

Auntie remarked that the first duty of a visitor was to conform to the rules of the house. Hitherto he had never opposed her, but now he said, "The rule of this house is that everyone does what they like."

"Breakfast is at half past eight."

"For those who like. Those who are sleepy like breakfast at nine or ten."

"No house could go on, Maurice. No servants would stop, as you will find."

"I'd rather servants went than my guests were treated like schoolboys."

"A schoolboy! Haw! He *is* one!"

"Mr Barry's now at Woolwich," said Maurice shortly.

Aunt Ida snorted, but Miss Tonks shot him a glance of respect. The others had not listened, intent on poor Mrs Durham, who would now only have the dower house. The loss of his temper left him very happy. In a few minutes Dickie joined them, and he rose to greet his god. The boy's hair was now flat from the bath, and his graceful body hidden beneath clothes, but he remained extraordinarily beautiful. There was a freshness about him—he might have arrived with the flowers—and he gave the impression of modesty and of good will. When he apologized to Mrs Hall, the note of his voice made Maurice shiver. And this was the child he wouldn't protect at Sunnington! This the guest whose arrival last night he had felt rather a bore.

So strong was the passion, while it lasted, that he believed the crisis of his life had come. He broke all engagements, as in the old days. After breakfast he saw Dickie to his uncle's, got arm in arm with him, and exacted a promise for tea. It was kept. Maurice abandoned himself to joy. His blood heated. He would not attend to the talk, yet even this advantaged him, for when he said "What?" Dickie came over to the sofa. He passed an arm round him. . . . The entrance of Aunt Ida may have averted disaster, yet he thought he saw response in the candid eyes.

They met once more—at midnight. Maurice was not happy now, for during the hours of waiting his emotion had become physical.

"I'd a latch key," said Dickie, surprised at finding his host up.

"I know."

There was a pause. Both uneasy, they were glancing at each other and afraid to meet a glance.

"Is it a cold night out?"

"No."

"Can I get you anything before I go up?"

"No, thanks."

Maurice went to the switches and turned on the landing light. Then he turned out the lights in the hall and sprang after Dickie, overtaking him noiselessly.

"This is my room," he whispered. "I mean generally. They've turned me out for you." He added, "I sleep here alone." He was conscious that words were escaping him. Having removed Dickie's overcoat he stood holding it, saying nothing. The house was so quiet that they could hear the women breathing in the other rooms.

The boy said nothing either. The varieties of development are endless, and it so happened that he understood the situation perfectly. If Hall insisted, he would not kick up a row, but he had rather not: he felt like that about it.

"I'm above," panted Maurice, not daring. "In the attic over this—if you want anything—all night alone. I always am."

Dickie's impulse was to bolt the door after him, but he dismissed it as unsoldierly, and awoke to the ringing of the breakfast bell, with the sun on his face and his mind washed clean.

30 This episode burst Maurice's life to pieces. Interpreting it by the past, he mistook Dickie for a second Clive, but three years are not lived in a day, and the fires died down as quickly as they had risen, leaving some suspicious ashes behind them. Dickie left on the Monday, and by Friday his image had faded. A client then came into the office, a lively and handsome young Frenchman, who implored Monsieur 'All not to swindle him. While they chaffed, a familiar feeling arose, but this time he smelt attendant odours from the abyss. "No, people like me must keep our noses to the grindstone, I'm afraid," he replied, in answer to the Frenchman's prayer to lunch with him, and his voice was so British that it produced shouts of laughter and a pantomime.

When the fellow had gone he faced the truth. His feeling for Dickie required a very primitive name. He would have sentimentalized once and called it adoration, but the habit of honesty had grown strong. What a stoat he had been! Poor little Dickie! He saw the boy leaping from his embrace, to smash through the window and break his limbs, or yelling like a maniac until help came. He saw the police—

"Lust." He said the word out loud.

Lust is negligible when absent. In the calm of his office Maurice expected to subdue it, now that he had found its name. His mind, ever practical, wasted no time in theological despair, but advanced to the grindstone. He had been forewarned, and therefore forearmed, and had only to keep away from boys and young men to ensure success. Yes, from other young men. Certain obscurities of the last six months became clear. For example, a pupil at the Settlement—He wrinkled his nose, as one who needs no further proof. The feeling that can impel a gentleman towards a person of lower class stands self-condemned.

He did not know what lay ahead. He was entering into a state that would only end with impotence or death. Clive had postponed it. Clive had influenced him, as always. It had been understood between them that their love, though including the body, should not gratify it, and the understanding had proceeded—no words were used—from Clive. He had been nearest to words on the first evening at Penge, when he refused Maurice's kiss, or on the last afternoon there, when they lay amid deep fern. Then had been framed the rule that brought the golden age, and would have sufficed till death. But to Maurice, despite his content, there had been something hypnotic about it. It had expressed Clive, not him, but now that he was alone he cracked hideously, as once at school. And it was not Clive who would heal him. That influence, even if exerted, would have failed, for a relation such as theirs cannot break without transforming both men for ever.

But he could not realize all this. The ethereal past had blinded him, and the highest happiness he could dream was a return to it. As he sat in his office working, he could not see the vast curve of his life, still less the ghost of his father sitting opposite. Mr Hall senior had neither fought nor thought; there had never been any occasion; he had supported society and moved without a crisis from illicit to licit love. Now, looking across at his son, he is touched with envy, the only pain that survives in the world of shades. For he sees the flesh educating the spirit, as his has never been educated, and developing the sluggish heart and the slack mind against their will.

Presently Maurice was called to the telephone. He raised it to his ear, and, after six months' silence, heard the voice of his only friend.

"Hullo," he began, "hullo, you will have heard my news, Maurice."

"Yes, but you didn't write, so I didn't."

"Quite so."

"Where are you now?"

"Off to a restaurant. We want you to come round there. Will you?"

"I'm afraid I can't. I've just refused one invitation to lunch."

"Are you too busy to talk a little?"

"Oh no."

Clive resumed, evidently relieved by the atmosphere. "My young woman's with me. Presently she'll talk too."

"Oh, all right. Tell me all your plans."

"The wedding's next month."

"Best of luck."

Neither could think of anything to say.

"Now for Anne."

"I'm Anne Woods," said a girl's voice.

"My name's Hall."

"What?"

"Maurice Christopher Hall."

"Mine's Anne Clare Wilbraham Woods, but I can't think of anything to say."

"No more can I."

"You're the eighth friend of Clive I've talked to in this way this morning."

"The eighth?"

"I can't hear."

"I said the eighth."

"Oh yes, now I'll give Clive a turn. Goodbye."

Clive resumed. "By the way, can you come down to Penge next week? It's short notice, but later all will be chaos."

"I'm afraid I can't do that very well. Mr Hill's getting married too, so that I'm more or less busy here."

"What, your old partner?"

"Yes, and after him Ada to Chapman."

"So I heard. How about August? Not September, that's almost certainly the by-election. But come in August and see us through that awful Park v. Village cricket match."

"Thanks, I probably could. You had better write nearer the time."

"Oh, of course. By the way, Anne has a hundred pounds in her pocket. Will you invest it for her?"

"Certainly. What does she fancy?"

"You'd better choose. She's not allowed to fancy more than four per cent."

Maurice quoted a few securities.

"I'd like the last one," said Anne's voice. "I didn't catch its name."

"You'll see it on the Contract Note. What's your address, please?"

She informed him.

"All right. Send the cheque when you hear from us. Perhaps I'd better ring off and buy at once."

He did so. Their intercourse was to run on these lines. However pleasant Clive and his wife were to him, he always felt that they stood at the other end of the telephone wire. After lunch he chose their wedding present. His instinct was to give a thumper, but since he was only eighth on the list of the bridegroom's friends, this would seem out of place. While paying three guineas he caught sight of himself in the glass behind the counter. What a solid young citizen he looked—quiet, honourable, prosperous without vulgarity. On such does England rely. Was it conceivable that on Sunday last he had nearly assaulted a boy?

31 As the spring wore away, he decided to consult a doctor. The decision—most alien to his temperament—was forced on him by a hideous experience in the train. He had been brooding in an ill-conditioned way, and his expression aroused the suspicions and the hopes of the only other person in the carriage. This person, stout and greasy-faced, made a lascivous sign, and, off his guard, Maurice responded. Next moment both rose to their feet. The other man smiled, whereupon Maurice knocked him down. Which was hard on the man, who was elderly and whose nose streamed with blood over the cushions, and the harder because he was now consumed with fear and thought Maurice would pull the alarm cord. He spluttered apologies, offered money. Maurice stood over him, black-browed, and saw in this disgusting and dishonourable old age his own.

He loathed the idea of a doctor, but he had failed to kill lust single-handed. As crude as in his boyhood, it was many times as strong, and raged in his empty soul. He might "keep away from young men", as he had naïvely resolved, but he could not keep away from their images, and hourly committed sin in his heart. Any punishment was preferable, for he assumed a doctor would punish him. He could undergo any course of treatment on the chance of being cured, and even if he wasn't he would be occupied and have fewer minutes for brooding.

Whom should he consult? Young Jowitt was the only doctor he knew well, and the day after that railway journey he managed to remark to him in casual tones, "I say, in your rounds here, do you come across unspeakables of the Oscar Wilde sort?" But Jowitt replied. "No, that's in the asylum work, thank God," which was discouraging, and perhaps it might be better to consult someone whom he should never see again. He thought of specialists, but did not know whether there were any for his disease, nor whether they would keep faith if he confided in them. On all other subjects he could command advice, but on this, which touched him daily, civilization was silent.

In the end he braved a visit to Dr Barry. He knew he should have a bad time, but the old man, though a bully and a tease, was absolutely trustworthy, and had been better disposed to him since his civilities to Dickie. They were in no sense friends, which made it easier, and he went so seldom to the house that it would make little difference were he forbidden it for ever.

He went on a cold evening in May. Spring had turned into a mockery, and a wretched summer was expected also. It was exactly three years since he had come here under balmy skies, to receive his lecture about Cambridge, and his heart beat quicker, remembering how severe the old man had been then. He found him in an agreeable mood, playing bridge with his daughter and wife, and urgent that Maurice should make a fourth in their party.

"I'm afraid I want to speak to you, sir," he said with an emotion so intense that he felt he should never accomplish the real words at all.

"Well, speak away."

"I mean professionally."

"Lord, man, I've retired from practice for the last six years. You go to Jericho or Jowitt. Sit down, Maurice. Glad to see you, shouldn't have guessed you were dying. Polly! Whisky for this fading flower."

Maurice remained standing, then turned away so oddly that Dr Barry followed him into the hall and said, "Hi, Maurice, can I seriously do anything for you?"

"I should think you can!"

"I've not even a consulting-room."

"It's an illness too awfully intimate for Jowitt—I'd rather come to you—you're the only doctor alive I dare tell. Once before I said to you I hoped I'd learn to speak out. It's about that."

"A secret trouble, eh? Well, come along."

They went into the dining-room, which was still strewn with dessert. The Venus de Medici in bronze stood on the mantelpiece, copies of Greuze hung on the walls. Maurice tried to speak and failed, poured out some water, failed again, and broke into a fit of sobbing.

"Take your time," said the old man quite kindly, "and remember of course that this is professional. Nothing you say will ever reach your mother's ears."

The ugliness of the interview overcame him. It was like being back in the train. He wept at the hideousness into which he had been forced, he who had meant to tell no one but Clive. Unable to say the right words, he muttered, "It's about women—"

Dr Barry leapt to a conclusion—indeed he had been there ever since they spoke in the hall. He had had a touch of trouble himself when young, which made him sympathetic about it. "We'll soon fix that up," he said.

Maurice stopped his tears before more than a few had issued, and felt the rest piled in an agonizing bar across his brain. "Oh, fix me for God's sake," he said, and sank into a chair, arms hanging. "I'm close on done for."

"Ah, women! How well I remember when you spouted on the platform at school . . . the year my poor brother died it was . . . you gaped at some master's wife . . . he's a lot to learn and life's a hard school, I remember thinking. Only women can teach us and there bad women as well as good. Dear, dear!" He cleared his throat. "Well, boy, don't be afraid of me. Only tell me the truth, and I'll get you well. When did you catch the beastly thing? At the Varsity?"

Maurice did not understand. Then his brow went damp. "It's nothing as filthy as that," he said explosively. "In my own rotten way I've kept clean."

Dr Barry seemed offended. He locked the door, saying, "Impotent, eh? Let's have a look," rather contemptuously.

Maurice stripped, throwing the garments from him in a rage. He had been insulted as he had insulted Ada.

"You're all right," was the verdict.

"What d'ye mean, sir, by all right?"

"What I say. You're a clean man. Nothing to worry about here."

He sat down by the fire, and, dulled though he was to impressions, Dr Barry noted the pose. It wasn't artistic, yet it could have been called superb. He sat in his usual position, and his body as well as his face seemed gazing indomitably at the flames. He wasn't going to knuckle under—somehow he gave that impression. He might be slow and clumsy, but if once he got what he wanted he would hold to it till Heaven and Earth blushed crimson.

"You're all right," repeated the other. "You can marry tomorrow if you like, and if you take an old man's advice you will. Cover up now, it's so draughty. What put all this into your head?"

"So you've never guessed," he said, with a touch of scorn in his terror. "I'm an unspeakable of the Oscar Wilde sort." His eyes closed, and driving clenched fists against them he sat motionless, having appealed to Caesar.

At last judgement came. He could scarcely believe his ears. It was "Rubbish, rubbish!" He had expected many things, but not this; for if his words were rubbish his life was a dream.

"Dr Barry, I can't have explained—"

"Now listen to me, Maurice, never let that evil hallucination, that temptation from the devil, occur to you again."

The voice impressed him, and was not Science speaking?

"Who put that lie into your head? You whom I see and know to be a decent fellow! We'll never mention it again. No—I'll not discuss. I'll not discuss. The worst thing I could do for you is to discuss it."

"I want advice," said Maurice, struggling against the overwhelming manner. "It's not rubbish to me, but my life."

"Rubbish," came the voice authoritatively.

"I've been like this ever since I can remember without knowing why. What is it? Am I diseased? If I am, I want to be cured, I can't put up with the loneliness any more, the last six months specially. Anything you tell me, I'll do. That's all. You must help me."

He fell back into his original position, gazing body and soul into the fire.

"Come! Dress yourself."

"I'm sorry," he murmured, and obeyed. Then Dr Barry unlocked the door and called, "Polly! Whisky!" The consultation was over.

32 Dr Barry had given the best advice he could. He had read no scientific works on Maurice's subject. None had existed when he walked the hospitals, and any published since were in German, and therefore suspect. Averse to it by temperament, he endorsed the verdict of society gladly; that is to say, his verdict was theological. He held that only the most depraved could glance at Sodom, and so, when a man of good antecedents and physique confessed the tendency, "Rubbish, rubbish!" was his natural reply. He was quite sincere. He believed that Maurice had heard some remark by chance, which had generated morbid thoughts, and that the contemptuous silence of a medical man would at once dispel them.

And Maurice went away not unimpressed. Dr Barry was a great name at home. He had twice saved Kitty and had attended Mr Hall through his last illness, and he was so honest and independent and never said what he did not feel. He had been their ultimate authority for nearly twenty years—seldom appealed to, but known to exist and to judge righteousness, and now that he pronounced "rubbish", Maurice wondered whether it might not be rubbish, though every fibre in him protested. He hated Dr Barry's mind; to tolerate prostitution struck him as beastly. Yet he respected it and went away inclined for another argument with destiny.

He was the more inclined for a reason that he could not tell to the doctor. Clive had turned towards women soon after he reached the age of twenty-four. He himself would be twenty-four in August. Was it possible that he would turn also . . . and now that he came to think, few men married before twenty-four. Maurice had the Englishman's inability to conceive variety. His troubles had taught him that other people are alive, but not yet that they are different, and he attempted to regard Clive's development as a forerunner of his own.

It would be jolly certainly to be married, and at one with society and the law. Dr Barry, meeting him on another day, said, "Maurice, you get the right girl—there'll be no more trouble then." Gladys Olcott recurred to him. Of course he was not a crude undergraduate now. He had suffered and explored himself, and knew he was abnormal. But hopelessly so? Suppose he met a woman who was sympathetic in other ways? He wanted children. He was capable of begetting children—Dr Barry had said so. Was marriage impossible after all? The topic was in the air at home, owing to Ada, and his mother would often suggest that he should find someone for Kitty and Kitty someone for him. Her detachment was amazing. The words "marriage," "love," "a family" had lost all meaning to her during widowhood. A concert ticket sent by Miss Tonks to Kitty revealed possibilities. Kitty could not use it, and offered it round the table. Maurice said he should like to go. She reminded him that it was his Club night, but he said he would cut that. He went, and it happened to be the symphony of Tchaikovsky Clive had taught him to like. He enjoyed the piercing and the tearing and the soothing—the music did not mean more to him than that—and they induced a warm feeling of gratitude towards Miss Tonks. Unfortunately, after the concert he met Risley.

"Symphonie Pathique," said Risley gaily.

"Symphony Pathetic," corrected the Philistine.

"Symphonie Incestueuse et Pathique." And he informed his young friend that Tchaikovsky had fallen in love with his own nephew, and dedicated his masterpiece to him. "I come to see all respectable London flock. Isn't it *supreme!*"

"Queer things you know," said Maurice stuffily. It was odd that when he had a confidant he didn't want one. But he got a life of Tchaikovsky out of the library at once. The episode of the composer's marriage conveys little to the normal reader, who vaguely assumes incompatibility, but it thrilled Maurice. He knew what the disaster meant and how near Dr Barry had dragged him to it. Reading on, he made the acquaintance of "Bob", the wonderful nephew to whom Tchaikovsky turns after the breakdown, and in whom is his spiritual and musical resurrection. The book blew off the gathering dust and he respected it as the one literary work that had ever helped him. But it only helped him backwards. He was where he had been in the train, having gained nothing except the belief that doctors are fools.

Now every avenue seemed blocked, and in his despair he turned to the practices he had abandoned as a boy, and found they did bring him a degraded kind of peace, did still the physical urge into which all his sensations were contracting, and enable him to do his work. He was an average man, and could have won an average fight, but Nature had pitted him against the extraordinary, which only saints can subdue unaided, and he began to lose ground. Shortly before his visit to Penge a new hope dawned, faint and unlovely. It was hypnotism. Mr Cornwallis, Risley told him, had been hypnotized. A doctor had said, "Come, come, you are no eunuch!" and lo! he had ceased to be one. Maurice procured the doctor's address, but did not suppose anything would come of it: one interview with the science sufficed him, and he always felt Risley knew too much; his voice when he gave the address was friendly but slightly amused.

33 Now that Clive Durham was safe from intimacy, he looked forward to helping his friend, who must have had a pretty rough time since they parted in the smoking-room. Their correspondence had ceased several months ago. Maurice's last had been written after Birmingham, and announced he should not kill himself. Clive had never supposed he would, and was glad the melodrama was over. When they talked down the telephone he heard a man whom he might respect at the other end of it—a fellow who sounded willing to let bygones be bygones and passion acquaintanceship. There was no affectation of ease; poor Maurice sounded shy, a bit huffy even, exactly the condition Clive deemed natural, and felt he could ameliorate.

He was anxious to do what he could. Though the quality of the past escaped him he remembered its proportions, and acknowledged that Maurice had once lifted him out of aestheticism into the sun and wind of love. But for Maurice he would never have developed into being worthy of Anne. His friend had helped him through three barren years, and he would be ungrateful indeed if he did not help his friend. Clive did not like gratitude. He would rather have helped out of pure friendliness. But he had to use the only tool he had, and if all went well, if Maurice kept unemotional, if he remained at the end of a telephone, if he was sound as regarded Anne, if he was not bitter, or too serious or too rough—then they might be friends again, though by a different route and in a different manner. Maurice had admirable qualities—he knew this, and the time might be returning when he would feel it also.

Such thoughts as the above occurred to Clive rarely and feebly. The centre of his life was Anne. Would Anne get on with his mother? Would Anne like Penge, she who had been brought up in Sussex, near the sea? Would she regret the lack of religious opportunities there? And the presence of politics? Besotted with love, he gave her his body and soul, he poured out at her feet all that an earlier passion had taught him, and could only remember with an effort for whom that passion had been.

In the first glow of his engagement, when she was the whole world to him, the Acropolis included, he thought of confessing to her about Maurice. She had confessed a peccadillo to him. But loyalty to his friend withheld him, and he was glad afterwards, for, immortal as Anne proved, she was not Pallas Athene, and there were many points on which he could not touch. Their own union became the chief of these. When he arrived in her room after marriage, she did not know what he wanted. Despite an elaborate education, no one had told her about sex. Clive was as considerate as possible, but he scared her terribly, and left feeling she hated him. She did not. She welcomed him on future nights. But it was always without a word. They united in a world that bore no reference to the daily, and this secrecy drew after it much else of their lives. So much could never be mentioned. He never saw her naked, nor she him. They ignored the reproductive and the digestive functions. So there would never be any question of this episode of his immaturity.

It was unmentionable. It didn't stand between him and her. She stood between him and it, and on second thoughts he was glad, for though not disgraceful it had been sentimental and deserved oblivion.

Secrecy suited him, at least he adopted it without regret. He had never itched to call a spade a spade, and though he valued the body the actual deed of sex seemed to him unimaginative, and best veiled in night. Between men it is inexcusable, between man and woman it may be practised since nature and society approve, but never discussed nor vaunted. His ideal of marriage was temperate and graceful, like all his ideals, and he found a fit helpmate in Anne, who had refinement herself, and admired it in others. They loved each other tenderly. Beautiful conventions received them—while beyond the barrier Maurice wandered, the wrong words on his lips and the wrong desires in his heart, and his arms full of air.

34 Maurice took a week's holiday in August and reached Penge according to invitation three days before the Park v. Village cricket match. He arrived in an odd and bitter mood. He had been thinking over Risley's hypnotist, and grew much inclined to consult him. It was such a nuisance. For instance, as he drove up through the park he saw a gamekeeper dallying with two of the maids, and felt a pang of envy. The girls were damned ugly, which the man wasn't: somehow this made it worse, and he stared at the trio, feeling cruel and respectable; the girls broke away giggling, the man returned the stare furtively and then thought it safer to touch his cap; he had spoilt that little game. But they would meet again when he had passed, and all over the world girls would meet men, to kiss them and be kissed; might it not be better to alter his temperament and toe the line? He would decide after his visit—for against hope he was still hoping for something from Clive.

"Clive's out," said the young hostess. "He sends you his love or something, and will be in to dinner. Archie London will look after you, but I don't believe you want looking after."

Maurice smiled and accepted some tea. The drawing-room had its old air. Groups of people stood about with the air of arranging something, and though Clive's mother no longer presided she remained in residence, owing to the dower house drains. The sense of dilapidation had increased. Through pouring rain he had noticed gate posts crooked, trees stifling, and indoors some bright wedding presents showed as patches on a threadbare garment. Miss Woods had brought no money to Penge. She was accomplished and delightful, but she belonged to the same class as the Durhams, and every year England grew less inclined to pay her highly.

"Clive's canvassing," she continued, "there'll be a by-election in the autumn. He has at last induced them to induce him to stand"; she had the aristocratic knack of anticipating criticism. "But seriously, it will be a wonderful thing for the poor if he gets in. He is their truest friend, if only they knew it."

Maurice nodded. He felt disposed to discuss social problems. "They want drilling a bit," he said.

"Yes, they need a leader," said a gentle but distinguished voice, "and until they find one they will suffer." Anne introduced the new rector, Mr Borenius. He was her own importation. Clive did not mind whom he appointed if the man was a gentleman and devoted himself to the village. Mr Borenius fulfilled both conditions, and as he was High Church might strike a balance against the outgoing incumbent, who had been Low.

"Oh Mr Borenius, how interesting!" the old lady cried from across the room. "But I suppose in your opinion we all want a leader. I quite agree." She darted her eyes hither and thither. "All of you want a leader, I repeat." And Mr Borenius's eyes followed hers, perhaps looking for something he did not find, for he soon took leave.

"He can't have anything to do at the Rectory," said Anne thoughtfully, "but he always is like that. He comes up to scold Clive about the housing, and won't stop to dinner. You see, he's so sensitive; he worries about the poor."

"I've had to do with the poor too," said Maurice, taking a piece of cake, "but I can't worry over them. One must give them a leg up for the sake of the country generally, that's all. They haven't our feelings. They don't suffer as we should in their place."

Anne looked disapproval, but she felt she had entrusted her hundred pounds to the right sort of stock broker.

"Caddies and a college mission in the slums is all I know. Still, I've learned a little. The poor don't want pity. They only really like me when I've got the gloves on and am knocking them about."

"Oh, you teach them boxing."

"Yes, and play football . . . they're rotten sportsmen."

"I suppose they are. Mr Borenius says they want love," said Anne after a pause.

"I've no doubt they do, but they won't get it."

"Mr Hall!"

Maurice wiped his moustache and smiled.

"You're *horrible*."

"I didn't think. I suppose that does sound so."

"But do you like being horrible?"

"One gets used to anything," he said, suddenly turning, for the door had blown open behind.

"Well, good gracious me, I scold Clive for being cynical, but you outdo him."

"I get used to being horrible, as you call it, as the poor do to their slums. It's only a question of time." He was speaking rather freely; a biting recklessness had come to him since his arrival. Clive hadn't bothered to be in to receive him. Very well! "After you've banged about a bit you get used to your particular hole. Everyone yapping at the start like a lot of puppies, Waou! Waou!" His unexpected imitation made her laugh. "At last you learn that everyone's far too busy to listen to you, so you stop yapping. That's a fact."

"A man's view," she said, nodding her head. "I'll never let Clive hold it. I believe in sympathy . . . in bearing one another's burdens. No doubt I'm unfashionable. Are you a disciple of Nietzsche?"

"Ask me another!"

Anne liked this Mr Hall, whom Clive had warned her she might find unresponsive. So he was in a way, but evidently he had personality. She understood why her husband had found him a good travelling companion in Italy. "Now why don't you like the poor?" she asked suddenly.

"I don't dislike them. I just don't think about them except when I'm obliged. These slums, syndicalism, all the rest of it, are a public menace, and one has to do one's little bit against them. But not for love. Your Mr Borenius won't face facts."

She was silent, then asked him how old he was.

"Twenty-four tomorrow."

"Well, you're very hard for your age."

"Just now you said I was horrible. You're letting me off very easily, Mrs Durham!"

"Anyhow, you're set, which is worse."

She saw him frown, and, fearing she had been impertinent, turned the talk on to Clive. She had expected Clive to be back by now, she said, and it was the more disappointing because to-morrow Clive would have to be really away. The agent, who knew the constituency, was showing him round. Mr Hall must be forgiving, and he must help them in the cricket match.

"It rather depends upon some other plans. . . . I might have to . . ."

She glanced at his face with a sudden curiosity, then said, "Wouldn't you like to see your room?—Archie, take Mr Hall to the Russet Room."

"Thanks. . . . Is there a post out?"

"Not this evening, but you can wire. Wire you'll stop. . . . Or oughtn't I to interfere?"

"I may have to wire—I'm not quite sure. Thanks frightfully."

Then he followed Mr London to the Russet Room, thinking "Clive might have . . . for the sake of the past he might have been here to greet me. He ought to have known how wretched I should feel." He didn't care for Clive, but he could suffer from him. The rain poured out of a leaden sky on to the park, the woods were silent. As twilight fell, he entered a new circle of torment.

He stopped up in the room till dinner, fighting with ghosts he had loved. If this new doctor could alter his being, was it not his duty to go, though body and soul would be violated? With the world as it is, one must marry or decay. He was not yet free of Clive and never would be until something greater intervened.

"Is Mr Durham back?" he inquired, when the housemaid brought hot water.

"Yes, sir."

"Just in?"

"No. About half an hour, sir."

She drew the curtains and hid the sight but not the sound of the rain. Meanwhile Maurice scribbled a wire. " 'Lasker Jones, 6 Wigmore Place, W.,' " he read. " 'Please make appointment Thursday. Hall. C/o Durham, Penge, Wiltshire.' "

"Yes, sir."

"Thanks so much," he said deferentially, and grimaced as soon as he was alone. There was now a complete break between his public and private actions. In the drawing-room he greeted Clive without a tremor. They shook hands warmly, Clive saying, "You look awfully fit. Do you know whom you are going to take in?" and introducing him to a girl. Clive had become quite the squire. All his grievances against society had passed since his marriage. Agreeing politically, they had plenty to talk about.

On his side, Clive was pleased with his visitor. Anne had reported him as "rough, but very nice"—a satisfactory condition. There was a coarseness of fibre about him, but that didn't matter now: that horrible scene about Ada could be forgotten. Maurice also got on well with Archie London—important, for Archie bored Anne and was the sort of man who could fix on to someone. Clive assigned them to each other, for the visit.

In the drawing-room they talked politics again, convinced every one of them that radicals are untruthful, and socialists mad. The rain poured down with a monotony nothing could disturb. In the lulls of conversation its whisper entered the room, and towards the end of the evening there was "tap, tap" on the lid of the piano.

"The family ghost again," said Mrs Durham with a bright smile.

"There's the sweetest hole in the ceiling," cried Anne. "Clive, can't we leave it?"

"We shall have to," he remarked, ringing the bell. "Let's shift our pianoforte though. It won't stand much more."

"How about a saucer?" said Mr London. "Clive, how about a saucer? Once the rain came through the ceiling of the club, I rang the bell and the servant brought a saucer."

"I ring the bell and the servant brings nothing," said Clive, pealing again. "Yes, we'll have a saucer, Archie, but we must move the piano too. Anne's dear little hole may grow in the night. There's only a lean-to roof over this part of the room."

"Poor Penge!" said his mother. All had risen to their feet, and were gazing at the leak. Anne began to probe the piano's entrails with blotting paper. The evening had broken up, and they were well content to make fun about the rain, which had sent them this hint of its presence.

"Bring a basin, will you," said Clive, when the bell was answered, "and a duster, and get one of the men to help shift the piano and take up the carpet in the bay. The rain's come through again."

"We had to ring twice, ring twice," remarked his mother.

"Le délai s'explique," she added, for when the parlourmaid returned it was with the keeper as well as the valet. "C'est toujours comme ça quand—we have our little idylls below stairs too, you know."

"You men, what do you want to do tomorrow?" said Clive to his guests. "I must go canvassing. Don't come too. It's beyond words dull. Like to take out a gun or what?"

"Very nice," said Maurice and Archie.

"Scudder, do you hear?"

"Le bonhomme est distrait," said his mother. The piano had rucked up a rug, and the servants, not liking to raise their voices before gentlefolk, misunderstood one another's orders, and whispered "What?"

"Scudder, the gentlemen'll shoot tomorrow—I'm sure I don't know what, but come round at ten. Shall we turn in now?"

"Early to bed's the rule here, as you know, Mr Hall," said Anne. Then she wished the three servants good night and led the way upstairs. Maurice lingered to choose a book. Might Lecky's *History of Rationalism* fill a gap? The rain dripped into the basin, the men muttered over the carpet in the bay, and, kneeling, seemed to celebrate some obsequy.

"Damnation, isn't there anything, anything?"

"—ish, he's not talking to us," said the valet to the gamekeeper.

Lecky it was, but his mind proved unequal, and after a few minutes he threw it on the bed and brooded over the telegram. In the dreariness of Penge his purpose grew stronger. Life had proved a blind alley, with a muck heap at the end of it, and he must cut back and start again. One could be absolutely transformed, Risley implied, provided one didn't care a damn for the past. Farewell, beauty and warmth. They ended in muck and must go. Drawing the curtains, he gazed long into the rain, and sighed, and struck his own face, and bit his own lips.

35 The next day was even drearier and the only thing to be said in its favour was that it had the unreality of a nightmare. Archie London chattered, the rain dribbled, and in the sacred name of sport they were urged after rabbits over the Penge estate. Sometimes they shot the rabbits, sometimes missed them, sometimes they tried ferrets and nets. The rabbits needed keeping down and perhaps that was why the entertainment had been forced on them: there was a prudent strain in Clive. They returned to lunch, and Maurice had a thrill: his telegram had arrived from Mr Lasker Jones, granting him an appointment for tomorrow. But the thrill soon passed. Archie thought they had better go after the bunnies again, and he was too depressed to refuse. The rain was now less, on the other hand the mist was thicker, the mud stickier, and towards tea time they lost a ferret. The keeper made out this was their fault, Archie knew better, and explained the matter to Maurice in the smoking-room with the aid of diagrams. Dinner arrived at eight, so did the politicians, and after dinner the drawing-room ceiling dripped into basins and saucers. Then in the Russet Room, the same weather, the same despair, and the fact that now Clive sat on his bed talking intimately did not make any difference. The talk might have moved him had it come earlier, but he had been so pained by the inhospitality, he had spent so lonely and so imbecile a day, that he could respond to the past no longer. His thoughts were all with Mr Lasker Jones, and he wanted to be alone to compose a written statement about his case.

Clive felt the visit had been a failure, but, as he remarked, "Politics can't wait, and you happen to coincide with the rush." He was vexed too at forgetting that today was Maurice's birthday—and was urgent that their guest should stop over the match. Maurice said he was frightfully sorry, but now couldn't, as he had this urgent and unexpected engagement in town.

"Can't you come back after keeping it? We're shocking hosts, but it's such a pleasure having you. Do treat the house as an hotel—go your way, and we'll go ours."

"The fact is I'm hoping to get married," said Maurice, the words flying from him as if they had independent life.

"I'm awfully glad," said Clive, dropping his eyes. "Maurice, I'm awfully glad. It's the greatest thing in the world, perhaps the only one—"

"I know." He was wondering why he had spoken. His sentence flew out into the rain; he was always conscious of the rain and the decaying roofs at Penge.

"I shan't bother you with talk, but I must just say that Anne guessed it. Women are extraordinary. She declared all along that you had something up your sleeve. I laughed, but now I shall have to give in." His eyes rose. "Oh Maurice, I'm so glad. It's very good of you to tell me—it's what I've always wished for you."

"I know you have."

There was a silence. Clive's old manner had come back. He was generous, charming.

"It's wonderful, isn't it?—the—I'm so glad. I wish I could think of something else to say. Do you mind if I just tell Anne?"

"Not a bit. Tell everyone," cried Maurice, with a brutality

that passed unnoticed. "The more the better." He courted external pressure. "If the girl I want won't, there's others."

Clive smiled a little at this, but was too pleased to be squeamish. He was pleased partly for Maurice, but also because it rounded off his own position. He hated queerness, Cambridge, the Blue Room, certain glades in the park were—not tainted, there had been nothing disgraceful—but rendered subtly ridiculous. Quite lately he had turned up a poem written during Maurice's first visit to Penge, which might have hailed from the land through the looking-glass, so fatuous it was, so perverse. "Shade from the old hellenic ships." Had he addressed the sturdy undergraduate thus? And the knowledge that Maurice had equally outgrown such sentimentality purified it, and from him also words burst as if they had been alive.

"I've thought more often of you than you imagine, Maurice my dear. As I said last autumn, I care for you in the real sense, and always shall. We were young idiots, weren't we?—but one can get something even out of idiocy. Development. No, more than that, intimacy. You and I know and trust one another just because we were once idiots. Marriage has made no difference. Oh, that's jolly, I do think—"

"You give me your blessing then?"

"I should think so!"

"Thanks."

Clive's eyes softened. He wanted to convey something warmer than development. Dare he borrow a gesture from the past?

"Think of me all tomorrow," said Maurice, "and as for Anne—she may think of me too."

So gracious a reference decided him to kiss the fellow very gently on his big brown hand.

Maurice shuddered.

"You don't mind?"

(175)

"Oh no."

"Maurice dear, I wanted just to show I hadn't forgotten the past. I quite agree—don't let's mention it ever again, but I wanted to show just this once."

"All right."

"Aren't you thankful it's ended properly?"

"How properly?"

"Instead of that muddle last year."

"Oh with you."

"Quits, and I'll go."

Maurice applied his lips to the starched cuff of a dress shirt. Having functioned, he withdrew, leaving Clive more friendly than ever, and insistent he should return to Penge as soon as circumstances allowed this. Clive stopped talking late while the water gurgled over the dormer. When he had gone Maurice drew the curtains and fell on his knees, leaning his chin upon the window sill and allowing the drops to sprinkle his hair.

"Come!" he cried suddenly, surprising himself. Whom had he called? He had been thinking of nothing and the word had leapt out. As quickly as possible he shut out the air and the darkness, and re-enclosed his body in the Russet Room. Then he wrote his statement. It took some time, and, though far from imaginative, he went to bed with the jumps. He was convinced that someone had looked over his shoulder while he wrote. He wasn't alone. Or again, that he hadn't personally written. Since coming to Penge he seemed a bundle of voices, not Maurice, and now he could almost hear them quarrelling inside him. But none of them belonged to Clive: he had got that far.

36 Archie London was also returning to town, and very early next morning they stood in the hall together waiting for the brougham, while the man who had taken them after rabbits waited outside for a tip.

"Tell him to boil his head," said Maurice crossly. "I offered him five bob and he wouldn't take it. Damned cheek!"

Mr London was scandalized. What were servants coming to? Was it to be nothing but gold? If so, one might as well shut up shop, and say so. He began a story about his wife's monthly nurse. Pippa had treated that woman more than an equal, but what can you expect with half educated people? Half an education is worse than none.

"Hear, hear," said Maurice, yawning.

All the same, Mr London wondered whether noblesse didn't oblige.

"Oh, try if you want to."

He stretched a hand into the rain.

"Hall, he took it all right, you know."

"Did he, the devil?" said Maurice. "Why didn't he take mine? I suppose you gave more."

With shame Mr London confessed this was so. He had increased the tip through fear of a snub. The fellow was the limit evidently, yet he couldn't think it was good taste in Hall to take the matter up. When servants are rude one should merely ignore it.

But Maurice was cross, tired, and worried about his appointment in town, and he felt the episode part of the ungraciousness of Penge. It was in the spirit of revenge that he strolled to the door, and said in his familiar yet alarming way, "Hullo! So five shillings aren't good enough! So you'll only take gold!" He was interrupted by Anne, who had come to see them off.

"Best of luck," she said to Maurice with a very sweet expression, then paused, as if inviting confidences. None came, but she added, "I'm so glad you're not horrible."

"Are you?"

"Men like to be thought horrible. Clive does. Don't you, Clive? Mr Hall, men are very funny creatures." She took hold of her necklace and smiled. "Very funny. Best of luck." By now she was delighted with Maurice. His situation, and the way he took it, struck her as appropriately masculine. "Now a woman in love," she explained to Clive on the doorstep, as they watched their guests start: "now a woman in love never bluffs—I wish I knew the girl's name."

Interfering with the house-servants, the keeper carried out Maurice's case to the brougham, evidently ashamed. "Stick it in then," said Maurice coldly. Amid wavings from Anne, Clive, and Mrs Durham, they started, and London recommenced the story of Pippa's monthly nurse.

"How about a little air?" suggested the victim. He opened the window and looked at the dripping park. The stupidity of so much rain! What did it *want* to rain for? The indifference of the universe to man! Descending into woods, the brougham toiled along feebly. It seemed impossible that it should ever reach the station, or Pippa's misfortune cease.

Not far from the lodge there was a nasty little climb, and the road, always in bad condition, was edged with dog roses that scratched the paint. Blossom after blossom crept past them, draggled by the ungenial year: some had cankered, others would never unfold: here and there beauty triumphed, but desperately, flickering in a world of gloom. Maurice looked into one after another, and though he did not care for flowers the failure irritated him. Scarcely anything was perfect. On one spray every flower was lopsided, the next swarmed with caterpillars, or bulged with galls. The indifference of nature! And her incompetence! He leant out of the window to see whether she couldn't bring it off once, and stared straight into the bright brown eyes of a young man.

"God, why there's that keeper chap again!"

"Couldn't be, couldn't have got here. We left him up at the house."

"He could have if he'd run."

"Why should he have run?"

"That's true, why should he have?" said Maurice, then lifted the flap at the back of the brougham and peered through it into the rose bushes, which a haze already concealed.

"Was it?"

"I couldn't see." His companion resumed the narrative at once, and talked almost without ceasing until they parted at Waterloo.

In the taxi Maurice read over his statement, and its frankness alarmed him. He, who could not trust Jowitt, was putting himself into the hands of a quack; despite Risley's assurances, he connected hypnotism with séances and blackmail, and had often growled at it from behind the *Daily Telegraph;* had he not better retire?

But the house seemed all right. When the door opened, the little Lasker Joneses were playing on the stairs—charming children, who mistook him for "Uncle Peter", and clung to his hands; and when he was shut into the waiting room with *Punch* the sense of the normal grew stronger. He went to his fate calmly. He wanted a woman to secure him socially and diminish his lust and bear children. He never thought of that woman as a positive joy—at the worst, Dickie had been that—for during the long struggle he had forgotten what Love is, and sought not happiness at the hands of Mr Lasker Jones, but repose.

That gentleman further relieved him by coming up to his idea of what an advanced scientific man ought to be. Sallow and expressionless, he sat in a large pictureless room before a roll-top desk. "Mr Hall?" he said, and offered a bloodless hand. His accent was slightly American. "Well, Mr Hall, and what's the trouble?" Maurice became detached too. It was as if they met to discuss a third party. "It's all down here," he said, producing the statement. "I've consulted one doctor and he could do nothing. I don't know whether you can."

The statement was read.

"I'm not wrong in coming to you, I hope?"

"Not at all, Mr Hall. Seventy-five per cent of my patients are of your type. Is that statement recent?"

"I wrote it last night."

"And accurate?"

"Well, names and place are a bit changed, naturally."

Mr Lasker Jones did not seem to think it natural. He asked several questions about "Mr Cumberland", Maurice's pseudonym for Clive, and wished to know whether they had ever united: on his lips it was curiously inoffensive. He neither praised nor blamed nor pitied: he paid no attention to a sudden outburst of Maurice's against society. And though Maurice yearned for sympathy—he had not had a word of it for a year— he was glad none came, for it might have shattered his purpose.

He asked, "What's the name of my trouble? Has it one?"

"Congenital homosexuality."

"Congenital how much? Well, can anything be done?"

"Oh, certainly, if you consent."

"The fact is I've an old-fashioned prejudice against hypnotism."

"I'm afraid you may possibly retain that prejudice after trying, Mr Hall. I cannot promise a cure. I spoke to you of my other patients—seventy-five per cent—but in only fifty per cent have I been successful."

The confession gave Maurice confidence, no quack would have made it. "We may as well have a shot," he said, smiling. "What must I do?"

"Merely remain where you are. I will experiment to see how deeply the tendency is rooted. You will return (if you wish) for regular treatment later. Mr Hall! I shall try to send you into a trance, and if I succeed I shall make suggestions to you which will (we hope) remain, and become part of your normal state when you wake. You are not to resist me."

"All right, go ahead."

Then Mr Lasker Jones left his desk and sat in an impersonal way on the arm of Maurice's chair. Maurice felt he was going to have a tooth out. For a little time nothing happened, but presently his eye caught a spot of light on the fire irons, and the rest of the room went dim. He could see whatever he was looking at, but little else, and he could hear the doctor's voice and his own. Evidently he was going into a trance, and the achievement gave him a feeling of pride.

"You're not quite off yet, I think."

"No, I'm not."

He made some more passes. "How about now?"

"I'm nearer off now."

"Quite?"

Maurice agreed, but did not feel sure. "Now that you're quite off, how do you like my consulting-room?"

"It's a nice room."

"Not too dark?"

"Rather dark."

"You can see the picture though, can't you?"

Maurice then saw a picture on the opposite wall, yet he knew that there was none.

"Have a look at it, Mr Hall. Come nearer. Take care of that crack in the carpet though."

"How broad is the crack?"

"You can jump it."

Maurice immediately located a crack, and jumped, but he was not convinced of the necessity.

"Admirable—now what do you suppose this picture is of, whom is it of—?"

"Whom is it of—"

"Edna May."

"Mr Edna May."

"No, Mr Hall, Miss Edna May."

"It's Mr Edna May."

"Isn't she beautiful?"

"I want to go home to my mother." Both laughed at this remark, the doctor leading.

"Miss Edna May is not only beautiful, she is attractive."

"She doesn't attract me," said Maurice pettishly.

"Oh Mr Hall, what an ungallant remark. Look at her lovely hair."

"I like short hair best."

"Why?"

"Because I can stroke it—" and he began to cry. He came to himself in the chair. Tears were wet on his cheeks, but he felt as usual, and started talking at once.

"I say, I had a dream when you woke me up. I'd better tell it you. I thought I saw a face and heard someone say, 'That's your friend.' Is that all right? I often feel it—I can't explain—sort of walking towards me through sleep, though it never gets up to me, that dream."

"Did it get near now?"

"Jolly near. Is that a bad sign?"

"No, oh no—you're open to suggestion, you're open—I made you see a picture on the wall."

Maurice nodded: he had quite forgotten. There was a pause, during which he produced two guineas, and asked for a second appointment. It was arranged that he should telephone next week, and in the interval Mr Lasker Jones wanted him to remain where he was in the country, quietly.

Maurice could not doubt that Clive and Anne would welcome him, nor that their influence would be suitable. Penge was an emetic. It helped him to get rid of the old poisonous life that had seemed so sweet, it cured him of tenderness and humanity. Yes, he'd go back, he said: he would wire to his friends and catch the afternoon express.

"Mr Hall, take exercise in moderation. A little tennis, or stroll about with a gun."

Maurice lingered to say, "On second thoughts perhaps I won't go back."

"Why so?"

"Well, it seems rather foolish to make that long journey twice in a day."

"You prefer then to stop in your own home?"

"Yes—no—no, all right, I will go back to Penge."

37 On his return he was amused to find that the young people were just off for twenty-four hours' electioneering. He now cared less for Clive than Clive for him. That kiss had disillusioned. It was such a trivial prudish kiss, and alas! so typical. The less you had the more it was supposed to be— that was Clive's teaching. Not only was the half greater than the whole—at Cambridge Maurice would just accept this—but now he was offered the quarter and told it was greater than the half. Did the fellow suppose he was made of paper?

Clive explained how he wouldn't be going had Maurice held out hopes of returning, and how he would be back for the match any way. Anne whispered, "Was the luck good?" Maurice replied, "So-so," whereupon she covered him with her wing and offered to invite his young lady down to Penge. "Mr Hall, is she very charming? I am convinced she has bright brown eyes." But Clive called her off, and Maurice was left to an evening with Mrs Durham and Mr Borenius.

Unusual restlessness was on him. It recalled the initial night at Cambridge, when he had been to Risley's rooms. The rain had stopped during his dash to town. He wanted to walk about in the evening and watch the sun set and listen to the dripping trees. Ghostly but perfect, the evening primroses were expanding in the shrubbery, and stirred him by their odours. Clive had shown him evening primroses in the past, but had never told

(184)

him they smelt. He liked being out of doors, among the robins and bats, stealing hither and thither bare-headed, till the gong should summon him to dress for yet another meal, and the curtains of the Russet Room close. No, he wasn't the same; a rearrangement of his being had begun as surely as at Birmingham, when Death had looked away, and to Mr Lasker Jones be all credit! Deeper than conscious effort there was a change, which might land him with luck in the arms of Miss Tonks.

As he wandered about, the man whom he had reprimanded in the morning came up, touched his cap, and inquired whether he would shoot tomorrow. Obviously he wouldn't, since it was the cricket match, but the question had been asked in order to pave the way for an apology. "I'm sure I'm very sorry I failed to give you and Mr London full satisfaction, sir," was its form. Maurice, vindictive no longer, said, "That's all right, Scudder." Scudder was an importation—part of the larger life that had come into Penge with politics and Anne; he was smarter than old Mr Ayres, the head keeper, and knew it. He implied that he hadn't taken the five shillings because it was too much; he didn't say why he had taken the ten! He added, "Glad to see you down again so soon, sir," which struck Maurice as subtly unsuitable, so he repeated, "That's all right, Scudder," and went in.

It was a dinner-jacket evening—not tails, because they would only be three—and though he had respected such niceties for years he found them suddenly ridiculous. What did clothes matter as long as you got your food, and the other people were good sorts—which they wouldn't be? And as he touched the carapace of his dress shirt a sense of ignominy came over him, and he felt he had no right to criticize anyone who lived in the open air. How dry Mrs Durham seemed—she was Clive with the sap perished. And Mr Borenius—how dry! Though to do Mr Borenius justice he contained surprises. Contemptuous of all parsons,

Maurice had paid little attention to this one, and was startled when he came out strong after dessert. He had assumed that as rector of the parish he would be helping Clive in the election. But "I vote for no one who is not a communicant, as Mr Durham understands."

"The Rads are attacking your church, you know," was all he could think of.

"That is why I do not vote for the Radical candidate. He is a Christian, so naturally I should have done."

"Bit particular, sir, if I may say so. Clive will do all the things you want done. You may be lucky he isn't an atheist. There are a certain amount of those about, you know!"

He smiled in response, saying, "The atheist is nearer the Kingdom of Heaven than the hellenist. 'Unless ye become as little children'—and what is the atheist but a child?"

Maurice looked at his hands, but before he could frame a reply the valet came in to ask whether he had any orders for the keeper.

"I saw him before dinner, Simcox. Nothing, thanks. Tomorrow's the match. I did tell him."

"Yes, but he wonders whether you'd care to go down to the pond between the innings for a bathe, sir, now that the weather had altered. He has just bailed out the boat."

"Very good of him."

"If that's Mr Scudder may I speak to him?" asked Mr Borenius.

"Will you tell him, Simcox? Also tell him I shan't be bathing." When the valet had gone he said, "Would you rather speak to him here? Have him in as far as I'm concerned."

"Thank you, Mr Hall, but I'll go out. He'll prefer the kitchen."

"He'll prefer it no doubt. There are fair young females in the kitchen."

"Ah! Ah!" He had the air of one to whom sex occurs for the

first time. "You don't happen to know whether he has anyone in view matrimonially, do you?"

" 'Fraid I don't . . . saw him kissing two girls at once on my arrival if that's any help."

"It sometimes happens that those men get confidential out shooting. The open air, the sense of companionship—"

"They don't get confidential with me. Archie London and I got rather fed up with him yesterday as a matter of fact. Too anxious to boss the show. We found him a bit of a swine."

"Excuse the inquiry."

"What's there to excuse?" said Maurice, annoyed with the rector for alluding so smugly to the open air.

"Speaking frankly, I should be glad to see that particular young man settled with a helpmate before he sails." Smiling gently, he added, "And all young men."

"What's he sailing for?"

"He is to emigrate." And intoning "to emigrate" in a particular irritating way, he repaired to the kitchen.

Maurice strolled for five minutes in the shrubbery. Food and wine had heated him, and he thought with some inconsequence that even old Chapman had sown some wild oats. He alone— Clive admonishing—combined advanced thought with the conduct of a Sunday scholar. He wasn't Methuselah—he'd a right to a fling. Oh those jolly scents, those bushes where you could hide, that sky as black as the bushes! They were turning away from him. Indoors was his place and there he'd moulder, a respectable pillar of society who has never had the chance to misbehave. The alley that he was pacing opened through a swing gate into the park, but the damp grass there might dull his pumps, so he felt bound to return. As he did so he struck against corduroys, and was held for a moment by both elbows; it had been Scudder escaping from Mr Borenius. Released, he continued his dreamings. Yesterday's shoot, which at the time had made little impression on him, began faintly to glow, and he realized that even during its boredom he had been alive. He felt back from it to the incidents of his arrival, such as the piano-moving: then forwards to the incidents of today, beginning with the five shillings' tip and ending with now. And when he reached "now", it was as if an electric current passed through the chain of insignificant events so that he dropped it and let it smash back into darkness. "Damnation, what a night," he resumed while puffs of air touched him and one another. Then the swing gate in the distance, which had been tinkling for a little, seemed to slam against freedom, and he went indoors.

"Oh Mr Hall!" cried the old lady. "How exquisite is your coiffure."

"My coiffure?" He found that his head was all yellow with evening primrose pollen.

"Oh, don't brush it off. I like it on your black hair. Mr Borenius, is he not quite bacchanalian?"

The clergyman raised sightless eyes. He had been interrupted in the middle of a serious talk. "But Mrs Durham," he persisted. "I understood so distinctly from you that all your servants had been confirmed."

"I thought so, Mr Borenius, I did think so."

"Yet I go into the kitchen, and straight away I discover Simcox, Scudder, and Mrs Wetherall. For Simcox and Mrs Wetherall I can make arrangements. Scudder is the serious case, because I have not time to prepare him properly before he sails, even if the bishop could be prevailed upon."

Mrs Durham tried to be grave, but Maurice, whom she rather liked, was laughing. She suggested that Mr Borenius should give Scudder a note to some clergyman abroad—there was bound to be one.

"Yes, but will he present it? He shows no hostility to the Church, but will he be bothered? Had I only been told which of your servants had been confirmed and which had not, this crisis would not have arisen."

"Servants are so inconsiderate," said the old lady. "They tell me nothing. Why, Scudder sprung his notice on Clive in just the same way. His brother invites him. So off he goes. Now Mr Hall, let's have your advice over this crisis: what would you do?"

"Our young friend condemns the entire Church, militant and triumphant."

Maurice roused himself. If the parson hadn't looked so damned ugly he wouldn't have bothered, but he couldn't stand that squinny face sneering at youth. Scudder cleaned a gun, carried a suitcase, baled out a boat, emigrated—did something anyway, while gentlefolk squatted on chairs finding fault with his soul. If he did cadge for tips it was natural, and if he didn't, if his apology was genuine—why then he was a fine fellow. He'd speak anyhow. "How do you know he'll communicate if he's confirmed?" he said. "I don't communicate." Mrs Durham hummed a tune; this was going too far.

"But you were given the opportunity. The priest did what he could for you. He has not done what he could for Scudder and consequently the Church is to blame. That is why I make so much of a point which must appear very trivial to you."

"I'm awfully stupid, but I think I see: you want to make sure that he and not the Church shall be to blame in the future. Well, sir, that may be your idea of religion but it isn't mine and it wasn't Christ's."

It was as smart a speech as he had ever made; since the hypnotism his brain had known moments of unusual power. But Mr Borenius was unassailable. He replied pleasantly, "The unbeliever has always such a very clear idea as to what Belief ought to be, I wish I had half his certainty." Then he arose and went, and Maurice walked him through the short cut through the kitchen garden. Against the wall leant the subject of their deliberations, no doubt awaiting one of the maids; he appeared to be haunting the premises this evening. Maurice would have seen nothing, so thick now was the darkness; it was Mr Borenius who exacted a low "Good night, sir" for them both. A delicate scent of fruit perfumed the air; it had further to be feared that the young man had stolen an apricot. Scents were everywhere that night, despite the cold, and Maurice returned via the shrubbery, that he might inhale the evening primroses.

Again he heard the cautious "Good night, sir," and feeling friendly to the reprobate replied, "Good night, Scudder, they tell me you're emigrating."

"That's my idea, sir," came the voice.

"Well, good luck to you."

"Thank you, sir, it seems rather strange."

"Canada or Australia, I suppose."

"No, sir, the Argentine."

"Ah, ah, a fine country."

"Have you visited it yourself, sir?"

"Rather not, England for me," said Maurice, strolling on and again colliding with corduroys. Dull talk, unimportant meeting, yet they harmonized with the darkness, the quietness of the hour, they suited him, and as he walked away he was followed by a sense of well-being which lasted until he reached the house. Through its window he could see Mrs Durham all relaxed and ugly. Her face clicked into position as he entered, so did his own, and they exchanged a few affected remarks about his day in town, before parting for bed.

He had taken to sleeping badly during the past year, and knew as soon as he lay down that this would be a night of physical labour. The events of the last twelve hours had excited him, and clashed against one another in his mind. Now it was the early start, now the journey with London, the interview, the return; and at the back of all lurked a fear that he had not said something at that interview that he ought to have said, that he had missed out something vital from his confession to the doctor. Yet what was it? He had drawn up the statement yesterday in this very room, and been satisfied at the time. He began to worry—which Mr Lasker Jones had forbidden him to do, because the introspective are more difficult to heal: he was supposed to lie fallow to the suggestions sown during the trance, and never wonder whether they would germinate or not. But he could not help worrying, and Penge, instead of numbing, seemed more stimulating than most places. How vivid, if complex, were its impressions, how the tangle of flowers and fruit wreathed his brain! Objects he had never seen, such as rain water baled from a boat, he could see tonight, though curtained in tightly. Ah to get out to them! Ah for darkness—not the darkness of a house which coops up a man among furniture, but the darkness where he can be free! Vain wish! He had paid a doctor two guineas to draw the curtains tighter, and presently, in the brown cube of such a room, Miss Tonks would lie prisoned beside him. And, as the yeast of the trance continued to work, Maurice had the illusion of a portrait that changed, now at his will, now against it, from male to female, and came leaping down the football-field where he bathed. . . . He moaned, half asleep. There was something better in life than this rubbish, if only he could get to it—love—nobility—big spaces where passion clasped peace, spaces no science could reach, but they existed for ever, full of woods some of them, and arched with majestic sky and a friend. . . .

He really was asleep when he sprang up and flung wide the

curtains with a cry of "Come!" The action awoke him; what had he done that for? A mist covered the grass of the park, and the tree trunks rose out of it like the channel marks in the estuary near his old private school. It was jolly cold. He shivered and clenched his fists. The moon had risen. Below him was the drawing-room, and the men who were repairing the tiles on the roof of the bay had left their ladder resting against his window sill. What had they done that for? He shook the ladder and glanced into the woods, but the wish to go into them vanished as soon as he could go. What use was it? He was too old for fun in the damp.

But as he returned to his bed a little noise sounded, a noise so intimate that it might have arisen inside his own body. He seemed to crackle and burn and saw the ladder's top quivering against the moonlit air. The head and the shoulders of a man rose up, paused, a gun was leant against the window sill very carefully, and someone he scarcely knew moved towards him and knelt beside him and whispered, "Sir, was you calling out for me? . . . Sir, I know. . . . I know," and touched him.

PART

Four

38 "Had I best be going now, sir?"

Abominably shy, Maurice pretended not to hear.

"We mustn't fall asleep though, awkward if anyone came in," he continued, with a pleasant blurred laugh that made Maurice feel friendly but at the same time diffident and sad. He managed to reply, "You mustn't call me sir," and the laugh sounded again, as if brushing aside such problems. There seemed to be charm and insight, yet his discomfort increased.

"May I ask your name?" he said awkwardly.

"I'm Scudder."

"I know you're Scudder—I meant your other name."

"Only Alec just."

"Jolly name to have."

"It's only my name."

"I'm called Maurice."

"I saw you when you first drove up, Mr Hall, wasn't it Tuesday, I did think you looked at me angry and gentle both together."

"Who were those people with you?" said Maurice, after a pause.

"Oh that wor only Mill, that wor Milly's cousin. Then do you remember the piano got wet the same evening, and you had great trouble to suit yourself over a book, didn't read it, did you either."

"How ever did you know I didn't read my book?"

"Saw you leaning out of the window instead. I saw you the next night too. I was out on the lawn."

"Do you mean you were out in all that infernal rain?"

"Yes . . . watching . . . oh, that's nothing, you've got to watch, haven't you . . . see, I've not much longer in this country, that's how I kep putting it."

"How beastly I was to you this morning!"

"Oh that's nothing—Excuse the question but is that door locked?"

"I'll lock it." As he did so, the feeling of awkwardness returned. Whither was he tending, from Clive into what companionship?

Presently they fell asleep.

They slept separate at first, as if proximity harassed them, but towards morning a movement began, and they woke deep in each other's arms. "Had I best be going now?" he repeated, but Maurice, through whose earlier night had threaded the dream "Something is a little wrong and had better be," was resting utterly at last, and murmured "No, no."

"Sir, the church has gone four, you'll have to release me."

"Maurice, I'm Maurice."

"But the church has—"

"Damn the church."

He said, "I've the cricket pitch to help roll for the match," but did not move, and seemed in the faint gray light to be smiling proudly. "I have the young birds too—the boat's done—Mr London and Mr Fetherstonhaugh dived splack into the water lilies—they told me all young gentlemen can dive—I never learned to. It seems more natural like not to let the head get under the water. I call that drowning before your day."

"I was taught I'd be ill if I didn't wet my hair."

"Well, you was taught what wasn't the case."

"I expect so—it's a piece with all else I was taught. A master I used to trust as a kid taught me it. I can still remember walking on the beach with him . . . oh dear! And the tide came up, all beastly gray . . ." He shook himself fully awake, as he felt his companion slip from him. "Don't, why did you?"

"There's the cricket—"

"No, there's not the cricket—You're going abroad."

"Well, we'll find another opportunity before I do."

"If you'll stop, I'll tell you my dream. I dreamt of an old grandfather of mine. He was a queer card. I wonder what you'd have made of him. He used to think dead people went to the sun, but he treated his own employees badly."

"I dreamt the Reverend Borenius was trying to drown me, and now really I must go, I can't talk about dreams, don't you see, or I'll catch it from Mr Ayres."

"Did you ever dream you'd a friend, Alec? Nothing else but just 'my friend', he trying to help you and you him. A friend," he repeated, sentimental suddenly. "Someone to last your whole life and you his. I suppose such a thing can't really happen outside sleep."

But the moment for speech had passed. Class was calling, the crack in the floor must reopen at sunrise. When he reached the window Maurice called, "Scudder," and he turned like a well-trained dog.

"Alec, you're a dear fellow and we've been very happy."

"You get some sleep, there's no hurry in your case," he said kindly, and took up the gun that had guarded them through the night. The tips of the ladder quivered against the dawn as he descended, then were motionless. There was a tiny crackle from the gravel, a tiny clink from the fence that divided garden and park: then all was as if nothing had been, and silence absolute filled the Russet Room, broken after a time by the sounds of a new day.

39 Having unlocked the door, Maurice dashed back into bed.

"Curtains drawn, sir, nice air, nice day for the match," said Simcox entering in some excitement with the tea. He looked at the head of black hair that was all the visitor showed. No answer came, and, disappointed of the morning chat Mr Hall had hitherto accorded, he gathered up the dinner-jacket and its appurtenances, and took them away to brush.

Simcox and Scudder; two servants. Maurice sat up and drank a cup of tea. He would have to give Scudder some handsome present now, indeed he would like to, but what should it be? What could one give a man in that position? Not a motor-bike. Then he remembered that he was emigrating, which made the problem easier. But the anxious look remained on his face, for he was wondering whether Simcox had been surprised at finding the door locked. Also had he meant anything by "Curtains drawn, sir"? Voices sounded under his window. He tried to drowse again, but the acts of other men had impinged.

"Now what will you wear, sir, I wonder?" inquired Simcox, returning. "You'll put on your cricketing flannels straight away perhaps; that rather than the tweed."

"All right."

"College blazer with them, sir?"

"No—never mind."

"Very good, sir." He straightened out a pair of socks and continued meditatively: "Oh, they've moved that ladder at last, I see. About time." Maurice then saw that the tips against the sky had disappeared. "I could have sworn it was here when I brought in your tea, sir. Still, one can never be certain."

"No, one can't," agreed Maurice, speaking with difficulty and with the sense that he had lost his bearings. He felt relief when Simcox had left, but it was overshadowed by the thought of Mrs Durham and the breakfast table, and by the problem of a suitable present for his late companion. It couldn't be a cheque, lest suspicions were aroused when it was cashed. As he dressed, the trickle of discomfort gathered force. Though not a dandy, he had the suburban gentleman's usual show of toilet appliances, and they all seemed alien. Then the gong boomed, and just as he was going down to breakfast he saw a flake of mud close to the window sill. Scudder had been careful, but not careful enough. He was headachy and faint when, clothed all in white, he at last descended to take his place in society.

Letters—a pile of them, and all subtly annoying. Ada, most civil. Kitty, saying his mother looked done up. Aunt Ida—a postcard—wanting to know whether the chauffeur was supposed to obey orders, or had one misunderstood?, business fatuities, circulars about the College Mission, the Territorial training, the Golf Club, and the Property Defence Association. He bowed humorously over them to his hostess. When she scarcely responded, he went hot round his mouth. It was only that Mrs Durham's own letters worried her. But he did not know this, and was carried out further by the current. Each human being seemed new, and terrified him: he spoke to a race whose nature and numbers were unknown, and whose very food tasted poisonous.

After breakfast Simcox returned to the charge. "Sir, in Mr

Durham's absence the servants feel—we should be so honoured if you would captain us against the Village in the forthcoming 'Park versus Village' match."

"I'm not a cricketer, Simcox. Who's your best bat?"

"We have no one better than the under gamekeeper."

"Then make the under gamekeeper captain."

Simcox lingered to say, "Things always go better under a gentleman."

"Tell them to put me to field deep—and I won't bat first: about eighth if he likes—not first. You might tell him, as I shan't come down till it's time." He closed his eyes, feeling sickish. He had created something whose nature he ignored. Had he been theologically minded, he would have named it remorse, but he kept a free soul, despite confusion.

Maurice hated cricket. It demanded a snickety neatness he could not supply; and, though he had often done it for Clive's sake, he disliked playing with his social inferiors. Footer was different—he could give and take there—but in cricket he might be bowled or punished by some lout, and he felt it unsuitable. Hearing his side had won the toss, he did not go down for half an hour. Mrs Durham and one or two friends already sat in the shed. They were all very quiet. Maurice squatted at their feet, and watched the game. It was exactly like other years. The rest of his side were servants and had gathered a dozen yards away round old Mr Ayres, who was scoring: old Mr Ayres always scored.

"The captain has put himself in first," said a lady. "A gentleman would never have done that. Little points interest me."

Maurice said, "The captain's our best man, apparently."

She yawned and presently criticized: she'd an instinct that man was conceited. Her voice fell idly into the summer air. He was emigrating, said Mrs Durham—the more energetic did—

which turned them to politics and Clive. His chin on his knees, Maurice brooded. A storm of distaste was working up inside him, and he did not know against what to direct it. Whether the ladies spoke, whether Alec blocked Mr Borenius's lobs, whether the villagers clapped or didn't clap, he felt unspeakably oppressed: he had swallowed an unknown drug: he had disturbed his life to its foundations, and couldn't tell what would crumble.

When he went out to bat, it was a new over, so that Alec received first ball. His style changed. Abandoning caution, he swiped the ball into the fern. Lifting his eyes, he met Maurice's and smiled. Lost ball. Next time he hit a boundary. He was untrained, but had the cricketing build, and the game took on some semblance of reality. Maurice played up too. His mind had cleared, and he felt that they were against the whole world, that not only Mr Borenius and the field but the audience in the shed and all England were closing round the wickets. They played for the sake of each other and their fragile relationship —if one fell the other would follow. They intended no harm to the world, but so long as it attacked they must punish, they must stand wary, then hit with full strength, they must show that when two are gathered together majorities shall not triumph. And as the game proceeded it connected with the night, and interpreted it. Clive ended it easily enough. When he came to the ground they were no longer the leading force; people turned their heads, the game languished, and ceased. Alec resigned. It was only fit and proper that the squire should bat at once. Without looking at Maurice, he receded. He too was in white flannels, and their looseness made him look like a gentleman or anyone else. He stood in front of the shed with dignity, and when Clive had done talking offered his bat, which Clive took as a matter of course: then flung himself down by old Ayres.

Maurice met his friend, overwhelmed with spurious tenderness.

"Clive. . . . Oh my dear, are you back? Aren't you fagged frightfully?"

"Meetings till midnight—another this afternoon—must bat a minute to please these people."

"What! Leaving me again? How frightfully rotten."

"You may well say so, but I really do come back this evening, then your visit really does begin. I've a hundred things to ask you, Maurice."

"Now, gentlemen," said a voice; it was the socialist schoolmaster, out at long stop.

"We stand rebuked," said Clive, but didn't hurry himself. "Anne's cried off the afternoon meeting, so you'll have her for company. Oh look, they've actually mended her dear little hole in the roof of the drawing-room. Maurice! No, I can't remember what I was going to say. Let us join the Olympic Games."

Maurice went out first ball. "Wait for me," called Clive, but he went straight for the house, for he felt sure that the breakdown was coming. As he passed the servants, the majority of them rose to their feet, and applauded him frantically, and the fact that Scudder didn't alarmed him. Was it meant for impertinence? The wrinkled forehead—the mouth—possibly a cruel mouth; head a trifle too small—why was the shirt open at the throat like that? And in the hall of Penge he met Anne.

"Mr Hall, the meeting didn't go." Then she saw his face, which was green-white, and cried, "Oh, but you're not well."

"I know," he said, trembling.

Men hate to be fussed, so she only replied, "I'm frightfully sorry, I'll send some ice to your room."

"You've been so kind to me always—"

"Look here, what about a doctor?"

"Never another doctor," he cried frantically.

"We want to be kind to you—naturally. When one's happy oneself one wants the same happiness for others."

"Nothing's the same."

"Mr Hall—!"

"Nothing's the same for anyone. That's why life's this Hell, if you do a thing you're damned, and if you don't you're damned—" he paused, and continued. "Sun too hot—should like a little ice."

She ran for it, and released he flew up to the Russet Room. It brought home to him the precise facts of the situation, and he was violently sick.

40 He felt better at once, but realized that he must leave Penge. He changed into the serge, packed, and was soon downstairs again with a neat little story. "The sun caught me," he told Anne, "but I'd rather a worrying letter too, and I think I'd better be in town."

"Much, much better," she cried, all sympathy.

"Yes, much better," echoed Clive, who was up from the match. "We'd hoped you'd put it right yesterday, Maurice, but we quite understand, and if you must go you must go."

And old Mrs Durham had also accrued. There was to be a laughing open secret about this girl in town, who had almost accepted his offer of marriage but not quite. It didn't matter how ill he looked or how queerly he behaved, he was officially a lover, and they interpreted everything to their satisfaction and found him delightful.

Clive motored him to the station, since their ways lay together that far. The drive skirted the cricket field before entering the woods. Scudder was fielding now, looking reckless and graceful. He was close to them, and stamped one foot, as though summoning something. That was the final vision, and whether of a devil or a comrade Maurice had no idea. Oh, the situation was disgusting—of that he was certain, and indeed never wavered till the end of his life. But to be certain of a situation is not to be certain of a human being. Once away from

Penge he would see clearly perhaps; at all events there was Mr Lasker Jones.

"What sort of man is that keeper of yours who captained us?" he asked Clive, having tried the sentence over to himself first, to be sure it didn't sound odd.

"He's leaving this month," said Clive under the impression that he was giving a reply. Fortunately they were passing the kennels at that moment, and he added, "We shall miss him as regards the dogs, anyhow."

"But not in other ways?"

"I expect we shall do worse. One always does. Hard-working anyhow, and decidedly intelligent, whereas the man I've coming in his place—"; and, glad that Maurice should be interested he sketched the economy of Penge.

"Straight?" He trembled as he asked this supreme question.

"Scudder? A little too smart to be straight. However, Anne would say I'm being unfair. You can't expect our standard of honesty in servants, any more than you can expect loyalty or gratitude."

"I could never run a job like Penge," resumed Maurice after a pause. "I should never know what type of servant to select. Take Scudder for instance. What class of home does he come from? I haven't the slightest idea."

"Wasn't his father the butcher at Osmington? Yes. I think so."

Maurice flung his hat on the floor of the car with all his force. "This is about the limit," he thought, and buried both hands in his hair.

"Head rotten again?"

"Putrid."

Clive kept sympathetic silence, which neither broke until they parted; all the way Maurice sat crouched with the palms of his hands against his eyes. His whole life he had known things but not known them—it was the great defect in his character. He had known it was unsafe to return to Penge, lest some folly leapt out of the woods at him, yet he had returned. He had throbbed when Anne said, "Has she bright brown eyes?" He had known in a way it was wiser not to lean out of his bedroom window again and again into the night and call "Come!" His interior spirit was as sensitive to promptings as most men's, but he could not interpret them. Not till the crisis had come was he clear. And this tangle, so different from Cambridge, resembled it so far that too late he could trace the entanglement. Risley's room had its counterpart in the wild rose and the evening primroses of yesterday, the side-car dash through the fens foreshadowed his innings at cricket.

But Cambridge had left him a hero, Penge a traitor. He had abused his host's confidence and defiled his house in his absence, he had insulted Mrs Durham and Anne. And when he reached home there came a worse blow; he had also sinned against his family. Hitherto they had never counted. Fools to be kind to. They were fools still, but he dare not approach them. Between those commonplace women and himself stretched a gulf that hallowed them. Their chatter, their squabble about precedence, their complaints of the chauffeur, seemed word of a greater wrong. When his mother said, "Morrie, now for a nice talk," his heart stopped. They strolled round the garden, as they had done ten years ago, and she murmured the names of vegetables. Then he had looked up to her, now down; now he knew very well what he wanted with the garden boy. And now Kitty, always a message-bearer, rushed out of the house, and in her hand she held a telegram.

Maurice trembled with anger and fear. "Come back, waiting tonight at boathouse, Penge, Alec": a nice message to be handed in through the local post-office! Presumably one of the house-servants had supplied his address, for the telegram was fully directed. A nice situation! It contained every promise of blackmail, at the best it was incredible insolence. Of course he shouldn't answer, nor could there be any question now of giving Scudder a present. He had gone outside his class, and it served him right.

But all that night his body yearned for Alec's, despite him. He called it lustful, a word easily uttered, and opposed to it his work, his family, his friends, his position in society. In that coalition must surely be included his will. For if the will can overleap class, civilization as we have made it will go to pieces. But his body would not be convinced. Chance had mated it too perfectly. Neither argument nor threat could silence it, so in the morning, feeling exhausted and ashamed, he telephoned to Mr Lasker Jones and made a second appointment. Before he was due to go to it a letter came. It arrived at breakfast and he read it under his mother's eyes. It was phrased as follows.

Mr Maurice. Dear Sir. I waited both nights in the boathouse. I said the boathouse as the ladder as taken away and the woods is to damp to lie down. So please come to "the boathouse" tomorrow night or next, pretend to the other gentlemen you want a stroll, easily managed, then come down to the boathouse. Dear Sir, let me share with you once before leaving Old England if it is not asking to much. I have key, will let you in. I leave per Ss Normannia Aug 29. I since cricket match do long to talk with one of my arms round you, then place both arms round you and share with you, the above now seems sweeter to me than words can say. I am perfectly aware I am only a servant that never presume on your loving kindness to take liberties or in any other way.

> Yours respectfully,
> A. Scudder.
> (gamekeeper to C. Durham Esq.)

Maurice, was you taken ill that you left, as the indoors servants say? I hope you feel all as usual by this time. Mind and write if you can't come, for I get no sleep waiting night after night, so come without fail to "Boathouse Penge" tomorrow night, or failing the after.

Well, what did this mean? The sentence Maurice pounced on to the neglect of all others was "I have the key." Yes, he had, and there was a duplicate, kept up at the house, with which an accomplice, probably Simcox—In this light he interpreted the whole letter. His mother and aunt, the coffee he was drinking, the college cups on the sideboard, all said in their different ways, "If you go you are ruined, if you reply your letter will be used to put pressure upon you. You are in a nasty position but you have this advantage: he hasn't a scrap of your handwriting, and he's leaving England in ten days' time. Lie low, and hope for the best." He made a wry face. Butchers' sons and the rest of them may pretend to be innocent and affectionate, but they read the Police Court News, they know. . . . If he heard again, he must consult a reliable solicitor, just as he was going to Lasker Jones for the emotional fiasco. He had been very foolish, but if he played his cards carefully for the next ten days he ought to get through.

41 "Mornin', doctor. Think you can polish me off this time?" he began, very flippant in his manner; then flung himself down in the chair, half closed his eyes and said, "Well, go ahead." He was in a fury to be cured. The knowledge of this interview had helped him to bear up against the vampire. Once normal, he could settle him. He longed for the trance, wherein his personality would melt and be subtly reformed. At the least he gained five minutes' oblivion, while the will of the doctor strove to penetrate his own.

"I will go ahead in one moment, Mr Hall. First tell me how you have been?"

"Oh, as usual. Fresh air and exercise, as you told me. All serene."

"Have you frequented female society with any pleasure?"

"Some ladies were at Penge. I only stayed one night there. The day after you saw me, Friday, I returned to London—that's to say home."

"You had intended to stop longer with your friends, I think."

"I think I did."

Lasker Jones then sat down on the side of his chair. "Let yourself go now," he said quietly.

"Rather."

He repeated the passes. Maurice looked at the fire irons as before.

"Mr Hall, are you going into a trance?"

There was a long silence, broken by Maurice saying gravely, "I'm not quite sure."

They tried again.

"Is the room at all dark, Mr Hall?"

Maurice said, "A bit," in the hope that it would become so. And it did darken a little.

"What do you see?"

"Well, if it's dark I can't be expected to see."

"What did you see last time?"

"A picture."

"Quite so, and what else?"

"What else?"

"What else? A cr— a cr—"

"Crack in the floor."

"And then?"

Maurice changed his position and said, "I stepped over it."

"And then?"

He was silent.

"And then?" the persuasive voice repeated.

"I hear you all right," said Maurice. "The bother is I've not gone off. I went just a little muzzy at the start, but now I'm as wide awake as you are. You might have another shot."

They tried again, with no success.

"What in Hell can have happened? You could bowl me out last week first ball. What's your explanation?"

"You should not resist me."

"Damn it all, I don't."

"You are less suggestible than you were."

"I don't know what that may mean, not being an expert in the jargon, but I swear from the bottom of my heart I want to be healed. I want to be like other men, not this outcast whom nobody wants—"

They tried again.

"Then am I one of your twenty-five per cent failures?"

"I could do a little with you last week, but we do have these sudden disappointments."

"Sudden disappointment, am I? Well, don't be beat, don't give up," he guffawed, affectedly bluff.

"I do not propose to give up, Mr Hall."

Again they failed.

"And what's to happen to me?" said Maurice, with a sudden drop in his voice. He spoke in despair, but Mr Lasker Jones had an answer to every question. "I'm afraid I can only advise you to live in some country that has adopted the Code Napoléon," he said.

"I don't understand."

"France or Italy, for instance. There homosexuality is no longer criminal."

"You mean that a Frenchman could share with a friend and yet not go to prison?"

"Share? Do you mean unite? If both are of age and avoid public indecency, certainly."

"Will the law ever be that in England?"

"I doubt it. England has always been disinclined to accept human nature."

Maurice understood. He was an Englishman himself, and only his troubles had kept him awake. He smiled sadly. "It comes to this then: there always have been people like me and always will be, and generally they have been persecuted."

"That is so, Mr Hall; or, as psychiatry prefers to put it, there has been, is, and always will be every conceivable type of person. And you must remember that your type was once put to death in England."

"Was it really? On the other hand, they could get away. England wasn't all built over and policed. Men of my sort could take to the greenwood."

"Is that so? I was not aware."

"Oh, it's only my own notion," said Maurice, laying the fee down. "It strikes me there may have been more about the Greeks—Theban Band—and the rest of it. Well, this wasn't unlike. I don't see how they could have kept together otherwise—especially when they came from such different classes."

"An interesting theory."

Words flying out of him again, he said, "I've not been straight with you."

"Indeed, Mr Hall."

What a comfort the man was! Science is better than sympathy, if only it is science.

"Since I was last here I went wrong with a—he's nothing but a gamekeeper. I don't know what to do."

"I can scarcely advise you on such a point."

"I know you can't. But you might tell me whether he's pulling me away from sleep. I half wondered."

"No one can be pulled against his will, Mr Hall."

"I'd a notion he'd stopped me going into the trance, and I wished—that seems silly—that I hadn't happened to have a letter from him in my pocket—read it as I've told you so much. I feel simply walking on a volcano. He's an uneducated man; he's got me in his power. In court would he have a case?"

"I am no lawyer," came the unvarying voice, "but I do not think this letter can be construed as containing a menace. It's a matter on which you should consult your solicitor, not me."

"I'm sorry, but it's been a relief. I wonder if you'd be awfully kind—hypnotize me once more. I feel I might go off now I've told you. I'd hoped to get cured without giving myself away. Are there such things as men getting anyone in their power through dreams?"

"I will try on condition your confession is this time exhaustive. Otherwise you waste both my time and your own."

It was exhaustive. He spared neither his lover nor himself. When all was detailed, the perfection of the night appeared as a transient grossness, such as his father had indulged in thirty years before.

"Sit down once again."

Maurice heard a slight noise and swerved.

"It is my children playing overhead."

"I get half to believe in spooks."

"It is merely the children."

Silence returned. The afternoon sunshine fell yellow through the window upon the roll-top desk. This time Maurice fixed his attention on that. Before recommencing, the doctor took Alec's letter, and solemnly burnt it to ashes before his eyes.

Nothing happened.

42 By pleasuring the body Maurice had confirmed—that very word was used in the final verdict—he had confirmed his spirit in its perversion, and cut himself off from the congregation of normal man. In his irritation he stammered; "What I want to know is—what I can't tell you nor you me—how did a country lad like that know so much about me? Why did he thunder up that special night when I was weakest? I'd never let him touch me with my friend in the house, because, damn it all, I'm more or less a gentleman—public school, varsity, and so on—I can't even now believe that it was with him." Regretting he had not possessed Clive in the hour of their passion, he left, left his last shelter, while the doctor said perfunctorily. "Fresh air and exercise may do wonders yet." The doctor wanted to get on to his next patient, and he did not care for Maurice's type. He was not shocked like Dr Barry, but he was bored, and never thought of the young invert again.

On the doorstep something rejoined Maurice—his old self perhaps, for as he walked along a voice spoke out of his mortification, and its accents recalled Cambridge; a reckless youthful voice that girded at him for being a fool. "You've done for yourself this time," it seemed to say, and when he stopped outside the park, because the King and Queen were passing, he despised them at the moment he bared his head. It was as if the barrier that kept him from his fellows had taken another aspect. He was not afraid or ashamed anymore. After all, the forests and the night were on his side, not theirs; they, not he, were inside a ring fence. He had acted wrongly, and was still being punished—but wrongly because he had tried to get the best of both worlds. "But I must belong to my class, that's fixed," he persisted.

"Very well," said his old self. "Now go home, and tomorrow morning mind you catch the 8.36 up to the office, for your holiday is over, remember, and mind you never turn your head, as I may, towards Sherwood."

"I'm not a poet, I'm not that kind of an ass—"

The King and Queen vanished into their palace, the sun fell behind the park trees, which melted into one huge creature that had fingers and fists of green.

"The life of the earth, Maurice? Don't you belong to that?"

"Well, what do you call the 'life of the earth'—it ought to be the same as my daily life—the same as society. One ought to be built on the other, as Clive once said."

"Quite so. Most unfortunate, that facts pay no attention to Clive."

"Anyhow, I must stick to my class."

"Night is coming—be quick then—take a taxi—be quick like your father, before doors close."

Hailing one, he caught the 6.20. Another letter from Scudder awaited him on the leather tray in the hall. He knew the writing at once, the "Mr M. Hall" instead of "Esq.", the stamps plastered crooked. He was frightened and annoyed, yet not so much as he would have been in the morning, for though science despaired of him he despaired less of himself. After all, is not a real Hell better than a manufactured Heaven? He was not sorry that he had eluded the manipulations of Mr Lasker Jones. He put the letter into the pocket of his dinner-jacket, where it tugged unread, while he played cards, and heard how the chauffeur had given notice; one didn't know what servants were coming to: to his suggestion that servants might be flesh and blood like ourselves his aunt opposed a loud "They aren't". At bedtime he kissed his mother and Kitty without the fear of defiling them; their short-lived sanctity was over, and all that they did and said had resumed insignificance. It was with no feeling of treason that he locked his door, and gazed for five minutes into the suburban night. He heard owls, the ring of a distant tram and his heart sounding louder than either. The letter was beastly long. The blood began pounding over his body as he unfolded it, but his head kept cool, and he managed to read it as a whole, not merely sentence by sentence.

Mr Hall, Mr Borenius has just spoke to me. Sir, you do not treat me fairly. I am sailing next week, per s.s. Normannia. I wrote you I am going, it is not fair you never write to me. I come of a respectable family, I don't think it fair to treat me like a dog. My father is a respectable tradesman. I am going to be on my own in the Argentine. You say, "Alec, you are a dear fellow"; but you do not write. *I know about you and Mr Durham.* Why do you say "call me Maurice", and then treat me so unfairly? Mr Hall, I am coming to London Tuesday. If you do not want me at your home say where in London, you had better see me—I would make you sorry for it. Sir, nothing of note has occurred since you left Penge. Cricket seems over, some of the great trees as lost some of their leaves, which is very early. Has Mr Borenius spoken to you about certain girls? I can't help being rather rough, it is some men's nature, but you should not treat me like a dog. It was before you came. It is natural to want a girl, you cannot go against human nature. Mr Borenius found out about the girls through the new communion class. He has just spoken to me. I have never come like that to a gentleman before. Were you annoyed at being disturbed so early? Sir, it was your fault, your head was on me. I had my work, I was Mr Durham's servant, not yours. I am not your servant, I will not be treated as your servant, and I don't care if the world knows it. I will show respect *where it's due only,* that is to say to gentleman who are gentleman. Simcox says, "Mr Hall says to put him in about eighth." I put you in fifth, but I was captain, and you have no right to treat me unfairly on that account.

Yours respectfully, A. Scudder.

P.S. *I know something.*

This last was the outstanding point, yet Maurice could brood over the letter as a whole. There was evidently some unsavoury gossip in the under-world about himself and Clive, but what did it matter now? What did it matter if they had been spied on in the Blue Room, or among the ferns, and been misinterpreted? He was concerned with the present. Why should Scudder have mentioned such gossip? What was he up to? Why had he flung out these words, some foul, many stupid, some gracious? While actually reading the letter, Maurice might feel it carrion he must toss on to his solicitor, but when he laid it down and took up his pipe, it seemed the sort of letter he might have written himself. Muddle-headed? How about muddle-headed? If so, it was in his own line! He didn't want such a letter, he didn't know what it wanted—half a dozen things possibly—but he couldn't well be cold and hard over it as Clive had been to him over the original *Symposium* business, and argue, "Here's a certain statement, I shall keep you to it." He replied, "A.S. Yes. Meet me Tuesday 5.0 p.m. entrance of British Museum. B.M. a large building. Anyone will tell you which. M.C.H." That struck him as best. Both were outcasts, and if it came to a scrap must have it without benefit of society. As for the rendezvous, he chose it because they were unlikely to be disturbed there by anyone whom he knew. Poor B.M., solemn and chaste! The young man smiled, and his face became mischievous and happy. He smiled also at the thought that Clive hadn't quite kept out of the mud after all, and though the face now hardened into lines less pleasing, it proved him an athlete, who had emerged from a year of suffering uninjured.

His new vigour persisted next morning, when he returned to work. Before his failure with Lasker Jones he had looked forward to work as a privilege of which he was almost unworthy. It was to have rehabilitated him, so that he could hold up his head at home. But now it too crumbled, and again he wanted to laugh, and wondered why he had been taken in so long. The clientele of Messrs Hill and Hall was drawn from the middle-middle classes, whose highest desire seemed shelter—continuous shelter—not a lair in the darkness to be reached against fear, but shelter everywhere and always, until the existence of earth and sky is forgotten, shelter from poverty and disease and violence and impoliteness; and consequently from joy; God slipped this retribution in. He saw from their faces, as from the faces of his clerks and his partners, that they had never known real joy. Society had catered for them too completely. They had never struggled, and only a struggle twists sentimentality and lust together into love. Maurice would have been a good lover. He could have given and taken serious pleasure. But in these men the strands were untwisted; they were either fatuous or obscene, and in his present mood he despised the latter least. They would come to him and ask for a safe six per cent security. He would reply, "You can't combine high interest with safety—it isn't to be done"; and in the end they would say, "How would it be if I invested most of my money at four per cent, and play about with an odd hundred?" Even so did they speculate in a little vice—not in too much, lest it disorganized domesticity, but in enough to show that their virtue was sham. And until yesterday he had cringed to them.

Why should he serve such men? He began discussing the ethics of his profession, like a clever undergraduate, but the railway carriage did not take him seriously. "Young Hall's all right," remained the verdict. "He'll never lose a single client, not he." And they diagnosed a cynicism not unseemly in a business man. "All the time he's investing steadily, you bet. Remember that slum talk of his in the spring?"

43 The rain was coming down in its old fashion, tapping on a million roofs and occasionally effecting an entry. It beat down the smoke, and caused the fumes of petrol and the smell of wet clothes to linger mixed on the streets of London. In the great forecourt of the Museum it could fall uninterruptedly, plumb onto the draggled doves and the helmets of the police. So dark was the afternoon that some of the lights had been turned on inside, and the great building suggested a tomb, miraculously illuminated by spirits of the dead.

Alec arrived first, dressed no longer in corduroys but in a new blue suit and bowler hat—part of his outfit for the Argentine. He sprang, as he had boasted, of a respectable family—publicans, small tradesmen—and it was only by accident that he had appeared as an untamed son of the woods. Indeed, he liked the woods and the fresh air and water, he liked them better than anything and he liked to protect or destroy life, but woods contain no "openings", and young men who want to get on must leave them. He was determined in a blind way to get on now. Fate had placed a snare in his hands, and he meant to set it. He tramped over the courtyard, then took the steps in a series of springs; having won the shelter of the portico he stood motionless, except for the flicker of his eyes. These sudden changes of pace were typical of the man, who always advanced as a skirmisher, was always "on the spot" as Clive had phrased it in the written testimonial; "during the five months A. Scudder was in my service I found him prompt and assiduous": qualities that he proposed to display now. When the victim drove up he became half cruel, half frightened. Gentlemen he knew, mates he knew; what class of creature was Mr Hall who said, "Call me Maurice"? Narrowing his eyes to slits, he stood as though waiting for orders outside the front porch at Penge.

Maurice approached the most dangerous day of his life without any plan at all, yet something kept rippling in his mind like muscles beneath a healthy skin. He was not supported by pride but he did feel fit, anxious to play the game, and, as an Englishman should, hoped that his opponent felt fit too. He wanted to be decent, he wasn't afraid. When he saw Alec's face glowing through the dirty air his own tingled slightly, and he determined not to strike until he was struck.

"Here you are," he said, raising a pair of gloves to his hat. "This rain's the limit. Let's have a talk inside."

"Where you wish."

Maurice looked at him with some friendliness, and they entered the building. As they did so, Alec raised his head and sneezed like a lion.

"Got a chill? It's the weather."

"What's all this place?" he asked.

"Old things belonging to the nation." They paused in the corridor of Roman emperors. "Yes, it's bad weather. There've only been two fine days. And one fine night," he added mischievously, surprising himself.

But Alec didn't catch on. It wasn't the opening he wanted. He was waiting for signs of fear, that the menial in him might strike. He pretended not to understand the allusion, and sneezed again. The roar echoed down vestibules, and his face, convulsed and distorted, took a sudden appearance of hunger.

"I'm glad you wrote to me the second time. I liked both your letters. I'm not offended—you've never done anything wrong. It's all your mistake about cricket and the rest. I'll tell you straight out I enjoyed being with you, if that's the trouble. Is it? I want you to tell me. I just don't know."

"What's here? *That's* no mistake." He touched his breast pocket, meaningly. "Your writing. And you and the squire— *that's* no mistake—some may wish as it was one."

"Don't drag in that," said Maurice, but without indignation, and it struck him as odd that he had none, and that even the Clive of Cambridge had lost sanctity.

"Mr Hall—you reckernize it wouldn't very well suit you if certain things came out, I suppose."

Maurice found himself trying to get underneath the words.

He continued, feeling his way to a grip. "What's more, I've always been a respectable young fellow until you called me into your room to amuse yourself. It don't hardly seem fair that a gentleman should drag you down. At least that's how my brother sees it." He faltered as he spoke these last words. "My brother's waiting outside now as a matter of fact. He wanted to come and speak to you hisself, he's been scolding me shocking, but I said, 'No Fred no, Mr Hall's a gentleman and can be trusted to behave like one, so you leave 'im to me,' I said, 'and Mr Durham, he's a gentleman too, always was and always will be.'"

"With regard to Mr Durham," said Maurice, feeling inclined to speak on this point: "It's quite correct that I cared for him and he for me once, but he changed, and now he doesn't care any more for me nor I for him. It's the end."

"End o' what?"

"Of our friendship."

"Mr Hall, have you heard what I was saying?"

"I hear everything you say," said Maurice thoughtfully, and continued in exactly the same tone: "Scudder, why do you think it's 'natural' to care both for women and men? You wrote so in your letter. It isn't natural for me. I have really got to think that 'natural' only means oneself."

The man seemed interested. "Couldn't you get a kid of your own, then?" he asked, roughening.

"I've been to two doctors about it. Neither were any good."

"So you can't?"

"No, I can't."

"Want one?" he asked, as if hostile.

"It's not much use wanting."

"I could marry tomorrow if I like," he bragged. While speaking, he caught sight of a winged Assyrian bull, and his expression altered into naïve wonder. "He's big enough, isn't he," he remarked. "They must have owned wonderful machinery to make a thing like that."

"I expect so," said Maurice, also impressed by the bull. "I couldn't tell you. Here seems to be another one."

"A pair, so to speak. Would these have been ornaments?"

"This one has five legs."

"So's mine. A curious idea." Standing each by his monster, they looked at each other, and smiled. Then his face hardened again and he said, "Won't do, Mr Hall. I see your game, but you don't fool me twice, and you'll do better to have a friendly talk with me rather than wait for Fred, I can tell you. You've had your fun and you've got to pay up." He looked handsome as he threatened—including the pupils of his eyes, which were evil. Maurice gazed into them gently but keenly. And nothing resulted from the outburst at all. It fell away like a flake of mud. Murmuring something about "leaving you to think this over", he sat down on a bench. Maurice joined him there shortly. And it was thus for nearly twenty minutes: they kept wandering from room to room as if in search of something. They would peer at a goddess or vase, then move at a single impulse, and their unison was the stranger because on the surface they were at war. Alec recommenced his hints—horrible, reptilian—but somehow they did not pollute the intervening silences, and Maurice failed to get afraid or angry, and only regretted that any human being should have got into such a mess. When he chose to reply their eyes met, and his smile was sometimes reflected on the lips of his foe. The belief grew that the actual situation was a blind—a practical joke almost—and concealed something real, that either desired. Serious and good-tempered, he continued to hold his own, and if he made no offensive it was because his blood wasn't warm. To set it moving, a shock from without was required, and chance administered this.

He was bending over a model of the Acropolis with his forehead a little wrinkled and his lips murmuring, "I see, I see, I see." A gentleman near overheard him, started, peered through strong spectacles, and said "Surely! I may forget faces but never a voice. Surely! You are one of our old boys." It was Mr Ducie.

Maurice did not reply. Alec sidled up closer to participate.

"Surely you were at Mr Abrahams's school. Now wait! Wait! Don't tell me your name. I want to remember it. I will remember it. You're not Sanday, you're not Gibbs. I know. I know. It's Wimbleby."

How like Mr Ducie to get the facts just wrong! To his own name Maurice would have responded, but he now had the inclination to lie; he was tired of their endless inaccuracy, he had suffered too much from it. He replied, "No, my name's Scudder." The correction flew out as the first that occurred to him. It lay ripe to be used, and as he uttered it he knew why. But at the instant of enlightenment Alec himself spoke. "It isn't," he said to Mr Ducie, "and I've a serious charge to bring against this gentleman."

"Yes, awfully serious," remarked Maurice, and rested his hand on Alec's shoulder, so that the fingers touched the back of the neck, doing this merely because he wished to do it, not for another reason.

Mr Ducie did not take notice. An unsuspicious man, he assumed some uncouth joke. The dark gentlemanly fellow couldn't be Wimbleby if he said he wasn't. He said, "I'm extremely sorry, sir, it's so seldom I make a mistake," and then, determined to show he was not an old fool, he addressed the silent pair on the subject of the British Museum—not merely a collection of relics but a place round which one could take—er—the less fortunate, quite so—a stimulating place—it raised questions even in the minds of boys—which one answered—no doubt inadequately; until a patient voice said, "Ben, we are waiting," and Mr Ducie rejoined his wife. As he did so Alec jerked away and muttered, "That's all right. . . . I won't trouble you now."

"Where are you going with your serious charge?" said Maurice, suddenly formidable.

"Couldn't say." He looked back, his colouring stood out against the heroes, perfect but bloodless, who had never known bewilderment or infamy. "Don't you worry—I'll never harm you now, you've too much pluck."

"Pluck be damned," said Maurice, with a plunge into anger.

"It'll all go no further—" He struck his own mouth. "I don't know what came over me, Mr Hall; *I* don't want to harm you, I never did."

"You blackmailed me."

"No, sir, no . . ."

"You did."

"Maurice, listen, I only . . ."

"Maurice am I?"

"You called me Alec. . . . I'm as good as you."

"I don't find you are!" There was a pause; before the storm; then he burst out: "By God, if you'd split on me to Mr Ducie, I'd have broken you. It might have cost me hundreds, but I've got them, and the police always back my sort against yours. You don't know. We'd have got you into quod, for blackmail, after which—I'd have blown out my brains."

"Killed yourself? Death?"

"I should have known by that time that I loved you. Too late . . . everything's always too late." The rows of old statues tottered, and he heard himself add, "I don't mean anything, but come outside, we can't talk here." They left the enormous and overheated building, they passed the library, supposed catholic, seeking darkness and rain. On the portico Maurice stopped and said bitterly, "I forgot. Your brother?"

"He's down at father's—doesn't know a word—I was but threatening—"

"—for blackmail."

"Could you but understand . . ." He pulled out Maurice's note. "Take it if you like. . . . I don't want it . . . never did . . . . I suppose this is the end."

Assuredly it wasn't that. Unable to part yet ignorant of what could next come, they strode raging through the last glimmering of the sordid day; night, ever one in her quality, came finally, and Maurice recovered his self-control and could look at the new material that passion had gained for him. In a deserted square, against railings that encircled some trees, they came to a halt, and he began to discuss their crisis.

But as he grew calm the other grew fierce. It was as if Mr Ducie had established some infuriating inequality between them, so that one struck as soon as his fellow tired of striking. Alec said savagely, "It rained harder than this in the boathouse, it was yet colder. Why did you not come?"

"Muddle."

"I beg your pardon?"

"You've to learn I'm always in a muddle. I didn't come or write because I wanted to get away from you without wanting. You won't understand. You kept dragging me back and I got awfully frightened. I felt you when I tried to get some sleep at the doctor's. You came hard at me. I knew something was evil but couldn't tell what, so kept pretending it was you."

"What was it?"

"The—situation."

"I don't follow this. Why did you not come to the boathouse?"

"My fear—and your trouble has been fear too. Ever since the cricket match you've let yourself get afraid of me. That's why we've been trying to down one another so and are still."

"I wouldn't take a penny from you, I wouldn't hurt your little finger," he growled, and rattled the bars that kept him from the trees.

"But you're still trying hard to hurt me in my mind."

"Why do you go and say you love me?"

"Why do you call me Maurice?"

"Oh let's give over talking. Here—" and he held out his hand. Maurice took it, and they knew at that moment the greatest triumph ordinary man can win. Physical love means reaction, being panic in essence, and Maurice saw now how natural it was that their primitive abandonment at Penge should have led to peril. They knew too little about each other—and too much. Hence fear. Hence cruelty. And he rejoiced because he had understood Alec's infamy through his own—glimpsing, not for the first time, the genius who hides in man's tormented soul. Not as a hero, but as a comrade, had he stood up to the bluster, and found childishness behind it, and behind that something else.

Presently the other spoke. Spasms of remorse and apology broke him; he was as one who throws off a poison. Then, gathering health, he began to tell his friend everything, no longer ashamed. He spoke of his relations. . . . He too was embedded in class. No one knew he was in London—Penge thought he was at his father's, his father at Penge—it had been difficult, very. Now he ought to go home—see his brother with whom he returned to the Argentine: his brother connected with trade, and his brother's wife; and he mingled some brag, as those whose education is not literary must. He came of a respectable family, he repeated, he bowed down to no man, not he, he was as good as any gentleman. But while be bragged his arm was gaining Maurice's. They deserved such a caress—the feeling was strange. Words died away, abruptly to recommence. It was Alec who ventured them.

"Stop with me."

Maurice swerved and their muscles clipped. By now they were in love with one another consciously.

"Sleep the night with me. I know a place."

"I can't, I've an engagement," said Maurice, his heart beating violently. A formal dinner party awaited him of the sort that brought work to his firm and that he couldn't possibly cut. He had almost forgotten its existence. "I have to leave you now and get changed. But look here: Alec, be reasonable. Meet me another evening instead—any day."

"Can't come to London again—father or Mr Ayres will be passing remarks."

"What does it matter if they do?"

"What's your engagement matter?"

They were silent again. Then Maurice said in affectionate yet dejected tones, "All right. To Hell with it," and they passed on together in the rain.

44 "Alec, wake up."

An arm twitched.

"Time we talked plans."

He snuggled closer, more awake than he pretended, warm, sinewy, happy. Happiness overwhelmed Maurice too. He moved, felt the answering grip, and forgot what he wanted to say. Light drifted in upon them from the outside world where it was still raining. A strange hotel, a casual refuge protected them from their enemies a little longer.

"Time to get up, boy. It's morning."

"Git up then."

"How can I the way you hold me!"

"Aren't yer a fidget, I'll learn you to fidget." He wasn't deferential any more. The British Museum had cured that. This was 'oliday, London with Maurice, all troubles over, and he wanted to drowse and waste time, and tease and make love.

Maurice wanted the same, what's pleasanter, but the oncoming future distracted him, the gathering light made cosiness unreal. Something had to be said and settled. O for the night that was ending, for the sleep and the wakefulness, the toughness and tenderness mixed, the sweet temper, the safety in darkness. Would such a night ever return?

"You all right, Maurice?"—for he had sighed. "You comfortable? Rest your head on me more, the way you like more . . . that's it more, and Don't You Worry. You're With Me. Don't Worry."

Yes, he was in luck, no doubt of it. Scudder had proved honest and kind. He was lovely to be with, a treasure, a charmer, a find in a thousand, the longed-for dream. But was he brave?

"Nice you and me like this . . ." the lips so close now that it was scarcely speech. "Who'd have thought. . . . First time I ever seed you I thought, 'Wish I and that one . . .' just like that . . . 'wouldn't I and him . . .' and it is so."

"Yes, and that's why we've got to fight."

"Who wants to fight?" He sounded annoyed. "There's bin enough fighting."

"All the world's against us. We've got to pull ourselves together and make plans, while we can."

"What d'you want to go and say a thing like that for, and spoil it all?"

"Because it has to be said. We can't allow things to go wrong and hurt us again the way they did down at Penge."

Alec suddenly scrubbed at him with the sun-roughened back of a hand and said, "That hurt, didn't it, or oughter. That's how *I* fight." It did hurt a little, and stealing into the foolery was a sort of resentment. "Don't talk to me about Penge," he went on. "Oo! Mah! Penge where I was always a servant and Scudder do this and Scudder do that and the old lady, what do you think she once said? She said, 'Oh would you most kindly of your goodness post this letter for me, what's your name?' What's yer name! Every day for six months I come up to Clive's bloody front porch door for orders, and his mother don't know my name. She's a bitch. I said to 'er, 'What's yer name? Fuck yer name.' I nearly did too. Wish I 'ad too. Maurice, you wouldn't believe how servants get spoken to. It's too shocking for words. That Archie London you're so set on is just as bad, and so are you, so are you. 'Haw my man' and all that. You've no idea how you nearly missed getting me. Near as nothing I never climbed that ladder when you called, he don't want me really, and I went flaming mad when you didn't turn up at the boathouse as I ordered. Too grand! We'll see. Boathouse was a place I always fancied. I'd go down for a smoke before I'd ever heard of you, unlock it easy, got the key on me still as a matter of fact . . . boathouse, looking over the pond from the boathouse, very quiet, now and then a fish jump and cushions the way I arrange them."

He was silent, having chattered himself out. He had begun rough and gay and somehow factitious, then his voice had died away into sadness as though truth had risen to the surface of the water and was unbearable.

"We'll meet in your boathouse yet," Maurice said.

"No, we won't." He pushed him away, then heaved, pulled him close, put forth violence, and embraced as if the world was ending. "You'll remember that anyway." He got out and looked down out of the grayness, his arms hanging empty. It was as if he wished to be remembered thus. "I could easy have killed you."

"Or I you."

"Where's my clothes and that gone?" He seemed dazed. "It's so late. I h'aint got a razor even, I didn't reckon staying the night. . . . I ought—I got to catch a train at once or Fred'll be thinking things."

"Let him."

"My goodness if Fred seed you and me just now."

"Well, he didn't."

"Well, he might have—what I mean is, tomorrow's Thursday isn't it, Friday's the packing, Saturday the *Normannia* sails from Southampton, so it's goodbye to Old England."

"You mean that you and I shan't meet again after now."

"That's right. You've got it quite correct."

And if it wasn't still raining! Wet morning after yesterday's downpour, wet on the roofs and the Museum, at home and on the greenwood. Controlling himself and choosing his words very carefully, Maurice said, "This is just what I want to talk about. Why don't we arrange so as we do meet again?"

"How do you mean?"

"Why don't you stay on in England?"

Alec whizzed round, terrified. Half naked, he seemed also half human. "Stay?" he snarled. "Miss my boat, are you daft? Of all the bloody rubbish I ever heard. Ordering me about again, eh, you would."

"It's a chance in a thousand we've met, we'll never have the chance again and you know it. Stay with me. We love each other."

"I dessay, but that's no excuse to act silly. Stay with you and how and where? What'd your Ma say if she saw me all rough and ugly the way I am?"

"She never will see you. I shan't live at my home."

"Where will you live?"

"With you."

"Oh, will you? No thank you. My people wouldn't take to you one bit and I don't blame them. And how'd you run your job, I'd like to know?"

"I shall chuck it."

"Your job in the city what gives you your money and position? You can't chuck a job."

"You can when you mean to," said Maurice gently. "You can do anything once you know what it is." He gazed at the grayish light that was becoming yellowish. Nothing surprised him in this talk. What he could not conjecture was its outcome. "I shall get work with you," he brought out: the moment to announce this had now come.

"What work?"

"We'll find out."

"Find out and starve out."

"No. There'll be enough money to keep us while we have a look round. I'm not a fool, nor are you. We won't be starving. I've thought out that much, while I was awake in the night and you weren't."

There was a pause. Alec went on more politely: "Wouldn't work, Maurice. Ruin of us both, can't you see, you same as myself."

"I don't know. Might be. Mightn't. 'Class.' I don't know. I know what we do today. We clear out of here and get a decent breakfast and we go down to Penge or whatever you want and see that Fred of yours. You tell him you've changed your mind about emigrating and are taking a job with Mr Hall instead. I'll come with you. I don't care. I'll see anyone, face anything. If they want to guess, let them. I'm fed up. Tell Fred to cancel your ticket, I'll repay for it and that's our start of getting free. Then we'll do the next thing. It's a risk, so's everything else, and we'll only live once."

Alec laughed cynically and continued to dress. His manner resembled yesterday's, though he didn't blackmail. "Yours is the talk of someone who's never had to earn his living," he said. "You sort of trap me with I love you or whatever it is and then offer to spoil my career. Do you realize I've got a definite job awaiting me in the Argentine? Same as you've got here. Pity the *Normannia*'s leaving Saturday, still facts is facts isn't it, all my kit bought as well as my ticket and Fred and wife expecting me."

Maurice saw through the brassiness to the misery behind it, but this time what was the use of insight? No amount of insight would prevent the *Normannia* from sailing. He had lost. Suffering was certain for him, though it might soon end for Alec; when he got out to his new life he would forget his escapade with a gentleman and in time he would marry. Shrewd working-class youngster who knew where his interests lay, he had already crammed his graceful body into his hideous blue suit. His face stuck out of it red, his hands brown. He plastered his hair flat. "Well, I'm off," he said, and as if that wasn't enough said, "Pity we ever met really if you come to think of it."

"That's all right too," said Maurice, looking away from him as he unbolted the door.

"You paid for this room in advance, didn't you, so they won't stop me downstairs? I don't want no unpleasantness to finish with."

"That's all right too." He heard the door shut and he was alone. He waited for the beloved to return. Inevitable that wait. Then his eyes began to smart, and he knew from experience what was coming. Presently he could control himself. He got up and went out, did some telephoning and explanations, placated his mother, apologized to his host, got himself shaved and trimmed up, and attended the office as usual. Masses of work awaited him. Nothing had changed in his life. Nothing remained in it. He was back with his loneliness as it had been before Clive, as it was after Clive, and would now be for ever. He had failed, and that wasn't the saddest: he had seen Alec fail. In a way they were one person. Love had failed. Love was an emotion through which you occasionally enjoyed yourself. It could not do things.

45 When the Saturday came he went down to Southampton to see the *Normannia* off.

It was a fantastic decision, useless, undignified, risky, and he had not the least intention of going when he left home. But when he reached London the hunger that tormented him nightly came into the open and demanded its prey, he forgot everything except Alec's face and body, and took the only means of seeing them. He did not want to speak to his lover or to hear his voice or to touch him—all that part was over—only to recapture his image before it vanished for ever. Poor wretched Alec! Who could blame him, how could he have acted differently? But oh, the wretchedness it was causing them both.

He got down to the boat in a dream, and awoke there to a new sort of discomfort: Alec was nowhere in sight, the stewards were busy, and it was some time before they brought him to Mr Scudder, an unattractive middle-aged man, a tradesman, a cad —brother Fred: with him was a bearded elder—presumably the butcher from Osmington. Alec's main charm was the fresh colouring that surged against the cliff of his hair: Fred, facially the same, was sandy and foxlike, and greasiness had replaced the sun's caress. Fred thought highly of himself, as did Alec, but his was the conceit that comes with commercial success and despises manual labour. He did not like having a brother who had chanced to grow up rough, and he thought that Mr Hall, of whom he had never heard, was out to patronize. This made him insolent. "Licky's not aboard yet, but his kit is," he said. "Interested to see his kit?" The father said, "Plenty of time yet," and looked at his watch. The mother said with compressed lips, "He won't be late. When Licky says a thing Licky means it." Fred said, "He can be late if he likes. If I lose his company I can bear it, but he needn't expect me to help him again. What he's cost me . . ."

"This is where Alec belongs," Maurice reflected. "These people will make him happier than I could have." He filled a pipe with the tobacco that he had smoked for the last six years, and watched Romance wither. Alec was not a hero or god, but a man embedded in society like himself, for whom sea and woodland and the freshening breeze and the sun were preparing no apotheosis. They ought not to have spent that night together in the hotel. It had now raised hopes that were too high. They should have parted with that handshake in the rain.

A morbid fascination kept him among the Scudders, listening to their vulgarity, and tracing the gestures of his friend in theirs. He tried to be pleasant and ingratiate himself, and failed, for his self-confidence had gone. As he brooded a quiet voice said, "Good afternoon, Mr Hall." He could not reply. The surprise was too complete. It was Mr Borenius. And both of them remembered that initial silence of his, and his frightened gaze, and the quick movement with which he removed his pipe from his lips, as if smoking were forbidden by the clergy.

Mr Borenius introduced himself gently to the company; he had come to see his young parishioner off, since the distance was not great from Penge. They discussed which route Alec would arrive by—there seemed some uncertainty—and Maurice tried to slip off, for the situation had become equivocal. But Mr Borenius checked him. "Going on deck?" he inquired; "I too. I too." They returned to the air and sunlight; the shallows of Southampton Water stretched golden around them, edged by the New Forest. To Maurice the beauty of the evening seemed ominous of disaster.

"Now this is very kind of you," said the clergyman, beginning at once. He spoke as one social worker to another, but Maurice thought there was a veil over his voice. He tried to reply—two or three normal sentences would save him—but no words would come, and his underlip trembled like an unhappy boy's. "And the more kind because if I remember rightly you disapprove of young Scudder. You told me when we dined at Penge that he was 'a bit of a swine'—an expression that, as applied to a fellow creature, struck me. I could hardly believe my eyes when I saw you among his friends down here. Believe me, Mr Hall, he will value the attention though he may not appear to. Men like that are more impressionable than the outsider supposes. For good and for evil."

Maurice tried to stop him by saying, "Well . . . what about you?"

"I? Why have I come? You will only laugh. I have come to bring him a letter of introduction to an Anglican priest at Buenos Aires in the hope that he will get confirmed after landing. Absurd, is it not? But being neither a hellenist nor an atheist I hold that conduct is dependent on faith, and that if a man is a 'bit of a swine' the cause is to be found in some misapprehension of God. Where there is heresy, immorality will sooner or later ensue. But you—how came you to know so precisely when his boat sailed?"

"It . . . it was advertised." The trembling spread all over his body, and his clothes stuck to him. He seemed to be back at school, defenceless. He was certain that the rector had guessed, or rather that a wave of recognition had passed. A man of the world would have suspected nothing—Mr Ducie hadn't—but this man had a special sense, being spiritual, and could scent out invisible emotions. Asceticism and piety have their practical side. They can generate insight, as Maurice realized too late. He had assumed at Penge that a white-faced parson in a cassock could never have conceived of masculine love, but he knew now that there is no secret of humanity which, from a wrong angle, orthodoxy has not viewed, that religion is far more acute than science, and if it only added judgement to insight would be the greatest thing in the world. Destitute of the religious sense himself, he never yet encountered it in another, and the shock was terrific. He feared and hated Mr Borenius, he wanted to kill him.

And Alec—when he arrived, he would be flung into the trap too; they were small people, who could take no risk—far smaller, for instance, than Clive and Anne—and Mr Borenius knew this, and would punish them by the only means in his power.

The voice continued; it had paused for a moment in case the victim chose to reply.

"Yes. To speak frankly, I am far from easy about young Scudder. When he left Penge last Tuesday to go to his parents as he told me, though he never reached them till Wednesday— I had a most unsatisfactory interview with him. He was hard. He resisted me. When I spoke of Confirmation he sneered. The fact being— I could not mention this to you if it weren't for your charitable interest in him—the fact being that he has been guilty of sensuality." There was a pause. "With women. In time, Mr Hall, one gets to recognize that sneer, that hardness, for fornication extends far beyond the actual deed. Were it a deed only, I for one would not hold it anathema. But when the nations went a whoring they invariably ended by denying God, I think, and until all sexual irregularities and not some of them are penal the Church will never reconquer England. I have reason to believe that he spent that missing night in London. But surely—that must be his train."

He went below, and Maurice, utterly to pieces, followed him. He heard voices, but did not understand them; one of them might have been Alec's for all it mattered to him. "This too has gone wrong" began flitting through his brain, like a bat that returns at twilight. He was back in the smoking-room at home with Clive, who said, "I don't love you any more; I'm sorry," and he felt that his life would revolve in cycles of a year, always to the same eclipse. "Like the sun . . . it takes a year . . ." He thought his grandfather was speaking to him; then the haze cleared, and it was Alec's mother. "It's not like Licky," she gibbered, and vanished.

Like whom? Bells were ringing, a whistle blew. Maurice ran up on deck; his faculties had returned, and he could see with extraordinary distinctness the masses of men sorting themselves, those to stop in England, those to go, and he knew that Alec was stopping. The afternoon had broken into glory. White clouds sailed over the golden waters and woods. In the midst of the pageant Fred Scudder was raving because his unreliable brother had missed the last train, and the women were protesting while they were hustled up the gangways, and Mr Borenius and old Scudder were lamenting to the officials. How negligible they had all become, beside the beautiful weather and fresh air.

Maurice went ashore, drunk with excitement and happiness. He watched the steamer move, and suddenly she reminded him of the Viking's funeral that had thrilled him as a boy. The parallel was false, yet she was heroic, she was carrying away death. She warped out from the quay, Fred yapping, she swung into the channel to the sound of cheers, she was off at last, a sacrifice, a splendour, leaving smoke that thinned into the sunset, and ripples that died against the wooded shores. For a long time he gazed after her, then turned to England. His journey was nearly over. He was bound for his new home. He had brought out the man in Alec, and now it was Alec's turn to bring out the hero in him. He knew what the call was, and what his answer must be. They must live outside class, without relations or money; they must work and stick to each other till death. But England belonged to them. That, besides companionship, was their reward. Her air and sky were theirs, not the timorous millions' who own stuffy little boxes, but never their own souls.

He faced Mr Borenius, who had lost all grasp of events. Alec had completely routed him. Mr Borenius assumed that love between two men must be ignoble, and so could not interpret what had happened. He became an ordinary person at once, his irony vanished. In a straightforward and rather silly way he discussed what could have befallen young Scudder and then repaired to visit friends in Southampton. Maurice called after him, "Mr. Borenius do look at the sky—it's gone all on fire," but the rector had no use for the sky when on fire, and disappeared.

In his excitement he felt that Alec was close to him. He wasn't, couldn't be, he was elsewhere in the splendour and had to be found, and without a moment's hesitation he set out for Boathouse, Penge. Those words had got into his blood, they were part of Alec's yearnings and blackmailings, and of his own promise in that last desperate embrace. They were all he had to go by. He left Southampton as he had come to it—instinctively—and he felt that not merely things wouldn't go wrong this time but that they daren't, and that the universe had been put in its place. A little local train did its duty, a gorgeous horizon still glowed, and inflamed cloudlets which flared when the main glory faded, and there was even enough light for him to walk up from the station at Penge through quiet fields.

He entered the estate at its lower end, through a gap in the hedge, and it struck him once more how derelict it was, how unfit to set standards or control the future. Night was approaching, a bird called, animals scuttled, he hurried on until he saw the pond glimmering, and black against it the trysting place, and heard the water sipping.

He was here, or almost here. Still confident, he lifted up his voice and called Alec.

There was no answer.

He called again.

Silence and the advancing night. He had miscalculated.

"Likely enough," he thought, and instantly took himself in hand. Whatever happened he must not collapse. He had done that enough over Clive, and to no effect, and to collapse in this graying wilderness might mean going mad. To be strong, to keep calm, and to trust—they were still the one hope. But the sudden disappointment revealed to him how exhausted he was physically. He had been on the run ever since early morning, ravaged by every sort of emotion, and he was ready to drop. In a little while he would decide what next should be done, but now his head was splitting, every bit of him ached or was useless and he must rest.

The boathouse offered itself conveniently for that purpose. He went in and found his lover asleep. Alec lay upon piled up cushions, just visible in the last dying of the day. When he woke he did not seem excited or disturbed and fondled Maurice's arm between his hands before he spoke. "So you got the wire," he said.

"What wire?"

"The wire I sent off this morning to your house, telling you . . ." He yawned, "Excuse me, I'm a bit tired, one thing and another . . . telling you to come here without fail." And since Maurice did not speak, indeed could not, he added, "And now we shan't be parted no more, and that's finished."

46 Dissatisfied with his printed appeal to the electors—it struck him as too patronizing for these times—Clive was trying to alter the proofs when Simcox announced, "Mr Hall." The hour was extremely late, and the night dark; all traces of a magnificent sunset had disappeared from the sky. He could see nothing from the porch though he heard abundant noises; his friend, who had refused to come in, was kicking up the gravel, and throwing pebbles against the shrubs and walls.

"Hullo Maurice, come in. Why this thusness?" He asked, a little annoyed, and not troubling to smile since his face was in shadow. "Good to see you back, hope you're better. Unluckily I'm a bit occupied, but the Russet Room's not. Come in and sleep here as before. So glad to see you."

"I've only a few minutes, Clive."

"Look here man, that's fantastic." He advanced into the darkness hospitably, still holding his proof sheets. "Anne'll be furious with me if you don't stay. It's awfully nice you turning up like this. Excuse me if I work at unimportancies for a bit now." Then he detected a core of blackness in the surrounding gloom, and, suddenly uneasy, exclaimed, "I hope nothing's wrong."

"Pretty well everything . . . what you'd call."

Now Clive put politics aside, for he knew that it must be the love affair, and he prepared to sympathize, though he wished the appeal had come when he was less busy. His sense of proportion supported him. He led the way to the deserted alley behind the laurels, where evening primroses gleamed, and embossed with faint yellow the walls of night. Here they would be most solitary. Feeling for a bench, he reclined full length on it, put his hands behind his head, and said, "I'm at your service, but my advice is sleep the night here, and consult Anne in the morning."

"I don't want your advice."

"Well, as you like of course there, but you've been so friendly in telling us about your hopes, and where a woman is in question I would always consult another woman, particularly where she has Anne's almost uncanny insight."

The blossoms opposite disappeared and reappeared, and again Clive felt that his friend, swaying to and fro in front of them, was essential night. A voice said, "It's miles worse for you than that; I'm in love with your gamekeeper"—a remark so unexpected and meaningless to him that he said, "Mrs Ayres?" and sat up stupidly.

"No. Scudder."

"Look out," cried Clive, with a glance at darkness. Reassured, he said stiffly, "What a grotesque announcement."

"Most grotesque," the voice echoed, "but I felt after all I owe you I ought to come and tell you about Alec."

Clive had only grasped the minimum. He supposed "Scudder" was a *façon de parler*, as one might say "Ganymede", for intimacy with any social inferior was unthinkable to him. As it was, he felt depressed, and offended, for he had assumed Maurice was normal during the last fortnight, and so encouraged Anne's intimacy. "We did anything we could," he said, "and if you want to repay what you 'owe' us, as you call it, you won't dally with morbid thoughts. I'm so disappointed to hear you talk of yourself like that. You gave me to understand that the land through the looking-glass was behind you at last, when we thrashed out the subject that night in the Russet Room."

"When you brought yourself to kiss my hand," added Maurice, with deliberate bitterness.

"Don't allude to that," he flashed, not for the first and last time, and for a moment causing the outlaw to love him. Then he relapsed into intellectualism. "Maurice—oh, I'm more sorry for you than I can possibly say, and I do, do beg you to resist the return of this obsession. It'll leave you for good if you do. Occupation, fresh air, your friends. . . ."

"As I said before, I'm not here to get advice, nor to talk about thoughts and ideas either. I'm flesh and blood, if you'll condescend to such low things—"

"Yes, quite right; I'm a frightful theorist, I know."

"—and'll mention Alec by his name."

It recalled to both of them the situation of a year back, but it was Clive who winced at the example now. "If Alec is Scudder, he is in point of fact no longer in my service or even in England. He sailed for Buenos Aires this very day. Go on though. I'm reconciled to reopening the subject if I can be of the least help."

Maurice blew out his cheeks, and began picking the flowerets off a tall stalk. They vanished one after another, like candles that the night has extinguished. "I have shared with Alec," he said after deep thought.

"Shared what?"

"All I have. Which includes my body."

Clive sprang up with a whimper of disgust. He wanted to smite the monster, and flee, but he was civilized, and wanted it feebly. After all, they were Cambridge men . . . pillars of society both; he must not show violence. And he did not; he remained quiet and helpful to the very end. But his thin, sour disapproval, his dogmatism, the stupidity of his heart, revolted Maurice, who could only have respected hatred.

"I put it offensively," he went on, "but I must make sure you understand. Alec slept with me in the Russet Room that night when you and Anne were away."

"Maurice—oh, good God!"

"Also in town. Also—" here he stopped.

Even in his nausea Clive turned to a generalization—it was part of the mental vagueness induced by his marriage. "But surely—the sole excuse for any relationship between men is that it remain purely platonic."

"I don't know. I've come to tell you what I did." Yes, that was the reason of his visit. It was the closing of a book that would never be read again, and better close such a book than leave it lying about to get dirtied. The volume of their past must be restored to its shelf, and here, here was the place, amid darkness and perishing flowers. He owed it to Alec also. He could suffer no mixing of the old in the new. All compromise was perilous, because furtive, and, having finished his confession, he must disappear from the world that had brought him up. "I must tell you too what he did," he went on, trying to keep down his joy. "He's sacrificed his career for my sake . . . without a guarantee I'll give up anything for him . . . and I shouldn't have earlier. . . . I'm always slow at seeing. I don't know whether that's platonic of him or not, but it's what he did."

"How sacrifice?"

"I've just been to see him off—he wasn't there—"

"Scudder missed his boat?" cried the squire with indignation. "These people are impossible." Then he stopped, faced by the future. "Maurice, Maurice," he said with some tenderness. "Maurice, quo vadis? You're going mad. You've lost all sense of—May I ask whether you intend—"

"No, you may not ask," interrupted the other. "You belong to the past. I'll tell you everything up to this moment—not a word beyond."

"Maurice, Maurice, I care a little bit for you, you know, or I wouldn't stand what you have told me."

Maurice opened his hand. Luminous petals appeared in it. "You care for me a little bit, I do think," he admitted, "but I can't hang all my life on a little bit. You don't. You hang yours on Anne. You don't worry whether your relation with her is platonic or not, you only know it's big enough to hang a life on. I can't hang mine on to the five minutes you spare me from her and politics. You'll do anything for me except see me. That's been it for this whole year of Hell. You'll make me free of the house, and take endless bother to marry me off, because that puts me off your hands. You do care a little for me, I know"— for Clive had protested—"but nothing to speak of, and you don't love me. I was yours once till death if you'd cared to keep me, but I'm someone else's now—I can't hang about whining for ever—and he's mine in a way that shocks you, but why don't you stop being shocked, and attend to your own happiness?"

"Who taught you to talk like this?" Clive gasped.

"You, if anyone."

"I? It's appalling you should attribute such thoughts to me," pursued Clive. Had he corrupted an inferior's intellect? He could not realize that he and Maurice were alike descended from the Clive of two years ago, the one by respectability, the other by rebellion, nor that they must differentiate further. It was a cesspool, and one breath from it at the election would ruin him. But he must not shrink from his duty. He must rescue his old friend. A feeling of heroism stole over him; and he began to wonder how Scudder could be silenced and whether he would prove extortionate. It was too late to discuss ways and means

now, so he invited Maurice to dine with him the following week
in his club up in town.

A laugh answered. He had always liked his friend's laugh, and
at such a moment the soft rumble of it reassured him; it suggested happiness and security. "That's right," he said, and went
so far as to stretch his hand into a bush of laurels. "That's better
than making me a long set speech, which convinces neither
yourself nor me." His last words were "Next Wednesday, say at
7.45. Dinner-jacket's enough, as you know."

They were his last words, because Maurice had disappeared
thereabouts, leaving no trace of his presence except a little pile
of the petals of the evening primrose, which mourned from the
ground like an expiring fire. To the end of his life Clive was not
sure of the exact moment of departure, and with the approach
of old age he grew uncertain whether the moment had yet occurred. The Blue Room would glimmer, ferns undulate. Out of
some external Cambridge his friend began beckoning to him,
clothed in the sun, and shaking out the scents and sounds of the
May term.

But at the time he was merely offended at a discourtesy, and
compared it with similar lapses in the past. He did not realize
that this was the end, without twilight or compromise, that he
should never cross Maurice's track again, nor speak to those
who had seen him. He waited for a little in the alley, then returned to the house, to correct his proofs and to devise some
method of concealing the truth from Anne.

TERMINAL NOTE

In its original form, which it still almost retains, *Maurice* dates from 1913. It was the direct result of a visit to Edward Carpenter at Milthorpe. Carpenter had a prestige which cannot be understood today. He was a rebel appropriate to his age. He was sentimental and a little sacramental, for he had begun life as a clergyman. He was a socialist who ignored industrialism and a simple-lifer with an independent income and a Whitmannic poet whose nobility exceeded his strength and, finally, he was a believer in the Love of Comrades, whom he sometimes called Uranians. It was this last aspect of him that attracted me in my loneliness. For a short time he seemed to hold the key to every trouble. I approached him through Lowes Dickinson, and as one approaches a saviour.

It must have been on my second or third visit to the shrine that the spark was kindled and he and his comrade George Merrill combined to make a profound impression on me and to touch a creative spring. George Merrill also touched my backside—gently and just above the buttocks. I believe he touched most people's. The sensation was unusual and I still remember it, as I remember the position of a long vanished tooth. It was as much psychological as physical. It seemed to go straight through the small of my back into my ideas, without involving my thoughts. If it really did this, it would have acted in strict accordance with Carpenter's yogified mysticism, and would prove that at that precise moment I had conceived.

I then returned to Harrogate, where my mother was taking a cure, and immediately began to write *Maurice*. No other of my books has started off in this way. The general plan, the three characters, the happy ending for two of them, all rushed into my pen. And the whole thing went through without a hitch. It was finished in 1914. The friends, men and women, to whom I showed it liked it. But they were carefully picked. It has not so far had to face the critics or the public, and I have myself been too much involved in it, and for too long, to judge.

A happy ending was imperative. I shouldn't have bothered to write otherwise. I was determined that in fiction anyway two men should fall in love and remain in it for the ever and ever that fiction allows, and in this sense Maurice and Alec still roam the greenwood. I dedicated it "To a Happier Year" and not altogether vainly. Happiness is its keynote—which by the way has had an unexpected result: it has made the book more difficult to publish. Unless the Wolfenden Report becomes law, it will probably have to remain in manuscript. If it ended unhappily, with a lad dangling from a noose or with a suicide pact, all would be well, for there is no pornography or seduction of minors. But the lovers get away unpunished and consequently recommend crime. Mr Borenius is too incompetent to catch them, and the only penalty society exacts is an exile they gladly embrace.

Notes on the three men

In Maurice I tried to create a character who was completely unlike myself or what I supposed myself to be: someone handsome, healthy, bodily attractive, mentally torpid, not a bad business man and rather a snob. Into this mixture I dropped an ingredient that puzzles him, wakes him up, torments him and finally saves him. His surroundings exasperate him by their very normality: mother, two sisters, a comfortable home, a respectable job gradually turn out to be Hell; he must either smash them or be smashed, there is no third course. The working out of such a character, the setting of traps for him which he sometimes eluded, sometimes fell into, and finally did smash, proved a welcome task.

If Maurice is Suburbia, Clive is Cambridge. Knowing the university, or one corner of it, pretty well, I produced him without difficulty and got some initial hints for him from a slight academic acquaintance. The calm, the superiority of outlook, the clarity and the intelligence, the assured moral standards, the blondness and delicacy that did not mean frailty, the blend of lawyer and squire, all lay in the direction of that acquaintance, though it was I who gave Clive his "hellenic" temperament and flung him into Maurice's affectionate arms. Once there, he took charge, he laid down the lines on which the unusual relationship should proceed. He believed in platonic restraint and induced Maurice to acquiesce, which does not seem to me at all unlikely. Maurice at this stage is humble and inexperienced and adoring, he is the soul released from prison, and if asked by his deliverer to remain chaste he obeys. Consequently the relationship lasts for three years—precarious, idealistic and peculiarly English: what Italian boy would have put up with it?—still it lasts until Clive ends it by turning to women and sending Maurice back to prison. Henceforward Clive deteriorates, and so perhaps does my treatment of him. He has annoyed me. I may nag at him over much, stress his aridity and political pretensions and the thinning of his hair, nothing he or his wife or his mother does is ever right. This works well enough for Maurice, for it accelerates his descent into Hell and toughens him there for the final reckless climb. But it may be unfair on Clive who intends no evil and who feels the last flick of my whip in the final chapter, when he discovers that his old Cambridge friend has relapsed inside Penge itself, and with a gamekeeper.

Alec starts as an emanation from Milthorpe, he is the touch on the backside. But he has no further connection with the methodical George Merrill and in many ways he is a premonition. As I worked at him, I got to know him better, partly through personal experiences, and some of them were useful. He became less of a comrade and more of a person, he became livelier and heavier and demanded more room, and the additions to the novel (there were scarcely any cancellations in it) are all due to him. Not much can be premised about him. He is senior in date to the prickly gamekeepers of D. H. Lawrence, and had not the advantage of their disquisitions, nor, though he might have met my own Stephen Wonham, would they have had more in common than a mug of beer. What was his life before Maurice arrived? Clive's earlier life is easily recalled, but Alec's, when I tried to evoke it, turned into a survey and had to be scrapped. He certainly objected to nothing—one knows that much. No more, once they met, did Maurice, and Lytton Strachey, an early reader, thought this would prove their undoing. He wrote me a delightful and disquieting letter and said that the relationship of the two rested upon curiosity and lust and would only last six weeks. Shades of Edward Carpenter!—whose name Lytton always greeted with a series of little squeaks. Carpenter believed that Uranians remained loyal to each other for ever. And in my experience though loyalty cannot be counted on it can always be hoped for and be worked towards and may flourish in the most unlikely soil. Both the suburban youth and the countrified one are capable of loyalty. Risley, the clever Trinity undergraduate, wasn't, and Risley, as Lytton gleefully detected, was based upon Lytton.

The later additions to the novel necessitated by Alec are two, or rather they fall into two groups.

In the first place he has to be led up to. He must loom upon the reader gradually. He has to be developed from the masculine blur past which Maurice drives into Penge, through the croucher beside the piano and the rejecter of a tip and the haunter of shrubberies and the stealer of apricots into the sharer who gives and takes love. He must loom out of nothing until he is everything. This requires careful handling. If the reader knows too much of what's coming he may be bored. If he knows too little he may be puzzled. Take the half-dozen sentences the two exchange in the dark garden when Mr Borenius has left them and avowal begins to hover. These sentences can reveal less or more, according to the way they are drafted. Have I drafted them appropriately? Or take Alec, when he hears the wild lone cry on his rounds: should he respond at once or—as I have finally decided—should he hesitate until it is repeated? The art called for in these problems is not of a high order, not as high as Henry James thinks, still it has to be employed if the final embrace is to be felt.

In the second place Alec has to be led down from. He has taken a risk and they have loved. What guarantee is there that such love will last? None. So their characters, their attitudes towards each other, the tests through which they are put must suggest that it may last, and the final section of the book had to be much longer than originally planned. The British Museum chapter had to be extended and a whole new chapter inserted after it—the chapter of their passionate and distracted second night, where Maurice comes further into the open and Alec daren't. In the original draft I had only implied all this. Similarly, after Southampton, when Alec too had risked all, I hadn't brought them to their final reunion. All this had to be written out, so that they might be ascribed the fullest possible knowledge of each other. Not until some dangers and some threats had been surmounted could the curtain prepare to fall.

The chapter after their reunion, where Maurice ticks off Clive, is the only possible end to the book. I did not always think so, nor did others, and I was encouraged to write an epilogue. It took the form of Kitty encountering two woodcutters some years later and gave universal dissatisfaction. Epilogues are for Tolstoy. Mine partly failed because the novel's action-date is about 1912, and "some years later" would plunge it into the transformed England of the First World War.

The book certainly dates and a friend has recently remarked that for readers today it can only have a period interest. I wouldn't go as far as that, but it certainly dates—not only because of its endless anachronisms—its half-sovereign tips, pianola-records, norfolk jackets, Police Court News, Hague Conferences, Libs and Rads and Terriers, uninformed doctors and undergraduates walking arm in arm, but for a more vital reason: it belongs to an England where it was still possible to get lost. It belongs to the last moment of the greenwood. *The Longest Journey* belongs there too, and has similarities of atmosphere. Our greenwood ended catastrophically and inevitably. Two great wars demanded and bequeathed regimentation which the public services adopted and extended, science lent her aid, and the wildness of our island, never extensive, was stamped upon and built over and patrolled in no time. There is no forest or fell to escape to today, no cave in which to curl up, no deserted valley for those who wish neither to reform nor corrupt society but to be left alone. People do still escape, one can see them any night at it in the films. But they are gangsters not outlaws, they can dodge civilization because they are part of it.

TERMINAL NOTE

Homosexuality

Note in conclusion on a word hitherto unmentioned. Since *Maurice* was written there has been a change in the public attitude here: the change from ignorance and terror to familiarity and contempt. It is not the change towards which Edward Carpenter had worked. He had hoped for the generous recognition of an emotion and for the reintegration of something primitive into the common stock. And I, though less optimistic, had supposed that knowledge would bring understanding. We had not realized that what the public really loathes in homosexuality is not the thing itself but having to think about it. If it could be slipped into our midst unnoticed, or legalized overnight by a decree in small print, there would be few protests. Unfortunately it can only be legalized by Parliament, and Members of Parliament are obliged to think or to appear to think. Consequently the Wolfenden recommendations will be indefinitely rejected, police prosecutions will continue and Clive on the bench will continue to sentence Alec in the dock. Maurice may get off.

September 1960

E(DWARD) M(ORGAN) FORSTER was born in England in 1879. He was educated at the Tonbridge School and at King's College, Cambridge. Soon after his graduation he began to write short stories, some of which appeared in the *Independent Review*. He then went to Italy, where he wrote the two novels, *Where Angels Fear to Tread* (1905) and *A Room with a View* (1908). His next novel, *Howards End*, was published in 1910. During World War I he traveled to Alexandria, where he did civilian war work and contributed a number of articles to the *Egyptian Mail*. After the war he returned to London; while there he was a frequent contributor to the *New Statesman*, the *Spectator*, and several daily papers, as well as literary editor of the Labor *Daily Herald*. In 1921 he went to India, and in 1924 *A Passage to India* was published, which won the James Tait Black Memorial prize in 1925, the first of many honors he has received. Principal among his other works are *The Longest Journey* (1907), *The Hill of Devi* (1953), *Two Cheers for Democracy* (1951), *Aspects of the Novel* (1927), and *Maurice* (1971), published posthumously. He died in 1970.

Stour Valley and Dedham Church   48.266   Constable, John   British, 1776–1837
Oil on canvas   55.5×77.8 cm. (21⅞×30⅝ in.)   Warren Collection
Courtesy, Museum of Fine Arts, Boston